SEAL of Protection
Collection One

SEAL of Protection

Books 1-3.5

Collection One

By Susan Stoker

Table of Contents

Protecting Caroline

SEAL of Protection
Book 1

By Susan Stoker

Acknowledgements

I would like to take the time to thank my awesome editor, Missy B., for polishing up my words and making Wolf and Caroline's story even better.

To my wonderful Stoker Aces…ya'll are the best street team ever. We might not be big, but you guys do such a great job in supporting me and pimping me out! Thank you!

To Connie N—Thank you for being my very first Beta reader for Protecting Caroline and giving me GREAT tips that I think helped make the story so much better.

To Amy H—Wow, you gave me the confidence I needed to really work to get this series out. Thank you for all your encouragement and tips, every day. It means more than you'll know.

To my friends and family, who I am sure are wondering when I'm going to be "over this writing thing"…thanks for putting up with me!

To all my readers, thank you for taking a chance on me. Without you I'm not sure I'd be putting my stories out there.

Prologue

MATTHEW "WOLF" STEEL couldn't be more proud of his five teammates, and friends. SEAL teams were notoriously tight, and his team was no different. The SEALs were exhausted. They'd just spent the last two weeks at an "undisclosed location" trying to ferret out the head bad guy in a nest of hundreds of other bad guys. It'd been a hell of mission, but one they'd ultimately succeeded in accomplishing.

Looking around the plane, Wolf observed the sleeping men. He really should be crashed as they were, but he still had way too much adrenaline coursing through his body to relax just yet. He knew he'd be out for the count later, but for now, he was wide awake.

Christopher "Abe" Powers was the first to catch Wolf's eye. Abe was probably his closest friend of the group. Wolf thought he was the only one of the group who knew even a little bit of Abe's background, but it was uncanny how well the nickname fit Abe. The man was as honest as the day was long and Abe demanded that same honesty in those he called his friends.

Wolf watched as Abe shifted in his seat and then settled once again. Wolf then looked over to Hunter "Cookie" Knox. Cookie had been the most recent addition to their team, but no one looked down on him as a result. Unlike many businesses, it didn't matter if a SEAL was fresh out of Seal Qualification Training or had been on a team for years, a SEAL is a SEAL.

The group was still getting to know Cookie, but he'd proven to be a great addition to their close-knit team. Cookie was the best swimmer out of all of them; he was funny, compassionate, and never hesitated to do whatever it took to get the job done.

Faulkner "Dude" Cooper's mutterings drew Wolf's attention. Dude hadn't taken any of his gear off and was sitting scrunched into the little seat on the military plane. Wolf remembered when Dude was almost blown up trying to secure a building. As their resident explosives expert, Dude found a booby trapped M14 mine duct taped to a door jamb during one of their missions. The mine was nicknamed "toe popper" because it was designed to maim and slow down people entering a room, rather than kill them.

Dude had immediately recognized the type of mine and had moved to re-insert the safety clip to disarm it, but something had gone wrong and the bomb went off. The mine did what it was intended to do; resulting in Dude losing parts of three of his fingers on his left hand. He had extensive scarring as well as missing parts of his hand as a consequence of being too close to the mine when it exploded.

Wolf knew Dude was more sensitive about his injury than he'd ever let on to any of his teammates. Wolf had seen Dude's face go blank and cold when a woman rejected him after seeing his mangled hand. Although he missed his friend's happy-go-lucky attitude at times, Wolf was thankful Dude was still with them. With the best instincts when it came to explosives, Wolf knew the team was better off because Dude was on it.

Thinking about Dude's issues with women caused Wolf to reflect upon Sam "Mozart" Reed. That was one man who certainly didn't have any problems with women. Mozart was popular with the ladies and never hesitated to turn any encounter into one which involved flirting and the possibility of a one-night-stand. As far as Wolf knew, however, Mozart had never been tempted into anything more.

Wolf figured Mozart's aversion to settling down with one woman had something to do with Mozart's little sister being murdered when he was a child, but Wolf never pried. A man was allowed to have his secrets.

Wolf chuckled to himself thinking about the last man on their team, Kason "Benny" Sawyer. Nicknames were a part of life on SEAL teams. Everyone got one and it wasn't necessarily something that was macho or even wanted by the recipient. Benny was a case in point. He'd been trying for years to get the guys to change his name, but they'd just laughed and ignored him. An inside joke with the team, they'd ask Benny if he liked some new name only to just laugh and say "too bad" when Benny agreed that he loved the new one. Benny had earned his nickname fair and square, and nothing he could say would change it.

Feeling tired for the first time since he'd climbed onto the plane, Wolf finally closed his eyes. He felt lucky he not only had one of the most interesting and exciting jobs in the world, but that he was able to work with such a great group of men. Each man had his strengths and weaknesses and there were no secrets within the group. Abe, Cookie, Mozart, Benny, and Dude were teammates, but they were also his closest friends.

Wolf sighed, settled himself into his seat and tried to get comfortable. The team would most likely have a few weeks stateside before being sent on another mission, but time off was never guaranteed. Wolf knew the night after they returned, the team would head to their favorite bar for a "post-mission" ritual of blowing off steam and shooting the shit.

Leaving the mission behind was sometimes difficult, but somehow their tradition of throwing back a few beers would break the team out of the military frame of mind and bring them back to what was important…friendship and women.

Wolf figured each team member knew they most likely wouldn't meet the woman of their dreams in a bar—especially not in a bar near the base where too many women were more than willing to sleep with a SEAL just to say she'd done it. But, it didn't stop the boys from enjoying what was frequently offered.

Wolf ignored the niggling little voice in his head that said he wouldn't mind settling down and finding someone to love. It wasn't as if he could plan it, he'd just have to go with the flow. Hopefully it happened sooner rather than later, but he wasn't going to act desperate about it.

Sleep finally came over Wolf, as it had the rest of his team, and they all slept the sleep of the exhausted as they flew toward California, and home.

Chapter One

L IKE A FANTASY brought to life, each woman in the bar was acutely aware of the table full of gorgeous men sitting in the corner. Obviously in the military, they were muscular and had a wariness about them that came from too many missions overseas. Every one of the women would have given anything to be able to go home with one of them—they were *that* good looking.

The group of six teammates and friends were enjoying a final beer together before some of them headed off on leave. Known for its excellent beer choices and as a good place to pick up women, the bar was where they spent quite a bit of time, especially after a mission. All six men had gone home with a woman they'd met there at one time or another. So far none of them had found "the one." It wasn't as if they didn't *want* to find someone to love, it just hadn't happened for any of them yet, and in the meantime they all enjoyed playing the field.

All of the men had played the pick-up game at one time or another, but Wolf was the least likely to hook up with a random chick who just wanted to bag a SEAL. He'd learned at a young age, by looking at the example his folks set, that true love was out there and could be found. Wolf wasn't a saint, but he also never flaunted his sexuality.

"You ready for your vacation?" Dude asked Wolf.

"Oh, hell yeah! I can't remember the last time I took some time off...hell, when *any* of us took time off."

"Where are you guys going again?" Dude questioned.

"Mozart, Abe, and I are headed out to Virginia to visit Tex. We've been using him on more and more missions lately because he's got some amazing contacts the Navy couldn't hope to replicate."

Taking a breath, Wolf continued, "After Tex lost his leg on that mission, he retired and it's been way too long since we've seen him. Since we're slated to leave out of Norfolk in a couple of weeks for our next mission, we thought we'd take some R&R and head out there beforehand."

Everyone around the table nodded at Wolf's explanation of where he, Abe and Mozart were going in Virginia. Benny, Dude, and Cookie also knew Tex well and were glad Wolf and the others would get to spend some time with him.

"That sucks he left the Navy," Benny said, "but I get it. If I couldn't stay with you guys and a team, I wouldn't want to stay in only to have to work a desk."

"Yeah, but can you imagine how much harder some of the shit we do would be if it wasn't for him?" Mozart responded. "Seriously, I have no idea how Tex gets the information he does, but I don't think we'd be as quick to get through some of our missions without him."

"Yeah, he seriously is scary with that computer shit," Cookie enthused. "Tex can find anyone, no matter where they are."

Mozart nodded. "I certainly hope that's true. He's working on something personal for me and I really need him to come through."

Wolf thumped Mozart on his back. "I'm sure he will. Given enough time Tex always comes through. Hey, you ready for Norfolk?"

Mozart's mood lifted immediately at Wolf's question. "Can't wait! Heard there are some awesome bars around the base out there and not as many SEALs to compete for the ladies."

Everyone laughed. The group knew how much Mozart loved finding "fresh meat" to convince to go back to his room with him.

The men sat in the bar until late in the evening, talking and enjoying their time together. Typically the conversation would veer toward women, alcohol, and their job. Because Wolf, Abe, and Mozart had get to the airport early in the morning, they eased off their typical competitive natures about who could drink the most and spent their time relaxing and playing the odd game of pool.

Finally, as the evening turned into night and the crowd began to get thicker and more uninhibited, Abe thunked his empty bottle on the table and sighed, "Damn, wish we weren't leaving so early in the morning, that chick at the bar's been checking me out all night."

Cookie laughed. "As much as I hate to agree with you, especially considering it makes me sound too much like Mozart, I think you're right. And if I'm not mistaken, her friend's been checking *me* out."

Everyone laughed because they'd noticed the duo at the bar making eyes at them all night. It was obvious the women didn't really care who they ended up with, as long as they went home with a SEAL, but their eyes followed Cookie and Abe more than the others.

"The one on the right is Adelaide and the one on the left is Michele," Mozart told them knowingly.

Wolf just raised an eyebrow at his teammate while everyone else demanded to know how Mozart knew who the women were.

"They come here all the time. I *might* have gotten to know them both reaaally well a couple of weeks ago. I'm sure they'll be willing to get to know you better when you get back, Abe."

Nobody was surprised at Mozart's words. Taking on two women at a time was just the type of thing they'd expect out of him. None of them doubted that Mozart was telling the truth and not just bragging. The group knew him too well.

"I'm a one-woman-at-a-time man," Abe told the group laughing. "But Adelaide looks like my kind of woman. I think I'll see if she might be interested in a few weeks when we get back home."

Everyone knew he was warning them off. Abe didn't stand for

poaching. The men chuckled at his claim, used to Abe's quirks when it came to women.

"As much fun as this has been, I'm gonna hit the road," Wolf announced to the group, not in the least abashed to be the first person leaving for the night.

"Yeah, me too," Mozart chimed in.

"We'll see the rest of you guys in a couple weeks in Norfolk," Abe told his friends and teammates as he stood up, joining Wolf and Mozart as they got ready to leave.

The three men smacked each other on the back good-naturedly as they said their good-byes to the rest of the group and headed out the door, disappearing into the night.

Cookie, Benny, and Dude pushed back their chairs not too much later to leave as well. "See you guys in the morning at PT," Dude told them as they walked out through the door of the bar.

"You'd think with the others gone we'd at least get a morning off from training," Cookie mock grumbled. Benny and Dude laughed, knowing Cookie loved to work out, never missing PT unless he was sick or recovering from an injury.

"Whatever Cookie, you know the CO has a ten miler scheduled. You'll be there before all of us."

Cookie just laughed. The men gave chin lifts to each other and faded into the parking lot to their cars and into the night.

A previous commander of the SEAL team once remarked to an Officer that had been visiting the base that this group of six men were one of the best teams he'd ever commanded, not because of the skills they'd learned during Hell Week or because of their strength, but because of the genuine respect they had for each other.

"Those men would do anything for each other. They're the epitome of the word "team." If ever I needed rescuing or protecting, those would be the men I'd want."

Chapter Two

CAROLINE SHIFTED UNCOMFORTABLY in her seat. She hated flying. She hadn't flown much and there were just too many people, too close together. She tried to ignore the people walking down the aisle to their seats. At least she'd gotten an aisle seat close to the front of the plane. Caroline watched the shoes of the people passing her. She felt too awkward to look into people's eyes as they lumbered past. The boarding process was one of the parts of flying Caroline hated the most...waiting to see who'd be in the seat next to her. Looking out the corner of her eye at the man sitting in the window seat, she noticed he was already settled in, reading a newspaper; not paying any attention to the rest of the passengers as they shuffled by their row.

Sneakers, flip flops, sneakers, loafers, sandals, boots....the boots didn't pass. She looked up and saw a man had stopped next to her seat.

"I guess I'm in the middle then," he said in a deep voice that sent shivers straight through her.

Caroline nodded and stood up to let him pass. Brushing against her as he moved past, he settled himself into the seat next to her. The dreaded middle seat. The man wasn't overweight, far from it, but he certainly wasn't small. It was a cozy fit. Caroline's shoulders literally rubbed against his when she sat back down—she wouldn't be using the armrest for the flight.

He was one hell of a man that was sure. He was tall, when she'd stood up to let him into the row she'd barely came to his shoulder. And holy hell, he was muscular. She wondered for a moment if he was a body builder. If she wrapped both hands around his bicep, Caroline didn't think her hands would touch. The man was wearing long sleeves, but she could see the fabric straining over his biceps. He was sporting a pair of cargo pants, the kind with the multitude of pockets. As they sat, Caroline could see his legs were just as muscular as the rest of him. She blushed a bit and tore her eyes away. Woah. He could be a model and would probably make a killing. She knew he probably wasn't though. He was too rugged, too masculine, too…well…manly to be any kind of model, no matter what he'd make doing it.

The man next to her shifted a bit and laid his head back on the head rest and closed his eyes.

Caroline fought with her conscience. She hated the middle seat. She really did, but there was no way this man would last the entire four hour flight squished in between her and the other man the way he was. With his knees hitting the chair in front of him, he looked scrunched. His muscular body sure didn't leave any extra room in the small cramped airline seat. He looked miserable. Caroline sighed, knowing what she had to do.

WOLF SAT UNCOMFORTABLY in the airplane seat. Outwardly he looked relaxed, but he was anything but. With eyes closed, Wolf processed the sounds around him. The passengers walking past his row to their seats, the sounds of the overhead bins filling up, the rustle of the newspaper from the man to his right, and the quiet sigh of the woman sitting to his left.

Flying commercial from San Diego to the base in Norfolk, Wolf, Mozart, and Abe were technically off duty at the moment, and were flying in civilian clothes. They'd booked this flight last minute, thus leaving him the middle seat and the others spread out in the plane. Wolf wanted to hop on a MAC flight, the free flight service offered by the military to members and spouses, but he knew there was no guarantee they'd get a space on the flight and the three of them wanted to get to Virginia to see Tex sooner rather than later. They talked to Tex all the time since he helped them get information when they needed it, but talking to him in an official capacity was way different than being able to sit down around a table, drink a beer, and talk about anything other than work.

Wolf, Abe, and Mozart were supposed to be on leave before their next mission started. They were leaving from Norfolk in two weeks, and the thought of being able to shut down and actually enjoy being around friends was a welcome one. They all spent way too much time hyped up and in danger. Spending two weeks before they had to risk their lives on another mission was just too tempting to turn down.

None of them had a lot of time off recently and Wolf, Abe, and Mozart were happy to get to pretend to be normal for a few weeks before they had to leave again. Wolf had been a SEAL for ten years, working with Mozart and Abe for the last eight. They hadn't been in BUD/S together, but that didn't matter. Bonded over firefights, scuba dives, and life threatening situations, they'd each saved each other's lives a few times and their connection was tighter than most siblings.

Wolf would've preferred to sit in the same row with his friends, but because they'd made their flight arrangements so late, they didn't have a choice and had to take seats that were available. Mozart offered to flirt with the airline employee in the hopes they'd be able to get upgraded, or at least be seated together, but they'd agreed to suck it up and sit where they were assigned. They all knew they wouldn't fit in the seats if they all sat in the same row anyway. Their shoulders were just too broad to fit comfortably side-by-side in a crunched airline row. Wolf knew his friends felt the same way he did—they didn't flaunt their SEAL status to receive preferential treatment. It was bad enough women hit on them back home in San Diego in the bars just because they were SEALs.

Wolf hated to admit it, but he'd gotten bored with the bar scene. He was picky in the first place, and he'd found too many women just wanted to sleep with a SEAL, it didn't matter *who* the SEAL was, just that they could brag later to their friends they'd done it with a legendary SEAL. The sadder part was that too many SEALs took advantage of it. Wolf could admit to himself that once upon a time he'd done that exact thing, but time and experience had shown him the encounters left him feeling dissatisfied and used. If someone had asked him right after he'd graduated from BUD/S if he'd ever feel used by a woman who wanted to sleep with him, he would've laughed himself silly.

Wolf knew what love looked like. His parents had been together for almost forty years. They were still as madly in love now as they were when they got married. It used to embarrass him, but lately it made him feel wistful. They'd still go on dates and hold hands wherever they went. His dad surprised his mom with romantic gifts and, every now and then, a special trip. Wolf wanted what his parents had. He wanted someone he could be himself with. He wanted someone to need him. He wanted to need someone. Wolf supposed it wasn't manly to admit any of those things, but it was what it was.

Wolf had no idea how to go about finding that special woman though, except he knew he wouldn't find her in a bar. The other issue was that he was a SEAL. He was sent off to crappy little countries to kill people and to keep the peace. Every now and then they were sent off on a rescue mission. He wasn't allowed to talk about the specifics of what he did with anyone. He had no idea how that would work in a marriage. He'd seen too many of his SEAL friends get married and then divorced because their wives just couldn't handle the secrecy and the uncertainty of when their husbands would be coming home, or even where they were going in the first place.

To be fair, not all of the marriages ended because of the secrecy and danger inherent in being a SEAL. Some ended because one of the people in the marriage cheated on the other. Sometimes it was the wife who cheated, and other times it was the husband. Wolf shrugged. There wasn't any use in obsessing about it. Hopefully he'd someday find someone to settle down with. If it didn't happen during his military career, perhaps it would once he was retired. There was no rule that said someone in their forties couldn't find true love and get married.

After drifting off and thinking about his lack of a love life, Wolf flinched when he felt a hand on his arm. He hadn't been paying attention and was actually startled. His team would get a kick out of that. Wolf was known to always be one step ahead of the enemy and to be able to have a good idea what they were going do before they did it. Now here he was letting a civilian take him by surprise.

He opened his eyes to look at the woman sitting in the aisle seat next to him. She was ordinary. He took in her jeans, sneakers, and long sleeve T-shirt at a glance. Her brown hair was pulled up into a messy knot at the back of her head. She looked to be in her early thirties. She wore no rings; had very little makeup on, her nails weren't polished; she had little gold studs in each ear and was looking at him expectantly. He inwardly sighed. When he was younger Wolf loved when women hit on him, now it had gotten old. Granted, this woman didn't look like she was the type to throw herself at a man, but he'd learned that looks were deceiving when it came to what women wanted.

Glancing in her direction, Wolf thought the woman appeared to be mulling over telling him something. This in itself was fascinating, since in his experience, women tended to get right to the point of what they wanted to say. Her hesitation made him more interested in hearing what she had to say to him and he waited, patiently, as she gathered her thoughts.

Chapter Three

CAROLINE WAS NERVOUS. She wanted to talk to the over-the-top masculine man sitting next to her, but she didn't want him to look through her as most men did. Caroline had faded into the woodwork most of her life. No boyfriend in high school, she hadn't gone to any of the school dances, not even prom.

One guy had the nerve to tell her that she wasn't "girlfriend material." Thinking back to that comment, made without thought, still hurt her today. Caroline knew she wasn't model beautiful, but she didn't think she was a troll either. She wasn't tall like men seemed to want in a woman, but she wasn't short and cute either. Caroline was average from the top of her brown-haired head to the bottom of her normal sized feet.

She'd always been the "friend" growing up. All the boys liked to talk to her, but only to get Caroline's opinion on the other girls and if they liked them. It was depressing as hell, but she'd gotten used to it. When she got old enough to really care and actually want to go to dances and dates, Caroline was firmly in the "friend" category and she'd sat at home while everyone else went out and had a good time.

The media's portrayals of the "perfect woman" didn't only affect women and girls, but it did the same with men. Men all seemed to want the skinny, perky, bubbly, woman they'd seen on television and in magazines all their lives. From reality shows to news casters and even to sit-coms, today's world was bombarded with flawless women, beautiful from sun-up to sun-down.

That just wasn't Caroline. She wasn't a genius, but she also wasn't dumb. She worked hard at her job and did her part to make the world go-'round. But she often wished, when she was lying in bed late at night, that she could find a man who would *see* her. See the real her.

Caroline's parents had her late in their life, and had recently passed away. She missed them. They'd been her staunchest supporters. Whatever she wanted to do, they'd encouraged her and told her she could do it. Without her parents and no close friends to keep her there, California didn't have the appeal to Caroline that it used to.

Caroline thought about the man sitting next to her. He probably had a lot of close friends. He looked trustworthy. Caroline almost snorted at her own thoughts. How the hell could someone "look" trustworthy? It was ridiculous. Didn't all the crime shows talk about how the killer always looked like the "guy next door?"

Caroline shook herself. She had to stop her line of thought or she'd depress herself even more than she already was. Who cared if this guy didn't "see" her? She'd only be sitting next to him for a couple of hours, and then they'd go their separate ways once they landed in Virginia. Hell, she knew he didn't really take note of her. He'd already met her, and when he'd sat down he'd looked right through her as if he'd never seen her before. It happened to her all the time, over and over. She should be used to it, but it seemed to hurt more this time.

Caroline had hesitated to touch him. She didn't really want to disturb the man, but it wasn't in her nature to let him suffer in that middle seat. Because he certainly was suffering. He looked jammed into the seat. Caroline knew he'd be stiff and uncomfortable by the time they landed in Virginia if he sat there the entire flight.

Caroline jerked her hand away after he flinched. She didn't mean to startle him, and for a second thought that if he decided he wanted to strike out at her, he could really hurt her. Not that she thought he would, but anyone that reacted that quickly and suddenly certainly wasn't used to being surprised.

Now he was looking at her expectantly. She'd gotten his attention and Caroline needed to follow through. She steeled herself and gave herself a quick pep talk. She just had to say it quickly before she lost her nerve.

"Um…Do you want to switch seats?"

He didn't answer, but raised his eyebrows as if to ask why she was offering.

Geez, even his eyebrow lift was sexy. "You don't look comfortable," Caroline told him bluntly and honestly. "I'll switch with you, that way you can at least have a little bit more leg room here in the aisle."

Wolf stared at the woman. Why was she offering? He wasn't sure, but he wasn't an idiot, he wasn't going to turn down her offer. He was miserable. If she made a move on him later in the flight he'd just have to politely rebuff her. Jesus, he was cocky and conceited. He decided to think that the nondescript woman sitting next to simply wanted to do something nice for a stranger. He'd believe that until he was proved wrong. If he *was* proven wrong, he'd figure out a game plan then. Arriving at his decision, he nodded once and told her simply, "Thanks."

Standing up and allowing the man to move out of the row, Caroline scooted past him and into the middle seat. There was something very intimate about sitting in the seat while it was still warm from his body. Especially when she thought about *what* body part had just been there. Caroline tried to put that out of her mind. Sheesh. *Get your mind out of the gutter!* Caroline admonished herself.

Caroline knew he didn't need her slobbering all over him. She figured he had women throwing themselves at him all the time. After throwing out the "body builder" thought she'd had earlier, she guessed he was probably in the military. She hadn't met one "normal" man who looked like him who wasn't in the military. Especially considering they were flying from San Diego, home of the one of the biggest naval bases in the United States.

When the man leaned down to grab his backpack he'd stowed under the middle seat, Caroline stopped him.

"It's okay, just leave it. It'll give you more room for your legs."

"Are you sure?"

"Of course. Your bag isn't even really blocking my legs at all, I'm short." She chuckled at herself.

Chapter Four

WOLF LOOKED MORE closely at the woman as he got comfortable and buckled his seat belt in the aisle seat. He was grateful for the extra room she'd just granted him by allowing him to leave his bag at her feet, but he didn't understand why she'd do it.

The woman turned away from Wolf to buckle her seatbelt. It didn't seem like she was trying to flirt with him or to get him to notice her. But the fact that she wasn't, only seemed to draw his attention to her more. Maybe that was her plan all along?

Wolf wasn't a man who was used to unselfish acts by other people. He lived in a world where people were deceitful and underhanded and would do anything they could to get ahead. Hell, in certain parts of the world they'd even kill someone if it meant more power, more money, or even more food to eat. Granted, giving up a comfortable seat on a plane wasn't even in the same league as what Wolf had seen people do to gain an advantage, but that was what made it so unusual.

Caroline could feel the man's eyes on her. It discomfited her. Shifting uneasily in her seat, Caroline wasn't used to men looking at her that closely. She was plain and uninteresting. She knew it and so did everyone else. Caroline wasn't the type of person who got special favors because of her looks, and she wasn't one to draw the attention of any man. She'd long ago learned to accept it. Caroline had a pretty healthy self-esteem, even with her plain looks. She'd had a tough time growing up, what teenaged girl didn't, but when all was said and done, Caroline learned to actually like herself. She was smart, had a good personality, and even if she didn't have men lining up to take her out, she was mostly content with herself and her life.

Thinking about her childhood and her parents made Caroline smile. Her mom and dad always encouraged her to be who she was. Remembering when she told her dad what she wanted to do after she graduated from high school, Caroline's smile grew wider. Some dads would've been disappointed, but not hers. All he'd done was kiss her on the forehead and say, "You can do anything you want to do Caroline. You're the smartest woman I know and I'm very proud of you." Caroline held that memory close to her heart and drew on it when she was feeling down.

Caroline snuck a peek at the man who was now sitting in the aisle seat and blushed, yup, he was still watching her.

Wolf watched as the woman glanced at him and then blushed furiously seeing his eyes on her. When was the last time he'd seen a woman blush? He couldn't remember. It was past time they introduced themselves. He held out his hand to her. "Matthew," he said softly. Wolf hadn't been around a lot of people who didn't have any connections to the military. He usually used his nickname when introducing himself, it was such an ingrained part of him, but he didn't want to freak this woman out. Wolf wasn't exactly a normal name for someone to call themselves in the civilian world.

Hoping she'd reciprocate and shake his hand, he waited for her to give him her hand. Wolf learned a lot about people by their handshake. Many women felt as if they shouldn't squeeze a man's hand when they met, so they just let their hand lay limply in his as they shook. He hated that. Wolf had no idea where that had come from, but if women knew how much it turned men off, they'd certainly stop doing it.

Caroline tentatively took his hand, but shook it with strength. She hoped he didn't squeeze her hand too hard in an effort to show off how strong he was. He could easily crush her fingers. She'd had that happen in the past too, especially since she worked with a lot of men. They'd exert what they thought was dominance, by clenching her hand too tight. It didn't exude dominance, only assholed-ness.

"Caroline," she reciprocated softly.

Wolf squeezed her hand and was pleasantly surprised at the softness interspersed with calluses on her palm. She obviously wasn't one to sit around; she worked with her hands in some way.

Of course thinking about the texture of her palm immediately made him think about how it'd feel caressing his body. Wolf was immediately ashamed of himself. Jesus, it'd obviously been way too long since he'd been with a woman if a simple handshake made him hard. He shifted in his seat trying to hide his arousal from the slight woman innocently sitting next to him.

Caroline was also pleased at their handshake. The man didn't squeeze her fingers too hard, and seemed to lighten up a bit after they dropped their hands. She noticed he shifted restlessly, but figured he was just trying to get comfortable in the cramped airplane seat.

They smiled at each other before directing their attention to the flight attendant at the front of the plane.

Another flight attendant came over the speaker and asked that all electronic devices be turned off, or put in airplane mode, and to prepare for takeoff.

Caroline watched as the attendant in the aisle went through the motions of showing the passengers how to put on their seatbelt, how to use the lifejacket in case of a water landing, and how to operate the flimsy oxygen thingies that would fall from the ceiling of the plane in case of depressurization. Caroline didn't want to think of the panic that would ensue in the plane if any of those things actually happened.

Caroline noticed that the flight attendant seemed extra bored. She figured giving the same demonstration to a plane full of people who were ignoring you could get old really fast, but wasn't it their job to at least *pretend* to have enthusiasm while doing it? She'd seen the video clips online of flight attendants who joked and danced, she'd never been on a flight with one who had done that, but these guys actually looked annoyed and uninterested about the entire pre-flight routine. It was weird.

Caroline mentally shrugged, it wasn't as if she could do anything about it, and turned her attention to the *SkyMall* magazine in the seat pocket in front of her. She idly flipped the pages, looking at the overpriced items as the plane taxied to the runway and took off.

After safely reaching cruising altitude, Caroline put the magazine back into the pocket in front of her and rested her head on the seatback, much as Matthew had done when he'd first sat down. She was tired, but the middle seat wasn't conducive to sleeping with nothing to rest her head against and there was no way she'd risk falling asleep with her head tilted back on the seat. She'd probably snore like an eighty year old man if she did. Even if the sexy man next to her wasn't interested, she still didn't want to embarrass herself. She had *some* standards after all.

Caroline looked over at Matthew and saw he also wasn't sleeping. He had one leg stretched out into the aisle and one under the seat in front of him. His eyes were closed and his hands were intertwined, resting on his stomach. Every now and then he'd shift in his seat, open his eyes, and close them again. She smiled. At least in the aisle seat he was more comfortable than if he'd been scrunched in the middle.

Wolf opened his eyes with a sigh; there was no way he was sleeping. Airplane seats sucked, another reason to not to fly commercial. Not knowing why he couldn't keep his eyes off of her, Wolf glanced over at the woman sitting next to him again, and caught Caroline's smile which lit up her whole face. Wolf thought that while she wasn't conventionally pretty, she was certainly interesting looking.

"So, you come here often?" He couldn't resist the cheesy pickup line. Something told him Caroline would think it was funny and not take him seriously. Hearing her soft laugh, Wolf knew he was right.

"Ha-ha. Actually, I don't fly too often, but I'm currently on my way to a new job in Norfolk. Normally I'd drive, but my new company is paying all my moving expenses, including shipping my car out to Virginia, so I figured instead of taking the extra days to drive cross country, I'd just fly and take the extra time to get to know Norfolk before I have to start work."

"Sounds sensible." Wolf agreed, happy to hear she seemed like a reasonable woman. He'd met too many women that were all about the money, or fame, or fashion, or whatever.

"What are you doing in Norfolk? Or is that just a stop-over to somewhere else?" Caroline asked curiously. She wasn't trying to pry, but since he was talking to her and seemed interested in what she had to say, she wanted to keep the conversation going.

Wolf knew he had to be careful about talking about his job, but he figured since they weren't on their way to a mission right now he could be mostly upfront. "I and two buddies are headed for some leave in Virginia. We're between missions...er...jobs right now."

"I figured you were military." Caroline told him matter-of-factly with no surprise or awe in her voice.

"How'd you guess?"

Caroline couldn't tell if he was being serious or just kidding with her. "I don't know if that was sarcasm or not, but I noticed you're very much in shape, you have combat boots on, and honestly, you just have the look of a military man."

Wolf laughed. "I was teasing you Caroline, but yeah, you're right. I'm in the Navy. I'm a SEAL." Wolf was surprised at himself. He didn't usually blurt out that he was a SEAL. There was something about this woman that invited confidences. He wasn't sure what to expect from her with his revelation, but was honestly surprised when she didn't say anything about it and continued their conversation as if Wolf never mentioned he was a member of one of the most revered and respected branches of their country's military.

"What are you going to do on your leave?"

"We have a friend who lives out there. He was medically retired after losing a leg in combat. We're just going to crash at his house and hang out. We'll probably go to the base and check it out, but we all decided we needed the down time and try to keep the shop talk to a minimum."

"Oh geez, that sucks about your friend. I'm so sorry. I'm so glad people today recognize what you guys do for our country. I knew someone in high school that told me when her dad came home from Vietnam he was spit on and generally treated like crap. It's such a shame and I love seeing the support all our country's soldiers get today. I think it's a good idea for you and your friends to take some time off and for you to try to keep talk about your job out of it," Caroline agreed. "It can be tough to really relax if all you do on a vacation is talk shop."

Enjoying the conversation more than he'd thought he would, Wolf asked, "So, what is this new job you're flying across the country for?"

Pleased he was showing interest in her, Caroline told him, hoping it wouldn't turn him off—some men didn't like smart women. "I'm a chemist. I decided I needed a change of scenery since my parents passed away. I researched where I wanted to work and applied for, and was hired, by a great company out east. I'm pretty excited to get started actually."

"So what does a chemist do exactly?" Wolf was impressed with what he'd heard so far.

Caroline laughed lightly. She wasn't exactly surprised at the question. It seemed like most people had no idea what she did most of the time, even when she explained it she could see their eyes glaze over.

Well, he'd asked, so she decided to tell him. She was enjoying talking to him and he seemed pretty smart. She had high hopes he'd understand.

"There are two basic 'worlds' when it comes to chemists. A macroscopic world in chemistry is the one that you'd probably think of when thinking of a chemist. It involves a lab and white coats and experimenting with different compounds and materials. You can actually see, hear, and touch things in the macroscopic world. On the other hand is the microscopic world. This involves things you can't actually touch or hear or see. It basically deals with models and theories mostly."

"Which do you work in?" Wolf asked, seemingly following her conversation without any issues.

"I'm a card carrying, lab coat wearing, chemist geek," Caroline answered laughing at herself.

Wolf didn't think, but reached over and took her hand in his. "You're not a geek sweetheart; you're a scholar in a lab coat who does magic with her hands."

Holy crap. This man was lethal. Caroline's stomach clenched at his words. Had any man, ever, said anything nicer to her than that? She didn't think so. She tried to blow off his words and airily joked, "Actually I have a wand that does the magic."

"Tell me more about your job. It sounds really interesting." Sensing Caroline's reluctance, Wolf begged, "Please?"

Embarrassed, but not sure why, Caroline hesitantly told him more. "I'm in applied chemistry; I work for a company and do short term research on whatever is on my plate at the time. It could be product development or improvement to something that's already out there. There are also pure chemists who do more long term research on whatever they want or can get funded and there's no real practical application in the short term with them."

"So what do you do all day at work?" Wolf found Caroline fascinating. He'd never met a chemist before. Oh sure, Wolf met people who were good at chemistry and had a knack for things like making bombs for the military, as well as defusing them, like Dude. But being a bomb ordinance technician wasn't the same thing as being a chemist. It wasn't like Wolf came in contact with someone like Caroline in his regular world.

"Well, it depends on the day and the project, of course," she told him, losing her self-consciousness since she was talking about a topic she loved. Caroline had no idea her enthusiasm made her prettier and that Wolf thought her excitement was a turn on.

"Sometimes I analyze substances, trying to figure out what's in it, how much of something is in it, or both. I can create substances too. Sometimes we make synthetic substances, trying to copy something that's in nature, and other times we work from scratch to create something new. And, sometimes I have to do boring things, like test theories."

They both laughed, Wolf knew she was probably never bored. The flush on Caroline's face as she spoke about what she loved was sexy as hell. Wolf couldn't believe he'd ever thought this woman plain.

It was during a lull in their conversation they both heard the man sitting by the window snort in his sleep. Caroline put her hand over her mouth to keep from laughing too loud and waking him up. She couldn't contain her giggles though and loved sharing a laugh with the big bad SEAL sitting next to her.

Caroline was pleasantly surprised with the conversation with Matthew, who was even more appealing now. Too many times good looking men thought they were God's gift to women and acted that way as well. She'd met some SEALs when she lived in California that were obnoxious because they thought every woman should be throwing themselves at them.

Matthew was interesting and he'd actually listened when she

talked. God, she had to get herself together. They were two strangers on a plane. Once they landed in Norfolk they'd go their separate ways and never see each other again. He was just being polite. It was disappointing, but it was just the way it was.

Continuing to talk while waiting patiently for the flight attendant to come by their row with their complementary drinks, Wolf and Caroline shared how they were both sad to leave the nice weather of San Diego—Caroline for good, and Wolf for whatever time he'd be on his new mission.

Finally the flight attendant made it to their row. Caroline was thirsty and was glad to see the drink cart. The attendant still seemed to be a bit sullen and didn't engage people in conversation. Asking the people in the row ahead of them what they wanted to drink and silently serving them, he did the same when he got to their row. The man next to the window had woken up and asked for vodka on the rocks. Caroline ordered a diet soda and Wolf requested an orange juice. Each was given a cup filled to the brim with ice and their drinks, while the flight attendant moved past them to continue serving the rest of the plane.

Caroline poured her drink into the cup and lifted it to take a sip. Suddenly, she stopped. What the hell? She brought the cup to her nose and inhaled deeply. Quickly placing it back on her tray, Caroline saw Matthew was about to drink from his plastic cup. Without thinking how intimate or odd it might seem, Caroline reached over, grabbed the top of Wolf's cup and lowered it to the small tray in front of him.

Chapter Five

W OLF TWISTED IN surprise as Caroline lowered his drink to the tray. What the hell was she doing? He'd thought they were getting along, but damn, he didn't really know her well enough for her to be touching his drink and invading his personal space like that.

He looked over at her, ready to question her, and was surprised to see she was quite pale.

"Don't...," was all she said at first. Wolf could tell Caroline was trying to get her thoughts together.

Wolf's senses went on alert. Whatever was going on had this woman on edge. Feeling bad about thinking she was overstepping her bounds a second ago, Wolf looked at Caroline more closely and saw goose bumps up and down her arms. Shit. Whatever she was thinking was serious.

Matthew gave her the time she needed to gather her thoughts, which Caroline appreciated. Without him asking again what was wrong, Caroline leaned close to him and cautioned in a soft urgent voice, "Something's wrong with the ice. I can smell it. It smells off, like something's in it."

Wolf picked up his drink again and raised it to his face. He could see Caroline wanted to stop him, but she didn't. Pretending to take a sip he smelled it as she had... nothing. He couldn't detect anything but the orange juice that was in the cup. He looked at her and said softly, "I don't smell anything."

Caroline was frustrated. She could tell Matthew wanted to believe her, but when he hadn't noticed anything off about his drink, he was having a hard time. She looked away. Great, now he thought she was nuts. But she wasn't. She was a chemist dammit, and this is what she did for a living. There was some other chemical in with the drink, she knew it. But how would she convince him without sounding crazy?

She turned back to Matthew, only to see him still looking at her.

"What is it?" he demanded softly. "Explain, so I can understand."

Caroline's respect for Matthew rose. He wasn't sure he should believe what she was saying, but he was smart enough to give her time to convince him, and she knew she'd have to explain it in a way he could understand.

Caroline knew she had to get through to him and did her best to convince him she knew what she was talking about. Lowering her voice even further so the people around them wouldn't hear her, she leaned into him and looked him in the eyes as she spoke. "I don't know, but as a chemist I'm trained to pick up on the different chemical smells of compounds. I don't know what it is, but it's not natural."

"Is it in mine too?" he asked her just as softly, passing his cup over to her.

She sniffed it and immediately nodded.

"Shit," Wolf said under his breath. He believed her. He wasn't a person to trust easily, but this woman didn't have any guile in her at all. She'd have no reason to lie to him. Caroline had too much pride as a chemist to pretend something was wrong, he could tell that just from talking to her for the last hour. Besides he couldn't think of what she'd get out of it even if she was lying, and she was obviously freaked the hell out.

His next thought was what the hell was going on with the plane? If Caroline was right, who was trying to drug the passengers on the plane? Who was in on it? Was it all the passengers or just him and Caroline? Was he targeted? Were Mozart and Abe targeted too? He thought about his teammates for the first time after he'd started talking with Caroline. How far back was the flight attendant with the drink cart? Had they drunk anything yet? Shit, he had to warn them.

Leaning in to avoid the possibility of being overheard, Wolf whispered, "Stay seated. I need to warn my men."

Caroline watched as Matthew put his drink on her tray and secured his tray back into the seat back. She didn't ask any questions as he stood up and reached into the overhead bin. He reached for his bag, took his time looking through the small duffle he'd placed up there, then latched the compartment and sat down again.

Wolf felt a bit better after settling back into his seat. He'd signaled to Mozart and Abe that there was danger and not to eat. They'd come up with the signal after being holed up while on a nasty mission and found that the food they were being served was drugged. His men would know something was up, but how to get word to them for sure?

Caroline was watching him closely. Could he use her? No, not use her, but have her help him? He hadn't refastened his seatbelt, so he turned in his seat so he was angled toward Caroline. He took one of her hands into his own, absently rubbing his thumb over the back of her hand as he thought about how he wanted to approach her with his plan. Finally he sighed and looked into her eyes. Caroline was watching him intently. Her big brown eyes were wide and slightly dilated. Her grip on his hand told him she was more scared than she looked.

Wolf's protective side was fighting to come out. He felt and could see the quivers taking over her body. He wanted to stuff her under the seat and tell her not to come out until they were on the ground safe and sound, but he also, unfortunately, knew that wasn't an option. He needed her.

"Caroline, I need your help," he admitted to her softly. He watched as she nodded immediately. Jesus, she didn't even ask what he needed help with, just immediately agreed. He felt something inside shift, but wrestled it down. Now wasn't the time.

"My men are seated in seats 18C and 24D. I need to tell them what's going on, but since we don't know what's really up or who's involved I need to keep it quiet. Will you help me?"

"Of course, Matthew," Caroline told him, her voice only shaking a little. "Although I'm not sure what I can do. I'm just a civilian…"

Wolf squeezed the hand he was still holding, "That's why this'll work. No one will think twice about you walking in the aisles. If I suddenly got up and went back to talk to my teammates, I would definitely be noticed. I'm going to write a short note, if you get up and go to the restroom in the back of the plane, you can pass it to Mozart, who's in 18C."

"Mozart?" was Caroline's comment.

Wolf smiled a bit, chuckling inside that in the middle of a serious scary situation, Caroline still had the presence of mind to question Mozart's name.

He explained quickly, "It's his nickname, we all have one."

Caroline nodded, she wanted to know what his nickname was, but knew this wasn't the time or the place. Maybe someday she'd pluck up the courage to ask him about it…if they got out of this…whatever *this* was. Remembering there were two of his friends on the plane she questioned, "What about your friend in row twenty-four?"

Wolf put his other hand over where their hands were still clutched together. "When you pass him, grab his shoulder instead of the seat and press your second and fourth fingers down hard." He demonstrated on the back of her hand he was holding. "He'll know what it means."

Wolf expected Caroline to ask what the gesture meant, but she didn't. She only nodded her head and demonstrated the hand signal back to him. "Like this?" she asked.

Wolf nodded with approval and couldn't help himself. He lifted her hand that was still clutched tightly in his own and kissed the back of it, holding his lips there for a moment longer than was socially acceptable, before letting go.

"That's all you need to do, then come right back here after you go into the restroom," he told her seriously, looking into her eyes, willing her to understand the danger she was in, that they were all in. "Don't try to be a hero. If something goes wrong, don't worry about it. Just continue on as normally as you can. Don't bring any undue attention to yourself. My guys know something is up and will look out for you. They can see you're sitting next to me so when you get up they'll be on alert. Do you have any questions?"

Caroline shook her head. She was nervous, but she could do this. She wanted to sit and digest the kiss Matthew had planted on the tender skin on the back of her hand, but she didn't have time. She knew if she *did* have the time, she'd probably overanalyze it, and besides she had to concentrate on not chickening out of what Matthew needed her to do.

Matthew quickly scribbled on a piece of napkin. His writing just looked like gibberish to Caroline, so she knew it was in code, but it didn't really matter. She knew he'd probably summed up the situation in a way his friends would be on alert and would be ready to do...whatever. Hopefully it made sense to the man in row eighteen. His other friend wasn't getting an actual paper message, but hopefully whatever pressing her fingers into his shoulder meant, he'd understand. There were so many "hopefullys" in what she was about to do, but they had no other choice. Matthew tucked the napkin into her hand and squeezed it closed gently.

"You can do this, Caroline," Wolf whispered.

It was time. Caroline stood up and flattened herself as much as she could to squeak past Matthew. He didn't want to get up again and bring too much attention to himself. She felt his hand on her waist as she squeezed by. The heat from his hand was intense, but she tried to ignore it. But holy hell, if they were anywhere other than here, in this particular situation, she knew she'd be a complete mess. As much as she wished Matthew was touching her in a sexual way, he was just trying to be reassuring; he wasn't putting the moves on her. She had to force her brain to concentrate though. It just wanted to replay his hands on her body.

18C, 18C, Caroline repeated to herself as she made her way down the aisle toward the back of the plane. She vaguely noticed the other passengers enjoying their free drinks without a care in the world. Caroline had no idea if their drinks were drugged as well, but she had a bad feeling they probably were. She had to make sure she delivered the note to the right person. The last thing she needed was to trip into the wrong person and have someone get the napkin with the weird code. She looked at the seat numbers as she passed them, concentrating hard on making sure she didn't screw up.

She knew right off who Mozart was. She shouldn't have worried about counting the rows. He looked as big and hard as Matthew. Just as she got near him she "tripped," and reached out with her hands to stop her fall, right into Mozart.

"I'm so sorry," she cried out apologetically as she extricated herself from his arms, taking her hands off of his chest where they'd landed. "I'm so clumsy!"

The man simply nodded and helped her right herself. He didn't actually say anything to her, and Caroline found herself blushing, as if she hadn't fallen into him on purpose. She had to get herself together. Sheesh. These sexy men were going to be the death of her.

She straightened, brushed herself off, and continued on her way to the restroom. She took a deep breath. One message delivered, one to go. She'd pressed the note into Mozart's chest when she fell, and she'd felt him grab it when he'd steadied her. She wanted to laugh; it seemed she was pretty good at this cloak and dagger stuff.

Caroline figured she might as well actually use the restroom while she was in the back of the plane. Who knew when she might get another chance with whatever was happening. The practical side of her mind never turned off. She arrived at the restroom in the back just as the flight attendants were finishing up the drink service. Squeezing past the guy who'd served their drinks with an apologetic smile, Caroline closed the restroom door, quickly got down to business, and washed her hands once she was done.

Just as she was going to leave the bathroom, Caroline heard two men talking right outside the door. She paled after hearing their conversation and waited until they'd moved away. Jesus. They were pretty dumb talking about their plan like that where people could overhear them. Caroline supposed they figured soon everyone would be passed out, so it didn't matter. She had to get back to Matthew and tell him what she'd overheard. Crap.

She left the bathroom and didn't look back at the galley; she just walked back toward the front of the plane, grabbing the seatbacks as she went down the plane. When she got to row twenty-four, without missing a beat, she nonchalantly grabbed the shoulder of the man sitting in the aisle seat with her right hand as she walked by, then continued up to her seat. Matthew was waiting and again, assisted her to her seat with a hand on her waist, looking at her questioningly. Caroline nodded once and sunk heavily into her chair. She reached for her seatbelt, but Matthew stopped her.

"Leave it off, just in case," he told her. Caroline nodded again. Crap, she should've thought about that. She wasn't thinking straight. She had to get herself together.

"Matthew," she stated urgently, "before I left the restroom I heard two of the flight attendants talking. They said everything was in place and as soon as the passengers were out, they'd start."

Chapter Six

WOLF DIDN'T SAY anything, just grabbed Caroline's hand, squeezed it and settled it on his leg. Holy crap, what had they landed in the middle of? He absentmindedly rubbed his thumb over the back of her hand while he thought about what the hell was going on.

He felt better knowing Mozart and Abe were alert and ready. Thank God they were on this flight with him. They had very little chance of breaking up whatever was going on here, but at least with all three of them they at least *had* a slim one. He was keyed up and ready to go, to do *something*, but they didn't know who the players were yet.

Obviously two of the flight attendants were in on whatever it was since Caroline had overheard them talking about their plan, but who else? They had to sit and wait and see. He hated that. Wolf thought about 9/11 and wondered if the people on the planes that had been crashed into the World Trade Center had known something was wrong. It was a helpless feeling. The passengers on the plane that had crashed that day in Pennsylvania obviously did what they could to prevent the plane from crashing into the White House, but unfortunately lost their lives in the process.

Wolf didn't want to die, but he knew he could at any time. His job wasn't the safest. Ironically, he was supposed to be on vacation and he was in just as much danger as he was when he was on a mission. It was crazy.

Wolf turned toward Caroline.

"You were amazing," whispered Wolf. "You pulled that off even though you were scared and you didn't bring attention back to yourself or me."

Caroline didn't respond with more than a quick smile. Wolf knew he wouldn't have been able to pull off what she did and not bring attention to himself. Hell, he wouldn't even *know* he was in the middle of a situation if it hadn't been for her. He hated she was going through this, and loathed even more the thought of her not making it through whatever was going on.

Wolf thought more about the situation and was aware the plane had gone pretty quiet. Oh, it hadn't been loud to begin with, but it was obvious what little conversation there had been, had dwindled off. He moved his head a fraction of an inch and saw the three people in the seats across from him had their eyes closed and were sleeping…or worse. He had no idea if they were unconscious, sleeping or even dead.

Just as he was about to tell Caroline they had to lay low and see what was going to happen next, she surprised him by beating him to it.

"Matthew, we have to pretend to have finished our drinks and that it affected us just like everyone else." She'd obviously noticed the other passengers' stillness as well.

Wolf nodded. "I was thinking the same thing. Great minds think alike." He watched as she blushed. She constantly amazed him. The women he'd known in his life didn't blush at a simple backhanded compliment. He thought it was a shame he didn't have the time at the moment to see what other compliments he could give her, just to watch her face light up in the charming blush that was currently covering her cheeks. He tamped down the thought of just how far down that blush went. Wrong time, wrong place, but God he wanted to know.

Caroline took her hand out of his reluctantly, and laid her head back on the head rest. She didn't dare open her eyes to try to see what was going on. They had to pretend to be just as unconscious as the other passengers. She knew Matthew had also tipped his head back and closed his eyes. They just had to wait.

Caroline hated waiting. She was terrible at it. She always got antsy. Her mom always teased her about not being able to sit still for even five minutes when she was little. She was always on the go. Caroline smiled internally at the memory of a story her mom loved to tell guests about when Caroline was about four years old. They'd been at an amusement park and there were long lines for everything; the food, the rides, and of course, the bathroom.

Apparently Caroline had had enough of waiting in the lines, and when they were waiting to use the restroom she'd gone right over to the grass alongside the building and pulled down her pants and peed right there. Caroline's mom was mortified, but everyone else around them had thought it was hysterical.

Caroline thought sadly of her mom. She missed her. So many times in the last year she'd wanted to pick up the phone just to talk. She'd known she would lose her parents far too early in her life, they were older, after all; but it was harder than she thought it'd be.

Pulled from her thoughts by Matthew shifting in his seat, Caroline admitted she was scared. Scared of what was going on and she had no idea how they'd get out of it. It couldn't be good to be trapped in a plane thousands of feet above the ground with people hell-bent on causing trouble. What that trouble was, remained to be seen.

Caroline thought about how glad she was Matthew was sitting next to her. At first she'd been apprehensive; he was a big man after all. But the gentle way he'd held her hand and how he'd immediately taken action to warn his teammates made her feel so much better. She had no idea if he and his buddies would be able to get them out of this, whatever *this* was, but just the fact he was here, made her feel not quite so lonely. She had no idea what she would've done if he hadn't been there. She would've noticed the smell of the ice, but wouldn't have known what to do and would've just had to have sat there, helpless. She shivered a little bit. God. This really sucked.

Thirty long minutes after they'd agreed to act passed out, the terrorists made their move. Almost all of the passengers sat in their seats not moving, either passed out or more. Wolf couldn't waste time thinking about them now. He thanked God for Caroline smelling whatever was in the ice. He shuddered to think about what would've happened if he hadn't been sitting next to her. Actually he knew what would've happened, he and Mozart and Abe would be passed out in their seats, just like all the other people around him now.

Wolf watched as two passengers and the two flight attendants passed by their row of seats and walked toward the front of the plane. He closed his eyes as the two of them then walked back through the plane, examining the passengers, making sure they were all unconscious. Wolf heard them talking quietly as they passed by him.

"Does Smythe have the coordinates?"

"Yeah, as soon as we contain the passengers that are awake, he'll go and take care of the pilots and put us on course."

Wolf tensed. Shit.

The few people the terrorists found awake, they made get up and go to the back of the plane to the galley. Wolf heard some women scream and cry, and grunting from of some of the men, but mostly it was a quiet operation. Eerily quiet. In all the battles and missions he'd been in, Wolf had never heard anything like it. Usually people were screaming and crying and there were the loud sounds of gunfire and mortars going off—not this silence and complete compliance from the passengers. It unnerved him, and with his history, that was saying a lot.

He kept his eyes opened only in slits, and watched as one of the terrorists, who'd been posing as a normal passenger, and one of the flight attendants made their way into the cockpit. It was easy since one of the flight attendants simply knocked on the door and requested to talk to the pilot. Since he had no reason to be alarmed, the co-pilot opened it without hesitation. He was immediately beaten bloody while the pilot was killed outright. It wasn't hard, just a quick slice to the jugular. His body was dragged out of the cockpit and thrown into the galley at the front of the plane—still jerking and bleeding out. The co-pilot was alive, but badly hurt. The other flight attendant calmly hefted up one of his legs and callously dragged him to the back of the plane with the other alert passengers.

Wolf's heart rate sped up in preparation for the fight to come. He had to be careful, as one of the terrorists was now at the controls of the plane. He'd been trained by the Navy the basics of flying almost any type of aircraft. He was most comfortable behind the stick of a helicopter, but he'd also spent some time in a big commercial plane like this one. He knew since he was closest to the cockpit, it'd be up to him to get up there and gain control of the airplane.

Mozart and Abe could also fly the plane, but Wolf would rely on them to take care of the other terrorists. He'd have his hands full as it was. He sincerely hoped none of the other passengers were hurt in the process of taking back over the plane, but he couldn't think about that now. His one and only goal was getting back control of the plane.

Wolf knew he had to get going, but for the first time as a SEAL he hesitated. He didn't want Caroline anywhere near what was about to go down, but he had no choice in the matter. He surreptitiously moved his hand and placed it on her thigh and squeezed, feeling her muscles clench under his palm. Caroline's hand came over slowly where it had been resting in her lap and covered his. They sat like that for a moment, both feeling better after the short, but intense contact. Wolf knew it was time to go. He couldn't wait anymore, all their lives depended on it. He turned his hand over so he could grasp Caroline's hand in his and gave it one hard squeeze. Seeing Caroline's small smile, she mouthed, "Good luck." Wolf immediately let go and took a deep breath. It was time.

Without looking around or saying another word, Wolf sprang from his seat and toward the front of the plane. In full battle mode, he blanked all extraneous thoughts out of his head, including the courageous woman he'd left sitting in his row. As he ran toward the front of the plane, Wolf heard a cry and managed a quick look back to see what the situation was.

Mozart and Abe were fighting with two of the terrorists at the back of the plane, but the third was headed right toward him. The look on his face was pure hatred. Shit. Wolf didn't have time to deal with him and make sure the fourth didn't crash the plane. For a second he hoped the guy now piloting the plane didn't know what was going on, but when he felt the plane lurch downward, he knew that thought was futile. Wolf had no choice but to continue toward the pilot. He'd deal with the guy coming up the aisle at him when he had to, which unfortunately might be sooner rather than later.

Wolf watched in amazement as suddenly a leg shot out from a row of seats and tripped the man coming toward him. Caroline! He turned around and ran full force toward the cockpit. Dammit. He wanted to go back to Caroline, but he couldn't stop now. He was scared for her, which was unheard of for Wolf to lose focus as he had, but there was nothing he could do for her now. He had to get control of the plane or they'd all be dead. Her actions just might give him enough time to subdue the man flying the plane before the other terrorist caught up to him.

Chapter Seven

CAROLINE COULDN'T BELIEVE she'd just tripped a terrorist. A freakin' terrorist! She was scared out of her mind. She'd sat next to Matthew and knew he was about to make his move. She could almost feel the tension in his body, the anticipation, the adrenaline being produced in his bloodstream. She wanted to beg him not to go, to stay with her and just let whatever was going to happen, happen. But he was a SEAL. She knew he wouldn't just sit around and let terrorists take over the plane. He'd be in the thick of it. Hell, he and his team would be the only reason any of them lived through this nightmare, *if* they lived through it.

When he put his hand on her thigh, she knew it was time. She couldn't have stopped herself from reaching out to Matthew at that moment if someone paid her a million dollars. She didn't know if she'd ever see him again, but somehow in the couple of hours they'd spent getting to know each other he'd become important to her. All she could do was smile and mouth to him "good luck"—how cliché. It was stupid. She was just another woman to him. Just one more woman who thought he was gorgeous and who wanted to take him home and spend hours in his bed getting to "know" him. Caroline hadn't admitted it until just now, but yes, she wanted him in the worst way. God, it was so inappropriate and it wasn't going to happen, but that didn't stop her from wanting him.

She didn't know what to do to help, she desperately wanted to do *something*, but she was just a chemist, not a kick-butt SEAL. Caroline watched as Matthew sprung up from his seat. A relaxed sleeping man one second and a raw on-a-mission SEAL the next. He leaped for the front of the plane and Caroline peeked back between the seats to see that Matthew's teammates were busy with two bad guys in the back of the plane. They'd clearly jumped into action right after Matthew had. Obviously Matthew was going up to the cockpit to deal with the terrorist flying the plane.

That left one bad guy unaccounted for. She watched in horror as he came running up the aisle of the plane, headed right toward Matthew. Caroline felt the plane tip down. Her heartbeat tripled. Crap. Crap. Crap. The guy flying was trying to crash the plane. Matthew was about to have to deal with two terrorists, she knew he needed all his concentration to take control of the plane so they didn't die.

Without thinking she slipped over to the aisle seat and when the terrorist was about to run by, she simply stuck out her leg. Damn, that hurt her more than she thought it would. She saw people trip people all the time on TV and in the movies, she had no idea that it'd hurt as much as it did.

The guy went down like a sack of flour. He landed hard on his hands and knees but Caroline knew he wasn't going to stay down for long, so without thinking about the consequences, she leaped out of her seat and latched onto his back. She just had to keep him busy until one of Matthew's teammates could come and help. At least she hoped one of the other guys would come up and help her soon...

Just as Caroline thought she had a good grip on the man, he flipped her over his head into the aisle and scrambled over her until he was on top of her and they were face to face. It'd all happened so quickly she didn't have time to get up or to avoid him.

Shit, Caroline thought looking up at the man. He was pissed, but she was pissed too. The bastard was trying to kill all of them. Caroline flinched away as his fist came toward her face. He managed to hit her in the side of the head, but it would've hurt a lot more if he'd actually made contact with her face. She threw her knee up as hard as she could, and managed to knee him in the thigh. Not where she was aiming, but it slowed him down a bit.

Caroline continued to struggle with the man, each trying to hit and scratch and gain the upper hand. The terrorist out-weighed and out-muscled her, but she didn't let it stop her. She fought like a wildcat. She had adrenaline on her side and a strong wish not to die as well.

Caroline scratched and struck out with her hands and knees and feet. Just as the guy thought he had the upper hand, she'd squirm out of his hold and get in a lucky strike. He was also getting his licks in as well, unfortunately. Caroline wasn't feeling too much pain now, she supposed the adrenaline was preventing any true pain from getting through to her panicked brain, but later she knew she'd hurt...if she had a later.

Any time now someone would come and help her...Caroline had to believe that. Suddenly the weight of the man on top of her lifted and Caroline saw the evil look in his eyes just as a knife cut through his neck. Caroline had to close her eyes as blood spurted out and splattered her chest and arms. It was warm and smelled coppery. Caroline supposed she should've been more freaked out, but she was just so thankful to be alive and to have prevented this man from getting to Matthew. Thank God one of his teammates had finally come to her rescue.

Caroline watched as the man Matthew called Mozart, yanked the man off her, practically threw the now-dead terrorist behind him into the aisle, and leapt over her toward the cockpit. He'd completely ignored her, but Caroline didn't care. She was just glad Matthew would have some help if he needed it. There was no time for introductions or questions in the middle of a terrorist attack. She vaguely heard some of the women in the back of the plane crying hysterically, and knew she had to get up off the floor. If nothing else, the aisle had to be cleared.

Caroline sat up slowly, only then realizing her side hurt. Well, actually, everything hurt, but her side *really* hurt. Caroline looked up and knew now wasn't the time to dwell on it. The women in the back of the plane were hysterical, Matthew's other teammate, from row twenty-four, was trying to calm the passengers in the back. She could see the two terrorists the SEALs had been fighting, lying dead in the back of the plane. Well, she just assumed they were dead. All she could see of the one dead guy was his feet sticking out into the aisle. He'd been partially dragged into one of the rows of seats. The other lay in the middle of the aisle, much as the dead guy she'd been fighting now was.

The entire scene was surreal. If she wasn't in the middle of it, she'd think it was all a bad dream. All around her the other passengers were either passed out or dead from whatever was in the ice. Other than the women in the back crying, it was creepily quiet. She looked toward the front of the plane; she could see Matthew and Mozart in the cockpit. The door laid smashed open on its hinges; Matthew must've broken it in order to get to the cockpit and the terrorist. Another man lay motionless outside the door, obviously the terrorist who'd been flying the plane. His head was turned toward her, his eyes blankly staring.

Caroline turned her attention away from the eerie stare of the dead man, only to have her eyes wander to the dead body next to her in the aisle. His blood was flowing out of the knife wound to his neck and slowly soaking into the cheap carpet underneath him. Caroline could see the puddle growing bigger with each second that passed.

Caroline slowly pushed herself off the floor, ignoring her aches and pains. She tried to ignore the blood on herself from the terrorist that Mozart had killed. Surprisingly she wasn't freaking out. She had no idea why. She *should* be, but she didn't want to be a nuisance to

Matthew and his team. It was vain of her, but she wanted them to think well of her.

Before Caroline could talk herself out of it, she leaned down and grabbed the man that had been trying to kill Matthew, and then her, by his ankles and slowly dragged him to the front of the plane. He was heavy, and it was harder than she thought it'd be to drag him. She watched, in a fog, as the blood oozing from his neck stained the aisle red as she drug him past the airline rows. She brought him into the galley and draped him over the other man that was already there. She had to get him out of aisle so when they did land, medical personnel could get through to the passengers.

After she'd completed that, she wasn't sure what else she should do. She heard Matthew saying her name from the cockpit. Caroline was still seeing and hearing everything as though she was in a long tunnel...she stuck her head into the cockpit.

"Are you all right?" she heard Matthew ask urgently.

Caroline just nodded numbly.

"Is any of that blood yours?"

Caroline shook her head at the question. She didn't really understand what he was asking, but just shook her head anyway.

"Is the co-pilot okay?"

"Uh, I'm sorry Matthew, I don't know." Caroline could barely string two sentences together. She hadn't even thought about checking on the copilot. Duh, she should have.

In a soft voice meant to soothe, Wolf asked, "Can you go back to check and see if he's in good enough shape to come up here and help?"

Caroline didn't look at Mozart, who was currently sitting in the co-pilot's seat and simply nodded. She spun around to go to the back of the plane, not seeing the concerned look on Matthew's face as she turned away and went to find the injured co-pilot. All she could think over and over was *Matthew needs the co-pilot, Matthew needs the* *co-pilot, Matthew needs the co-pilot...*she kept repeating it to herself so she wouldn't forget.

When she got to the back of the plane, the other SEAL turned towards her. Caroline couldn't remember if Matthew had told her his name, it was enough that she remembered her errand.

"Matthew needs the co-pilot," she said woodenly to the man. Caroline had no idea if she was making any sense, but he must have understood her because he nodded and turned toward the people huddled in the back of the plane. Caroline didn't know what to do, and eventually just headed back to her seat.

She was scared and the adrenaline she'd been operating on for the last thirty minutes was wearing off. Caroline took the unused napkins from their drinks that they'd stuffed into the pockets in front of their seats and tried to wipe some of the blood off her shirt and arms. She was impressed with her clean up job, thinking she'd been surprisingly successful. As she watched, the co-pilot unsteadily made his way back up toward the cockpit. Mozart came out of the small space not long after and headed back toward his teammate in the back of the plane. On his way through, he noticed her and stopped.

"Are you sure you're all right ma'am?" Mozart asked politely.

"Yes, thank you," she replied not elaborating or looking up from her continued attempt at cleaning the blood off of herself. She just didn't have it in her at the moment.

Mozart paused a moment and stared hard at her. Sensing he hadn't left, Caroline finally looked up and stared right back. What did he want her to say? That she wasn't fine? That she was hurting and scared and wanted *off* this stupid plane? Even though it was all true, none of that would be helpful at the moment, so she kept quiet. She was hanging on by the thinnest thread, willing herself not to freak out. Finally Mozart nodded and continued down the aisle.

Caroline sat in the aisle seat in her row with her feet on the seat and her arms wrapped around her legs. Feeling rebellious, she'd refused to put on her seat belt. If she lived through a damn terrorist attack, she could take the risk of sitting unbelted. She knew it was ridiculous to feel like she had to sit in her assigned seat, it wasn't as if anyone would care where she sat, and most of the other seats still had people in them. She would've sat back in her seat in the middle, but couldn't stand to sit next to the guy at the window. He was slumped over. She could see his chest rising and falling, so she was glad for that. It would be horrifying if all the people all around them were all dead. On the other hand, she was glad they hadn't been conscious for everything that had happened. If the reactions from the few people in the back of the plane were anything to go by, it wouldn't have been a good scene. It would've been a lot harder to deal with everything if there had been hundreds of hysterical and panicking people.

The next thirty minutes were some of the longest in Caroline's life. Somehow they felt longer than when they'd been waiting for the terrorists to make their move. Maybe they felt longer because she didn't have Matthew sitting next to her? He made her feel safe and feel like nothing could hurt her. Now she just felt disconnected and shell-shocked.

Feeling the plane start to descend, Caroline knew they weren't in Norfolk yet, not enough time had gone by, so they must be making an emergency landing somewhere. She looked around again, most of the passengers still hadn't moved. Not able to help herself, and having to know one way or another, Caroline lifted her hand, leaned over and checked the man's pulse sitting by the window. He still had one, although it was faint and weak. Hopefully wherever they were landing had a good hospital. These people didn't deserve to die.

The plane finally touched down. It wasn't the smoothest landing, but they were on the ground. Caroline waited and heard the co-pilot come over the loudspeaker and explain what was happening in a wobbly voice.

"This is the co-pilot. We've made an emergency landing in Omaha, Nebraska. Everyone who can, please move to the back of the plane. There'll be emergency personnel coming aboard as well as Federal Agents. We'll get everyone off as soon as we can and anyone who needs medical help will get it. Thank God, we all made it."

The plane fell silent. Caroline pushed herself to her feet and made her way to the back of the plane. There were eight civilians in the back besides her—five woman and three men. The men looked like businessmen, and the women…the women were gorgeous. Jesus, where were the ugly people? Oh crap, was *she* the ugly person here? The women were all tall and slender. One had attached herself to the SEAL that been sitting in row twenty-four…Caroline still hadn't learned what his name was, and another was hovering close to the man Caroline knew as Mozart. The other women were huddled with the civilian men. It looked as if they'd all bonded over the horrifying experience, while Caroline was once more left sitting on the outside looking in.

The SEALs had moved through the cabin checking the statuses of the other passengers, but there wasn't a lot they could do for them. Caroline eased past the women hanging all over the SEALs without looking at them, and moved to the back corner of the galley.

The jump seats in the back were already occupied, one with a man and a woman on his lap, and the other with another one of the women, who didn't look inclined to move, so Caroline put her back to the wall and slid down until she was sitting. Curling her knees up in front of her and laying her head on her knees, Caroline figured it'd be a while before they'd be leaving and she just wanted to rest.

Caroline didn't see Mozart and the SEAL whose name she never learned, exchange glances. She was just tired and scared. She wanted a shower to get the rest of the dead guy's blood off of her, but knew that wasn't happening anytime soon.

Hearing the medical personnel arrive on board and organizing the removal of the passengers, Caroline overheard Brandy, one of the women standing in the back with the other conscious passengers, exclaim over Mozart and an apparent knife wound he had.

"Don't worry about me," he'd told her. "It's only a flesh wound, I should know, I'm a medic. Besides, the hospital will have enough to worry about with the other passengers. I'll look at it myself, or get one of my buddies to take a look at it. I'll be fine, don't worry about me, but make sure the EMTs get a good look at *you*, sweetheart, to make sure you're all right."

Caroline silently agreed, admiring him. Thinking about her own throbbing side, the SEAL was right. Even though she was hurting, she was alive and didn't want to be a bother. It probably wasn't even a big deal, just a scratch. The other people on the plane needed medical care more than she did—*they* were unconscious and had ingested who knew what. Caroline wished she could've been more help. If she'd been able to figure out what chemical was put into the ice the doctors would be able to help the passengers quicker, but without her lab, she had no idea.

Finally all of the passengers had been taken off to local hospitals. Caroline had fallen into a half-conscious state—awake, but barely aware of all that was going on around her.

After the plane was emptied of the other passengers, the police and FBI herded the little civilian group in the back of the plane outside so the EMTs could look them over. Caroline watched with detached interest the reactions of the other women and men to the dead terrorists scattered around the plane. They were now covered in sheets, but the blood was still clear on the floor as they walked past and over it.

Caroline didn't think anyone was really hurt, but there was no way the police were going to let anyone get off the plane without at least being looked over. There were too many sue-happy people in the world today for them to let that happen.

When it was Caroline's turn, the EMT wasn't happy with her.

"Look, I can see you're favoring your side, let me look at it."

Caroline tried to wave him off. "No, really, it's nothing. I just hit it when I fell on the plane—it's fine."

"I should at least look at it," he insisted.

"Well…" Caroline was about to give in when Brandy, one of the civilian women, piped up from next to the young man.

"Sir? I'm feeling a bit dizzy…do you think I can sit down somewhere?"

When Caroline looked at her, she didn't think she looked sick at all. The woman had her hand wrapped around the EMT's bicep and she was leaning into him, crushing her ample boobs against him.

"Uh, yeah, okay, let me finish up here and I'll be right with you. Please sit on that bumper right there so you don't fall and hurt yourself."

Caroline wanted to roll her eyes. When the EMT turned back to her she could see he was already thinking about Brandy. She put him out of his misery.

"Look, just give me some alcohol wipes or something. I'm not hurt that badly and you can go and see what Brandy needs."

It was ridiculous at how quickly the man agreed with her and pulled out some antiseptic wipes. Caroline thought meanly that it was a good thing she wasn't hurt more badly, she'd probably be lying on the ground bleeding to death and the men around her would still probably ignore her.

After each of the conscious passengers were looked at, the police reassured that no one had any life threatening injuries, and they'd all signed paperwork refusing transportation to the hospital, the group was herded onto a little bus.

As the shuttle bus headed toward the airport, away from the tarmac, Caroline was a little depressed. Matthew, Mozart, and the other SEAL had left in a separate bus to who-knew-where. She watched closely as the SEALs walked to their shuttle to see if Matthew would acknowledge her in any way, and of course he didn't. He and his teammates had their heads together as they walked away without looking back at the plane. She shouldn't have been surprised. It happened to her every day.

It was just the eight passengers left, plus herself. Caroline followed the other passengers onto the shuttle. They were driven toward the terminal and hustled in through a side door into a room in the airport. The federal agents wanted to hear their side of the story.

Two hours later Caroline was ready to scream. She wanted to get away from here. She just wanted to be in Norfolk and have all this behind her. They'd been questioned as a group, then separately. The other passengers had no clue what had happened. They'd told the authorities they were sitting in their seats one minute and the next, men with knives had herded them to the back of the plane and while they heard yelling and such, they hadn't seen anything. No one knew what had made the other passengers pass out.

Caroline just nodded along with whatever the others said. No one paid too much attention to her. She was used to it though and, in fact, had counted on it now. She explained the blood on herself away by saying she'd slipped and fallen in the blood of one of the terrorists. She didn't want to say anything because she knew SEAL missions were notoriously secret. And while this wasn't a mission, they were in the wrong place...or was that the right place, at the right time? She didn't want to spill any of their secrets or anything. She wasn't sure what she was supposed to say or not say. The FBI and whomever else would learn what they needed to from the SEALs themselves, not from her. She wasn't even a player in the whole drama, she told herself. She was just Caroline Martin, a regular citizen.

After the authorities had heard everything the awake passengers knew about the attempted hijacking, they were free to go, after being warned not to talk to the press. *Yeah, right!* thought Caroline... A plane hijacking was big business for the media, *huge*. And she knew there was no way Brandy wouldn't use this experience to get herself on television. Caroline had been glad to hear Brandy and the others didn't know what Matthew and his friends did for a living, but of course there was speculation that they were some kind of military secret agents or something.

Caroline wasn't sure where they were free to go *to*. It was dark outside. The airline employees weren't even there anymore. The airport was deserted except for the odd janitor or two. It was a small town and a regional airport. There were no late night flights out. The group was told flights would resume the next morning and they should be able to get on another plane at that time. Caroline sighed. She didn't have her purse; it was still on the plane. She'd have to wait until they released their luggage so she could use her identification to book another seat to Virginia.

Apparently the airline wanted to put all of them up in a local hotel. The airline employees had told the police when they were done interviewing the witnesses to let them know they could get the shuttle to the hotel and stay free-of-charge. Caroline was glad to hear it, since she didn't have any money, but one look outside the airport made her change her mind.

It was complete pandemonium. There were news trucks and people standing around everywhere. It was a madhouse. The reporters were trying to talk to anyone that was around, hoping they'd have some information about the hijacking they could use on their morning news program. Caroline even saw a CNN truck amongst all the other vehicles.

She wanted absolutely nothing to do with the media. It wasn't as if she was afraid to talk to them or anything, she was just exhausted from everything that had happened that day. The fight with the terrorist in the aisle was finally taking its toll on her—she was tired and hurting. All Caroline wanted to do was find a dark corner and shut her eyes. No, what she really wanted was a bath and to talk to her mom, but since she couldn't have either, she'd have to make do with a dark corner where she wouldn't have to talk to anybody.

Caroline watched as Brandy and the other women tried to straighten their already impeccable hair and clothing and got a light of determination in their eyes. They'd seen the media vultures and were thrilled to be able to be in the spotlight. Ignoring the orders not to talk to the press, the small group of witness quickly left the lobby and entered the fray. No one looked back at the quiet, plain woman walking back into the depths of the airport.

Chapter Eight

WOLF, MOZART, AND ABE settled into a booth at the bar at the hotel. They'd spent an hour going over what had happened over the phone with their commander, then another hour going over it again with the FBI agents. Most of their actions were downplayed as their profession required, so the story the FBI received was a watered down version.

But now they were alone and could debrief amongst themselves. While they'd discussed what had happened with the authorities, now they could talk to each other and get the real story, something they hadn't had time to do before now.

"How did you know what was going on Wolf?" Mozart asked in a low voice so no one around would overhear. They all knew if they'd taken a drink most likely everyone on the plane would be dead—them included. It was a sobering thought, but nothing they hadn't been through before.

Wolf shook his head. "I didn't. It was Caroline."

"Who?" Abe asked confused.

"The woman sitting next to me. The brunette."

"The one who gave us the messages," Mozart offered with certainty.

Wolf nodded. "She's a chemist and smelled something off with the ice. She wouldn't let me drink my orange juice."

The men were quiet and digested what Wolf said, realizing they owed their lives to the woman. While they were used to using whatever they had to in order to be successful, none of them could remember a time when a civilian woman's actions had unequivocally saved their lives.

The threesome continued to discuss what had happened. Abe and Mozart had also seen the effect the drinks had on the other passengers and were biding their time until Wolf was ready to move. They'd instinctively known Wolf would take the terrorist in the cockpit out since he was closest to the front, just as the others would take out the remaining men.

"What happened to the third man while you were taking care of the other two?" Wolf asked.

"He was in the aisle fighting with that woman," Mozart answered. "I took care of him and went up to assist you. You know the rest, she was up front and you asked her to get the co-pilot."

"Was she hurt?" Wolf asked Mozart, regretting he hadn't been able to talk to Caroline after everything had started happening.

"I don't think so. I asked if she was okay when I went to the back, she nodded, but I didn't get to talk to her after that." Mozart replied nonchalantly.

"What do you think she said to the Feds?" Abe asked quietly. They knew they hadn't done anything wrong, but at the same time, they didn't want to be the subject of the media's attention either. They had a job they had to do in a couple of weeks and media attention wouldn't be good.

"I have no idea, but they didn't come in asking us more questions, and there was no media when we checked in," Mozart said thoughtfully.

"About that...did you guys sense anything weird about the Feds that interviewed us?" Wolf asked his teammates.

"Yeah, I was going to bring that up. They seemed more interested in how we knew what was going down than about who the terrorists were or how they managed to get those knives on board." Abe had spoken, but all three men knew something was off.

Mozart added his say as well. "It's obviously important to know how we found out about their hijacking attempt, but it's also very strange they didn't spend as much time trying to figure out how it was all planned."

"I'll talk to the commander when we land in Norfolk. Tell him our concerns and see what he can figure out. It's horrible timing with our upcoming mission though. We don't have time to look into it ourselves. Besides there's no way the Feds will talk to us about it. We'll have to leave it in the commander's hands." Wolf was frustrated. They were missing something, but he didn't know what. If they were back at the base, they'd be able to spend more time trying to figure it out. Wolf had been so looking forward to this vacation, and now he didn't think he'd be able to enjoy it. He'd do what he could from Virginia to look into it though. His gut was screaming at him, there's no way he could drop it.

The men heard a commotion at the bar. They looked over and saw a couple of the women from the plane and two of the businessmen. They were laughing loudly and had obviously imbibed a few too many alcoholic beverages. Obviously this was the hotel the airlines had sent them to after they were allowed to leave the airport. The SEALs had been quietly offered a free room after they'd talked to the authorities, and they'd gladly accepted it. It was obvious the other passengers had also most likely been put up for free as well.

"They are *hot*," Abe said, watching the women, always on the prowl for a one night stand. "Until we had to leave the blonde on the right was into me." He laughed. "Guess she found someone else huh?"

"Where's Caroline?" Wolf asked, more to himself than to his teammates, but they heard him anyway.

"I'm sure she's here somewhere. Man I'm tired and could use a few hours sleep. You guys coming up?" Abe asked, dismissing Wolf's concerns about Caroline as if he didn't even remember meeting her.

As the three men headed up to their rooms Wolf couldn't help but continue to ponder why Caroline wasn't around. She'd been amazing. She was the hero in the whole situation in his eyes. Without her, they'd all be dead. Hell, hundreds of passengers would be dead.

He recalled when he'd looked back and saw her fighting with a terrorist, a *terrorist* dammit. He couldn't believe she'd actually stuck her leg out into the aisle to trip the guy as he made his way toward him. It was a stupid thing to do, and he knew it had to have hurt.

Wolf had been scared for her and felt helpless because he couldn't aid her. He wished he'd been able to talk to her before they'd left, but he didn't have time. As soon as he landed the plane he, Mozart, and Abe had to get their story straight before they met with the Feds. He hadn't even thought about checking up on Caroline before he'd left the plane. Suddenly he felt bad about that. Had she watched him leave? What did she think? Did she even care?

Wolf wondered again where she was. Was she okay? He suddenly felt an urgent need to talk to her. To make sure she was all right. Everything had happened so quickly and he just wanted…he didn't know what he wanted. He hoped he'd see her tomorrow. She said she was going to Norfolk, so she had to be at the airport tomorrow. Their commander told them he was sending a military bird to pick them up in the morning, but maybe he'd see Caroline at the airport before they left. He made a vow to himself to leave early enough in the morning so they'd have time to scope out the civilian side of the airport and see if he could find her and thank her.

CAROLINE WASHED AS much of her face and hands and arms as she could in the restroom at the airport. It was mostly deserted with the occasional passenger here and there, and of course the cleaning crews busily going about their business. She was hungry and wanted to brush her teeth, but had no money, and certainly no toothbrush, but it didn't matter if she had a thousand bucks...the stores were all closed.

Caroline turned her shirt inside out to try to hide some of the dried blood. She didn't really want to put the terrorist's dried blood next to her skin, but she also wanted to blend in. And blending in with others trumped feeling squeamish. Besides, she didn't have any other clothes to wear, so she had to deal with the shirt she had.

The cut on her side was bleeding sluggishly, even after she'd used the antiseptic wipes the EMT had given her, but Caroline didn't think she was in any imminent danger. It hurt, but again, there wasn't anything she could do about it now. She'd go to the doctor when she got to Norfolk. She'd be just fine. Thinking for a moment about heading to the hospital there in Nebraska, Caroline dismissed the thought almost as soon as she had it. All they'd do was probably put a few steri-strips on it and it'd be fine in a few days anyway.

One reason she didn't want to go to the hospital here was that it'd probably be absolutely crawling with reporters trying to get the scoop on the passengers. Second, just as Matthew's friend had said to the woman on the plane, the hospitals were too busy here to need to deal with her little cut. Third, at this point she just wanted to get to Norfolk. Caroline also hated hospitals. If she could at all avoid having to go to one, she would. She'd spent enough of her life cooped up in one for her to voluntarily check herself into another now. As long as she was upright, mobile and her arm wasn't hanging off, she'd self-medicate.

Wadding up some paper towels and holding them to her side as she left the ladies room, Caroline searched for a place to lie down for the night. Thank God the airport police were keeping the reporters out. Maybe, just maybe she'd be able to sleep a couple of hours. She found a dark empty gate and made her way to the edge. Crap. The seats all had arm rests that weren't removable, and she had no desire to sleep sitting up.

Giving up on finding a comfortable seat, Caroline eased herself down to the floor, turned onto her side and made sure the wadded up paper towels were pressed to her side against the floor. Hopefully the pressure of her body against her side and the paper towels would have the sluggish bleeding stopped by morning.

Caroline closed her eyes and tried to block out the images that bombarded her. She saw the terrorist's eyes right before his throat was slit; she saw the stranger sitting next to her slumped over against the window; she saw herself tripping a freaking terrorist and watching as he flew through the air. She saw the sightless eyes of both the pilot and the terrorist that had been flying the plane. Also whipping through her mind as if she was watching a movie and not simply recalling events that had actually happened to her were scenes of Matthew holding her hand and running his thumb over her knuckles. She saw the tender look in his eyes as he asked if she was okay while he was sitting in the cockpit. Finally she saw him walking away from the plane without a second glance.

Chapter Nine

THE MILITARY PLANE wasn't leaving until early afternoon so the SEAL team had a leisurely breakfast—as leisurely as it could be with the shouts and lights from the media outside the small hotel—and watched as two women from the plane and the men headed out the door to go back to the airport to see if they could catch another flight.

Abe heard them talking before they left about how irritated they were that the airline and Feds hadn't given them their bags back yet. The men had their wallets in their pants pockets, but the women's purses were still on the plane. That got Abe thinking about the woman who'd saved all their lives. He'd been thinking more about her last night. Yesterday had been crazy, but he'd had time to think now, and he was ashamed of himself and his fellow teammates.

"About the woman…" he blurted out when they'd all sat down at breakfast.

Wolf and Mozart looked at him with surprise.

"What about her?" Wolf snapped, somehow knowing Abe was talking about Caroline and Wolf was feeling possessive for no good reason he could think of. But he knew there was no way he was letting Abe make a move on Caroline if that was what he was getting at. He was way too slick with the ladies and hadn't ever had a lasting relationship. He didn't want to think of Caroline being just another conquest for Abe.

"SEALs don't leave SEALs behind. Ever." It was their motto. The thing that every SEAL learned throughout Hell Week and BUD/S training. "Why do I feel like we've left a team member behind?" Abe asked quietly. Neither of the other men said anything.

"We all heard the women this morning say they didn't have their purses with them. They weren't able to get their stuff from the plane. We didn't see Ice last night and she's not been down for breakfast this morning. Where did she stay?"

"Who?" asked Mozart.

Abe smiled for the first time that morning. "Ice. That's her nickname."

They all nodded, understanding at once how she'd earned the moniker. Without Caroline smelling the ice and knowing something was wrong, they'd all be dead.

Wolf still hadn't said anything, but stood up and gathered his stuff quietly. Mozart and Abe didn't even have to ask what he was doing. They'd been together long enough to know when Wolf decided on a course of action he was all about getting it done. After throwing some bills on the table to pay for the food they'd barely touched, they followed his lead. They were going to find their teammate.

CAROLINE STOOD LEANING against the wall of the airport and watched the chaos around her. She'd slept like crap the night before. Even though the airport was basically deserted, the stupid recording about not parking in the white zone and the possibility of being towed was replayed all night over and over. She had no idea why they bothered to keep it going when there weren't any passengers around to hear it. The recording, along with her nightmares and the pain in her side, kept her from getting a good night's sleep.

When Caroline had woken up that morning she'd felt light headed and weak and wasn't thinking straight. When she'd gone to the restroom and checked out her side, she was dismayed to see that as soon as she took the paper towels away from her side, she started bleeding again. It was red and obviously infected as well. Nice. *The least the terrorist could've done was made sure his knife was clean,* Caroline thought grimly, wincing as she poked the reddening wound on her side.

At least she had some good news that morning—she'd finally gotten her purse back. Since she was already at the airport she was first in line to reclaim her belongings. All of the passenger's bags were still sitting in the belly of the plane. The airline couldn't release them yet; they were still investigating how the terrorists had smuggled their weapons on board, so everyone's luggage was being searched. She'd been reassured that the bags would eventually be flown to Norfolk once the investigation was over and the airline employee handed her a business card with a small apologetic smile.

Caroline bought a bottle of water and a bagel as soon as the little coffee shop in the airport opened, but when she'd started to eat, she felt nauseous. She hoped she'd be hungry later, so instead of throwing the food away, she tucked it into her purse.

Many of the relatives of the passengers on the plane had been arriving in the little airport all morning. A lot of the passengers had been released from the hospital already. Caroline watched for a while as they ran the gauntlet to try to get into the airport. If possible, it looked like there were even more media trucks and people standing outside. Of course this was a huge media event. An attempted airplane hijacking after the September 11 attack was a huge deal and it was getting coverage from what looked like every country in the world.

All of the passengers who'd decided to brave flying again, and their relatives, were standing in line to talk to someone from the airline. Everyone wanted to get to Virginia, or at least get to *somewhere*, but of course the airline was putting them all on standby. It seemed to Caroline that the least the airline could do was get another plane here to take care of them all. But she didn't really know anything about how the industry worked, and most likely, it was easier said than done.

Caroline stood against the wall eyeing the line at customer service, waiting for it to go down. She should've gotten in line first thing this morning, that was one of the reasons she'd stayed the night in the airport instead of the hotel, but she'd been hungry and feeling sick, so she'd put it off. Now the line was too long for her to be able to stand in it–not with how much her side hurt. If she'd been thinking clearly she would've realized the line wasn't going to get shorter anytime soon because people were arriving at the airport steadily. So as soon as one person would get seen, another would arrive and get in the back of the line.

Caroline had to get a seat on another plane east, but wasn't sure when the next one would be leaving. Hell, it wasn't as if she'd be able to get on it anyway. Flying standby sucked. She closed her eyes. She'd just rest here against the wall and wait for the line to go down. Surely it couldn't take too long.

Mozart, Abe, and Wolf stalked into the airport not knowing if they'd find Ice there or not, but they had to try. The reporters were crazy aggressive outside the small building, but the friends waded through the people, refusing to stop and talk to anyone. When they entered, they stopped and looked around the baggage claim area. It was a zoo. Obviously the relatives of the passengers had started to arrive.

"Let's split up and see if she's down here," Mozart said. "Meet back here in ten."

They all set out. Ten minutes later they were all back; there was no sign of Caroline. The airport wasn't that large and the baggage claim area only had three carousels.

The three men headed upstairs to the ticketing area. At the top of the stairs they looked around. There was a customer service desk that had a line that was at least an hour long and two ticket counters, which also had long lines. There were also a few small shops and the entrance to the gates where security screening was set up. The area wasn't large and they could see almost everyone in it. There was a chance Caroline had already gotten past security and was waiting at a gate for a plane, but they had no way of knowing or getting past security to look for her.

Looking around and not seeing any sign of Ice, Mozart said dejectedly, "I really thought she'd still be here."

"We should probably go and catch our ride," Abe added quietly as disappointed as Mozart was at not finding the woman who'd saved their lives.

Wolf gave them an incredulous look. "Are you guys blind? She's right there," and he turned his back and headed for Caroline. She was standing by herself near a wall with her eyes closed. She was obviously wearing the same clothes as the day before. Guilt hit Wolf hard. Damn.

Even though she looked exhausted and miserable, Caroline looked great to him. Wolf was so damn relieved she was still here he felt his toes tingling. He couldn't wait to talk to her again. He was so gone.

Abe and Mozart were close on Wolf's heels as he headed toward her.

"Damn, I didn't even see her," Abe apologized to Wolf quietly.

"Me neither, Abe," Mozart commiserated. "She doesn't draw any attention to herself does she?"

Wolf reached Caroline first. She hadn't heard him walk up and he didn't want to scare her.

"Caroline?" He whispered.

Caroline was in her own world. Imaging she was sleeping in a big bed when she heard her name. Her eyes flew open. Crap. How had someone snuck up on her? She was obviously more tired than she'd thought.

Her brain realized it was Matthew before her body did, but she couldn't stop herself from lurching to the side and away from the perceived threat. Wolf was ready for her reaction and grabbed her arm to keep her from falling. Caroline could feel his hand brush against her wounded side as he held her arm gently. It took everything in her to not flinch with pain. For some reason she didn't want this incredible man to know she'd been hurt. Caroline and Wolf just looked at each other for a moment then Mozart and Abe were there.

"Here you are! We've been looking for you, Ice," Abe exclaimed.

"For me?" Was all Caroline could get out she was so surprised. "Why?"

"SEALs don't leave SEALs behind. Ever." He said with complete seriousness.

"And? I'm not a SEAL," Caroline said befuddled.

"Maybe not in truth, but you saved our lives, that makes you one of us in our eyes," Mozart answered, completely serious.

Caroline looked back and forth between the three men, confused. She cleared her throat and finally commented, "I assume you guys are all okay?"

Wolf chuckled. "Of course we are. Are *you*?"

"Uh, yeah, I'm okay too," she answered and just looked at them waiting for...something. She still had no idea what they were doing there. She didn't really understand the whole "you're a SEAL" thing. Duh, of course she wasn't. Had they lost their minds?

"What are you doing over here? Do you already have another ticket to get to Norfolk?" Mozart asked breaking the silence between them.

Caroline shook her head to clear it. He'd asked her something. Oh yeah...

"I'm waiting for the line to go down so I can see if I can get on another plane," she explained. "I have to fly standby, but I thought I'd wait a bit for the crowd to thin out."

"Doesn't look like it's going to thin out anytime soon, Ice," Mozart said. "Why don't you come and sit with us for a while?"

Caroline knew she couldn't sit with them. She wasn't used to attention from a man, nonetheless three men who looked like they should be on the cover of *GQ* or *Soldiers of Fortune.* They were gorgeous and were attracting attention by just standing there in the airport. Caroline could see women do double takes as they walked by. She had no idea how they were able to blend in when they were on a mission. There was no way these men could go anywhere unnoticed.

She also knew she didn't feel good, and didn't want them to know. Caroline was embarrassed that a little scratch on her side was making her feel so terrible. She was obviously a wuss. They were strong men, they thought she was one of them, she couldn't show any weakness. Then something Mozart said finally sunk in.

"Ice?"

All three men chuckled again. Geez, having all three of them smiling at her like that made her feel like she was only woman in the room, and that scared her to death.

"Yeah, Abe named you that for your super sniffing skills smelling that ice and knowing what was up," Mozart explained.

Caroline smiled a bit at that. Funny. Then something else occurred to her. This was the first time she'd heard the third SEAL's name. "Abe?"

Abe came forward and took the hand on the arm Wolf wasn't holding, and brought it up to his lips. "I'm Abe. It's good to meet you sweetheart. Thanks for saving our lives."

Caroline nervously pulled her hand back and ignored his over the top flattery. Somehow she knew he probably treated all women the same way. She wasn't special. She also knew if she wasn't able to deal with it when she was one hundred percent, she definitely couldn't deal with it today.

She looked at the three gorgeous men standing around her looking at her with concern. The concern felt good, but she knew it wouldn't last, it never did.

"I can't call you guys by your nicknames. Sorry. It's just too weird. What are your real names?"

Not letting them answer, Wolf told her, "Abe is Christopher and Mozart is Sam."

"Okay, that's easier for me to remember. I'll call you guys that."

They all smiled at her as if they thought she was cute. Mentally rolling her eyes, Caroline couldn't go around calling these masculine men by the silly nicknames they'd given each other for probably asinine reasons.

Seeing their smiles reminded her that she needed to make them leave. They'd leave soon enough, she might as well hurry them along so she could go and find a seat and feel miserable in solitude.

She looked at each of the men and said in a tone that projected dismissal, "Well, thanks for coming to check on me, but I'm okay and I have to go get in line now. I'm glad you're all okay too. Good luck on your upcoming mission and stay safe. All right?"

She peeled herself away from Matthew and turned toward the line. She waved lamely at the three men, turned her back on them and went to get in line. She couldn't let them stay. She didn't belong with them, she was just plain Caroline. Not Ice, not a part of their team. She was nowhere near their league. She had to leave now before her heart decided it wanted more. Before she let Matthew break her heart.

Mozart, Abe, and Wolf watched as Caroline walked away from them without a second glance and got in line.

"Well, that didn't go well did it?" Mozart asked no one in particular.

Wolf grunted and headed toward the stairs. Fine. If she didn't want them around, they'd go. He didn't understand his feelings of hurt, but he'd never chased after a woman, and wasn't going to start now, no matter how much he wanted to. A little part inside told him he was being an ass, but he ignored it. He'd thought they had a connection, but if Caroline was able to walk away from him that easily, he was obviously wrong.

Caroline held her breath. She didn't really want them to go, especially didn't want Matthew to go, but she didn't think she had a choice. They weren't really interested in her; they were just following up on the incident. She was glad to see that none of them seemed to be hurt though. That was good. Caroline hoped they'd be safe in their upcoming missions. The more she thought about those missions, the more she panicked a little inside. She had no right to worry about them—no right to be concerned. She was a passing oddity for them. Once they got to Norfolk they'd laugh about the entire thing and come to their senses. *Matthew* would come to his senses. He'd realize she was a nobody, a geek, and move on with his life.

Once she knew they were gone, she'd go back and sit down. She couldn't stand in this line much longer. She already felt dizzy and was still nauseous. She swayed on her feet trying to calculate how much time they needed to disappear and how much time she had left before she fell on the floor in a dead faint.

Abe and Mozart followed Wolf down the stairs. They didn't say anything to him, but they knew he was fighting some sort of demon they didn't understand, so they didn't push him. Of course they figured it was about Ice, but since neither of them had seen him act like that before, they weren't sure what was going on. Wolf was a ladies man, like most of them. He didn't have to work hard to attract women, but lately he seemed out of sorts. He hadn't been out with them for a while and he just didn't seem interested in women...until now. Until Ice.

Mozart took a hard look at Wolf. His hands were clenched at his sides and he strode purposefully down the stairs. They were headed out of the building to another part of the airport where their military bird waited for them. Suddenly Mozart noticed something else, something Wolf and Abe seemed to have somehow missed. He knew they'd be pissed they'd overlooked it. After all they'd been trained to be observant. Mozart couldn't wait to rub it in.

"I'll meet you at the plane," he promised Abe and turned and ran back up the stairs taking them two at a time without any other explanation. Abe had no idea where his buddy was going, but shrugged and followed Wolf out the door. He'd be back soon no doubt.

Wolf sat in the seat on the military airplane brooding. He wasn't sure why Caroline had gotten to him so much, but she had. She was smart and brave and...dammit. He didn't want to leave her. But what choice did they have? Did *he* have? They had a plane to catch. Did he have to leave? What if he stayed and flew commercial with her? He still had some leave time. Shit. His commander had said they had to get to Norfolk and debrief in person. They had to meet with someone there and go over what happened. Wolf knew the entire episode was a security breach and someone had to answer for it.

But Wolf still had a thousand questions for Caroline. What did she tell the authorities, where did she spend the night last night, what had really happened with the terrorist Mozart had killed when he was on top of her? And maybe most importantly, did she want to see him again? Wolf was still brooding about the entire situation when he looked up and saw Mozart escorting the woman he couldn't get out of his mind onto their plane.

What the hell? Mozart knew civilians weren't allowed on official military flights. Wolf stood up to chew him out when Mozart signaled him to "wait." Wolf ran his hand through his hair in frustration. What had he missed? Why did Mozart go back and get Caroline? He wasn't someone to buck authority, ever. But he was now. What was going on? Wolf sat back down and bided his time. He trusted his team, but he wanted to know what was going on now.

He wasn't sure he could handle spending more time with Caroline only to have her rebuff him again. It hurt enough the first time. Yes, it hurt, Wolf admitted to himself. Every instinct he had was screaming at him to get up and go to Caroline, but if Mozart wanted him to wait, it was for a damn good reason. He'd give him a bit of time, but as soon as they were in the air he was going to find out what the hell was going on.

Caroline tried for the tenth time to get Sam to let go of her arm. He wasn't budging. He'd come back up the stairs, straight to where she was standing in line, took her arm and led her away. Away from the airport and to here, this plane. To where Matthew was.

She tried to tell him to let her go, tried reasoning with him, tried making him mad, tried everything she could think of, but he just held on and kept walking. He didn't say anything to her other than, "Come on, Ice, you're traveling with us back to Norfolk." That was it. Nothing else. She didn't even know where they were going once they got to Virginia, but she supposed anyplace beat sitting in the airport going nowhere.

Caroline sat in the seat Sam led her to gingerly. He helped her get buckled in, then walked further back into the plane to find his own seat. Thank God he hadn't put her next to Matthew. She didn't want him to know she was hurt. It hurt to lean back, so she sat upright in the seat. Surprisingly enough, none of the SEALs came and sat next to her. She'd seen both Matthew and Christopher on the plane, but neither one approached her.

She was glad, but also sad too. Mostly she was confused. As the plane taxied down the runway she tried to relax and not think about hijackers. Nothing was going to happen on this flight. It was a military plane, flown by military personnel with three SEALs on board. There were no flight attendants, only the four passengers and the pilots. She tried to relax, but couldn't. She couldn't get the thoughts of the terrorists out of her mind.

As soon as the plane was airborne and at a relatively safe altitude, Mozart stood up and went to Ice. On his way he signaled to both Wolf and Abe, "injured."

Wolf watched as Mozart got up. He wasn't going to go to Caroline. She didn't want to come with them. With him. He'd be damned if he....just as he was working up a good temper toward her, he saw Mozart's signal. Fuck. Injured? How the hell did he miss it? He got to Caroline about the same time as Mozart. He didn't remember getting up and moving forward, but there he was. *Caroline was injured? What the fuck?*

Mozart let Wolf squeeze by, and as he did told him quietly, "I saw the blood on your shirt from where you grabbed her in the airport." Sure enough, Wolf looked down and saw the tiny smear of blood. He'd missed it. Jesus. Thank God Mozart hadn't. He'd never live it down, but at the moment he couldn't give a damn.

Wolf kneeled down next to Caroline's seat. Her seat belt was buckled, but she was sitting up straight, unnaturally straight. Now that he knew she was hurt, he could see how uncomfortable her position was.

"Caroline, where are you hurt? Let me see."

Caroline shook her head, but didn't look at Matthew. "I'm fine, really..."

Wolf gave a chin lift to Abe and Mozart and signaled for them to get the makeshift cot in the back ready. Like most military planes, this one was equipped with a space in the back for injured soldiers.

"Come on Caroline, up you go. We're going to the back. Let me take a look and make sure you're all right." He reached out and quickly unbuckled her seatbelt, brushing her hands aside when she tried to prevent him from taking care of her.

"Seriously Matthew, I'm okay. I just want to sit here. I'm tired."

Caroline whined, trying to resist, but she was too tired and hurting too much to put up more than a token resistance.

"Caroline, please. Let me help you."

It was the please that finally got to her. She sighed and nodded, defeated. He was going to have his way no matter what she said. Besides, they were already airborne; it wasn't as if she could ignore them or walk away.

Wolf helped her to the back and sat her down on a cot. He sat next to her and put his hand over hers on her knee.

"Mozart here is going to take a look." When she struggled a bit and looked like she'd stand up, Mozart leaned down toward her.

"Look at me, Ice," Mozart demanded. At the tone of his voice, Caroline looked up at him, panic in her eyes.

"I'm just going to look. I'm sure you're fine, but at least let me see…okay? I won't hurt you. I *am* trained you know," Mozart said with humor in his voice.

"It's not that…" At their expectant looks she sighed and quipped sarcastically, "Okay, but if you suddenly have the urge to jump me, don't blame me!" She knew what kinds of women these men were used to, tall skinny women without an extra pound on them. She wasn't that, no way, no how. Usually she didn't care, but baring herself to them, especially to Matthew, wasn't something she wanted to do in this lifetime. She couldn't seem to lose the last fifteen pounds that clung stubbornly to her stomach and thighs. She didn't tan, and …she couldn't think of anything else because Mozart was lifting up her shirt and exposing her stomach and side. She tried to suck in her breath and her stomach at the same time.

"Relax," Wolf murmured next to her head. He tilted her head up so she had to look him in the eyes. "Talk to me Caroline," he commanded.

"Wh-what do you want to know?" She stuttered trying to ignore what Mozart was doing.

"Tell me what happened after I got up to go into the cockpit," Wolf insisted.

Caroline was quiet for a moment, then tried to downplay what had really happened.

"When you got up, the other guy was coming for you so I tripped him. It stopped him for a moment, but you were still busy and he was getting up. I grabbed him to stall him and then Sam came up and killed him." She finished in a rush and looked away from Wolf's eyes.

"Now tell me what *really* happened," he growled. "You're a terrible liar." He paused and when she didn't continue he added, "Please tell me. Caroline, I've been on hundreds of missions for my country, but I don't have the words to express how thankful I am that you were sitting next to me on that plane. Not Mozart, not Abe...*you*. You did what you had to do and you saved my life and the life of everyone on that plane not once, but twice. Now tell me."

Caroline ducked her head. Crap. She hadn't done anything she was ashamed of, but for some reason she really didn't want to tell Matthew what had truly happened. She couldn't help but feel as if she should have done more. She inhaled a quick breath when Sam did something to her side that really hurt. Damn. She quickly stumbled over her explanation to get it out of the way and to try to take her mind off of Sam's probing.

"The terrorist was on the ground but getting up and you were still trying to get into the cockpit. I knew I had to do something or we'd all die. So I jumped on his back. I tried to keep him down, but he was too strong for me. He flipped me over and we had a kicking and hitting match. I didn't know he had a knife, which was dumb I suppose, but he must have gotten me while we were fighting."

"Why didn't you say anything afterward? Either before we landed or when the paramedics were there? Didn't you see an EMT?" Abe asked suddenly from somewhere off to her uninjured side. Caroline shifted her gaze over to him.

"For the same reason you didn't, Christopher," she explained slowly. "I heard what you told that woman on the plane. She asked why you weren't going to get help. You said the hospitals were busy enough with the other passengers. They wouldn't have had time for you and it wasn't fair to the other passengers. I agreed, and besides it was just a scratch. I got some antiseptic wipes from the EMT and tried to clean it last night. It wasn't until this morning that it started looking red."

There was silence. The three SEALs were actually stunned into silence. Jesus, this woman was braver and less self-serving than a lot of the people they worked with on a daily basis.

Finally Mozart broke the silence and told Caroline, "It looks like the knife missed penetrating very deeply, Ice, but you have a good slice across your side. It's more than a scratch. It's infected. I think you need stitches as well as antibiotics."

Caroline took a deep breath and didn't say anything. She looked up at Matthew and saw him clenching his teeth and working his jaw. She looked away. Why was he mad at her?

"I don't want to go to the hospital. I-I don't like hospitals." Caroline begged, a little desperately. She kept her eyes on the man hovering above her, not able to look at the disappointment she knew she'd see on Matthew's face.

Wolf turned her head back toward him again so she was looking him in the eyes. "Mozart can sew you up, if you'll trust him."

Caroline didn't hesitate, "I trust him. I trust all of you. I just...." She paused. Took a deep breath and continued on. "I just don't want you guys to think I'm a wuss."

She hadn't hesitated to say that she trusted them—that went a long way toward making Wolf feel better. But a wuss? Seriously?

"Ice," Abe said firmly before Wolf could get a word out, "You're not a wuss. In fact I would go so far to say you've held up better than some of the SEALs in training back in San Diego. Let us take care of this for you. You'll be up and around in no time."

Wolf looked at his teammate. Interesting. Abe wasn't known for being the most patient man, especially with women. He knew Abe respected woman and tried to be polite with them, but most of the time he tended to be short and abrupt with women, wanting to be with them sexually, nothing else. But there was something about Caroline that brought out the protective instincts with all of them.

"We'll be right here with you, Ice," Abe promised firmly. Caroline nodded and shut her eyes. Wolf had to distract her. He could see that every muscle in her body was scrunched up tight in preparation for whatever it was she thought Mozart was going to do to her.

"Where did you go last night, Caroline?" Wolf asked.

Caroline answered without opening her eyes. Her eyebrows were still scrunched together as she was waiting for Sam to do something. "Nowhere. I spent the night in the airport."

Wolf's eyes met Abe's eyes guiltily. Abe had been right.

"Why? Why didn't you go to the hotel? Didn't they offer you a comped room?" Wolf asked knowing what the answer was already, but asking anyway.

"Yeah, but I thought I'd just stay at the airport since I'd hoped to leave first thing this morning. Besides, I didn't have any money for anything like food when I got there. They gave us the room for free, but I didn't know if the food came with it or not." Caroline grunted as Sam inserted the needle that would put the anesthetic into her side.

"Hell, why didn't you just ask, Caroline? If you did need money, I'm sure one of the men would have given it to you." Wolf chastised her gently.

Caroline opened her eyes at his tone. She looked him straight in his eyes. She wanted him to *hear* what she was saying. Without looking away from Matthew she asked Christopher a simple question.

"Christopher, when did you first notice me?"

Abe answered without hesitation and laughed a bit. "When you fell on top of Mozart as you walked down the aisle on the plane."

"Sam, when did *you* first notice me?" Mozart was waiting for the anesthetic to take effect and told her honestly. "Same as Abe, I saw you walking down the aisle and of course when you about fell in my lap."

Caroline hadn't looked away from Matthew while the others were answering her question. She directed the same question to him.

Wolf thought back and suddenly he knew where she was going with her question and opened his mouth to lie when she interrupted him, as if she could tell what he was thinking. "And don't lie, Matthew."

Shit. Wolf sighed. "I noticed you when you offered to switch seats with me."

Caroline nodded as if they'd given her the answers she expected.

"Christopher, you and I met at the lunch counter in the airport in San Diego. I was standing right in front of you. You dropped your fork and I picked it up for you. You thanked me and continued to your seat." Abe flushed, remembering the incident now that she'd brought it up, but Caroline wasn't done.

"Sam, you were sitting at the end of a row of chairs with your feet out, I tried to step over your legs without disturbing you, but you noticed anyway, apologized, and moved out of the way. I said it wasn't a big deal, you nodded and I went and sat down in the same row of chairs as you." Caroline still hadn't looked at the other men, but heard Mozart's low, "damn."

Caroline took a deep breath. "Matthew, you and I met on our way into the airport. I was having problems getting my suitcase in the door because one of the wheels was broken and..."

Wolf interrupted her, "...And I helped you carry your suitcase through the door and up to the check-in kiosks." Caroline nodded a bit sadly. "You said you hoped I had a good flight and walked off down toward the security check-point." Except for the roar of the engines there was silence.

"You asked why I didn't ask for help, Matthew," Caroline continued after a beat, "it's because I'm not the kind of woman people notice. The three of you all talked to me, but still didn't remember me. I'm not the kind of woman people recollect or go out of their way to help." All three men went to interrupt her, but Caroline weakly held up her hand to stop them and continued.

"It's okay. I know what I am and what I'm not. What I'm not is like one of those women on the plane. You know Christopher, the blonde that was cozied up to you? The ones that got the men to fawn all over them? Even if I'd asked for help I'd most likely have been turned down. Politely I'm sure, but turned down. In a room full of people, no one notices me. That's just the way it is, and it's *fine*." Caroline emphasized. "So don't any of you feel sorry for me. I didn't ask for help because I knew I'd be fine in the airport for one night. Hell, people spend the night in airports all the time. I just didn't have the energy to care last night. And I don't have the energy right now to be embarrassed about telling you all of this. So don't go reminding me later, okay?" She tried to make the men feel better. She knew they felt guilty, but she didn't want them to. That wasn't why she told them what she had. "I just want you guys to know that I understand why you feel like you have to help me, but I'm fine. I'll be okay." She shut her eyes, not able to look at the guilt she could see in Matthew's eyes anymore.

"I don't think you understand anything about us, Caroline," Wolf countered. He didn't elaborate.

Caroline didn't open her eyes or say anything else. Wolf knew she'd heard him; she just wasn't acknowledging what he'd said.

Mozart poked at her side for a moment and when Caroline didn't flinch, declared to everyone that her side was numb enough to put in the stitches. Wolf stood up and carefully helped Caroline lie down on the cot then kneeled on the floor next to her. She lay on her side. She had one hand under her head and the other was curled up against her chest, as if anticipating the stitches going in.

Mozart actually looked to Wolf for approval before he leaned down and started stitching her side. It wouldn't take too many, but he wanted to be as careful as he could be. Since it was Ice, he wanted to spare her as much pain and make the scar as small as possible.

Abe had left their side for a moment while Mozart stitched her up but he was back with another needle as soon as Mozart was done with his handiwork. Abe also looked to Wolf for his okay before proceeding. Wolf nodded at him. With Wolf's approval, Abe leaned down and stretched out Caroline's arm that had been clenched tightly against her chest. He found a vein on the inside of her elbow and administered the drug before she could do more than put up a token protest.

Caroline turned to look at Matthew in surprise.

Wolf's chest expanded at the fact she'd looked at him for reassurance, not at Abe or Mozart. At her questioning look, Wolf simply said, "To help you sleep."

Caroline nodded but laughed. "I don't think I need any help sleeping, Matthew. I didn't sleep very well last night."

Wolf leaned close to Caroline's head. Damn, she hadn't complained once. She'd been in pain, was in a plane getting stitched up, and she'd let a man she didn't really know inject an un-known drug into her system. Wolf would've beaten her ass if he hadn't been so proud of her for being so strong.

Wolf figured he'd get to ask one more question before she was out. They hadn't had a chance to talk to her about what went on in the interrogation by the Feds. He hated to do it now, but they had to know what everyone said in the civilian's debriefing before they met with the commander in Norfolk.

"What did you say to the FBI about what happened, Caroline?" He wanted to put off the uncomfortable question and possibly bring back bad memories for her, but he knew, as the team leader, this was something they needed to know before any of the personal things could be said.

"Nothing, Matthew," she said sleepily.

"Nothing?" Wolf pressed skeptically.

"Nothing." Caroline confirmed. "They were more interested in the stories from the other passengers. They were willing to talk and say what they knew, which wasn't a lot. They thought you guys were most likely some sort of military, but since they were in the back when most of what happened, happened, they didn't have much to say. While they questioned me, no one really seemed interested. I already told you about me and people not noticing me."

While he was happy she hadn't said anything, it'd make it easier for them to stay under the radar, and he was still baffled by this woman. All three men looked at each other over Caroline's drowsy form. If she'd kept quiet as she'd claimed that should help with whatever was going on with the Feds. They'd been very interested in how and why the terrorist's plan failed; to the point of suspicion. None of the SEALs wanted Caroline put in the middle of whatever was going on.

Mozart asked the question they were all thinking. "Why didn't you tell them what you did, Ice?" he asked quietly from her side.

Caroline tried to open her eyes, but they were just too heavy. *Jesus what was in that shot?* "I didn't *do* anything, *you* guys did all the hard work...and I didn't want to get you guys in trouble." She murmured. "I know what you SEALs do is usually kept hush-hush and I didn't want to say anything that you guys didn't already explain, so I told them nothing. Figured it'd be better." Her voice slurred more and more. "Believe me, I wanted everyone to see how sexy you guys are, and know you're heroes and what you did, but I know that's not how you operate…" Her voice trailed off. She was out.

The three SEALs said nothing as they got Caroline cleaned up and comfortable on the cot. They had to strap her in so when they landed she wouldn't roll off. Mozart had given her enough of the sedative to keep her asleep for a while. Wolf stayed by Caroline's side holding her hand, while Abe and Mozart went and sat in empty seats.

They all had a lot to think about. This slip of a woman had touched each of them in different ways. None of them would be the same. All of them knew they'd protect her with their lives if need be. They didn't know what would happen next, but somehow they knew it wasn't over. Their instincts were screaming at them that something was wrong, but they didn't know how or why. None of them wanted to see Caroline disappear from their lives. She'd become important to them by just being herself. She was unassuming and they were so damn proud of her they couldn't stand it.

Chapter Ten

C AROLINE WOKE UP slowly, feeling like her head was filled with cotton. She rolled over and gasped in pain. Ouch, she'd forgotten about her side. She lifted up her shirt and saw the neat row of stitches. Sam had done a good job. She was a bit surprised it wasn't covered with a bandage, but figured Sam knew what he was doing. Thank God they hadn't brought her to a hospital. She really did hate them. She thought back to the one time she'd had to spend time there and shuddered. She'd rather have Sam stitch her up any day of the week then go through that again.

Looking around, Caroline could tell she was in a hotel room, but not where or which one. She should've been freaking out, but the last thing she'd remembered was the three SEALs staring down at her tenderly as she passed out on the cot on the plane. If she couldn't trust a SEAL, then she couldn't trust anyone.

She carefully got out of bed and stumbled to the bathroom as if she was drunk. She couldn't remember the last time she'd eaten and she felt pretty weak and unsteady on her feet. Caroline used the toilet gratefully, then noticed the brand new toothbrush and toothpaste on the counter. She pounced on them and brushed her teeth thoroughly. She'd never take that for granted again.

Seeing the shower, she suddenly had an intense urge to get clean. She knew she probably shouldn't get her stitches wet, but she *had* to have that shower. She figured she'd try to keep her injured side out of the water, but if it got wet, it got wet. She could still *feel* the blood splatter from the terrorist's neck. She felt itchy and didn't want to even think about the germs she'd picked up from rolling around on the floor of the plane and then sleeping on the ground at the airport.

She tore off the shirt that she never wanted to see again, throwing it in the trash. She thought briefly about the fact that she wasn't wearing any pants. Someone, hopefully it had been Matthew, had taken them off of her before putting her to bed. The thought made her tingly inside, but she pushed it aside. He'd obviously been gentlemanly enough not to remove her shirt, and even though she didn't really know Matthew, figured he'd probably turned his head when he undid and removed her pants.

Caroline took a much quicker shower than she really wanted to, just enough to get clean and wash her hair, but she did take the time to wash her hair twice. She would've stayed in the shower all day enjoying the beat of the hot water on her back, but she had to figure out what was going on and where she was. She stepped out of the shower and wrapped herself up in a fluffy bathrobe that was on the back of the door.

She stepped back into the room and noticed for the first time her suitcase sitting on the floor. What the hell? How had that gotten here? The last thing she remembered was that the airline had said they would send all the luggage to Virginia when they were done with it. Damn. She hated not knowing what had happened. Caroline remembered being on the plane with Sam, Christopher, and Matthew, but nothing after Sam started stitching her up. That shot was definitely stronger than anything she'd ever taken before. She'd always reacted strongly to drugs, something they couldn't have known.

She sighed and sat on the side of the bed. She noticed a piece of paper on the table next to the bed and leaned over gingerly, not wanting to tweak her side, to grab it.

Caroline. If you're reading this I'm not there to tell you what's up. Don't worry, everything is fine. You were out of it when we landed yesterday. We met up with the Feds and they released your bag to us (guess there's an advantage to being a SEAL after all huh?). I brought you here since I didn't know what plans you made for when you got here.

You slept all night and I really wanted to talk to you when you finally woke up. Mozart assured me that you were fine, just sleeping. He said you'd wake up when you were ready.

We had to get to the base this morning to go over what happened on the plane. I haven't left for good though. I'll be back as soon as I can. I made sure there was some food in the hotel fridge, you're probably hungry. The coffee is all ready to go, just hit the on button.

I hope you feel better today. We'll talk when I get back from the base.

Matthew

Caroline held the note to her chest. Wow. It didn't really say anything romantic, but somehow it was the most romantic thing she'd ever been given by a man, okay, hell, it was the only note she'd been left by a man. She hadn't received any notes in high school, or in general. Matthew had been thinking about her. She glossed over in her mind the fact that he would've had to have carried her into the hotel room and concentrated instead on how he'd said he'd be back later.

She had no idea what time he'd left. She looked at the clock; it was currently eleven in the morning. She leaped up, as gracefully as she could with the stitches in her side, and fumbled through her suitcase for something appropriate to wear. She wanted to look casual, but at the same time neat and put together. Caroline finally decided on a pair of jeans and a fitted top. She usually wore T-shirts when she was at home, but she didn't want to see Matthew again in one.

She put her hair up with a barrette and went over to the kitchenette. There was a little refrigerator as well as a microwave and a little coffee pot. She checked, and yup, Matthew had filled it up with fresh grounds and water. She turned it on and set about tidying up the room.

She opened the refrigerator and saw that Matthew *had* made sure there was some food in there, it wasn't a lot, but it should take the edge off her hunger. She grabbed a yogurt and a pre-packaged strip of cheese. She ate those while she waited for the coffee to be done.

Caroline sat on the bed and sipped the coffee once it had filled the little cup. God, it tasted good. She wasn't sure what to do with herself. She generally was a very "busy" person. She didn't have a lot of down time, but since her job didn't start for a week or so and she had nowhere to go and nothing to do at the moment, she found herself actually enjoying the coffee she was drinking for once.

Done with her drink, she got up and put it on the table. She then lay back on the bed and relaxed.

Just as she was about to fall back asleep she heard the click of the door lock being disengaged. She sat up carefully to see Matthew entering the other room of the suite. She could tell he was trying to be quiet.

"Hello," She greeted him softly.

Wolf turned around and smiled at her. Woah. His smile was lethal. His teeth were straight and when he smiled she could see the wrinkles crinkle up by his eyes. And if Caroline thought he was good looking in jeans and a shirt, he was positively deadly in his uniform.

"Hey, how do you feel?" Wolf asked with a happy glint in his eyes.

Wolf was glad to see Caroline was awake. As he'd told her in his note, he'd been worried about her. Mozart had assured him she was fine, but until he'd actually seen her awake he wasn't sure he believed him. She'd been completely knocked out when they'd arrived at the hotel.

"Pretty good, all things considered," Caroline told him. "How'd this morning go at the base?"

"Good. We wanted to keep your name out of it, but we had to tell the commander here in Norfolk your part in the whole thing."

Caroline nodded. "I figured you'd have to. It's fine. I'll talk to whomever I have to in order to help. If they think I can help prevent this from happening again, I'm happy to do it."

Somehow Wolf knew she'd say that. He smiled broadly at her. "Everyone is really interested in who those guys were and what they wanted to accomplish. We didn't give them time to tell us where they were going. You said two of them were talking about coordinates right?"

At her nod he continued. "We don't know if they were planning on crashing into something like the terrorists did on 9/11, or if they were planning on landing the plane somewhere."

Wolf went over and sat next to Caroline on the bed. Just the fact they were both sitting on a bed together seemed very intimate. Caroline couldn't stop the blush that crept up her face.

Wolf took one finger and ran it lightly over her cheek. When she blushed further and bit her lip with her teeth, but didn't pull away, he leaned in closer. He watched her lips and when her tongue darted out to moisten them he nearly groaned. God, how could he ever have missed seeing her? Really seeing her before he got to know her.

He ran his index finger lightly over her bottom lip where she'd been biting it and had just licked. He could feel the hot wetness on his fingertip.

"I'm going to kiss you Caroline," he informed her somewhat gruffly. When she didn't say anything he growled out a warning. "If you don't want this, now's your last chance to say something."

Wolf could see the pulse in her neck beating hard. She swallowed, but didn't stop him. He leaned toward her and used the same index finger that had just been caressing her lip to lift her chin. He wanted to look into her eyes to ascertain if she really wanted this, but he couldn't tear his eyes away from her delectable mouth. Finally his lips met hers.

Her lips parted immediately to let him in. He didn't plunge into her mouth right away; instead he ran his tongue over her top lip, stopping to tease the same lip with a quick nip of his teeth. He pulled back a fraction of an inch to look at Caroline. She had her eyes shut and was clutching the front of his uniform with both hands.

He decided to stop messing around and went in again. This time when their lips met, Wolf thrust his tongue into her mouth and rejoiced when she met it with her own. They caressed each other over and over. Wolf retreated and she followed, then he pushed her tongue back and explored her mouth with his.

Finally, when Wolf knew he had to stop, not risk pushing them further than they were ready to go, he pulled back. One of his hands had made its way behind her neck and he'd been holding her against him. His other hand was low on her back. If they'd been standing or lying down he would've been pushing her pelvis into his own. Wolf took a deep breath, but didn't move his hands.

Caroline slowly opened her eyes. Holy Hell. Matthew was delicious. She'd been kissed before, but she'd never been kissed like that. Like Matthew needed her to breathe. Like she was precious. She didn't know what was different about that kiss from every other kiss she'd had in her life, but deep down she knew it *was* different.

Caroline loved the feel of Matthew's hands on her body—the hand behind her neck held her still and she could feel the heat of his hand on her back. She laid her forehead against his shoulder. Matthew didn't remove his hand from her neck, just followed her in and held her against him.

"Wow," was all Wolf could say at the moment.

"Wow indeed," he heard Caroline's muffled voice against his shoulder.

He chuckled. He felt great. Better than he had in a long time. Strangely, knowing she was just as affected as he was went a long way toward calming him down.

"What do you say we take today to sightsee?"

Caroline lifted her head from where it was resting against Matthew's chest and looked at him. "Sightsee?"

"Yeah, sightsee. You know the thing people do when they aren't working and are on vacation?"

Caroline chuckled. "Yeah, okay." If he wasn't going to talk about their kiss that was fine with her. "What is there to do around here?"

Wolf could tell she was relieved he wasn't rehashing their kiss. He'd give her time to digest it and come to terms with what happened, but he knew they'd have to discuss it sooner or later. He wanted more, a lot more.

"Well, I could give you a tour of the Naval Station, or we could go to the Norfolk Zoo, or the Botanical Gardens. If you like museums, there are several here. What are you in the mood to do and what can you physically do? I don't want you hurting yourself further."

Caroline went to sit up straighter and couldn't help but flinch as the move stretched her side and pulled at her stitches.

Of course Wolf saw. "All right, before we go, I want to check your side. Then how about I show you the base then we grab something to eat. We can then come back here and watch a movie. That way I don't have to keep asking you how you're feeling and you won't feel the need to lie to me."

Caroline laughed out loud. Crap. How could he know her that well so soon? "Sounds good."

When Matthew made no move to get up Caroline smiled and

pointed out, "You'll have to let go of me if we're going to go anywhere."

Matthew leaned down and whispered, "What if I don't want to?"

Caroline didn't have anything to say, but the goose bumps that rose on her arms were answer enough. Matthew smiled at her, took his arm from the back of her neck and ran it down her arm, kissed her hard, then stood up. He held out his hand to help Caroline up.

He didn't let go of her hand once she was standing but merely turned and led her to the bathroom. He helped her sit up on the counter, and had her hold up her shirt so he could see her side.

Wolf tried to keep his hands from wandering all over her creamy flesh, but it was difficult. She wasn't skinny, but she wasn't fat. She was…soft, and squishy, and Matthew loved it. He'd had all sorts of women, but this woman made him lose his legendary control faster than anyone ever had before.

Not able to resist, he ran the back of his hand up her side to just below her breast. At her sharp intake of breath he smiled and let his fingers trail back down to her side and her stitches. They looked good. Mozart had said to leave the wound unbandaged, as long as it wasn't bothering her.

"Does it hurt? Do we need to cover it up?"

Caroline shook her head. "It doesn't hurt. Sometimes the stitches catch on my shirt, but it doesn't hurt."

Wolf nodded, then ran his finger around the stitches one more time. He loved seeing her shiver in reaction. He reluctantly smoothed her shirt down and said, "Let's go before I decide we're better off staying here and getting to know each other better."

Wolf watched as Caroline gathered her stuff she needed for the day and they finally headed out the door.

Caroline couldn't remember a nicer day. The weather was behaving and it was beautiful outside. They'd spend the early afternoon strolling slowly around the base. Matthew pointed out important buildings and historical plaques. They'd even been able to get a guided tour of one of the huge ships. She couldn't remember what kind it was, but was fascinated at how everything worked on board. They had their own post office and kitchen and even jail on the ship.

After the tour, Caroline was feeling tired. She'd had a tough forty eight hours and was still feeling the effects of the sedative. Matthew noticed, of course, and insisted they stop and grab take-out instead of eating in a restaurant.

When Caroline didn't complain about eating in, Wolf knew she was probably hurting more than she was letting on. The more time he spent with her, the more he got to know her. She'd probably fall flat on her face before admitting she was tired or hurting.

They'd come back to the hotel and spread their dinner out on the coffee table. She'd snuggled into Mathew's side after eating and they found an action adventure movie on the television to watch.

Wolf smiled down at the woman in his arms. Caroline fit perfect-ly against him. He couldn't remember having a date where he'd had a better time, especially when sex hadn't even been on the table. He knew they'd have to wait. She physically wasn't up for it for one, and Wolf didn't want to rush it. He loved just sitting and talking to her and getting to know her. Perhaps that was what was missing on his other dates—the connection, the getting to know each other outside the bedroom.

"Why the nickname Wolf?" Caroline murmured softly from be-side him, asking the question out of the blue.

Wolf looked down. It actually sounded strange to hear his nick-name coming from her mouth. He was so used to her always calling him "Matthew," in fact he preferred it.

"I'd love to tell you it came about because I'm stealthy or that I have the patience of a wolf, but alas it's nothing so manly as that."

Caroline picked her head up so she could see Matthew better. "Now I'm really interested. Go on."

"Many times in the military nicknames come from a soldier's name. Like, if my last name was Wolfgang or Wolfowitz, drill sergeants and the other guys would start calling me Wolf."

"But your last name isn't Wolfgang or Wolfowitz." Caroline said giggling, stating the obvious.

Wolf chucked Caroline under her chin. "Yeah, well my nickname came from boot camp. It was a completely new experience for me and I was worked harder than I've ever been worked in my life. I was always hungry. Apparently every time we went in for chow I ate my food so fast I finished way before everyone else. I'd also be happy to eat anything the other guys didn't want."

Caroline sat all the way up, fully awake now. "Oh my God, don't tell me. You were *Hungry Like a Wolf?*"

Wolf laughed and grabbed Caroline so she fell back against him. He loved how she snuggled back down into him, shifting around until she was comfortable, like an animal burrowing down into their bed for the night. "I haven't thought about that old song in forever. Jesus. And actually, yes, I was always 'wolfing' down my food. The name stuck."

He loved hearing Caroline giggle. He knew she hadn't had a lot of reasons to laugh recently.

They both settled back down into watching the movie. When Wolf shifted about twenty minutes later, Caroline murmured under her breath and snuggled deeper into him. The fact that she was asleep, but still turned toward him, made his heart clench. Wolf was amazed she was such a heavy sleeper. In his line of work it didn't pay to sleep as heavily as she apparently did, so it'd been a long time since he'd seen it.

For the second night in a row, Wolf picked Caroline up and brought her to bed. He laid her down and pulled the covers up to her shoulders. He didn't dare remove her clothes. It was bad enough seeing as much of her as he had that morning while checking her stitches and the night before. He hadn't wanted her to be uncomfortable by sleeping in her pants. He'd reached under her shirt and had unbuttoned her pants. The warmth of her skin was heavenly next to his fingers. He thought about removing her shirt and pants now to help her into something more comfortable but knew if he started, he wasn't convinced he'd be able to stop, and he wasn't going to take advantage of her.

She'd just have to sleep in her jeans tonight. He wasn't strong enough to remove them again and leave her alone in the bed.

Wolf sat by the edge of the bed and simply watched Caroline sleeping. He studied her and tried to figure out what made her different from all the other women that had come before her. After a while he gave up. It was what it was and he wasn't going to analyze it anymore. He just wanted to enjoy it.

He still had a lot of time left before he had to leave for the next mission. While he wanted to visit with his friend, Tex, he wanted to spend most of his vacation time with Caroline. His priorities had shifted in a blink of an eye. Wolf didn't fight it.

He leaned down and kissed Caroline on the forehead. Wolf closed the hotel door softly and headed down the hall to the elevator. He'd meet back up with Mozart and Abe at Tex's house then come back early the next morning. He couldn't wait to spend another day with Caroline.

Chapter Eleven

CAROLINE ROLLED OVER the next morning and groaned. Shit. She'd done it again—fallen asleep—and Matthew had to put her to bed. She yawned and stretched, thinking she was such a lame date.

She got out of bed and instead of heading straight for the bathroom, Caroline checked the coffee pot…and smiled. It was set and ready to go. Matthew had obviously set it all up before he'd left last night. Caroline liked knowing he thought about her comfort that way. It had been so long since someone had done something so simple for her. She liked being taken care of. Caroline turned the switch to on and went back to the bedroom to get ready for the day.

After showering and checking her stitches—which were healing nicely—Caroline poured herself a cup of coffee and settled on the couch to watch TV. She was enjoying the free time to be lazy and not have to rush off to work. That time would come soon enough, so for now she was happy to lounge around.

Glancing around the room, Caroline did have to see about checking out of the hotel though. She figured Matthew had to be paying for it, as she certainly didn't give the front desk her credit card. She'd ask the hotel to switch to her card when she checked out; it wasn't fair for Matthew to pay for her room.

Since she rented an apartment before she left California, Caroline had planned on staying in a hotel for a few nights anyway until her stuff arrived. This hotel was just as good as any other. Figuring she had another couple of days before her furniture arrived from California, she relaxed against the couch again. Ahhhh, it felt so good to lounge around and be a bum. She didn't get to do it very much and it was a luxury now.

The phone ringing next to her startled her so badly she spilled her coffee. Crud. She rubbed at the coffee that had fallen on her jeans at the same time she leaned over to answer the phone. It had to be Matthew, she didn't know anyone else in the area.

"Hello?"

"Good morning, Caroline. How are you feeling today?"

God, if Caroline thought his voice was sexy in person, over the phone, rumbling in her ear? Panty melting. "I'm good. I'm sorry I conked out on you again last night. You're always taking me to bed." She blushed as soon as she said it. It sounded much dirtier out loud than it had in her head.

Wolf laughed. "Believe me, Ice, I love putting you to bed. I'm hoping sometime in the near future I can join you there."

Caroline was stunned into silence. Hell, she'd been thinking about how much she wanted him to join her in bed, but she didn't think he'd come right out and say it. She didn't know what to say.

"Caroline? You still there? Too soon?"

"Yes...er...no..." Shit. She was beyond flustered. She heard Matthew chuckle and tried to clarify. "Yeah, I'm still here, and...a bit...but I think I want that too." She still couldn't get over that Matthew, looking like he did, tall, dark and handsome, a man who could get any woman in his bed, seemed to want *her*.

She must have said that bit out loud because Matthew retorted, "Hell yeah I want you, Ice. You're smart, you're level headed, and I've wanted you since I shook your hand on the damn plane."

"Uh..." was all Caroline could get out. Holy. Shit.

Matthew continued as if he hadn't just blown her mind. "So, I'm coming over in an hour to get you. I thought I'd take you to meet my friend, Tex. The one I told you about on the plane? He's having a mini-get together with us, Abe, and Mozart and some of his friends here in town. I want you to meet him. It's casual, so don't dress up. Okay?"

Knowing this was a huge deal, meeting his friend, all Caroline could do is say, "Okay."

"I'll come up when I get there. See you soon, Caroline."

Caroline hung up the phone. An hour. She couldn't wait to see him again.

CAROLINE THREW HER head back and laughed unselfconsciously at Matthew's friend, Tex. His name was really John, but since he'd been from Texas when he joined the SEALs his nickname was naturally, Tex. He still had a thick southern accent and was just as brawny as all the other men standing around.

Tex had been on a mission and in a building which had been hit by an IED. The men downplayed the incident, but Caroline instinctively knew there was a lot more to it than they'd talked about.

Tex had lost his leg after several surgeries to try to repair it. He told her one day after he'd been admitted to the hospital again for a severe infection, he begged the doctors to just take it off. He figured it'd be better than dealing with the pain of infections and numerous surgeries to try to heal it, when he most likely wouldn't be able to walk on it again anyway.

Tex was hysterical, constantly saying outrageous things to make her laugh. Caroline didn't think she'd laughed so hard in all her life. Caroline liked all of Tex's friends as well, and had enjoyed hanging out with Christopher and Sam. The guys had told her to call them Abe and Mozart, but as she'd told them earlier, it felt weird to call them by their nicknames when she wasn't a part of their team. They'd argued with her about it, claiming she *was* a part of their damn team, but she'd gotten stubborn and crossed her arms and told them in no uncertain terms that she'd call them what she wanted and they could just deal. Abe and Mozart merely laughed and told her she could call them whatever she wanted, but she'd always be "Ice" to them.

Nobody talked about what Tex did now that he was medically retired from the Navy. Caroline had asked once and noticed the subject was quickly changed. She'd merely shrugged, figuring it was a secret Navy thing or he was embarrassed about it. Either way, it didn't matter as she probably wouldn't ever see him again.

Caroline tried not to feel self-conscious at the get together. There were some other women around, but she kept herself glued to Matthew's side. It was hard for her to open up, and she felt most comfortable with Matthew. He certainly wasn't complaining and was constantly touching her. He'd put his hand at her waist to steady her, brought her a plate of food once it was done, and brushed his hand against hers. Once he even kissed her on the top of her head when she was feeling bad for Tex and what he'd gone through. Caroline loved it, but she was still cautious. She'd never understand what Matthew saw in her.

After leaving Tex's house, Matthew had taken her to the Botanical Gardens. The gardens were beautiful. Caroline didn't know the name of many of the flowers, but she loved seeing the artistic way they'd been arranged and grown on the grounds. Matthew bought her a bouquet of some exotic type of flower and they'd made their way back to her hotel room.

Matthew came up with her to the room and settled them on the couch. They'd ordered room service and had eaten it enjoying each other's company and the relaxed conversation about nothing in particular.

As night fell, Caroline got more and more nervous. She couldn't help but think about what Matthew had said that morning about taking her to bed. One side of her, the hussy side, wanted it. The other more practical side, knew it was too soon.

"What are you thinking about so hard?" Wolf asked, putting his finger under her chin and lifting it so she had to look him in the eye.

"I…just…I want you." Caroline couldn't believe she'd just blurted it out like that.

"I want you too," Wolf returned without hesitation.

"It's just…well…"

"It's too soon." Wolf finished her sentence for her.

Caroline nodded. "I like you Matthew, but I don't know about this. About us. You're…you and I'm me…and you live in California and I just moved here…"

Wolf drew Caroline into his body. She felt so right there. He couldn't believe how right she felt. She had some valid points. They had a lot going against them, the least of which was that they lived on opposite sides of the country.

"Shhhh, Ice. I know this is crazy. We just met, but I'll tell you this, I've never, in all my life, felt about someone the way I feel about you. There's something about you that I'm having a hard time resisting."

He felt her nod against his chest and smiled.

"I'd love to spend my leave time with you and see if we think this thing between us can work out. I'm not going to say we won't make love, because I want that more than I can tell you, but I'll try to keep it easy for now. Okay?"

At her soft, "okay," he let out the breath he'd been holding. Wolf didn't know what he would've done if she'd disagreed with him.

"But that doesn't mean I'm not going to kiss you, hold you and touch you as much as I can while we're 'taking it slow.' I want to make sure you're good with that."

Caroline lifted her head from his chest and looked him in the eyes. "I'm very good with that, Matthew."

He smiled and turned and stretched her out under him on the

couch. Touching from their toes to chest, Wolf could feel Caroline's heart beating quickly under him. He could see her breathing increase and felt her hands grip his shirt at his waist.

Wolf leaned down, brought his lips low until they remained a breath above hers, and waited. She didn't disappoint him. She stretched her neck up until she could reach his mouth. He sighed in contentment. Caroline wanted the same thing he did. Thank God. It was important to him that she come to him. While he wasn't shy or usually all that concerned about being the aggressor in a relationship, with Caroline, he wanted her to be sure. He wanted her to want him as much as he wanted her.

While his lips caressed hers, his hands roamed her body gently. He kept his hands on top of her clothes, knowing he wouldn't be able to stop himself if he felt Caroline's creamy skin against his hands. Wolf was careful not to touch her injured side, but otherwise he didn't hold his roaming hands back.

He skimmed his hands over her breasts lightly, feeling her nipples peak under his touch. He kept moving, gentling her when she bucked under him and holding her tight against him so she could feel how excited he was. Wolf didn't want her to think she was alone in what she was feeling, alone in her attraction.

Finally with one hand at her hip holding her close and one hand lying over her heart, he pulled his lips away from hers reluctantly.

"Jesus, Caroline. You're perfect. Perfect for me."

As he expected, she blushed a rosy pink.

"You're not so bad yourself, Matthew."

He smiled and pulled them upright. Caroline's hair was mussed and her lips were swollen from their passionate kisses. She looked amazing. Wolf fitted her body next to his and kissed her on top of her head.

"Snuggle in, Ice. I don't want to leave yet, but we have to stop...that...so we'll watch a movie. Sound good?"

Caroline smiled. Hell yeah it sounded good.

WOLF JERKED AWAKE. He could go from asleep to being one hundred percent awake, thanks to being a SEAL. He didn't know what had woken him up until he heard a whimper. Caroline was jerking in his arms. It was obvious she was having a nightmare.

"Wake up, Ice." Wolf tried to talk her out of her dream, but Caroline just whimpered louder at his words. "Caroline." Wolf said loudly and firmly. "Wake up. You're dreaming."

Wolf wasn't ready for her reaction. She fought against him as if she was back on the plane fighting the terrorist.

Caroline fought with all her might. The terrorist was going to hurt Matthew, she had to make sure he didn't get to him. It was up to her to save Matthew. She batted at the hands that were grabbing at her, ignoring his words. She had to fight, if she didn't, he'd kill her.

Her struggles had made them tumble off the couch—luckily he'd hit the floor first and prevented Caroline from landing on her back. Wolf's heart hurt at the expression on her face. She was terrified and his hold on her wasn't helping.

"Caroline!" Wolf yelled. She stilled, he was getting to her. He turned her over so she was lying on her back on the floor. He hovered over her, not putting his weight on her, but close enough he could still feel her body heat. "Wake up! You're safe, you're fine. You're here in Virginia, not on the plane. Come back to me. It's Matthew."

"Matthew?" Caroline's voice was soft, disbelieving.

"Yes, open your eyes."

Caroline forced her eyes to open and saw that it was, indeed, Matthew. He was straddled over her, leaning down peering into her eyes intently.

"Oh shit," Caroline whispered.

"Come on, let's get you up off the floor." Wolf helped her sit up and situated back on the couch. As soon as she was, he sat next to her and pulled her into his chest.

"You're okay. It was just a dream."

Caroline shook with the aftereffects of the images that had been flitting through her head. It had seemed so real.

"Want to talk about it?"

She shook her head against his chest, not looking up.

"Okay. I'm assuming it was about what happened on the plane?" At her nod he told her, "You need to talk to someone about it, Caroline. If you don't, the dreams won't stop. Believe me, I know."

At that, Caroline looked up at Matthew. "You know?"

He looked grim, but met her eyes. "Yeah, in my line of work there's no way I can keep it all bottled in. It's true most men in the military don't like to admit to weaknesses when it comes to night-mares and PTSD, but we're required to debrief anytime we have a heavy mission. In fact, Abe, Mozart, and I are required to meet with someone here to talk about what happened on the plane."

Caroline could only stare up at him in amazement. "Really?"

Wolf chuckled and brought her into his chest again. She tucked her head under his chin and wrapped her arms around his waist. He changed position until he was lying with his head on the armrest of the couch, shifting Caroline until she was lying with her front settled along his side. Her arm came to rest on his chest, where she idly drew shapes over his heart.

"Yeah. Can't say I like all the shrinks they make us see, but hon-estly, it works. We might grumble about it, but if it keeps us sane, and ready for our next mission, we'll do it."

"I was fighting that guy. I knew if he got the better of me or if I let him go, he'd go and kill you. I didn't want you to die." Caroline spoke quietly and from the heart.

"Oh, sweetheart." Wolf tightened his arms around her. "You were so brave. I'm so proud of you. But..." he waited until she raised her eyes to his. When she was looking at him, he continued. "I can take care of myself. Don't ever put yourself in danger again for me. Promise me."

"But Matthew, this is just…I don't…" Shit. She'd never had a hard time expressing what she wanted to say before. But the right words just wouldn't come to her.

He shook his head. "No buts. Just promise me Caroline. Look after you first. Always."

She could only nod. The look in his eyes was intense. She broke eye contact and laid her head back down. She gripped him harder and brought the hand that was lying on his chest up and curled it around the back of his neck and squeezed.

"Sleep now. I'm here. I'll make sure nothing happens to you."

"Thank you. I feel safe here with you."

Caroline fell asleep still clutching him. Wolf had never felt more content in all his life. Usually he felt antsy sleeping with a woman; never letting her cuddle into him, and leaving as soon as it was socially acceptable. But with Caroline all bets were off.

Long after the sun fell from the sky Wolf eased out from under her. He once more carried Caroline to bed. He laughed quietly to himself. This was becoming a habit for him—one he liked.

As he spread the comforter over Caroline, Wolf heard the shrill ring of his phone in the other room in the suite. Crap. His phone didn't ring unless it was work. No! They still had over a week before they were supposed to leave. Maybe it was about the terrorist incident? With one final look at Caroline and one last light kiss to her forehead, Wolf closed the bedroom door softly and went to answer his phone, hoping against hope it was nothing important.

CAROLINE STRETCHED CAREFULLY as she woke, amazed at how quickly her side was healing, and looked around. Crap. Really? Third time in a row? Once again she didn't remember how she'd gotten to bed. She *did* remember her nightmare and the intense make out session with Matthew though.

Smiling at the memory, Caroline immediately looked at the pillow next to her and saw a piece of paper folded up.

Her heart raced and she couldn't wait to see what he had to say. Caroline reached over and grabbed the unassuming little note and opened it.

Caroline, you have to know I hate having to write you another note. Hopefully one day I can be right there next to you when you wake up...Now that you're blushing...

Jesus, this man knew her so well. Caroline kept reading.

...You know Mozart, Abe, and I came out here to Norfolk for vacation before our mission started; unfortunately that mission came sooner than we thought it would. I've had a great time spending time with you over the last couple of days. If it's okay, I'd like to get in touch with you when we get back. I'd like to get to know you better. I know we have some things to work out, mainly the distance between our homes, but I still want to explore what's happening between us. I'm not sure how long it'll take for us to get back to Norfolk. Sometimes our missions are short, but other times they can drag on much longer than we'd like. I'm leaving my cell phone number so you can call me. If you'd like to get together when I get back (and I hope you will!) just call and leave me a number where I can reach you. I'll call as soon as we get back. Good luck with your new job. Knock 'em dead! Matthew. PS. Abe and Mozart say hello and they're sorry they didn't get to hang out with us last night. I didn't tell them I wasn't...

Caroline read the letter twice and hugged it to her chest. She wasn't sure what to do about Matthew. It was a heady feeling, one she'd never experienced. No one ever wanted to get to know her better. It was almost too good to be true.

Caroline carefully put the letter in her purse and took a deep breath. Time to get back to her real life. She wasn't a SEAL and needed to contact her employer to let him know what was going on. She could even start work early if he wanted her to and she almost hoped he did. She needed something to take her mind off of Matthew and everything that had happened recently.

Caroline packed up and took one last look around the hotel room on her way out. She was headed to the apartment she'd rented before coming out to Virginia. Before she left, she pulled out both letters Matthew had left her and read them one more time. On impulse she added his number to her cell phone contacts. Not that she was going to call him...they couldn't possibly work out...it was better to end things now before she fell in love with him...wasn't it?

Chapter Twelve

Two weeks later.

FOR THE MOST part, Caroline was enjoying her job. It was much the same as she'd done in San Diego. A chemist's work really wasn't that exciting to most people no matter where it was done, but Caroline loved it. It was hard to explain to someone else why or even what she did. She was just fascinated how the mixing of chemicals could make something useful and lifesaving, or it could make it destructive and deadly. She recalled how Matthew had seemed interested when she'd tried to explain what it was she did to him.

She'd actually dialed Matthew's cell phone a few times in the last few days. Each time she planned to leave a message agreeing to see him when he got back, but she chickened out each time. Heck she had no idea if he was even back already. What if he'd changed his mind and decided a relationship was too much trouble? Did he even want a relationship? She was driving herself nuts.

Caroline decided to give Matthew the benefit of the doubt and believe he was still out of the country. So she'd called him. Just hearing his voice on his voice mail was enough to snap her to her senses. What was she doing? They had a great time in those couple of days together, but what if he was just feeling grateful she'd help save his life, or he was just concerned about her in the way someone would be concerned about a sister?

Of course the kisses they shared didn't *feel* like a brother/sister kiss to her. She sighed. She usually wasn't this indecisive. When she wanted something she went for it. But then again, she'd never had someone who looked like Matthew show her any attention before.

Caroline thought about the three SEALs quite a bit over the last two weeks. She supposed you didn't go through something like what they had and not feel some sort of connection. She did want to know if Matthew, Sam, and Christopher were all okay and back safe from wherever they'd gone, but she was embarrassed to actually leave him a message. Matthew was the kind of man a woman only dreamed about. He was the type of man that tall gorgeous women dated, not someone like her; a geeky scientist.

The media had been going crazy over the hijacking. Every time she turned on the TV a story about it was on. Caroline had seen Brandy all over the various news channels. Brandy had no idea what she was talking about, as she'd hidden in the back of the plane while everything was happening, but the news outlets were still clamoring to talk to her.

There was a lot of talk about the "mysterious" men who'd saved the day, but from what Caroline had seen, so far no one knew who they were. And there had been no mention of her name that she could tell, thank God.

One thing Caroline did hear when she'd watched one of the stories that made her extremely nervous, was when the hijacking was called a "trial run" for a bigger operation of taking over planes that was supposed to have happened later on. *That* had certainly riled the country up. Airline security had been tightened, and people were obviously scared to fly. But what made Caroline nervous was knowing it wasn't just four people acting alone. There was someone, or some *people* out there who wanted to do it again and possibly hurt and kill more innocent people. Caroline wouldn't wish what she'd gone through on anyone else.

After seeing that news story Caroline had tried to not watch anything else on the hijacking. She'd lived it, and knew the truth, and honestly it was just freaking her out hearing all the political reasons why it might have happened. She started listening to the oldies radio station for noise factor instead of turning on the television.

Caroline's new apartment wasn't too far from where she worked, so she didn't need to drive to get there. She took the bus most places she had to go, but Caroline would drive to the beach or up the coast. She enjoyed the Virginia countryside. It was soothing to her frazzled nerves.

As far as getting to work, Caroline varied her travel times and routes, any single woman alone knew it was a smart thing to do, but she still felt extraordinarily nervous. A few times she'd thought she was being followed, but when she tried to figure out by whom, she couldn't find anyone who looked suspicious. Caroline had also been getting hang up calls at work—answering the phone to no one there, or at least they weren't saying anything.

Caroline hadn't given much thought to the episodes before she'd seen the news reports about the attempted hijacking she'd been involved with. With the potential threat for other planned hijackings, now she couldn't *not* think about them! What if somehow the terrorist group, knew who she was and about her part in the failed hijacking? What if they were following her?

A few days after watching the news reports about the hijacking, Caroline was late leaving the office—working late on a project that was having a breakthrough. Her coworkers had stayed as well, but they'd all left in their cars to head home. Caroline actually watched them walk to their cars, leaving her standing in the doorway of the office building. She mentally shook her head. She was the only one who used public transportation and no one thought to ask if she wanted a ride home. Too independent for her own good sometimes, Caroline knew she should've just asked for a ride—now it was too late.

Caroline wistfully thought about Matthew. She knew he was the type of man that would never let a woman take any type of public transportation this late at night alone. At the very least he'd escort her home. She sighed. Caroline never thought about this sort of thing until she'd met Matthew and his team. She'd just taken it as status quo and gone about her business.

Caroline got out her cell phone and walked with a purpose toward the bus stop. She only had to go three blocks, but it was dark out. Luckily the bus arrived not too much after she arrived at the bus stop, which was good because Caroline didn't want to stand in the dark waiting for it. She was too freaked out.

The feeling she was being watched didn't abate once she was on the bus. Once again she didn't see any passengers that looked out of place, but she couldn't get rid of the creepy feeling.

She hurried off at her stop and power walked all the way to her apartment building. She didn't relax until she'd made it inside and had closed and locked the door. Keeping her phone in her hand so she could beat herself up over whether or not to call Matthew later that night, she put her purse and bag down and headed toward the bathroom. She wanted to splash some cold water on her face and change out of her work clothes. The anxiety about her uncertain relationship with Matthew, her feelings of being watched, along with the stress of the aftermath of the hijacking were messing with her big time. She wasn't sleeping well and she was exhausted.

As she reached the bathroom, she heard a noise behind her. She looked back and saw the doorknob of her apartment being turned. The door was locked, but someone was out there. Holy crap. She wasn't losing her mind. Someone *had* to have been following her. If it was someone who wanted to talk to her legitimately they would've knocked. No one came up to a door and grabbed the doorknob to open it; they knocked and announced themselves…unless they were up to no good.

Caroline didn't wait to see who was at the door, or if they got through it or not. She bolted into the bedroom and opened the window at the fire escape. She had no idea if it would trick the person at the door into believing she'd left that way or not, but maybe, just maybe they'd think she fled and wouldn't take the time to search the rest of the apartment.

She raced back toward the bathroom just as she heard the creak of the front door notifying her that someone had just opened it. They'd obviously used some sort of lock pick to get in; otherwise she would've heard the door being broken down. They were trying to sneak up on her to surprise her. They also obviously didn't want to make a ruckus so others in the complex would hear and become suspicious.

Heart racing, she entered the bathroom and left the door open. She prayed the open bedroom window would make whoever it was think that she left that way. The open bathroom door would hopefully also make them think no one was in there. She climbed into the tub and eased the shower curtain most of the way shut. She didn't close it all the way, again in the hopes that it would look like no one was in the shower.

Caroline noticed her cell phone in her hand. Thank God. She almost cried in relief. She quickly dialed 911 and waited for someone to answer.

"Hello, 911, what is your emergency?"

Caroline heard the voice on the other end of the phone and literally sagged in relief. She had no idea who the person was, or what they looked like, and she didn't really care. All she cared about was that someone was there to help her.

Whispering in a voice so low she had no idea if the woman on the other end of the line could hear her, she said, "I'm in my apartment, someone broke in. I'm hiding in the shower. Please. Hurry!"

"Okay, I've got your address. The police are on the way. Stay put, stay quiet, they'll be there as soon as they can."

Caroline sighed in relief. The 911 operator's voice was calm and soothing, just what she needed at that moment. Still whispering Caroline said, "Thank you," then hit the off button on the phone. She knew she probably was supposed to stay on the line until the cops got there, but she couldn't, she wanted to hear Matthew's voice.

Caroline hit his name in her address book and dialed his cell, almost on autopilot. She didn't know who was in her house, but whoever it was, wasn't going to let her live if they were somehow related to the terrorist incident. She knew it.

Caroline didn't want Matthew thinking she never wanted to see him again. If he got back from his mission and didn't hear from her that's exactly what he'd think. He'd probably never know she'd been thinking about him and how much she'd enjoyed the time they'd spent together. It was time to leave that message for him.

She waited through his message, tearing up at hearing his low, grumbly voice. After the beep she whispered, "*Hi Matthew, it's me, Caroline…um…Ice. I wanted to let you know I would've loved to have gotten together with you again when you got back. I didn't want you to think that I didn't….but I don't know if I'll be here…..I'm in my apartment, but someone just broke in. I'm hiding in the bathroom. I've called 911, but if they don't get here in time… I wanted you to know that I desperately wanted to see you again…*"

Caroline hit the disconnect button to end the call and turned off the phone entirely. She didn't want the concerned sounding emergency operator calling her back and having the phone ring at the wrong time. Even on vibration mode, the ringing could still be heard.

She tried to slow her breaths and be as quiet as she could. That was harder than she thought. It was scary that she was actually hoping it was just someone that wanted to rob her, or God forbid assault her, but deep down she knew whoever it was would kill her if he found her. She listened as whoever it was in her apartment went into her bedroom and closed her window. Caroline thought she heard him swear, then she heard him going through her drawers. She couldn't even be embarrassed. He could look at her undies all he wanted, if he just *left*.

At one point, he actually came into the bathroom, looked through her medicine cabinet and even used the toilet. Caroline was afraid to breathe. She was more scared now than she was on the plane. All it would take is one breath, one wrong movement, one cough, one sneeze, to alert him she was there. Matthew and his team weren't there to help her. Caroline was on her own and she suddenly realized how out of her element she really was. She thought she was brave, but when push came to shove, she realized she wasn't brave at all. She'd never felt so alone in all her life.

Finally whoever it was left the bathroom. Caroline heard sirens in the distance, running feet and her door close quietly. Jesus, he didn't even slam the damn door. That said a lot about his control and level of professionalism. She didn't move. What if there were two of them in her apartment? What if the person wasn't really gone and only wanted her to *think* he left the apartment to try to draw her out.

Caroline stood silent and quiet even when she heard the police banging on her front door. She was frozen in fear, but desperately wanted to rush to the door and throw herself into the officers' arms. But the more she thought about it, the more she realized she couldn't trust even the police, what if it wasn't really the cops? She didn't move until she heard the officers in her little apartment. Knowing she couldn't stay cowering in her shower forever, she slowly moved the curtain aside and called out to the officers.

Chapter Thirteen

WOLF COULDN'T WAIT until the ship he was on got closer to land. He wanted to check his voice mail, but knew it wouldn't work until they were in range of a cell phone tower on American soil. For the thousandth time he wished he had a satellite phone, but of course that was impractical for everyday use. He shook his head and laughed at himself. He was worse than a high schooler with his first crush.

Mozart and Abe had given him a hard time, but he knew they were just as anxious to hear from Caroline, to make sure she was all right. They'd really taken to her and had told Wolf all the time how lucky he was.

Cookie, Benny, and Dude hadn't met Caroline, but they'd certainly heard all about her from the team. They'd been stunned at her actions on the plane and had asked a million questions about her job as a chemist. Wolf knew they'd find her as amazing as he did. As long as they kept their hands to themselves, all would be well.

Wolf should've been surprised at how possessive he felt about Caroline, but he wasn't. It just seemed right. He couldn't be freaked out about it when she felt like *his*.

It went against everything Wolf knew to leave Caroline in that hotel bed without talking to her first, but he didn't have a choice. As soon as he'd answered his phone he knew he'd have to leave. His boss had notified Wolf the situation had changed and they had to go right away. No one argued with him, such was life as a Navy SEAL, but

Wolf hadn't liked it. For the first time in his life there was someone in his life that came before his job.

Being a Navy SEAL had always come first. Always. At no time had he allowed a woman to dictate what he did when. It felt weird because in the past when a woman tried to tie him down, he got antsy and broke things off. Now, he *wanted* Caroline to tie him down. He didn't know if he loved her, but he figured with the way he felt about her after the short time he'd spent with her, he was well on his way.

When he'd made it to the ship Mozart and Abe wanted to know how Caroline was doing. How was her side? Were the stitches okay? Wolf had answered their questions and told them how much he'd enjoyed his time with her. Expecting the guys to give him crap, he was shocked when they'd just smiled at him and told him it was about time he found a woman who was good enough for him.

Even Tex had pulled him aside at his house and told him how much he liked Caroline. Tex had always been an easy-going guy and never, not once, had he commented on Wolf's choice of woman...until Caroline. His team's approval meant a lot to him. That wasn't to say Wolf would've listened to them if they didn't like her, but he was glad they did. They'd hopefully be seeing more of Caroline in the future.

Finally the phone in Wolf's hand vibrated. They'd sailed close enough to the United States to be able to receive a signal. Thank God he had a message! He eagerly drew the phone up to his ear, hoping to hear Caroline's voice saying she wanted to see him again.

"Hi Matthew, it's me, Caroline...um...Ice..." At first Wolf was thrilled to hear her voice, but confused about why she was whispering. Then his blood ran cold. *What the hell? Oh shit.* His Caroline was in trouble. Listening to her soft voice quavering in fear was heart wrenching. She'd been in trouble and called to reassure *him.* Jesus. She knew he couldn't help her, but she'd called anyway. Wolf

couldn't even think. *Him*, the Navy SEAL, had no idea what to do.

He spun, took the stairs two at a time, and burst into the day room. All five members of his team looked up sharply, instantly alarmed. They'd never seen Wolf so frazzled and it put them on high alert.

"Caroline," was all he could get out. He was breathing hard and was definitely panicked. Mozart and Abe came over to him and Wolf just held out the phone. Abe grabbed it and played the message on the speaker for them all to hear.

No one said a word until Mozart uttered, "Fuck." It looked like she'd called about twenty-four hours ago. Twenty-four freaking hours ago. There were no other messages from her. No one wanted to say it, but they all knew that wasn't a good sign.

They couldn't get off the ship for at *least* another four hours. They had to dock and get clearance. Benny, Cookie, and Dude hadn't met Caroline, but with everything they'd heard enough about her from the others, they were just as concerned about her as Mozart, Abe, and Wolf were. Well, maybe not as concerned as Wolf.

Wolf immediately dialed the number Caroline had called from. He listened to it ring and ring and ring. When her message came on, he didn't bother to listen to it. As much as he wanted to hear her voice again, he wanted to hear her in person, not a recording. He hung up and called back. He had no idea how many times he would've kept calling her back, probably until one of his team members confiscated his phone, but luckily the third time he'd hit her number she finally answered.

"Hello?" She answered tentatively.

"Caroline?" Wolf said urgently, hoping like hell it was her. How she'd become so important to him in such a short time, he had no idea. But there it was. It was the moment he'd heard her whispered voice and realized he wasn't there and couldn't help her that he knew she was his. Period. His.

"Yes, this is she," Caroline said shakily. She hadn't recovered from the break in at her apartment and didn't recognize the voice on the other end of the line.

"It's me, Wolf...er...Matthew. Are you okay? Jesus, Caroline. Talk to me."

"Matthew!" Caroline breathed a sigh of relief. Oh my God, she was so relieved to hear his voice she had to sit down. She collapsed on a chair that luckily was nearby, then remembered the message she'd left for him. "Are you back? Are you calling to see when we can get together?" Caroline tried to play dumb and pretend Matthew was calling about a date. Maybe he hadn't checked his voice mail yet. She wasn't thinking straight because he wouldn't know her number if he hadn't checked his messages. She also knew by the tone of his voice when he'd asked if she was all right, he'd heard the panicked message she'd left.

"What the hell, Caroline?" He practically roared at her. "Are you all right woman? What the hell is going on?"

Caroline winced. Shit. Maybe she shouldn't have called him from her apartment after all. He sounded pissed, not excited to hear from her. She leaned over in the chair clutching her stomach. Her lower lip trembled and she closed her eyes.

Abe grabbed the phone from Wolf and glared at him as he brought it up to his ear. Abe knew Wolf was frantic, but Jesus, he was going to piss Ice off or scare her away if he didn't get control of himself.

"This is Abe, Ice. What Wolf *meant* to say was that he got your message and he wanted to make sure you were all right," he said quietly gesturing at Wolf to "relax" and shooting daggers at him with his eyes.

Caroline sighed and choked back a sob. "I'm okay, Christopher. Thanks. Can you put Matthew back on? Please?" Caroline was impressed she remembered his real name. She'd been afraid she'd forget them, so she'd repeated them to herself several times over the last few weeks, making sure she knew them backward and forward.

Abe looked over at his team leader. Wolf was sitting on a chair with his head resting on his clenched fists. He could see the whites of Wolf's knuckles and could tell he was in no condition to talk rationally yet.

"Um, no, sorry, not just yet. Why don't you tell me what's going on."

Caroline sighed. Christopher had asked her to tell him what was going on, but she knew it wasn't really a question. It was a demand.

"I didn't mean to upset him, Christopher. God, can you tell him that? I just...hell...If something happened, I didn't want Matthew to think I didn't want to see him again. That's all. He's the best thing that's happened to me in my life." She paused, took a deep breath, and continued. "Then I ...got busy...and forgot to call him back." That was a lie, but she figured it was safer for the moment to stretch the truth. She didn't want to blurt out that she missed Matthew terribly and had wanted to call him every day, every hour. That was a little too "stalkerish," even for her.

Abe repeated his question. "What's going on? I can tell you aren't telling me everything. You *know* I hate it when people lie. Tell me, Ice. Tell me now."

Caroline didn't like the hardness in Christopher's voice, but she knew she wouldn't be able to beat around the bush for much longer. She told him a watered down version of what had happened at her apartment.

"I got home from work and someone tried to break in. I hid in the bathroom until the cops got there and whoever it was left."

Abe knew there was more to what happened than what she'd told him. Hell, she'd tried to downplay wrestling with a damn terrorist; there was no way that two sentence explanation was anywhere *close* to what had happened. Deciding to let it rest until they could see her in person, he informed her, "It'll take us a bit to get over there, probably about five hours or so, but don't you *move* from your apartment until we get there. Okay?"

Caroline hesitated.

"Okay, Ice?" Abe asked again impatiently when she didn't immediately agree.

"I'm not at my apartment, Christopher." Caroline told him in a small voice.

"Where the hell are you then?" Abe practically shouted at her.

Caroline flinched at the other end of the phone as she sat up in the chair. Her stomach hurt. This was horrible. She wanted Matthew and his team there, but she wanted them to be safe more. Why were they yelling at her? Crap. She drew her feet up and sat them on the chair by her butt. She grabbed her knees with one arm and held the phone to her ear with the other hand. She couldn't deal with this on top of everything else. A new voice came on the other end of the phone.

Dude had taken the phone from Abe. "Ice? My name's Dude and I'm on Wolf's team. I take it you aren't at home? Why don't you tell me where you are and we can come and see in person that you're okay."

Caroline shook her head. "Sorry Faulkner, it *is* Faulkner right? I'm trying to match up everyone's given names with nicknames. Matthew told me all about you guys, and I think I have it, but I could make a mistake." Caroline knew she was stalling so she continued, "I don't really know you though. I'm not telling someone I haven't met where I am, even if you *are* in the same room as Matthew and Christopher."

Silence followed her pronouncement, and yet another voice came at her from the other end of the phone.

"Ice, this is Mozart. You remember me right?"

Caroline snorted, and it came out as a half laugh and half sob. It looked they were going to keep passing the phone around until everyone on the team spoke with her. "Duh. Of course I do. You did such a pretty embroidery job on my side, Sam." She tried to keep it light.

"That's right. Now where are you?" Mozart cut to the chase, glad to hear her voice and know she seemed to be okay, but not happy at the way she was prevaricating. "Why aren't you at your apartment?"

"It's a long story, Sam, but I can't tell you right now."

"Why not, Ice? Please, you know you can trust us, we'll help you."

"I know, but I'm not allo…..I just can't. Okay?"

"Allowed? You aren't allowed to tell us? What the *hell*, Ice?" Mozart sputtered, getting more and more incensed and worried about her.

Wolf finally had himself under control and gestured for his phone back. Mozart saw that Wolf did indeed seem to have himself back under his iron control and handed the phone over while whispering urgently, "Find out what the hell's going on and do it now. Something's wrong."

Wolf nodded curtly and tried to soften his tone when he spoke into the phone again. "Caroline? It's Matthew."

"I know," Caroline told him softly, "I recognize your voice now."

"I need to know where you are, honey," Wolf pleaded, emotion coating his words, "Please."

"Matthew, I'm not allowed to tell anyone. I'm not even supposed to be on the phone."

Ignoring the "allowed" comment for the moment, Wolf tried to back up a bit. She'd get to it; he just had to make her feel safe with him again. In a tender voice, he urged, "Tell us what happened Caroline. Please. I'm going to put you on speaker so we can all hear you and you don't have to repeat it."

Caroline sighed. When Matthew spoke to her in that low urgent voice she really couldn't deny him anything. She wasn't happy about being on speaker, and having his entire team hear what had happened, but Matthew had a good point. She didn't want to repeat her story a million times either.

"It was dark when I headed home from work and all the way home I felt like someone was watching me. Actually I felt that way all week."

Before she could continue, Wolf interrupted her. "Why'd you leave work so late? Why didn't anyone make sure you got home all right?"

Caroline hesitated; she didn't want Faulkner, Hunter, or Kason to have to hear about how she was. "Matthew, I *told* you about me already. You *know*."

Wolf gritted his teeth. Dammit.

Abe broke in before Wolf could say anything. "Caroline, it's Abe. We might not have noticed you in the airport before we knew you, but any man who's any kind of man would've made sure you got home all right."

Caroline shook her head. They just didn't understand. They were *there*. They'd seen the men on the plane leave with the pretty women and ignore her when she'd decided to stay at the airport. Hell, *they'd* left her there too. She willed the tears back. Now wasn't the time. She had to get through this story.

"Anyway, so I felt like someone was following me, but I didn't see anyone. When I got home, I heard someone at my door trying to get in. I opened the bedroom window that leads to the fire escape in the hopes whoever it was would think I heard him and went out that way. I then hid inside the shower in the bathroom and called 911. The lady that answered was so nice. She kept calm and tried to make sure *I* was calm."

Wolf could hear the way her voice wobbled as she'd talked about calling for help while hiding in her damn shower. "You called me too," he murmured in a low voice.

Forgetting she was on speaker and all of his team could hear her, she admitted, "Yeah. All I could think of is that if you'd been there, I'd have felt so much safer and you would've taken care of it...me."

Jesus. Wolf tried to reassure her. He could hear in the tone of her voice how scared she'd been. "I'm sorry I wasn't there. You're right, I would've taken care of you." After letting that sink in he urged her to continue. "Go on, tell us the rest."

"Well, the police came and I told them what happened. The next thing I knew the FBI was there talking to me, telling me I had to go to a safe house." She lowered her voice, "I don't understand what's going on, Matthew. The FBI wouldn't really say why they thought I had to be put here. I don't know who to trust and I don't know what's going on. I don't think it had to do with the plane, but even if it did, I didn't tell the FBI anything. I swear I didn't, Matthew."

"Shhh, I know you didn't, hon. I promise we'll figure this out. You trust us right? You trust me?"

"I do, Matthew. Out of everyone throughout this I trust you and Christopher and Sam."

"Caroline, you can trust Benny, Cookie, and Dude too. Don't trust anyone else but my team. No one. Understand?"

Caroline nodded, then remembering that he couldn't see her, said, "Yeah, I understand. But I've never met your teammates, so I don't know what they look like. How can I trust them if I wouldn't know them on the street if I saw them?"

Wolf hadn't thought of that. Abe spoke up.

"Ice, remember the code you used to let me know on the plane that something was wrong?"

Caroline had forgotten Christopher and the others could hear her conversation with Matthew.

"Yes," she told him slowly.

"When you meet any of our team, we'll use that signal in our handshake to you. So if someone says they're Dude or Cookie or Benny, and you shake their hand and they don't give you the signal, you'll know it's not really them. Understand?"

"Okay, but is this really all necessary? You're scaring me." She said in a soft voice. "I'm just a chemist. Why me? I'm not cut out for any of this."

Cookie cut in. "Ice, this is Cookie, first of all, thank you for saving my team's sorry butts on the plane that day. And I understand why you're having trust issues and that's okay for now. But know while you're deciding on whether or not you can trust us, we'll be figuring out what's going on and we'll keep you safe. Okay?"

Caroline took a deep breath. "Okay, but *you* guys stay safe. I don't know what's going on, but you'd better not get hurt or caught up in whatever this is. I'm sure the FBI has it under control…Oh…someone's coming. I have to go."

Before she could hang up Wolf said softly. "We're coming for you, Ice. Stay strong." The phone connection was cut.

Wolf's team sat there for a moment looking at each other.

Finally Cookie said, "We'll figure this out, Wolf. We'll keep your woman safe. We'll stake our lives on it."

"I'm counting on it Cookie. I'm counting on it," Wolf responded softly, realizing again what his team already knew. Caroline was his. And he'd protect what was his. His team would protect her too. All because she was Wolf's.

Chapter Fourteen

CAROLINE SAT IN the room in the little cabin not sure what was really going on. She'd talked to one of the FBI agents who was guarding her. He hadn't told her much, but it was enough for her to make some deductions.

Apparently the hijacking attempt *was* part of a larger terrorist plan. The fact it hadn't succeeded and airline security was heightened pissed off the terrorists and now they were after her. She wasn't clear on how they even *knew* she was on the plane, nonetheless what had happened since all four of the terrorists on the plane were dead. That was the scariest part. Someone knew, and that person had passed her name along to terrorists. *Terrorists* for God's sake.

Caroline felt as if she was in a movie. These things just didn't happen to people like her. She was painfully ordinary. She wasn't brave, she wasn't a hero, she wasn't cut out for this.

She worried about her job. She'd just started and now they were saying she couldn't go back to it until they caught whoever was behind the threats and caught the people who were after her. Jesus, that could be any number of people. Caroline hated to think she might have to give up her profession, her job and be stuffed away into the Witness Protection Program. She had no idea what her new boss thought. He'd probably written her off by now and was looking into hiring someone new.

The worst thought about having to go into the Witness Protection Program was losing Matthew. She was just getting to know him.

She wasn't naïve enough to think they'd end up married or anything, they'd only started seeing each other and getting to know each other, but the thought of leaving and never getting the chance to get to know him better was depressing. Figures, just when she found the sexiest man she'd ever seen, and he seemed interested in her, she'd have to disappear forever.

She sighed. She couldn't even *talk* to Matthew because the FBI agent caught her when she hung up with Matthew and his team and took her phone away. The FBI agent had been mad, but she was mad too. It wasn't fair. What was she supposed to *do* in this stupid cabin? Why couldn't she talk to anyone? How many times had people been brought to cabins for their safety only to die because someone snuck up on it? She didn't know if she'd feel any safer in the city in an apartment, but out here she felt exposed.

She'd heard the phone ring a few times while she was in her room, but ignored it. It was the FBI agent's phone. Caroline stayed on her bed. She wasn't sleeping, but she was so tired. She wanted nothing more than to be able to fall into a dreamless sleep, but every time she closed her eyes, she relived the hijacking and had other dreams about faceless enemies shooting at her and trying to kill her. She hadn't had the nightmares since she'd been with Matthew in the hotel, but after the break-in they'd returned with a vengeance.

It had been a couple of days since she'd spoken with Matthew and his team. When she'd talked to him, he'd said it'd take about five hours to get to her apartment, but she hadn't told them where she was now. She wouldn't, even if she knew exactly where she was. If anything happened to them because of her, she'd never forgive herself. Caroline didn't know what was going on, but she certainly didn't want to bring anyone else into it. And besides, she tried to tell herself, they'd just gotten back from a mission and needed their rest too. She was on her own, just as she'd always been.

Caroline didn't know how long she'd been sitting on her bed

zoning out when she heard voices in the other room. She didn't get up. It was just the agents switching out. She waited for one to knock on the door, introduce himself and to check on her. It'd been what had happened every other time someone new had come. When she continued to hear the voices she went to her door and opened it. She was shocked. Matthew! What was he doing here? How had he found her? What was going on?

Wolf smiled at Caroline. She looked great...well, not really. She looked tired and stressed, but he was so very glad to see her. He turned back to the agent. It'd taken his team a while, with Tex's help, to track Caroline down, and none of them liked what they'd found out in the process.

Wolf had talked to their commander back in San Diego, and convinced him there was something big going down and that he and his team needed to be here. His commander agreed there was a leak somewhere, in the FBI most likely, and promised he'd look into it discretely.

His commander told Wolf their actions wouldn't be sanctioned by the Navy, but he'd do what he could to keep the heat off of them. He also allowed them to stay in Virginia and unofficially officially work the case. He'd greased some wheels with people he knew in both the FBI and the Navy, and they were now officially working together.

There was a double agent in the FBI. That was the only thing that made sense. Someone had leaked information back to the terrorist organization about what had happened on that plane, and had told them Caroline had a role in the failure of the mission. As a result, Caroline had a bounty on her head. The terrorists wanted her dead. They figured if they couldn't reach the SEALs responsible, they'd kill Caroline. Wolf was furious. Unknowingly he'd been responsible for her being in the damn safe house and being in danger.

Wolf was also scared. Being scared was a new feeling for him. He wasn't scared for himself, he never was. He knew what he could and couldn't do and he knew he could handle anything the terrorists threw at him. He was scared for Caroline. He'd never felt that way about another human being before in his life. He always could take or leave women, but not Caroline. In the short time he'd gotten to know her he was impressed as hell by her outlook on life and how she'd handled herself on that plane.

Wolf knew there weren't a lot of people that could've done what she'd done.

So he and his team, thanks to his commander back in San Diego pulling strings, were now a part of the team protecting Caroline. They had no idea who the double agent was, but at least this way they could protect Caroline while searching for the bastard.

Abe, Benny, Dude, Mozart and Cookie were currently checking out the lay of the land around the cabin the FBI had stashed her in. They were setting up perimeters and making sure that nothing could get to the cabin without first alerting them. The men would take turns being on watch. There was no question about who would be in the cabin with Caroline. That was Wolf's woman in there, and they'd all protect their team leader and his woman.

Caroline didn't know what the hell was going on, only that she'd been thinking about Matthew and suddenly he was there. He looked wonderful. Strong, capable...and completely out of her league. Caroline smiled back at Matthew absently then went back into her room and shut the door. This was going to kill her. She wasn't sure what he was doing there, but obviously the FBI agent was expecting him.

After a bit of time had passed, Wolf knocked softly on Caroline's door.

"May I come in, Ice?" he asked. When there was no answer he turned the knob and opened the door. Caroline was sitting on the bed, her back against the wall, knees up to her chest with her arms grasping them tightly. She looked heartbreakingly vulnerable.

Wolf left the door open and walked over where she was sitting. He sat down gingerly at the end of the bed. It took everything he had not to take her in his arms and hold her tight. She scared the hell out of him with her phone message and it wasn't until right now, seeing she was okay, that he could slightly relax.

"What are you doing here, Matthew?" She asked softly.

"I'm here because you're here," he answered honestly.

Caroline just shook her head. "I don't understand. You don't really know me. I don't understand why you'd be here. You can't be here."

Matthew knew she was confused. Hell, he was a bit confused himself. He tried to explain. "There's something between us, Caroline," he said honestly. "I can't explain it any better than you can. The kisses we shared were the most honest and arousing I've ever had in my life. You *know* how badly I wanted to lay you down and love you all night long. You have no idea how you tested my willpower every night when I tucked you into your bed. I wanted to join you there and show you how much I liked you, being with you."

Caroline sucked in a breath, not believing what he was saying.

"Yeah, you heard me right. I got harder just kissing you than any other time I've been with a woman. But it's not only sex. I like you. You're intelligent, fun to be around, and I want to know everything about you. When I heard you were in trouble, there was no place I needed to be more than here with you. Protecting you. Making sure you're safe." When she didn't say anything, but continued to stare at him with her big brown eyes, he asked, "Why did you really call me that day in your apartment Caroline? Be honest."

Caroline sighed. He was right. Matthew deserved the truth. She didn't know what was going on with the two of them, but whatever it was, at least he seemed to feel it too.

Her voice trembling with emotion and just above a whisper, she told him honestly, "I called you because you were the first person I thought of when I was scared. I called you because if I died, I wanted you to know I was thinking about you, that I wanted to see you again. I didn't want you to come back to Norfolk and think I didn't want to go to see you again. I wanted it more than you know, and I thought I wouldn't have a chance..." Her voice trailed off.

Wolf didn't say anything, just did what he'd desired to do the first time he saw her in the room. He reached over and gathered her into his arms. She was stiff at first, then she melted into him. She smelled of some sort of flowers. Maybe it was her shampoo, maybe it was a lotion she used, but it went straight to his head. He tightened his arms around her and Caroline lost it. She cried. She cried for being scared on the plane, she cried for being hurt, she cried remembering how alone and scared she felt in her apartment when only a thin piece of plastic kept a killer from knowing she was in the bathroom, she cried in relief that Matthew was back from his mission. Matthew rocked her and held her tight. He wasn't used to a woman's tears, but there was no way he was letting her go.

Finally her tears dried up and she only sniffed here and there. Wolf drew back a bit and looked at her face. She wasn't a "cute crier"—her face was red and blotchy. She refused to raise her eyes. Wolf rubbed her cheeks with his thumbs and then lifted her chin up so Caroline had to look at him. He didn't say anything just leaned down and touched her lips with his. It wasn't a passionate kiss, but it felt right. It was a comforting kiss. It was exactly what she needed from him at that moment.

He pulled back and looked into her eyes. "You're safe now. I'll do everything in my power to make sure you stay that way."

Caroline believed him. He was an honest-to-God hero. And for the moment, he was *her* hero. She tipped her chin up, reaching again for his lips with hers.

The second she moved, he was there. Wolf had tried to hold back with her. She was feeling vulnerable and he didn't want to take advantage of her. But with the first touch of her lips against him, he was lost.

He devoured her. He stroked her tongue with his and she stroked his right back. He fell back on the bed taking her down with him. He could feel every inch of her delectable body against his. She was curvy and soft and he could feel her nipples harden against his chest.

He wrapped his hand in her hair and moved her head where he wanted it. He took complete control of the kiss and rolled them until she was under him. Wolf felt her leg bend and it opened herself up to him even more. He settled into the vee of her legs and felt his erection burrow into the heat in Caroline's center. Christ. He had to stop. Now. Or there'd be no stopping. It was the thought of the FBI agent in the other room that finally made Wolf stop. Hell, he hadn't even shut the door behind him. When he took Caroline it wouldn't be in some crappy cabin with someone who may or may not be a traitor to their country listening nearby.

Wolf eased back, but couldn't bear to break contact with her. He buried his head into her neck and licked and suckled at her earlobe. The whimpering that came from her throat made him grow even harder. She arched into him, trying to get closer. She was sexy as hell.

"Jesus, sweetheart. I'd give anything to take this where we both want to go, but I can't, not now, not here, and not while you're in danger." He hoped like hell Caroline wouldn't be offended by his words.

Caroline shut her eyes tightly. God, Matthew felt so good against her. She was wet. She hadn't ever gotten so wet so quickly with any other man before. Just Matthew. Only him. When she felt him shift above her she slowly opened her eyes. Jesus. He was so sexy, and he was here, with her. That alone was a miracle. She saw the hard line of his jaw and his kiss-swollen lips. She wanted nothing more than to have him strip off all her clothes, but unfortunately, she knew he was right.

"I-I know. Will you stay? Here? With me?" Caroline was a little embarrassed to even ask, but she needed him. She needed his closeness; she needed the safety his embrace promised.

"Of course, sweetheart." Without letting go, he moved them up further onto the bed and turned them on their sides. Wolf tucked Caroline into his big frame. Her back was to his front and they lay there in silence for a few minutes. Wolf had one arm under her head and the other was wrapped around her tightly. His forearm rested between her breasts and his hand rested on her shoulder. She was cocooned in his arms, and it felt heavenly.

"What's going on, Matthew?" Caroline asked sleepily.

"Shhhhh. I'll tell you everything tomorrow," he told her. "Just sleep now. I've got you."

Caroline fell asleep almost immediately. She felt safe for the first time in a long time. Matthew was here, he wouldn't let anything happen to her. Even while unconscious, in the depths of sleep, her body knew she was safe. She didn't have one nightmare that night.

Chapter Fifteen

THE NEXT FEW days went by without anything interesting happening. Matthew came by the cabin each night, but left early each morning. He'd told her, he and his team were here and they were keeping watch, but she hadn't seen anyone but Matthew. She would've liked to have talked to Christopher and Sam, but she was way out of her element. She didn't ask Matthew any questions, outside of the obvious ones. She didn't ask where his team was, she trusted him to make sure she was safe.

Matthew slept with her each night. They'd shared more of those soul searching kisses, but he hadn't let anything more happen. On one hand it was driving her crazy, but at the same time she understood he was "working"—they'd have to wait. For now, it was enough to be able to fall asleep cuddled up in his arms, safe. She wasn't convinced Matthew could *really* want someone like her, but she held out hope. He was convincing her one night at a time. She hoped the bounty on her head would be taken care of soon and then they could figure out where they stood.

Caroline thought sometimes it was all just too ridiculous. She lived in Norfolk now and Matthew lived in San Diego…when he was even in the country. She didn't begrudge him his job, but knew it was tough to be involved with any military man, but most especially a SEAL. But at this point in their relationship, Caroline could honestly say she wanted to give them a shot. Matthew was the best thing to happen to her in a long time, she didn't want to give it up yet.

It wasn't just because of the way he looked either. Caroline supposed that was a part of it, but it was more the kind of man he was. He was loyal, smart, and attentive. Matthew paid attention to her as if she was the most important thing in his life. She knew if they stayed together, she'd come first in his life—before his friends and even before the military...if at all possible. She'd be an idiot to let him go. If Matthew wanted to see where their relationship could go after all the crap with this was over, she was all for it.

Caroline wasn't sure what had woken her up, but when she went to roll over she felt Matthew's large hand cover her mouth. She stiffened. She knew it was Matthew behind her because she could smell his unique scent, but he was as still as a statue and was as tense as she'd ever felt him. She felt him lean down toward her head.

"Don't make a sound. Okay?" he whispered tonelessly, directly into her ear.

Caroline nodded and he lifted his hand from her mouth. He rolled off the bed soundlessly, a pistol materializing in his hand. Caroline didn't know where the gun came from, but was glad to see he was armed. She watched as he took the time to push his feet into a pair of boots.

She was afraid to move, but forced herself to sit up and scoot over to the edge of the bed. If she had to move quickly, she wanted to be ready. She also leaned over and slipped on her shoes sitting next to the bed. Caroline couldn't hear anything at all, but he'd obviously heard something out of the ordinary.

Wolf listened at the bedroom door. He eased the bedroom door open and still didn't hear or see anything. He looked back at Caroline sitting on the bed. The last few days had been hell, holding her, kissing her, but not making love to her. He wanted to bury himself so far inside her she'd *know* she was his, but he held back. It wasn't the time or the place, but he hoped it would be soon. They were making progress. Each day he and his team met and went over documents, and he felt they were narrowing in on the double crosser.

Wolf held his finger to his lips and motioned for Caroline to stay where she was. He saw her nod once and eased out of the room. He was very proud of her. She hadn't panicked and didn't ask any questions. She understood what was at stake and trusted him to do his job. That trust made him feel ten feet tall. He wouldn't let her down.

Wolf pushed thoughts of Caroline out of his head and concentrated on figuring out what was wrong. He had a job to do and he knew he couldn't do it if he was thinking about her. The gut feeling that something wasn't right was what had woken him up. He thought he'd heard something, but wasn't sure. He wasn't willing to let it go, not when it meant Caroline's safety.

He eased his way into the small outer room, trying to figure out what, if anything was wrong. He looked right and left, then stopped suddenly. Shit. He smelled gas. Just as he took a step back toward the bedroom door, the front of the cabin went up in flames in one big *whoosh*.

Wolf was knocked backwards by the wave of heat. He lay on the floor for just a moment getting his bearings. Before he could get up again, the wall on the other side of the cabin went up in flames. Matthew couldn't catch his breath. The flames had sucked all the oxygen out of the room in an instant. He tried to crawl back down the hall toward Caroline. He had to get to her. Where the hell was his team? He had no idea what had gone wrong, but it was obvious something bad had happened to them. There was no way anyone could've slipped by them in order to torch the cabin.

The terrorists had done their job well, and cut off both exits from the cabin, they were trapped. The last thought he had before he passed out from breathing the super-heated toxic air, was of Caroline, and disgust with himself that he'd let her down.

Caroline didn't move from her spot on the bed until she heard the first explosion. She leaped from the bed and ran for the bedroom door. What the hell? The heat coming from the main room almost drove her back. She got on her hands and knees and, without thinking twice about what she was doing, crawled into the burning room.

She saw Matthew on the floor and then the other wall burst into flames. Caroline ducked and covered her head with her hands. Shit. Shit. Shit. She'd managed not to squeal like a little girl, but a terrified croak escaped before she could call it back.

She looked up and saw Matthew try to crawl toward her and then fall down unmoving. Caroline didn't stop to think. She fast-crawled over to him, grabbed him under the arms, much like she'd done with the terrorist on the plane, and hauled him back to the bedroom. It was a slow process because Matthew was heavy and the exertion plus the smoke filling the room was making it tough to move quickly.

The cabin was quickly filling with smoke. It wasn't until she'd gotten Matthew back into the room and shut the door she realized they were trapped in the house. She ran to the attached bathroom grabbed a towel, quickly soaked it in water from the tap, and stuffed it along the bottom of the door to the bedroom. It reduced the smoke coming into the room a bit, but not all the way. The bedroom was going to fill with smoke sooner rather than later, and it wouldn't be long before the flames were burning through the entire wall.

Caroline grabbed two of her T-shirts from the drawer. She ran into the bathroom, well aware of the time that was ticking by, and soaked them with water in the sink. She put one around her nose and mouth and ran back to Matthew. He was still lying where she'd left him on the floor. She tied the other T-shirt awkwardly around his head. She had to protect him from the smoke making its way into the room. Caroline was operating completely on auto-pilot now.

She ran to the only window in the room. She cautiously drew back the curtain and looked out.

BAM

Caroline leaped back and crouched down just as the window shattered. She couldn't help but scream out in fright this time and she covered her head as the glass from the window rained down on her. Crap. She crawled over to where Matthew lay on the ground motionless.

"This would be a really good time to wake up Matthew," she said shakily as she pried the pistol out of his hand. She shook him once, hard. He didn't respond and Caroline allowed one desperate sob to escape before she beat it back. If she started crying now, she wouldn't be able to stop.

It looked like the terrorists had found her. They'd set the front and side of the cabin on fire to force her into this room, and the only escape was the window…only there were obviously men out there waiting for her to leave that way. She was going to die. She didn't want to die and she definitely didn't want Matthew to die either. She wasn't going to give up until it was too late. She wasn't a SEAL, but was there anything she could do?

She tried to think like a soldier, what would Matthew do if he was conscious? As she eased her way back to the window and couldn't see any bad guys she deflated a bit. How was she supposed to defend herself with the gun she now held in her hand, if she couldn't even see who she was supposed to shoot?

Caroline allowed a few stray tears to leak out of her eyes. What was the best way to die? Burning to death? Smoke inhalation? Getting shot? Shit. None of the choices were good ones. She had to get herself together. Matthew wouldn't just give up. If it was her lying uncon-scious on the ground he'd do whatever he had to do to keep her safe. She'd do the same.

She tried to think. Caroline had to believe Matthew's team would get to her. He'd said they were patrolling around the cabin. They'd get here soon; she'd act as if they were out there right now figuring out how to get both her and Matthew out. She risked a glance out the window again. There! She finally saw someone, a man off to the right. She stuck the pistol out the window and pulled the trigger. The kickback of the gun was more than she was ready for and she fell backward with the force of it. She heard yelling outside, then silence again. Had she hit him? She doubted it. She risked another glance. Nope, they were still there.

The smoke in the room was getting thicker. She went back to Matthew and drug him closer to the window, trying to avoid the glass on the ground. She wasn't sure how they were going to get out of this, but she wasn't leaving Matthew behind. Wasn't there some SEAL code on that? She tried to think back. Yeah, Christopher had said something about it to her in the airport when they'd come to find her.

Well, she wasn't a SEAL, but she wasn't leaving Matthew behind to die in this stupid cabin. The only reason he was there was because of *her*. She wouldn't be able to live with herself if he was killed because of her. Shit. She had to stop thinking about Matthew being dead.

Just as she was gearing up to look out the window again she heard more shots. She hoped it was a good sign. She reasoned that since there were no bullets coming through the walls of her prison, it had to be. Hopefully it was the Calvary coming to their rescue. After a short period of time she heard a voice calling urgently from outside.

"Wolf? Ice?"

Caroline risked peeking out the window again. It was Sam. He was standing outside the window. She stood up and blurted, "Here!"

Mozart was never as glad to see anyone as he was to see Ice. When the cabin had gone up in flames he'd been surprised. Someone, or some people, had obviously made their way past their recon around the perimeter of the cabin. He'd immediately set out to find the culprits and get Wolf and his woman out of the cabin.

"Where's Wolf?" he demanded urgently.

"He's here, but he's unconscious." Caroline stopped to cough. She had no idea trying to breathe when in a burning building would hurt so much. Again, stupid, but how was she supposed to know?

"Let's get you out, then we'll get him." Mozart ordered. He'd holstered his pistol and reached up for her. The window was on the first floor, but since the land sloped down on this side of the cabin, it was about a five foot drop to the ground. Caroline shook her head.

"No. Matthew first."

Mozart started to disagree, but Caroline disappeared from the window. Damn. He didn't have time to argue with her. He wasn't sure if there were any other terrorists around, but he knew Ice and Wolf were running out of time. The roof was on fire and the entire cabin was about to go up in flames. He saw Ice struggling with Wolf's inert body near the window. He grabbed the window sill to pull himself in and help, but let go quickly. The metal around the window was red hot.

"Careful, Ice," Mozart said urgently. "It's really hot."

Caroline nodded. She heard him, but didn't take her eyes off Matthew. He'd groaned a few times, she hoped he was coming out of it. She quickly dragged him as close as she could to the window and untied the T-shirt from around her face and laid it over the window sill. She heard it sizzling as the wet cloth met the red hot metal of the sill. She pushed as hard as she could until Matthew was lying on his stomach right under the window.

Caroline grabbed Matthew again and hauled him up as close as she could get him to the open window. She draped his arms outside and yelled at Sam to grab him. With Sam's help, she pushed, and Mozart pulled, and Matthew slid out of the house. Caroline quickly looked out and saw that Sam had mostly caught him and was easing him to the ground taking the T-shirt off his face as he laid him on the ground.

"Okay, come on, Ice. I've got you." Mozart held up his arms to help her get out of the burning cabin.

Caroline shook her head again, "No, take Matthew and go, I'm right behind you. I don't need help. Just get him out of here and safe."

Mozart was frustrated, but she was right. He had to get Wolf out of there. He leaned down and put his teammate over his shoulder in a fireman's carry.

"Okay, I've got him; get your ass out of there. *Now!*" Mozart bellowed at Ice.

Caroline ignored the ire in Sam's voice. She knew he was stressed and wasn't really yelling at her. She turned around to look around the room to see what she could use to help her get out of the window and not get burned. The T-shirt she'd laid there to protect Matthew had slid out with his body.

She grabbed a pillow off the bed. She laid it over the hot window sill and watched as it too immediately started to smoke. It was now or never. She didn't have any time to spare. She stuck one leg, then the other out the window and sat on the pillow on the sill. She took one more look behind her and saw the bedroom wall collapsing. She let out a small shriek and jumped. It wasn't too far to the ground but she fell sideways when she landed anyway. She immediately got up and headed after Sam.

Mozart took the time to turn and look at Ice as they ran away from the burning cabin. She was next to him. She had cuts on her arms and legs from the glass from the window, her face was covered in soot, she was coughing like a forty year old smoker, but she was mobile and running. It had to be good enough for now.

"Why didn't you get out of there, Ice?" Mozart asked, not even out of breath. He was obviously in good shape and this was just another little run for him.

"SEALs don't leave SEALs," Caroline panted and said between coughs. "I couldn't leave him. I just couldn't."

Just as they were reaching the nearby tree line, a man stepped out from behind a tree, holding a pistol pointed right at them.

"Stop right there," he said menacingly.

Mozart knew he could take him. No problem. As he was leaning over to set Wolf on the ground he saw more men come out of the trees, all with rifles or pistols pointed at them. Shit. He was good, but he wasn't *that* good. Where was the team?

"I bet you're wondering where your team is, aren't you?" The man sneered, seemingly reading his mind. "They aren't coming. They've been 'indisposed,'" he threw his head back and laughed in the most evil laugh Caroline had ever heard.

"You've been a pain in my butt for a while now bitch, but now it's my turn to be one step ahead. You SEALs think you're indestructible, but you aren't."

Before any of them could do anything, the man raised his pistol and shot at Mozart. Mozart felt the bullet graze his head and he fell sharply to the ground. Hell, that hurt. He heard Ice screaming. God, Ice. He felt Wolf's bodyweight heavy on his back. He tried not to pass out. He needed to stay awake and get Caroline out of there. He needed to protect her and make sure Wolf was all right.

Caroline screamed as she watched Sam fall to the ground still holding Matthew. Two men came out from the trees toward her and grabbed her before she could even think about running or fighting back. She struggled and tried to kick them, but they had her arms bound behind her back before she could do anything.

The zip ties they'd used immediately bit into her flesh. They'd tightened them to the point of cutting off her circulation. They obviously weren't concerned about her comfort. That scared her more than anything.

"No, stop it. What are you doing?" She said, still struggling in the grip of the two men and against her bindings. They walked her toward the man that had shot Sam.

"You're coming with us, bitch," the man smirked and backhanded her hard across the face. Caroline would've fallen to the ground if she wasn't being held up by the other two men. Dammit, that hurt. Her head swam. She coughed. Jesus, she was in trouble here.

Mozart struggled on the ground. He'd heard what the man had said. Shit, he had to get to Ice; he couldn't let this guy take her. His head was swimming and he couldn't get his arms to work right. He was going to pass out; he wasn't going to be able to help her.

The man turned his attention back to Sam and Matthew on the ground. He held the pistol toward them.

"No. No. *No!*" Caroline screamed, struggling even harder, ignoring the pain in her arms from the awkward way she was being held. "Leave them alone. What do you want? Me? You've got me, leave them alone!"

The man turned back toward Carline with a glint in his eye. "You don't want me to kill them?" He said with venom.

Caroline shook her head vigorously.

The man laughed evilly. "What will you do for me if I let them live?"

Caroline was scared out of her mind. She had no idea what this man had in store for her, but she knew he wasn't really asking for her permission. He'd kill them in a heartbeat if he wanted to. "Whatever you want. I'll do whatever you want. Just don't kill them. They're only here because of me." She'd drop to her knees if she thought it would help, but the man didn't even give her a chance to offer.

The man turned his back on her and went over to Sam and Matthew. He pulled a knife out of his pocket and leaned down toward Sam. Before Caroline could beg the man not to hurt him he'd sliced into Sam's cheek. Laughing he did it again, and again. Standing upright again he brought his boot down and ground it in Sam's face as if he was squishing a bug under his foot.

Turning toward Caroline, who was now watching in horror, he

sneered, "Fine, I won't kill them, but they'll wish they were dead when my men get through with them. They've got other ways to make them suffer." He nodded at two other men nearby and they headed for Sam and Matthew.

Caroline struggled with all her might but all it did was make her wrists bleed sluggishly. The last thing she saw as she was led away was the two men kicking Sam and Matthew who lay unconscious on the ground.

Chapter Sixteen

WOLF PACED THE room. It'd been six hours since Caroline had been taken. His throat was still raw from smoke inhalation, and he was still coughing, but he was alive. He was glad he didn't remember the beating he and Mozart had been given on the field. The rest of the team had arrived in time to prevent the two thugs from killing them.

The terrorists were good. They'd created a diversion that had Benny, Dude, and Cookie headed off on a wild-goose-chase. Wolf only knew what his team had told him they'd seen when they came across the terrorists beating the crap out of him and Mozart, which wasn't much. He had no idea what had happened to Caroline and how they'd gotten out of the cabin. Mozart had most likely rescued the both of them and they'd been overwhelmed while escaping.

Mozart was still unconscious. A bullet had grazed his head and that, along with the beating, had him laid up in the hospital. Wolf was especially worried about Mozart's face as well. Someone had carved him up and there was enough dirt and crap in his wounds to cause a massive infection. Mozart had always been the "pretty" one of their crew and Wolf worried that his days of being a flirt would be over. His face wasn't pretty, but at this point that wasn't what was concerning the doctors. They'd all just have to wait and to see how long it'd take him to pull out of it. Dude, Abe, Benny, Cookie and himself were now trying to figure out what the hell happened and where the fuck Caroline was.

Wolf hurt, but he ignored his injuries. He'd suffered worse in the past and continued on. This time was different though, they had his Caroline. He closed his eyes in despair, then quickly opened them again. He didn't have time to feel sorry for himself or to panic. He had to figure out what the hell was going on and where Caroline was. It was time to call Tex. If anyone could find her, it was Tex.

CAROLINE OPENED HER eyes slowly. She hurt. Everywhere. She had no idea where she was. The man who'd kidnapped her had stuffed her into an SUV and one of the other men had knocked her out with a cloth over her nose and mouth. She knew it was chloroform, and fought as hard as she could, but inevitably, couldn't fight its effects.

When she'd come to, she was restrained to this stupid chair. The damn zip ties were still on her wrists, but now they were attached to the arms of the chair she was sitting in. She could see the blood oozing over the edge of the armrests and dripping onto the floor. Jesus, it was like a bad movie. The chair, the zip ties, the chloroform…if it hadn't been happening to her and if she wasn't so scared, it would've been laughable.

The man who'd cut Sam and ordered both him and Matthew beaten—she hoped they weren't killed, despite what he'd said—came into the room. She was in some sort of warehouse. He came right up to her and spit in her face. Caroline was so surprised she didn't do anything to try to avoid the spittle. She felt it ooze down her cheek as he yelled at her.

"You stupid bitch," the man growled at her. "You cost me *everything*! I had it all planned. It was gonna work, and you blew it. *You*. It's all *your* fault! Those dumb ass country hick SEALs wouldn't have known what was going on if it wasn't for you."

The man continued his ranting. "You'll tell me everything that happened on that plane. I want to know exactly how you knew about the ice and how you overpowered my men!"

Caroline didn't want to tell him anything. It was enough he knew she was involved. She'd never been so scared in all her life. Even when she was hiding in the shower afraid to breathe too loud, she hadn't been *this* frightened. Jesus, each situation she'd been in was worse than the last. This time she knew she was going to die. The government didn't make deals with terrorists and besides that, no one even knew where she was. Matthew and Sam had been unconscious when she'd been dragged out of the clearing by the cabin, and she hadn't seen anyone else around. If his men *had* been around, they would've prevented them from taking her...wouldn't they?

Even as the brief thought flashed through her head that maybe they let the terrorists take her to save their teammates, she dismissed it. She hadn't met the rest of the team yet, but if they were anything like Matthew, hell, like Christopher or Sam, they wouldn't have let them take her. She had to get control of herself. Thinking irrationally wasn't going to save her life. If she had any chance of getting out of this clusterfuck, she had to use her brain.

Even though she was scared, she vowed to herself she wasn't going to tell this maniac anything that would help him take down another plane or hurt more people. She looked away from the man and around the room instead. To even have a chance, she had to start trying to figure out how to get out of there.

"You aren't going to talk, bitch?"

Caroline's eyes went back to the crazy man standing in front of her. She just looked at him without saying a word.

He leaned in toward her. Caroline could smell the foul body odor coming off of him. It was as if he hadn't showered in days, no weeks. He leaned in as a lover would, and whispered into her ear.

"You tell me what happened or I'll make you so miserable you'll be begging me to let you tell me every little thing I want to know. Then you'll beg me to kill you." He licked the side of her neck up to her ear with a long slow brush of his tongue against her. Then he bit her earlobe so hard Caroline was afraid he'd torn it in two. She couldn't help but whimper and try to pull away from the pain. She didn't want to tell him anything, but she wasn't tough. She was just…her.

The man stood up and backhanded her. He didn't give her a chance to recover from his strike before hitting her again, then again. Then he kicked her shin as hard as he could. He continued hitting her and slapping her and occasionally biting her. He tried everything he could to get her to talk, but Caroline kept her mouth shut.

Caroline started off stoic and not giving any reaction to each strike, but she was soon crying out with every hit and she could feel the tears coursing down her cheeks. The man knew he was hurting her, but he didn't stop. He laughed as he beat her.

Caroline knew she was going to die, but she'd be dammed before this crazy man used her knowledge to hurt or kill others. She said nothing throughout his beating, just kept trying to avoid his fists and feet when she could, which wasn't often.

Finally he stopped. Caroline knew it wasn't because of anything she'd done, but more because he was tired. He was breathing hard, and panting as if he'd run a couple of miles. He was sweating profusely and his face was bright red.

"You're a stupid bitch. Don't worry, I'm leaving you for now, but I'll be back. We'll start up where I left off. I'll bring some of my buddies back with me. You can just sit there and think about all the ways I can make you hurt before I kill you, slowly. I'll give my men a go at you as well. Have you ever been gang banged? No? Well you just sit there and think about it. You can save yourself the pain and misery if you'd just tell me what I want to know. If you do, I'll kill you quickly. If not, you'll die a horribly painful death. I can promise you that. My men will make sure you're bleeding out of every hole before they kill you. They'll watch you bleed and laugh." He spit on her once more and left the room.

Caroline's head bobbed. She closed her eyes and tried to process everything. She was still tied up in the chair and had blood dripping from her head somewhere. Her eyes were almost swollen shut. But she was still alive...for now. She completely believed the man when he said he'd make her suffer. She'd seen the look the men who'd roughly pushed her into the SUV had given her. They wouldn't be gentle at all with her. She was scared shitless. She didn't want to die slowly, or otherwise, but she just couldn't, and wouldn't, condemn other innocent people to die.

Caroline tried to figure out more about where she was. If she had a shot at all to get out of there she had to pay attention. She couldn't see that well through her swollen eyes and the blood blurring her vision, so she tried to listen.

There...what was that? Seagulls. The nasty birds always made those cawing sounds as they flew through the air. She had to be by the sea. She felt proud of herself for a moment, but then realized most of Norfolk was by the ocean. Crap. That wasn't going to help anyone. She could hear what sounded like ship horns blowing. She tried to concentrate more, but finally just closed her eyes. She was so tired...

It could have been minutes or hours later when she heard the door squeak open in the cavernous room. A man came in, not the same man that had beaten her before. She'd never seen him before, but he was wearing a three piece black suit. His hair was slicked back and not a piece was askew. He looked as out of place in the dungeon-like atmosphere of the filthy room as he would've at a rodeo in the heart of Texas. He was followed by three other men, including the guy who'd beaten her earlier. *Oh shit. Was this it?* Caroline held in a sob. She regretted with every fiber of her being not making love with Matthew. She suddenly fervently wished she'd put her concerns about moving too fast with him aside and had gone for it.

The man in the suit didn't look at her, didn't say anything. He got busy setting up what looked like a tripod. Oh God. Was he going to *film* the men raping her? He mounted the video camera on the tripod and turned it around so it was facing her. He stood behind it and gave a chin lift to the three other men. Caroline saw the red light blinking on the camera and shuddered, watching as the men came toward her, cracking their knuckles. No, no, no, she couldn't do this. She screeched as they reached for her.

WOLF SAT AT the table, his hands clenched in his lap. He was a SEAL. He was supposed to be able to save the world, but he felt helpless because he couldn't save the one person who'd quickly come to mean everything to him. He and his team had discussed for what seemed like hours what they were going to do next. Tex was working frantically with his hacker friends to try and track down where the men had taken Caroline. They had some clues, but no location, not yet. Cookie's phone rang and he answered it quickly.

"Yes, sir. Got it. I'll tell him." He hung up. "Check your email, Wolf." Cookie said. "That was the commander, he just received a video. He told me to tell you they were tracing it now."

Cookie called Tex to update him on the email and to have him get to work tracing it. They knew the commander was tracing it as well, but more often than not Tex could get results faster than anyone else. Wolf quickly brought up his email on the laptop and the team gathered around to watch.

The five men watched in horror and anger. It wasn't anything they hadn't seen or experienced for themselves in the past. But this was Caroline. Wolf's Ice. That made all the difference in the world.

The video showed Caroline strapped to a chair. She'd obviously been beaten. Her wrists were bleeding where the zip ties held her to the chair and she had blood dripping from her head somewhere. But her face. Jesus. They'd beaten the hell out of her. Her eyes were swollen almost shut, and her face was already bruising. The T-shirt she was wearing was ripped and hanging off of one shoulder. They could see her bra strap vividly white against her skin. She was breathing quickly and erratically.

There was a man speaking, but Wolf barely heard him. *His* woman was hurt. Christ. He couldn't handle this. He pushed pause on the video and locked his hands behind his head. He paced back and forth rapidly. He took a deep breath. He *had* to handle it. He couldn't let Caroline down. He had to focus.

His teammates let him be. No one tried to talk to him. No one gave him false reassurances. They didn't know what they were going to see on the rest of the tape. It was up to Wolf on when, and if, he wanted to watch the rest of the video.

Wolf paced, trying to gather up the courage to watch the rest of the video. If his woman was killed in front of his eyes, he didn't know how he'd react. He had to lock it down. Wanting to go back to the previous night when he'd held Caroline's soft sweet body in his arms, Wolf took a deep breath. *"Fuck."* All his anguish and dread were put into that one word. The room was quiet. No one said anything; they could feel Wolf's anguish.

He finally spun toward the laptop and clicked the mouse that would start the awful video again.

"Tell me what happened!" The man beating her screamed. At her silence he continued screeching at her. "How did you know the ice was drugged? I *know* it was you. Those dumb ass SEALs don't have the smarts to know their head from their ass. I know it wasn't them. What tipped you off? How did they get the jump on my men?"

The SEALs could see the man getting more and more agitated as he continued to ask Caroline questions and she refused to answer. At one point Wolf heard Cookie say under his breath, "Jesus, just tell him sweetheart. God, just tell him what he wants to know."

She didn't.

Abe paced behind the men. He couldn't watch anymore. Those bastards. How could they do that to a woman? To their Ice? Why didn't she just tell him and save herself some agony?

They watched as the man yelling at Caroline stopped asking her what she'd done and looked up toward the camera. Then he lost it, ranting at the SEALs, at how they all thought they were God's gift to the world and thought they were invincible.

The man continued to berate and hit at Caroline, but they heard a disembodied voice come from behind the camera. They hadn't realized someone else was in the room. They could only see the three men taking turns beating Caroline. "How does it feel watching my interrogation? I'm finding it quite…entertaining." The chuckle that followed the flat statement was horrifying. It suddenly became clear.

"That's the traitor," Benny said, hate clear in his tone. "That's the bastard that's behind everything."

Before anyone else could say anything, the camera was jostled and the team realized the mysterious traitor was now holding the camera.

The SEALs all watched as the unknown man carried the camera close to Caroline. He zoomed in on her face, speaking directly to the SEALs the entire time.

"How does it feel to watch them beat her? How does it feel to see the blood falling from her skull, knowing I ordered it?" He zoomed in on her wrists. "Look at how she's struggled trying to get away from me. The zip ties are cutting off her circulation. See how her fingers are turning blue?"

He laughed then—an evil nasty laugh that sliced through Wolf and his team.

The man stood back so they had a wide angle view of Caroline in the chair. They all saw the other men come up on either side of her.

"Jesus no," Wolf moaned. He couldn't take this anymore. He turned away from the computer screen. They were going to kill her and he couldn't watch. He wouldn't stop the video again, but he'd be damned if he watched his love die. Then, changing his mind he abruptly turned back to the screen. No, he wanted to watch. He needed the motivation to keep him going after she was gone. He needed a reason to find every one of the men, and every one of the terrorists in their organization and make them pay.

The team watched as one of the men struck out and knocked her over, still tied to the chair. She fell hard on her side. All the men could hear her grunt as her head bounced off the hard floor as she landed.

The man in charge just laughed in the background.

"That was awesome. I'm surprised her head didn't split open." The camera came close to Caroline's face again. The disembodied voice sounded again. "You want to tell me what I want to know yet, babe?" he taunted her.

"I'll tell you," Caroline mumbled while bloody saliva dripped from her battered and torn lips.

Abe moaned, actually moaned. "No, Jesus, don't." None of them knew if it was better if she kept her mouth shut or if she told this demented man what he thought he needed to know. Who knew what he'd do after she told him how she knew the ice was drugged.

Wolf leaned toward the screen as if he could will the man behind the camera to make a mistake, to step in front of the video camera just once. All he needed was one split second. Tex would do his magic and have a photo to them in no time if that happened. He saw Caroline spit some blood out of her mouth and try to lift her head off the ground. She still lay on her side, suspended in the chair she was tied to.

She sounded horrible. Her words were slurred and she mumbled her words. "You want to know what happened, asshole?"

At the man's affirmative grunt, she continued, "Well fuck you. You and your army of *gull*ible terrorists can get back on whatever party boat you sailed here on and go to hell!" She'd looked right at the camera while saying it, not at the man standing next to her, not into the eyes of the man holding the camera. It was as if she looked right into the eyes of each of the SEAL team members as she'd spoken. There was silence in the room for a moment, then the man behind the camera nonchalantly commented, "Tsk. Tsk. Tsk. Your bitch isn't very bright is she, Wolf? We'll be in touch." And the video went dark.

Wolf tried to hold it together. He was losing it. They had nothing. Nothing. He growled and kicked at a stool. It went flying across the room.

In the silence of the room Abe unexpectedly urged, "Play that last part again."

Wolf turned to him incredulously. "You want to watch that shit again? What the *fuck*, Abe?"

Abe wasn't listening. He reached over Wolf, ignoring his incredulous question and grabbed the mouse, not waiting for him to do what he'd asked. They watched Caroline being kicked and watched her stare eerily at the camera again and heard her recorded voice say, *"Well fuck you. You and your army of gullible terrorists can get back on whatever party boat you sailed here on and go to hell!"*

Abe played it again. Then again. Wolf was about to beat the hell out of his teammate. He couldn't watch it one more time without losing his shit. He couldn't hear her slurred words full of pain. He felt like his heart was breaking.

Abe turned to his teammates. "Did you catch that?"

"Hell yeah," Dude said urgently. "It's not a lot to go on, but it's a start."

Wolf shook his head and stared at his teammates. What was he missing? What had Dude and Abe caught that he'd missed? As much as he didn't want to see Caroline's battered and bruised face or hear her tortured voice one more time, he had to hear it for himself.

"Well fuck you. You and your army of gullible terrorists can get back on whatever party boat you sailed here on and go to hell!"

Suddenly he got it. Caroline was giving them clues. Gulls and party boats....she had to be somewhere near the ocean. She'd looked right at them and willed them to understand. It wasn't a lot to go on, as Norfolk was an ocean port, but the party boat remark had to mean *something*. Caroline knew the difference between the Navy ships, the container ships, and pleasure boats. They'd even had a conversation when they'd toured the base about the difference between a ship and a boat. She'd teased him about not wanting his manly SEAL ship to be called a boat. Her wording to them couldn't have been coincidence.

The men all got up from the table. Cookie was already on the phone with their commander, and Abe was on the phone with Tex. They'd find her, they had to.

Wolf thought of his woman. He loved her. Caroline was his everything. She was amazing and if he lost her he didn't know what he'd do. She could be dead right now, they could've killed her after they shut off the video, but he didn't think so.

Wolf thought again about how the guy behind the camera called him by his name. He knew him, or at least knew *of* him. They had to figure out who he was and fast. Right now Caroline was his main concern, but Wolf knew they had to stop the leak as a matter of National Security. The man would want to keep Caroline alive to taunt him. Wolf didn't know how he knew that, but if they hadn't killed her on the video, she was still alive. They were going to use her somehow; they just had to get to her before that happened.

"Hang on, Ice. We're coming for you." Wolf hoped his fervent words somehow made it through the cosmos into her heart.

Chapter Seventeen

CAROLINE DIDN'T OPEN her eyes when she heard the men return to the room. They hadn't bothered putting her upright after turning off the video camera earlier, so all she could do was lie on the floor and concentrate on breathing.

She didn't think she could take much more of the attacks. She was having trouble breathing; she thought she most likely had a broken or cracked rib or two from the last beating she'd received. She wondered if Matthew and the others had gotten her message. She didn't think it was all that clever or helpful, but maybe they could figure it out.

While she'd been waiting for the men to come back and start beating on her again, she'd realized the sounds she was hearing outside weren't sounds like she heard on the Naval docks when Matthew had taken her there. She also didn't hear anything like she'd seen at the shipping yard. So she could only conclude she was at some smaller dock. That's why she'd made she'd said 'boat' and not 'ship.' She knew Matthew would understand, she'd joked with him about living on a boat and he'd made sure to correct her. He'd been on a ship, not a boat. It was a long shot, but she had to try to give them something.

She couldn't think straight anymore. They hadn't given her any-thing to eat or drink. Her mouth was beyond dry and she'd kill for a drink of water. She supposed it was too much bother to feed people you were going to kill. She figured if Matthew and his team didn't find her *really* soon, it wasn't going to matter anyway.

She felt two men pick up the chair she was strapped to and set it upright again. Caroline sagged against the ropes binding her to the chair. Ouch. She felt the ropes being loosened and she almost fell back onto the floor. Her wrists were still zip-tied to the armrests so she wasn't going anywhere. She didn't try to move, she couldn't anymore. She was all out of fight. She pried her swollen eyes apart and looked at the man crouched in front of her. It was the dirty smelly one that had first threatened her with rape. The polished man in the three piece suit wasn't anywhere she could see.

"Not so arrogant now are you, bitch?" he spat, then continued as if they were having a real conversation. "It really is a pity you know. My men really wanted to take their turn with you, but they aren't interested anymore. They wanted to see if you were as much of a spitfire while being taken from behind as you would be when they raped you on your back."

Caroline didn't even flinch. Nothing this man could say to her would faze her anymore. She knew he probably wasn't kidding, but all she cared about was how he was going to kill her. She knew it'd be unpleasant and she was trying to brace herself for any possibility. She tuned him out thinking about whether having her throat slashed open would hurt.

The man continued to talk while one of his men shoved a pair of scissors under one zip tie on her wrist to cut it off. Caroline gasped at the pain that tore through her, but she refused to cry out. She knew they were being extra brutal with her just to see if they could get her to beg them. She tried to pay attention to the smelly man as the other zip tie was cut off cruelly.

"It's too bad you wouldn't cooperate with us. We'll still succeed without you. I'll figure out what tipped you off. I'm done with this. He's done with you. I'll be sure to tell your boyfriend how pathetic you were. We're going to go for a little boat ride...I'll give you one more chance…"

When she looked away from him, refusing to consider telling him anything, he grunted and stood up. He motioned to one of his men and he came forward, leaned down and hauled her over his shoulder. Caroline screamed out in pain. Agony shot through her body. The ribs she'd *thought* might be broken, she now knew were. The pain shooting up from her ribs was almost unbearable. She gasped, it was the worst pain she'd ever felt in her entire life. She wished she could pass out.

She'd watched television in the past and felt sorry for women who'd been beaten by their boyfriends or husbands, but she'd never really thought about the pain they went through. She'd seen their black eyes and heard them say how much it hurt, but until you experienced it first-hand there was no way to describe the feeling.

Caroline wished with all her heart Matthew was here. She knew it was irrational and impossible, but she wanted him. She'd never been the type of person to rely on a man, but God, she'd do anything for him to hold her and tell her everything would be all right. He'd know what to do.

She would've cried if she had it in her, but all she could do was try to hold on to the man who was carrying her and try to breathe shallow careful breaths. With her luck he'd drop her just to laugh at her reaction. She shut her eyes. God, would this ever end?

WOLF WATCHED THE warehouse closely. They'd lucked out. Tex had sent out word to be on the lookout for suspicious activity to his vast network of military members, private investigators, cops, and hackers. After only half an hour, one of his contacts had mentioned there'd been some activity at a warehouse near where his boat was docked in the old section of Norfolk. There was a large marina nearby that had boats that cost up to a million dollars right alongside small fishing vessels.

Tex had taken that lead and followed up with it himself, finding cell phone pings and other electronic activity coming from the area. He'd hacked into a security camera on the dock and had confirmed that at least one of the men that had been beating Caroline on the video was in the area.

Wolf's team headed out there immediately, set up a perimeter, and watched for a while. They saw two of the men from the video enter the building. This was it. Wolf wanted to race in and snatch Caroline away from the lunatics, but he knew he couldn't. He had to let this play out. He'd actually put Abe in charge of the mission because he knew there was no way he could be objective. This was Caroline, *his* Ice, they were going to rescue.

The team had been on many rescue missions together in the past, and they'd most likely go on many more in the future, but they all understood at a gut level it was different this time. They were essentially rescuing one of their own. Ice belonged to Wolf; they all knew it and they all were one hundred percent devoted to getting her back alive. Not one of them was unaffected by watching her bravery on the tape.

They'd been trained how to deal with interrogation tactics and how to mitigate the effects of a beating. Hell, their time in basic training and BUD/S was more torture than most people would ever have to face. They'd had years of experience. Caroline had none, yet she'd taken what they'd done to her better than any civilian. She was as innocent as anyone else they'd ever met. She was theirs. She was Ice.

Abe had no problems with being in charge. Wolf knew that he, out of all the rest of his team, knew how much Caroline meant to him and how badly he wanted to get her back safely as well. Abe had seen her bravery in person. While Cookie, Dude, and Benny appreciated her bravery from watching the video and from what they'd heard from the others, they didn't *know* her yet. While it wasn't "just" a job to them, it was more personal for him and Abe.

They knew they couldn't just rush in. They had to wait and get the traitor behind the camera. That was the only way this would end and Caroline could be free to live her life. Wolf didn't want to think of Caroline walking away from him, but he wanted her to be able to live free of fear. This whole incident might make her think twice about having anything to do with him. If he thought it was in her best interest, he'd even push her away. But he wanted to her to live. He *needed* her to live.

He hadn't thought much past getting back from his mission and seeing Caroline again, but everything that had happened in the short time they'd been back in the States had changed his outlook, especially now that he'd held her in his arms for a few nights. He didn't want to let her go. He wouldn't let her go if she showed even half the interest in him that he had for her.

As the group watched the warehouse, two men exited with Caroline thrown over one of their shoulders. Wolf watched as she tried to prop herself up with her arms on the guy's back, but she was having trouble. It took Abe's hand on his arm for him to realize he'd been about to rush the men right then and there. It went against every protective bone in his body to allow the men to carry her further and further away from him and not do anything about it. He *knew* they had to find the man behind the attempted hijacking of the plane, but knowing almost wasn't enough. They watched as the trio headed toward the boats lined up on the dock on the other side.

Wolf and Abe moved around the building silently. Wolf trusted Benny was still in position. On a hunch, they'd set him up undercover. Hopefully the scumbags wouldn't recognize him from the cabin. No one knew if the terrorists had actually seen the other members of the team or not, but they had to take the chance. Wolf figured even if they did see Benny, they wouldn't recognize him the way he was disguised.

Bennie had dressed as a fisherman who was cleaning his fish near the dock. They wanted to get as much information as they could before they moved in. If the terrorists tried to move Caroline, they wanted Benny there to listen and see what he could find out. If they did transport her by water, they needed to know which boat she was on. There were too many boats for them to have to guess where she was. They all knew they wouldn't get another chance to find her. This was it.

They watched as the terrorists drew near to where Benny was.

"She had too much to drink, huh?" Benny laughed, acting as if he'd had one too many beers that day while fishing.

The man carrying Caroline made sure to keep her head away from Benny. He smacked her ass and said, "Yeah, something like that." They didn't stick around to chat, but kept walking, keeping their eye on Benny.

Benny stood up as they passed him. He made no move to interfere with their movements, knowing he was out numbered, and essentially on a recon mission. After they passed he sat back down and pretended to go back to work on his fish again.

Seeing the fisherman do nothing suspicious, the men turned around and walked briskly toward the dock.

Caroline lifted her head to try to get the drunken fisherman to notice her. She had to make someone see that this wasn't normal, that she was hurt; she had to get some message out. When she lifted her head, she saw the fisherman staring back at her. She didn't want anyone else drawn into this, but she had to do something. She opened her mouth to say something; she didn't know what, but something. But before she could get anything out, they started around a corner of the dock.

Just before they went around a small building she thought she saw the fisherman raise his hand. It looked like he was trying to tell her something, but it was too late. They'd turned the corner and he was out of sight. Caroline was too tired to cry. She'd blown her last chance, she knew it. Her head drooped. She didn't know how much more she could take.

Benny watched as the group disappeared around the corner. Shit. He'd tried to let Ice know they were there, they were coming for her, but he'd waited too long and he didn't know if she knew what he'd been trying to tell her. He'd signaled the sign for "help is coming," but didn't see any recognition in her eyes and no acknowledgement of his signal.

Benny gathered up the fish and the basket he'd been pretending to clean and walked seemingly nonchalantly toward the warehouse. He had to meet up with his team and get their speedboat ready. He'd seen the boat they were taking her to. One part of him was glad the rescue was moving to the water. SEALs were generally always prepared for any kind of fight, but there was nothing better than bringing a battle to the water. It was what they were trained for.

CAROLINE BARELY WINCED as she was thrown onto a seat on a small motor boat. She was beyond pain at this point. Oh she still hurt, but her upcoming death was overcoming her feelings of pain.

The men didn't spare her a glance as they readied the boat to leave. She thought about jumping overboard, but didn't think that would help her much. She knew she was a good swimmer, but they'd just fish her right back out. Besides, she wasn't sure how well she'd fare in the water with her injuries. With her luck, the blood still oozing from her wrists and head would attract a shark and she'd get eaten.

The men were planning on continuing to torture her, she had no doubt. They didn't want her to die a nice, painless death. She decided she'd be better off biding her time and waiting to see what they had planned. If she had the opportunity, maybe she could slip overboard when they weren't looking. Once they got out to sea she had a better chance. It was getting dark and the lack of light would help her. She just had to wait and try to be patient.

She watched the men bumble around the boat getting it ready to push off from the dock. Just as they were about to leave, the smelly man and the man in the suit joined them. The smelly man walked right over to her and smacked her hard across the face, then laughed. The fancy man, as she dubbed him, ignored her and went into the small pilot room. She was dead. She knew it.

WOLF WAS GLAD the sun was going down. It'd work in their favor. His skin was crawling. He was ready to have Caroline back in his arms and out of danger. They followed the motor boat from a distance. It wasn't as if they'd lose them on the open ocean. It made it trickier to follow them without their knowledge, but after a while it wouldn't make a difference if the terrorists knew they were there or not. It'd just be a matter of catching up to them before they could kill Caroline.

Wolf knew their boat was more powerful than the one the terrorists were in, but again, he wanted to wait and see what they were going to do. In any rescue, the goal was to get the captured person back alive. Until they knew what the terrorists had up their sleeve, they couldn't guarantee Caroline's safety.

Wolf and his men watched from a distance as the traitor boarded the boat. They weren't close enough to see him clearly though. Wolf sat silent and still, almost too still. Every fiber of his being was focused on the boat slicing through the choppy water ahead of them. All of the men who'd hit his woman were on that boat. If he had his way, they'd all die today; after he got Caroline safely away.

CAROLINE HUNG ON to the side of the seat, wincing every time the boat hit a wave. Her ribs hurt like hell. She tried to ignore it and concentrate on where they were. If she had to swim back to shore, she wanted to be sure she was going the right way. It would be just her luck to escape from terrorists only to swim *out* to sea instead of toward shore.

After navigating what seemed like miles, the boat finally stopped. The man in the suit came out of the wheelhouse and watched silently as one of the other men grabbed her ankles. Because Caroline wasn't thinking clearly and was distracted by the cold demeanor of the man in the suit, she didn't have a chance to fight or to jump overboard. She didn't notice the chains they were putting around her ankles with the weights until they were firmly attached. She tried to kick at the nearest man, but it was too late. Oh. My. God. She really was going to die. In one corner of her brain, she'd kept the hope alive she'd be able to escape, but it was obvious what they had in store for her.

The fancy-man was holding the camera again.

"Say goodbye to your SEAL, bitch. It didn't have to come to this. You could still tell me what I want to know." He paused as if giving her a chance to talk and to save her life.

Caroline glared at him, refusing to talk. She knew even if she spilled her guts now, he'd still kill her. He was crazy. He looked sane in his pressed and flawless suit, but it was obvious he was the craziest one of the bunch. Caroline didn't want to die, but at this point she didn't think she had any other option.

"That's what I thought. Brave to the end aren't you? Well, we'll see how brave you are when you're sitting on the bottom of the ocean. Oh don't worry, I'll make sure your SEAL sees your last minutes alive. I'm sure he'll blame himself for the rest of his life." He chuckled under his breath, laughing at himself. Then he nodded at the smelly man. He grabbed her under her arms and one of the other men grabbed her legs. The third man picked up the weights. They moved in tandem toward the side of the boat.

Caroline thrashed and fought against their hold. She raked her nails down the side of the closest man's face in desperation. She finally found her voice and started screaming. She pleaded with them not to do it and promised she'd tell them whatever they wanted to know. At the realization that her death was imminent all thoughts of being noble and brave flew out of her head. The men her just laughed at her feeble attempts to get away and threw her over the side of the boat like they were throwing out the garbage.

Caroline gasped and tensed, knowing hitting the water was going to hurt...badly. She choked and sucked in a bunch of water when she hit. Damn, it *did* hurt; she landed on her side with the broken ribs. She felt herself sinking quickly. They hadn't tied her hands, so luckily she could use them to try to help get to the surface. Luckily, she was naturally buoyant. She'd never regret those extra fifteen pounds again.

She took a gasp of air before sinking downward again. She tried again and managed to tread water quickly enough to keep from sinking. The weights they'd tied to her ankles fortunately weren't too heavy. They'd underestimated her. She knew she wouldn't have the energy to keep it up for long though. She was heavy, in pain, and tired, and while she was a good swimmer, she knew she couldn't keep herself above water indefinitely. There was no way she'd survive if they left her in the middle of the ocean.

The waves were crashing over her head as she bobbed up and down. Caroline didn't know why she thought the water would be calm out in the middle of the ocean. It was a good thing she was a chemist and not an oceanographer. She swallowed water each time she took a gasping breath, but since she was getting some air, she didn't think she could complain.

She heard the fancy man call out from the boat. It was keeping near her, but not near enough for her to grab the side. They circled her, as if taunting her further.

"We'll pull you back in if you tell me about the plane. All you have to do is tell me how you knew about the ice and you'll live."

He was screwing with her and she knew it. She'd promised to tell them everything she knew before they threw her overboard. If he'd really wanted to know, he would've made the guys put her down and listened to her.

"Screw you!" Caroline cried out at the man, even though it wasn't much of a yell. She watched as the stupid red light on the camera kept blinking. The bastard was still filming her. The man next to him raised his arm. Oh geez. Really? Now they were going to shoot her? She choked back a sob. This would be so much easier if she didn't want to live so badly.

Caroline took a deep breath and let herself sink. She'd be damned if she'd be shot on top of everything else she'd gone through. Hijacked, stabbed, stalked, blown up, kidnapped, beaten, thrown overboard, and *then* shot? No. Just frickin' no.

She vaguely remembered a television show where the hosts proved that ducking underwater would protect a person from a bullet because once the bullet hit the water it slowed down or was deflected or something. She couldn't really remember the science behind it, but she hoped they hadn't made it all up.

She sank quickly. The weights around her ankles helped. Caroline stopped thinking and just sank. It was almost like floating. The silence was heavenly.

ABE FLOORED THEIR boat and headed straight at the other boat, now bobbing in the water. They'd watched in horror as Caroline was thrown overboard, screaming, then in relief when she came back up.

It was now or never. Wolf and Benny were ready on board, Dude and Cookie were in their wet water gear and ready to go overboard. They'd discussed the plan and each of them knew their role. They'd worked together so long they could almost read each other's minds. They were a SEAL team, and they were here to do their job. Failure wasn't an option. It *definitely* wasn't an option when one of their own was involved. And Ice was theirs. One hundred percent.

They heard the shots as they pulled up near the terrorist's boat. Wolf's heart was in his throat. Caroline had to be okay, she just had to.

"Put down your weapons, United States Navy," Abe hollered through the loudspeaker of the boat. He aimed the floodlight at the other boat, partially blinding them. They saw two men hurry into the relative safety of the wheelhouse. At least the gunshots stopped with their actions. One of the men who'd run into the pilot house had been the one who'd been shooting at Caroline. The man in the suit just laughed and turned the handheld camera to them. The fourth man, the one who'd been on the video beating Caroline the most, just stood there arrogantly.

"You think you'll save her?" The suited man yelled. "I don't think so. Didn't you see the chains that were attached to her ankles? You'll never find her now. The bitch is on the bottom."

Keep him talking, keep him talking, Wolf said to himself over and over, refusing to rise to the bait of the other man. He had to distract him. He had to do his job. Caroline's life depended on it.

"Give yourself up now and you'll be spared." He responded loudly, knowing it wasn't going to happen, but he tried to convince the man anyway.

The man finally put down the camera.

"No way in hell!" He yelled back and pulled a pistol from his pants. He pointed it at the SEAL's ship and fired. Wolf ducked just in time and swore he heard the bullet pass over his head.

"I'll give you one more chance, asshole," Wolf yelled again, making sure to stay low in the boat.

When there was no answer, Benny gave Abe the signal to pull back from the terrorist's boat. They'd have to do this another way. They always had a Plan B. In fact most of the time Plan B was really Plan A, everyone knew it, but they'd always tried to go the "nice" route first.

Wolf knew the commander would be pissed, but they had other things to be concerned about, namely Caroline. They'd given the traitor a chance to give up, but he hadn't. They'd wanted to interrogate him, find out more about his connections and how ingrained the terrorist cell was, but now they had no choice. Everyone on the team hoped this was a fed working independently, but until they got back to base and analyzed the videotape of what was going on tonight, they'd never know.

It was standard operating procedure to film their missions when possible. Benny had hooked up the camera before they'd left the dock. Tex would be able to check it out and they'd see just how deep the traitor's reach had gone. Hell, Tex probably already knew who the traitor was by analyzing the security tapes at the marina. The man was spooky good at what he did.

There wasn't a lot of time to save Caroline and deal with these assholes. It was them or Caroline, It wasn't even a choice. It was time to make their move.

Making the terrorists think they were giving up, the SEALs backed off. One of the men on the terrorist boat started its engine and began to peel away. Wolf and Abe could just hear his cackled laughter before he put the boat into full throttle. Counting down three seconds, Wolf turned his head to protect his eyes just as the boat exploded.

Pieces of the terrorist's boat rained down in the water around them. Wolf and Abe knew the terrorists wouldn't be an issue anymore.

Wolf didn't spare a second's thought for the four men who'd literally just exploded in front of his eyes. He didn't give a rat's ass about them. All he cared about was Caroline. Had they taken too long? Was she still alive?

CAROLINE FELT HERSELF sinking further and further down in the water. Her ears popped and it brought her out of her stupor. Shit, she'd sunk too far. She didn't think she was going to make it back to the surface before she ran out of air…or energy.

She hurt all over, but she had to try. She'd started to use her arms to swim back up to the surface when someone grabbed her from behind. Caroline panicked. She kicked out with her bound legs, she tried to get her arms to move to hit whoever it was, but her arms were pinned to her sides. Oh Jesus, she was gonna die. She was going to die right here, after all she'd been through, after all her fighting and struggling. It wasn't fair. She might as well inhale as much water as she could to try to make it quick.

Caroline felt something being put over her face and tried to get away from whoever held her, but she couldn't fight her body's natural reaction of inhaling for the need of oxygen. This was it, she was dead….but somehow she wasn't.

She inhaled again. Oxygen. It was a diving mask over her face. She sucked in the oxygen greedily. She was still terrified, but at least for now, she had air. She tried to turn her head, but the hand holding the mask over her face was too strong. She started to panic again. Was she being kidnapped by the terrorists again? Had they laid in wait in the water making her think she was going to die before they caught her again? Was this some new kind of torture?

Just before a full-blown panic could set in, Caroline felt the person behind her take one of her hands in his and press his second and fourth fingers down hard. Caroline almost sobbed in relief. Matthew....no, it wasn't Matthew, but it was one of his team. She grabbed the man's hand and squeezed it has hard as she could, which probably wasn't really very hard in her condition, to let him know she understood. That she knew he was with Matthew. She was just so glad they'd found her. She wanted to cry, but she had to concentrate on breathing.

She had no idea how whoever it was behind her had ended up in the water with her just when she needed him, but she couldn't think about it now. She'd appreciate it later. She tried to relax. She went limp in the man's arms so he'd know for sure she understood he was there to help her.

He lifted one of her hands to the mask on her face and pressed hard. She nodded. She got it; she had to hold the mask on. She could do that.

Cookie relaxed a little. She'd understood. He was afraid Caroline would've been too far gone in her panic and pain and wouldn't remember what Wolf had told her about the signal to let her know who he was. After everything he'd heard about her from Wolf, Abe, and Mozart, he should've known she'd keep her head and trust him to do what he needed to do to make sure they both made it out alive.

Cookie had been prepared to knock her out if he had to, but it was so much easier with her cooperating with him. He was doubly thankful he'd gotten to her before she'd gone unconscious. It would've been much harder if he had to worry about doing CPR under water. It wasn't something any of them wanted to have to do, but they'd been trained on the lifesaving technique. Cookie wasn't sure what was going on above their heads, but knew he was working on limited time.

Cookie couldn't do anything about the weight around Caroline's ankles right now, but the extra weight and the fact she couldn't use her legs wouldn't slow him down. He kicked away from the terrorist's boat. He had to get them moved a good distance before Dude blew it up. The shockwave under the water could kill them as easily as a bullet or inhaling water would.

He kicked hard; checking every now and then to make sure Ice was still holding the mask to her face and breathing the lifesaving oxygen.

Every time he looked down at her she was still breathing. He knew she'd had a close call. Even now he could tell she was using all her remaining energy to hold the mask on her face. She wasn't trying to help him swim. She was deadweight in his arms.

WOLF LOOKED AROUND. It was hard to see anything with all the parts of the exploded boat floating around them. Where was Dude? Where was Cookie? Where was Caroline? Fuck. He'd never been this anxious about the outcome of a mission before. Benny joined him at the side of the boat while Abe maneuvered slowly around the main wreckage site. They all scanned the surface for a glimpse of their teammates. Abe saw the signal first. It was Dude. He eased the boat over next to the man and Wolf and Benny helped pull him on board.

Dude pulled off his mask.

"Have you picked them up yet?" he asked, just as anxious as Wolf was. Wolf shook his head, knowing Dude meant Ice and Cookie then stood back up to scan the surface of the water again. Dude stood up and joined him.

"Cookie and I split up about two hundred feet from the boat. He went after Ice who'd ducked underwater right before that asshole shot at her. I went around to the front of the boat. Just as we planned, while you guys distracted them, I put the explosives on the bow and backed off just as they gunned it to leave. You know the rest."

Wolf nodded absently. He knew what the plan was and recognized Dude's part in the plan went off exactly as planned. Even with his busted up hand and missing fingers, Dude was the best demolition expert he'd ever seen. There wasn't a bomb around today he couldn't figure out how to disarm and there wasn't a type of explosive he couldn't use to its best advantage. Even with the thoughts running through his mind about how grateful to Dude he was for ending the standoff, he wondered where Cookie and Caroline were. He desperately needed to know she was okay and alive.

As COOKIE SWAM Ice away from the boat she'd been thrown off of, he felt the explosion. It was close, but not too close. They'd made it. He continued swimming underwater to make sure they were safe from any flying debris. After everything she'd been through, Cookie didn't want them to be hit by anything either above or under the water. He swam a bit further than what he figured was safe just to make sure they were in the clear and cloaked by darkness. He didn't know exactly what had gone down above their heads…he knew what was *supposed* to have happened, but he also knew that wasn't always what *did* happen.

After judging they'd gone far enough, Cookie eased them slowly toward the surface. It was pitch dark now. He saw the SEAL boat about five hundred yards off to his left, its lights bobbing up and down in the waves, but didn't immediately signal. He had to make sure it really was safe and that Ice was all right. He knew Wolf would be pissed at the delay, but he wasn't going to risk Ice's life after everything she'd been though.

He still held her firmly with one arm. She was heavy from the chain around her ankles, but she wasn't in danger of sinking. Cookie was the best swimmer of all of them. That was part of the reason he was chosen to be in the water in the first place. Wolf had volunteered to go, but they all knew he had to be on the boat. The man on the tape knew who he was and it'd be better if he was there to try to negotiate with him. Cookie knew it killed Wolf to back off and agree. Unspoken was the fact that if Caroline hadn't survived whatever the terrorists had done to her, Wolf would lose it. It was better to have Cookie in the water, just in case.

Cookie held Ice's back to his front with one arm, and tried to ease her hands down from the mask with the other. She was still holding it in place with a death grip.

Caroline repeated to herself, *Don't let go. Don't let go. Don't let go.* It was her mantra. She was so tired and hurt so much, but she knew she had to keep holding that mask to her face, otherwise she'd die. Caroline heard something…she tried to concentrate, but she was so tired…finally she realized it was someone talking to her.

"It's okay, Ice, you're okay. You can let go of the mask now, you're all right. You made it. I've got you. We're not underwater anymore…you're safe…" Cookie kept talking to her soothingly. He'd keep it up as long as it took for her to come out of her stupor.

Caroline opened her swollen eyes as far as they'd go. She couldn't see much, as it was dark, but she could see a light bobbing off in the distance. She could feel herself bobbing up and down in the waves. She tried to relax her arms, but they wouldn't move. Finally she forced her screaming muscles to let go of the mask. Cookie reached up and removed the mask from her face as soon as she let go, and Caroline took a shallow breath, any more deeply hurt her ribs. She grabbed on to the arm that was across her chest holding her up. She couldn't see the man behind her, but she knew he was one of the good guys; he was one of Matthew's teammates.

"Th-th-thank you," she got out in a low cracked voice.

Cookie squeezed her chest gently in response. "You did all the hard work, Ice. I was just there at the end when you needed a little help. How about we get out of here?" he asked softly. He felt her nod and smiled. He activated the signal light and waited.

"LOOK!" BENNY SAID while pointing off into the distance. They all looked and saw a light bobbing in the water about five hundred yards away.

"Thank God," Wolf muttered, knowing that Cookie would have found Caroline. He refused to think differently. He turned to make sure Abe had seen Cookie, but Abe was already turning the boat and heading in their direction. Wolf watched as the light got closer and closer. Finally he could see Caroline safe in Cookie's arms. He thought he'd lost her for good. God. When they didn't immediately find either her or Cookie, Wolf had begun to think the worst. He should've known she was too stubborn to die. Abe pulled the boat up next to them.

"Careful, Wolf," Cookie said softly. "She's hurt pretty badly. She also has that chain around her ankles."

Wolf clenched his fists. He wanted to go back and kill the men again. He nodded stiffly signaling he'd heard his buddy's words.

Cookie leaned in close to Caroline again.

"Ice, you have to let go of my arm. Wolf is here…he'll help you on the boat…okay?"

Caroline nodded and opened her puffy swollen eyes again but shut them quickly. The light from the boat hurt her eyes. She cautiously uncurled her fingers from around Cookie's arm and waited.

She couldn't help herself. She just waited for someone to haul her butt on the boat. Finally she felt Matthew's arms go around her waist and felt Cookie let go. She felt really heavy…oh yeah, she still had the weights around her ankles.

Wolf gingerly took Caroline by the waist and grasped her to him. She was heavy, and he saw it was because of the chain and weight around her ankles. He eased her over the side of the boat and when he saw she'd cleared it, he lay backward on the deck with Caroline on top of him. The water from her clothes quickly soaked him, but he didn't even notice. Her arms hadn't reached around him, but stayed clenched together in front of her, against his chest. He could hear her shallow breathing.

"My God, Caroline," he whispered to her. "Thank God. Thank God. I've got you. You're safe." He was babbling and couldn't stop. All he knew was that his Caroline was in his arms, battered and bruised, but safe.

Caroline heard Matthew in the recesses of her mind. She somehow found the strength to open her eyes to slits. She couldn't lift her head from the crease of his neck, but she managed to unfurl one fist and lay it flat on his chest. She could feel his heart beating under her hand, and it calmed her. She was finally safe. "I'm getting you all wet," she said softly, then promptly passed out.

Benny and Dude cut the chain off her ankles as they headed back to shore. Wolf didn't move. He couldn't. He wrapped his arms around his woman and held on tight. He could see her swollen eyes and saw that blood was still oozing from her head somewhere. She'd been through hell, but she was here, and alive.

Cookie covered Ice and Wolf with a blanket. Wolf nodded his head in thanks at his teammate. He held Caroline close to his chest and prayed she'd be okay. He counted her breaths, taking solace in the fact that she was actually breathing after everything she'd been through. She felt so fragile in his arms. He was scared to move her. He knew she was hurt. This happened to her because of him. He knew she wouldn't agree, but he knew the truth. He had some decisions to make.

Chapter Eighteen

CAROLINE GROANED. SHE hurt. She tried to remember what she'd done that had made her so sore. It came back to her in a flash. The cabin, Matthew, the warehouse, the boat…she opened her eyes, or at least tried to. Wow, her face hurt. She reached a hand up to her face and felt how swollen it was. Oh man. Finally she got her eyes open a crack and looked around. A hospital room. She was in the hospital. She *hated* hospitals. She looked around. It was empty except for her. She tried to push down the disappointment she felt. Matthew had no reason to be there when she woke up, but she'd hoped he would be anyway. Where was everyone? She wanted out of there…she wanted…hell. She closed her eyes and was asleep again in seconds.

AFTER DROPPING CAROLINE off at the Navy hospital, Wolf and his team called their commander. They'd explained all that had happened that night. Tex had analyzed the tapes and enhanced them. Surprisingly, the man in the suit was easy to identify. When Tex had sent the picture to Wolf, he'd recognized the man immediately.

He was an FBI agent, and they'd actually talked to him in Nebraska after they'd landed the plane. It was no wonder he'd been close enough to be able to come and talk to them. He'd arranged for the plane to crash in the first place. He'd obviously volunteered to come to Nebraska and interview them. Wolf, Abe, and Mozart had felt something was off about the interrogator after they'd been interviewed. Their instincts were dead on.

They had no idea what his real motives were behind his double-cross, but at this point it didn't really matter. The only thing that mattered to Wolf was that they'd rescued Caroline. It was up to the rest of the Feds to see how deep his betrayal went. For the country's sake, Wolf hoped he was working alone. God only knew their job was hard enough without having to constantly battle domestic terrorists as well as foreign ones.

Wolf was thankful they'd kept what had really happened close to their chests. The only person they'd told all the details about the flight and Caroline's role in it had been their own SEAL commander. They'd have to report all that had happened in Virginia, and the repercussions would be long lasting most likely, both for the FBI and the SEAL team, but Wolf couldn't bring himself to regret it. Not as long as Caroline was safe.

WOLF TRIED TO ignore his teammates. They weren't happy with him. Not happy was an understatement, they were pissed. They'd argued most of the night and he still wasn't swayed. He was no good for Caroline. Look what had happened to her after she met him. Nothing but bad things. She'd almost died in a plane hijacking, her apartment had been broken into, she was put in the witness protection program, she'd been kidnapped, beaten up, shot at, and then almost drowned. It wasn't safe for any SEAL to be in a relationship. Why couldn't his team members see that?

They'd wanted to wait for Ice to wake up when they'd brought her into the hospital. Cookie, Benny, and Dude needed to meet her while she was conscious, not half conscious on the bottom of a boat. Cookie more than the others. Caroline seemed to affect everyone the same way. She impressed the hell out of Cookie, and that was a hard thing to do. He told them all how she'd panicked, but recognized their signal to her right away. How she relaxed and let Cookie swim them to safety, and even how she'd thanked him while floating in the middle of the damn ocean.

They were pissed Wolf was seemingly giving up on her. They couldn't understand how Wolf could just leave Ice to recuperate alone in the hospital after all of his angst about rescuing her. They *knew* he loved her, but for some reason he was being stubborn now that she was safe.

Wolf could only think about all that Caroline had been through. She had two broken ribs and too many cuts, bruises, and scrapes to count. Her wrists were heavily bandaged and she'd received eight stitches in a cut on her head. She was dehydrated and weak from not eating or drinking anything. She'd taken a hell of a beating and still had her wits about her. When she was delirious in the boat and on the way to the hospital she kept repeating, "I didn't talk, I swear I didn't tell him anything," over and over. Wolf had been able to reassure her, but as soon as he let go of her and placed her on the gurney in the hospital, she started saying it again. It literally broke his heart to leave her there, but he *knew* it was the right thing to do, no matter what his team said.

COOKIE, BENNY, AND DUDE tiptoed into the hospital room, as much as three grown men could tiptoe. They went over to the woman lying in the hospital bed by the window. She was sleeping. She looked horrible. Her face was covered in bruises, her arms weren't much better. They couldn't see the rest of her, but they knew she had a couple of broken ribs and was most likely covered in bruises everywhere else as well.

The three men had wanted to stay with her when she was brought in, but Wolf refused to let them. They'd come today without him knowing. They had to meet her in person. They'd heard so much about her from Mozart and Abe, and even watching Wolf with her on the boat.

Women weren't something they'd ever given much thought to in the past. They loved women, loved *sleeping* with women, but had never thought much about them beyond that. They wondered why this woman was so special, what was it about her that made their teammates do things they never would've done before meeting her? Cookie and Benny sat on one side of her and Dude sat on the other.

Caroline stirred, restless. What had woken her up? She opened her eyes and kept herself from shrieking, barely. There were three men sitting around her bed. Big men. Were they there to harm her? Had Wolf captured all the terrorists? She tried to think…did she have any weapons? Just before she went into a full blown panic one of the men held out his hand to her.

"Nice to meet you Ice, I'm Dude."

Caroline looked at the man and his outstretched hand. Dude. One of Matthew's men? She reached out and grasped his hand in hers cautiously and shook his hand. She decided to give him the benefit of the doubt. "Nice to meet you, I'm Caroline." Her voice came out scratchy and low.

She waited, and finally felt it. His second and fourth fingers pressed harder than the rest of his hand against hers. She smiled. "Faulkner, right?" Caroline asked the big man.

He nodded and smiled, but said, "Dude."

"I'm Benny," another one of the men said to her softly. Caroline turned toward him to shake his hand and received the same signal from him. They were Matthew's teammates. Thank God. She didn't think she had it in her at the moment to escape another damn terrorist.

"Benny…" she thought for a moment then tentatively said, "Kason?"

Benny brought her hand up to his lips and kissed it gently. "That's me."

Caroline turned to the third man as Kason let go of her hand. "And you have to be Hunter," She said shakily, feeling emotionally raw at meeting the man who'd literally held her life in his arms.

He nodded and instead of holding out his hand to her he stood up and leaned over. He gathered her carefully into his arms and into a tight comforting hug. It felt right to Caroline. It still hurt a little bit, but she ignored the pain and concentrated on showing her appreciation to the big SEAL holding her.

"Thank you, Hunter," she said earnestly in his ear. "Thank you." She didn't have to say anything else. She felt Hunter nod and then carefully, he laid her back down on the bed.

Caroline looked at the three men sitting around her.

"It's so good to finally meet you guys. Are you all okay? I'm not sure what happened out there. I know Hunter saved me when I was under the water, but I only have flashes here and there of what went on after that. What happened to the fancy-man?"

Dude knew who she was talking about and could hear the fear in her voice. "It's over, Ice. You don't have to worry about him ever again. He was the man behind everything. He was a disgruntled FBI agent. It looks like he was working on his own and didn't have an entire network or anything. He can't send anyone else after you. You're safe." Dude wasn't one hundred percent certain that was true, but there was no way in hell he'd say anything to worry Ice in any way. She'd been through enough.

Caroline let out a breath of relief. "Thank God. But are you guys okay? Everyone else is all right?"

Benny nodded. "We're all fine Ice. It's *you* we're concerned about."

Caroline tried not to cry. It was nice to be worried about, but if she was honest with herself, these weren't the men she really wanted to see. She wanted to see Matthew, to make sure he was okay...hell, to just be with him. But he hadn't been by at all. She hadn't seen him since the boat, and she hardly remembered much of that. It was obvious he'd decided she wasn't worth it. It hurt. She'd thought he really liked her. He was damn good at acting that was for sure.

"How's Sam?" Caroline asked quickly, trying to hide her pain that Matthew didn't want to see her.

"He's good." Cookie told her. "Bitching to get out of the hospital and back to work. He'll be coming back to San Diego with us in the next few days." He didn't mention the scarring on Mozart's face and how bad it was. Cookie knew Caroline probably felt bad enough as it was.

Caroline's heart sunk after hearing Hunter's words. So they were leaving. Soon. In the next few days. She knew they would be, but she'd hoped to see Matthew, or at least talk to him before they left. She tried to pull herself together.

"I'm sure he is," she said with a forced laugh. "Tell him I said hello?"

"Of course, Ice. He'd be here if he could." Benny told her.

"I know. I'm just glad he's okay."

There was a moment of silence in the room. Caroline didn't want to ask where Matthew was, or why he hadn't come to see her. But she *so* wanted to know. As if he could read her mind Cookie told her gently, "He doesn't know we're here."

Caroline nodded, even though it felt like her heart was being ripped out. Matthew didn't want to see her and didn't want his friends seeing her. That hurt more than she'd ever admit to anyone.

Benny continued, trying to make her feel better, "We wanted to meet you...*really* meet you. It's weird not knowing one of our own teammates." He smiled at her.

Caroline tried to smile back, but figured she'd failed miserably when Kason didn't smile back at her. "Thanks guys, but you know

I'm not a part of the team. I just got in the way of *your* team."

Not one of the three men cracked a smile.

Cookie reached into his pocket and pulled something out. He took one of her hands, placed whatever it was in her palm, and gently closed her hand around it before she could see what it was. When he sat back without a word, Caroline opened her hand and looked down. It was his SEAL trident pin.

"You *are* a part of this team, Ice." He told her. "I can't think of any other person, male or female, that would've been as tough as you've been these last few weeks. You didn't break, you didn't hesitate to do what you thought was right, even when you were scared. Most importantly you've saved our teammates lives...more than once. If you need us, all you have to do is ask."

He put one finger under Caroline's chin and lifted her eyes up to his and put his hand over hers as she gripped the pin tightly. "I don't know if you know anything about The Budweiser pin and what it symbolizes." When she shook her head, Cookie continued. "Every SEAL gets their pin after they've finished BUD/S training, completed SEAL Qualification Training, and can officially call themselves a SEAL. It symbolizes that we are brothers in arms that we train together and fight together. It's the one thing most of us are most proud of."

"But..." Caroline tried to interject, but Cookie spoke over her.

"You're one of us. You earned your Budweiser pin, Ice. You *more* than earned it."

Caroline felt a tear slip from her swollen eye and her lip quiver. All she could do was nod. She was so touched by Cookie's gesture. She wanted to throw her arms around him, but she knew it'd hurt too much. She probably should say something profound, but she just had one thought running through her mind. She knew the guys would help her.

"Can you get me out of here?" She pleaded softly, choking back a sob, "I hate hospitals."

★ ★ ★

ABE SAT DOWN next to Wolf. He wanted to beat the hell out of his friend, but decided to try to talk some sense into him instead.

"I talked to Mozart yesterday," he said quietly.

Wolf nodded. Mozart was okay. He'd finally woken up and seemed to be all right. His face would always be scarred and it'd still be quite a while before it healed, but overall he'd been lucky. He'd be joining the team again when they got back to San Diego.

"We talked about what happened at the cabin." Wolf winced. He didn't remember any of it. He only remembered the fire and trying to breathe, and then nothing else. Since the only people that had been there were Caroline and Mozart, he hadn't known what had happened to get Caroline kidnapped, except that he hadn't protected her. He hadn't done his job. He was having a hard time getting over the guilt of that.

Abe gave his team leader a quick rundown of what Mozart had told him went on when he arrived.

"After Mozart shot the two terrorists waiting at the window to kill anyone that came out, he saw Ice. He tried to get her out, but she wouldn't leave without you. She dragged you to the window and made Mozart get you out first. He asked her what the hell she was thinking and she told him that SEALs don't leave SEALs behind."

Abe let Wolf absorb that, then continued. "She was in a house that was burning down around her. Instead of getting out as fast as she could, she made sure *you* got out first. She wouldn't leave you. She fought as hard as she could, and when she realized the only way to protect you was to go with that asshole willingly...she did."

Abe watched his team leader struggling with the truth of Caroline's actions for a moment.

"The way I see it Wolf, is that if she wouldn't leave you behind in a fucking burning building…why are you leaving her behind now? You *know* she doesn't like hospitals. Remember when we tried to make her see a doctor after she got hurt on the plane? Remember how she'd reacted? Jesus, Wolf, we all know you two are crazy about each other. We know she's yours. Why are you doing this to Caroline and to yourself?"

"She's in there because of me," Wolf admitted out loud for the first time.

"Bullshit," Abe said immediately, surprising Wolf with his emphatic assessment.

"She's in there because she's one tough chick. Most women I know would've given up and died. Hell, most women I know would've cowered in the back of that plane and done nothing. Think about it. If I *ever* find a woman who puts me first, who looks out for me before she looks out for herself, I'm grabbing her and never letting go. If Ice wasn't as tough as she was, she would've died five different ways. But she didn't. She's still alive and wishing you were there with her. You have one hell of a woman, and you're throwing her away. She's loyal as hell and doesn't take any shit from anyone. Just the kind of woman you need. You'll never find another like her. She's yours. You just have to be brave enough to go and take what you want for once in your damn life. There's no guarantee any of us will be around tomorrow. We could fall down a flight of stairs or be hit by a car walking across a street. There are no guarantees in life, but I can guaran-damn-tee if you don't go to her now, you *will* regret it the rest of your life."

Abe waited and let that sink in. Then he continued. "Benny, Dude, and Cookie went to meet her yesterday."

At that, Wolf looked up quickly. He didn't want to ask, but then again he didn't have to. Abe knew what he wanted to know.

"She looks like hell. She's beaten up and depressed. Cookie gave her his Budweiser pin. Said she was a part of this team."

Wolf clenched his teeth. *He* wanted to be the one with her. *He* wanted to be the one welcoming her to the team with his pin. But he couldn't. It was the only way he could think of to protect her.

"She asked a favor of them," Abe told him. "She wanted their help in getting her out of the hospital."

"She's not ready to be released!" Wolf burst out furiously. "What the hell is she thinking? Tell me they didn't!"

Abe continued calmly, ignoring Wolf's outburst. "Did she ever tell you why she didn't like hospitals?"

Wolf shook his head, remembering back to when Mozart had stitched her up in the plane, she'd told them she didn't like hospitals.

"While you've had your head up your ass, I've had Tex do some digging for me." Abe told him testily. "When she was twenty two she was in a car accident. She spent three months in traction in the hospital. Her parents couldn't come to her because her dad had just started a new job and wasn't able to take any leave. They were older, and her mom didn't feel comfortable traveling by herself. Besides, Ice told her she was fine. Unsurprisingly, she downplayed her injuries to her mom. Apparently she had a lot of complications, but the hospital was overcrowded and busy. She had *two* visitors the entire time she was there. One was the lawyer of the guy that hit her, and the other was a man she'd been dating. He came once, and never returned. She sat in that room day and night and suffered through bed sores and other 'minor' ailments because no one was there to fight for her. No one cared about the single, ordinary woman sitting alone in her room day after day." Abe fell silent, letting what he'd said sink in.

Wolf clenched his teeth hard. No wonder his Caroline was so strong. She had to be.

Abe could see Wolf was hurting. He hadn't meant to upset him, but he had to make him see what he was throwing away.

"The guys sprung her from the hospital and took her back to her apartment. She told them she'd be fine, and they left. Then they came to see me." He paused. "A SEAL doesn't leave a SEAL behind. Ever, Wolf. Would you really leave her behind and go back to San Diego thinking that she means nothing to you? Would you really leave here letting *her* think she was a burden to you…to us? Because that's what she thinks. She thinks the same thing that you do, that it's *her* fault we were even involved in anything that happened. I *can* tell you this; if you don't want her, that's fine, but know that the rest of the team will be keeping in touch with her. We like her. We respect her. We'll take care of her if you don't."

"Don't *want* her Abe?" Wolf said incredulously, not able to stand the harangue anymore. He stood up abruptly and paced the room. "God there's nothing I want more. But…"

Abe interrupted him. "But nothing, Wolf. If you want her, you'd better go and get her. Otherwise she'll find someone else."

Abe clasped Wolf on the shoulder in the way that men did, and walked away. He'd said what he had to say. If Wolf didn't listen to him, he'd request a transfer to another team. He couldn't work for a man that wouldn't do what was best for himself and the woman he loved.

Ten minutes later Abe watched as Wolf left the building and got into a rental car. He sure hoped Wolf was going to get his woman. Abe had done everything he could; it was up to Wolf now.

CAROLINE HEARD THE ringing of her doorbell, but she ignored it. She snuggled down deeper into the couch. She didn't want to see anyone. She didn't want to talk to anyone. She'd even put off calling her boss. She had no idea if she still had a job or not, but she didn't feel good enough to deal with anyone yet. All she wanted to do was close her eyes and forget the last few weeks ever happened, well most of it at least.

When the ringing of her front door bell didn't stop, Caroline drew the blanket up over her head gingerly. She figured it was probably someone trying to sell her something, because she couldn't imagine who else would be at her door. Hell, she didn't *know* anyone other than the SEAL team, and she'd sent Hunter, Kason, and Faulkner away the day before firmly. She told them she was fine, felt great, and that she'd keep in touch with them.

The fact was she wasn't okay. She was depressed and still in quite a bit of pain. She wasn't hungry and hadn't bothered to get dressed. Finally the ringing of her doorbell stopped. Thank God. She closed her eyes, maybe if she slept long enough, the pain, both emotional and physical, would go away.

Wolf made quick work of the lock on Caroline's door. She really needed to get better security. Anyone who knew anything about picking locks, like him, could get in. No wonder the damn terrorist had been able to get in so easily. He closed the door softly behind him and walked into Caroline's apartment. Everything was quiet. He walked through her kitchen into the living room and saw Caroline bundled up on the couch. The blanket covered her from head to toe; all he could see was the top of her head. He went over and kneeled down next to her.

"Caroline," he said softly.

Caroline wasn't quite asleep when she heard her name. She opened her eyes and sat up quickly. She saw Matthew as the blanket slid off her face, then groaned and fell back onto the couch. Damn. That hurt.

"I'm so sorry sweetheart," Wolf fretted, "I didn't mean to scare you."

"How'd you get in here? Oh, never mind," Caroline whined petulantly. He was a SEAL; a locked door wouldn't keep him out. "What do you want?"

"You," Wolf said simply. He was sick of beating around the bush with this woman.

Caroline opened her eyes and looked at the man kneeling next to her. "What?" She questioned, not believing what she'd heard.

"You. I want you." Wolf repeated. "I've been an idiot. Every day since I left you in that hospital I've been kicking myself and wanting to get back to you. I'm not the most romantic guy you'll ever meet, but you won't meet one more devoted to you. I'm sorry I was a jerk, but I'm here now and I don't want to let you go."

Caroline lay there stunned. Matthew was saying everything she'd ever wanted a man to say, but was he serious? Of course he was. He wouldn't have said it if he wasn't.

"I thought you'd left," she murmured sadly, looking Matthew in his eyes.

"I couldn't," Wolf told her honestly. He stood up and gathered Caroline carefully in his arms, sat on the couch, and settled her onto his lap. He rejoiced when she didn't complain, but instead curled up into his chest and shut her eyes.

Caroline thought he smelled so good and she was so tired.

"It's okay, go ahead and sleep, baby, I'm not going anywhere."

Caroline realized she must've said that last bit out loud about being tired. She nodded and was out within seconds.

Wolf sat with Caroline on his lap for about an hour just watching her sleep and stroking her hair. He was so thankful she hadn't thrown him out yet, but he also knew she was exhausted and probably not thinking straight. Finally he laid her back on the couch carefully, brushed his finger down her still healing face, took off his jacket, and went into the kitchen to get to work.

When Caroline woke up she smelled something delicious. She sat up slowly and groaned. Jesus, she was sick of feeling helpless. Suddenly Matthew was there, he was actually still there.

"You need to eat Caroline," he told her gently. "I've made you some soup."

"You're still here." The words popped out without her even

thinking about them.

"I'm still here. Now, come on. Up you go." He helped her up and into the little dining area off the kitchen. He settled her into a chair and shook out two pain pills.

"I don't like taking those," Caroline told him petulantly.

"Doesn't matter," he retorted. "You need them, you're in pain."

"They make me drowsy and I feel weird when I take them," Caroline whined feeling grumpy and out of sorts.

"Ice. You need them. Please. I'll be here to help you, and you can sleep as long as you want to."

"What do you mean?" She asked him carefully.

"I mean I'm here for as long as you need me."

"Then what?" She asked Matthew sternly. "What about when I'm all better and don't need you here anymore?"

"I'm hoping you'll always need me as much as I need you."

Caroline sat in stunned silence. Her heart lightened a little bit. He *sounded* serious, but was he really?

Wolf continued as if his words hadn't just changed her life. "I know we'll have to work some things out with our jobs, but all I know is that I don't want to let you go. I want to spend all my time with you when I'm not working. I want to come home to you, and only you, after a mission. Please say you'll give us a chance."

Wolf stopped and waited. She held his heart in her hands.

A tear slipped down Caroline's face. "Yes, Matthew. I want that too. I'm scared. I know what you do is dangerous as hell. I don't want to lose you."

"You won't lose me. I won't allow it."

Caroline smiled. She had no idea how they'd make things work, but she knew she'd do whatever it took. She loved this man.

"I love you, Matthew." She suddenly realized she'd never told him.

"I love you too, Caroline. And you'll give Cookie back his damn

Trident. If you're going to keep anyone's Budweiser pin, it'll be mine."

Caroline smiled. She knew the pin was a big deal, but obviously she hadn't worked out in her head just *how* important it was. "Okay, Matthew," she told him contentedly. Caroline knew everything would all work out. Matthew would make sure of it.

Epilogue

"**S**ERIOUSLY, HUNTER, QUIT it. I'm not an invalid. I can carry some of my stuff."

"I know you're not an invalid, Ice, but this box is too heavy for you. I got it."

Caroline huffed and let Hunter take the box out of her arms and watched as he carried it into the house. She really couldn't stay mad at any of Matthew's friends. She loved them all. Not as much as she loved Matthew, but she didn't know what she'd do without them. They'd done their best to make sure she and Matthew had time together while they'd been living on opposite sides of the country. She knew they'd taken some assignments for him and had let him take extra time off just so he could fly out to see her.

The first time she'd seen Sam's face she'd broken down in sobs. She hadn't been crying because of his looks, exactly. She'd told him flat out, "It's my fault."

Mozart had been pissed and had held her face in his hands and sternly said, "Bull. Ice, *you* didn't do this. The terrorists did. If I had to do it again, I'd do it all exactly the same way."

"But your poor face..." Sam didn't say anything but just crossed his arms and glared at her.

Finally he put two fingers over her lips and wouldn't let her continue her thoughts. "Seriously, I'm all right. Yeah, I have scars. Yeah, women sometimes look over and through me as a result, but it doesn't mean a damn thing to me, Ice. Now I don't want to hear you ever apologize to me about it again. Hear me?"

Caroline could only nod. "Okay, but you *will* let me find some of that cream that can help reduce the scarring. I know some women get it when they have C-sections. You'll put it on every night until I tell you you're done with it." She tried to sound bossy, but didn't know how well she'd succeeded when Sam just laughed at her and brought her toward him with a hand at her neck and kissed her forehead.

Caroline had watched Sam after that, and it looked like he'd told her the truth. He didn't seem to care about his face, and as time went on it had healed somewhat, but he'd never be as "pretty" as he'd been before. She'd given him the tube of cream she'd threatened to get for him. He'd grumbled about it, but had promised he'd been using it. Caroline knew it'd never be enough to completely make the feelings of guilt subside, but she'd promised not to bring it up again.

After five months of dating, Caroline had had enough of her long distance relationship with Matthew. She told him while they were lying in bed one night that she didn't want to waste any more time. She'd contacted her old boss back in California and he'd agreed to let her have her old job back. They hadn't been able to find a replacement for her yet, so he was thrilled to have her back in the fold.

Matthew didn't waste any time. The second she said she wanted to move back to California, he'd contacted a real estate agent and gotten to work trying to find them a place to live. They'd finally agreed on a small house with a full basement. It wasn't her dream house, but she'd live anywhere as long as Matthew was with her.

They'd spent some hilarious nights with the team. Caroline thought, as she had the first time she'd seen them, they were sex-on-a-stick, and apparently the ladies in California did too. They all rotated girlfriends as often as she changed her shoes, which was a *lot*. Even Sam's scars didn't seem to deter many women, much to her relief. Caroline tolerated the skanky women as best she could. Luckily Matthew knew how she felt and when they all met up on date night, he'd excuse them early.

They'd go home and make love until the wee hours of the morning. That was one of the best things about being in the same town as Matthew. She could have him whenever she wanted. And she wanted him a lot. They were well matched as far as their libidos went. Matthew never seemed to get tired of her and always complimented her lavishly. In return she'd let Matthew get bossy in bed. But when he got bossy, she never went to sleep unsatisfied. It was a good tradeoff.

Caroline's life was wonderful and she couldn't be happier. She found it extremely nerve-racking whenever Matthew and his team had to head out on a mission, but one night, seeing her stressing about it, Matthew had tried to reassure her.

"Caroline, I know it's not easy to be with me, but you have to know I'll do whatever it takes to get back to you. How could I do anything less when you fought so hard to stay alive until I could find you and rescue you? Trust me. Trust in the team."

She'd understood. She *had* fought to live, for him. If she hadn't loved him she would've given up long before she found herself in the middle of the ocean struggling to stay afloat.

All was well in her life. She had almost everything she ever wanted. The only thing missing was girlfriends. She hadn't had any close friends in her life, but she wanted that. All around her she saw moms shopping with their daughters, friends at the spa enjoying the day, or women sitting down for a quick lunch during the work week.

She hoped Matthew's team would find women to love, women she could be friends with, but she was losing hope. The bitches the men hung out with were definitely *not* the kind of people she wanted to associate with. She had no idea what they saw in them...okay, well she *did*, but she knew none of them were good enough for them outside the bedroom.

Caroline thought about Christopher. He was dating one of the worst of the bunch, some chick named Adelaide. She acted like she was so much better than Caroline and it drove her crazy. She figured she must be *really* good in bed, because the Christopher *she* knew deserved so much better. She knew part of his past, and it was time he found a good woman. Someone who'd put him first. She sighed. She might as well wish for the moon. Adelaide knew she'd latched onto someone so much better than her. Who knew what she'd do to keep him?

Caroline felt arms come around her and pull her backward. She leaned back into Matthew.

"Happy?"

"You have to ask?" Caroline scolded him. She laid her head on his shoulder and felt him turn his head to kiss her temple.

"The house isn't too small for you?"

Caroline turned in Matthew's arms. "I couldn't care less where we live. I just want to fall asleep in your arms every night and wake up in them in the morning. I love you. I'd go thorough everything all over again as long as it meant I'd end up right here again."

Wolf didn't say anything, just leaned down and kissed her. Hard.

"Hey you two, quit it! Come help us carry more boxes in."

They laughed as Faulkner bitched at them. Caroline smiled up at Matthew. She had no idea how she'd been lucky enough to end up with this man, but she wasn't giving him back. He was hers. Now and forever.

Protecting Alabama

SEAL of Protection
Book 2

By Susan Stoker

Chapter One

Age 2

"OUT! WANT OUT!"

"Shut *up* you stupid whore! I'll let you out when you shut up and not a second before! You hear me, brat?"

Alabama Ford Smith only cried harder. She didn't understand why Mama wouldn't let her out of the closet. She was hungry and it was dark and scary inside the small room.

"Maaaaamaaaaaa."

Alabama stopped and listened against the door and couldn't hear anything. Was Mama still there? Alabama tried to reach the doorknob, but her little, two-year-old fingers couldn't grasp it. The knob wouldn't turn anyway; it was locked from the outside.

After an hour of wailing and crying, Alabama laid down on the floor amongst the shoes, boxes, and musty smelling hats and gloves. She sniffed. Mama had been serious. Alabama wasn't going to get to come out of the little room until she shut up. She didn't know what a whore was, but it had to be a bad little girl like her. She would try harder to please Mama.

Age 6

"ALABAMA FORD, HOW many times do I have to tell you to shut the hell up? Too damn many. If I hear one more word out of you, you'll be sorry!"

"But Mama…"

"Dammit, I warned you…"

Alabama felt her mama's hand hit the side of her face right before she went sailing down the three stairs that led from the kitchen into the family room. She watched as Mama came at her with murder in her eyes. She couldn't quite dodge the foot that was aiming at her head. It glanced off of her and she could see that just made Mama madder. The next hit came from the same foot into her side. Alabama curled into the smallest ball she could and tried to protect her head. She knew she wasn't the smartest girl, but Alabama figured if she had any chance of being able to walk in the morning, she had to protect her knees as well. Mama loved to kick them and then laugh as she tried to hobble around the house.

"Stupid whore bitch. Why do you have to be so stupid? I *said* to shut up. I'll teach you to speak out of turn. Don't. Ever. Speak. Again. Unless. I. Ask. You. Something."

Spittle flew from Mama's mouth as she enunciated and kicked at Alabama with each word spoken. Alabama finally got it. She shut up. Even as a six year old, Alabama knew Mama was serious. Mama meant every word that came out of her mouth. That was the year Alabama stopped talking unless she was asked a direct question.

Age 11

"ALABAMA, DO YOU want to talk to the nice policeman?"

Alabama looked up at the stern looking officer. He was tall and muscular and looked so strong. She sniffed a little and tried to be brave. Mama had walloped her this morning with the skillet she'd been holding. Alabama knew it was her fault. She'd made the mistake of asking Mama when she'd be home later that day. She *knew* better. How many times had Mama told her never to talk to her? Too many. And Alabama asked anyway. She knew Mama had been aiming at her head, but Alabama turned at the last minute and the skillet collided with her arm instead. Over the course of the day it had turned a nasty shade of purple. Of course a teacher noticed and insisted on taking her to the principal's office.

The principal was a nice enough lady, but she had no idea what Mama was like. No one did. Alabama was beginning to think Mama was crazy. It wasn't a nice thing to think about your own mama, but she couldn't think anything else. After eleven years of living with her, Alabama finally figured out that other little girls didn't have to worry about their mama's hitting them if they spoke out loud at home. They didn't have to worry about skillets coming at their heads if they so much as coughed too loud.

Alabama figured this was her chance. Maybe this officer would protect her. Policemen were supposed to protect people. She told him everything. How Mama would lock her in the closet when she went out. How she wasn't allowed to talk at home. How Mama hit her all the time with whatever was handy. Alabama spilled her guts to the police officer in the hopes he'd take her away and give her to a nice family, one with a nice mama. When he kneeled down in front of her, took her hands, and smiled at her, Alabama knew she could finally relax. This man would help her. He'd protect her.

Age 12

ALABAMA LISTENED TO the mutterings of the people around her. She lay on the bed with her eyes closed. She thought back to the day at school about a year ago. She felt as if she'd aged ten years since that time. Twelve was too young to have to deal with this.

"Did you hear what happened? That her mother did this to her?"

"No way! Holy crap. Do you think she's done it before?"

"Hell yes. Look at her, Betty. No one does this the first time. I bet she's been waling on this child for years. She can't go back. You know it, I know it. Hell, even her mom knows it. I think that's why she did it."

There was silence. Alabama couldn't fall back to sleep, even though it's what she wished with all her heart. She wished she wasn't there anymore. She'd trusted the police officer last year. He said it'd be okay. He said she wouldn't have to worry about her mama anymore. He lied. Seven days after she told the policeman everything, she was back at home. Mama didn't like it that she'd told. Apparently she'd gone through interviews with the police and Child Protective Services who were checking to make sure Mama was a good mama. Alabama knew Mama could be nice when she wanted to. Apparently she'd convinced everyone Alabama was a typical almost-teenager who was just rebelling. Mama told everyone she'd hit herself with the skillet in order to get attention. So Alabama was sent back.

Things got worse at home after that. Alabama learned never to say a word. She kept her mouth shut. Mama was scary. Alabama learned she'd have to protect herself. No one else would do it for her.

Mama had finally lost it tonight. Alabama had been in her room with the door shut when she'd gotten home from the bars. Mama had burst into her room and started waling on her. Mama yelled such horrible things. She'd told Alabama she was a mistake—that Alabama never should've been born, that she wasn't wanted. Mama yelled how she'd even given Alabama the stupidest name she could think of; how Alabama was named after the state Mama had gotten pregnant in and even gave Alabama the middle name of the stupid car she'd been conceived in. Alabama hadn't even known that Smith wasn't Mama's last name. Mama made it up because she didn't want her baby to have *her* name.

Alabama remembered Mama leaving the room and coming back a moment later with the dreaded skillet. It wasn't until Alabama woke up in the ambulance she realized, based on what the EMTs were saying, that Mama had broken her jaw. Okay, Mama had broken most of Alabama's face too—nose, cheekbone, and even her eye socket had been cracked.

Lying in the hospital bed with her jaw wired shut, Alabama made a vow to her twelve year old self. No matter what happened in the future, Alabama would never trust anyone to protect her again. If her mama didn't want her, if the police couldn't or wouldn't protect her…who would? She was nobody. Alabama had a made up last name and a first name based on the state her mom had sex in.

Age 16

SIXTEEN YEAR OLD Alabama walked down the hall of the high school with her head down, clutching her books. Another birthday had passed with no one knowing. No one said "Happy Birthday," no one gave Alabama any presents. She was the "weird" kid in school. She never spoke to anyone. She kept her head down and didn't make trouble. She aced all her tests and loved English, but she refused to answer any questions in class. Alabama never talked to her classmates. She went to school every day, minded her own business, and kept to herself. She didn't cause any trouble at school or at her foster home.

Alabama's foster mom tried to engage her, tried to get Alabama to open up, with no luck. Alabama had learned her lesson. She spoke only when spoken to and only when absolutely necessary. She got a job at the local library stocking shelves. Alabama saved her money for the day she'd turn eighteen and would move out on her own. She'd never rely on anyone again. Alabama was on her own.

Chapter Two

C HRISTOPHER "ABE" POWERS looked around the room and sighed. It was time to break it off with Adelaide. After dating her for about three months, Abe realized he didn't really even like her all that much. He supposed he'd stayed with Adelaide this long because she was good in bed, and he was lazy. The hunt for women had gotten old. It was all just a game. Abe knew he was good looking. He wasn't conceited, but he'd had his share of women over the years...too many, truth be told.

Abe was a Navy SEAL. He was used to women hearing that term and practically begging to go home with him. He'd seen how his buddy Matthew, also known as Wolf, had settled down with the love of his life. Caroline was different from almost every woman Abe had ever met. She was smart and pretty, even if she didn't think of herself that way, and stronger than he would've guessed. She also hated Adelaide. He supposed he should've listened to Caroline when she'd tried to tell him Adelaide wasn't good enough for him, but he'd enjoyed the things Adelaide could do with her tongue too much to call it off.

Abe met Caroline on an airplane, of all things. In fact, she'd saved his life, along with everyone else's on the plane. If it wasn't for Caroline's chemist background, they all would've been drugged and the terrorists would have killed everyone on the plane for their own agenda. Caroline and Wolf had been through hell, but they'd come out all right on the other side.

Abe thought about Wolf and Ice. They hadn't had an easy time of it, that's for sure. Surviving the terrorist hijacking was just the tip of the iceberg. The SEAL team had just returned from a mission and learned that Caroline had been taken into Federal custody after an attempt on her life. The team had joined her protection detail, but the terrorists had found her again. They'd taken Caroline captive and tortured and beaten her trying to find out how she'd figured out the terrorist plot on the airplane. The team had to actually rescue her from the ocean after the terrorists had thrown her overboard with weights tied around her ankles.

It had been a sobering time for the team, knowing how much Wolf loved Caroline and how they'd all felt helpless watching her be tortured and almost killed.

While Abe wanted a relationship like Caroline and Wolf had, he definitely didn't want his woman to have to go through the hell Caroline lived through. Abe didn't think he'd be able to stand it. He hated to see women and children hurt—they should be protected by any means necessary.

He supposed that was why he was a SEAL. Abe wanted to join the military and serve his country, but it wasn't until basic training and seeing the SEALs in training that he decided he wanted to be one of the best of the best.

Abe's team *was* one of the best. The team had been on too many missions to count and while they weren't fun, the missions were certainly necessary.

Abe met Adelaide while out at *Aces Bar and Grill,* their usual hangout, after a mission one night.

He and Wolf and Mozart and the other guys had gotten hammered. Abe supposed it was partly because his friends were with him, but he'd taken Adelaide up on her proposition and gone home with her. He'd refused to take her girlfriend as well. Some of the other guys enjoyed that sort of thing, but Abe was a one-woman-at-a-time man. He always had been and always would be. He knew it was partly because of his father, but he'd never analyzed it.

Abe and Adelaide spent most of the night in bed. She'd been willing to try just about anything, and at the time, it'd been just what he was looking for. He needed to blow off steam and having sex, lots of it, was a great way to do that.

But now, he was realizing, Adelaide was a total bitch. He hated to compare every woman he met to Caroline, but he couldn't help it. He was standing there listening to Adelaide gossip with her coworkers and wishing he was anywhere else. How had he stooped this low? This wasn't like him at all.

"Can you believe she brought *that*?"

"I know, ridiculous!"

"I guess she can't cook at all. But seriously, why didn't she cater something?"

Abe sighed loudly. Shit. Why did Adelaide and her catty coworkers even care that someone apparently brought a bowl full of vegetables instead of making a dish or bringing something catered to the pot luck? Jesus. Didn't they have anything better to do?

"Adelaide, I'm going to head over and grab something to eat. Do you want anything?" Abe might be ready to ditch her, but he'd treat Adelaide right in the meantime. It was hard wired into Abe's very being. He'd never disrespect Adelaide by breaking up with her in front of her friends and coworkers, but it was coming…and soon.

"No, but thanks, sweetie, you know I'm watching my weight." Adelaide snuggled up and leaned into him, making sure to brush her breasts against his arm. "I'll show you what I *want* later. Hurry back, I'll be waiting for you."

Abe shrugged out of her hold and managed to escape without having to endure being kissed. He eyed the lipstick she'd caked on her mouth earlier that night with disgust. Didn't she know how horrible that stuff tasted? Not to mention how Abe hated having it smeared all over his lips when Adelaide kissed him. He suspected she did it on purpose, a kind of ownership thing on her part. He snorted. *He* was supposed to be the dominant in the relationship, but Adelaide took the word to a whole new level. The more Abe thought about it the more he realized she didn't care about *him* per se, he could be anyone. Adelaide only cared that Abe was a SEAL and good looking. Yup, it was definitely time to break it off.

Abe walked over to the overflowing food table. Adelaide's company was having their annual banquet to thank their employees for a job well done over the past year. Wolfe Family Realty was the top realty company in their small town of Riverton and Adelaide was one of the most successful realtors they had. Abe supposed Adelaide had a teensy right to be entitled, but it wasn't enough for him to want to stay with her.

The Wolfe Family had been in the real estate business for years. They tried to keep their company close-knit, but it was obviously more of a wish than an actual fact. Abe had lived in Riverton a long time and didn't know most of the people at the event.

Abe grabbed a plate and got in the short line of people waiting to make their way down the line of delicious looking food. Abe took a step backward to avoid being run into by a man not paying attention where he was walking, and stepped on the foot of the person standing in line behind him.

Turning around Abe apologized, "I'm so sorry. Are you all right?"

Getting a good look at the woman who he'd stepped on made him forget what it was he was saying.

The woman was gorgeous. Abe didn't think she'd even tried to fancy herself up for the event, and that just made her stand out more. She came up to about his chin and had brown shoulder length hair, pulled back away from her face by a headband, but wisps of hair had escaped the wide swath of leather to frame her face. Abe thought she looked like she was wearing a bit of makeup—mostly around her eyes, and her lips were shiny with what looked like gloss. The lack of lipstick was a huge turn on for him, especially considering Adelaide's penchant for caking it on.

Abe continued his perusal of the fascinating woman standing behind him. She was wearing a pair of jeans with a top that had some ruffles on the sleeves. It was cut low in front, but not so low to be provocative—sexy because it left what was there mostly to the imagination. Abe could see only a hint of her curves. She was wearing a pair of flip-flops with flowers on the band and her toenails were painted a pale pink. Everything about her had Abe's complete attention.

Abe suddenly realized he'd asked her a question, but she hadn't answered. He tried to look her in the eyes, but she was looking at the ground. He could see the faint blush on her cheeks. God, blushing? When was the last time he'd seen a woman blush? The Alpha male inside him stood up and took notice. She was obviously shy and that made her even more endearing.

Abe repeated himself as they shuffled forward in the line. "I'm really sorry. Did I hurt you with my big feet?" He willed her to look up at him.

The fascinating woman just shook her head and refused to look up.

"Hey, if you don't look at me I'll think you're lying to try to spare my feelings," he teased, hoping he'd get to see the color of her eyes.

"I'm fine," she said in a voice so low he almost didn't hear her.

Her voice was raspy, as if she hadn't used it in a long while and the low tone just made it sexier. The sound of it went through Abe and settled in his heart. Amazingly, he felt the hair on his arms stand up on end. Whoa.

Abe scrunched down and tried to look her in the eyes. She gave him a small chin lift as if to say, *"look."* Abe turned and saw the line had moved forward and it was his turn to shuffle down the food table. He grabbed a plate and turned to the mysterious woman and held it out to her. Abe finally got to see her eyes when she looked up at him in confusion. Her eyes were a pale gray with streaks of blue. He figured in a different light they'd probably look more blue than gray. To answer her unasked question, Abe told her while waggling the plate, "For you."

Abe watched as she took the plate gingerly, as if it was a bomb he'd offered her instead of a simple dish. Abe took one off the top of the stack for himself and tried to engage the woman as he walked through the food line.

"What's good? What did you bring?" When she didn't answer, but concentrated instead on serving herself, Abe tried to joke with her. "Let me guess, which one is yours…hmmm, the homemade rolls? No? What about the macaroni salad there? Oh, I know… the lame bowl of vegetables?"

Realization dawned about the same time she bit her lip and looked away from the table in consternation. Oh shit.

"Ah fuck, I'm sorry. I didn't mean anything by that."

When she didn't say anything but only shrugged and continued to look as if she wanted to be anywhere but standing next to him, Abe tried desperately to backpedal.

"Seriously, I'm sorry. That was beyond rude. Jesus. You must think I'm the biggest asshole. I love veggies."

When she still didn't say anything, Abe transferred his plate to one hand, grasped her elbow lightly with the other, and pulled her away. They'd both filled their plates and had reached the end of the table. "Look at me."

At the commanding tone in Abe's voice, she looked up, finally.

Abe tamped down his feeling of triumph at her reaction to his demand. God, now wasn't the time for his Alpha side to come out, but deep down he reveled in her continued reactions to his words.

"I'm sorry. Okay?"

"Okay," she again said in a soft voice, nodding at the same time to reinforce her answer.

Loving the sound of her voice, even if he'd only heard her say a few words, Abe firmly stated, "Look, that's more than I brought. I'm being a mooch. At least *you* contributed." The hesitant smile that crept across her face was worth any embarrassment Abe felt at putting his foot in his mouth.

"I can't cook. Believe me, it's better I brought vegetables than if I tried to actually make something," she admitted sheepishly, again speaking to him in her soft husky way.

Somehow knowing her speaking to him was a victory of some sort, but not knowing exactly why, Abe gave her a huge grin.

Still holding his plate in one hand, Abe held out his other hand and said, "I'm Christopher. My friends call me Abe, but you can call me Christopher."

"Alabama." The woman replied politely, but didn't reach for his hand to shake and didn't ask any questions about his name, or nickname. Alabama was gripping her plate with both hands as if her life depended on it. It didn't faze Abe though. Trying to keep the conversation going, Abe simply nodded at her and said, "It's very nice to meet you, Alabama. I guess you work here too?" He watched as her face lost all animation and her eyes darted away from his, as if looking for something to distract her. Alabama's teeth came out to nibble at her lower lip. Abe knew she was going to bolt right before she spoke.

"I gotta go."

Alabama didn't even apologize or try to change the subject. She literally just fled away from him.

Abe watched her go. He had no idea what it was about her, but he knew he wanted to get to know Alabama more than anything he'd wanted in his life recently. There was something about her that made all of his protective instincts come flying to the surface. There was a story there, and he wanted to know it. Abe wanted to know all about Alabama.

Chapter Three

A LABAMA FLINCHED AS she scurried away from the hottest guy she'd ever seen. If her hands were free and she could've smacked herself in the forehead, she would have. God. She was *such* a dork. Seriously. Alabama didn't think she'd ever been so mortified in her life. Ok, she *knew* she'd never been so embarrassed before. Probably because she always avoided people and never tried to engage them in conversation.

Christopher. *Christopher*. Not Chris, but Christopher. His name was even hot. Alabama didn't know what his last name was, but she was sure it was something equally cool. She didn't like the sound of "Abe" at all. He didn't look like an "Abe"—even if that was what his friends called him, Alabama knew she never would.

She hadn't meant to really engage him in conversation; it went against every instinct she had. Alabama wasn't a talker. She wasn't ever going to be a talker. She'd gotten better as she'd gotten older, but when Christopher said he was sorry so sweetly and contritely, Alabama couldn't stop herself from trying to make him feel better. *She* was trying to make *him* feel better. Crazy. And when Christopher demanded in *that* voice for her to look at him, she couldn't help herself.

All her life, Alabama tried to please people—Mama, teachers, foster parents…but it never did any good. No one had ever been happy with Alabama. She spoke too much, she didn't talk enough, she was weird, she wasn't engaging enough…why couldn't Alabama stop trying to make others happy now? You'd think she'd have learned her lesson by now.

Alabama scooted over to the corner of the room and sagged into a chair, put her plate on her lap, and tried to regain her composure. What time was it? Could she leave yet? Yes, she was invited to the party by the Wolfe's, Alabama *did* work there after all, but she wasn't a realtor. She was a janitor. She cleaned the offices after everyone else had gone home. It wasn't glamorous, but she did it well. Alabama took pride in making sure everything was spotless. She actually liked the job because she didn't have to talk to anyone. She could put in her iPod and jam out to her favorite music as she cleaned.

Alabama knew every nook and cranny of the office. She probably knew more about what went on there than even the Wolfe's did. It was amazing what people would throw away, thinking that once it was in the trash it was "gone." She'd seen used condoms, antacids, sticky notes with love poems on them, and she'd even had to empty a trash can full of vomit. Alabama shook her head. If only they all knew what she had to deal with in cleaning the office.

Alabama knew most of the relators didn't even know she existed, and that was all right with her. She'd never made friends easily. Oh, she figured she was a nice enough person, she just wasn't very social. Alabama didn't enjoy idle chitchat and most women thought she was strange. Besides, making friends meant opening up and making herself vulnerable. Alabama tried one year after she'd moved to Riverton. There was another janitor who Alabama *thought* she'd befriended.

They'd been out to dinner a few times and spent some time to-gether at work. Alabama had even started picking her up for their shift and driving her home as well. One night, Alabama overheard her talking on the phone to someone about what she really thought about their friendship. She'd only been using Alabama for the rides so she could save money. She'd told whoever was on the phone she thought Alabama was weird and she was glad she'd be getting her car back the next week. That was the last time Alabama had offered to drive her to and from work and the last time she'd tried to make friends.

Coming back to the present, Alabama looked at Adelaide across the room. She wished Adelaide didn't know she existed. The woman hadn't liked Alabama on sight. Alabama had no idea why. She'd been in the office, cleaning as usual, when Adelaide had come in late one night. They were both surprised to see each other, but Adelaide had ordered her out of her office and shut the door. Adelaide was in there for about thirty minutes before exiting again and telling Alabama she didn't need to clean her office that night.

Alabama just shrugged and continued on with her cleaning. That was it. Ever since that night, Adelaide shot daggers out her eyes every time she'd seen Alabama. Alabama had no idea what Adelaide hid in the office that night, but obviously it'd been something she didn't want anyone to know about. Alabama thought about searching the office and seeing what she could find, but she didn't bother. She honestly didn't really care. Whatever it was would only cause more trouble for her, she was sure of it.

Alabama had heard Adelaide's snide comments about her veggies before she'd gone to get in line. She knew that was where Christopher had heard about them, but she tried not to hold it against him. He'd been trying to joke with her, not be mean, and had no idea she'd brought them.

Alabama nibbled on the food she'd put on her plate unenthusiastically and watched the people all around her. There were, as usual, too many people in the small space, but the Wolfe's didn't want to hear about having their annual "get together" anywhere else. It was tradition to have it in their business space, so that was where it was going to be, period. Most of the people were laughing and talking easily. The volume was loud in the room because of the size of the crowd. But at least everyone seemed happy and relaxed.

Alabama watched as Christopher made his way back to Adelaide's side. It really was too bad he was with her. Adelaide certainly didn't deserve Christopher. Alabama remembered back to when he'd handed her a plate. He'd done it so nonchalantly, as if he did that sort of thing all the time, and he probably did. It seemed to be ingrained in him to take care of others, but, she couldn't help but think, who took care of him? Adelaide certainly didn't. She didn't even notice that when she grabbed his arm when he came up beside her again, it jostled his hand and punch spilled over the edge of the cup to land on his shirt. Adelaide didn't even look up from the conversation she was having to notice his scowl or to help him mop up the spilled drink.

Even with her actions, Alabama noticed that Christopher continued to watch out for Adelaide. Alabama watched as he pulled her out of the way of two men who were trying to get past the group of women and how he took the empty glass out of her hand when she was done with it. Adelaide ignored him and hadn't even thanked him. Alabama could watch and appreciate Christopher's actions, but she had no idea how it actually felt to be treated that way.

Did Adelaide even recognize how much Christopher did for her? Did she realize how he protected her in so many little ways? Alabama tried to put herself in Adelaide's shoes; if Christopher was her boyfriend would she take advantage of the things he'd do for her? She mentally shrugged. She'd never had anyone in her entire life bother to look out for her so she couldn't imagine what she'd do. Whatever. Alabama didn't need anyone. She got along just fine by herself, at least that was what she tried to tell herself.

Alabama was so engrossed in covertly watching Christopher with Adelaide she missed the first sign of alarm. It wasn't until she saw Christopher actually drop the plate he was holding, ignore the food splattering all over their legs, and grab Adelaide by the arm, that she realized something might be wrong.

Alabama looked over toward the buffet table and saw that the table, and the curtain behind it, was on fire, and the fire was spreading fast. The room, which was overfull to begin with, was quickly filling with smoke and she could hear people screaming in panic. Alabama quickly dropped her own, now almost empty, plate and looked around at her exit options.

Ever since she was young and needed to try to escape Mama when she was pissed, Alabama made sure to make note of where the exits were in whatever situation she was in. That knowledge had saved Alabama from a beating more than once in her life and now it might just save her life.

Most of the people were heading toward the front door, the same door they'd entered earlier in the night. It was human nature to head for the door you knew about rather than trying to find an alternative exit.

Alabama knew there was a side door, but it was in the opposite direction from where most of the people in the room were trying to get out and it was down a short hall off the main room. It couldn't be seen from the main area where the party was taking place and thus it wasn't even an option for the panicking crowd. The smoke was billowing up from the curtains and was black and heavy. Alabama could feel the air thinning and it was becoming harder and harder to breathe.

Alabama had actually taken two steps toward the hall, and freedom, when she stopped. She thought about all the people who most likely wouldn't be able to get out the other exit because of the crowd of panicked partygoers. They'd surely block the door once they lost air. She'd seen enough news footage of crowded bars and nightclubs that had caught fire and the resulting carnage resulting in the press of people trying to get out a blocked door. If everyone continued to push and shove and try to get out the main door, it would soon be unpassable. Christopher wouldn't be able to get out.

Before she'd even made the conscious thought to move, Alabama was headed toward where she'd last seen Christopher. She quickly realized she wouldn't be able to stay upright if she wanted to breathe. Alabama dropped to her knees and started crawling as fast as she could. Thank God she was wearing pants. Alabama headed to the other side of the room, away from the freedom the side exit offered, but toward Christopher. He'd never been in this building and would have no idea about that other door. Somehow Alabama also knew he wouldn't leave Adelaide and the other women he'd been standing near. Christopher would do what he could to get them out.

Alabama lost precious minutes trying to get her bearings in the room, which seemed so much bigger when she couldn't see and when it was filled with smoke. She coughed once, then coughed again. She tried to hurry. Alabama knew time was running out. Finally, she reached the place where Christopher had been standing with Adelaide—they weren't there, but she saw a group of people huddled against the wall nearby.

Alabama scurried over to them but grabbed the arm of the man she passed along her way. She pointed toward the other side of the room where the hallway was and said urgently, "There's another door. Through the hall—over there... Go!"

The man didn't hesitate; he simply grabbed the hand of the woman next to him and left to go to where Alabama had pointed. They disappeared into the smoke filled room in a matter of seconds. If Alabama hadn't touched him she would've wondered if she'd dreamed him. She continued along the wall looking for Christopher and steered anyone she met along the way toward the other side of the room. They all looked thankful for her assistance, but none encouraged her to come with them. They just turned around and headed where she'd pointed.

After pointing the way out to several groups of people, she finally reached Christopher and Adelaide. They were on their knees huddled against the wall. Christopher had taken off his sports coat and put it around Adelaide. He'd also taken off his white dress shirt and tied it around Adelaide's head to try to help her breathe more easily. He'd tucked Adelaide into his front and was hovered over her protectively. Alabama could see him trying to take in the room, most likely to find an escape.

Alabama took half a second to admire Christopher's physique before snapping herself back to the emergency at hand. She didn't have time to gawk at how muscular he was and ignored how her stomach actually clenched at her first view of Christopher's six pack abs.

"Christopher," Alabama yelled as she grabbed his bicep, feeling it bulge under her fingertips. "There's another door over there." She pointed toward the other side of the room and the hallway that she'd been directing people to.

Expecting him to immediately snatch Adelaide up and head for safety, Alabama was surprised when he ignored her words and instead gripped her arm urgently. "Are you okay, Alabama?"

While she loved that he'd asked about her, now wasn't the time. They had to get out of there. It was getting hard to talk and hear anything with the noise of the fire.

Alabama simply nodded. "The door is that way." She pointed again and tried again to get him to go.

"Are you sure?" Christopher asked—his voice gritty with the smoke he'd inhaled.

Alabama nodded urgently. Crap, if he wouldn't go on his own, she'd have to make him. "Follow me," she ordered.

They turned to crawl across the floor but Adelaide refused to budge.

"Where are you going? No! The door is here, we have to stay here. It'll clear in a second." Adelaide started harshly coughing—her voice muffled from the shirt Christopher had wrapped around her.

Christopher turned back to Adelaide and spoke harshly to her. He was trying to convince her to go toward the other exit. Alabama could see the embers from the walls and other flammable material floating down and landing on Christopher's bare back as he kneeled next to and over Adelaide. He wasn't wearing a shirt and he was going to get burned if he crawled all the way across the room like that.

Alabama looked around desperately and spied a discarded suit coat lying on the ground, obviously thrown off in the panic of the other people. She scrambled over to it and grabbed a pitcher of water still sitting forlornly on a festive tablecloth. She walked on her knees back to Christopher and without warning, dumped the water over his head and watched it cascade over his hair and down his back.

She felt badly for just a moment, but then decided it was better he be pissed at her than be burned. Ignoring Adelaide's shrieks of outrage at her actions, Alabama thrust the jacket she'd pilfered off the floor at Christopher.

"To protect your back." She watched as Christopher didn't even quibble or say anything about the way she'd drenched him and shrugged on the jacket. It was a tight fit, and not only because he was now wet. He was obviously much broader and muscular than the man who'd discarded the jacket. Christopher simply nodded at her then slicked back his now dripping hair. He turned back to Adelaide.

Having grown tired of her tirade, Christopher grasped Adelaide's upper arm tightly and simply demanded in that no nonsense voice of his, "Move."

Seeing he was serious, and finally deciding moving was the better course of action than just kneeling against a wall inside a burning room, Adelaide finally stopped her bitching and meekly nodded. Christopher dropped his hand from Adelaide's arm and gestured for Alabama to lead the way. Alabama did without any hesitation. She could feel Christopher right at her side. He hadn't just allowed Alabama to take the lead, he was right there next to her, as they moved across the room to the exit, but not letting her get out of his reach. His shoulder would every now and then brush against her butt, he was that close.

The room was scary now. It was loud. Really loud. And it was dark. Alabama knew the air in the room was almost depleted. All thoughts of how hot Christopher looked without a shirt on and how nice he'd been to her were now gone from her head. Alabama was concentrating solely on getting out of the building which was burning down with them still inside it.

Alabama was coughing nonstop and could feel Christopher jerking against her, coughing as well. As they crawled, Alabama's hand touched a piece of cloth on the ground. Without thinking she snatched it up and kept going. She reached back briefly and pressed it to Christopher's arm. He grabbed it and she hoped he was using it as a filter to breathe through, as she intended it to be. Alabama might not be thinking about how good-looking the man was, but that didn't mean she hadn't stopped worrying about him. Christopher needed to cover his face so he wouldn't inhale any more smoke then he already had. She didn't even think about herself. Alabama only wanted to protect Christopher.

As Alabama and Christopher crawled, they came across a few other people seemingly lost in the confusion and Alabama grabbed on to them and urged them to crawl along with them. By the time the group made it to the hallway and then to the door, they were a group of about ten people, all in one long line. Alabama stopped and pushed on the door. She panicked for just a second when it didn't budge, but Christopher came up beside her and put his strength to it alongside hers. Their combined weight made it spring open. Fresh air swept into her face and Alabama took a deep breath.

The fresh air felt great, but the influx of oxygen into the hallway and toward the burning room just seemed to piss the fire off. Black smoke rolled out the door and the motley crew which had crawled across the fiery hell didn't waste any time getting out. One by one, they crawled through the door, got to their feet, and ran away from the burning building as fast as they could.

Alabama sat next to the door and helped everyone get out. She steadied them as they crawled out the door and tried to stand up. She couldn't stop coughing, but then again, neither could anyone else. Deep hacking coughs echoed in the air around them. If the fire hadn't been raging around them, all she would've heard was people coughing. As it was, she barely heard herself, nevertheless everyone else. She saw Christopher hesitate before he left, but Adelaide latched on to his arm, pulled him away and he disappeared out into the clean air.

Looking inside one more time after the last person in their group crawled out, Alabama didn't see anyone else. The fire was licking the ceiling and it was hot. Hotter than anything she'd ever experienced before. If anyone else was still inside, she didn't think there was any way they'd survive.

Alabama hadn't had time to think before, but what she'd just done scared the hell out of her and she started shaking. It was okay. She was okay. She'd gotten Christopher out. She'd gotten others out. Thank God, she knew about this exit.

Finally stumbling away from the door, Alabama looked around at the total chaos that was around her. There were fire trucks pulling up at the curb and people sitting and standing around the building in shock. She saw some news trucks driving in as well. This would be a huge story, she knew.

Alabama continued to cough, but ignored it as she frantically looked around. Finally seeing Christopher with Adelaide made her tense muscles relax a fraction. He was here. He was safe. Why that meant so much to her, she couldn't say. Hell, she didn't even know the man. There was just something about how Christopher talked with her as if he was interested and how he'd treated Adelaide that struck a chord within Alabama.

Something deep inside her that had hoped and prayed for someone to take her side, to protect her from Mama, sat up and took notice of Christopher. He was the kind of man she wanted. He was the kind of man that would look after his woman. Christopher would never let anyone hurt her. She knew firsthand that kind of man didn't come along every day. Even though he wasn't hers, she knew the world was a better place because he was in it.

She watched as Adelaide buried her face against Christopher's throat and wailed. Nastily, Alabama thought if Adelaide had the energy and ability to cry that hard and not cough up a lung, Adelaide was in better shape than most of the people sitting around her, including Christopher. Adelaide should've been more interested in how Christopher was than losing her shit.

Alabama watched as Christopher tried to comfort the woman in his arms while attempting to catch his own breath at the same time.

Alabama noticed two EMTs making their way through the people sitting haphazardly around on the grass trying to ascertain who needed help first. Everyone was coughing, but for the most part most people seemed to be all right. When one of the men made his way over to her she quietly and succinctly spoke her concerns to him, while brushing off his questions about her own well-being.

Finally understanding what she wanted, she watched as the EMT left and walked over to Christopher. Seeing he was going to be treated sooner rather than later, Alabama turned her attention toward getting out of there and back to her small apartment. It was a piece of crap, but it was home, and she desperately wanted to go home.

Alabama would figure out what was going on with her job later. The cleaning crew would be the last thing the Wolfe's would be concerned about right now. She'd wait a bit before contacting them to see what her next steps needed to be. She *needed* that job, but she didn't want to be selfish when others were hurt and everyone would be concerned about their jobs and livelihoods.

Alabama didn't look back toward the man she wished was hers. She simply walked away from the chaotic scene. There was no use wishing for something that would never happen. It was what it was. She'd learned her lesson a long time ago. Alabama had to be satisfied with their brief encounter and that Christopher was being cared for.

Abe looked up at the EMT that came toward them. Thank god, the EMT could take over caring for Adelaide and he could get the hell out of there. Abe wanted to find Alabama and thank her. He was surprised when the guy spoke to him specifically and didn't even look at the semi-hysterical woman trying to bury herself in his arms.

"Sir? I've been told you were burned? I'd like to take a look and make sure it's just superficial."

"Burned?" Abe was confused. Who said he was burned? Was he hurt and just didn't realize it?

"Turn around, sir, let's get this coat off and see how bad it is."

Abe coughed and let go of Adelaide who was cutting off the circulation in his arm. She resisted, but the EMT firmly instructed her to let go so he could check his back. The coat burned a bit as it slid off his back, but Abe showed no outward sign of discomfort. As far as pain went, it was low, especially compared to some of the injuries he'd received on his missions.

"Okay, it doesn't look too bad, sir," the EMT said briskly. "It looks like some of the embers landed on your back while you were getting out of there. I'm assuming you didn't have this jacket on the entire time? It's a good thing you put your coat back on, that's for sure. You would've been burned a lot worse if you hadn't. Look at the back of this."

Abe looked at the jacket the man held out and was amazed. He hadn't felt anything hitting his back while he'd been against the wall with Adelaide, adrenaline he supposed. But if Alabama hadn't had the presence of mind to douse him with water and to give him that coat…Alabama! Where was she? All of a sudden he desperately wanted to find her, to make sure she was all right, to thank her, hell…for all sorts of reasons he didn't understand.

Abe looked around and didn't see her anywhere. Did she get out?

"Who did you say told you to check me out?" Abe knew the man hadn't said, but it had to have been Alabama, no one else would have known he'd been burned. He needed to make sure.

"The lady over there…" The EMT pointed where he'd last seen Alabama and she wasn't there. "Well, she *was* over there. She was wearing jeans and wasn't very tall."

Abe nodded, a little irritated at his less-than-flattering description of the woman he found fascinating and gorgeous. "I know who it was. Thanks, man."

Abe didn't notice the snarl on Adelaide's face as he confirmed Alabama's presence.

"You know she's a janitor right?" Adelaide said malevolently, making herself known for the first time since the EMT had joined them. "She's weird and cleans toilets for a living."

"*You* know she just saved your life right?" Abe said without missing a beat. "Hell, she saved a *lot* of lives today, including mine. I don't care if she's an escaped felon or the queen of fucking England."

Adelaide just turned her head away and coughed dramatically.

"Come on, let's go and clean off your back, then you'll be good to go," the EMT said uncomfortably, not liking being in the middle of their disagreement.

Abe wanted nothing more than to leave Adelaide sitting on the ground, but he couldn't. It wouldn't be right, no matter how upset he was over the whole situation. He helped her up and put his arm around her waist and assisted her to the back of one of the ambulances that was lined up at the curb.

Feeling Adelaide's thin waist did nothing for Abe anymore. He couldn't even believe he used to think she was sexy. When he'd first seen her at *Aces* in her little black dress he'd been infatuated. She'd seemed like the perfect woman. Now he knew better. She was mean, and mean trumped looks every day of the week.

Knowing this wasn't really the place; he couldn't, and wouldn't, wait any longer.

"Adelaide, this isn't how I wanted to do this, but it's time we moved on. We had a good time together, but I don't see us going anywhere."

"You're dumping me?" Adelaide shrieked not even coughing. Obviously Abe's shirt had adequately protected her while they were in the fiery hell. "What the hell? I thought you were this great protector, this great Alpha male. But when I'm at my lowest and hurt you're telling me we're over? Are you dumping me for the *janitor?*"

When he didn't say anything but only stared at her with derision, she sneered, "You prick. You'll regret this."

"I already do." Abe walked away shaking his head. He'd never understand women. Never. Walking away, he was already making plans in his head on how to find Alabama. She didn't know it yet, but she'd be seeing him again very soon. He'd contact Tex if he had to. Tex could find anyone. Tex used to be on a SEAL team, but after losing his leg on a mission he'd moved to Virginia and started his own independent private investigator business.

Tex was still close to all of the team and he'd helped locate Caroline when she'd been kidnapped by terrorists earlier that year. Tex would help him find Alabama, and then Abe could get to work seriously getting to know her.

Abe hadn't been this excited to get to know a woman in a long time; too long. He couldn't wait. Alabama wouldn't know what hit her. She'd be his.

Chapter Four

ALABAMA COUGHED AND watched the news the next night sadly. The anchorman was covering the fire. Apparently one of the cords to a crock pot on the buffet table shorted out and caught the cheap paper tablecloth on fire. Alabama couldn't help the mean thought that at least her veggies didn't burn the place down; it was someone's fancy catered food they'd brought.

By the time someone noticed, the small flame had spread and the curtains were already on fire. Luckily no one was killed, but there were still about a dozen people in the hospital. They were being treated for smoke inhalation and burns. Too many people were trapped trying to shove out the door. The news people had interviewed a few bystanders standing around. Most had said how scared they were and how they thought they were going to die.

Alabama recognized one couple who she'd pointed towards the hall and the door. They'd talked about how the room was dark and scary and even mentioned how someone had pointed them toward the side door so they could get out. They had no idea who it was though. The person interviewing them seemed interested at first, but then someone was wheeled by on a gurney, and apparently that was more interesting than the unhurt bystanders.

A part of Alabama was glad. She had no interest in being interviewed or pointed out. Anyone would have done what she'd done. At least she thought they would. She hated being in the spotlight. But another part of her was a little hurt. If someone had saved *her* life, she sure as hell would've made sure she noticed who it was and at the very least thanked them. Oh well.

Alabama's lungs still hurt, but she honestly couldn't complain, she was here and alive, *and* she'd helped many others get out. She hadn't bothered to go to the hospital. Once she saw Christopher was being seen for the burns on his back, she'd just left. Cleaning offices for a living didn't give her a lot of extra money, and Alabama figured a trip to the hospital and paying a co-pay for a doctor to tell her she was fine wasn't a good way to spend her hard-earned money.

She snuggled down into the blanket on her couch. The little apartment was all Alabama could afford on her salary. She was saving up her money for a down payment for a house of her own. She didn't know what house, or where, but she'd do whatever she could to have her very own space. Growing up the way she did made her crave a place of her very own. Her own safe place. Even though she'd made the apartment as cozy as she could, Alabama would never feel safe until she had her own house and her own space.

Her foster homes had never felt safe. Alabama always had to be careful of the other foster kids and even sometimes the parents. Lord knew she never felt safe with her mama. Her current apartment was perfect for now; it was small and cheap and allowed her to save money each month.

Alabama was proud of the amount of money she'd been able to save so far. She was sure some people wouldn't think it was a lot, but it was a huge deal to her. She scrimped and saved and tried to shop at second-hand stores to save even more. Even this tiny apartment was a conscious effort to be frugal.

Her landlord was a slimy bastard named Bob. Alabama didn't even know what his last name was. He'd only introduced himself as "Bob" before he listed the rules of his place when she'd first inquired about renting. No pets. No parties. No Subleasing. No smoking. Rent was due on the first every month. No extensions. One month deposit up front. The apartment was partially furnished, but Alabama had bought her own small bed. No way was she sleeping where someone else had done who-knew-what. She'd had to do that throughout her childhood. Alabama swore to herself once she'd graduated from high school and set out on her own that she'd never sleep on a used mattress again. So far, she'd managed it.

The one room apartment Bob advertised was really a misnomer, as the only "room" in the place was the bathroom, but that was okay with her. Alabama lived alone and didn't really need any more space.

Just as she was nodding off to sleep, there was a knock at the door. Alabama bolted upright. What the hell? No one came to her apartment. She didn't have any friends. No one ever just dropped in. Was it one of her neighbors? She'd seen the old lady who lived on the same floor as her. They'd smiled at one another, but hadn't really spoken to each other. That had to be who was at her door.

She looked down at herself. She was wearing sweats and a large T-shirt. She shrugged. It wasn't as if she needed to impress anyone. It was either her neighbor or someone who was knocking on the wrong door anyway.

Alabama went to the door and cracked it open an inch. Of course Bob hadn't spent the extra money to install doors with peepholes in them. Cheapskate.

The absolute last person she expected to see standing outside her door was Christopher. She suddenly realized she didn't even know his last name. She just stood there like an idiot staring at him through the crack in the door. What the hell was he doing here?

"Hey, Alabama. I wanted to stop by and make sure you were all right."

After staring at him for a few moments, Alabama shook herself. At the rise of his eyebrows, she bravely ignored her self-imposed no talking rule and couldn't help but ask, "How did you find me?"

She was amazed to see a rosy hue rise up his face. Holy hell, was he blushing? She'd never in a million years have thought a man like him would blush.

"Yeah, well, I figured since your name was pretty unusual you wouldn't be too hard to find…and I was right. Did you know you're the only person in Riverton named Alabama? I was all ready to ask the Wolfe's about someone who worked for them named 'Alabama' when my buddy called back about two point three seconds after I sent him your name and city. You're apparently really easy to find, probably too easy, we need to talk about that… Anyway, he found you and here I am."

Alabama could only stare at him in disbelief. Christopher actually tracked her down? Had one of his buddies track her down? Why? If he wanted to thank her he could've just called and left a message with the Wolfe's or something. Alabama had so many things she wanted to ask, but her brain wasn't cooperating.

"Yeah, so anyway, I did want to come by and thank you and see if you wanted to have a cup of coffee with me sometime."

When she didn't say anything in reply Christopher continued as if she'd agreed with him. "Okay, great. So how about I pick you up tomorrow around eleven? We'll go to that little coffee shop downtown and we'll chat." He chuckled at himself in amusement. "Well, maybe I'll chat and you'll listen." He got serious and leaned in. His voice was pitched low and demanding.

"I want to sit down with you and thank you properly for saving my life, and saving countless others as well. I don't know you, but I want to *know* you. You probably don't want any thanks, but you're getting it anyway, at least from me. Will you be here tomorrow when I come to pick you up?"

Alabama nodded immediately. When Christopher lowered his voice like that she couldn't *not* agree with anything he said. He was right, she wasn't comfortable with being the center of attention and she didn't want any thanks really. Alabama was just happy *he* was here and in one piece. She had a lot of things she had to do, the first of which was to contact the Wolfe's and figure out what she was going to do about her job, but she also wanted to sit down and have a cup of coffee with this man. Alabama just wanted to feel normal for once.

Abe straightened up and held out his hand. "We never really introduced ourselves did we? At least our full names. I'm Christopher Powers. I already told you my friends and teammates call me Abe." He waited, hoping Alabama would follow his lead.

Alabama looked down to the hand being held out to her. Christopher had well groomed nails and his hand looked strong. How could a hand look strong? She shook her head as if to clear it of her foggy thoughts. She opened the door a bit more and finally tentatively reached her hand to his. "Alabama Smith."

Abe caught her hand and shook it as she intended, but he then brought it up to his lips and gently kissed the back of it. "I'm honored to make your acquaintance." Abe couldn't believe how great her hand felt. Her *hand* for God's sake. Her nails weren't painted and he could feel the rough spots on it, obviously from the cleaning she did. But it was soft and felt so dainty enclosed in his. He never wanted to let her go. He wanted to pull her close to him and wrap his arms around her back. He resisted the urge, barely.

Alabama chuckled out loud before she could stifle it. She wasn't sure why she was laughing. She figured she was laughing at the situation—at the fact that there was a gorgeous man standing on her doorstep kissing her hand. That sort of thing just didn't happen to her.

"I'll see you in the morning, Alabama Smith. Sleep well."

Alabama watched as Christopher backed away from her door. He kept eye contact with her for as long as he could. Finally he turned around and headed down the hallway. Right before he went out of sight he looked back and winked at her. Alabama closed the door in a daze. Oh crap. Did she just agree to a date with the best looking man she'd ever met? What the hell had she done?

ABE COULDN'T SLEEP. He'd risked a lot tracking Alabama down. He usually wasn't so aggressive. Hell, who was he kidding? He couldn't remember the last time he'd had to chase a woman. It was pathetic that asking a woman out for coffee was aggressive for him. He'd gotten way too used to women throwing themselves at him. No wonder he was bored with women. He'd gotten complacent. He'd gotten lazy.

Caroline had scolded him for just that earlier that week. She'd hated Adelaide and wasn't afraid of letting him know.

Alabama was different. He couldn't put his finger on it, but somehow he knew it. It wasn't just that she was a bit shy, or that he'd had to track her down. She certainly wasn't a chatterbox, and he found he liked it. In fact he didn't think she'd said more than her name the entire time he'd been at her door. But that lack of nervous talking was calming. He didn't have to pretend to be interested in inane conversation.

Growing up as the only male in a family full of women made solitude hard to come by. He'd never associate "calming" with women, at least he hadn't before Alabama.

He loved his sisters to death, but they sure could talk. Their family dinners were always full of stories and laughter. He'd had a great childhood. He loved his family. His sisters drove him crazy, but he wouldn't change anything about them. Susie was the youngest at twenty five. Alicia was the middle child and was twenty eight. Abe was thirty four. Abe figured the six years of age difference between him and Alicia made him the way he was today. He felt it was his responsibility to protect her. He'd spent most of his school years looking out for her and fighting her battles when he could. He'd honed his protective Alpha instincts from an early age and hadn't looked back.

He didn't begrudge his sisters or mom anything. Abe loved being the man in the family. He'd never really known his father. Even though Susie was nine years younger than him, his dad hadn't been around much. There was a reason, but it wasn't one he liked to think about.

His dad would be around for a while, then he'd be gone for a month or more. When he'd come back his mom hadn't seemed to care. Abe wasn't even really sure what he'd done for a living. A part of him felt bad about that.

All he knew was when he was eleven his mom took him aside and told him his dad had passed away. He tried not to think about what his dad had done to his mom…and him. He knew his father's actions were why he was the way he was today and Abe figured some psychologist would have a field day analyzing him and his protective personality. They'd link it back to his dad, and try to get him to talk about it, but he was who he was and he wasn't going to change.

Abe had always looked after his family. Family was the most important thing in his life and he'd protect them to the end of his days. Nothing was more important than his sisters and mom. Abe once brought a woman home for a family dinner and at the end of the night knew the relationship was over. His date had been rude and hadn't veiled her contempt at his mom's homeliness. He knew he turned sappy when he was around his sisters and mom, but he loved them more than anything and he'd be damned if anyone would feel it was all right to belittle that. He'd dumped her on the way home and wouldn't listen to her attempts at explaining her words had come out wrong.

He hoped like hell Alabama would get along with his family. It was way too early to be thinking anywhere along those lines, but Abe couldn't help it. He knew he'd bring her around to meet them before too long. He hated it was a test of sorts, but he was getting old enough now to want what he wanted and the hell with anyone who thought he was inflexible.

Abe was ready to have someone of his own, especially after seeing Caroline and Matthew and how happy they were. He hadn't even thought about Adelaide being his. He'd known he was biding his time with her. Adelaide was good in bed and had been enough for him. Other than her being catty and pretentious, he hadn't even known what it was that really bothered him about her or any other relationship he'd been in.

It struck Abe in the middle of that inferno with flames licking at the walls and the air in the room running out—what it was that made Alabama different from any other woman he'd ever dated. Abe's entire life he'd taken care of others. He didn't begrudge anyone that, it was the way he was. It was second nature for him to open doors, buckle a woman's seatbelt, pull out chairs, and basically be courteous and helpful. Abe's job with the SEALs only reinforced that protectiveness. He was always the one rushing in to save someone else. He performed best on missions where they'd been sent in to save someone's life or rescue them. It was his job, his duty, and he did it well.

But Alabama's simple act of taking the time to douse him with water and find a coat to cover him up with floored him. Alabama startled the hell out of him when she'd dumped the pitcher of water on his head, but luckily he'd known immediately what she was doing. He'd never have forgiven himself if he'd retaliated against her for thinking she was a threat.

But what sealed the deal for Abe was when they were crawling across the floor and Alabama had reached back and handed him something to breathe through. She hadn't said anything; she hadn't wanted anything from him. She'd simply acted to do something *for* him. That was it.

Abe doubted she even realized how momentous her actions were to him. No one "took care" of him. He took care of others, always.

Even his mom hadn't taken care of him in a long time, since he was little. He still called her every week when he wasn't on a mission to make sure she was all right, to see if she needed anything. He'd do little chores around the house and generally make sure all was right in her world.

It was the same with his sisters. Abe would always take care of them. He loved them, of course, but it was more than that. He didn't want them to suffer any hardship if he could prevent it. He went all out on their birthdays and the holidays.

But no one took care of him. Abe hadn't even noticed it until Alabama and that damn napkin she'd handed him. Even when he was sick, he cared for himself. Once when he'd gotten in a minor car wreck, his family and SEAL team were there in the hospital for him, but as soon as he was discharged, they'd gone back to their homes and lives. Abe didn't feel slighted at the time, but now? That damn napkin meant everything to him. He wished he still had it. He'd frame it and put it on his wall.

He wanted to ask her why she'd done it. The thing that really struck him was that they were in the middle of a life-and-death situation and she'd done it. Hell, they didn't even *know* each other. Abe couldn't name one other woman that would've taken the time look out for him in that same situation. It was human nature to look out for yourself first. He'd seen it over and over on some of the rescue missions he'd been on and in all the foreign countries he'd been to over the years.

He chuckled bitterly. Adelaide certainly hadn't cared how he was or what he was doing. It wasn't until they were outside and safe and the EMT had come over to them, that she'd even tried to pretend to have any kind of concern for him. It had been too late for that. Way too late.

Abe still had a lot of unanswered questions, but the bottom line was that he had an urgent drive to find Alabama. He had to get to know her better. He had to see if this feeling was mutual. Tex had made fun of him and wanted to know more about the mysterious Alabama, but Abe told him to mind his own business.

Abe had hunted her down and was taking her out for coffee in the morning. It was almost pathetic how excited he was. He hoped to get to know her better. Abe wanted to know everything. How old she was, where she was from, if she had brothers or sisters…hell, he wanted to know anything she'd tell him. He chuckled to himself. He'd be lucky if she said anything. Alabama was quiet as a mouse. He couldn't deny a part of him wanted to be the one to bring her out of her shell. To hear her call out his name in her quiet melodious voice while be brought her to orgasm.

Hell, Abe was already picturing them in bed together and they hadn't even had a first date. He tried to reign in his overactive imagination. There'd be time for that later. For now he had to think about how he was going to get Alabama to go on a second date with him.

Chapter Five

A LABAMA DIDN'T SLEEP well that night. She tossed and turned and couldn't stop wondering why Christopher had asked her out for coffee. She worried he might be doing it on a dare, or because he thought she was a challenge. She really had no idea why he'd ask *her* out. Adelaide was beautiful, and it was obvious they were dating. Was he cheating on Adelaide? If so, Alabama would be extremely disillusioned. She wanted him to be the gallant man she'd dreamed about.

She started worrying again why he'd be asking her out. Once in high school one of the boys on the football team had asked her if she wanted to meet him at the skating rink. She'd been ecstatic. She wasn't the type of person guys noticed. She'd spent a long time getting ready and trying to make herself look as pretty as possible. She'd even shown up at the rink early, she'd been so excited.

As she sat and waited for the boy to show up, she'd quickly realized it was a set up. Every other football player had been there along with most of the cheerleading squad. They'd skate by her table and giggle and laugh. After an hour of sitting by herself enduring the stares and giggles, she'd slunk out of the building, humiliated. She'd found out later it had been a type of initiation for the guy. The rest of the team had dared him to ask out the school "weirdo." He had, and the joke lived on in infamy in the halls of her high school.

Alabama had honestly thought he'd asked her out because he saw something in her worth dating. It wasn't until she was out of high school that she'd dared to try to go out with a guy again. Unfortunately, that had been a disaster as well. She'd lost her virginity to that man, only to find out he'd been trying to make his ex-girlfriend jealous, and he'd really not even liked her all that much. Of course he'd "stooped" to sleeping with her, even though he hadn't wanted to see her again. The whole experience was embarrassing and just another disappointment in a long line of them when it came to men.

With Alabama's history she just couldn't understand why Christopher would ask her out and be serious about it. She was just a cleaning lady, he was....hell, she had no idea what he was, but she was sure whatever it was, he was good at it.

After a few hours of twisting and turning in her bed and worrying herself sick, she made the decision that he probably asked her to coffee to some way to get back at Adelaide. She decided she just wouldn't answer the door when he got there in the morning. She'd pretend to not be at home. He'd knock then go away. Alabama could avoid any embarrassment and humiliation he was sure to be trying to pile on.

Alabama was way too nervous to eat any breakfast in the morning. She'd gotten up very early and paced the house. She finally decided to put on a pair of jeans and a long sleeved V-neck shirt. She wasn't expecting to see Christopher, but just in case, she wanted to be prepared.

At the last minute Alabama figured she probably should've left the house altogether instead of staying inside and pretending to be out, but it was too late by the time she'd thought about it.

At ten fifty five sharp, Christopher knocked on her door. Alabama sat on her couch staring at the door, wishing he'd give up and leave. He knocked again and she heard his voice through the door.

"Alabama? Are you there? Come on, sweetheart. Open the door."

Alabama stayed silent and bit her lip in trepidation.

"I know you're in there. Open the door and talk to me, well, at least let me see you so I know you're all right. If you don't come to the door I'll assume you're sicker from the fire than you let on and I'll have to break the door to get in to make sure you're okay."

Alabama wrestled with herself. Damn. She had to open it. She didn't want to have to pay to have the stupid door replaced. She figured he'd do just what he said; he'd break it down if she didn't open it. Christopher was certainly strong enough to do it without even breaking a sweat.

She walked quickly to the door and cracked it open, just as she had the night before. Christopher was leaning against the doorjamb looking way sexier than anyone had the right to look. He was wearing a faded pair of jeans and a scruffy pair of tennis shoes. He had on a polo shirt with a few buttons undone at the collar and a light windbreaker was over his shoulder to top off his outfit. His hair was messy, as if he'd run his hand through it a couple of times.

"Hey, Alabama. You ready to go?" Abe acted as if he hadn't just told her he'd break her door down if she didn't answer it.

Alabama knew she should be scared of him, he'd just kinda threatened her after all, but she couldn't be. She knew he wouldn't hurt her. How she knew that she had no idea, but she did. She nodded at him and backed away from the door to get her purse.

Abe gently pushed the door open and took a step inside her apartment. It wasn't very big, but it was clean and homey looking. She had placemats set out on the tiny kitchen table and there were two stools pushed under the table. There was a vase with some wildflowers in it. The one room didn't have a lot of furniture in it, but it still seemed a bit cramped. There was a small bed up against one wall with a blanket thrown over it. There was a tattered loveseat couch across from the bed. It was obviously a second hand piece of furniture because it had a sheet thrown over it and he could see the legs on the thing were chopped off.

There was a small television across from the couch that was sitting on an, again, obviously second hand table. Even though he could tell many of the things she had were hand-me-downs, it didn't look ragged. Alabama had gone to great lengths to try to clean and polish everything up. She'd put in a lot of effort into her home and he actually liked it much more than Adelaide's large, polished, perfect apartment.

Abe watched as Alabama walked over to the kitchen counter and grabbed a small purse. When she turned around he couldn't help but be dazzled by her. The V-neck T-shirt she was wearing wasn't provocative at all, but she still looked sexy as hell in it. He could see a hint of cleavage and being a breast man, he could tell she was all natural. He hadn't realized until this very moment how much he disliked fake boobs.

Alabama turned back toward Christopher, who was now standing just inside her front door. She was embarrassed he'd seen her little apartment. She knew it was nothing special, but it was all she could afford. She'd worked hard at finding just the right furniture for her home. She'd spent a few weeks going to the different thrift shops and garage sales to find what suited her. It wasn't new, but it was comfortable, that was all that mattered to her.

But now, looking at it through Christopher's eyes Alabama was embarrassed. It was old. It was beat up, and it was obvious. She headed back toward him looking at the floor hoping she'd make it through the morning and whatever humiliation was in store.

Abe took Alabama by the elbow when she got close to him. "I like your place, Alabama." He was surprised when she snorted in response. He smiled. God that was cute. "No seriously, you've done a great job at making this place comfortable. Oh I know, it isn't fancy, but it's you. It's cozy and lived in. I'd much prefer that to living in a place that was hard and stilted and way too fancy. You've done a good job."

Alabama looked up at him. Was he serious? She saw the small

grin on his face as he looked down at her. Whoa. He *was* serious. "Thanks," she said softly returning his smile with a tentative one of her own.

Satisfied that she'd taken his compliment gracefully, Abe steered her out the door and held out his hand. "Keys." He chuckled at Alabama's look of confusion. "Give me your keys, sweetheart. I'll lock your door for you."

Alabama looked down at the keys she was holding tightly in her hands. Why did he want to lock her door? She could do it. She didn't say anything though, and dropped her key ring into his outstretched hand and watched as he put the key in the lock and turned it. When he put her keys into his pocket after he was done, she couldn't keep quiet.

"Give them back," she said as sternly as she could, not looking into his eyes and trying not to panic.

Abe had put her keys in his pocket without even thinking about it. He'd naturally kept them, planning on being around to open her door for her when he brought her home again. At her tone of voice he took a second look. Alabama was panicking. It was obvious, especially to him, as he'd been trained to read body language. He immediately put his hand in his pocket to retrieve her keychain.

"Don't panic, sweet, here they are. I'm sorry; I didn't mean to scare you. I didn't even think about it. I wasn't trying to keep you from your home."

Alabama breathed in a sigh of relief and closed her fingers around her keys again. He was right, she *had* been panicking. She'd once stayed at a foster home where the parents didn't give the foster kids keys to the house. She'd had to sit on the stoop all the time waiting for them to get home and unlock the door. She felt like a stranger in her own home. One evening she'd been locked out all night because they'd gone on an overnight trip and hadn't told her they were leaving. She didn't like to ever be without a way to get into her house ever since. She nodded at him in embarrassment and thanks, and dropped her keys into her purse.

Abe walked them to his car, an ordinary four door sedan. For some reason Alabama thought he might have owned something a bit more flashy.

He must have read her confusion because he told her without a bit of embarrassment, "I know it's not anything fancy, but I prefer reliable over flash."

When they got to the passenger side of the car Abe opened it and waited until she sat down. Then he grabbed the seatbelt and handed it to her.

Alabama took the belt without a word and watched as Christopher walked around the front of the car. She continued watching him as he sat in the driver's seat and got comfortable.

When he looked over at her and saw she was looking at him he smiled a small smile and asked, "What?"

Alabama just smiled shyly at him and shook her head. She couldn't put into words what she was feeling, even if she wasn't reticent to talk.

Abe didn't push the issue; he just started the car and pulled away from the apartment complex. They didn't talk during the ride, but the silence wasn't uncomfortable. Alabama felt safe with him. He was a good driver. He wasn't reckless, he wasn't driving the speed limit, but he also wasn't being a speed demon.

They pulled up to the local coffee shop. It was a cute little building and the shop was called simply *Coffee and More*. Alabama had stopped in a few times in the past and enjoyed the little snacks and the flavored coffees they offered.

Abe parked the car and turned to Alabama. "Stay put, I'll come around and open your door for you." He waited until Alabama nodded before getting out and walking around to her side. He opened her door and held her elbow as she climbed out of the passenger seat.

On their way to the front door, Alabama felt Christopher's hand on the small of her back. He wasn't groping her, just confidently leading her where he wanted her to go, without being in front of her. It felt good. It'd been so long since she'd been touched. She led a solitary existence and hadn't ever been touched affectionately. She hadn't missed it until right this moment with Christopher's hand warming her back.

Abe opened the door and followed Alabama into the small shop. The décor was just as cute as the outside of the shop.

One side of the room had the counter and the kitchen area. The rest of the room was filled with seats. There were a few loveseats with big fluffy pillows. There were also some tables scattered around the room. Some were square and others were circular shaped. There was even a long table against the wall that had electrical outlets along the back side, for those that wanted to sit and use their computer while they enjoyed their coffee. The floor had two big circular rugs in bright colors. It brightened up the room and made it seem more homey.

The pictures on the wall were obviously done by children. They were framed and matted as if they were done by a master painter. Alabama had heard the owner held a contest every year and whichever child won got to see their picture up on her wall. The place was comfortable. The music wasn't playing loudly. It was a place people could relax in. She'd always loved the coffee shop and was happy Christopher picked it.

She still wasn't sure why he'd chosen to bring her here, but for now she was going with it.

"What can I get for you, sweet?" he asked leading her up to the counter.

"Vanilla latte, please."

"No problem. Do you want anything to snack on?" At the shake of her head he told her, "Okay, I'll take care of this. Go ahead and choose a place you want to sit, I'll be there in a sec."

Alabama hesitated for just a moment. She felt as if she should offer to pay or something, but she knew he'd probably be offended. She mentally shrugged. It was only a coffee after all.

She headed over to a small circular table that was near the wall on the other side of the restaurant and sat facing the room. Alabama watched as Christopher strode over to the table not too much later. He had two coffees and a small bag.

When he got to the table, Alabama expected him to take a seat and get right down to business telling her what he wanted her to know.

Abe put the drinks on the table and set the bag of muffins down as well. When he didn't sit down Alabama looked up at him. Abe looked uncomfortable. He ran his hand over the back of his neck. Finally he said, "Sweet, I don't want you to feel uncomfortable here, but I can't sit with my back to the room."

Alabama didn't understand. She gave him a quizzical look.

"I'm a Navy SEAL. I've been trained to be aware of my surroundings at all times. I can't sit with my back to the room. I need to sit where I can see what's going on. Will you switch seats with me?"

Alabama got it. Of *course,* he was in the military. She should've known. She'd taken the seat with her back to the wall, leaving the chair on the other side of the small table for him. She quickly stood up and mumbled, "Sorry," as she went to scoot around Christopher to take the other chair.

Abe blocked her maneuver and put his hand under her chin, forcing her to look up at him. "Don't apologize, sweet, you didn't know. We could both sit on that side if you wanted." He didn't give her a chance to agree or disagree, but put his hand at her waist and gently nudged her back from the table. He grabbed the chair she'd just vacated and pushed it over a foot. Then he leaned over and took hold of the other chair and pulled it to sit against the wall next to the first one.

Then he again put his hand at her waist and steered her into the furthest chair. After she'd sat down, he settled himself in the chair next to her. It was a close fit. His knee brushed against hers and his arm touched hers as they sat. He reached over to the bag and brought out two muffins. He put one on a napkin in front of her and placed the bigger of the pastries on it. He pushed the vanilla latte over in front of her before getting his own food set.

Then he turned to her and said, "So, tell me everything about yourself. I want to know it all."

Chapter Six

ALABAMA LOOKED AT Christopher in shock. Tell him everything about her? No way in hell. He didn't really want to know.

At her look of disbelief, Abe chuckled. "Too fast? Okay, how about if I go first?"

Alabama didn't know what was going on. She thought he just wanted to thank her. Now he wanted to know everything about her? And he wanted to tell her about him? She couldn't wrap her mind around it all.

"You know my name is Christopher Powers. I have two sisters, both younger than me. I'm thirty four years old. I'm a Navy SEAL. My buddies call me Abe. I love my job because I love my country. I don't like what I see while I'm doing my job sometimes though. I've never been married, never even come close. I've had one serious girlfriend in my life, when I was sixteen." He paused and smiled then continued. "I've seen a lot in my life, and I've done a lot of macho things, but nothing impressed me more than you in the middle of that room burning down around us. You kept your head, saved a lot of lives, saved *my* life. Thank you."

Alabama didn't know what to say. She looked away from him down at the table and the muffin she'd been shredding with her fingers while he talked.

Abe reached out and put his finger beneath her chin and raised her head so she'd look him in the eyes once more. God, she was amazing. Most of the women he'd known in the past would have simpered and cooed and taken his words as an invitation to snuggle up to him and get closer to him. Not Alabama. His words made her uncomfortable and she tried to hide from him. The skin under his finger was warm and smooth. He wanted to cup her cheek in his hand, but knew that would be too much for her right now. Soon.

"I didn't say that to embarrass you, sweet. I just wanted to let you know how much I appreciate what you did for me. I'm a big bad SEAL, no one takes care of me. But when you did it, it felt great. So thank you."

Alabama just nodded. God. This was…she didn't know what this was. Every time he called her "sweet", she felt her heart lurch. She'd never had a man speak to her as if she was important, as if he didn't want to be anywhere other than in her company. Goose bumps broke out over her arms. Christopher's hand felt good on her skin. She wanted to lean into him, to feel his hand running over her hair, but she didn't know him. She figured he was just grateful to her, he'd just said so after all.

"I…you're welcome." She managed to squeak out.

Abe let go of her chin and reached for her hand. He threaded his fingers with hers and squeezed her hand. "Okay, your turn. Tell me about yourself."

Alabama froze. She couldn't. She wasn't interesting at all. She looked around nervously out of habit. She'd always made sure growing up Mama wasn't anywhere nearby when she needed to say something. Alabama hated that she still did it today, but she couldn't break the habit. There were just too many times she'd been caught unaware by Mama to be able to stop herself. Seeing no one that resembled Mama, Alabama cautiously turned back to Christopher.

"I'm Alabama Smith. I'm thirty. I've lived here for several years. I don't have any siblings or family. It's just me." She stopped. What else could she tell him? She didn't have anything else. She didn't have a good job. She was just…her.

"Go on, sweet," Abe encouraged. "Tell me more. I want to know everything."

"That's it. There isn't much to know about me."

"I highly doubt that. Alabama, you're amazing. You've made a home out of a tiny little apartment that most people would scoff at. You saved the lives of dozens of people this week. You're beautiful. I want to know everything about you. Your favorite color, your favorite food, what you like to read, where you went to school...everything. Maybe not today, but I'd like to see you again. I want to get to know you."

Alabama could only gape at him. What the hell did this gorgeous man want with her? Was he messing with her head? Like high school? She couldn't stop the next words from coming out of her mouth.

"Did you lose a bet?"

Abe watched as Alabama blushed. She was so damn cute, but he didn't like the implications of her question. He squeezed her hand again and ran his thumb over the back of her hand. He definitely didn't like her lack of self-esteem and what might have happened in her life to make her that way.

"No sweet. I'm here because I see you. I'm here because I like what I see. I want to get to know you better because no one has ever affected me the way you have. I'm not a boy who plays games, I'm a man. I'm a man who saw a woman who caught his interest, and wants to get to know her better."

"I don't get it." Alabama was frustrated she couldn't put into words what she meant. She knew what she looked like. She wasn't a troll, but she also didn't look like Adelaide. She wasn't fashionable, she wasn't gorgeous, she wasn't...she just wasn't like the women she imagined he'd be with.

Shifting so he sat sideways in his chair, Abe turned Alabama as well. He just reached out and shifted her chair with her sitting in it. He scooted his chair closer to her so she had no choice but to part her legs to give him room. Their position was intimate. He took hold of her other hand and they sat facing each other. Alabama could feel her breathing speed up and her heart race. Holy moly. He was intense, but intense in a good way.

"Alabama, look at me. Does it look like I have a problem finding a woman?" He wasn't being cocky; he just wanted to make a point to her. When she shook her head emphatically, he chuckled and then continued.

"Exactly. I'm here because I want to be here. Women like Adelaide are nice to look at sure, but they aren't nice inside. They want me because I'm a SEAL. They want me because I have muscles. They want me because they think I can give them something. I don't think that's the way you see me. Am I right?"

Alabama slowly nodded her head. That definitely wasn't the way she saw him. If she had any brains she'd choose a man who was nerdy and would fade into the woodwork, just like her. She had no idea why she had the instant attraction to Christopher, she only knew she did.

"Adelaide isn't a good person, Alabama. I knew it before last night and was going to break it off with her. She only invited me to that shindig because she wanted to show me off. But you, you *saw* me. Even when I was being an ass, you forgave me on the spot." Abe switched topics abruptly, trying to get his point across to the shy woman sitting across from him.

"I've saved hundreds of lives. I've gone into situations you'd only think about in your nightmares. The fire that night was nothing compared to what I've lived through. I saw the direction the other people you spoke with were crawling and was about to head that way myself when you appeared out of the smoke. No one, other than my mother when I was a baby, and my teammates, have ever had my back the way you did. You put your life at risk for me. *Me.* You think I didn't notice that you came across the room to me instead of getting your ass out of there? I did. That's why I want to get to know you. That's why I think you're so much better than women like Adelaide. You're a good person inside and that's what I saw that night. That's who I want to get to know. You'll let me right? You'll let me take you out on a real date?"

Alabama could only stare at the beautiful man in front of her. She still didn't one hundred percent believe he was telling the truth. She was just Alabama. A broken woman who'd had a crappy childhood, but she couldn't help but *want* to believe him. *Want* to have the fairytale.

There was no denying Christopher was a beautiful man. He was tall. She'd prefer his hair be a bit longer, but couldn't deny the short military cut looked good on him. He was muscular all over. He probably didn't have an ounce of fat on him anywhere. Christopher was definitely fit and ready to go on whatever mission he and his team were called on. But besides all the outside trappings, she wanted to believe he was a good man. When he'd spoken about his sisters she could hear the pride in his voice. Alabama knew being on a SEAL team was one of the toughest jobs in the military. He put himself on the line every day for his country, and most of the time no one would ever know how dangerous his job was.

"Thank you for your service to our country," she blurted out before thinking. Alabama mentally slapped her forehead. God, she was such a dork. There he was asking if he could see her again and she'd gone and said that.

Abe simply smiled and brought one of their clasped hands up to his mouth. He kissed the back of her hand and left his lips there for a moment while looking into her eyes. "Thank you sweet. Now…about that date…"

"Yes."

The smile that broke out over his face was dazzling. "That wasn't so hard now was it? We can exchange cell numbers and I'll make the arrangements and call you." At her immediate frown he asked, "What? What's wrong?"

"I don't have a cell," she admitted sheepishly. She couldn't afford one. The hundred dollars a month that it cost was too much. Alabama was embarrassed. *Everyone* had a cell phone these days. Since she didn't have a lot of friends she didn't see the need. She had a land-line in her apartment, but hadn't ever owned a cell phone.

"But you have a phone? At home?" At her nod, Abe continued. "No problem then, just give me that number and I'll give you mine and I'll call you. Okay?"

Christopher could tell she was embarrassed about not having a mobile phone and he tried to downplay it as best he could. He was surprised actually. He'd never met anyone that didn't have a cell phone. There was no way he'd let her know though. He didn't want to embarrass her any more than she already was.

Abe didn't like the thought of her not having a way to contact someone in case she had an emergency. Anything could happen, her car could break down, she could have an accident, someone could break in…the bad things flashed through his mind one after another. He thought about Caroline, hell, someone *had* broken into her apartment. If she hadn't had her cell phone the police might not have gotten there in time.

Abe couldn't help but see Alabama stranded somewhere with no way of getting a hold of anyone…specifically him, when she needed help.

Seeing the look on his face made Alabama want to explain. "I have plans to get one of those pay-as-you-go phones for emergencies, I just haven't yet."

"It's okay sweet. No need to explain to me. People today are way too dependent on cell phones. They don't stop to actually talk to people, always looking down at their little screen to see what the next tweet is from some overpriced actor in Hollywood."

He smiled at Alabama when he saw her relax a bit. God, he wanted nothing more than to wrap her up in his arms and take her home and hide away from the world. Nothing in his life had prepared him for her. But he wasn't backing off, no matter how much he was pushing his luck. And she'd be getting that phone before she knew it, that was for sure. He'd take care of it for her.

"Okay, so I'll call you tonight?" Waiting for her affirmative nod, he then continued. "I'll plan something for Friday. Are you busy that day? I have to check in on base in the morning for PT, but then I have the weekend free, as long as we don't get called in. That's always a possibility. Does that bother you?"

Alabama thought about it. Did it bother her? Yes, but not in the way he was probably thinking. She looked around furtively again, checking to make sure it was safe to speak, then told him with more honesty then she probably should've shared at that point in their relationship, whatever that relationship was.

"Yes, but not because you won't be able to take me out, but because if you get sent on a mission I know it'll be dangerous. And I'll worry about you."

Not liking the way she constantly scanned the room before speaking, Abe put that aside for the moment, instead concentrating on what she'd said. "Thanks for worrying about me sweet. I'm trained. My teammates are trained. They have my back and I have theirs. I know we don't know each other that well yet, but understand this. I'll do everything in my power to get back safely. I think I've just discovered another reason to make sure I come home safe."

Alabama blushed hotly. Holy crapola. He was intense. This whole conversation was intense. It was crazy. How in the hell could he feel those things about her when he didn't even know her? Hell, how could she feel that way about him?

Abe loved the blush that crept up Alabama's face. Jesus, she was cute. Trying to lighten the mood he reluctantly let go of her hands and scooted his chair back a bit. "Come on, let's finish up our breakfast and I'll take you home. Unfortunately, I have some things I have to do on base today, but I'll call you later tonight."

Alabama leaned on the inside of her apartment door and listened as Christopher walked away down the shabby hallway of her apartment complex. They'd finished their muffins and coffees and he'd brought her home. He'd insisted on escorting her back up to her doorway. She was nervous, wondering if he'd kiss her. He hadn't, but he had taken her face in his hands and leaned his forehead against hers briefly.

"Lock the door behind you sweet. Okay? I want to hear the chain going on."

It was an odd thing to say in such an intimate position, but all she could do was nod. Christopher had taken a deep breath and stood up straight, not taking his hands off her face. Finally he'd run one hand up and over her hair and the other moved to lightly squeeze her shoulder. "I'll talk to you later."

Alabama knew he'd waited outside her door until he'd heard her locking the door and putting the security chain on. Then he'd walked away down the hall.

She slid down the door holding her knees. Whoa. This morning had been surreal. She smiled to herself. Good surreal. No, *great* surreal.

Chapter Seven

ALABAMA HAD MADE it through the day on auto pilot. She hadn't contacted the Wolfe's yet about her job, but it was first thing on her to-do list for the next day. She'd been putting it off, but couldn't any longer.

She piddled around all day doing nothing important in her apartment. She cleaned it from top to bottom, did all of her laundry, including her bed sheets and towels, she'd even scrubbed the toilet. She'd tried to read for a while, but the romances she usually read just weren't holding her attention.

Would Christopher call? He *said* he'd call, but she still didn't really believe he would. Even with everything he'd told her that morning, it was hard for her to believe. At one point she put in the movie *Drop Dead Gorgeous* to try to keep her anticipation down. She'd bought a bunch of movies at a garage sale once, and had never regretted it. She'd gotten some great oldies including *The Princess Bride, Ever After,* and even some of the *Little House on the Prairie* seasons.

Alabama thought about the supposed-impending call. While it was true she had an issue talking with people, speaking on the phone was easier...as long as she could close herself off in a small room. She felt safe that way. If she was in her own house, locked away where Mama couldn't possibly find her, she was okay with talking. Alabama knew she probably needed therapy of some kind, but it just wasn't a priority at this time for her.

Just as the movie got to the point where the first pageant was starting, her phone rang. It scared the crap out of her, even though she was half expecting it. It had to be Christopher, no one else called her. Ever.

Alabama stopped the movie, grabbed her cordless phone and climbed into her small bed. She looked around the apartment one last time making sure she was alone. Of course she was. She was always alone.

She snuggled down under the covers and lay on her side and huddled into herself before finally pushing the talk button on the phone.

"Hello?"

"Hey, sweet. It's Abe."

Alabama giggled. "I know. I recognized your voice."

"You should do that more often," Abe told her.

"What?"

"Laugh. You have a beautiful laugh."

Alabama blushed; even when he wasn't in front of her he could embarrass her. "Thanks, I think. How was your day?"

Abe was thrilled she was talking to him. He wasn't sure she would after getting to know her a bit that morning. She wasn't a talker, that was obvious. He was half afraid he'd be talking to himself when he called. He was pleasantly surprised. "It was good. I worked out with my team, sat in on a few meetings, then had dinner with my friend Wolf and his woman, Ice."

"Wolf? Ice?" Alabama asked.

"Yeah, remember how I told you I was called Abe? Well, Matthew's nickname is Wolf. His girlfriend's name is Caroline, but she earned the moniker 'Ice.' Everyone on the team has a nickname. Most of the time it has to do with something about that person. Matthew earned the name Wolf because of the way he ate while training to become a SEAL. He'd scarf down all his food and come back for more. He was always wolfing down his food. The name stuck."

Alabama loved hearing Christopher talk about his friends. He had such passion in his voice. It was obvious he loved what he did and really liked the people he worked with. "Why Ice? Is she on your team too?"

"Not exactly. We met her a little bit ago when we were flying to Virginia. She saved all the lives on the plane we were on. Terrorists had drugged the ice they used to make the drinks with and were planning on hijacking the plane. She's a chemist and realized what was going on. Wolf happened to be sitting next to her and was able to let us know what was going down and we were able to foil the plan. They went through some other shit too, but all's well that ends well. They're blissfully happy and I'm proud to call both of them my friends."

Alabama smiled. She was scared to death to hear that he'd almost died, but happy he had such great friends. "I remember seeing that on the news. I'm so glad you guys are all okay. Why are you called Abe?"

Abe laughed. "The guys started calling me that because I can't stand it when people lie. I'd much rather people be honest with me. Even if it's crap I don't want to hear, I want the truth."

Alabama hesitated. She wasn't sure she wanted to be one hundred percent honest with him. She was ashamed with her history. On one hand she knew it wasn't her fault, but if her own mama didn't want her, how and why would anyone else?

"Sweet? You still there?"

"I'm here."

"You okay?"

"Yeah."

"You're freaked aren't you?" When she didn't say anything Abe went on. "Please don't be. I don't expect you to spill your guts with me right off. I do want to know everything about you, but I don't want you to lie to me. When you feel comfortable enough, you can talk to me."

"How do you know I have something to spill in the first place?"

"Sweet, I've been around enough people with Posttraumatic Stress Disorder to recognize it when I see it." When she started to interrupt him to protest, he wouldn't let her. "No, it's okay. I don't know what happened to you, but it doesn't matter to me. I like you. I like that you're soft-spoken and think about your words before you say them. I don't like that you look around the room to see who's there before you speak, and I hope you'll tell me about that someday, but rest assured, I won't hold it against you. Okay?"

"Are you for real?" Alabama couldn't believe what she was hearing. How could this man know her, without really knowing her? It was eerie really.

"I'm for real, sweet." Christopher knew Alabama was getting freaked out, and it was the last thing he wanted to do. "Tell me about your day," he changed the subject, hoping to make her feel more comfortable.

Alabama talked to Christopher for two hours straight. They talked about nothing really, non-important stuff that most people spoke about when they were getting to know each other. She learned his favorite food was a thick juicy steak, and he learned that she loved to go the movies by herself on the weekends and get lost in a good thriller.

"I've really loved talking to you," Abe told her quietly. "But I do need to get going. I've got training in the morning and you need to get some sleep."

"Okay, Christopher. Thank you for calling. I've really enjoyed it."

"It was my pleasure. The only way this would've been better is if we'd been face to face. I'll get back with you soon about our date on

Friday, all right?"

"All right."

"Sleep well, sweet. I'll be thinking about you."

"Good night."

"Bye."

Alabama clicked off the phone and held it to her chest. She'd never felt like this in all her life. She felt as if she mattered. She'd never mattered to anyone before. It felt good.

Chapter Eight

ALABAMA HAD JUST spoken with Stacey Wolfe. She'd been glad to hear from her and had expressed her thanks for what she'd done to help save lives the night of the fire. She'd reassured Alabama that she still had a job. The Wolfe's were working on renting a building near the one that had burned down until they could rebuild. Within a week they'd be ready and Alabama could go back to work.

The company was even going to pay her for the week of work she wouldn't be doing. It was more than generous of them. Alabama almost didn't know what to do with the surprising time off. She would've preferred to have stayed busy so she wouldn't have to think about her upcoming date.

She hadn't seen Christopher since their coffee date, but they'd talked on the phone two more times. The first time it was a short conversation. Christopher had called in between meetings just to say hello. Alabama had been so bamboozled, she hadn't had much to say, but luckily Christopher didn't seem to mind.

The second time was another late night phone call and they talked for another couple of hours. Alabama learned more about his sisters and mom and how much they meant to him. He'd even told her he wanted them to meet her. He knew he'd made her uncomfortable and had rushed to reassure her that they'd love her.

They'd talked for a bit more before ending the call. Alabama even admitted to him partly why she was able to talk to him on the phone, but wasn't comfortable talking in public. She'd told him she didn't have to worry about if anyone was around listening to her or judging her. Christopher had tried to tell her that it didn't matter what others thought about her, but since that wasn't the only reason she was more comfortable talking to him on the phone in the safety of her own house, Alabama didn't argue with him.

Christopher had again told her that he'd be thinking about her before he let her hang up the phone.

Now it was Friday and time for their date. Christopher wouldn't tell her much about where they were going, he'd only told her to be sure to wear comfortable clothes and to bring a sweatshirt of some sort.

Abe was feeling antsy. He hadn't felt this way about a woman in a long time. His buddies, especially Wolf, had teased him unmercifully. They'd all wanted to meet Alabama, but he'd told them they'd have to wait. He knew Alabama was shy around others and didn't want her to be overwhelmed with his friends before he could make sure she was his.

Abe planned an interesting day for them, knowing if she'd enjoyed the day, she really was the woman for him. He felt a little bad about testing Alabama the way he was planning, but he'd been snowed too many times by women who he'd thought liked him for him, but were only pretending interest in what he liked. Deep down he knew Alabama wasn't like that, so this wasn't so much a test as it was a way to spend some quality time with an amazing woman.

Abe shook his head as he pulled up to her apartment complex. It really was a piece of crap. He wouldn't say anything her though, because he figured she didn't make a lot of money. He hoped she'd open up to him today and tell him more about herself. He didn't even know what she did for a living, except that it had something to do with Wolfe Realty.

He moved the package on the seat next to him to the backseat before exiting his car and walking up to her floor. He knocked once and the door was opened almost immediately. He smiled. She looked great. Alabama was wearing a pair of well-worn jeans and a fitted V-neck T-shirt, the kind she usually wore. It was a deep purple color and plunged deep into her chest. Holding a white sweatshirt over one arm, she'd dressed just like he'd asked. He loved it.

Alabama was nervous as all get out. She had no idea what they'd be doing today, but she trusted Christopher. She probably shouldn't, but hell, if she couldn't trust a Navy SEAL, who could she trust? Alabama tried on three different shirts before settling on the purple one. She thought it made her chest look "perkier," and she'd always loved the color.

Christopher looked good. He was wearing a pair of khaki cargo pants and a long sleeved shirt. It wasn't tight like he was trying to show off, but it was snug. Alabama could see the definition of his arms. He was built. God, was he built. He was wearing a pair of combat boots on his feet. He was leaning against the doorframe of her apartment when she opened the door. If he'd been selling something, she would've bought whatever it was on the spot.

Alabama stepped out of her apartment and wasn't surprised when Christopher held out his hand for her keys. She remembered he'd done that the first time he'd picked her up too. She dropped her keys in his hand and watched as he locked her door. When he was finished, instead of putting the keychain in his pocket as he'd done the last time, Christopher turned and held it out to her. She smiled shyly at him as she took the keys and put them in her purse. He'd remembered how she wasn't comfortable in letting him keep her keys and hadn't pushed the issue. She liked that about him. Heck, so far she'd liked everything about Christopher.

Abe took Alabama's elbow as they walked down the hall. He winked at the old lady who was peeking out her door at them as they walked by. She winked back and smiled, then closed her door after they'd passed.

As they settled into the car, Abe looked at Alabama. She hadn't asked where they were going, although he could tell she was curious.

Before starting the car, he leaned behind them and picked up the package. He handed it to Alabama and leaned one arm on the steering wheel and watched her.

Alabama looked at Christopher in bewilderment. He'd gotten her a present?

"Go ahead, open it." Abe urged gently.

Alabama carefully peeled back the paper on the package and looked into the box. It'd been a long time since she'd gotten a gift. Hell, she couldn't remember when anyone had ever wrapped something up for her. She almost wanted to keep it wrapped and stare at it all day, but Alabama knew she'd look like a freak if she did that.

After lingering over opening the gift for as long as she could she stared down at what he'd given her. It was a phone. Not one of the crazy expensive smart phones, he must've known she wouldn't accept one of those, but a flip phone that you paid for as you used the minutes.

Alabama bit her lip and tried not to cry. Mama hadn't ever celebrated Christmas with her and certainly hadn't bought Alabama anything for her birthday. Once Alabama entered into the foster care system, none of her foster-parents had cared enough to bother either.

"I'm not taking it back, Alabama. You need it. *I* need you to have it. I need to know you'll be safe when I'm not around."

Alabama looked around quickly, and seeing no one blurted, "I've never gotten a present before." Tears sprang into her eyes and she tried to blink them back.

"Hey, look at me, sweet." Abe couldn't believe what he'd just heard. He knew Alabama must've had a tough upbringing, but it'd obviously been worse than he'd imagined. When she wouldn't look up, he put his hand under her chin gently. "Please?"

Alabama finally looked up. She'd controlled her tears enough that they wouldn't fall, but tears were still pooled in her eyes. "Thank you, Christopher," she managed.

"You're welcome. You'll keep it?" Abe wanted to demand to know what had happened and how it was that she'd never been given a gift before, but he also didn't want to make her cry. He could see she was holding on by a thread.

At her nod he told her, "Okay then. When we get home tonight you can plug it in and charge it up. Be sure you take it with you wherever you go just in case you need it. I've loaded it up with five hundred minutes to get you started."

"That's too much," Alabama managed to get out.

"No, it's not. It's not enough for my peace of mind, but I knew you wouldn't accept it if I'd put as many minutes on there as I wanted to. Besides, you'll probably use all those up in the first week talking to me. At least I hope you might."

Alabama smiled. Jeez, he was amazing. "Okay. Thank you, Christopher. Seriously."

Abe didn't think, he just tipped Alabama's chin up higher with his finger, leaned in, and gave her a quick kiss on the corner of her mouth. He didn't linger, although he wanted to. The quick taste he'd gotten of her was enough to drive him crazy. Alabama tasted like peppermint, and he wanted more. Abe forced himself to drop his hand, caressing her chin before letting go, and then turning toward the steering wheel. He started the engine and headed out of the parking lot.

Alabama couldn't believe Christopher had just kissed her. It *did* count as a kiss right? It was short and sweet, but it was awesome. Much better than the sloppy French kisses she'd received in the past. She could still feel the touch of Christopher's fingers against her jaw. Alabama leaned back into the seat, trusting Christopher to get them wherever they were going safely. She looked down at the phone in her lap. He made her feel safe. She'd never felt that way before.

★   ★   ★

THE DAY HAD been awesome. Alabama didn't think she'd ever smiled so much in her entire life. Christopher had first driven them to the beach. Riverton was a suburb of San Diego and Alabama hadn't had a lot of time to spend at the beach. Alabama loved the water, but this was the first time she'd experienced a picnic in the sand. The beach wasn't one of the touristy ones. In fact she'd only seen a handful of people the entire time they'd been there.

Christopher had brought a light blanket and a thermos of coffee and some fruit. They'd sat on the beach and watched the water. They'd talked a bit, but mostly they'd just enjoyed the morning air and being in each other's company.

Next they'd gone to the San Diego zoo. Alabama generally didn't like zoos. She'd always felt sorry for the animals. She didn't think they were being abused in any way, but she just thought it was sad to see the majestic animals cooped up behind the bars of their cages. But Alabama wasn't thinking too much about that while visiting with Christopher.

He'd taken hold of her hand as they walked around and hadn't let go. When the crowds got bigger Christopher brought her to his side and protected her from being jostled by the other people rushing here and there. A man accidentally dropped his drink and it splashed onto her jeans and shoes. Alabama thought Christopher was going to lose it. When he looked like he was going to go after the man and beat the crap out of him, all Alabama had to do was put her hand on Christopher's arm and he'd stopped. She watched as he visibly controlled himself. It was fascinating.

Christopher kissed her hand and tucked her deeper into his side. He'd glared at the man as they walked by, but otherwise let it drop.

After spending most of the day at the zoo, and eating way too much junk food, he'd driven them to the end of an air strip near his base. Of course Christopher was able to get onto the base with his credentials. He'd parked the car and helped Alabama get out. Christopher spread the blanket they'd used on the beach on the trunk of his car, and they'd settled on it. They leaned back against the back window and watched the planes take off and land.

Abe interlaced their fingers together on one hand and brought them to rest against his belly. They'd talked softly about nothing in particular.

When it began to get dark, Christopher helped her off the car and back into the passenger seat. They'd picked up Chinese food to go and gone back to her apartment.

After eating dinner, they'd settled on the couch and Alabama put in *The Princess Bride* for background noise. She'd seen it so many times she'd memorized all the lines.

They'd been watching for about twenty minutes before Christopher broke the silence. "Tell me more about you, Alabama. Tell me about why you look around before you talk to me when we're in public, but at night, when you're here, in your own space, you become much more talkative. Is it only because no one is here to overhear you and judge you? Or is there more?"

Alabama tried to pull her hand away from his instinctively. Abe wouldn't let go, and instead pulled her toward him and into his side. He tucked her head into his chest and murmured "Shhhh sweet. You're safe here. Talk to me. Let me in."

It was crazy. She was seriously considering it. No one else had ever cared enough to notice or ask. Was she just feeling this way toward Christopher because she hadn't ever felt this way before? Or was it real? Alabama had no idea, but she wanted to try. She *wanted* to trust him.

"I..." she paused. Jesus. She couldn't do this.

Christopher didn't say anything, just continued to rub her arm up and down and rub his thumb over the back of her hand as it rested against him.

His silent support, along with the fact she didn't have to look at him while she told him her pathetic story, gave her the courage to continue.

"You're right. While it's true I'm not comfortable with others overhearing my thoughts when I talk to people...that's not the only reason. My mama wasn't...nice. She...she didn't want me, but for some reason didn't give me up for adoption. I wish she had."

"Jesus," Abe murmured. "Come here, sweet."

He shifted on the small couch until he was prone and Alabama was lying against him. The back of the couch was behind her and Christopher was half under her and half beside her. One arm was around her waist holding her close. The other arm was wrapped around her shoulders and tangled into her hair. He pressed her head to his chest. "Close your eyes, feel me here with you. You're safe. Tell me."

He was demanding, but Alabama didn't feel threatened. She'd never been held like this. She'd spent the night with a guy before, but as soon as he'd had sex with her, he'd rolled over and she waited a miserable six hours for the sun to rise so she could get out of his apartment.

Christopher was warm and smelled so good. She wasn't sure what he smelled like, just that it was comforting. She closed her eyes as he'd demanded and burrowed closer to him.

"Mama named me Alabama Ford Smith. Alabama because that's the state she got fucked in...her words, not mine...and Ford because that's *where* she got fucked. Her last name wasn't even Smith. She didn't want me to have her last name." Alabama gripped the sleeve of Christopher's shirt with her left hand without even realizing it and continued.

"My earliest memory is being locked in a closet and having Mama yell at me to shut up. I don't know why I was crying, but she couldn't stand it. Anytime I'd speak to her, she'd lock me in the closet. I learned not to talk to her if I wanted to eat or even sleep in my bed. But sometimes I'd forget. Or I'd talk not knowing she was around to hear me. I still hear her yelling at me to shut up over and over again."

Abe wanted to tell Alabama to stop, that he couldn't bear it, but he knew she had to get it out. He couldn't believe she was as sweet as she was. Other people who'd gone through what she had wouldn't have turned out half as adjusted as Alabama was, and he knew she was probably downplaying it anyway. Even knowing her for the short time he had, he knew she wouldn't tell him everything.

"When I was eleven, she hit me with a skillet because I'd asked her something. A teacher noticed and I trusted a police officer when he said he'd help me. He didn't, and they sent me back to her. When I was twelve, she beat me with that same skillet and broke my jaw, along with most of my face. She swore, as she was hitting me, that she'd teach me not to talk."

Alabama stopped and cleared her throat. She'd never talked so much at one time in all her life. But it felt good to get it out. To tell someone. To tell Christopher. She finally noticed Christopher's hand clenched in a fist at her side. He'd bunched up her shirt and was holding it tight. She lifted her head and brought her hand up to his face.

"Are you all right?"

Abe snorted. Of course she'd try to comfort *him*. *He* should be comforting *her*. He tried to relax; unclenching his fist and soothing it over her side. "I'm okay, sweet. I'm just pissed as hell at your mother and trying to understand how you turned out to be the sweetest woman I've ever met with your upbringing."

Alabama just shook her head and put her head back on his chest.

Abe didn't make her look up at him, but told her quietly, "Seriously, sweet. You don't have to say a word and your goodness comes through loud and clear. I could sense it standing at that damn table at the party." When she didn't say anything else Abe decided not to push. "What then? Where did you go after she beat you?"

"Into foster care."

"Was it…okay?"

"I guess. Mama had told me to shut up so many times in my life I'd finally taken her words to heart. Everyone thought I was weird and I didn't talk to many people. Even today when I hear the words 'shut up,' I cringe. It brings me back to sitting in that damn closet and listening to my mama screaming at me to 'shut up, shut up, shut up.' You said something to me once and I think you were right."

"What's that?"

"You said I had Posttraumatic Stress Disorder. I hadn't thought of it that way, but you're probably right. I think I need to talk to someone about it. I mean…other than you."

"I'll help you with whatever you need. If you want me to help you find someone, let me know. There are lots of counselors on base that have experience with PTSD. If you'd prefer to talk to someone who specifically deals with child abuse, I can help with that too. But sweet, you'll never know how much it means to me that you trusted me with your story. I know we're still getting to know each other, but you mean something to me. I won't let you down. I won't tell you to 'shut up' now that I know it's a trigger for you. I've told you this before, and I'll keep saying it, you're safe with me. I promise.

"Also, your mother might have tried to give you a name that didn't mean anything, but you should own it. You *are* Alabama Ford Smith. You've survived. You've persevered. Don't let her own petty actions stain you. Those are *her* issues, not yours. You're unique and amazing and you have a unique and amazing name. Besides, I *like* your name. I like you."

Alabama turned her face into Christopher's shirt and inhaled deeply. God, he was awesome. She tried not to cry, but it was no use.

The tears came out of her eyes and leaked down onto his chest when she turned her head back to the side so she could breathe.

"Let it out sweet. Let it out. I'm here. I'm not going anywhere."

Alabama cried for her lousy childhood. She cried because her mama had never loved her. She cried for her loss of trust in people in general. Finally when she was all cried out, she sniffed once and settled on Christopher's chest. She relaxed into him, thinking how comfortable she was and she never wanted to move.

Abe was furious. He tried to stay relaxed under Alabama, but he didn't know how successful he was at it. He decided to share some of his life with Alabama, so she didn't feel awkward about sharing something so intimate about herself with him.

"I didn't really know my dad growing up." Abe felt Alabama's head lift as she looked at him, but he kept talking. "He would come around every now and then, but just as we were used to him being around, he'd leave again. My mom would cry every time he left. She never knew I knew about it, but I'd sit outside her bedroom and listen to her bawl her eyes out. I swore I'd take care of her. I did what I could. I did my chores without being asked, I helped my sisters with their homework, and I gave my mom every cent I earned from mowing lawns and other small jobs I did for the neighbors."

Abe stroked Alabama's hair, not sure if he was comforting her or himself. "We didn't have a lot of money, because my dad certainly didn't contribute, but we did okay. I'd do anything for my sisters and mother, and it hurts me that you didn't have that in your life. I wish I'd known you when you were growing up, Alabama."

Alabama didn't say a word, but lay in Christopher's arms, loving the feel of his arms around her. She thought about what he'd just told her about his family. Alabama understood more about what made him how he was today. "You need to take care of people," she told him drowsily.

"I take care of those that mean something to me."

Alabama didn't say anything else, but his words settled into her soul and she could almost feel the crack in her heart healing.

Abe continued to run his hand over Alabama's hair until she finally fell asleep on his chest.

He'd never wanted to hurt a woman before, but Abe wanted to hurt Alabama's mother more than he'd ever wanted anything before in his life. How could she do that to her own child? How could she take someone as sweet as Alabama and abuse her that way? He was amazed she'd turned out as well as she had. It said a lot about Alabama's inner strength.

Abe lay under Alabama enjoying her softness, enjoying her trust in him. He'd never forget this moment. It was the moment he knew he could easily fall head over heels in love with a woman for the first time in his life.

Chapter Nine

A LABAMA OPENED THE door to the temporary offices of Wolfe Realty. The building was much like the old one. The offices were all on one floor, but this time the realtors had to share offices until the new building was constructed.

It was actually easier to clean this building than the old one because everything had been destroyed in the fire and there wasn't as much clutter around.

Alabama pushed her new cleaning cart as she moved through the building. She'd always loved the quiet of the evening when she'd worked. Some people didn't like empty buildings and thought they were creepy, not Alabama. She loved the solitude.

She thought back over the last week. She and Christopher had spent every evening together. He had to work during the days, but had come over each night for dinner before she headed to work and to spend time with her.

One evening when she'd had the night off, they'd gone to his quarters on the base. They weren't anything special, but to Alabama it was a whole new world. She didn't know anything about the military, and in fact being on the base itself made her nervous. There were unwritten rules she had no idea about. In order to get inside the grocery store you had to prove you were affiliated with the military and you had to show your identification. The same was true of a lot of the services on the base. It wasn't that anyone was unfriendly, it was just overwhelming.

Christopher sensed her unease and hadn't asked if she wanted to come to his place on base after the first time they'd been there, telling her since she was more comfortable at her apartment, he'd come to her. He hadn't seemed unhappy about it, simply telling her it wasn't a big deal.

Alabama loved hanging out with him. It was easy. It wasn't until the third evening they'd spent some time together that Christopher had asked if he could kiss her.

Alabama stood in the hallway of the building she was cleaning and closed her eyes recalling how perfect that first kiss was. They'd been sitting on her small couch watching some movie when she'd felt him looking at her. She turned to him and the look on his face was intense. When their eyes met his hand came up and cupped her cheek. She tilted her head and rested her cheek into his hand.

"I want to kiss you, sweet. Will you let me?"

Alabama simply nodded.

The hand at her cheek shifted to the back of her neck. Christopher cupped her in a firm, but strangely gentle grip, and shifted closer to her. He'd rested his forehead against hers and just held her there for a moment.

"I've been wanting to do this since you opened your door to me last week. You have no idea…"

Then he brought his other hand up to her face and cupped it. Alabama was sandwiched between the hand at the back of her neck and the one on her face. She didn't feel trapped, she felt protected. Christopher tilted her head just so and swooped in for his kiss. For some reason, Alabama had thought he'd take it slow. Everything he'd done so far had been easy and gentle, but this kiss wasn't either of those.

It was a confident kiss, a kiss that demanded she open and let him in. And she did. Alabama didn't hold back. Their lips met and immediately parted. She felt his tongue do an initial sweep of her mouth, then retreat to tease and caress her lips before plunging back in. Alabama tried to keep up, swirling her tongue around his, and at one point taking his tongue and sucking on it. She thought she'd feel awkward and uneasy, but she'd been so aroused, she didn't have time to be embarrassed.

At that point, Christopher took the hand that had been on her cheek and put it on her back and laid her down against the cushions of the couch. He kept his hand at her neck supporting her head as he eased her down. Alabama didn't even notice...until she felt his hardness against her. Christopher never stopped his sensual exploration of her mouth, but she could feel his strength over her. He wasn't crushing her, in fact, his body felt good pressing against hers. She could feel his length against her leg—he was hard, all over.

Alabama breathed in through her nose and pressed her head back, breaking contact with his lips. Without missing a beat, Christopher leaned down and put his mouth against her neck, nipping and sucking lightly. Her breath came out in pants and she tried to get her brain to start working again.

"Now *that* was a kiss," she'd said breathlessly. She heard him chuckle against her throat before he moved up and nipped her earlobe.

"You make me lose my mind, sweet."

One part of Alabama wanted to do nothing more than stand up and lead him to her small bed in the corner, but the other part of her was terrified. She'd trusted before and been let down. She didn't think Christopher would break her trust, but she wasn't certain yet.

Alabama brought her hands down from his back where she'd been clutching at him and put them on his chest. He'd immediately reared up so he could see her face. Of course that pushed his erection harder into her thigh, making her blush. Christopher laughed and kissed her lightly on the nose. He sat them both up and brought her into his side.

"Thank you, Alabama. That was the best kiss I've ever had."

They hadn't said much more that night, they'd simply finished the movie. When it was over and time for Christopher to leave, she'd walked him to her door and he'd taken both of her hands in his and held them loosely in between them. Christopher leaned forward and touched his lips to hers. What started out as a short, sweet goodnight kiss turned into something hotter and longer.

He hadn't let go of her hands while they were kissing and it was interesting to be touching him with nothing more than her lips and tongue. Just that contact made her squirm. She'd never felt anything like she did when she was with him...kissing him.

"Good night, sweet. Lock the door behind me," was all he'd said. Then he'd kissed her once more on the tip of her nose, squeezed her hands, and walked out.

Alabama took a deep breath and opened her eyes. She'd zoned out in the middle of the hallway of the realty office. She'd been clenching the handles of the cleaning cart so hard, her fingernails had bit into her palms. She had it bad.

She laughed at herself and continued down the hall. Alabama had just entered one of the agent's offices when she heard the front door open. It wasn't too late, but late enough that there really shouldn't be anyone working. Feeling her heart jump with fear, Alabama stood stock still, not knowing what she should do. She reached in her pocket for the phone Christopher had given her, feeling better knowing she had some sort of way to call for help. She pulled it out and flipped it open. She pushed a nine and a one and her thumb hovered over the last one. She'd wait to see what was going on before she actually dialed for emergency help.

She watched down the hall and soon she saw someone walking toward her. It was Adelaide. Alabama let out a breath of relief. She didn't want to see the woman, but at least it wasn't a crazed killer. She shut the phone and slipped it back into her pocket.

Adelaide looked up when she was a few doors down from Alabama and finally noticed her.

"What are you doing here?" She asked nastily.

Alabama thought it was a pretty dumb question considering she was the janitor and was standing in front of a cleaning cart. She gestured toward the cart and didn't answer verbally.

"Yeah, I forgot you don't talk much do you?" Adelaide sneered. "I came in to get some papers for a client that I left here by accident. Get out of my way."

Alabama moved to the side and watched as Adelaide brushed past her into the office she'd been about to clean.

"By the way, I know all about you and Abe, bitch. He was mine and you stole him. But don't worry; he'll come back to me. After all, look at *you*, then look at *me*. There's no way he's serious about you. You're short and plain. You can't hold his attention for a millisecond."

Alabama had enough. At no time had Christopher made her feel as if he was playing with her or just clocking time. He'd mentioned to her several times that he hadn't been serious with Adelaide. She was just being mean and jealous and taking it out on her.

Alabama looked around, still not being able to break the habit, and responded quietly and firmly, "I didn't steal anything. *He* came to *me*. I might not be as pretty as you, but it doesn't seem to matter to him. He likes me, and I like him. So back off and leave us alone."

As far as comebacks go, it was pretty lame, but Adelaide actually took a step back in surprise. She hadn't expected the meek little janitor to fight back. Maybe no one had ever talked back to her, although that was unlikely. It seemed Adelaide was the kind of woman who'd make enemies, and surely someone had protested being talked down to.

Adelaide narrowed her eyes and glared at Alabama. Alabama glared right back.

"You'll regret this, bitch," Adelaide finally hissed. She turned toward the desk and grabbed a folder that was sitting on it. "And get out of my office. I don't trust you to keep your hands off my stuff."

That hurt Alabama more than Adelaide's previous words had. She might not be the prettiest person in the world, but she wasn't a thief. Even at her lowest, when she'd turned eighteen and had gotten free of the foster care system, she hadn't resorted to shoplifting. There were times she would've killed to have something to eat other than cheap noodles, but she'd never taken something that wasn't hers.

Without looking behind her, Alabama pushed her cart down the hall. Fine, if Adelaide didn't want her office cleaned, she wouldn't bother. Hopefully the spiders and dust took over the space and made Adelaide miserable.

Alabama entered the office next to Adelaide's and heard the bitch stomp down the hall and exit the building. Once Adelaide left, Alabama sat down wearily on the chair next to the desk. Damn. She didn't like confrontations, but she felt good for finally sticking up for herself for once. Adelaide was a bitch, but luckily she didn't have to work with her. Hopefully she'd remember her papers from here on out and Alabama could avoid another nasty encounter with her.

Chapter Ten

THE NEXT COUPLE of weeks were some of the best in Alabama's life. She'd been spending a lot of time with Christopher and tonight they were going to go out with his SEAL teammates and their girlfriends.

Alabama was beyond nervous. She wasn't good in crowds, especially out in public, but she wanted to do this for Christopher. He'd been so good to her. He hadn't pushed her to have sex, even though it was obvious he was ready. They'd had a few serious make out sessions on her couch and she knew it'd been hard for him to stop. Hell, it'd been hard for *her* to stop.

The last one ended with both of them with their shirts off and he'd actually made her explode with just his lips on her breasts. She'd never experienced that kind of passion before and it had freaked her out. Christopher had immediately noticed, and instead of pressuring her to continue, he soothed her. He pulled her into his chest and just held her. He'd been so good to her. She knew she was in way over her head with him. Alabama was pretty sure she loved Christopher. She wasn't sure she really knew what love was, but not a minute went by during the day that she didn't want to talk to him, to see him, to spend time with him.

The first time she'd called him on her new mobile phone, Christopher had been so happy. He didn't try to hide his excitement and joy that she'd actually called him. When he'd calmed down to find out what she needed, he was speechless for a moment when she'd told him she'd just wanted to say hi.

So tonight they were going to a local bar, called *Aces Bar and Grill*, that apparently catered to military members, especially SEALs. Alabama had heard a lot about Matthew, also known as Wolf, and his girlfriend, Caroline. But apparently there were four others on the team that were like brothers to Christopher. There was Sam, whose nickname was Mozart, Hunter, whose nickname was Cookie, Kason went by Benny, and finally Faulkner who they called Dude.

There was no way she'd remember everyone's name, but she'd try to go with the flow. Christopher had promised to help her. When Alabama asked about the team's nicknames and their history, he'd only chuckled and told her that it was up to each man to explain it, if they so choose.

She shrugged. That was the least of her worries.

Alabama clutched Christopher's hand, desperately, as they headed toward the entrance of *Aces*. Before they went inside, Christopher stopped and pulled her to the side of the door and backed her against the wall.

Christopher bought his hand up to her face and cupped her cheek. He did that a lot when he wanted her to look into his eyes while he spoke to her. It should irritate Alabama, but it didn't. It made her feel warm inside. She loved his hands on her.

"It's going to be fine, sweet. I'll be right there with you. You'll be safe. They'll like you, I promise."

At her nod, he held her eyes for a moment then leaned forward and brushed his lips over her eyebrows, then her nose, then finally her lips. He didn't linger, but nipped her bottom lip gently once, and drew back. "You're the bravest person I've ever met. Come on; let's go in before you have a heart attack."

Alabama could feel her heart beating double time in her chest. She was nervous, but having Christopher there helped. She wanted his friends to like her, but she didn't really know how to make friends. She wasn't good at it.

They walked toward a large table in the back of the room. There were a group of people already seated and laughing together.

There was a pretty waitress standing at the table taking drink orders. She was about normal height and was wearing a pair of sneakers, unlike the other waitresses who were all wearing high heels. She also stood out from the other servers in the bar because she was wearing a modest tank top and a pair of jeans, instead of a skimpy shirt and a mini-skirt. Her attire did nothing to distract from how pretty she was.

She had long black hair which was pulled back into a braid that ended midway down her back. She finished up taking everyone's drink order as they arrived at the table.

"Hey! You got here just in time, what can I get you from the bar?"

The nametag on the waitress' tag read, 'Jess.'

Abe turned to Alabama and gestured for her to order.

"Coke please," Alabama said softly.

Christopher squeezed her hand to reassure her and Alabama tried to relax. "Hey, Jess. I'll take whatever you have on tap tonight." It was obvious Christopher knew the waitress, probably because the group of friends came to the bar frequently.

"No problem. I'll be back soon," Jess said in a confident voice.

Alabama watched as the waitress limped away from the table. She had just a second to wonder what was wrong with the pretty waitress before Christopher put his hand on the small of her back and turned her to the table.

Alabama looked up to see that everyone was looking at them. She gripped Christopher's hand as if it was the only thing keeping her above water.

"Hey guys," Abe said easily. "This is Alabama. She's nervous to meet all of you, so go easy all right?" He said it lightly, but there was steel running through his words.

He'd had a talk with his team that day and they all knew how shy Alabama was, just as they knew how important she was to Abe. Abe had also told them a little of her childhood and they'd all been taken aback. They all knew such abuses happened all the time, but they hated it'd happened to someone who was so obviously important to their teammate.

Finding a good woman was new to the team. They'd all been there when Caroline had almost died at the hands of terrorists and had seen how hard Wolf had struggled to finally get the nerve to claim her.

None of them would admit it, but they were all a bit jealous. Seeing the close relationship they shared had finally brought home to them all how meaningless their one night stands were. They were all itching to find someone for their own, and it looked like Abe just might be the next in line to find a woman for himself.

Tamping down the impulse to look around the room, Alabama gripped Christopher's hand so hard she knew he'd have indentations from her fingernails, and simply said, "Hi."

"Hey, Alabama, glad you could make it," said a gorgeous man who'd stood as they'd arrived. The other men also added their greetings and Christopher led her to a seat at the end of the table against the wall. He waited until she was seated and then settled next to her. He put his arm on the back of her chair and leaned in.

"Okay, sweet?"

Alabama looked at Christopher and nodded. He really was a good guy. She vaguely noticed how all the men were seated in such a way that they could see the rest of the room. Obviously they all felt the same way Christopher did about putting their back to a room.

"I guess we should all introduce ourselves," a beautiful woman sitting in the middle of the table said in Alabama's direction. "Don't worry, if you don't remember everyone's names. It took me forever to remember them myself!"

Everyone around the table laughed.

"And I'll do it, 'cos if the guys do it you'll only hear their nick-names and you'll never learn their real names. I'm trying to get them to use their given names, but they're hopeless! I'm Caroline and I'm with this big lug, Matthew. Sitting at the end is Sam and his girl-friend Molly. Next to them is Faulkner and Brittany. Then there's Kason and Emily, and finally, across from you, is Hunter and Michele."

When she'd introduced them, everyone said hello at once and then started talking again. Alabama breathed a sigh of relief that no one seemed to want to draw her into conversation yet.

Alabama listened as the men joked with one another. It was tough to keep everyone straight, especially when the men called each other by their nicknames and the women used their real names. It was if there were double the number of people sitting at the table.

"Hey, Christopher, how did you guys meet?" Alabama thought it was Kason's girlfriend that had asked, but she couldn't remember her name.

"Remember that fire a month or so ago?" Christopher asked. When the women all nodded he continued. "Alabama saved my life. She was there and helped get me and a bunch of other people out of the building."

"Whoa, that's intense," Michele said. "Didn't you go to that par-ty with Adelaide?"

Abe's eyes squinted like they did when he was pissed. Alabama didn't know what was up with Michele and her attitude, but it obviously pissed Christopher off.

"Yeah, I did, but it didn't work out. I met Alabama that night and things went from there."

Michele obviously didn't know when to stop, because she contin-ued, "What did Adelaide have to say about that?"

Cookie didn't give Christopher time to respond because he jumped in. "What the hell Michele? Abe's with Alabama now, give it a rest."

Alabama was confused and freaked out. She'd never met Michele, but it seemed as if she didn't like her...at all.

"We all know you and Adelaide are tight, but Jesus, woman, Abe dumped her because she was acting crazy. I told you to let it drop and here you are bringing it up in front of his new woman." Cookie was obviously pissed. Strangely enough him being pissed seemed to calm Abe down.

"Let's go," Cookie told the woman at his side. "We're done. Abe man, sorry. Alabama, it was nice meeting you. You're way too good for an asshole like Abe here, but damn glad you're overlooking that. Hope to see you again soon." With that, Cookie forced Michele up with a hand on her elbow and without giving her a chance to say anything, led her away from the group.

Alabama didn't know what to say, so she just sat there embarrassed.

"Jesus, sorry about that Abe, Alabama," Benny said softly, leaning across the table toward his teammate and his date. "Alabama, he's been seeing Michele for a while. She and Adelaide are friends. Obviously it was a mistake to bring her tonight."

Abe nodded stiffly. Jesus, he'd wanted to make sure Alabama would meet his friends in as stress-free of an environment as possible, and Cookie's girl-of-the-month had to go and ruin it. He looked down at Alabama.

Feeling Christopher's eyes on her, Alabama looked up. He looked tense and pissed on her behalf. She giggled a small quiet giggle and watched as his eyebrows rose questionably.

Alabama knew she had to grow a backbone. The whole thing was pretty funny if she thought about it. She wanted to reassure Christopher that she was all right. She didn't want him to think she'd cry every time some woman brought her claws out. Hell, with the way he looked, she'd be crying all the time. She knew every woman in the place was jealous as hell of her, and it strangely cheered her up.

Not being able to stop her eyes from scanning the interior of the bar before reassuring Christopher she paused, then leaned up toward him and whispered in his ear teasingly, "Any other friends of your ex-girlfriend I have to worry about tonight?"

She pulled back and smiled at him, making sure he knew she was teasing him. She watched as his eyelids fell and his pupils dilated. "Shit, Alabama, I was worried you'd be freaked."

Not breaking eye contact she told him quietly, "I *am* a little freaked, but you're here with *me*, not her. Hunter didn't let her stay, and I like your friends. I'm determined not to let it bother me."

Abe let out the breath he'd been holding. He'd been ready to escort Michele out himself. Damn her. She'd brought up Adelaide purposely, just to be catty. He hoped Cookie wouldn't be seeing her anymore. Anyone that deliberately set out to hurt someone else wasn't someone anyone on the team wanted to be around.

Before Abe could pull Alabama into his arms and kiss the hell out of her, Emily piped up, "So, Abe huh? I've heard the stories about the others, but what's the story of your nickname?"

Normally the guys would leave it up to their friends to explain their own names, but Dude jumped in before Abe could say anything.

"Abe, like Honest Abe," he explained. "There was this one time in BUD/S when this one loser decided he was too tired to clean his own shit, and in the middle of the night swapped it with Abe's gear. Dumbass didn't realize the gear had serial numbers on it. So in the morning when inspection was going on and Abe saw his gear wasn't his own, he went on a mission to find out who'd swapped it. Didn't take long. Abe made sure to teach him a lesson he wouldn't forget. Asshole rang out that morning."

There was a lot about the story Alabama didn't really understand, but she nodded as if she did.

Dude continued the explanation. "Ever since then anytime anyone stepped out of line and tried to get out of something by lying or stealing, Abe called 'em on it. The name stuck."

Abe revealed more when he continued. "I can't stand it when people lie or steal. There's just no need for it. We've seen some crazy shit on missions. People in poor countries stealing food from women and kids. People lying their asses off just to get an extra cup of water or bread. On one hand, I know desperation makes people do things they might not otherwise do, but it sticks in my craw every time. I hate it. I'd rather people be honest and upfront about what they need or want them to lie about it."

Benny jumped into the conversation agreeing. "Yeah, remember that one chick you...er...dated that was wearing that smokin' hot dress, but when you got her home you found she still had the tag on it? She was gonna bring it back to the store and get her money back after wearing it..."

He stopped because Caroline had smacked his arm, hard. "Jeez, Kason, have some class. You can't talk about previous uh...girlfriends when his current girlfriend is sitting right next to him!"

Looking confused, Benny sputtered, "What?"

Alabama giggled again and looked at Christopher. He just shook his head and murmured, "Jesus, this was a bad idea." Alabama laughed at him again and put her hand on his thigh.

Loving the feel of Alabama's hand on his leg, Abe put his hand over hers and intertwined their fingers. He then tried to clarify what his friends were bungling so badly. "What my so-called 'friends' here are trying to say is, that I don't like liars, and I don't like people who steal. Even buying a dress with the intention of wearing it and then returning it is a type of stealing. It's not right and it's not cool."

Alabama got what he was saying and gripped his thigh harder, making him look down at her. "I don't lie or steal."

Abe smiled. "I know, sweet. You're too nice to do either."

The night continued and Alabama relaxed. She was actually having a good time and no one seemed concerned she wasn't talking much. At one point, when she'd stood up to go to the restroom, Caroline joined her. "You know us women can't go by ourselves. We'll be back," she'd exclaimed to the group at large.

Then she'd taken Alabama's hand and they'd walked toward the restroom. Upon arriving they'd done their business and when they were washing their hands, Caroline said what she'd obviously been wanting to say all night.

"Christopher's a good man. He was on the plane with me, Matthew, and Sam when the terrorists tried to take it down. He was the one who gave me my nickname. He was the one who convinced Matthew to fight for me. I'd do anything for him. *Anything*."

Alabama flinched. Here it came. Caroline obviously didn't think she was good enough for Christopher.

"That being said, I like you. You're just what he needs. I've never seen Christopher so relaxed. The way he looks at you is how Matthew looks at me. If you're just using him for whatever reason, please let him go now. But if you really like him, and I think you do, please protect his heart. These guys are tough. They're strong and macho, but they're marshmallows inside. You can hurt him. I'm just asking you not to."

Taking a quick glance around the empty bathroom, Alabama forced herself to answer and to try to reassure the other woman. "I'm not going to hurt Christopher. I like him. I know I'm not good enough for him, but until he figures that out, I'm staying."

The smile that came across Caroline's face was blinding. She reached out and pulled Alabama into a hug. Alabama was too surprised to do anything other than awkwardly put her arms around the other woman.

"Welcome to the family, Alabama," Caroline gushed. "I'm so glad Christopher has found someone who's worthy of him. Not some skank who just wants in his pants."

Alabama did something she'd never done in her life before, she blurted out, without thinking, without looking around to make sure Mama wasn't lingering nearby, "Oh, I want in his pants all right."

Caroline pulled back in surprise, then leaned back and laughed as if Alabama had just said the funniest thing she'd ever heard. "Oh man, you guys haven't done it yet?"

Embarrassed now, Alabama could only shake her head.

"Now I know he *really* likes you. Hang on tight, girlfriend. Hang on for the ride of your life. If you ever need me, don't hesitate to contact me. Us old ladies have to stick together."

Alabama could only nod as Caroline grabbed her hand again and they walked back toward the table.

When they arrived, Caroline gave her another secret smile and sat down next to her man. Alabama watched as Matthew leaned toward Caroline and kissed her. It wasn't a polite "I'm-in-front-of-company" kiss either. It was passionate, and it lingered. Alabama was almost embarrassed to be a witness to it. But on the other hand it was amazing. It was the kiss a man gave to his woman. A kiss that showed her how much he loved her, how much he couldn't wait to get her alone. It was beautiful.

Looking away, Alabama caught Christopher's eye. Whoa. His eyes bored into hers. "Everything go okay in the restroom? She didn't scare you away?"

Alabama shook her head. "No, she was great actually. You have amazing friends."

"I do, don't I?" He paused. "You ready to go?"

"Go? But it's still early…"

"I want to be alone with you. I want you, Alabama."

Alabama's stomach did flip flops. Did she want this? If they left now, she knew they'd end up in bed together. She didn't want to overanalyze it. "I want you too."

At her words Abe's breathing sped up. He put his hand on her elbow and immediately stood up. "It's been real guys, we're headed out. See ya later."

Without giving her a chance to say much more, he threw some bills on the table to cover their drinks and headed for the door.

Alabama looked back at the table to see Caroline wink at her. She smiled back.

THE RIDE BACK to Alabama's apartment was done mostly in silence. Alabama had told Christopher she'd been glad to meet his friends and he'd only grunted in response. Alabama almost laughed. It seemed as if their roles were reversed—he was the one without the verbal ability at the moment.

He drove quickly, but safely, through the streets back to her little apartment. Alabama knew what was coming and was nervous, but excited. It was time. She was ready to make love to Christopher.

Christopher parked his car and silently got out and met her at the front of the car. Alabama was too impatient to wait for him to come and get her out of the car. They walked hand in hand up the stairs to her apartment. Alabama handed over her keys when they reached her door and he unlocked it for them. Christopher placed the keys in a basket by the door and slipped her purse off her shoulder. He took her face into his hands and leaned down to kiss her.

Abe was holding on by a slender thread. Alabama was sexy as hell and he couldn't wait to get inside her. She was everything he'd ever wanted in a woman. She was sweet and kind and beautiful. He kissed Alabama deeply while walking her backwards into the room. He hadn't dared pay any attention to her small bed in the corner before. He knew he wanted her there, but he'd been taking things slow. They were finally ready.

He backed her toward the bed until her knees touched the mattress. Abe wanted nothing more than to push her back on the bed and strip her naked, but he had to make sure she was on the same page as he was. "You want this right, sweet? It's not just me?"

"Make love to me, Christopher. I'm yours."

Abe didn't hesitate. Alabama's words were all the permission he hadn't known he'd been waiting for. He grasped her shirt at the hem and drew it upward, not breaking eye contact. He wanted Alabama to know he saw *her*. That he wasn't stripping just another woman's body, but he was stripping *his* woman's body.

Alabama's heart skipped a beat as she watched Christopher's eyes as he drew her shirt up and off. It wasn't until he threw it behind him on the floor that he took his eyes from her face and ran them down her body. Of course, he'd seen her before in their make out sessions, but this was different. This was more intimate, more personal. More everything.

"God, sweet. You. Are. Beautiful."

Abe took Alabama's hands in his and held them out away from her body. She *was* beautiful. Her bra was a basic black cotton piece, but it fit her personality. The dark fabric against her light skin made for a wonderful contrast. "Take if off for me," he murmured letting go of her hands so she could obey him.

Alabama blushed, but did as he asked without question. Whatever he wanted, she'd do. She reached behind her and unclasped the hooks of her bra. She dropped her arms and the straps fell down her shoulders and then down and off her arms. She caught the garment with her hand and let it drop to the floor.

Abe inhaled. He wasn't going to last long. She was perfect. He watched as her nipples beaded as he took her in. She was breathing hard, but he could tell it wasn't in fear. Alabama wanted him as much as he wanted her.

He took her hands in his again and once again held them out to her sides. "Beautiful," he murmured as he leaned forward and took one of her pouty nipples into his mouth.

Alabama groaned. Abe knew how sensitive her breasts were from their earlier sessions on the couch. She tugged at her hands, wanting to touch him. Wanting to make him feel as good as he was making her feel. Abe didn't let go, and instead tightened his hold on her. She'd do as Abe wanted, if he let her do what *she* wanted, he'd never last.

Abe knew he was on the edge. He couldn't wait anymore. This first time was going to be quick, but he consoled himself with the thought that they had all night.

He finally dropped her hands and reached for his own shirt. "Get undressed and get on the bed. I can't wait." His voice was low and hard, and sexy as hell.

Alabama watched as Christopher tore off his own shirt and bent down to undo his boots. She quickly unbuttoned her own jeans and shimmied out of them. She peeled her undies off and dove under the covers.

She watched as Christopher stood up and toed off his boots. He undid the buttons on his cargo pants and quickly shed them. Looking her in the eyes for the first time since they'd started undressing, he asked, "You ready for me?"

God yes, she'd been ready for him for a while now. "Yes, I want to see you. Please."

Alabama inhaled as Christopher took off his boxer briefs. He was beautiful. He was larger than the only other man she'd slept with. She knew she didn't have a lot to compare him to, but he was long and obviously hard…for her. It was difficult for her to wrap her mind around everything that was finally happening between the two of them.

Before she'd gotten her fill of looking at him, Christopher threw back the covers and joined her.

"Don't hide from me. I want to see every inch of your delicious body."

He crushed her to him and growled into her mouth. He wanted to take his time and learn Alabama's body, but he couldn't, not this first time.

While kissing her, Abe brushed his hand down her body. Alabama moaned under him and opened her legs to him. Feeling she was just as excited as he was, Abe separated their lips by a scant inch and murmured, "You're so ready for me. I love feeling how wet you are, and it's all for me, isn't it?"

Alabama nodded and thrust her hips up into his hand as he caressed her deeper. "I'm ready. Please, Christopher."

Possessiveness shot through him unexpectedly. He never felt possessive toward any of the women he'd been with in the past. He guessed he'd been using them to get off just as they'd used him for the same. But with Alabama, it was different. She was his.

"This is gonna be quick. I had plans to take this slow. To make sure I memorized every inch of your body before making love to you, but I'm not gonna last. I'll make it up to you later. I can't wait. You're mine."

Alabama just nodded and gripped his biceps harder.

"Say it, Alabama. Mine."

Alabama gasped. "Yours, Christopher. Please."

"Are you protected sweet? I'm clean. I have to get tested by the Navy regularly."

Alabama tried to get her thoughts together. They should've had this talk already, but neither of them had been able to wait and she'd been too embarrassed to bring it up before.

"I'm on the pill. I needed to regulate my...er...you know."

Abe thought she was cute. She was embarrassed to talk about her period, but they were in bed about to do the most intimate thing two people could do with each other. Adorable.

Alabama continued, embarrassed. "And…uh…I'm clean too…I've only been with one other guy and it was a while ago…so…uh…"

"Shhhh, I know you are. I never thought differently. I want to come in you bare. But it's your choice. Whatever you want, it's up to you."

"You, I want *you*, Christopher, please," Alabama begged. She'd never felt this way before. The last time she'd slept with a guy, he'd barely gotten her wet and then shoved himself in. It had hurt, and he didn't seem to care. He just grunted and pumped in and out of her until he'd gotten off. Then he'd had the nerve to ask if it'd been as good for her as it had been for him. Thank God, she'd made him wear a condom.

She hadn't known how good sex could really be. Hell, she and Christopher hadn't had much foreplay either, but she was ready for him. More than ready. She was soaked. One kiss was all it took for her to want him more than her next breath.

Then he was there. Christopher eased up on his knees and looked down at Alabama. She lay before him naked with her skin gleaming from the sweat popping over her body. He ran his hands from her shoulders down to her belly and then up again. Squeezing and caressing. Up and down he went. "Beautiful," he exclaimed breathlessly. "Mine."

Alabama could only nod and watch as he spread her legs wider and scooted closer to her core. He raised her up until her ass was propped up and resting on his knees. He took hold of himself with one hand and placed the other on her pubis, right above where she wanted him most. He held her still as he slowly pushed the head of his cock into her tight center.

They both hissed at the pleasure.

"Please, Christopher, more."

Abe eased more of himself into her until his hips met hers. He put both hands on her hips and hauled her higher up on his thighs until they were fused together as close as two people could be. Abe leaned over her then and put his hands on the mattress next to her shoulders. "Hold on to me." He ordered hoarsely.

Alabama reached up and grabbed hold of his biceps again. She loved the way they flexed and moved with him. She couldn't reach all the way around them, and it made her feel tiny and small under him. She wrapped her legs around his hips and urged him on. "Please," was all she could get out.

Abe moved. God, she was hot and wet and all his. He looked down and saw Alabama had her head thrown back and her eyes were closed. "Look at me," he demanded. "Open your eyes and see who it is that's making love to you."

Alabama's eyes popped open at his request. Christopher was looking straight at her intensely. She gasped as he thrust harder.

"That's it. Look at me and know it's *me* that's here with you. You're mine. I'm not letting you go."

Alabama said the first thing that popped into her head. "Promise?"

"I promise. You're not going anywhere. Hell, I'm not going anywhere."

Alabama kept her eyes on Christopher as he loved her. Time seemed to stand still and at the same time, fly by.

Abe watched as Alabama eased closer and closer to the edge. He brought one of his hands down to where they were joined and pressed, hard, right on her clit. That was just what she needed to fly over the edge. At his demand, she kept her eyes on his until the last minute, then she arched her back and thrust her hips into his harder and groaned his name.

That was all it took for Abe to lose it as well. He thrust into her one last time and held still as he emptied himself into her soft core.

After a minute or so, Abe took a deep breath and eased down next to Alabama, not leaving her. He loved the feel of her aftershocks clutching his body and wanted to keep that connection with her as long as he could.

Alabama was sprawled under him as if she was a rag doll. He'd ridden her hard, but she'd taken everything he'd given her. He couldn't hold his words back if his life depended on it.

"I love you."

Alabama's eyes popped open. It would've been comical if they were in any other position than what they were. Alabama couldn't believe what she'd just heard. She had to have heard him wrong.

She closed her eyes, enjoying the feel of being still intimately joined with Christopher, and sighed happily. She had no idea. None. No wonder sex was so popular in books and movies if it felt like this.

"Did you hear me, sweet? I love you." Abe said it again, enjoying the clenching of her inner muscles at his words.

Alabama opened her eyes again and looked up at the gorgeous man hovering over her. He traced one eyebrow with his finger. "You're everything I've been looking for in a woman. I know it's been fast with us, but it's real. I know it. I won't let you go. You're mine. You admitted it. I'm not letting you renege on that."

"You love me?" Alabama couldn't wrap her mind around what he was saying.

Abe smiled. He'd say it over and over again until she got it. "Yes, sweet. I love you."

Alabama felt like she'd lost all her brain cells. The orgasm she'd just experienced must've sucked them all out of her head, because she'd never have said what she did next if she'd been thinking properly. "I've never been loved before."

Abe groaned and eased down beside her. He shifted so he was lying on his back and Alabama was cuddled up against his side. He slipped out of her and they both moaned at the loss. "I love you,

Alabama Ford Smith. You might never have been loved before, but you are now. Get used to it."

"Bossy," Alabama murmured, half asleep. She'd never felt this good, this safe, this protected, this…loved in all her life.

Abe squeezed her. This is where she was meant to be. In his arms.

Just before he slipped off to sleep he heard her murmur softly, "I love you, too."

He smiled, and slept better than he had in weeks.

Chapter Eleven

ALABAMA SMILED AS she cleaned. It'd been three weeks since Christopher had told her he loved her and Alabama could still hardly believe it. Her life had changed so much in the short time she'd been dating Christopher. She'd come out of her shell more and more, and she actually enjoyed spending time with his teammates.

Of course it seemed like each time they'd gone out, Faulkner, Kason, Hunter, and Sam had a new girlfriend, but she'd loved getting to know Caroline. She was funny and so smart. Alabama felt awkward around her at first. Caroline was a freakin' chemist, for God's sake, and Alabama was merely a janitor, but Caroline never made her feel less because of it.

Alabama hadn't wanted to tell Christopher what she did for a living, but it seemed absurd not to. She'd stressed about it for a week before finally just blurting it out after they'd made love one night. He'd only laughed and asked her how long she'd been trying to gain the courage to tell him. She'd blushed. He knew her too well.

All he'd said was, "I love you, sweet. I don't care what you do, just that you enjoy it. I bet you're the best damn janitor the Wolfe's have ever had." She'd laughed and admitted that Greg and Stacy Wolfe had begged her to stay with them after the fire. They'd even paid her for a week's worth of work when there'd been nothing to clean.

Caroline had been the same way. She'd not even cared what Alabama did for a living. She brushed over it like it wasn't a big deal and proceeded to ask what she thought of Hunter's new girlfriend. After he'd dumped Michele, he'd seemed even more restless than before. Not one to gossip, Alabama had just shrugged and listened as Caroline proceeded to tell her all the gossip about the guys on the team.

Alabama hadn't seen Adelaide much after their run-in in the offices a few weeks ago. It wasn't unusual, after all Alabama did clean after regular work hours were over, but she did run into some of the other agents and they were pleasant. Overall the job wasn't hard. It wasn't what Alabama wanted to do for the rest of her life, but for now it suited her. And Christopher was right. She was good at it. She took pride in her work and made sure the offices were spotless each evening before she'd left.

Alabama left the offices with a spring in her step. Her nights were better now that she had Christopher in her life. She thanked her lucky stars every day she'd found him.

Christopher made her life easier in many ways. He'd changed the locks on her door and made sure she felt safe when he couldn't be there. He was always bringing her flowers and other small gifts. When she'd protested, he just kissed her until she stopped complaining.

Alabama took care of him in return too. She'd become more comfortable on base and he'd gotten her a guest pass. She was able to come and go as she wanted and she took advantage of that by stocking up his refrigerator with his favorite foods and drinks when he was out.

The night he'd asked her to hold out her hand and he'd placed a key in it, was one of the most amazing in her life. Christopher explained it was a key to his place and that he wanted Alabama to feel as comfortable coming and going there as she did in her own place. It meant a lot to her. She'd promptly made him a copy of the key to her place as well. Alabama had no idea Abe already had one since he'd changed the locks, and he wasn't going to tell her.

Abe loved the little things Alabama did for him. He didn't think Alabama even realized how much they meant to him. He'd tried to tell her once, but she'd blushed so hard and had gotten so flustered, Abe just let it go.

One day he'd come out of his office at the base to see his car had been detailed. She'd taken his spare set of keys and spent the morning cleaning it from top to bottom for him. When he went to Alabama's apartment from work, most of the time she'd have something made for them to eat. She hadn't lied when he'd first met her when she'd said she didn't really know how to cook, but that made the simple meals she'd made for him all the more special.

Alabama did countless other things that the other women he'd dated hadn't bothered to do as well. Abe hadn't missed them at the time, but he noticed everything Alabama did for him. She picked up his dry cleaning, she'd learned how to polish his boots for him, once she'd even borrowed Caroline's bike and rode behind him while he ran one morning. She'd been sore as hell for the next couple of days and they'd had to get creative in the bedroom, but it'd been worth it. She'd told him she just wanted to be with him and if that meant she had to exercise with him, so be it.

Abe made it clear Alabama was his, but she'd turned around and made sure Abe knew he was hers as well. He loved it. He loved her.

Abe was waiting in her apartment when she'd gotten home from work. He'd made her a big dinner, complete with steak and mashed potatoes. She'd once told him that she had no idea how to grill steak or cook meat and that she never bought it anyway because of the price.

Alabama was thrilled to see Christopher when she got home. They tried to get together each night, but sometimes it wasn't possible with his work schedule.

She went right up to him as he stood in front of her stove and put her arms around him. "Hi. Did you have a good day?"

Abe was so proud of the way she'd opened up. Very rarely did she look around the room for her evil mother before she'd speak. With him, in their homes, she never hesitated and talked all the time. Abe loved he could give Alabama that feeling of safety.

"Yeah, sweet. You? Have a good night?"

"Yeah. The offices were all empty. No issues."

"Good, I made steak for us tonight. Have a seat and I'll dish it up."

"You spoil me, Christopher."

"Good, it's about time someone did."

God, Alabama loved this man.

They ate dinner making small talk. When Alabama took the dishes to the sink to wash them, Christopher took her hand. "Those can wait; I need to talk to you."

Alabama immediately tensed. That didn't sound good. No wonder men hated it when women would tell them, "We have to talk."

"It's not as bad as I'm sure you're thinking. Come on, come sit with me."

Abe led her to the couch and sat down in his usual corner, pulling her into his arms at the same time.

"I want you to meet my family."

Alabama flinched. Whoa, that hadn't been close to what she'd thought he was going to say. "Your family?"

"Yeah, my mom and my sisters. I've told them all about you and they're dying to meet you and get to know you. I want you to meet them, too. You didn't have a good mom, and I'm sorrier than you'll ever know about that. So, I want to share mine with you."

At his words, Alabama immediately started tearing up. As far as romantic words went, it wasn't much, but they meant the world to her. He knew what she'd gone through growing up and in his own way, Christopher wanted to try to make up for it.

"What if they don't like me?" Alabama couldn't help but ask.

"Oh, sweet. They'll love you. You're the best thing that's ever happened to me. They'll see that and love you because of it."

Alabama laid her head on Christopher's chest and curled into him, tucking her hands against her cheek. She could feel his arm tighten around her. He didn't pressure her; just let her work through his request on her own.

She did want to meet them. She'd heard so much about his sisters, Susie and Alicia, and of course his mom. She'd never had a family and would do almost anything to be a part of one.

"Okay."

"Okay?"

"Yeah, okay."

Abe smiled and squeezed Alabama harder. "I'm proud of you sweet. You've made me so happy. I hope you know that."

When she didn't answer, he just smiled. "I'll call them and see what I can set up."

Alabama nodded.

"Come on. Time for bed. I need you."

Alabama sat up quickly and pulled out of his arms and headed for the bed. She needed him too. She ignored his chuckle and pulled off her shirt on the way to the bed. That stopped his laughing quickly. She giggled as he scooped her up and dropped her on her back on the bed.

Her fears of meeting his family were forgotten as Christopher showed her just how much he loved her.

Chapter Twelve

A BE WATCHED ALABAMA try to control the shaking of her hands as they walked up to his mom's little house. Abe had helped his mother buy the house after he'd been in the Navy for a while. She hadn't been able to afford anything very big when he and his sisters were growing up, and Christopher wanted to make sure she was comfortable. He wanted to return the love she'd shown to him and his sisters their entire lives.

Abe didn't ring the doorbell, but instead simply opened the door and walked in. Alabama trailed behind him, nervously clutching the bouquet of flowers she'd insisted on stopping to get before they'd arrived.

She heard feminine voices as they made their way into the house.

"Mom? We're here!" Abe called out, not stopping.

Alabama couldn't help but think back to her own childhood. If she *ever* had yelled out anything like that she'd have gotten beaten. She shuddered and tried to bring herself back to the present.

Two women came rushing from the back of the house toward them. One was short but slender. She had brown hair that swung freely around her shoulders. She was wearing a pair of shorts and a henley T-shirt. She wore tennis shoes on her feet. The other woman was a bit taller and was wearing jeans and a light sweater. She had a short pixie haircut that was extremely flattering.

The shorter woman leaped at Abe and he caught her up and swung her around.

"It's so good to see you!"

"You too squirt!"

Abe put her down and turned to greet the other woman. "Hey Leesh, it's great to see you too!"

The taller woman hugged Abe hard and said, "You too bro."

"It's about time you got here!" They heard from behind them. Everyone turned to see Christopher's mom. Alabama thought she looked exactly like what a "mom" should look like. She was average height and was carrying more weight than was socially acceptable. She looked healthy and happy.

"Mom!" Abe took a step and folded his mother into his arms. He kissed her on the cheek and pulled back, still holding her. "You look great, as usual."

"Oh, you. Introduce us to your woman." She didn't waste time on pleasantries. It was obvious she'd been waiting on them.

Abe stepped away from his mom and turned toward Alabama who'd been waiting a few steps away. He reached out, grabbed her free hand and pulled her toward them.

Alabama stumbled, not expecting his move, but Abe steadied her and brought her against his side.

"Mom, Suse, Leesh, this is Alabama."

"We're so glad to finally meet you!" Susie, the shorter woman exclaimed.

"Yeah, it's about time Chris brought you out from the rock he's been hiding you under." Alicia joked smiling.

Alabama smiled back shyly. Both his sisters were funny. She loved the ease in which they joked with Christopher.

Mrs. Powers came forward and held out her hands to Alabama.

Alabama looked up at Christopher who nodded encouragedly to her. She turned toward Bev Powers and held out her free hand.

Christopher's mom grasped her hand with both of hers and squeezed. "You have *no* idea how happy I am to meet you, Alabama."

Alabama blushed, not knowing what to say. She couldn't help but look around before answering. She was uncomfortable enough to fall back into her old habits. "Thanks, Mrs. Powers. I'm happy to meet you too."

"It's Bev. You call me Bev."

"Okay. Bev."

She beamed.

Alabama didn't know what to do. She felt awkward and Christopher's mom was still holding her hand. Christopher came to her rescue, as usual, taking the flowers she'd still been clutching in her other hand and holding them out to his mom.

"We brought these for you, Mom."

Finally letting go of Alabama's hand, Bev took the flowers. "They're beautiful. Thank you. Now, let's not stand out here in the hall. Let's go sit down so we can get to know each other better."

Abe claimed Alabama's hand and held on tight as he let his sisters and mom precede them so he could have a bit of privacy before joining them.

"You doing okay so far, sweet?"

Alabama looked up at him and answered, "Surprisingly yes. I'm still nervous, but they're really nice. You're very lucky, Christopher."

Abe smiled back. He knew she'd learn to love his family as much as he did. She was tender hearted and he knew all it'd take was a bit of friendliness and she'd open up.

They headed into the living room to join his sisters and his mom.

ALABAMA SAT ON the couch next to Susie and laughed as she pointed to pictures of Christopher when he was young. They were pouring through the photo album his mom had unearthed after dinner.

His sisters were hysterical. They had no problem laughing at themselves, as well as each other. They'd shown her naked pictures of both themselves and Christopher, but obviously took great pleasure in showing off embarrassing moments of their brother's childhood.

The stories they'd shared all night were also precious to Alabama. She had no such memories of her life, and she loved that Christopher had them.

"Hey, Chris, remember that time you came home to visit when I had a date and you actually threatened him?" Alicia recalled.

"Hey, I didn't threaten him!" Abe returned laughing. "All I did was tell him if he didn't get you home safe and sound by curfew, he'd regret it."

"Yeah, and you were sitting on the porch cleaning your gun when we got home. He didn't even kiss me good-night. He actually shook my hand. *Shook my hand!* God, it was so humiliating!"

Everyone laughed. Alabama could just imagine it. Christopher had obviously learned to be protective at a young age, but she loved it. She'd never had anything like that in her life and she would've done anything to have experienced it just once growing up. Before she thought about what she was saying she blurted out, "You guys were so lucky to have a protective older brother."

"Oh, they didn't think so at the time," Bev said laughing, "but you're right, Alabama. We're all very lucky. I don't know how I managed it, but Chris turned out all right."

Alabama could feel Christopher's eyes on her. She raised her head and saw the intense way he was looking at her. He *knew* what she was thinking. He *knew* how she grew up and how she would've done anything to have had a brother like him.

"Mom, Suse, Leesh, we're gonna have to get home." He'd said it without looking away from Alabama.

She blushed. She was embarrassed, but she was ready. The night had been stressful. Nice, but stressful. Alabama was ready to go. She wanted to come back though.

They all stood up and Alabama watched as Christopher hugged each of "his girls," then came back to her side.

"It was great meeting you, Alabama. I hope you'll come back soon. We're thrilled you're lowering yourself to date our brother." Alicia said, laughing once again.

Bev also put her two cents in. "Yes, please, come back soon. I was going to try to talk to you alone at some point tonight, but I see that Chris doesn't want to leave your side. I hope you know how much my son likes you. He's only brought one other woman home to meet us, and she wasn't nice."

Alabama blinked. Huh?

"You're nice. We like you. He wouldn't have risked bringing you here if you were only a passing fancy for him. I'm looking forward to many more dinners and lunches and get-togethers. If my son knows what's good for him, he'll put a ring on your finger sooner rather than later."

"Mom!" Abe admonished. Jesus. Now *he* was embarrassed.

"What?" Bev said not-so-innocently. "I just wanted to make sure Alabama knew this wasn't an everyday occurrence for you."

"Jeez, Mom, do you think I haven't already told her that?"

Alabama tried to smother a laugh. For once it was nice to see Christopher embarrassed instead of her. She squeezed his hand. "It's okay, Christopher." She tried to soothe him.

Everyone laughed, breaking the tension.

"Okay, we're leaving. I'll call you guys as soon as I can. Stay safe."

Everyone got hugs, including Alabama, which was a bit awkward for her, but she returned the embraces as if they were her due.

Abe settled Alabama into the passenger seat of his car then walked around and climbed into the driver's seat. Before starting the car, he turned toward Alabama and wrapped his hand around the back of her neck and pulled her toward him. He rested his forehead against hers and whispered, "Thank you, sweet."

Alabama grasped his wrist with her hands and said, "For what?"

"Thank you for coming with me today. It means more to me

298

than I can say that you like my family."

"They're good people, Christopher. I'm just glad they didn't hate me."

"There's no chance they would've hated you, baby. They loved you. They would've moved you into my place today if you'd given them half a chance."

She laughed. "I'm not sure about that, but I loved seeing you guys together. You have no idea how lucky you are."

"I know, Alabama. Believe me, I know. I spend too much time in crappy countries and see way too many examples of horrible things people do to one another to take advantage of my family...or you."

Alabama caressed the back of his neck with one of her hands. "I know you do, Christopher. You deserve your family."

"You deserve my family too, sweet."

They sat in the car for another moment before Abe closed his eyes and touched his lips to hers. The kiss was light and sweet, but wasn't short.

They pulled back and sat for a few seconds looking into each other's eyes.

"You ready to head home?" Abe asked with an intense look in his eyes.

Alabama knew exactly what was on his mind, and it was on hers too. She nodded.

Abe kissed her one more time, then let go and turned the key in the ignition. "Let's go home, sweet. I'll show you how much I 'like' you." He smirked.

Alabama couldn't wait.

Chapter Thirteen

THE NEXT NIGHT after cleaning the offices, Alabama entered Christopher's quarters on the base. He'd told her to come to his place because he wanted to make her dinner. She much preferred it when he made dinner because she sucked at it. She could make packaged noodles or stew, but that was about the extent of her culinary skills.

The moment she opened his door she smelled the delicious scent of garlic and other spices. He was making spaghetti and it smelled heavenly.

Abe couldn't wait for Alabama to get off work and get home. He'd started thinking about anyplace they were sleeping each night as "home." He wanted to spoil her tonight because he'd gotten the news he'd been dreading for a while. He knew it was going to come sooner or later, and today their commanding officer told them they were slated for a mission.

They were leaving the next morning, which wasn't surprising. Most of the time when they got called away, it was with little-to-no notice.

Now Abe had to tell Alabama he was leaving. He was nervous. It was the first time the team had been called away on a mission since he and Alabama had gotten together.

Abe wasn't stupid. He knew the statistics of relationships of Navy SEALs. They were abysmally low. But if Caroline and Wolf would make it work, Abe had hope that he and Alabama could as well.

This first time he had to leave Alabama would be tough, he knew it. For the first time in a long time, Abe wasn't looking forward to leaving. Usually he was the first person on the plane and was the most enthusiastic about completing the mission successfully.

This would be the first time Abe didn't spend the night before they left going over the intelligence they'd received. He wanted to spend every second with Alabama, not thinking about work. Abe wanted to answer any questions Alabama had, that he was allowed to answer, and he wanted to spend his last hours with her wrapped in his arms.

"Hey, sweet, did you have a good day?" Abe went to meet Alabama as she came into the room.

"Yeah, same ol', same ol'. You?"

"I missed you."

"Well, duh," Alabama returned with a smirk.

Abe laughed and grabbed her. He bent her over his arm and leaned her backwards until her head was below her shoulders.

Alabama shrieked and grabbed his biceps tightly. Abe put his mouth on her neck and nipped. "You missed me?" He asked between bites.

"Yes, yes, you know I did! Let me up!"

Abe chuckled and brought her upright, not letting go.

Alabama could feel how happy he was to see her. His hard length pressed against her as he held her close.

"Kiss me, sweet. It's been almost eight hours since I've tasted you."

"With pleasure."

After a few moments Abe reluctantly pulled away. "If I don't stop now, we don't get to eat."

"That's okay with me," Alabama murmured before pulling his earlobe into her mouth and sucking, hard.

Abe shuddered and thought about saying the hell with dinner

before remembering he had to tell her he was leaving in the morning.

He set Alabama away firmly and laughed as she pouted. "Come on, let me feed you, woman."

Dinner was delicious, as usual. Christopher was a wonderful cook and Alabama always enjoyed whatever he made. The sauce for the noodles was spicy, but not overwhelmingly so.

When they'd finished, they both cleared the table and Christopher washed the dishes while Alabama dried them.

"Want to watch television for a while?" Abe asked, knowing she'd decline.

"No, I want you."

Alabama had come out of her shell and Abe loved it. She didn't seem shy with him anymore and she was confident in bed. He loved that she let him be as bossy as he needed to be. She'd do whatever he told her to with no questions asked. He'd told her one night that if there was ever anything he asked of her in the bedroom that she didn't feel comfortable doing, she should tell him and he'd back off. Abe had been surprised by her response. Alabama told him that she trusted him. That she loved when he took charge and she'd loved everything they'd done together. Abe knew they were meant to be together.

Abe grabbed Alabama and slung her over his shoulder in a fireman's hold. At her surprised shriek, he laughed.

"Put me down, Christopher, I'm too heavy!"

"Are you kidding me? Baby, you know I'm a SEAL right? The equipment I have to carry weighs more than you do!"

She laughed with him. He stopped laughing when he felt her hands gripping his butt. He walked faster toward his bed. He had to be inside her. Now.

He stalked into his bedroom and dumped Alabama in the middle of his bed. Abe loved the sound of her laughter, loved being the one to give that to her. He knew she hadn't laughed enough in her life.

"I love seeing you here."

"Where?"

"In my bed."

Alabama smiled up at Christopher and sat up. Without a word she lifted both arms above her head.

Abe reached for Alabama and slowly tugged her shirt over her head. Without looking to see where it landed, he threw it behind him. He reached for her breasts and caressed them. "God, Alabama, you are so fucking sexy."

Alabama just smiled up at Christopher. She could see the evidence of how sexy he thought she looked, by the hard ridge in his pants. She laid back, dislodging his hands. Resting on her elbows on the bed, she told him playfully, "These pants are awfully uncomfortable. Care to help me with them?"

Abe loved when Alabama got playful. "Of course, sweet. Wouldn't want you to be uncomfortable…" Running his hands over her stomach he took his time in getting to the button on her jeans. He released it and slowly eased the zipper down. "Lift up," he ordered hoarsely and swallowed hard when Alabama lifted her hips up at him.

Abe put his hands inside her jeans at either side of her hips and eased the material down, taking her undies with them at the same time. "Whoops, looks like your panties accidentally came off with your jeans."

Alabama just laughed and reached behind her back and unclipped her bra. She quickly removed it and laid back, hands over her head, and arched her back. "One of us is overdressed."

Without a word Abe pulled Alabama's hips to the side of the bed. She shrieked in surprise, but he didn't hesitate. He looked up and caught her eyes with his and lowered his head.

"Christopher," Alabama moaned in ecstasy.

Finally taking his eyes from hers, Abe looked down at the perfection that was Alabama's sex. "You're so wet." He took one hand from her hips and ran his finger lightly through her wetness and up to her clit, then he lowered his head. While his finger caressed over and around her hot spot, his tongue explored every inch of her folds.

Alabama moaned. She never dreamed oral sex could feel this good. She and Christopher had played and explored each other's bodies, but this was different somehow. He was still completely dressed and she loved it. She felt wanton and sexy and she loved every second of his mouth on her. "God, that feels so good."

Abe moved his mouth up to her clit, and lightly sucked. He eased his finger inside her at the same time and searched for the soft spot on the front wall of her sex. When Alabama jumped in his grasp, he knew he'd found it. He eased another finger inside to join the first while his other hand gripped her hip tightly. Abe lifted his head long enough to murmur, "Let go, sweet. I want to feel you come around my fingers. Give me all you got, don't hold back." He lowered his head and set about driving her crazy.

Alabama writhed in Christopher's grasp. She put one hand on the back of his head and gripped what little hair he had. Her other hand gripped the sheet at her side tightly. She'd orgasmed with Christopher inside her before, but this was different somehow. It seemed more intimate, more intense…just more.

Abe could feel Alabama was close. He stroked her inner wall and sucked hard on her clit at the same time. With one last twist of his hand and a little hum under his breath, Alabama was coming for him.

He didn't let up as she thrashed under him, but kept going until she shuddered again. Finally when she moaned, "God, please, Christopher," he eased up. He licked her one more time and slowly removed his fingers. Waiting until she looked down at him, he brought his fingers to his mouth and slowly cleaned off her juices. "Beautiful and delicious," he told her with a gleam in his eye.

"I want you."

"You have me, sweet."

"No, inside. I want you inside me. Now."

Abe slowly backed away from the side of the bed where he'd been kneeling and stood up. "Scoot back, sweet. Give me some room."

Alabama did as he asked, and moved to the center of the bed, not taking her eyes off of Christopher. As she moved, he whipped his shirt up and over his head, then removed his pants and underwear without taking his eyes off of her. Within moments he was moving over her on the bed.

She looked up at his as he came over her. His eyes were intense and dilated with lust. Without a word he finally broke eye contact and leaned down and captured one breast in his hand and the other with his mouth. He alternated sucking and pinching her nipples. Finally when Alabama was ready to attack him, he said, "I can't wait anymore."

"Then don't. Jesus, Christopher. Take me already."

"Guide me in."

Alabama moaned. Everything out of his mouth was sexy as hell and turned her on even more. She reached down and caressed Christopher's impressive hard on. When he growled at her, she just smiled.

"Do it."

Alabama would've teased him further, but she wanted him inside her as much as he apparently wanted to be there. She guided his length to her opening and they moved at the same time. She thrust her hips up just as he pushed into her with one quick movement.

"Oh yeah," he moaned at the same time Alabama said, "God, yes!"

Abe held himself still over Alabama for a moment. She felt amazing. Every time they made love felt like the first time all over again. She gripped him tight and she was soaking wet. He pulled out to the tip, then thrust in to the hilt. He wanted to lose himself in her, to somehow make them one. He pulled out again, slowly, then slammed inside once more.

"Yeah, Christopher. Again. Harder."

Abe did as Alabama asked, and repeated his movement. Over and over, he slowly pulled out, then slammed back inside her. When her hips started thrusting up to meet his on each down stroke, he flipped them. Alabama faltered at the change in position and leaned up to look down at him. Her hands rested on his chest and he could feel them flex into little claws.

"Ride me, Alabama. Take me."

Without a word she moved. She pulled herself up, then back down. It look her a few strokes to get into a rhythm, but once she did, they both groaned.

"You are beautiful. Look at you." Abe couldn't believe how lucky he was. Alabama *was* beautiful. Her breasts bounced with her movements and her head was thrown back. He ran his hands down over her chest and gripped her hips tightly in his. "Harder, Alabama. I'm yours. Take me."

When Abe knew he was on the verge, he reached down and ran his thumb over Alabama's clit as she rode him. Three strokes was all it took before she exploded. He took over and held her hips tight as she shook above him and slammed himself into her. After five strokes, he too was coming. Abe held Alabama to him as they rode out their orgasms. Finally Alabama collapsed on top of him.

"I'm too heavy," Alabama murmured and tried to slide off to the side of his body.

"No, you're perfect. Stay. I don't want to lose you yet." That too was a new experience for Abe. In the past he couldn't wait to retreat from a woman's bed and clean himself up. He couldn't take a shower soon enough after he left the bed. But with Alabama, he reveled in their combined scent, her touch, the feel of himself softening inside of her. He was going to miss this. He was going to miss her. Fuck, he didn't want to leave her.

They lay in bed entwined and sated. Every time they'd made love it seemed to get better and better. Alabama had finally slid to the side and her head was now resting on his shoulder and she had one leg thrown over his. Her arm was tight around his abdomen and she was snuggled into his side as if she was attached.

Abe knew it was time. He couldn't put off the news of his leaving any longer. He hated to do it when they were both so relaxed, but it had to be done.

"Sweet, our commanding officer called the team in today with news. I have to leave tomorrow on a mission. I can't tell you where we're going or how long we'll be gone, but I swear to you, I'll be back as soon as I can."

Tears immediately sprung to Alabama's eyes. She knew this day was coming. They'd been lucky so far, the team hadn't been called out in a long time. She didn't let go of Christopher, but tilted her head back so she could see his face.

"Don't cry sweet, I'll be back soon," Abe begged.

"That's not why I'm upset," Alabama choked out.

"Talk to me."

"You'll be careful, won't you?"

"Oh, baby." Abe knew immediately what she was scared of. "Of course. You know my team is the best of the best. Besides, I have *you* to come back home to. I won't be taking any chances. I want to come home to you."

"Promise?"

Abe smiled. She'd made him promise all sorts of things since they'd been dating, and he hadn't hesitated to promise whatever she needed to hear. He'd lasso the moon if he could for her.

"I promise, sweet."

She sniffed loudly and tried to bring herself under control. "Maybe I'll call Caroline and hang out with her while you guys are gone."

Abe tilted her chin up and kissed her passionately. He loved how sensitive Alabama was. She went from being upset he'd be gone, to immediately thinking about her friend and how she'd need some support as well.

"That's a great idea. I know she'd love to have some company while we're gone. You know you could also call Susie or Alicia too. I'm sure they'd love to get to know you better."

Alabama nodded and cuddled deeper into Christopher's arms. She wasn't ready to meet with his sisters by herself. She knew it'd take a few more visits with Christopher with her before she'd be ready to go out with them on her own.

They were silent for a while, lost in their own thoughts. Finally, Abe turned Alabama until she was on her back and he loomed over her. He smiled. Yeah, he didn't want to leave, but the sooner he left, the sooner he could get back and have out-of-this-world "welcome home" sex. In the meantime he meant to leave his woman so satiated they'd be able to make it through their separation.

Chapter Fourteen

A LABAMA SAT AT her small kitchen table twirling a fork around her fingers while she waited for her microwave dinner to finish. It'd been ten days since Christopher had left and she felt bereft. She and Caroline had gotten together several nights and talked. Alabama got a better idea what it meant to be with a SEAL. Many times the SEAL team had to leave at a moment's notice. Caroline never knew where Matthew was or when he'd be back.

But Caroline had explained while it was tough, very tough, she also knew it was what Matthew was meant to do. Because of her experiences with the team, she knew they were competent at what they did. Caroline had told Alabama the entire story about how she'd been kidnapped and thrown overboard in the ocean. The SEAL team had come together and not only saved her life, but brought down the bad guys at the same time.

Alabama had been horrified at what Caroline had been through, but understood what Caroline was trying to tell her. Caroline trusted the team to take care of each other—she'd seen them first hand in action.

Caroline loved the other men on the team like brothers. There was no one she'd rather have at Matthew's back then the men on the team. Alabama figured if Caroline could trust them to keep Matthew safe, then she could do the same with Christopher.

Alabama came back to the present. Work that night had been weird. She'd shown up as usual at the Realty building, but Adelaide had been there with another agent, Joni. Alabama didn't really know Joni that well. She'd joined the company after the fire. Alabama had seen Adelaide and Joni hanging out, so she hadn't bothered to try to get to know her. She figured if Joni was hanging out with Adelaide, she had no desire to *get* to know her. Maybe that wasn't fair, but it was what it was.

Alabama had gone to get her cart ready for the night's cleaning when Joni had come up behind her. She'd scared the crap out of Alabama, but she tried to brush it off.

"Hey, Alabama. How're you tonight?"

Alabama was surprised Joni was talking to her, even more surprised than she'd been at seeing them in the office after hours.

"I'm good. How are you?" She'd gotten so much better at small talk since she'd started dating Christopher and hanging out with his team.

"Good. So, how long do you usually work each night? It has to suck working nights huh?"

"It's not so bad. I'm usually done in a couple of hours."

"Ah, yeah, that's not too bad. Okay, well, I'm out of here. Have a good night."

Alabama watched warily as Joni walked back down the hall. Not too much later she saw Adelaide and Joni leaving together. She shrugged and continued with her work. She couldn't care too much about them. She'd learned what really mattered in life. Christopher. He was out working to protect their country; she couldn't worry about catty women like Adelaide.

ALABAMA CHANGED INTO her flannel pajamas and snuggled down into her bed. She'd had to do laundry yesterday and she felt so hollow lying in her bed now. While the sheets smelled fresh and clean, she missed smelling Christopher. His scent had permeated the pillowcases and sheets, but tonight she couldn't smell him.

It wasn't only the lack of his scent that made her melancholy. They'd done so many wonderful things in her bed. Alabama had gotten used to sleeping with Christopher; she'd had a hard time adjusting to sleeping alone again.

Alabama jerked awake when she heard a key in her lock. She sat up straight in bed and watched as the door opened. She shrieked a girly shriek, seeing it was Christopher. He was home!

Abe braced himself as Alabama leaped across the small room and threw herself at him. He grunted as she made contact with his body and went back on a foot. He dropped his duffel bag and gathered her close. God he'd missed her. She smelled so good. He was tired. When they'd gotten back to the base, he'd thought about going back to his place to get some much needed sleep and coming over to her apartment in the morning, but he couldn't make himself do it. He hadn't even taken a shower before coming to her apartment.

He needed to see her. He needed to feel her in his arms. The mission hadn't been terribly difficult, but it seemed twice as long this time. Now that he had Alabama waiting for him back at home, the mission seemed harder. He'd talked to Wolf about it and they'd had some good discussions about what it meant to have someone at home. Wolf had gone through the same thing.

Every single thing they did while fighting for their country had a deeper meaning now that they had someone waiting for them. It wasn't that they were careless before, but now, every single decision they made could mean their woman would never see them again. It was tough. Wolf helped Abe try to work through it in his mind.

Alabama didn't hesitate to wrap her arms and legs around Christopher. Thank God he was home. She buried her nose in his neck…then drew back. Whoa. He stunk. He certainly didn't smell like the man she knew and loved. She watched as Christopher grinned.

"I gotta shower, sweet."

"Yeah, I can see and smell that."

"I had to see you. I didn't want to wait."

Okay, that was sweet. She smiled, dropping her legs and standing, but not letting go of him. "I'm glad you didn't. I love you."

"Jesus. I love you too." Abe gathered her close again and they stood there for a bit enjoying the feel of being back in each other's arms.

"Okay, to the shower with you. Do you have clothes that need to be put in the wash? Do you want something to eat or drink?"

"No sweet. Thank you. It can wait until morning. All I want is to get clean then get in you." He watched as she blushed. He loved she could still blush at his frank talk. "Go crawl in bed and get naked, I'll be there in a second."

Alabama nodded and backed away from him. She'd never get used to his dirty talk, but secretly she loved it. She brought her hands up to the buttons on her shirt and started unbuttoning them from the bottom. "Hurry up, Christopher. I'll be waiting."

She laughed as he stumbled on his way to the small bathroom in her apartment. She loved being able to surprise him. It didn't happen very often so when it did, it was awesome.

Abe took the quickest shower he could and still get the stink and grime off of him. The bandage on his shoulder had to come off, since it had gotten wet, but he didn't think he needed another after he was done. He whisked the towel over his body and quickly shaved the stubble off his chin. As much as he enjoyed the thought of leaving his mark on Alabama, he didn't want to hurt her. He strode out of the bathroom with the towel draped around his waist and stopped dead in his tracks at the sight of Alabama in the bed.

She was completely naked and lying on top of the covers. She'd propped herself against the pillows and was reclining against the headboard. Her knees were bent and her legs were open. She was running her hands over her chest, up and down and occasionally running her fingers down her inner thigh. "It's about time."

Abe strode quickly to the bed, losing the towel on the way. It fell forlornly onto the ground, immediately forgotten. "Hell, you are amazing."

Alabama was all ready to seduce her boyfriend. She felt awkward as hell touching herself, but if his reaction was anything to go by, it was worth it. Just as he got to the bed and put a knee on the mattress to crawl over to her, she saw the wound on his shoulder.

Alabama gasped and immediately closed her legs and stopped touching herself. "Oh my God! Christopher, you're hurt!"

"No, sweet, it's nothing. Now come here."

"No! You're hurt. Let me see."

Abe sighed. He really needed her, but it didn't look like she was going to cooperate, at least not yet. He could've ordered her to get back in place, but he didn't have it in him at the moment. It'd actually feel good to have her fuss over him.

Alabama leaned over and turned the light on next to the bed. She seemed to have no idea how sexy she was fussing over him totally nude. Abe tried to ignore how her body swayed and jiggled in all the right places, but it was no use. He'd spent the last week and a half in a hell hole on the other side of the world missing her. He wasn't going to be able to wait to be inside her for long.

Alabama inspected Christopher's shoulder. He was right, it wasn't bad, but it did look deep. "What happened?" She inquired softly, running her fingers lightly over the stitches in his shoulder.

"A bad guy with a knife got a bit closer than I'd have liked."

Ignoring all the implications of what he'd said, Alabama tried to tamp down her curiosity. Most likely she really didn't want to know what really happened. She'd probably have nightmares if she did know.

"Did you guys win?"

Abe chuckled. He'd been prepared to deflect her questions about the mission itself. He couldn't talk about it, even with her. But she'd surprised him again. He shouldn't have been though. It seemed she understood.

"Yeah, sweet, we won." It wasn't like it was a contest, but he didn't bother to explain that to her. He figured she knew that though, her words just came out wrong.

Abe clenched his teeth as Alabama leaned toward him and kissed the ten stitches in his shoulder. He'd killed the man even as the knife was glancing off his shoulder. It'd gotten him where the Kevlar vest hadn't quite covered him. It was a lucky strike, too bad it wasn't lucky enough. The man was dead before he'd hit the ground.

The feel of Alabama's tongue on his skin was the last straw. Abe flipped her over and pinned her under him. She smiled up at him.

"I missed you, Christopher," she said sweetly. "I'm glad you're home."

"Me too, sweet. Me too."

They spent the next few hours showing each other how much they'd missed each other. The sun had just started to peek over the horizon when they finally fell into exhausted slumber, both secure in the fact the other was close and safe.

Chapter Fifteen

A LABAMA SAT IN the hard chair shaking. The tabletop in front of her was a shiny stainless steel, without even a single fingerprint on it. She wondered how they got it so clean. Vaguely, she also wondered what kind of cleaner they used on it. She tried not to think about how long it'd been since she'd been told Christopher had been called. The police officer hadn't let her call him herself, but said he'd pass the word along she was here and she wanted to see him. He'd come soon, Alabama just had to keep telling herself that.

She was freezing. They must keep the temperature unnaturally cool so people would confess or something. She had no idea, she only knew she was cold and couldn't wait for Christopher to come and help her make sense out of what was going on. He'd told her again and again he'd look after her. She definitely needed him to "look after her" now.

That morning was one of the best of her life. She'd woken up in Christopher's arms much later than usual after their late night of passion. He'd sleepily kissed her and told her he loved her. He'd been exhausted. She supposed missions would do that, not to mention their late night antics in bed.

She'd gotten up and made him brunch. He hadn't had to go in early because of their late night return, but he'd told her he had to go in to debrief that afternoon. They'd made plans to get together later after her shift at work.

When she'd arrived at Wolfe Realty, it was to find the place in an uproar. She wasn't sure exactly what had happened, but the next thing she knew, she was in handcuffs and being brought to the police station.

Alabama was terrified. Nothing like this had ever happened to her before. Her experience with police officers wasn't the best, and she was scared. She'd begged to be able to call Christopher, and they hadn't let her. Finally, seeing she was losing it, she was told they'd call and explain things to him. She didn't like that, but she supposed it was the best deal she'd get at the moment.

Alabama knew something wasn't right when the officer who'd said he'd call Christopher re-entered the room without him.

"Is he coming?" Alabama asked nervously. He'd come. He'd be there. He promised to take care of her.

"Uh, he's on his way, but first he's answering some questions."

"You can't do that!" Alabama immediately exclaimed. "He doesn't have anything to do with this. Leave him alone! He's a hero to his country, he just got back from a mission. You can't do that!"

The officer was obviously taken aback by her outburst. She knew he hadn't expected her quick and passionate defense of Christopher.

"Calm down, lady. He was the one who wanted to have some words with my boss before he came in to talk to you."

His words did calm Alabama down. Okay, she got it. Christopher was trying to figure out the best way to get her out of this. He'd know this was all bullcrap and he'd get her out of here. They'd be laughing about it later tonight.

When the door opened a second time Alabama looked up and sighed in relief. Finally.

Alabama watched as Christopher opened the door and kept one hand on the knob and stood by the door. She nervously stood up. She looked at him and tensed. He was pissed. She didn't know at who or why, but it was obvious he was holding his anger in check by his fingernails.

Alabama took one step towards him. "Christopher?"

He looked away from her and at the officer still standing in the room. "Can I have a minute?"

"Sure, but you know protocol." He pointed up at the little camera in the corner of the room. Obviously they'd be taping whatever conversation she had with Christopher.

Abe nodded tightly and stepped out of the way so the officer could leave the room.

"Thank God, you're here!" Alabama exclaimed in relief and took another step in Christopher's direction. She was stunned to see him take a step sideways, away from her. She stopped in her tracks a good four feet from him. What the hell? Her heart sped up in her chest. What was going on?

"Why'd you do it, Alabama?" Abe asked tensely. "Why'd you steal that crap? You know I'd give you anything you wanted. There was no reason to take it."

Alabama stood stunned. He actually thought she'd *done* what they accused her of? She wasn't sure what to say, but it obviously didn't matter to Christopher, he was still talking.

"I *told* you how I feel about stealing. You heard how my nickname came about. We talked about it. You *knew* and you still did it. It feels like you purposely were trying to sabotage our relationship. What was last night about then? One last fuck? Can you explain why the hell you threw us away? Huh? Can you?"

"Threw us away?" Alabama asked incredulously in a shaking voice. What was he saying? She couldn't gather her thoughts. If she thought she was scared before, now she was downright terrified. Christopher was supposed to be here helping her figure out what the hell happened. He should be holding her tight in his arms. In all the time they'd been together he'd always protected her from this sort of thing. He'd never let anyone raise their voice to her the way he was doing right now. What happened between the time when they'd last seen each other that afternoon, and now?

"Christopher, I…"

"*Shut up*, Alabama, I don't really want to hear your excuses right now."

Alabama could literally feel her heart shrivel up and die at his words. She took a step back as if he'd punched her. She felt like throwing up. He knew what his words would do to her. He *knew*. He was right, they *had* talked about it. She'd spilled her guts about her mama and the things she'd said to her. Christopher knew telling her to "shut up" was the one thing she couldn't handle. He knew it and did it anyway, shattering her in the process.

"All I ever wanted from you was an honest relationship. I was ready to give you everything I had. You could've had it all. I would've laid it all at your feet. My protection, my love, my family; but instead you *had* to have that money. I hope it was worth it."

Alabama really had nothing to say. After all they'd been through. She'd told him she loved him. He'd claimed to love her in return, but it was obviously all a ploy to get her into bed, or something. He was so ready to listen to others and not even to hear what she had to say and it killed her. But him telling her to shut up, gutted her.

"You promised." The words came out soft and tortured. She looked him in the eyes and repeated, "You promised, Christopher."

She watched as he slightly flinched at her words. But she didn't care. She was done. She was empty inside. She'd thought she'd finally found someone who would be there for her. Who loved her as she was. Who would stand by her and help her make her way through the world and be her refuge. *Shut up, Alabama. Shut up, Alabama. Shut up, Alabama.* His words echoed through her brain over and over. Every time slicing at her as if it was the first time she'd heard them.

Alabama turned around and sat in the chair she'd so eagerly vacated at his entrance into the room. She calmly pulled the chair up to the table, clasped her hands in her lap and stared at the wall on the far side of the room blankly. Christopher's voice morphed into her mama's. *Shut up. Shut up. Shut up.* She cringed, remembering the feel of Mama's fists and feet as she hit her over and over.

Alabama couldn't think. She just had to make it through the next five minutes. Then the next. Then the next. It was how she'd made it through those awful times Mama had locked her in the closet. It was how she'd made it through most of her life before Christopher had crashed his way into her heart. She counted her breaths. One. Two. Three. She had to keep breathing.

She vaguely heard Christopher talking, but she blocked him out. Nothing he said mattered anymore. Alabama could feel her heart beating unnaturally fast, but sat still, not saying anything.

Finally she heard the door shut. She was alone in the room. She was alone, as she should've remembered she'd always be. It was her against the world. No matter what anyone said. No matter what anyone tried to convince her otherwise. She'd forgotten for a while. She'd forgotten the lessons Mama had taught her. That the high school football player who'd humiliated her so long ago had taught her.

Abe smacked the door to the police station hard as he left the building. Damn Alabama to hell. He'd woken up this morning happier than he'd ever been in his life. The debriefing of the mission had been tough. They'd all had to rehash their actions and make sure they'd done everything right. Through the debriefing they'd discovered some things that could've gone better and Abe knew those things were *his* fault. His head wasn't one hundred percent in the game. He'd messed up.

Then he'd gotten a call from Cookie, who'd heard from his old girlfriend, Michele, that Alabama had been arrested at her job. Apparently Michele had gotten the whole sordid story from Adelaide. Alabama had been stealing money from the agents for a while now.

She'd clean their offices at night and take stuff from their desks. At first it was little things, candy from candy bowls, pens, that sort of thing. Then money started going missing. Jewelry.

They'd found some of the missing items on her cleaning cart. There was a secret pocket sewn into the side of the material. She was caught red-handed.

His Alabama was a thief. His heart broke and he felt sick. How could she do this? *Why* was she doing it? Wolf had tried to talk to him, but Abe's phone rang. It was an officer at the police station calling to tell him Alabama had requested to see him.

He'd gone straight to the station without telling Wolf and his other teammates what had happened. He was too pissed, too embarrassed that his girlfriend was apparently a thief.

He'd spoken to the chief when he'd arrived at the station. He'd outlined the charges against Alabama and what evidence there was. They were doing interviews with some of the witnesses now, then they'd interrogate Alabama.

Jesus. Interrogate her.

Abe had seen red. All of it had been a lie. What else had she lied about? Was her pitiful story about her childhood even true? Did he even *know* her? He'd stormed into the room where she was being held and confronted her.

Abe sat in the front seat of his car with his head on the steering wheel. His heart hurt. What had just happened?

He'd been so *pissed*. He'd gone into that room not knowing what he was going to say to her and every time she'd opened her mouth to try to explain, he'd cut her off. He didn't want to hear her lies.

Abe recalled the look on Alabama's face when he'd told her to "shut up." He'd seen her close down right in front of him. One minute she was there trying to talk to him, the next it was like she was gone. A veil had come over her eyes and she was just gone. She'd spoken two words to him, *you promised*, and the Alabama he'd known over the last few months was gone. He'd known she wasn't hearing him after that. She'd gone and sat back down at the table and refused to look at him. It had to be an admission of guilt; she was ignoring him because everything he'd said was right on the money.

He rubbed a hand over his eyes a few times and then back over his head. God he was tired. He hadn't caught up on the sleep he'd missed on the mission, and last night's passion filled night with Alabama hadn't helped. He couldn't think. He didn't want to think.

Abe pulled out of the parking lot and headed for the base. He'd think tomorrow. Tonight he just needed to sleep.

ALABAMA HADN'T SAID a word since Christopher left. There was no point. She had nothing. No one. The officers tried to get her to talk, but she sat stonily in front of them staring off into space. They'd showed her the evidence against her, including pictures of the hidden pocket sewn into the cleaning cart.

When they'd gotten no reaction, they'd tried to scare her into confessing. Still, she sat as still as a statue, not saying a word. Finally, they had no choice but to book her into the county jail.

As Abe was settling into a restless sleep in his room on the base, Alabama was being fingerprinted and booked. She'd had to change into a pair of county-issued orange elastic pants and scrub-type shirt. She'd been roughly led to the third floor of the county building in Riverton, and locked into a small dank room that smelled slightly of body odor. Her roommate tried to talk to her, but getting no response, shrugged and settled back on her mattress.

Alabama lay on the top bunk in the jail cell wondering how her day had gone from the best day of her life to the worst in a matter of hours. A lone tear fell down her temple before she locked it down. *Shut up. Shut up. Shut up.* She squeezed her eyes shut and tried to block out the words. She counted her breaths. One. Two Three...

Chapter Sixteen

ABE HAD HAD time to think about everything that had happened in the last few days and knew he made a mistake. *Knew* he'd made the biggest mistake in his life. Problem was, he had no idea how to fix it. He shouldn't have opened his mouth. He should've let Alabama talk to him. He'd never forget the look in her eyes when he'd told her to shut up if he lived to be a hundred. He knew what he was doing when he'd said it, and that made him even more of a bastard. Abe knew he'd marked Alabama when he saw the shield fall down over her eyes. It as if one minute she was there, and the next she wasn't.

He wasn't thinking straight when he'd left the station. It wasn't until a couple of days later that he wondered what was happening to Alabama. He thought she would've tried to call him by now. Now that he'd gotten some sleep, he'd begun to be able to think clearly again. He'd gone through the last couple of days in a haze. Cookie had called asking what was up his butt and Abe told him the entire sordid story.

"So when I went to the police station I was pissed. Pissed at myself, pissed at my dad, pissed at her. After everything she'd been through in her life, I didn't let her explain. I cut her off and told her to shut up."

Abe heard Cookie's indrawn breath and quickly defended himself. "I heard my dad's words ringing in my ears. His excuses. I didn't mean it."

"You didn't mean it, but you said it anyway. You can't take something like that back. Once it's out there, it's out there. You know it Abe," had been Cookie's response, and he'd hung up on him. That was two days ago and Abe hadn't heard from anyone else on the team since then.

Abe now knew deep in his gut that Alabama was innocent and that Adelaide was behind whatever had happened. He didn't know how he knew it, but it had to be the reason Alabama had been arrested. Adelaide been pissed at Alabama for supposedly stealing him away from her. That hadn't been the case, but there was no reasoning with a jealous woman.

As soon as Abe realized Alabama was innocent, he'd thought in horror about what she was going through. What had happened when he left that night? Had she been arrested? Did they send her home? What if they'd arrested her? Panic started clawing through Abe. Cookie was right, he *was* a dumb ass.

Abe started trying to fix the wrong he'd done by calling Cookie. He didn't answer. He systematically tried each of his other teammates and no one answered. He even called the police department and was told Ms. Smith had bonded out. Abe wanted to throw up. Bonded out. Fuck. That means they'd arrested her. He hoped she'd been able to pay the fine that night, but when he'd inquired about when she left, he was told Alabama had spent three nights and two days locked up.

Shit. Just shit. This was his fault. He had to fix it.

You promised.

The words wouldn't leave his head. They repeated over and over. He *had* promised, and at the first sign of trouble he'd left her high and dry. Some hero he was. He felt horrible. He had to fix this.

He headed over to her apartment. He'd find her there and they'd talk. He wouldn't let her take no for an answer. He'd apologize and then set about fixing what he'd broken between them. Abe couldn't imagine another scenario. He loved her. She had to forgive him.

Abe stood inside Alabama's apartment and looked around in shock. It was empty. All her things were gone. The couch was still there. The bed too. But the little vase that had been sitting on the kitchen table and had held the many flowers he'd brought her was gone. The bright blanket that had covered her bed, gone. The movies they'd watched together that had been stacked up against the TV stand, gone.

You promised.

Abe walked over to the refrigerator and opened it. Empty. Suddenly in a flurry of motion he threw open cabinets, hoping against hope to find some sign of Alabama. There was nothing.

He sagged against the counter. Jesus. Where had she gone?

Abe startled badly when a voice came from the open door. It was the old woman who he'd winked at several times as he saw her peeking out her door as he and Alabama would pass by.

"She's not here, boy," she said disapprovingly holding tight to the cane that looked like was the only thing holding her upright.

"What do you mean?"

"I mean she's not here. She left. She's gone. Old Bob came to her door and told her she had four hours to get out. He said he wouldn't rent to no felon."

Abe blanched. Shit. This was one more thing piled on his head. "Where'd she go? Do you know?"

"Have no idea. We tried to talk to her, but she hasn't said more than three words to anyone since she got arrested. All her neighbors know she didn't do what those bitches said she did, but seems like no one else cares." She glared at Abe. "Besides, I'm not sure I'd tell you where she was, even if I knew."

Abe flinched but knew he deserved her ire. "I have to find her."

"Whatever." The lady turned around and hobbled back into the hall.

More determined than ever to find his love, Abe knew he'd have to rely on his SEAL contacts to help him. It might be unethical or even illegal, but he'd find her. He had to. He promised. Tex had helped him find her before, he'd do it again.

You promised.

He couldn't get Alabama's anguished words out of his head. They haunted him.

"You HAVE TO help me, Cookie," Abe pleaded with his teammate.

"I don't have to help you do shit."

Abe flinched, knowing he deserved that, and anything else Cookie had to say to him. He paced as Caroline, Cookie, and Wolf sat at a table and glared at him. Abe had called Cookie and Wolf and begged them to meet with him. They'd finally agreed. Caroline was also there when he'd shown up.

Abe knew he deserved the cold shoulder they were giving him, but he didn't care. He'd do whatever he had to do to find, and fix, what he'd done to Alabama.

After Cookie had talked with Abe and heard what happened, he'd immediately called a lawyer and gotten the bond paid so Alabama could get out of jail. He'd gone to pick her up at the station and had been appalled at what he'd found.

He'd found Alabama, but not the Alabama they'd grown to love as a friend. She was broken. She didn't say more than a few words to Cookie or Caroline. She'd been locked behind bars for two long days. Cookie couldn't imagine what she'd been though. No, that wasn't right. He could all too well imagine it. Jail wasn't a good place to be, even if it was the local county lockup. He couldn't imagine shy, sweet Alabama in a place like that, and yet she had been. For three nights and two long days. If Abe had called Cookie sooner he could've gotten her out before she had to spend so long behind bars, but Abe had waited a few days before pulling his head out of his ass.

"We tried to get her to come home with us," Caroline spat at Christopher, "but she just shook her head sadly. She wouldn't even let us come up to her apartment with her. God, Christopher. I've never seen anyone broken like that before. I wanted to crush her up in a hug, but she wouldn't let any of us touch her. When we went back the next day to talk to her, to figure out what's going on, she was gone. All her stuff was there, but she was gone. A neighbor told us her landlord was going to throw all her stuff out since he'd evicted her and she hadn't taken it with her. So we packed it all up and put it in storage for her. What an asshole."

With every word Caroline spoke, Abe's heart hurt more and more. Wolf picked up where Caroline left off.

"I called my contact on the force and had a long talk with him. All off the record, of course. He told me he didn't believe Alabama had done it. The "witnesses" seemed too eager and knew just where to look on that damn cleaning cart to find the hidden pocket. He thought it seemed way too easy. He's been looking into it. Currently, he's going over the security tapes at Wolfe Realty to see what he can find. What do you want to bet he'll find Adelaide and her sidekick planting evidence?"

"God dammit!" Abe roared, punching the wall as hard as he could. He barely felt the pain in his knuckles. He turned until his back was against the wall and slid down until his ass touched the ground. Ignoring the blood trickling down his fist, he ground his fists into his eye sockets.

Caroline looked over at Wolf, who was frowning. She was still pissed at Christopher, but she couldn't stand witnessing his pain. She walked over to him and squatted down.

"We'll find her, Christopher."

When he looked up at her, Caroline was shocked to see tears in his eyes. She'd never seen her husband or any of the other SEALs cry.

326

Ever. She couldn't imagine the pain Christopher was feeling.

"I've lost her. I don't deserve her. God, you don't even know."

Caroline sat down on the floor with her friend. "We'll find her."

Taking a deep breath Abe tried to get himself under control. "I'll find her. She won't want me anymore, but I'll make sure she's okay. I promised." His voice broke and he looked at Caroline. He remembered when she'd lain broken in a hospital bed. Remembered all she went through and how she was here with his friend and teammate today. Anguished, he repeated, whispering, "I promised, Ice, I *promised.*"

Caroline reached up and put her arms around the big SEAL. She couldn't do anything but hold him as he sobbed in her arms. She couldn't berate him anymore. Christopher was beating himself up more than any of them could. She had no idea where Alabama was, but she knew Christopher would do everything in his power to make sure she was safe, and that Adelaide and her minion would pay.

Chapter Seventeen

ALABAMA HUDDLED ON the cot in the homeless shelter. She was broke. All the money she'd saved up over the years was gone. She'd had to use some of it to pay the bond to get her out of jail. Hunter had paid it at first, but once she'd been able to get her hands on her own money, she emptied her savings account and given most of it to him.

He hadn't wanted to take it, but she'd refused to take it back. That had been eight days ago. Eight of the longest days of her life.

She had nowhere to go. No job. No money. No Christopher. *No*. She refused to allow herself to go down that mental road. She had to figure out what she was going to do. It was time to leave the west coast. Maybe she'd go to Texas...well, when she earned enough money for a bus ticket.

The only things she had with her were what she could fit into her one suitcase. She hadn't been able to take her little vase. She hadn't been able to take any of the belongings in her house that reminded her of better times. Hell, she hadn't wanted to take any of them at the time, but now...now she'd kill for one of her pillows that smelled like *him*.

It was harder than she'd ever imagined to let him go. Even though Christopher gutted her, she still loved him.

Alabama looked down at the one thousand two hundred and twenty three dollars in her hands. It was all the money she had left, but she couldn't keep it. She put it in the envelope sitting on the cot and reached for the pad of paper and pen lying nearby.

She penned the note, putting all her bitter feelings into her words. It didn't have to be this way, but she didn't know what she'd done to make Christopher dump her so brutally. Mama had been right all those years ago. Alabama was unlovable. If her own mama couldn't love her, no one could.

She finished the note and folded it carefully. It felt like her heart was breaking all over again. She stuffed it into the envelope with the money inside and wrote on the front.

For Christopher Powers, Navy SEAL.

She didn't know his address, but when she met with the lawyer Hunter had hired for her later that day, she'd give it to her to deliver. Once that was done, she'd feel better.

She had no idea what was going on with the case. She knew she hadn't stolen anything, but Alabama had no idea if anyone would believe her. It would be her word, a janitor, against Adelaide's, who was a respected realtor in the area. It was hopeless.

Alabama knew she'd run before going back to jail. It'd been horrible. Oh, she hadn't been beaten up or raped or anything, but it was an awful place. She'd been watched at all times. The guards were broken down bitter men and women who had no empathy toward any of the inmates. The people behind bars with her, were just plain scary.

Alabama had stayed away from everyone, which wasn't hard considering it was just the local county jail. She'd taken meals in her cell and tried to figure out what to do. She didn't know how the justice system worked, so all she could do was wait.

She'd never been so glad to see Hunter in all her life. She wanted to cry, but she felt dead inside. She was nobody. Caroline had tried to talk to her, but Alabama shut her out too. She couldn't. Just couldn't. They were Christopher's friends. She didn't know why they were helping her. Hadn't Christopher told her what she did? She didn't ask. Just nodded at them when they dropped her off at her apartment and went inside without looking back.

Of course Bob had been waiting for her to kick her out. She knew he'd loved it. He stood at her door and watched her pack her meager belongings and demanded her key when she was done. She hadn't looked back, just walked out of the building and into the night.

Alabama stood up and grasped the handle of her suitcase. She couldn't leave it behind at the shelter while she met with her lawyer; if she did she might never see it again. A homeless shelter wasn't a place to leave anything unattended if you wanted to see it again when you returned. With the envelope in one hand and her suitcase in the other, she walked out of the room to meet with her lawyer in the common space downstairs. One way or another, Alabama hoped this nightmare would soon be over.

ABE LOOKED DOWN at the note and saw his hand was shaking. Actually shaking. He'd received a call from his commanding officer and he and Wolf had gone down to see him. Abe had been shocked when he'd been handed a thick envelope and that it had been delivered by Alabama's lawyer. He'd thanked his CO and he and Wolf had gone back to Wolf's office.

Now he sat looking at the envelope, knowing he wasn't going to like what was in it.

"Do you want me to open it?" Wolf asked seriously.

Abe shook his head and tore open the seal. Money spilled out onto his lap falling onto the floor as well. He looked up at Wolf then back down to the dreaded envelope. He ignored the bills and took out the plain piece of paper. It was a note from Alabama.

Abe read her words once then re-read them and read them a third time. He could almost feel the pain radiating from the words on the page.

Christopher,

Enclosed you'll find $1,223. I have no idea if this is exactly what I owe you, but it's as close as I can figure. I wouldn't want you to think I stole anything from you, so this is reimbursement for most of the things you did for me while we were...dating. Included in the $1,223 is: three pizzas delivered, four alcoholic drinks, two dinners, gas money for the times you picked me up from work and traveled to and from your place to mine, $157 for the flowers you gave me, and $400 or so for the groceries you bought when you made me dinners and lunches. I included some extra for things that didn't cost anything but your time, but time is money as they say. So for all the times you took me to work, held open my door, held my hand, and let me spend time with your friends and family, I've included reimbursement.

You might be thinking that I spent an awful lot of time remembering every single thing you did for me, and you'd be right. I only remember because you're the first man to do anything like that for me. Every single thing you did left its mark on me. I only wish I'd realized before now it was all payment for services rendered. I wish I'd known you were paying for me to sleep with you, I would've said no thanks.

I'm sorry I misunderstood. My fault. I hope I've returned everything. I wouldn't want to be accused of stealing from you.

–Alabama

Abe realized he'd been rubbing his chest while he'd been reading her letter. He knew he should be pissed at her. The Alpha man inside him wanted to punish her for throwing all of his gestures back in his face. On the surface, sending the money seemed like a petty thing to do, as she'd stated, but Abe knew Alabama well enough to know how much he'd hurt her. She was only trying to protect herself.

He leaned down and gathered up the money tucking it back into the envelope. He'd return it as soon as he could. In the meantime he'd have to figure out how he was going to help his woman.

"Help me, Wolf. Help me find her."

"You got it, Abe."

Chapter Eighteen

THEY'D BEEN SEARCHING for Alabama for two days straight, with no luck. It was amazing how someone could just disappear. Abe would've been impressed, if he hadn't been so worried about her. Even Tex hadn't been able to dig up any reliable information to help find her. It was as if she'd disappeared off the face of the earth.

The team had split up around the city, each of them taking a different section. They hadn't found her, but they'd heard stories. The first time Abe had heard someone talking about Alabama, he'd been excited, thinking they were close, but it wasn't the case.

They'd gone into a small "mom and pop" grocery store with Alabama's picture asking the owners and workers if they'd seen her. They had. The clerk explained how she'd purchased five packets of those cheap packaged noodles college students were notorious for buying. Five. The total came to a dollar and forty two cents. She'd counted out the money from the change in her pocket. The clerk went on to tell them how he'd noticed her because after she'd made her purchase, he'd watched her walk across the street, kneel down next to one of the local homeless guys and give him one of the packets, and apparently the rest of the change she'd had in her hand.

So they'd left the store and tried to find the homeless guy. They hadn't found the exact person, but they'd talked to two other homeless women who'd said they'd met Alabama. They'd told Abe how sweet she'd been to them and how they'd let her stay with them on the street one night.

Abe was going out of his mind. He had over a thousand dollars of her money in his pocket and she was literally sleeping on the street and eating freeze dried-fucking-noodles. He wanted to howl his frustration. His woman shouldn't be living like that. She should be in his bed tucked in next to him. Safe. But he'd put her on the street. Him.

That night, after another day of searching with no luck, Wolf was fed up. "Jesus, we've had better luck finding terrorists inside third world countries! It's time to stop messing around. We need to trick her."

"No way," Abe immediately protested, not liking the thought of deceiving Alabama in any way.

Wolf immediately countered, "Do you want to find her, Abe? Or do you want her to spend another day and night on the street eating who knows what, meeting who knows what kind of people?"

Hell, when he put it that way, Abe was all about doing whatever Wolf wanted to do if it meant finding her. "What do you suggest?"

"We need to get her back with her lawyer. Alabama trusts her. We need to talk to her and get her to set up a meeting. Hell, she needs to meet with Alabama anyway. She has to get her to sign the papers acknowledging her freedom and the fact the case against her as been dropped. We have no idea if Alabama even knows Adelaide and Joni were arrested for making false statements. Those security tapes proved Alabama didn't steal anything and that Adelaide and Joni set her up from the start."

"Good idea."

"I'm not sure you should be there when we meet with her, Abe," Benny said.

"Oh hell no!" Abe said vehemently. "I have to be there. I started this and I'll finish it. I need her."

At the anguished tone in his friend's voice, Benny relented. "At least let us make sure she won't bolt before you can talk to her."

Reluctantly Abe nodded. He knew as well as the others did, if Alabama saw him first, that's exactly what she'd do, bolt. He deserved it, but he just hoped she'd give him a chance to grovel. "All right, set it up. Let's do this."

IT WAS TWO days before the lawyer could manage to get word to Alabama, and another day before the meeting was set up. The SEALs were impressed with the lawyer. As much as they hated it, she was able to find Alabama within forty eight hours.

Abe didn't care how she'd done it, just that he'd finally be able to see Alabama. He hadn't slept well since he'd realized what an ass he'd been. He fell asleep each night wondering if she was okay, and he'd wake up wondering the same thing each morning. His commanding officer was getting fed up with him *and* his team. They'd been worthless at work, and everyone knew something had to give. Abe didn't give a fuck though. Alabama came first in his life now. Before work, before his country, before everything.

Abe paced the hallway at the homeless shelter waiting for Wolf to give him the all clear. Alabama was supposed to meet with her lawyer in ten minutes. They all held their breaths hoping she'd actually show up.

The plan was to let the lawyer talk to Alabama first and break the news about the charges being dropped. Once she did that, Wolf and Dude would enter the room and let Alabama know they were there to talk to her. Once she settled from their arrival, Abe would go in. They had it all planned out, but no one knew what her reaction would be to it all.

ALABAMA WAS TIRED. She was dirty, sore, hungry, and perpetually scared out of her mind. Living on the streets was scary. It wasn't like the movies where everyone you met was nice and concerned about your welfare. People were on drugs and desperate and wouldn't hesitate to do whatever it took to get what they wanted. It wasn't all *Pretty Woman-esque* either. Alabama had been trying to avoid a local pimp for the last two nights. She knew if he could, he'd have her flat on her back working for him in no time.

She'd spent as many nights here in the shelter as she could, but when she'd heard Abe was looking for her, she'd bolted. She didn't want him to find her. It'd hurt too much. She was trying to figure out what to do, where to go, and how to get there.

When she'd heard her lawyer was needing to talk to her, she agreed to meet her today. Alabama couldn't wait to get the hell out of Riverton, but she had to make sure she was in the free and clear to leave. As much as she'd like to get out of town now, she knew she'd never make it far if she was wanted for skipping bond and leaving the state. So she'd stuck around.

The last time Alabama had talked to her lawyer, the woman had been convinced the charges would soon be dropped. She'd told Alabama there was a security camera in the Realty building. She'd point blank asked Alabama if she'd stolen anything. At Alabama's firm shake of the head, she'd simply nodded and said, "I didn't think so."

Alabama thought at the time it was pretty sad that a jaded lawyer had believed her with no questions asked, and Christopher, the man who'd told her he loved her, hadn't even given her a chance to explain. Alabama refused to let her mind go back down that road again. That part of her life was over. She was moving on. Of course it was easier said than done, but she was trying.

Alabama sat in the chair at the table in front of her lawyer. She'd left her suitcase near the door as she'd walked in. She felt dirty. Hell, she *was* dirty. She hadn't had a proper shower in days and her hair needed washing, badly. All she wanted to hear was that she was free to go, and she was out of here.

"Alabama, I've got great news," her lawyer gushed, not making her wait. "Those security tapes showed just what we thought they would. Adelaide and Joni planted the money on your cart and it's all on tape. I just got back from the District Attorney's office and all the charges against you have been dropped."

She paused, as if waiting for Alabama to leap up in joy or something.

Alabama just sat there. Whoopee. She was innocent. Big deal. She'd been innocent the entire time. She *was* glad at the decision, however, because it meant she was free to go. She tilted her head at her lawyer as if to ask, *"Are you finished?"*

"I'm not done." She'd interpreted Alabama's nonverbal head tilt well enough. "There are some friends of yours here who've been looking for you. I agreed to let them join us in our meeting today."

At her words Alabama leaped to her feet. *No!* She didn't want to see anyone. She couldn't.

Just as the lawyer finished dropping her bomb, Matthew and Faulkner walked into the room. Their eyes took in everything about her with one glance. They saw her battered bag by the door. They saw her tired, haggard appearance. They saw the panic in her eyes.

"Sit down, Alabama," Wolf said sternly. "We want to talk to you."

Alabama didn't want to sit. She wanted to go. She glared at her lawyer. Why had she done this to her? Alabama had thought she'd liked her. Dammit.

Faulkner came over to her and firmly took hold of her arm and led her back to the seat she'd just vacated. He sat on one side of her while Matthew sat on the other side. Faulkner put one arm on the back of her chair and rested his other on his knee. Matthew just turned his chair toward her and put his elbows on his knees and leaned toward her.

"Are you okay, sweetheart?" Matthew asked softly. He wanted to touch this broken woman in front of him, but knew it wasn't his place. This was Abe's woman. He had to try to fix what Abe had done. Granted, Abe hadn't told them exactly what had happened when he'd gone to see Alabama at the station, but obviously whatever it was had broken Alabama. When she didn't answer him, Wolf looked up at Dude for a moment then tried again.

"Okay, dumb question. Of course you aren't all right. Hear me out, okay?" Not giving her a chance to agree or disagree he continued. "I've known Abe for most of his adult life. We were in BUD/S together. BUD/S is where we learned to be SEALs. I've saved his life and he's saved mine. Several times over. He's the one who got me to get my head out of my ass when I was ready to leave Caroline. He made me see I was being stupid and letting my head get in the way of my heart."

He stopped to reach over and take Alabama's hand in his. He noticed how much dirt there was under her nails and he winced. Jesus. It wasn't fair.

"He fucked up, Alabama."

At that, Alabama raised her head and looked at Matthew for the first time. She'd expected him to plead with her to forgive Christopher. To tell her what a great man he was. To take his side and tell her a sob story about what he'd been going through. She was ready for that. She could resist that. She wasn't ready for Matthew to so bluntly disparage his friend.

"Yeah, I know. You thought I'd come in here and tell you all about what a great guy he is and how you should take him back. Hell, I *do* think you should take him back, but I'd totally understand if you didn't. He made a huge mistake, Alabama. He knows it. You know it. We know it. But what you don't know is how much he regrets it."

When Alabama started shaking her head he squeezed her hand.

"I know. Regret doesn't change what happened to you. It doesn't change the fact you lost your home, that you spend three nights in jail. It doesn't change the fact you're currently homeless and penniless. It doesn't take away what he said to you, the hurt you feel. But it *could* change your future. What Abe won't tell you is the *real* story about how he came to be known as Abe. I will. If you'll listen…"

Alabama didn't want to. She really didn't want to. She wanted to hate Christopher. She wanted to despise him, but she couldn't. She loved him. Still. Even with what he'd said to her, she still loved him. She remembered every second they'd spent together. She remembered all the nights they'd spent loving each other.

Her heart was beating wildly in her chest. She was scared to death, Christopher could hurt her. He *had* hurt her. But if there was a one percent chance she'd get him back, she'd have to take it. She tilted her chin at Matthew to continue.

"Good girl. I'm so proud of you. You're the bravest woman I've ever met…well except for my Ice." He smiled so she'd know he was teasing her. Then he sobered and continued.

"When Abe was a little kid, he didn't know his father very well. The man would come to the house, then leave for months at a time. Abe never understood what was going on. That sort of thing would be confusing to any little kid. When he was eleven his dad left and never came home. His mom told him he'd died. It didn't really hurt Abe because he didn't know his dad that well. It wasn't until he was a teenager that he'd found out his mom had lied to him. She'd lied to protect him, but it still changed him fundamentally."

"His dad had a second family. Yup, a whole second family. He spent most of his time with that other family and not with Abe's. He'd come home every now and then to pretend, but then he'd be off again. He'd been killed when the brother of a *third* woman he'd set up and had kids with found out about his double, well triple life, and shot him. Abe wasn't upset with his mom. They're still close to this day, as you know. But the fact his father had lied to all of them, hell had lied to three different women and a total of eight kids, did something to him."

"Abe told me all of this one night when he was completely drunk, mind you. His dad's betrayal helped to formulate the man he is today. It's true he doesn't like it when people steal, but it's more the lies he can't abide. Here's where I try to explain what happened that day. Please know I'm not excusing his behavior in any way shape or form. But it might help you understand where his head was at."

Alabama didn't know if she wanted to hear it. This whole situation was crazy. She looked over at Faulkner who'd been sitting with his arm on the back of her chair the whole time. He simply nodded at her, encouraging her. Faulkner's jaw was tight and he looked pissed. Alabama didn't think it was at her, but the control that oozed out of every pore of Faulkner's body was daunting. Alabama turned back to Matthew.

He continued. "As you know, we'd just spent ten days in a third world country hellhole. I can't tell you what we were doing or why we were there, but as I'm sure you can guess, it wasn't to be diplomatic and "talk" to anyone. But while we were waiting to get home, Abe and I talked. This was the first mission since you guys had gotten together. He was missing you and worried about you. It drove him crazy because he'd never felt that way while on a mission before. He made mistakes. Nothing that would get him or us killed, but mistakes nevertheless. It was eating at him. We talked about how to handle it. I did the same thing on my first mission after getting together with Caroline. He was glad to be going home, to you. We hadn't had much sleep. In fact, I think he'd been awake for forty four hours or something like that. He went home straight to you, and the two of you probably didn't get much sleep that night either." Wolf smiled.

Alabama blushed. Wolf didn't comment on it, but squeezed her hand. "We'd just gone over the mission and discussed the mistakes that were made. He was feeling raw. He felt as if he'd let us all down.

Then he heard about you, what you'd allegedly done. He was running on adrenaline and about three hours sleep in the last three days. He'd just learned how many mistakes he'd made because he'd been thinking about you and not about the job. He wasn't thinking straight, and he was hurting and embarrassed. He couldn't separate what his dad did in his mind, with what you were accused of. I know what he said to you was unforgiveable, Alabama. We're all pissed at him."

Alabama looked up at that. She was embarrassed all the guys knew what had happened, but she also suddenly felt bad for Christopher. These were his friends. She was a newcomer to their group, shouldn't they be on his side?

"Can you forgive him Alabama?"

Alabama looked down at her lap. If it hadn't happened to her she could've forgiven him in an instant. But it *had* happened to her.

Faulkner squeezed her shoulder without a word and got up from the chair next to her and left the room. Alabama looked over and saw that her lawyer had also left. She took a deep breath and looked at Matthew.

"I don't know." She whispered, answering Matthew honestly.

"Try, Alabama. Try. True love only comes along once in your life. That man loves you. He'd die for you. Trust me. I know." Matthew stood up, took her hands in his, kissed the back of both, ignoring the dirt, and left the room.

Alabama sat at the table thinking. What should she do now? She had no idea. She was a free woman, but still didn't have any money to her name. She looked toward her bag which she'd left by the door and gasped.

Christopher stood by the closed door silently watching her. How long had he been there? She watched as he slowly slid to the ground and finally came to a rest with his back against the door, his legs drawn up in front of him. He didn't say anything, but continued to stare at her intently.

Alabama stood up on shaky legs and crossed to the other side of the table. She wasn't scared of him physically, but putting distance between them was the only thing she could do at the moment to feel safe.

Abe cringed at her actions. He closed his eyes briefly then opened them again. "I deserve your mistrust. I do. I know it. But it kills me to see it. If it takes me the rest of my life I'll make it up to you, I swear."

Alabama didn't know what to do. One part of her wanted to leap out of her seat and rush to Christopher. The other part, the six year old who'd been locked in a closet over and over and had learned not to expect kindness, kept her standing in place and silent.

Abe sighed. Jesus. He hadn't let himself think about what he'd said to her that day in the interrogation room. She'd been scared to death and so relieved to see him, and he'd done the unthinkable. He'd thrown her love back in her face as if it meant nothing.

"If it matters, you should know I've ruined Adelaide."

When he said nothing more, Alabama raised an eyebrow at him.

"She might be facing charges for making that stuff up about you, but she'll definitely find out soon enough she shouldn't have messed with you."

"Christopher." Alabama's voice was tortured and rusty from lack of use. She never wanted him to do something like that for her. What if he got in trouble because of what he'd done? She didn't know *what* he'd done, but he obviously had the connections to do all sorts of things.

"Jesus, sweet." Abe choked out. He hated hearing how wobbly her voice was. She'd gone from speaking freely, to not talking at all in the space of a few weeks. And it was all his fault.

Alabama forced the tears back. She'd missed him calling her "sweet," but she wasn't ready to trust him again yet. She couldn't.

"I hate that you don't feel safe around me, Alabama. I know it's my own fault. I know it, but I hate it. I want you to feel safe. I'll do whatever it takes for you to have that again. I hope to Christ I can be in your life when it happens, but if not, I'll deal. It's more important for me to know you're safe, happy, and protected."

Now Alabama was crying.

Abe continued, forcing himself to stay seated and not rush across the room to hold her and tried to ignore her tears. Each one gutted him. "For what it's worth, I'm sorry. I was wrong. I was an asshole. I hurt you and I should've trusted you. It was inexcusable for me to say what I did. You know what I'm talking about."

She did. Alabama wasn't ready to forgive him, but his simple, straightforward apology went a long way. She didn't know many people who could come right out and admit they were wrong. Not to mention apologize for it in the same sentence.

"I'd do anything, and I mean *anything* to take it back, but I can't. All I can do is move forward and let you know it won't happen again. I know you won't believe that now, but I can say with one hundred and twenty percent certainty, I won't let you down again."

Abe took a deep breath. He knew Alabama wouldn't come running into his arms, but it still hurt to see her cowering behind the table on the other side of the room.

"Caroline is here to take you to her house. They got all your stuff that was left in your apartment and put it in storage when you were evicted. They went and got it all yesterday and moved you into their basement. You can stay there as long as you want. I talked to one of the Navy counselors on base and told her a little about you. She'd really like to talk to you…if you want. I left her information with Caroline. I'll stay away. You don't have to run to escape talking to me."

He took another breath and stood up slowly and gripped the doorknob to keep himself in place. "I know you hate me, sweet, and I don't blame you. But rest assured, I hate myself more. You didn't deserve this. You deserve someone better than me. You deserve someone who won't let you down. I hope like hell you can forgive me someday though."

Abe opened the door and gestured to Caroline that he was done. Wolf had allowed her to come with him and she'd been waiting in the hallway. She brushed by him, completely ignoring him, and rushed into the room to her friend.

Wolf stood off to the side in the hallway waiting for Abe as he exited the room.

"So?"

"She listened."

"And?"

"Don't know. It's up to you to convince her to stay. I'm sure she wants to bolt. I can't say I blame her. Take care of her, man."

"Oh, don't give me that shit, Abe. You aren't giving up on her. You can't. You wouldn't let me give up on Caroline; I won't let you give Alabama up."

"It's not up to me, Wolf. Ball's in her court. It's not the same as with you and Ice. I wouldn't blame her if she never said another word the rest of her life, that's how badly I screwed up. But I hope you and Caroline can get through to her. Get her to see that counselor."

Wolf put his hand on his friend's shoulder. "We'll do what we can. She'll come around. She loves you."

"And I love her. More than I ever thought I could ever love someone. But I hurt her. No, I devastated her. I'm not sure, if I was in her shoes, that I'd forgive me."

"She will, Abe. She will."

"I hope so. I sure hope so."

Chapter Nineteen

ALABAMA SLEPT FOR eighteen hours straight. Caroline had brought her to her house, given her a big hug, and left her alone in the basement apartment. It was just what Alabama needed. She needed some time alone to process all that had happened in the last month. She needed a safe place to hole up and get her balance back. She'd been through so many emotions, she was exhausted. She'd been scared, confused, hurt, sad, uncertain, and just plain tired.

Alabama took a long hot shower, scrubbing her skin raw, then, barely taking the time to dry herself off before putting on a T-shirt, collapsed into bed.

She'd woken up disorientated and confused, before remembering where she was. Her mouth felt like cotton and she knew if she breathed on anyone, she'd knock them over with her horrible breath.

Alabama groaned and rolled out of bed and staggered into the bathroom. After another long, hot shower Alabama felt more like herself. She'd forgotten she didn't have any clean clothes, all her clothes had been sitting in storage and needed to be washed, but when she walked out into the room she saw a pile of clothes on a chair in the corner. Caroline had obviously brought her some of her own things to wear.

Alabama pulled on the pair of sweat pants and the simple T-shirt, sans underwear. She debated with herself on whether she should go upstairs or not. Caroline had made it clear she was more than welcome, but Alabama wasn't sure she was ready to talk…or not talk. All it had taken was two little hurtful words from Christopher's mouth to put Alabama right back where she'd been when she'd met him. Wary and uncomfortable when talking to people. She reverted back to her old habits of keeping her mouth shut unless absolutely necessary.

She sighed. It'd be rude to stay shut up in the basement, besides she'd honestly missed Caroline. She'd become a good friend in the short time they'd known each other.

Alabama made her way up the stairs and opened the basement door and entered the kitchen. The smell of steaks grilling made her mouth water. She was suddenly starving.

Alabama didn't see anyone around, but knew Caroline and Matthew had to be there somewhere. Instead of snooping around, she pulled out a chair from the kitchen table and sat.

Not too much later, Caroline came in from the other room.

"Alabama! You're awake!"

Alabama smiled shyly and nodded.

"I'm so glad you came up. Hungry?"

Again, Alabama nodded, a bit more enthusiastically.

"Okay, Matthew is grilling steaks. I swear he always makes enough meat for a hockey team. There's more than enough for you to have one too. Is that all right?"

Alabama forced herself to do more than just nod this time. "Yes, that sounds heavenly."

Caroline looked sad for a moment, then came toward Alabama and kneeled on the ground in front of her and engulfed her waist in a huge hug. Her head was buried in Alabama's lap and her voice was muffled when she spoke. "We were so worried. Thank God, we found you and you're okay."

Alabama was shocked. She had no idea Caroline had felt like that. Before she could respond, Caroline lifted her head, keeping her arms around Alabama and kept talking.

"Don't you ever do that again. If you're scared, or hurt, or *any-thing*...you call me. I'll come and we'll work it out...okay?"

Alabama didn't understand. "But, I hardly know you."

"Bull. We know each other, Alabama. I like you. You're my friend. I'd like to think I'm your friend too. Let me put it this way, if I called you and said my car ran out of gas, would you help me?"

"Of course." Alabama didn't even have to think about it. Caroline had been nicer to her than almost anyone she could think of in her life before now.

"See? We're friends. That's what friends do for each other."

Alabama got it. For the first time she got it. She slowly wrapped her arms around Carline and belatedly returned her hug."

Caroline smiled and squeezed tight, then let go and stood up and held out her hand. "Come on; let's get some veggies together to go with Mr. Caveman's meat."

Alabama smiled and got up to help her friend.

LATER THAT NIGHT, Alabama sat on the bed in the basement with Caroline. After eating, Caroline had announced they'd have a slumber party. Alabama hadn't ever had a sleepover with anyone, and strangely enough, was looking forward to it.

It was silly really. She was thirty years old, but she needed someone to talk to. She wanted to talk about everything that had happened to her. She needed another opinion. She didn't trust her own feelings.

Matthew had been great throughout dinner. He hadn't brought up Christopher's name or talked about anything heavy. He'd talked and laughed with Caroline and tried to make Alabama feel as comfortable as he could.

Caroline changed clothes and wandered down the stairs later that night to join Alabama. Alabama had been sitting cross legged on her bed waiting. She could've watched television, but didn't really feel like paying attention to anything.

Caroline sat down next to Alabama on the bed and smiled.

"You look better. The sleep and food did you good."

Alabama made a conscious effort to talk to her friend. "I feel better. Thank you for everything. I mean it."

Caroline waved her thanks off. "Talk to me, Alabama. I know the basics of what happened from Matthew, and I saw how miserable Christopher looked, but I want to hear from you. What happened?"

"I honestly don't know, Caroline." Alabama told her. "I'd just had one of the best nights of my life, Christopher had come home safe from whatever scary mission he'd been on, and the next thing I knew, I was in an interrogation room waiting for him to come and get me out. But he didn't. He left me there."

Alabama took a deep breath. It was hard to talk about her childhood, but it'd be even harder to tell Caroline what Christopher had done.

"My mother abused me when I was little. She locked me in a closet and refused to let me out. She told me to shut up all the time, and if I spoke, at all, she'd beat me. I can't hear the words 'shut up' without remembering the terrifying nights I spent huddled on the bottom of a closet. Or feeling her hitting me."

"Oh, Alabama," Caroline said, emotion coating her words. "I'm so sorry."

Alabama knew she had to get the rest out before she lost her courage. "I thought Christopher was there for me. He wouldn't let me explain. He just kept ranting. Then when I tried one more time to talk to him, he told me to shut up." Ignoring Caroline's indrawn breath, Alabama continued. "He said the one thing that was guaranteed to rip my heart out and he left. He *left* me there. I spent three of the most terrifying nights of my life in jail, and believe me, that's saying something."

Caroline reached over and grasped Alabama's hand. "I've known

Christopher for a while now, and while I can't imagine how you feel, how you *felt* hearing those words coming out of his mouth, it's obvious he's suffering."

When Alabama stiffened, Caroline continued quickly. "I know, you're suffering too. I'm not defending him, but he loves you, Alabama. He loves you so much. He sat in front of me and sobbed after hearing you'd had to spend the night in jail. The question is, did those two words kill your love for him?"

Alabama nodded immediately. Then changed her mind and shook her vigorously. Then she put her head in her hand and mumbled, "I don't know."

"You do," Caroline said with conviction.

"How do you know?"

"Look at what you're wearing, Alabama."

At the strange question, Alabama looked down at herself. She hadn't realized what she'd put on. She was wearing one of Christopher's T-shirts. She'd obviously grabbed it when she was packing up necessities in her apartment before she'd been evicted. One of Christopher's shirts had been folded up in her drawer and she'd packed it.

Alabama realized she'd worn it every chance she'd had. She felt closer to him when she was wearing it. For a while it had even still smelled like him.

Caroline pressed her point. "Could you see yourself walking away today, actually leaving Riverton and moving across the country, never to see him again?"

"Maybe it'd be best. I don't know if I can ever trust him again, nevertheless forgive him."

"Let me put it this way. What would you feel if he left on a mission and never came back? What if he was killed in action?"

Alabama didn't think. "Don't say that, Caroline! Jesus, don't *say* that sort of thing! You can't….he won't…" Tears came to her eyes.

"I'm sorry, Alabama. I had to make you *think*. He lives on the edge every day. *Every* time they leave the house there's a chance they might not come back. Don't you think I hate it too? I live with the worry every time Matthew leaves. But I trust him. I trust in his team. I trust in his love. You have to find a way to forgive him. You love him. Let that love guide you."

"But…"

"No buts, Alabama. I can guarantee you that Christopher will never, *ever*, say that to you again. He won't let anyone else say it either. He won't let anyone even *think* it. He learned his lesson. If you thought he was protective before, you haven't seen anything."

"What do you mean?" Alabama asked. Her mind was going in a million different directions. She loved Christopher. She was still beyond hurt by what he'd done, but she knew if she never saw him again, she'd be devastated.

"That man tore this city apart looking for you. Anytime anyone hinted he let you go, he lost it. Every time someone even *suggested* you might've been guilty, he lost it. That lawyer of yours? Hunter might have originally hired her, but Christopher harassed her every day trying to get information on you when they were trying to find you. He made sure she concentrated on your case and your case alone. And I don't know if he told you, but Adelaide is going to wish she never messed with you too, I'll tell you that."

Alabama was stunned. She had no idea he'd been that concerned about her. She'd thought he'd dumped her, made a clean break. "He told me she'd wish she didn't mess with me, but not what that meant specifically. What'd he do to Adelaide?"

"Well, I don't know exactly, but Matthew told me some of it. They have a good friend out in Virginia named Tex He knows a lot of people and is really good with a computer. *Really* good. Adelaide's now broke. Her identity was 'stolen.' He told all her friends what she'd done and he had a talk with the Wolfe's. She doesn't have a job anymore and I'd be surprised if any of her friends stood by her."

"But that's…that's mean."

Caroline laughed harshly. "Alabama, that's not mean. What that bitch did to *you* was mean."

"But…Christopher's not like that. He protects people. He's a hero."

"Hon, she threatened you. She hurt you. *She* did that to you. Christopher is a trained killer, he could've done worse, and I have a feeling he would've if Matthew and the rest of his team hadn't reined him in."

At the shocked look in Alabama's eyes, Caroline continued in a softer voice. "He loves you. He loves you so much. He'd do anything for you, give you anything you want. He'll protect you with his life. You just have to forgive him and let him back in."

A lone tear finally dropped from Alabama's eye and spilled down her cheek. "I want to, but…"

"No, no buts. Give it a few days. Let everything sink in. You're safe here. You can be alone for as long as you need to be. You can stay here for as long as you want. I have the name of that counselor on the base if you want to talk to her as well. When you're ready, let me know, and I'll arrange for you guys to talk. Okay?"

"Okay. Caroline?"

"Yes?"

"I've never had a best friend before. Hell, I've never even had a close friend before. But I'd like to call you my friend."

"Oh girl…If you didn't, I'd have to bitch slap you."

The two women laughed together breaking the tension. Finally, being tired, they drew the covers back on the bed and climbed in. The heavy talk done, they giggled and gossiped for a long while before finally drifting off to sleep.

Chapter Twenty

WHEN ALABAMA WOKE up, Caroline was gone. Alabama didn't blame her. If Christopher had been nearby, she probably would've climbed into his bed too. She had a lot to think about. She wanted to forgive Christopher, she still loved him, but she had no idea *how*.

She might still love him, but she wasn't sure she trusted Christopher anymore. He'd broken her trust in the most brutal way possible. He'd left her to face the false accusations by herself, not to mention leaving her to spend time in jail.

Alabama sighed. As Caroline had told her last night, she wanted to think about things for a few days. She hadn't completely decided if she was leaving or staying in Riverton, but she was pretty sure she was staying. She wanted to get to know Caroline better and besides, Christopher and his team were stationed near here.

Alabama got out of bed and took a shower. She lovingly folded and put Christopher's shirt under her pillow for when she got ready for bed again. She wandered upstairs, hoping to see Caroline again.

Caroline wasn't around when she made her way to the kitchen, but Matthew was. He told Alabama Caroline had to work that day, she was making headway into a new chemical process. Matthew admitted easily he had no clue what it was, but Caroline wanted him to tell Alabama she'd be home for dinner.

"What is it Alabama? I can tell you're thinking heavily about something. Spit it out."

"It's just…I don't understand why you guys are letting me stay here. Don't get me wrong, I'm thankful, and I really like Caroline, but I don't get it."

"Abe has saved my life more than once. He even saved my woman's life. Caroline told me a little about what you went through when you were a kid and I already knew what Abe said to you. It was unacceptable and hurtful, we all know that and we're all more than pissed at Abe because of it. But the thing is, you're still his. Being his, makes you, by default, mine; and Mozart's, and Cookie's, and Benny's and Dude's. We made a vow to protect each other with our lives, and that extends to our families."

"But…"

"No buts," Matthew said interrupting her. "You're ours to protect, and that means protecting you against hurtful words too, no matter who they come from. Until you're ready to talk to Abe, you're under my protection. No one will get near you without my say-so. When I'm not here, one of the team will be. We're giving you the time you need to work through what happened in your mind. If at the end of your thinking, you decide you don't want to stay, we'll respect your decision. But fair warning, we'll still probably try to convince you otherwise."

Alabama just stood there staring at Matthew. He couldn't be serious. "But, you guys have to work."

"Yeah, we do, but we've worked out a rotation and got it okayed by our commander. Anywhere you want to go, anything you want to do, you've got one of us to help you do it."

Alabama just shook her head. "You guys are crazy."

Wolf smiled. "Get used to it."

THE NEXT FEW days were surreal for Alabama. Every morning when she made her way upstairs she found a different member of Christopher's team waiting for her. One morning Hunter was standing at the stove flipping pancakes. He'd calmly asked her what she wanted to drink. Another morning Kason was sitting at the table eating doughnuts from a huge box. The third morning Alabama thought she'd finally been left alone, only to find Faulkner sitting outside the house in his car. When she'd left the house to take a walk he'd gotten out of his car and walked with her.

Matthew was right. They were there, looking out for her, simply because they thought she belonged to Christopher.

Finally, after a week had passed since she moved into Caroline and Matthew's basement, she thought she was ready. She'd gone over and over what had happened in her mind. She didn't *think* she'd been at fault, except maybe she could've talked faster and *made* Christopher listen to her. But the bottom line was that she still loved him. She wanted to see him; she wanted to hear what he had to say.

It was Saturday. Caroline had picked up some cute clothes for her yesterday on her way home from work. She apologized to Alabama for not thinking about it earlier and swore they'd soon spend all day at the mall making sure Alabama had everything she needed.

Alabama took advantage of the cute clothes she now owned and put on a pair of jeans with a tank top. The tank top wasn't sexy per se, but it showed more than Alabama was used to showing. She knew she was stressing over seeing Christopher again, but she couldn't help it.

When she entered the kitchen, Caroline and Matthew were sitting on a chair at the table. Caroline was in his lap and they were so busy kissing each other they didn't even know she'd entered the room until she cleared her throat loudly.

Alabama laughed at the blush that spread across Caroline's face. She watched as Matthew's hand eased out from under her shirt and grasped her around the waist. He wouldn't let her jump up off his lap though.

"Good morning, Alabama," he said in his low rumbly voice. "Did you sleep well?"

Alabama simply nodded. She didn't want to go through the niceties this morning. She got right to the point. "I'm ready."

The couple knew exactly what she was talking about.

"Awesome." Caroline exclaimed quietly.

"Thank God," Matthew said fervently. He leaned forward with Caroline on his lap and reached into his back pocket for his phone. Alabama watched as he swiped the phone to turn it on and pushed some buttons, obviously sending a text message. In just a moment, he put the phone on the table in front of him and said, "He'll be here in a few."

"What?" Oh my God. Already? Even though Alabama had said she was ready, now that Christopher was actually going to be here, she was panicking.

"Yeah, he's been spending every night in the driveway, in his car."

Alabama thought her head was going to explode. She felt like a parrot repeating everything she heard. "What? He's been spending every night in the driveway, in his car?"

Matthew chuckled and settled Caroline deeper into his chest, her head tucked under his chin. "Yeah, he wanted to watch over you himself. We tried to tell him you were safe and nothing would happen to you in our basement, but he insisted."

"That's...insane."

"No, hon," Caroline finally chimed in, "that's love."

Alabama didn't have time to say anything because the doorbell pealed throughout the house. She looked at Matthew and Caroline. They hadn't moved.

"Are you going to get it?" She asked them.

Matthew laughed. "We all know who it is, Alabama. Go and put him out of his misery...and yours."

Alabama took a deep breath and slowly walked toward the door.

She knew she'd said she was ready, but now she wasn't so sure.

She slowly opened the door. She put a hand on her chest. Just the sight of Christopher was enough to bring back the pain she'd felt when he'd told her to shut up in the police station.

Abe stood in front of Alabama with his hands in his pockets. He was nervous as hell. He'd screwed up so badly, but all he wanted was a chance to talk to her, to apologize.

"Hey."

"Hey."

"Thank you for agreeing to see me."

Alabama just nodded. She suddenly felt tongue tied again. She knew he wouldn't disparage her again, but it was still hard for her to talk to him as she'd once done.

"Will you come with me today? Will you trust me enough to keep you safe for the day?"

Alabama nodded automatically. It wasn't that she didn't trust him…exactly. Okay, that wasn't completely true. She knew he'd keep her safe from physical danger; it was her emotional safety she was more concerned about.

Abe let out a long breath, as if he'd been holding it waiting for her answer. "Do you need to get anything before we go?"

Alabama nodded. "I'll meet you at your car?" She didn't know why, but she wanted to talk to Caroline and Matthew again before she left.

"Okay, sweet, I'll wait for you out here. Take your time." He took a step back. He seemed to understand her uncertainties.

Alabama shut the door and went back into the kitchen. Her friends hadn't moved. "I'm going out."

"Good. Remember what we talked about, Alabama," Caroline told her seriously. "Give him a chance."

"Can I…" She paused, biting her lip.

"What is it, Alabama? Can you what?" Wolf sat up straighter as he asked.

"Can I call you to come get me if I need to?"

Wolf felt Caroline about to answer and squeezed her hip hard. She kept silent and he slowly put her aside so he could stand up. He kissed Caroline lightly, then walked over to Alabama.

Wolf reached out for her, watching for signs of her pulling away. She didn't and he enfolded her into his embrace. "Of course you can, Alabama. I don't care where you are, when it is, if it's today, or ten years from now. You need me, or Caroline, or anyone on the team, you call. We'll come running. Okay? You're not alone. You have all of us now. We aren't letting you go no matter how this turns out today. You'll be fine, but if you need us, we're here. Just call and we'll come. Okay?"

Alabama nodded. Wolf pulled back and kissed her on the forehead. "Now, go on. Try to enjoy the day. Get the heavy stuff over with so you can enjoy being with your man again. Make him grovel, but in the end, take him back."

Alabama gathered what little strength she felt she had around her, and pulled away. "Okay, thanks. Have a good day, guys."

She grabbed her little purse and went back toward the door and Christopher.

Wolf snatched up his phone and quickly tapped out a text to Abe before Alabama had even made it to the front door.

Alabama opened the door and stepped out, watching as Christopher put his phone into his back pocket before he started toward her.

Abe felt sick inside. He'd read the text from Wolf. Jesus. She'd gone back inside to ask if they'd come and get her if she asked. He wanted to kick his own ass. He'd done this to her. She didn't trust him and he couldn't blame her. Today was the first step at getting her trust back. Abe didn't know what he'd do if he didn't earn it, but he'd spend the rest of his life trying, if only she'd let him.

"You ready, sweet?" The endearment slipped out without any

thought on his part.

Alabama nodded and allowed Christopher to open the passenger door of his car. He helped her in and held out the seatbelt for her. Once she was secured, Abe closed her door and walked around to the driver's side.

Starting up the car, he turned and looked at Alabama. She was beautiful. He'd missed her, but it was his own fault. He'd done a lot of things he regretted in his life, but hurting Alabama was at the top.

"I thought we'd go downtown, have some lunch, then maybe walk along the beach. Does that sound okay?" He didn't want to do anything she'd be uncomfortable with.

"Yes." Alabama answered softly, but at least she'd answered.

Abe found a parking spot downtown and they entered the small trendy café down by the water. He asked for a table outside, hoping being unconfined would help her relax. He even let her have the seat against the wall.

Alabama knew how badly Christopher was trying to make her feel comfortable the second he offered the seat against the wall to her. She recalled the conversation they'd had the first time he'd taken her out for coffee about sitting against the wall so he could see the room.

She shook her head and took the other seat instead. He wouldn't admit it, but she could see the relief in his eyes. Christopher hadn't wanted to take the other seat, but he would've if she'd wanted him to.

They ordered drinks and sandwiches and sat in awkward silence for a couple of minutes. Finally, after their drinks were delivered, Abe broke the silence.

"I know I've already apologized, but I hope you'll let me do it again. I'm sorry. Jesus, I'm so sorry."

When Alabama didn't say anything, but remained looking at him with sad eyes, he continued.

"I have nothing to say to defend myself. I hadn't had a lot of sleep, I heard what you'd been accused of and I immediately thought about my asshole of a father. If I'd only stopped to think for half a second I would've known the truth. But I didn't. I rushed to the station and said shitty things to you. I didn't believe it."

At her look of disbelief he swore. "I didn't, sweet, I swear to God. I was confused and hurting, and I took it out on you."

When he stopped talking and just looked at her, Alabama knew she had to tell him of her experiences. She looked at the tabletop instead of at him while she spoke. "I thought you were there to help me. I was so scared. I asked for them to call you and I was so relieved when you walked in the door. Then you said...that...I couldn't believe it. I didn't understand."

Abe made a choking noise, but she didn't look up. "Every night when I was in that cell I was scared to death. Some of the other inmates said some...things...to me. I didn't know if I was going to get out of there or not. I couldn't eat. I didn't sleep more than twenty minutes at a time. Throughout it all, all I could think of, all I could see was your face, all I could hear were your words, as you came into that interrogation room."

Alabama risked a look up at the man who'd hurt her so badly. He looked anguished. She continued quickly wanting to get it all out in the open. "I didn't take a shower while I was in there because I was afraid to take my clothes off. When Bob was yelling at me calling me a felon, I didn't know what to do. All I could do was grab some things and get out. You hurt me Christopher. No, you devastated me."

Alabama continued quickly, before Christopher could say any-thing. "I was ready to leave. I wanted to get away from here, away from the hurt I'd felt." She paused, then looked up and stared Christopher in the eyes. She was amazed to see they were swimming in tears. "But then Caroline asked me a simple question and I knew I had to see you again. I had to give you another chance."

Abe blew out the breath he'd been holding. He'd never hurt as badly as he had in the last few minutes listening to Alabama talk about what she'd been through, what *he* had put her through. He'd been shot, stabbed, beaten, and starved, but nothing had hurt as badly as her words.

"What'd she ask you, sweet?" Abe asked softly, dreading her answer, but wanting to hear it nevertheless.

"She asked how I'd feel if you left on a mission and never came back."

The air between them cackled. Neither broke eye contact when the waiter brought their lunches and set down the plates on the table.

Abe waited for her to continue.

"I knew then that I still loved you. You hurt me, but God, I love you, Christopher."

Abe pushed his chair back from the table and took a step toward Alabama. He knelt down on the floor and lightly put his hands on her knees. Alabama was shocked. She hadn't expected him to get on the floor. She could feel the heat from his hands seeping through her jeans and she soaked it in as if she was a plant that had been in the darkness for months.

"I don't deserve you, Alabama. Lord knows I don't, but I love you too. I don't want you to go. I want to woo you." At her half laugh, half snort, he grinned, then sobered up again. "Yeah, it sounds silly, but I want to show you that you can trust me again. I want to show you how important you are to me. I know SEALs aren't known to have lasting relationships, but I'll do everything in my power to make sure you know you come first in my life. Yes, I might have to fly off at the last minute for an assignment, but if push comes to shove, you'll come first. I'll go AWOL or tell my commander to take me off the mission list if I have to. You're it for me, sweet. I'll spend the rest of my life earning your trust back."

"I've never come first to anyone before," was Alabama's timid response.

Abe wasn't expecting it. He didn't know what he expected, but it wasn't that. He picked up one of her hands and kissed the back of it. He wanted nothing more than to haul her into his arms and kiss her deeply, but he knew he hadn't earned her back yet. "You're the most important person in my life, Alabama."

They grinned at each other and Abe slowly got up off the ground. He kept hold of Alabama's hand and went back to his seat. They ate lunch and both were glad of the decreased tension in the air between them.

After lunch, Abe took her to the beach as he'd promised. They'd wandered up and down the sand laughing at the antics of the seagulls that were constantly looking for food.

The trip back to Caroline and Wolf's house was made in comfortable silence. Abe wanted to reach out and hold Alabama's hand, but knew it was too soon. It could've been weird, knowing they loved each other, remembering the times they'd spend loving each other in bed, feeling the distance between them now, but Abe was happy for whatever she'd give him.

Now that Abe knew Alabama still loved him, he knew he had a chance. He'd go as slowly as she needed him to. All he wanted was her trust. Love was one thing, but trust was what made a relationship solid.

He pulled up to Wolf's house and shut off the car's engine. Abe turned to Alabama. "Thank you, sweet. I don't deserve you. I know I told you this before, but I'll say it once more. I'll never give you a reason to distrust me again. You need me, I'm there. No matter what. I don't care if someone tells me you've killed someone. I'll never doubt you, and I'll always give you a chance to explain, whatever the situation is. I'll never walk out on you again. I know you don't trust me now, but you will. I swear."

Alabama gave him a sad smile. "I hope so, Christopher. I need you. I need your trust. I don't think I can get through the rest of my life without it."

"Come on, sweet. Let's get you inside. I'm sure you're tired."

They walked up to the porch and stood in front of the door. "I feel like I'm on a first date," Alabama tried to joke.

"In a way we are." Abe leaned toward her and lightly kissed her lips. He then moved to her nose, then her forehead, before stepping back.

Alabama couldn't stand it anymore. She looked up at the man she loved with every fiber of her being and stepped into him. He immediately put his arms around her and clasped her to him. Alabama snuggled into his body, wrapping her own arms around his waist. They stayed like that for a couple of minutes, neither wanting to let the other go.

Finally Alabama straightened and pulled away. "I'll see you later?"

Abe brushed his knuckles down her cheek. "Of course, sweet."

"Go home, Christopher. You don't need to sleep in your car. I'm okay. I'll talk to you tomorrow, okay?"

He smiled. She was so cute. "I'll talk to you tomorrow." He ignored her request. He'd sleep outside Matthew's house until she was back in his arms, and bed, for good. He'd promised to put her first, to look out for her, and dammit, that's what he was going to do.

Alabama just shook her head at him. She reached for the door handle and turned it. With one last look at him, she disappeared into the house.

Abe breathed in a sigh of relief. He'd been so scared she wouldn't forgive him, that she wouldn't love him anymore. He was thankful Alabama was so forgiving. He wasn't sure he'd be the same way if he was in her shoes, but he wasn't looking a gift horse in the mouth.

He turned to head back to his car and his bed for the night. He had a "wooing" to plan. He couldn't wait.

Chapter Twenty-One

THE NEXT FEW weeks went by fairly quickly. Christopher had been true to his word and had been doing his best to woo Alabama. He'd come over to the house at least twice a week to spend time with her and Caroline and Matthew, and they'd also spent almost every weekend together. He'd even encouraged her to spend time with his mom and sisters. The Saturday they'd gone shopping was one of the most fun times Alabama had ever had.

His family was hysterical. They'd been horrified at what had happened to her. She appreciated they hadn't defended what Christopher had done; in fact, they'd all cussed him out. Alicia even took her phone out to call him and tell him what an ass he'd been.

Luckily Alabama was able to calm her down. They'd talked through everything that had happened over lunch. There were still swear words thrown out, but there were also tears. Alabama hadn't realized how much she needed to be able to talk through what happened with someone that wasn't directly involved.

The three Powers ladies had commiserated with her and supported her. After their initial shock, they'd also supported Christopher. They didn't tell Alabama anything she didn't already know, but they'd told stories about Christopher when he was little. Alabama got a better idea of how he'd made himself into the man he was today, and how much the actions of his father had affected him.

Christopher came over that night and they'd had another long talk. Alabama told him all about how his family had reacted and while he winced only once, all he said was, "I'm glad you were able to talk to them, sweet."

Alabama had just started working again. She didn't go back to Wolfe's, and none of her friends blamed her. Greg and Stacey had come to see her to apologize and beg her to come back, but Alabama knew she wouldn't be able to. They'd let her down. They'd believed Adelaide and Joni over her, without asking any questions.

Christopher's commander had given her a reference and used his contacts to get her a cleaning job with a local office building. It held several different businesses. The best thing about the job was that she didn't have to work evenings anymore. While she preferred cleaning when others weren't around, no one really spoke to her as she went about her cleaning duties.

She'd been embarrassed to tell Christopher, after all she was only a janitor, but when he'd heard, he was thrilled for her. He told her there was no shame in what she did for a living. She was still a bit embarrassed, after all he had such a larger-than-life job and she didn't, but she changed the subject when he'd tried to talk to her about it again.

Alabama's life was settling down. She had good friends for the first time in her life, and she loved hanging out with Christopher and his teammates. She'd gotten to a point where she was ready to get back to where they'd been before, but she had no idea how to get there with him. It wasn't as if she could come out and say, "Hey, I'm ready to sleep with you again."

ABE WAITED OUTSIDE Wolf's house. He'd worked really hard to get Alabama to trust him again. It seemed as if he was making progress, but he didn't want to rush her.

Alabama opened the door and his breath caught in his throat. Damn, she was so beautiful. She wasn't wearing anything overtly sexy. In fact, he knew she'd probably be embarrassed if he told her how hot she actually looked.

She was wearing a pair of shorts that came down to her knees, and her usual V-neck T-shirt, today it was pink, and a pair of flip flops with a giant pink flower on them. Her toes were painted a bright pink as well. Obviously she liked the color and had gone all out to accessorize on her shopping trip with his sisters and mom.

"Hey, sweet, you look beautiful."

As if on cue, she blushed.

Alabama didn't say anything, but held the door open for him to enter the house. Abe had never heard her say so much to anyone at one time as she had to him when she'd explained how she'd been affected by his actions when they'd been at lunch. She'd never be comfortable speaking in public or large crowds, but Abe knew she was getting more and more relaxed when speaking with him or to others when he was around.

Abe leaned in and kissed her on the side of her mouth when he got close enough. He took the door out of her hands and shut it.

"Where's Wolf and Caroline?" Abe knew they weren't going to be there, Wolf had given him a head's up that day at work.

"They went out to dinner and then they were going to go to a movie afterward."

Abe put his hand on the small of her back and steered her toward the kitchen. "So, it's just you and me tonight huh?"

Alabama blushed again. Jesus, she had to stop. It wasn't as if he'd announced he was going to throw her on the sofa and make love to her all night long…not that she'd complain. They'd already explored and tasted every inch of each other's bodies, it shouldn't be embarrassing to think about making love with him. Alabama simply nodded, affirming they'd be alone most of the night.

Entering the kitchen, Abe saw a pot of water boiling on the stove. He chuckled. "What're you making me tonight?" It was a running joke between the two of them now. She'd never be a gourmet cook, but she could make a mean pasta dish.

"Just spaghetti."

"Aw, sweet, it's never 'just' spaghetti. I love your spaghetti."

Alabama rolled her eyes at him. He laughed and put his arms around her waist while she stirred the noodles.

"Don't you know? I don't care what you make us to eat. I'm just happy to spend time with you. Anything you make, I'll eat with a smile on my face."

Alabama smiled weakly up at him. She knew she wasn't the best cook, but she'd kept herself alive this long, they wouldn't starve.

They talked while the sauce bubbled on the stove and they chopped vegetables for the salad. When the noodles were ready, he drained them while Alabama got the dressing out of the fridge. They served themselves and set their plates on the small table in the kitchen. They ate the simple, yet delicious, meal in comfortable silence.

After putting the dishes in the dishwasher they sat on the sofa. Alabama wanted to bring Christopher downstairs to her little apartment, but she had no idea how to bring it up, so she stayed silent.

Abe put in a movie and they watched it for about an hour. Just as Bruce Willis was about to blow something else up, the doorbell rang. Alabama looked at Christopher in surprise.

Seeing that Alabama wasn't expecting anyone, Abe told her, "Stay put sweet, I'll see who it is."

Abe opened the front door and saw two police officers standing there. They were slightly overweight and had their hands on their belts, as if ready to defend themselves. Abe hadn't heard Alabama come up behind him, but he heard her indrawn breath.

"Oh my God," she exclaimed softly, "Is it Matthew and Caroline? Are they all right?"

Abe had been thinking the same thing, but the brown haired cop quickly reassured them.

"No, no, it's nothing like that. Are you Alabama Ford Smith?" He peered at Alabama suspiciously.

Abe put his hand around Alabama's waist and pulled her to his side and partially behind him as she said simply and cautiously, "Yes."

"You'll need to come with us ma'am. We have some questions we need to ask you at the station."

Abe felt Alabama go stock still. He could feel the tension course throughout her body. Oh hell no. "What's this about?" He demanded, not so gently.

"There's been a reported burglary at the building down on Main and Third. We have some information that Ms. Smith works there and has been arrested in the past for theft. We only need to ask her some questions."

"Fuck no." The answer was swift and growled with menace.

Alabama looked up at Christopher. She couldn't control her breathing. Her breaths were coming out fast and hard. It was happening again. Oh God…

"You have no idea what you're talking about. If you'd read those reports a bit more carefully you'd have known she was falsely accused. You'd have known she has one of the best lawyers this city has ever seen."

"Sir, all we want to do is ask her some questions." The shorter of the two police officers was getting visibly irritated.

"She didn't do it."

"You don't know what it is…"

Abe interrupted the man. "No, because whatever you think she did, you're wrong. She didn't do it. She didn't steal dick."

Alabama kept her eyes on Christopher's face. She couldn't look at the officers. She was shaking hard enough as it was—she couldn't look at their uniforms, it would bring back too many memories. Listening to Christopher defend her from…hell, she had no idea what it was he was defending her from, but it was as if a warm blanket straight from the dryer had been wrapped around her. Christopher was defending her. He was pissed on her behalf. This was what she'd expected all those weeks ago. *This* was the man she'd fallen in love with.

"You want to ask her questions? Fine, we'll come down in the morning, with her lawyer. And, if you don't have probable cause to question her, you'll be wishing you hadn't bothered us."

"We can't just..."

Abe wasn't letting them get a full sentence out. "You can, and you will. Is she under arrest?" At the negative response, he continued, "Then, we'll see you in the morning at the precinct."

Abe slammed the door in the officer's faces and turned Alabama into his body. He pulled her until she was belly to belly with him. He could feel her trembling. It infuriated him. How dare they come here and scare her. How *dare* they assume she had anything to do with whatever was missing. Abe was pissed, but he tried to stay calm. He needed to stay calm for Alabama.

The warmth of Christopher's body felt so good. He'd wrapped his arms around her—one arm around her waist pulling her into his body and the other against her back. He placed his hand on the back of her head, pushing it into his chest. Without moving, she mumbled, "Can you even do that?"

"Hell yes. And I just did. They had no evidence. They had no reason to come over here this late at night. They only wanted to scare you. Assholes."

They stood there for a few more minutes, then Abe said through clenched teeth. He was nowhere near calm. "I gotta call Wolf and the rest of the team, sweet. Let me tell them what's going on, they'll take care of it and will get your lawyer to meet us at the station tomorrow."

"You didn't let them take me."

"What, sweet? I couldn't hear you." Abe leaned his head down until his ear was near her mouth.

"You didn't let them take me," Alabama repeated.

Abe took the hand that had been on her head and put it under her chin. He tipped her head up until she had no choice but to look him in the eyes. "I told you I'd never doubt you again. I love you. I'll protect you with my life if I have to. You don't *ever* have to deal with anything by yourself ever again."

Alabama's breath hitched. He *had* said that, but she hadn't believed it until right then. All she could do was nod. She stood on her tiptoes to brush her lips against his.

At the first touch of her lips Abe swooped in. The kiss wasn't sweet, it wasn't gentle. It was a claiming. Abe claimed his woman again. She was his and he wasn't letting her go.

Alabama let Christopher take the lead; she'd follow him wherever he wanted to take her. She was his.

ALABAMA SNUGGLED INTO Christopher's side. It'd been a long night. Christopher hadn't let go of Alabama throughout the evening. He'd kept her close to his side, touching her, soothing her, calming her. After the intense kiss they'd shared, he'd called Matthew. He and Caroline had rushed home and set up a sort of command post on their dining room table.

Soon the house was overflowing with testosterone. The entire team had banded together. It was the most amazing show of support Alabama had ever seen in her life. Personally, she thought it was a bit of overkill, especially since she'd spent the day with Matthew and Caroline and hadn't even been alone all day, so she had a pretty good alibi, but she'd never say anything to the men who were discussing their next steps.

Christopher had called her lawyer and she'd agreed to meet them at the station in the morning. She was going to call and see what had happened before they met up so they'd have a head's up as to what was going on.

Every one of the men had told her she had their support before they'd left. When Hunter had hugged her tight and told her if she ever wanted to leave Abe, he'd be right there ready to snatch her up, she finally lost it.

At the sight of her tears, Abe had almost gone ballistic. It wasn't until he realized she was crying tears of happiness at all the support she'd been shown, that he finally calmed down.

Now they were lying on her bed in the basement. He was wearing jeans and his button up shirt and she'd changed into the T-shirt of his she'd been sleeping in for the last few weeks. He didn't say a word about it, only smiled possessively when he'd seen her. Christopher was on his back with his arm around her and she was on her side. Her head was resting on his chest and one of her legs was thrown over one of his. She was surrounded by him, and she loved it.

"I love you."

Christopher's arm tightened around her. Alabama could feel the muscles in his bicep twitch on her back. It was the first time she'd said it outright to him since the day she'd been arrested.

"Sweet," his voice was tortured. "I don't deserve you. You're way too good for me, but I can't let you go. I won't."

"You don't have to, Christopher. I'm yours for as long as you want me."

He rolled toward her until she was on her back looking up into his eyes. They were intense. "I'll always want you. You're mine."

His head dipped and for the second time that night he kissed her with all the dominance he'd been holding back for the last few weeks.

Alabama's hands went to his head and clenched his hair as he ravaged her mouth. Finally he pulled back, just enough to look into her eyes.

"Don't worry about tomorrow, sweet. Trust me to take care of it, of you."

Alabama couldn't believe he'd stopped. She was ready for him to make love to her again. "I know you will…now shut up and kiss me."

She loved seeing the smile creep over his face.

"Whatever you want. Whatever you want."

Epilogue

CAROLINE AND ALABAMA sat on the couch and tried to pay attention to the movie that was playing. Neither was doing a very good job of it. Finally Caroline shut off the television.

"When were they supposed to land again?" Alabama was more than ready to see Christopher again.

The team had been called out on a mission to Mexico. They weren't able to tell them where exactly they were going or what they were doing, but both Caroline and Alabama knew whatever it was, it was dangerous.

Each mission had been easier and easier for Alabama to take, but she knew it'd never be *easy*. Every time Christopher walked out of the house, whether it was for a mission or for a simple trip to the grocery store, she worried.

Christopher had been steadfast in his support of her. He'd taken care of the "misunderstanding" the night they'd gotten back together. The police officers had even apologized for bothering her that night. Alabama knew Christopher was behind that, but he'd never admitted it.

Alabama had quit the cleaning job she'd had, with Christopher's urging and support, and decided to go back to school. She wasn't sure what she wanted to do, but for now she was taking general education classes. She had time to decide later. She hadn't wanted to not work, but Christopher had convinced her after one long night in bed, that she'd be better off concentrating solely on her studies.

She'd gotten closer to his friends and teammates, and she worried almost as much about them as she did about Christopher, almost.

Caroline watched as Alabama paced. Caroline missed Matthew just as much as Alabama missed Christopher, but she'd been with him longer, so she'd had more experience in the agony of waiting for him to return from a mission.

"They'll be home as soon as they can, Alabama."

"I know, I just miss him."

Finally after another hour passed, the women heard a truck in the driveway. They both raced to the front door and out into the yard.

Alabama had eyes only for Christopher. He met her in front of the truck and held her to him in a hard, possessive embrace. As usual, she burst into tears.

"Jesus, sweet. I'm fine. Wolf's fine. Everyone's fine."

"I know," Alabama said between sniffs, "I'm just so happy you're home. I missed you!"

Christopher picked her up, carrying her toward the door. Every time they came home from a mission Matthew invited them to stay in her old basement bedroom. They'd always agreed because driving to their townhouse seemed as if it would just take too long.

"I missed you too, sweet."

Alabama inhaled Christopher's scent as he carried her into the house. She didn't bother to look up at Caroline and Matthew; she knew they'd be doing the same thing she was.

As Christopher carried her down the basement stairs she quickly asked, knowing if she didn't, she'd be way too preoccupied to ask for the next few hours. "Everyone okay?"

Abe loved how she was always concerned for his teammates. They were like brothers to him and it showed just how sweet Alabama was that she always asked. "Yeah, everyone's okay. We got the girls out, they're gonna be okay."

"Girls?"

"Well, women. I'm not supposed to talk about it, but in nutshell this woman had been kidnapped a few days ago. We went in and found her easily, but there was another woman there too…she'd been there for a couple of months. Cookie stayed back in Texas with Benny and Dude to help her…acclimate."

"God, I love you, Christopher. You know that right?"

"I do, sweet. I love you right back."

"I'm proud of what you do. Those women are so lucky you and your team do what you do."

"It's missions like that that make our job easier. Even though it was tough, it's always nice to be able to save people." Abe stopped talking. Alabama was obviously done rehashing his mission. She was unbuttoning his shirt and kissing every inch of his chest as she bared it. He grinned to himself, he'd let her have her fun for a bit, he knew soon it'd be his turn.

He'd make contact with Cookie and check on the woman…later. Much later.

Protecting Fiona

SEAL of Protection
Book 3

By Susan Stoker

Acknowledgements

I think many times people think writing a book is done in isolation, when in reality it's done with the help and support of many people. I just want to acknowledge some of those people here, if you'll indulge me.

Patrick. My husband does a good job of leaving me alone when I'm writing and letting me just...write. Thank you for being my own military man.

Amy. Holy Hell, what would I do without you? You're my cheerleader, my "reader of 1 star reviews", my sounding board, my beta reader, and my friend. Thank you, woman. #youhavenoclue

My Facebook friends. Seriously. All I gotta say is, "I need some help," and I have so many people willing to jump right in and give me suggestions and get my brain working in the right direction. So thank you to all of you for being there for me online.

Michele. Thank you for letting me "steal" your baby's name for my book. The second you told me what you were naming him, I knew I had to use it. Hopefully one day Hunter will see this and know he was "famous" before he was even born!

Dad. I love that you aren't afraid to carry around romance novels with almost-naked men on the cover and hand them out as "tips" to waitresses, hairdressers, and anyone else you come across. Thanks for being one of my biggest fans.

Kathleen Murphy. Thank you for your assistance in my research. I love when friends of friends can connect.

Chris. My graphic designer. Every time someone sees something you've made, they tell me how lucky I am to have a great designer.

For someone who has *never* designed anything for a romance author, you've certainly entered a new realm, and knocked it out of the park.

Missy. My editor who makes me feel good by "wanting to throat punch" the mean women in my books even a week after she's read it! And who gives me such great advice. Thank you.

To my readers. Thank you for being interested in my world of hunky, military men. A world where the most important thing in their lives...are their women. If only we lived in a world where every man felt that way. I wish for you all to find your very own "Protector" and to live Happily Ever After.

Special Note from the Author

Protecting Fiona is a made-up story about two women who have been kidnapped and brought to a foreign country with the intent to sell them for sex. While this is a fictional account, this same thing happens all over the world day in and day out. Sex trafficking exists, and there are millions of women and children who have no hope of being rescued.

The International Labor Organization estimates that there are 4.5 million people trapped in forced sexual exploitation globally.

At least 20.9 million adults and children are bought and sold worldwide into commercial sexual servitude, forced labor and bonded labor

Women and girls make up 98% of victims of trafficking for sexual exploitation

An estimated 80% of all trafficked persons are used and abused as sexual slaves.

These statistics are *not* okay.

So while in this story, Julie and Fiona are rescued, there are millions of other women and children out there who are being sexually exploited and will never be rescued. Educate yourself and learn more. You might not feel as if you personally can do anything, but if everyone thought that, how would any of us live in a safe and lawful world?

No matter what country you live in, sexual exploitation and trafficking exists around us. It's a horrifying fact with even more horrifying statistics like I've listed above.

Below are a few websites where you can learn more information. No matter what country you live in, if you do an Internet search, you will find information about trafficking.

http://www.fbi.gov/about-us/investigate/civilrights/human_trafficking
http://www.dhs.gov/blue-campaign
http://ctip.defense.gov/
http://www.equalitynow.org
www.sharedhope.org
http://www.state.gov/j/tip/rls/tiprpt/2014/index.htm
http://www.polarisproject.org/

<u>Warning</u>: Recovering from a sexual assault is not something that happens overnight. It can take years of therapy and help and understanding from family and friends. While this book doesn't describe any kind of sexual assault or rape in detail, reading it might trigger some uncomfortable feelings and thoughts in some readers who have experienced sexual trauma.

Prologue

SIX MEN SAT around a table on the military plane studying a map of the Mexican countryside closely. They were called in for a special assignment. A Senator's daughter had been drugged and kidnapped while she was partying in Las Vegas with friends and hustled over the border before anyone knew she was missing. No ransom note had arrived and that meant the kidnappers were most likely sex traffickers. They wanted a pretty woman they could sell as a sex slave in the bowels of Mexico or beyond.

Wolf, Dude, Abe, Mozart, Benny, and Cookie were all members of the SEAL team that had been chosen to do some recon and see if they couldn't find out where the woman was taken…and bring her home.

The seventh unofficial member of the team, Tex, was in Virginia working his magic with his contacts and computer. In today's day and age, no one was completely off the map. Even terrorists and kidnappers used electronics to communicate with each other. The second they logged onto the Internet, or used a cell phone, Tex would find them.

"Benny, you and Dude will be in charge of extraction. Wait with the helicopter and be ready for the signal," Matthew "Wolf" Steel commanded.

The men nodded in agreement. Benny and Dude had the most experience in flying a helicopter and were the best choices to man the multi-million dollar aircraft. Wolf was the unofficial leader of their group. Every man respected the hell out of him and would follow him into Hell if he asked.

"Abe, you and I will head into the closest village and see what we can find out from the locals. Cookie, you and Mozart will need to check out both of the possible holding sites we've mapped out. This will have to be a 'divide and conquer' mission. We don't have the time to be a hundred percent sure where they're keeping the girl. If you find her, radio back to Benny and Dude, they'll report back to the rest of us and we can all meet up at the coordinates we discussed. Make sure you have the extra set of clothes her father sent, and travel light and fast. We can't afford to fuck this up, and not just because 'Daddy' is a Senator."

Everyone nodded solemnly. They didn't give a rat's ass about what the government or the Senator thought, it was all about the woman. If they didn't find her, and fast, she'd disappear, probably forever, and become just another horrifying statistic.

"Okay, we'll land in about twenty minutes. If I hear anything else from Tex, I'll radio it forward. Let's do this."

Every man nodded in agreement, but not much more was spoken. They were all focused on the upcoming mission.

Hunter "Cookie" Knox cracked his neck and went over in his head his role in the extraction. He was headed toward one of two possible camps where the woman could be. They'd gotten intel that the scumbags who'd usually holed up there were communicating with some known human traffickers. Unfortunately there was *another* group in the same area, one that ran drugs and was known for also selling the occasional woman. This group had also been active recently and the team was looking into them as well.

Mozart would take one group and Cookie would take the other. Cookie hoped like hell he'd find the woman. Orders were to snatch and grab her, but he wouldn't be opposed to taking some of the assholes out. Anyone who thought it was okay to kidnap and sell women deserved to die a slow painful death.

The SEAL team had been on too many rescue missions to count, so unfortunately, this was nothing new, but for some reason Cookie's skin felt too tight. He was way too wound up for this one. He couldn't wait to get boots on the ground and get the woman the hell out of dodge.

The plane started its decent, it was time.

Chapter One

COOKIE WALKED SILENTLY through the jungle, every now and then looking down at the GPS clipped to his LBV, Load Bearing Vest, to make sure he was still heading in the right direction. He could feel the sweat dripping from his forehead and he was constantly wiping it away as he continued ducking and dodging trees and obstacles in his path. Cookie was able to cover a good distance every hour, something he knew he wouldn't be able to do once Julie was with him…if Julie was with him.

Even though their intel told them that it was likely she was being held in one of the two camps, Cookie hoped like hell their information was correct. Sex trafficking wasn't anything that followed patterns. One time a group might keep a woman for weeks, another woman might be held for only hours. It depended on where, and who, she was headed for.

Even though Cookie was paying attention where he was placing his feet, he still found himself stumbling over roots and mud on the ground. The jungle wasn't anyplace anyone would ever take a pleasure hike, and Cookie knew the walk back to the extraction point with Julie wasn't going to be easy. Hell, it wasn't easy for him, and he was trained, and dressed, for it.

The Senator had given them clothes for his daughter, but even a long sleeve shirt and a pair of pants couldn't keep the mosquitos out of their eyes and the heat from permeating the very morrow of their bones as they walked back to the extraction point. Cookie knew he'd never take air conditioning for granted again.

He slowed his pace as he got close to his target. The camp was noisy and bustling. The men were consuming large quantities of alcohol and it was obvious they were celebrating something. Cookie kneeled down in the darkness the jungle provided and bided his time. He wanted to rush to the most likely building, sitting off to the side, but he made himself wait. He only had one chance to do this right, and Julie was counting on him to get her out of there. Cookie would wait until the right time. Then he'd make his move.

FIONA SAT IN the dark, eyes straining. She wasn't sleeping well, as usual, and had listened while her captors had partied the night away. They'd grown quiet an hour or so ago and she knew morning was on its way. Fiona had been thinking about how quiet it was, now that the men were most likely passed out, when she thought she heard something. She wasn't sure if it was her imagination or the drugs they'd been forcing on her, but she didn't think it was either. Fiona knew every creak and moan in her hellhole, and the sound she heard was out of the ordinary.

Julie, the other woman, was finally silent. She'd cried nonstop for two days. It wasn't as if Fiona was cold hearted, but Julie wouldn't listen to her and wouldn't be consoled. Fiona tried to remember back to when she was first brought here, but it was impossible. It was just too long ago. She thought it had been around three months, but she couldn't be sure. Fiona had tried to keep track, but she knew there were some days that she'd been out of it from the drugs her captors been forcing on her. Ninety days, one hundred days…whatever it was, it was a lifetime.

There. A small beam of light in the corner. Fiona knew it wasn't the guards, they weren't going to sneak around, and they certainly wouldn't just have a small flashlight. Who was it? What was it? Fiona was afraid to hope.

Fiona knew no one was coming for her. She didn't have any family back home, and her friends were more acquaintances than anything else. She knew how these things worked. When someone was kidnapped, the family would do whatever it took it get back their loved one…but in her case, she had no one. Fiona was at the mercy of the kidnappers, had been at their mercy for three long months, and no one was going to rescue her.

Her mind almost veered toward the hell she'd been through at the kidnappers' hands, but Fiona clamped it down. She couldn't go there. Didn't know if she'd ever be able to go there again. Her new mantra was to survive one day at a time, but even that little rebellion against her captors was on shaky ground. Fiona had slowly picked up some Spanish during her captivity, and the words she'd been able to translate, namely, drug, die, bitch, and dirt, weren't making her think happy thoughts. But Fiona would much rather face death head-on then suffer through whatever the men had in store for Julie. No contest.

COOKIE HAD BEEN dropped off five miles away by Dude and Benny in the chopper. The plan was to grab the woman, and set off back through the jungle. Cookie was prepared for anything, or so he thought. He half chuckled to himself. Hell, they *tried* to be prepared for anything, but as they usually found out Plan A usually didn't work, and Plan B typically became the new Plan A. Every now and then the team would have to come up with a Plan C on the fly when both the other plans became FUBAR, fucked up beyond all recognition.

Cookie stealthily made his way toward the ramshackle building at the edge of the camp. It was early in the morning, and pitch dark. He'd watched as the men in the camp drunk themselves into a stupor and staggered around the camp. Some fell in the dirt and their so-called buddies just left them there to sleep off the alcohol.

They'd been partying for a reason; these types of men didn't have money to waste on getting drunk every night. Cookie hoped like hell he was in the right place. They could be celebrating selling the woman he was here to find. He hoped he wasn't too late. If they'd already sold Julie, there was little chance the team would be able to get her back. She'd disappear, just as hundreds of women did every year.

Cookie turned his penlight on for just a moment so he could get his bearings. There was no noise coming from the small rectangular building. His intelligence said the woman could be here, and the men's actions outside seemed to confirm it. Mozart was about twenty clicks north of his location, checking out a second possible site. The twelve miles or so between them might as well have been a hundred. Mozart was too far away to provide backup, and the reverse was true as well.

If the building was empty, Cookie would fade away back into the jungle and meet back up with Wolf and Abe who were waiting in the closest town for the results of their investigations.

The woman that he'd come after, Julie, had been missing for five days. Five days of Hell. Five days too long in Cookie's opinion. Hell, *one* day was too long.

Cookie and his SEAL team brothers had seen all of this before. He'd never get used to the fact that humans were sold for sex slaves. It was so barbaric. Cookie thought about his teammates' women being in this type of situation and it made his skin crawl. Caroline and Alabama were two of the strongest women he knew. Caroline had saved Wolf's life twice. Cookie knew women were stronger, in general, than most men gave them credit for.

But this, being kidnapped and knowing you were to be sold into a life of abuse and sexual depravity never to be free again, that was something Cookie didn't know how anyone could survive with their sanity intact.

Julie was the daughter of a Senator, and probably one of the only reasons Cookie and his team were in Mexico. If it had been anyone else, any other less-rich, less-politically motivated father, the family would've had to try to work with the local police, or private investigators, and gotten nowhere. Cookie went back to his thought that no woman, no *human*, should have to go through what Julie what had inevitably gone through since she'd been kidnapped. Cookie figured she'd probably been raped repeatedly to try to scare her into submission. She was probably starved and scared out of her mind. Cookie knew Julie would most likely need years of counseling to help her become normal again...*if* he could find her and get her out of the jungle safely.

If Julie could walk, it'd make his job easier, but he was prepared to carry her if he needed to. Cookie knew she was a small woman, only about five feet two inches tall and weighing about a hundred and ten pounds. He figured she'd probably lost weight the week she'd been in captivity, so he knew he wouldn't have any issues carrying her through the jungle if he needed to.

The pack he normally carried on missions weighed about what Julie did, but Cookie had gone light for this trip. He carried only the bare necessities for their trek back through the thick trees. He wanted to be able to move quickly and silently, and that'd be easier if he had less weight to carry.

Cookie also had his first aid kit so he could help Julie in any medical way if she needed it, and she probably would. Human traffickers weren't known to be the nicest of people. The change of clothes he'd brought in her size would protect her from the insects and plants as they cut back through the jungle to the extraction point. He was carrying extra water and food rations for the two of them for a day or two as well.

Cookie moved silently to the building and shone his light briefly on the corner. Bingo. The boards were rotted here from the heat and wetness of the jungle. They'd be easier to remove. Cookie knew the kidnappers were in the other buildings, most of them passed out, but he wasn't taking any chances. He wanted to get Julie and get the hell out of there without anyone noticing. If luck was with him, he and Julie would be long gone before the kidnappers realized she'd escaped.

Cookie removed two boards, just enough for him to squeeze through, and eased himself into the room, not knowing what he'd find. He didn't want to just shine his light into the room because if it wasn't where Julie was being held, he could be in a rash of shit.

Fiona held her breath. She could hear whoever it was working on the wall in the corner. She'd thought many times that if she could only reach the walls she could escape out into the jungle…but since she was chained to the floor, she couldn't get anywhere near them. She watched as a man, Fiona assumed it was a man, eased himself into the room.

There was only the light coming in from the moonlight through the hole he'd made in the wall, but since Fiona's eyes were adjusted to the darkness, she could see surprisingly well. The man was big, and had a large pack on his back. He wore all black and was focused on Julie, who was lying on the floor on his side of the room. Since she was on the other side of the rectangular building, Fiona didn't think the man could see her through the inky blackness of the night.

Cookie tried to breathe through his nose. The smell in the room was putrid. It smelled like urine, sweat, blood, and fear. Some people would scoff at his saying he could smell fear, but Cookie had been in enough hell holes, and seen enough bad shit in his career, to know that fear had an odor. It wasn't something he could readily explain to someone else, but anyone who'd been in combat and had seen the things he had, would know immediately what he meant.

He'd been in a lot of bad places with his SEAL team, but this was one of the worst. Cookie hadn't thought the sex traffickers had the woman long enough for it to get this bad, but he supposed anything was possible. Everyone dealt with the shit that happened in their lives differently, and because Julie was from a rich, powerful family, Cookie supposed she didn't have the coping mechanisms other people did.

Cookie saw a shape on the floor that had to be Julie. His pulse shot up even higher than it already was. The adrenaline coursed through his body. He'd found her. Thank God.

"Julie," Cookie whispered, while briefly touching her shoulder.

The woman rolled over, looked up and took a huge intake of breath. Knowing what was coming, Cookie quickly put his hand over Julie's mouth to stifle her scream. He quickly tried to reassure her.

"My name is Cookie, I'm an American Navy SEAL. I'm here to take you home." His words were toneless and quiet. They barely penetrated the few inches from his mouth to her ears, but she heard them nonetheless.

Julie nodded frantically and started to cry. "Thank God," she whispered brokenly after Cookie had removed his hand from her mouth.

Cookie didn't waste any time trying to reassure her further, but instead got to work freeing her. He was pissed. Julie was attached to the floor by a short chain attached around her ankle. She had some freedom of movement, but not a lot. There was a bucket nearby, Cookie assumed for Julie to relieve herself in.

"Can you stand? Can you walk?" Cookie asked Julie, again in the toneless quiet voice he'd used before.

Julie nodded, but swayed when she stood up. Cookie dug in his pack and got out the black long sleeved shirt he'd brought for her. She was small, almost dainty, and fragile looking. Cookie helped Julie put each arm through the sleeves. He then took out the black cargo pants. Eying Julie's build, he thought they might actually be a bit big, but he hoped they'd do.

"Julie, take off your shorts and put these on, quickly." Cookie wasn't known as being a gentle man, and he couldn't help it if he sounded short. He knew time was against them, they had to get out of there and disappear into the jungle before the kidnappers started sobering up and came to haul Julie out of there and give her to her new owner.

"What?" Julie said huffily, "I couldn't possibly with you here…"

Cookie cut her off with a hand over her mouth again. "Look, do you want to get out of here or not? You can't walk out in that jungle with shorts on, just put the damn pants on."

Cookie half turned to give Julie as much privacy as he could. He didn't like the whiny tone of her voice, but tried to give her the benefit of the doubt. She was scared out of her mind. He could try harder to be pleasant. Cookie tried to imagine Caroline or Alabama in Julie's shoes. The thought made him soften his voice. "I'm sorry, I didn't mean to be so abrupt. Let me know when you're ready."

"Please, let's just go," was Julie's response. Cookie turned and saw that she'd put the pants on and was holding onto the waist with one hand. The pants fit, but barely. Cookie steadied her when she stumbled as she lurched toward the corner of the room where he'd entered. Julie's hand gripped his shirt into a ball as they headed for the exit.

As Cookie turned to leave the room, he took one last glance around the long room and stilled and narrowed his eyes. He thought he saw something at the other side. Was he seeing things? Cookie cocked his head and strained to listen. Were they about to be caught? Was it one of the men? Cookie gripped the knife at his waist and waited, every muscle ready to leap into action.

Chapter Two

FIONA WATCHED DISPASSIONATELY as the man who'd snuck into their prison helped Julie into a long-sleeved shirt. Fiona didn't move a muscle. It was obvious that the man had come for the slight woman and not for her. Even though Fiona hoped and prayed someone would find her, it hurt that he'd come for Julie and not her. She was a big girl; she'd survived everything they'd done to her so far, she'd survive this too.

All Fiona could do was look on helplessly. She wouldn't cry, she wouldn't beg. She thought about calling out to the man, but he was obviously trying to be quiet and last thing she wanted to do was alert the kidnappers of what was going on, that their latest slave was being rescued.

Fiona watched as the man turned away to give Julie some privacy to put on the pants he'd brought her. She couldn't hear what he'd said to her, his voice was pitched too low for it to carry across the room. Fiona hadn't known many men that were honorable, but it seemed that this soldier was one; at least he understood Julie might be embarrassed or traumatized about taking off her shorts in front of him after everything she'd been through.

She watched as the pair turned to leave through the now-missing boards in the corner. Fiona held her breath. She tried to tell herself it was a miracle that at least one of them would get out of this hellhole. Maybe Julie would tell someone about her once she was away from there and safe.

Just as the pair was about to leave, the man turned to take one last look around the room. Fiona watched as he went perfectly still, while seemingly looking right at her. She knew she hadn't made any noise. Had she? Had she unconsciously moved or done something to gain his attention? Had he seen her? How had he known she was there?

Cookie put his hand on Julie's arm and whispered, "Wait right here. I thought I saw something."

"Where are you going?" Julie screeched quietly and grabbed his arm desperately. "No, don't go over there....we have to go; please I want to go right now!"

Cookie put up his hand to silence her and pried her hand off his arm. "Quiet. Do you want everyone in camp coming in here to see why you're making so much noise?" At Julie's quick head shake, he continued. "Right. Now stay here for a second, I'll be right back."

Cookie slipped into the darkness toward the other side of the room. He thought he'd seen someone else in the room, his knife at the ready. If it was one of the bad guys, he'd have to take him out. He couldn't leave any witnesses as to what happened to Julie. As soon as he'd had the thought he dismissed it. It couldn't have been one of the kidnappers, he would've been confronted by now. Cookie was confused, if it was another prisoner why hadn't the person said anything? Was he seeing things? If it was another person, why hadn't Tex said anything about a second prisoner? Tex had been illegally monitoring the area with the highly sensitive government satellites, he should've known about a second person in the building with Julie.

Cookie and his team were always prepared for anything, but if it *was* another person, or God forbid, more than one person, this rescue just got one hundred percent more complicated. They hadn't counted on more than Julie, not even Plan B had accounted for more than one prisoner. Cookie tried to mentally calculate the provisions he had with him, along with the extraction procedures as he crept on silent feet to the other side of the long empty space. Everything would have to be altered depending on what he found.

Cookie moved silently along the wall toward where he thought he'd seen something. As he moved, the stench in the room got stronger. If there was someone else here, they'd been here a lot longer than Julie had been, based on the smell alone. He tried not to gag, to react, as he moved closer. Cookie stopped suddenly. Holy shit. It *was* another person, another prisoner. It was a woman.

She looked horrible. She was also chained to the floor, but she'd been chained by the neck instead of by the ankle, as Julie had been. She was sitting with her legs to the side on the floor, with one hand propping her up. She was covered in dirt and filth. He could see the whites of her eyes shining through the grime on her face. The light was almost nonexistent back here, but Cookie could see all too clearly the shape she was in.

She was wearing a raggedy T-shirt, cut off jean shorts that had seen better days, and there was a pair of flip flops sitting next to her on the floor. She sat there staring at him silently.

Fiona watched the man approach her. As she guessed, he was some sort of soldier. She suddenly had the horrible thought that maybe he wasn't here to rescue Julie, but instead to steal her from their captors to sell her himself. Fiona took a deep breath. No, she had to believe he was there to save Julie, not put her through more hell.

Fiona saw the man take her in in a single glance. She could only guess what she looked like. She knew she was filthy and smelled horrid. Her captors hadn't allowed her to shower and the only way to see to her needs was the bucket nearby, which hadn't been emptied in way too long.

They'd tortured her by shortening her chain and attaching it to her neck rather than her ankle so she didn't have much freedom of movement. Fiona only had enough room to stand up if she hunched over, and only enough to move two feet from one side to another. She was still wearing the same clothes they'd taken her in. She was disgusting, Fiona knew it. She hadn't worried about it before, rightfully thinking it helped keep her abuse to a minimum, but now...now she cared.

Fiona wasn't sure what to say to the man. She was embarrassed and desperately wanted to get out of there, but she knew that no one had paid for him to get *her* out, only the other woman. Maybe she could convince him to tell the government or the Army, or *someone*, that she was there so they could come back and get her. Fiona knew there was no way this man could take her with him too. It was okay; she tried to tell herself, really.

Cookie couldn't help but be shocked. And he wasn't easily shocked. The types of missions he and his team had been on had, for the most part, all been awful. While some had good outcomes, none were anything he ever wanted to re-live. This trumped them all.

The woman sat on the floor, surrounded by filth, chained to the floor, and just looked at him. Cookie couldn't believe she hadn't said anything the whole time he was there. He almost left without knowing she was there.

"Do you speak English? What's your name?" Cookie asked softly as he kneeled down next to her and reached for his knife.

"Fiona," she said softly, with no discernible accent.

American, Cookie thought to himself, *probably from the Midwest.*

"We've got to hurry, Fiona," he said to her distractedly. He said it as much to her as he did to himself. Cookie wasn't thinking much about her at the moment, his mind was preoccupied with coming up with a new plan on how to get both her and Julie out of the jungle unscathed. He had no clothes for this woman. They'd only planned on Julie. Cookie thought about what he had in his pack. He could give her the extra shirt he'd brought for himself, but he couldn't do anything about her shoes or her shorts. *Shit, this was going to be tough.*

In the midst of thinking through a new escape plan, Cookie also thought back to Julie's actions. She was going to let them walk out of the room without once saying anything about another person being held with her. Julie was going to let this woman, Fiona, die, or at least be put through more hell. Cookie had met some selfish people in his life, but he'd never thought that anyone could be as callous as Julie had just been. Cookie tried to concentrate back on Fiona and not think about Julie for a moment.

Fiona put out her hand to touch the man, then changed her mind and put it back in her lap. She was amazed the soldier was going to try to break her chain, but he really didn't have the time. They had to get out of there before they were discovered.

"It's okay, Sir," Fiona said as softly as she could. "I know you're here for her," she gestured toward Julie who was a dark blob on the other side of the room, impatiently waiting by the corner, "and don't have time for me, but if you could maybe tell the Army, or police, or *someone*, that I'm here when you get home, I'd appreciate it."

Cookie stilled and looked at the woman. Had he heard her right? "Pardon?" he asked before he could stop himself.

Fiona almost cried. He sounded mad. She didn't want to make him mad. She stuttered a bit in responding, and dropped her voice a bit more. Fiona was embarrassed for Julie to hear how pathetic she really was. "I-I-I don't have any money to hire you to get me away too, so if you could just tell someone when you leave…" she trailed off as the man continued to stare at her.

Finally he said in a clipped tone, "If you think I'm leaving you here, you're crazy."

As Fiona opened her mouth, he quietly shushed her and got to work on the chain around her neck.

Cookie was pissed. What the hell? Why would this woman think he'd leave her here? As much as having her along was going to be an inconvenience, it wasn't impossible. Nothing was impossible, every

SEAL had that pounded into them from day one of their training. Cookie couldn't carry both this woman and Julie, so he hoped one of them would be able to walk on their own. Fiona was painfully thin, but tall. As Cookie leaned toward her, he tried to breathe through his mouth. The stench was horrific, but he knew it would embarrass her if he made any mention of it, consciously or unconsciously.

"I'm sorry that I stink," Fiona told him softly, as if she could read his mind.

Cookie quietly shushed her again. He didn't know how else to respond. He couldn't deny that she stank, but he also didn't want to say that it didn't bother him. Cookie didn't have time to get into all the things he wanted to say to her and to ask her.

He concentrated harder on the chain. He knew time wasn't on their side. Finally Cookie said to her, "I can't get the metal collar off right now, but I can break the chain."

Fiona simply said, "Okay," as if the heavy metal collar around her neck was a beautiful gold delicate necklace instead of a torture device that had to be causing her pain.

When the chain finally fell free, Cookie eased it to the ground so it wouldn't clank loudly. He quickly turned back to his pack and dug deep until he came up with his extra shirt. It was long sleeved and black, just like the one he had on. He held it out to Fiona.

"I don't have any extra pants, but I do have a shirt, it'll be big on you but it'll help some. It's better than nothing."

Fiona nodded, inordinately pleased to have even that. "Thank you. Seriously, I…it'll be perfect."

Cookie continued speaking. "I don't have any shoes that will fit you or an extra pair of pants," he told her, voicing his worries out loud.

Fiona knew that walking through the jungle in shorts and flip flops was going to suck, which was probably the understatement of the century, but she certainly wasn't going to complain. The collar around her neck hurt. It had rubbed her skin raw and she thought she was bleeding, but again, Fiona would volunteer to wear the thing forever if it meant getting out of this hellhole.

"I can manage with just the shirt, thank you," Fiona told him honestly. At his look of disbelief that she misinterpreted, she straightened a bit and vowed, "I won't slow you down. I know you don't have to help me, but I swear I'll be quiet and I'll keep up. I'll do whatever you tell me to, I'll do anything to get out of here."

Cookie looked at Fiona in surprise. She kept impressing the hell out of him. She could've been hysterical, but she had a quiet dignity about her. He wished he could take the time to get to know more about what the hell had happened to her and how she'd gotten there, but he was quickly running out of time.

"That's good to hear, Fiona. Just talk to me as we go," Cookie told her. "I'll do what I can to help you, but if you don't tell me something is wrong or that you need assistance, I can't help you."

Fiona nodded and told him, "If I *do* slow you down too much, just go on without me. I'll either catch up or you can send someone back for me later."

Cookie just shook his head. "Not gonna happen, Fiona," he told her. "We're all getting out of here together."

Cookie stood and reached down to help Fiona up. He grasped her by the upper arm. He shouldn't have been surprised at how fragile she felt, but he was. Her quiet strength as she'd spoken had distracted him to her true physical state.

He felt her sway a bit, but she caught herself and straightened quickly. Cookie heard her take one quick inhale of breath and then quiet herself. He watched as Fiona hobbled awkwardly over to her flip-flops and slipped them onto her feet. She nodded awkwardly, because of the metal collar, as if to tell him she was ready to go.

Cookie grabbed her hand and squeezed, something he didn't have to do, and normally didn't do, but he wanted to show this woman that everything would be all right. There was just something about her that made him want to reassure her. The team had been taught when rescuing civilians from uncertain situations, not to touch them unnecessarily. They had no idea what they'd been through and what might be a trigger for them. The last thing the team needed was someone flipping out or reacting badly in the middle of a volatile situation.

Cookie had no idea if everything would work out all right, they were far from safe, she was far from being rescued, but he needed Fiona to know he was impressed with her. He wanted to convey so much with that one small hand squeeze. Cookie didn't know her story, but he would soon. He just had to get them all out of here in one piece.

Fiona fought back her tears. Jesus, she had to get it together. His small sign of approval and encouragement was all it took for her to want to fall into his arms and never let go. She couldn't do anything to distract or irritate this man. He was all that was standing between her and freedom.

She trudged behind him as quietly as she could as they crossed back to the hole in the corner of the room. Fiona flinched as her shoes made a *thunking* noise every time she took a step. Flip-flops weren't exactly quiet. She began to shuffle her feet instead, and the noise quieted.

Fiona watched as the soldier lay on his stomach and scooted out the hole first. He'd told both her and Julie to wait until he'd checked out the immediate area to make sure it was safe. Fiona took the moment to sit on the floor and rest. Jesus, even the short walk across the room tired her out. She had no idea how she was going to make it out in the jungle, but she'd do her best as long as she could.

As if reading her mind, Julie leaned over and grabbed Fiona's arm with a surprisingly strong grip and dug her nails in. "You better not screw this up for me. My daddy sent him for *me*, not for your sorry ass."

Fiona jerked her arm out of Julie's grip and scooted away from the other woman. She didn't say anything. She couldn't. Every vile word out of Julie's mouth was the truth and couldn't be refuted.

Cookie found the camp much the way it was when he'd entered the building the women had been held in. No one was up and about; they were all still sleeping or passed out. They didn't have much time before the sun started rising and they had to be long gone by then. Cookie headed back to the building and helped Julie slither out of the hole. He motioned for her to crouch by the wall, then he turned to help Fiona.

After both women were out, Cookie propped the boards back up in their original places. It wouldn't pass a close inspection, but hopefully the kidnappers weren't that smart and wouldn't have any idea how their prisoners escaped for a long while, giving them a nice head start.

"Come on, ladies, let's get out of here."

Cookie watched as both women nodded enthusiastically, and they all headed off into the unforgiving jungle.

Chapter Three

FIONA TRUDGED ALONG behind the soldier and Julie silently. She'd vowed not to do anything to hold them up, and she was doing her damnedest to keep that vow. It was still dark out, but the sun had just started to make its way above the horizon. Fiona could barely see Julie ahead of her. The other woman was holding on to the backpack of the soldier for dear life. Julie hadn't let Fiona get anywhere near the man, she'd claimed him for herself.

He was setting a good pace and Fiona could hear herself breathing too hard and too loud. She'd stopped swatting at the bugs on her legs a while back, it was useless and pointless. As soon as she swatted one away, two more would land. Fiona knew she'd have bug bites all over, but she'd be alive. Her feet also hurt. She'd stubbed her toes more than once on the logs and other things on the forest floor, but she wasn't going to complain. Fiona refused to bitch about it. She was out of that hellhole and she'd endure whatever she had to in order to get out of the country altogether.

Fiona *was* worried about the drug withdrawal she knew she was going into. Her body had started to shake and she knew it was only a matter of time before the craving for the drugs her captors forced into her system would get bad. She had no idea what the hell they were shooting into her body, but hated every second of it. The feeling of some mysterious cocktail being shoved into her veins was awful. She'd fought her captors like a wildcat every time they came in with another syringe. They'd just hold her down as they shoved the needle into her arm. Fiona had gone through withdrawal several times since they'd begun shooting her up, and her captors had just laughed at her. They'd watched her, waiting for her to beg for the drugs, but Fiona refused. No way in hell was she gonna beg the assholes to put more poison in her body. Finally they'd gotten bored of their little game, and injected the drug into her body regularly, not caring that she fought them every time.

Fiona had to take her mind off of the drugs and her body's reaction...she did what she had done while chained to the floor...she started concentrating on counting backward from one thousand slowly. If she concentrated on the numbers everything else seemed to be better. *One thousand, nine hundred ninety nine, nine hundred ninety eight.*

When Fiona had counted down to the three hundreds, the soldier came to a stop. The morning light was peeking through the trees now, heating the area up quickly.

"We'll stop here for a break," he told the women.

Julie immediately sat down. "Please," she said in a whiny voice. "I'm so hungry, do you have any food?"

Cookie looked at the woman sitting at his feet. Of course she was hungry, but he'd wanted to get them as far away from the compound before stopping. He remembered back to the hellhole he'd found Julie in and thought about how she'd wanted to leave Fiona behind. He tried to hold back his annoyance. Julie *had* been kidnapped for Christ's sake.

"Of course, Julie. I've got some granola bars."

Julie snapped, "That's it? Only granola bars? Do you know how long it's been since I've had any kind of *real* food?"

Cookie paused in the act of reaching into his pack and simply stared at the woman. He was getting pissed. Was she serious? Of course she was. He tried to stay civil.

"Yes, that's it. You'll be away from here soon enough and will be able to have a full meal then. It's not a good idea to eat a big meal right now when your stomach isn't used to it. You'll want to start out slowly and get used to regular sized meals again. I've also got some water. You both," he continued, including Fiona in his gesture, "will need to be sure to drink some."

Fiona's mouth watered uncontrollably. She stood off to the side of Julie and the man, leaning against a tree. She hadn't wanted to sit down, knowing she might not be able to get up again. Besides, as sore as she was, it felt great to stand fully upright, something she hadn't been able to do for a while. The chain around her neck had prevented it. Her back hurt from the walk and unaccustomed exercise, but it felt so good to be in the fresh air and upright, she wasn't about to complain about it.

And granola bars. God. It'd been so long since Fiona had eaten real food, just as Julie had said. Of course *her* "long time" was quite a bit longer than Julie's had been. Sometimes her captors would bring her some potato chips or something, but usually they'd just throw in a piece of hard bread. Fiona wasn't sure how long it had been since she'd had something that wasn't moldy or stale.

And fresh water? She was in heaven. It was amazing how the little things meant so much more when you didn't have them. She'd been drinking crappy water for longer than she remembered. At first she was sick as a dog from drinking whatever her captors brought to her, but eventually her body got used to the bacteria and whatever other organisms were swimming in the water. Her stomach still hurt sometimes from the parasites Fiona knew were probably coursing through her body, but at least she wasn't constantly sick anymore. Fiona wanted to jump the man, grab the food, and stuff it in her mouth as fast as she could. But she couldn't. She didn't know how much food he had brought, and she was extra baggage. Fiona figured she'd waited this long, she could wait a bit longer to get something to eat if there wasn't enough…maybe.

Cookie walked over to where Fiona was leaning against a tree. If he thought she looked bad before, in the light of the new day he could see she looked worse than he'd thought. He hadn't been able to see her very well in the building, and they'd been walking in the dark since then, but now that Cookie had the chance to really look at her, he wasn't sure how she was still standing.

The metal collar was partially hidden by his black T-shirt, but he could see Fiona's skin around the top of it was red and painful looking. Cookie couldn't see any blood, but it wouldn't surprise him if she was bleeding where the collar dug into her neck. Her legs were filthy, and he could see they were covered in welts from bug bites. Her feet in the flip-flops were absolutely disgusting, covered in mud and caked with black stuff up to her knees. She'd pulled back her hair at some point and secured it with a vine from one of the trees they'd passed. It was stringy and limp and badly in need of some soap. Her face and hands were also covered in dirt and she had rivulets of sweat running down her temples.

She was also very skinny, too skinny. She'd obviously not had enough to eat in far too long. Cookie held out a wet-wipe that he'd pulled from his bag and offered it to Fiona without a word.

Fiona looked at the man and at the wet wipe he held out. She wanted to snatch it up and revel in the cleanness of it, but she hesitated.

Cookie saw her hesitation and said softly, misunderstanding her reticence. "I know it's not much, but until we can get further away, we can't risk a full bath." Fiona nodded. It was silly, but she didn't want to be partially clean. It'd just bring home to her how awful the rest of her felt and smelled if she cleaned just a part of her.

As if he could read her mind, the gorgeous man in front of her said, "At least your hands, Fiona. Then you can eat without worrying about germs."

Fiona laughed without humor. "I don't think I have to worry

about germs. I don't want to take your last one," she told him being honest.

"I have plenty," Cookie told her, still holding out the cloth.

Fiona finally reached out for the wet wipe slowly, embarrassed at how badly her hands were shaking. She tried to smile at the man, hoping he wouldn't notice. Of course he did.

"Are you okay?" Cookie said softly, narrowing his eyes, "Your hands are shaking."

Fiona concentrated on rubbing her hands and wouldn't look him in the eye as she tried to scrub three months of crud from her hands. "I'm good. I'm just really ready to get out of here."

Cookie watched the woman in front of him. Holy Hell. Where did she get her strength from? He knew of a lot of men that could endure great pain and had awesome endurance. He'd seen it time and time again with his own teammates. But standing there, watching this woman nonchalantly try clean her hands and ignore her hunger and the fact she'd just escaped after being held captive for who knew how long... Cookie thought she had to be one of the most mentally strong women he'd ever met, and that included Wolf's woman, Caroline.

Cookie almost forgot he'd brought her a granola bar, but finally remembered. "When you're done, be sure to give me back the wipe. We don't want to leave any sign we've been here." He watched Fiona nod, still not looking at him. "Then you can eat your granola bar and we can be on our way."

Cookie watched as she did finally look up at that, not at him, but at the food he held out toward her. Fiona's eyes were locked on the food in his hand as if she blinked, it would disappear. He could almost see her salivating. The muscle in her jaw ticked as she ground her teeth together and Cookie could see her swallow several times. She might outwardly act like it didn't matter if she ate anything or not, but he could see in her eyes how desperate she was for the little piece of food he held out to her. Her breathing had increased and he could almost see her heart beating in her chest. She swallowed twice more, struggling with herself.

Fiona wanted that granola bar more than she'd ever wanted anything before, well maybe not more than getting out of this jungle. She dropped her eyes and shrugged, trying to look disinterested. She looked back down at her hands, now absently rubbing them, and told him, "It's okay, I'm not hungry, you can save it for later."

Cookie barely kept his mouth from dropping open. The woman was skin and bones, he knew she was hungry, starving in fact, and she was refusing the food? What the hell?

"Fiona, you need the strength to continue. You need to eat."

Just as Fiona opened her mouth to respond, Julie interrupted. "I'll eat it if she doesn't want it."

Fiona swallowed hard and tried not to cry. Her stomach rebelled at the thought of giving the granola bar away, but she controlled herself and forced herself to whisper to Cookie, "Julie can have it. I'll just have some water."

Uh, no. Cookie took Fiona by the arm and led her a bit away, saying sternly over his shoulder to Julie, "We'll be right back, stay put."

"What is *up* with you?" Cookie asked Fiona with little patience in his voice. He didn't have time for this. This was why he didn't have a steady girlfriend. He'd never understand the games women played if he lived to be a hundred. "I have to get you both to the extraction point. I need you to walk, I can't carry you *and* her at the same time," Cookie scolded bluntly. "I can only carry one of you at a time."

"You won't need to carry me. I told you I won't slow you down. I know I'm extra baggage you didn't expect. I won't get in your way, I won't slow you down and I won't eat the food so that there isn't enough. You only planned for two, you didn't plan for me."

Cookie calmed down. So that was it. She wasn't trying to play him in any way, she wasn't playing games, she was trying to fly under his radar. He didn't want to burst her bubble, but it wasn't working.

"Look," Cookie tried to reassure Fiona, putting a hand on her shoulder briefly, "it's not that far to the extraction point. I have plenty of food for us all, even though I didn't expect you. Eating one granola bar will not deplete my resources. I was going to wait to tell you both this at the same time, but I obviously need to let you know now. I'm part of a Navy SEAL team that was dropped here to get Julie out. My teammates are nearby. We'll meet at the extraction point and get the hell out of here. No more talk about being 'extra' okay? Now, please, you need the energy and the calories, Fiona. Take it."

Fiona didn't look like she believed him, either about the help coming or about the amount of food he had for them, but she was literally starving. Cookie almost chuckled at the obvious indecision on her face, but he saw the moment she made her decision.

Fiona couldn't make herself reach out for the granola bar when he again held out it out to her, but she knew she needed it so she'd be able to continue. She looked up at the man, not knowing how her eyes pleaded with him to take the decision out of her hands.

Cookie reached out and gently took one of her shaking hands and held on when Fiona would've jerked it back. He waited until she looked up at him. "I swear to you, Fiona, you are *not* extra baggage. Yes, we were sent here for Julie, but I would've come by myself if I had known you were there. I would have come for *you*."

Fiona just stared at him, willing her tears away. After not hearing a kind word in so long, his words felt like balm to her blistered soul. He'd never know how much what he'd just said meant to her.

Cookie wanted to say more. He wanted to say that he admired her, that he was amazed by her, but he knew it wasn't the time or the place. He dropped his hand and Fiona was left holding the granola bar. Cookie watched as she tried to open the snack. She fumbled with the thick plastic and couldn't grip it hard enough to rip it open. Cookie took it and tore it open for her, then handing it back to her without the wrapper.

Fiona took a small bite and closed her eyes. It was the best thing she'd ever eaten, *ever*. She tried to savor the flavors and not chew too fast. She finally finished the first bite, swallowed, and opened her eyes again to take another small bite and met the man's eyes. Fiona turned away in embarrassment. God, she was such a dork. She should just eat the stupid thing and be done with it, but it'd been so long, she wanted to savor the granola as long as she could.

Cookie swallowed his anger. He was furious. Not at Fiona, but at the creeps who'd held her for so long. The pleasure on her face from that one small bite hit him hard. He'd never been so hungry that one bite of food was total bliss. Of course during SEAL training and BUD/S, he and his buddies had *thought* they were going to die of hunger, but from the look on Fiona's face just now, he knew they hadn't even been close.

He turned away to give Fiona some privacy and went back over to where he'd left Julie resting. Cookie knew he sounded harsher than he wanted when he told the women a little while later that it was time to continue on. Julie groaned and whined about how much she hurt, but she got up, grabbed onto his pack, and they were ready to go again.

Chapter Four

FIONA KEPT QUIET as they walked. She concentrated on making the granola bar last as long as she could. She took tiny bites and counted every chew she made. It not only made the food last longer, but it took her mind off of how horrible she felt.

Her stomach hurt, but Fiona knew she had to keep eating something. It had been empty for so long, it actually physically hurt to eat. The water the soldier had given her was the best she'd ever had. She watched as Julie gulped hers down, but Fiona savored hers. It wasn't cold, not even close, and it wasn't designer, but it was clean, and that was a huge step up from what she had been drinking. Fiona didn't feel any grit in her mouth after drinking it and while it had a slightly metallic taste from whatever cleansing tablet the soldier used to make sure it was clean and healthy, it still tasted awesome.

It was easier for Fiona to take her time eating the granola bar when Julie and the man weren't watching her every move. Fiona had no idea what his name was, he hadn't told them. She desperately wanted to call him something other than "the man" or "the soldier" in her head, but she thought it'd be rude to outright ask him. Fiona suddenly had a thought. If he was a Navy SEAL she probably shouldn't even be calling him "soldier." Didn't they call themselves "sailors," or was it "seamen"? Damn. Fiona's head hurt. If he wanted to let them know what his name was, he'd tell them. Maybe he wasn't even allowed to tell them. Maybe it was some top secret thing that SEALs weren't allowed to tell the people they rescued who they were.

Fiona knew her brain was flitting from one subject to the other with no rhyme or reason, but she couldn't help it. She was hanging onto her sanity by a thread. All she wanted to do was drop to the ground and curl into a little ball, close her eyes, wiggle her nose, and find herself back in her apartment in El Paso...but she couldn't. Of course she couldn't. Fiona had sworn to the soldier that she wouldn't be any trouble. She could hang on for a bit longer...maybe.

Her hands still shook, and Fiona's body's craving for whatever drugs she'd been given was still there, but as long as she could concentrate on something other than having more of the toxic cocktail injected into her body, she could stave off the drug withdrawal reaction just a bit longer. Fiona didn't want the man to know what was happening. He'd certainly leave her behind then. He had to get Julie out of there and back to the States. Or maybe he'd decide they shouldn't continue on if she just stopped on the trail, and that wasn't acceptable. Fiona wanted out of this jungle. She could hold on just a little bit more. It wasn't that far until they'd get to where he said someone would come and pick them up.

They'd been walking for what seemed like a long time, but after a while the man stopped and signaled for she and Julie to crouch down in a clump of trees. Fiona sensed something was wrong. She watched the soldier closely. He hadn't said anything, but he looked tense. He was crouched down beside them and there was a cleared section of the forest just beyond the trees. It wasn't quiet, there were too many animal noises for it to be called silent in the forest, but Fiona still thought it was eerie...obviously the soldier did too.

He kept looking at his watch and up at the sky. Fiona figured their transportation was late, or wasn't coming. She absently scratched a bite on her leg with shaking fingers. Her withdrawal symptoms were getting worse. If they didn't get out of here, he was going to notice. Fiona didn't know what he'd do. Leave her? Be disgusted? Get pissed at her? She couldn't risk telling him. She'd just have to ride it through, just like everything else she'd gone through.

"What are we waiting for?" Julie whined softly. "My butt hurts and I want to go home."

Cookie sighed. Shit. When things went bad, they did it in grand style.

He turned toward the women. Julie had crocodile tears running down her face and Fiona just stared at him as if she knew he was going to say something was wrong.

"Change of plans," he said bluntly, making his decision. "The helicopter didn't show and I can't get through to my teammates. We have to move to the back-up extraction point."

Cookie knew some people would assume the team was just running late, but SEALs didn't "run late." Something was wrong and it was time to move to the backup plan they'd rehearsed before the mission started. Cookie deliberately didn't tell the women where the backup extraction point was, but Julie wasn't having any of his vague explanations.

"But where is it? How much further do we have to go? I thought we were going to be picked up here."

Julie's voice was whiney and it grated on Cookie's last nerve. He held on to his temper by the skin of his teeth. He was used to having his team with him as a buffer. Anytime a rescued person became too much, they'd take turns with the person. He missed his team. Cookie always preferred working with his friends than by himself. It was how the SEALs normally operated and this mission was making it clear to Cookie, once again, why. He was having a hard time dealing with Julie.

He sighed and scrubbed his face with one of his hands. "It's a ways away, but we don't have to get there today. We have a few days…"

Cookie was interrupted by Julie. "A few days?" she screeched too loudly for the quiet jungle. "What the hell are you talking about? I thought you were here to rescue me, we need to get out of mmph..."

Cookie moved quickly for a man with a huge pack on his back. His hand was over Julie's mouth before the last syllable came out.

"Shhhhh," he ordered furiously. "The men who kidnapped you could be anywhere. Besides them, this jungle is crawling with drug runners and other men we definitely don't want to run into. We aren't safe here. You need to remember that and keep it down." Cookie watched as Julie nodded fearfully, her eyes wide.

Fiona could see the solider was upset. The entire rescue had been full of surprises, and not good ones. The least of which was her presence, and now apparently their ride hadn't arrived. She wanted to reassure the man, but wasn't sure what to say, so she kept silent.

Cookie slowly removed his hand from Julie's mouth. "Here's the plan. We'll walk south toward the river, then double back again and head west. They'll figure that we'll follow the river, so we'll do the opposite. Just stay close to me and you'll be fine," he said to Julie, knowing he didn't have to tell Fiona to stick close. He knew she'd do it or die trying.

Cookie glanced at Fiona. She hadn't taken her eyes off of him and something eased inside him with her calm acceptance of the situation. At least he wouldn't have two hysterical women to deal with. He gave Fiona what he hoped was a reassuring nod and said, "Let's go."

Cookie had no idea where Mozart was, he couldn't reach him on the satellite radio and obviously something had gone wrong with the helicopter, otherwise Dude and Benny would've been there by now. It could be that they had to pick Mozart up because he ran into trouble. Whatever the reason was, Cookie didn't waste time dwelling on it. The team had made the alternate arrangements for pick up for just this reason. Sometimes things just didn't go as planned and they'd have to adjust their plans.

The trio headed back into the jungle. They had a long way to go before they were safe.

Julie had finally ceased complaining about an hour before they stopped for the night. Cookie figured she had the right to be tired, but they were all in the same boat…actually they weren't. He glanced at Fiona. He hadn't heard her say anything for a while. She'd kept quiet and had kept up with them, as she'd promised. He could only wish Julie had the same inner fortitude as Fiona did.

Cookie didn't know how long Fiona had been in captivity, but he was certain it was a hell of a lot longer than Julie had been. He knew something was up with her, but he hadn't had the time to figure it out…until now.

They'd stopped and Julie had immediately sat on the ground and brought her knees up to her chest and clasped her hands around them. She laid her head on her knees and hadn't moved as he set up their make-shift camp for the night. It wasn't much; they couldn't afford to light a fire, possibly alerting anyone lurking in the dark jungle where they were. Cookie recalled the short conversation he'd had with Fiona as they'd settled in. She'd asked if she could help him in any way. He'd thanked her, but told her honestly that she'd just slow him down. She hadn't pouted or sulked; she'd just nodded, as if she'd expected his response, and sat against a nearby tree, out of his way.

He'd talk to her now that they were stopped for the night. It hadn't been a big deal to set up three lean-tos instead of the two that he'd planned. Supplies were plentiful in the jungle, leaves and sticks. Cookie was traveling light and didn't have any tents. He hadn't thought he'd need them in the first place, but even if he'd planned on spending several nights in the jungle, he preferred to keep his pack as light as possible, and tents would've added quite a bit of weight. Cookie had handed out another granola bar to each of the women, and had heated up two Meals Ready to Eat. They'd all split the food, with Fiona only eating a little bit, claiming her stomach hurt from the heavy food that she wasn't used to, and now both women were resting.

Cookie looked over at Fiona now. She was still propped up by the tree with her arms around her legs. Her head was resting on her knees and her eyes were closed. She was in much the same position as Julie had been, but somehow she looked more vulnerable than Julie had.

Cookie thought again as to what was "off" about Fiona. Was it her feet? They were pretty beat up. Had she been hurt by the branches and shit they'd walked through? She wasn't wearing pants. Maybe the men had hurt her last night before he'd gotten there. Shit, she had to have been raped and was probably scared to be around him.

That last thought made Cookie visibly flinch and feel physically sick. He'd been around rape victims before, but for some reason this time was different. Maybe it was because he was the only one around. Maybe it was because Fiona was trying so hard to be brave. Whatever it was, all Cookie knew was that something inside him completely rebelled at the thought of her being violated that way.

Unfortunately, they had about ten more miles to walk before they'd get to the second extraction point. Ten fucking miles. They had two more days to get there, which meant two more days of hard walking. If someone had told him he'd have to have two kidnapped women hike over ten miles through the Mexican jungle, he'd have told them they were crazy. But here they were. Cookie wasn't sure either woman would make it, and that worried him.

Julie was the stronger of the two, but she was soft. She wasn't used to the exercise and she complained every step of the way. It was obvious in her "real" life, anytime something was "hard," she was allowed to quit. Not able to keep the mean thought out of his head, Cookie wasn't sure *he'd* make it another two days if he had to listen to Julie's incessant complaints the entire time.

He thought Fiona should be able to make it, but he wasn't positive. If she'd been at one hundred percent, Cookie had no doubt she would've made the ten mile hike look easy. Hell, she probably could've done it in a day. But she *wasn't* a hundred percent. Hell, she probably wasn't even at fifty percent. She'd been captive a hell of a lot longer than Julie, and she didn't look good. But she hadn't given up. She'd soldiered on all day without one word of complaint. Cookie was fucking impressed.

The flip flops Fiona was wearing worried him. Fuck, who was he kidding, everything about her worried Cookie. Her lack of long pants, the collar around her neck, her shaking hands, her dehydration, her obvious hunger...Cookie needed to find out what was going on with her tonight, so he could make better decisions for all of them.

Once Julie was settled for the night, Cookie walked over to where Fiona was sitting. She was still resting against the tree silently. If Cookie didn't see her back lightly moving up and down he would've been afraid she was dead. As he walked up to her she opened her eyes, but didn't otherwise move. Cookie sat down beside her.

"How are you holding up?" Cookie asked quietly.

"I'm fine," Fiona told him. "I won't slow you down."

Cookie nodded and told her, "I know, you've done great so far." He paused, then continued. "I don't think I've introduced myself to you yet. I'm Cookie." He didn't bother reaching out his hand for her to shake. They'd gone beyond the social niceties.

"Cookie?" Fiona stared at the handsome man sitting next to her trying to make small talk. She felt like crying. He was trying to make her feel normal, and she appreciated it more than she could say.

"Yeah, everyone on my team has a nickname. There's Dude, Mozart, Wolf, Abe, Benny, and me...Cookie."

"Are you going to tell me why you're called Cookie?"

"Are you gonna laugh if I do?"

Fiona loved the easy-going banter. Hell, just hearing someone talk to her in English felt awesome. "Probably. Especially since you seem to be reluctant to tell me."

Cookie chuckled. He knew it was inappropriate, but he was enjoying the hell out of this conversation, especially after the tension and complaining from Julie all day. He'd obviously taken too long to respond because Fiona continued talking.

"Are you going to make me guess?"

"You'd never guess, Fee."

Fiona jerked her head off her knees to look at him. What had he called her?

"What? You think you *can* guess?" Cookie had noticed her reaction, and correctly guessed it was in a result of him calling her "Fee." He didn't know where it came from, but it sounded right in his head. She looked like a "Fee."

"Uh, okay, your mom sent you cookies every week while you were in basic training?"

"I went to boot camp, not basic. And good guess, but no. Strike one." Cookie watched as Fiona's eyes narrowed. She obviously had a competitive spirit. He'd have to remember that and use it to keep her going later if he had to.

"When you were little, you ate too many cookies one Christmas and puked your guts out?"

A low surprised laugh escaped from between Cookie's lips before he could keep it back. "Wow, I think I'm hurt. Nope, that's not it either. One more guess left."

Fiona's whole body hurt, she was exhausted and thirstier than she could ever remember being, but for some reason she was having fun. This man had surprised her. She thought he'd be all business and gruff, but she liked this side of him. Let's see…why would someone have the nickname Cookie? Fiona decided to really mess with him. What the hell, she had nothing to lose.

"You were a virgin when you joined the Navy and after *boot camp* your buddies took you out on the town and paid an eighty year old whore named Cookie to deflower you."

Cookie started laughing, quietly, and couldn't stop. It was several moments before he could speak.

"Jesus, Fee, I'll have to remember not to piss you off in the future. First, I was *deflowered* when I was fourteen by my seventeen-year-old date to the Homecoming Dance. So, your last guess is also wrong. Although you're much more creative than what the reason for my nickname really is. I was the last member to join the team. Typically newbies are called nuggets, FNGs, or cookies. Cookie stuck."

They sat there for a moment just looking at each other.

Not knowing what a "FNG" was, Fiona decided to let it go. It didn't really matter anyway. "Do you have a real name?" Fiona didn't know why she wanted to know, but she did.

"Hunter. Hunter Knox."

"Are you serious?"

"Dead. Why?"

Fiona couldn't believe that was really his name. "Because it's the kind of name a stripper or superhero would have." She immediately blushed. Oh crap. Had she really just said that out loud? Jesus, she was *such* a dork.

"I think I'll take that as a compliment, Fee, but I prefer to strip for a party of one."

"Please, just ignore me. I don't know what I'm saying. Let me try again." Fiona looked up. She was embarrassed, but determined to say it. "It's nice to meet you, Hunter. No, it's fucking *awesome* to meet you. I've never been so glad to meet anyone in my entire life."

Cookie's eyes lost their humor and he got serious immediately. He understood what she was saying. "I'm happier to have met you than anyone I've met in *my* entire life, Fee."

A comfortable silence fell between them. Fiona put her head back on her knees, and closed her eyes again.

Noticing her white knuckles from squeezing her hands tightly Cookie finally asked what had been on his mind for most of the day. "I need to know what's up, Fee." He watched as she flinched. "I don't know what's going through your head, but I'm not going to leave you. I'm not going to get mad, I just need to know so I can be sure we all get through this and get home. If your feet are bothering you, I can wrap them with tape to help with that. Shit, I should've already done it. We can coat your legs with mud to try to protect them a bit more. I can see all the welts from the bug bites. I wish I had an extra pair of pants for you."

Fiona didn't say anything, just continued to sit next to him silently. Cookie was frustrated. He wanted to help her, but he couldn't if she wouldn't talk to him. Finally, he thought he knew what to say to get Fiona to open up to him. Cookie knew she was stubborn and tough just from being around her for a day and for surviving her kidnapping ordeal. He thought of what he could say that would get to her. Finally he knew. It'd be the same thing that, if said to him, would get him to open up and be honest.

Cookie lowered his voice and spoke from his heart. "No bullshit, Fiona, my life depends on you. I will *not* leave you. If I don't know what's going on with you, and you fall behind or can't continue, that could end up hurting me as well, because I'll stay with you and try to help you. There's no way in hell I've brought you this far to leave you behind now. You're stuck with me. No matter what."

He waited. Cookie thought maybe Fiona had fallen asleep or that she was going to refuse to talk to him.

Finally Fiona spoke softly, without opening her eyes. "I'm going through withdrawal."

Chapter Five

WHATEVER COOKIE THOUGHT Fiona was going to say, it wasn't that.

"What?" he asked more harshly than he'd intended. His mind whirled. How could he have missed that? Cookie couldn't believe it. Well, it was dark in the room he'd found her in and she was now wearing a long sleeve shirt, so he'd never gotten a good look at her arms.

Fiona kept her eyes closed and continued, "They'd been shooting me up with something. I'm not sure what. Not enough to freak me out, but enough to control me, to keep me complacent. I think they thought they could get me to do what they wanted if they got me hooked, that I'd do anything for another fix. But I refused to beg or behave for them. It's been a while since they last gave me anything, I don't know for sure how long. I swear if it gets bad enough, that if I slow you down, I'll let you go ahead. I know you didn't bargain on this, or me…I'm sorry. I'm so sorry. I should've told you before we left that hut." Fiona's voice trailed off. She'd kept her eyes closed throughout her entire confession. Fiona waited for Hunter to get up and walk away in disgust. Not only was she disgusting and filthy and smelly, she was an addict too.

Cookie swallowed once. He had to swallow again before he could talk. He was relieved it wasn't something more serious on one hand, but at the same time, he knew sometimes getting off of drugs was the worst part. He knew what he said now was important.

"Can I see?" Cookie waited, and when Fiona nodded slightly, moved so he was kneeling in front of her. He gently unclasped her hands and took hold of one and threaded his fingers with hers. Cookie waited until Fiona opened her eyes to check on what he was doing.

He kept eye contact with her while he pushed the sleeve on her right arm up past her elbow. It wasn't until it was all the way up that he looked down. He clenched his teeth at the needle marks inside her elbow. He could clearly see them, even with the waning light of the evening. He lowered that sleeve, and pushed up the other one to see the same thing. The bruising on her arms was an indication of how she'd fought her captors and how they hadn't been gentle when injecting her.

Cookie smoothed her shirt down and took both her hands in his. Fiona was watching him now warily. He could feel the tremors in her hands.

He met her eyes and said, "Fee, I'm so sorry. I'm sorry I didn't get there quicker. I'm sorry I didn't know you were there. I'm just so damn sorry."

When Fiona took a breath ready to say something, Cookie interrupted her. "No, don't say anything, and *don't* fucking apologize again. Listen to me. I've only known you for a day, but you're one of the strongest people I know. Not just the strongest *woman* I know, but one of the strongest *people*. You haven't told me how long you were in that damn building, but I know it was a while. You've walked a shit ton of miles today, on your own, without complaint. I don't know how long it's been since you've had something decent to eat or drink. All you care about is this mission and not being in the way. You are *not* in the way. If there were ten women in that hovel, I would've rescued all of them, even though I was only expecting one."

Cookie paused and let his comment sink in, then continued, "We have two more days of hard walking. We only have two days before our next scheduled backup pickup. I obviously don't have anything to give you to help you with the withdrawal. Without knowing exactly what drugs they were giving you, I don't want to risk injecting you with the wrong thing. I've got some pain killers in my pack, but it's not a good idea to mix them with unknown narcotics. While I don't have anything to counteract your withdrawal symptoms, I can certainly help distract you or do anything else you think will help. Okay? Don't shut me out." Then Cookie chuckled and pleaded softly, humor coating his words, "Please don't leave me with Julie as my only conversation."

Fiona smiled at his words, but sobered quickly, staring at Hunter with big eyes, her concern and worry clearly showing.

Cookie continued on. "I'm not a therapist and I can't imagine what you've been through, but if you need someone to talk to…"

Fiona nodded, cutting Hunter off. She knew she'd never tell him what she'd survived. It'd been bad enough to have gone through it; she couldn't bear for him to feel any more sorry for her then he already did. She liked Hunter. Genuinely liked him. She hadn't known many military people, but she imagined them all to be either grunting, sex-hungry jerks or assholes who thought they were more important than anyone around them. Obviously she'd been stereotyping, because Hunter wasn't either. At least she didn't think so. He'd sounded genuinely concerned for her. That concern felt wonderful.

Cookie squeezed her hand. "Try to get some sleep, Fee. We'll be starting off early tomorrow. I want to get going before it gets too hot. And remember, I'm here if you need to talk."

Fiona squeezed his hand back and then dropped it to clasp her legs again. She couldn't rely on him. She knew she'd probably be out of her head before too much longer, and she had to concentrate to keep herself under control. She scooted into the little lean to Hunter had made for her without saying anything else and curled into a ball.

Fiona could tell she was getting worse. Her captors had never let her go this long before. She knew Hunter said he'd help, but there was nothing he could do. Fiona needed to distract herself; she started counting backward from one thousand again.

At four the next morning, Cookie woke the women up. Each got another granola bar and he checked their water. He eyed Fiona warily. She didn't look good. She refused to look him in the eyes, and the tremors in her hands were worse, even though she tried to hide it from him. She was also very pale. She ate the granola bar with the same enjoyment she had the day before, just as Julie ate hers with the same disgust. When they were done, and had relieved themselves in the bushes nearby, they set off.

The heat was brutal. The fact they weren't walking near the river meant they didn't have to worry as much about animals who'd go there to drink, but it also meant they had to conserve what water they had. It also meant that it was hot; hotter than it might have been if they'd been able to cool off with a dip in the fast flowing water now and then.

Julie didn't talk much, but when she did, it was to whine about how much further they had to go and how hot she was. She also complained about her feet hurting, the bugs, the leaves smacking her in the face…the list was endless. But Fiona was quiet. Too quiet. She trudged along behind Julie without a word. Cookie looked back to check on her often and saw Fiona was making it…barely. He knew she was weak, but now knowing about the drugs her captors had forced on her, he was even more concerned.

When they stopped for a short food break, Fiona uncharacteristically laid down in the shade of a tree and curled into a ball, her preferred resting stance now. Cookie was busy with his pack and didn't notice until Julie groaned sarcastically, "Oh great, we'll never get there now."

Cookie saw Fiona start to sit up upon hearing Julie's words. He went over and put his hand on her back.

"Stay. Rest. We'll get going soon enough." He looked at Julie and said in a harsh tone, without bothering to try to tone it down. "You should lie down and take a nap too. We've still got some ground to cover today."

Fiona looked up at Hunter with misery in her eyes as he turned back toward her. "I'm sorry."

Cookie cut her off. "None of that. Shit, Fiona, you aren't superwoman. Just rest a bit and we'll leave in a while. And before you say it, you aren't holding us up. We all need a break and it's safe enough."

Fiona nodded and squeezed her eyes shut again. She heard Hunter walk away. She knew he was probably lying for her sake, but she couldn't make herself care at the moment. Fiona felt like crap. Her whole body was rebelling against her. She wished those damn kidnappers were there to give her the drugs. She was ready to beg for them now. She'd finally gotten to the point where she'd do whatever they wanted in order to get them. Fiona knew they were bad, even without knowing exactly what crap they'd been shoving into her body, but she'd do anything to get rid of the crawling sensation under her skin and the horrible nausea.

The shakes she could deal with, but the feeling of bugs crawling on her was horrible. She itched something fierce as well, but she tried to resist the urge to scratch. Fiona knew that once she started she wouldn't stop. Hell, half of the itch was probably from bug bites and not from the drugs, but it didn't matter right now. Itchy was itchy.

Fiona choked back a sob. Why hadn't they killed her? Why? They had the chance. More than once. She couldn't think straight. She took a deep breath. She had to stop thinking that way. She knew Hunter wouldn't leave her in the jungle, and if he wouldn't leave her, then none of them would get out anytime soon, maybe not at all. She couldn't live with that on her conscience. Fiona took a deep breath to get herself together and not give in to the despair desperately trying to suck her down and started counting backward...this time from two thousand.

Cookie watched Fiona. She wasn't sleeping. He could see her lips moving. He finally realized she was counting. Around the same time he figured it out, he heard Julie say with malice, "That's all she did when we were in that fucking building. She counted backwards. It nearly drove me crazy."

Cookie just looked at Julie incredulously. She couldn't really be that callous could she?

"Well? It did!" Julie retorted defensively after seeing the look on Cookie's face, but fell silent under his continued scathing glare.

Yup, she could be that callous. Finally Cookie knew they couldn't wait any longer. It was time to move. He stood up and was going to go over to help Fiona, but he saw she was sitting up on her own. She'd heard him moving around and knew it was time to go. The pitiful little group gathered up their belongings and started out again.

A couple of hours later, Fiona started dry heaving. She didn't have any food in her stomach to really throw up, other than a few bites of granola, but her body tried to get rid of anything that was there anyway. She stopped in the middle of the path and dry heaved. She'd tried to stop it, but it was impossible. The retching noises she made were horrifying.

Julie screeched and jumped out of the way yelling, "Gross!"

While Cookie wasn't sorry he'd rescued Julie, she was a human being, and a woman at that, he *was* wishing she'd just be quiet for one fucking second. She was obviously spoiled and wasn't dealing with the logistics of being rescued that well. Cookie didn't analyze his thoughts too much. He'd probably had former captives act worse than Julie was, but when he compared Julie's actions to Fiona's, he was hard pressed to have much sympathy toward Julie.

Cookie went to Fiona. She held out her hand as if to ward him off, but he just took her hand and kept coming. He led her away from where Julie was standing and just held her upright as her stomach spasmed.

Fiona was so embarrassed. She wanted nothing more than to lie down on the jungle floor and die, but she couldn't. She took a deep breath, and with Hunter's strength straightened.

"I'm okay," she whispered. "We need to keep going."

"Jesus, Fee, just rest for a second. I've got you."

Fiona would've cried if she had any extra liquid in her body. She stood, shaking, with her side against Hunter. He was holding her sideways in case she had to throw up again, but she knew she was done...for the moment.

Cookie pulled away, just enough, so that he could lean over and look in Fiona's eyes. "I wish like hell I could take this for you."

Fiona could only say quietly, "I wouldn't wish this on my worst enemy."

Cookie ran his hand over Fiona's head and smoothed her hair down. Without a word he leaned over and kissed her lightly on the top of the head before asking quietly, "Ready?"

Fiona nodded briefly, deciding she couldn't deal with understanding Hunter's actions right then. Maybe later she'd remember his touch and his kiss and analyze it. But for now, she had to concentrate on staying upright and mobile. For Hunter's sake.

Cookie knew Fiona was right when she'd said they had to keep going, but he wasn't happy about it. She needed a medical care, immediately. But that wasn't going to happen anytime soon. He hadn't meant to kiss her, but he been unable to control himself. Cookie wanted to take Fiona in his arms and whisk her away, but it was impossible. He'd consoled himself with the caress of his hand and the brief kiss.

When they started off again, Cookie walked beside Fiona, this time with his arm around her waist. He had to stop with her several more times as she dry heaved. Finally Cookie calculated they'd walked far enough for the day. They were mostly on track to get to the extraction point on time, and he stopped to let them all settle for the night. They'd made his goal of five miles, but he'd secretly hoped they'd get further so they'd have less to go tomorrow.

When Cookie had Julie settled, thank God she wasn't trying to cling to him, and was satisfied they were as safe as they could be for the moment, he went to join Fiona. She hadn't moved much since he'd helped her to the ground, and he was worried about her.

She also hadn't eaten anything, not wanting, in her words, to "waste it" by throwing it up as soon as she ate it. Cookie didn't know what it was that made him want to be by Fiona's side, well, actually he *did* know. It was her courage and inner strength.

Cookie had seen it before, with Caroline. When Wolf's woman had been kidnapped by terrorists and thrown overboard in the middle of the ocean with her feet tied together and weighted down, he'd been the one to get to her and give her lifesaving oxygen while Wolf and the team took down the terrorists. Cookie had been amazed at Caroline's fortitude and strength then, and still was today. He hadn't met anyone like her, until Fiona.

Cookie had promised himself that if he *did* meet someone like Caroline, he'd snatch her up and never let her go. When Cookie made that silent vow to himself, he hadn't expected to actually find a woman he admired as much as he admired Caroline. But it wasn't admiration, exactly, he was feeling about Fiona.

Cookie had been on hostage recovery missions that were way worse than this one. Bullets flying was the worst, but most of the time they were hard because of the lack of inner fortitude of the person, or people, being rescued. Cookie and the team never blamed them, after all, being kidnapped wasn't ever a good experience, but the fact that this woman, held longer than anyone he'd ever rescued before, was dealing with a reaction to a withdrawal of some sort of drug, and knew she was only being rescued because someone else had been sent for….it made him respect her. Respect and pride. That was what he was feeling about this woman.

There were very few people in his life that Cookie truly respected. The fact that he'd known Fiona for two days and respected her said a lot. He was also fucking proud of her. Fiona was holding her own in a horrible situation. She deserved a fucking medal. Cookie eased down beside her.

Fiona was on her side curled into a ball, as usual. The woman stunk to high heaven, was covered in dirt and filth, and was wearing a metal collar around her neck. Cookie wanted to get as close as he could to her to offer comfort, regardless of all that. To let her know she wasn't alone. He supposed that he shouldn't do it, especially with Julie shooting daggers at them from across the way, but he couldn't help but offer this woman comfort.

Fiona felt Hunter ease himself onto the ground beside her and fit himself around her. His front to her back. He didn't try to move her, she was still curled into a protective ball, but she fit in the crook of his body better than she thought she ever would with a man. Fiona was pretty tall for a woman, around five nine, and had never found a man that had "fit" her as Hunter had.

Fiona knew that Hunter could feel her trembling, but she couldn't stop it.

Cookie felt helpless. He was a Navy SEAL. He could solve almost any problem thrown his way. He could fight the meanest bad guy, swim the widest ocean, fall from the sky and come out shooting, but he couldn't do anything for the woman trembling in his arms. Not one fucking thing. The only thing he could do for her was talk to her.

"You're doing fine, Fee."

Fiona shook her head in denial. "I don't think I'm going to make it, Hunter," she whispered, scared if she said it too loud, it'd somehow make it true.

"Are you kidding me? You've already made it."

"What are you talking about? Did you eat a bad mushroom at some point in the last day?" Fiona tried to joke with Hunter. If she didn't make a joke, she'd probably cry.

Cookie ran his hand over Fiona's head, wiping the sweat off her forehead in the process. "Funny girl. I mean, you've already made it away from those jackasses. *That* was the hard part. *This* is a piece of cake."

Fiona closed her eyes and whispered her greatest fear out loud. "What if I freak out and get you killed?"

Cookie's heart about broke in his chest. Fiona hadn't said, "What if I freak out and they take me back," she'd been more concerned about him. Jesus fucking Christ.

"You won't freak out, Fee."

"You don't know that."

Cookie turned her head just enough and got up on an elbow so he could look into Fiona's eyes. "I know we've just met, but I know you. You'll hold on until we're safe. I *know* you will." Cookie watched as Fiona closed her eyes, but continued anyway, keeping his hand on her face, liking the connection it gave him to her. "And even if you don't hold on, and you *do* freak out, you won't get me killed and I won't allow them to take you back. I swear."

"Don't get hurt on account of me, Hunter. You're so much more valuable than I am."

Cookie couldn't take it anymore. Every time he tried to reassure Fiona, she turned around and said something else that slayed him.

"Shhhh, Fee. Rest. You're safe. Just relax."

They laid on the ground for a while longer. Cookie knew Fee wasn't sleeping. "What do you count to?" he asked her unexpectedly.

"What?" Fiona stammered, feeling embarrassed. She hadn't realized Hunter had heard her counting. It was the one thing that had kept her sane in the pit they'd held her in, but now it was the *only* thing that kept her from falling into hysterics with the withdrawal.

"I know you've been counting to distract yourself," Cookie said softly. "Let me help."

"Really, Hunter," Fiona complained, "you should get some rest…I smell horrible, you have other things to worry about…"

Cookie cut her off. "What do you count to?" His words were hard and unrelenting.

Fiona sighed to herself. She didn't know how Hunter counting would distract her, but she finally told him. "I usually start at one thousand and count backwards, but lately I've been starting at two thousand."

Cookie said nothing, but leaned down and kissed her temple, holding his lips against her skin for a moment. Then he brought his lips to her ear and softly started counting. "Two thousand, One thousand nine hundred ninety nine, one thousand nine hundred ninety eight…"

Fiona counted in her head with him, loving the low, rumbly sound of Hunter's voice. It was deep and soft and soothing. Her exhausted body soon fell into a troubled sleep with the sound of Hunter's voice still counting in her head.

Chapter Six

THE NEXT MORNING Cookie woke up early again. He enjoyed the feel of Fiona in his arms, even in their present not-so-good situation. He hated to wake her up and that they had another tough day of trekking through the jungle. Fiona had just about broken his heart last night with her words. She was trying desperately to hold on and be brave, but Cookie could tell she was struggling.

The situation wasn't ideal. Fiona wasn't at her best, hell that was the understatement of the year, but Cookie was still drawn to her. Even smelly, sweaty, covered in dirt, and suffering from withdrawal from who-the-hell-knew what drugs, Cookie thought she was amazing. He gently eased off the ground and removed his arm from around Fiona's waist and got up. Cookie slid a lock of hair off Fiona's cheek and tucked it behind her ear gently, then turned to get ready for the day. Knowing they had one more day of grueling travel before they could reach the extraction point, Cookie wanted to let the women sleep longer before having to wake them.

After stalling as late as possible, Cookie finally woke them up. Julie was irritable and had no problem letting Cookie know it. She bitched about the hard ground, the lack of good food, even about not having a damn toilet. Cookie ignored her as much as he could. He only had to get through one more day before she'd be someone else's issue. It was a terrible thing to think after what she'd been through, but he couldn't help it.

Once Fiona was up and moving, Cookie thought she actually

looked a bit better than the day before, but she still in no way looked good. He could still see her hands shaking. She was able to keep half of a granola bar down and Cookie took that as a good sign. He was running low on food, but hopefully it wouldn't make a difference after tonight. There was no way Cookie was letting Fiona know they had just one more granola bar left. She'd insist that he or Julie eat it, when it was obvious she was the one who needed the nutrients the most.

Fiona was glad she'd been able to eat something and not immediately throw it back up; she hoped she was coming out on the other side of the worst of the withdrawal symptoms she'd been experiencing, but she wasn't sure. She still smelled horrible and most likely looked like a refugee from a third world country. Fiona was glad she hadn't seen a mirror. She didn't think she wanted to see her reflection anytime in her near future. She was covered in bug bites as well. They were maddeningly itchy. Her feet were not faring well in the flip-flops either, but Fiona knew she had no choice there. Hunter had tried to wrap them in tape before they set off yesterday, but the tape would only last so long. She had blisters between her first and second toes because of the plastic on the flip flops between them, but honestly, they were the least of her problems at the moment. Fiona purposely hadn't asked Hunter how long they had to walk today, not wanting to know.

After their lunch break, Cookie told the women they were coming to the most dangerous part of their trip. There was a reason this was Plan B. First, it was a lot further from the kidnapper's camp, but second it was in a more populated area and near a well-known drug runner's hangout. They all had to keep quiet and not talk unless absolutely necessary. Cookie told them to watch where they were walking and try to make as little sound as possible. He didn't think they'd have to worry about the kidnappers finding them this far out, but the last thing he wanted to happen was to run into drug runners while escaping from sex traffickers.

Finally, after a long quiet couple of hours of walking, Cookie stopped. "Okay, ladies, here's the plan," he told them quietly. "The chopper should be here in about an hour. We need to sit tight and wait. You can rest and get your strength back as much as possible. Be ready for anything when the chopper comes into range. If anything happens, and I mean *anything*, you two are to get your butts to that chopper. I'll cover your backs and make sure you get there. Got it?"

Julie, not surprisingly, nodded enthusiastically, agreeing to anything as long as it got her out of the jungle. Fiona wasn't as quick to agree. Somehow Cookie knew she'd protest.

Fiona had been feeling better earlier, but started feeling shaky again when they stopped to wait for the helicopter. She didn't like what Hunter was saying and let him know in no uncertain terms. "No, not okay," she said defiantly.

"Shut up," Julie hissed meanly, not waiting for Cookie to say anything. "He's here because of *me*, if it wasn't for *me*, you wouldn't even have been rescued. So let him rescue us and shut the hell up!"

Fiona looked at Julie incredulously. "You're right; if not for Hunter, *you'd* still be in that stinking building or on your way to be some guy's sex toy. You're willing to let him *die* for you?"

Without waiting for an answer, to what was obviously a rhetorical question, Fiona turned to Hunter. "There's no way we've come this far to leave you behind now. Tell us what to be on the lookout for and we can help you."

Cookie shook his head and kept his voice even, yet firm. He couldn't deny it felt good to have Fiona stand up for him, even if he didn't need it. Not many women had the guts to go to bat for him. At least none in the recent past that he could remember.

"No, Fiona, that isn't how this works. I'm the professional, you're not. You'll follow my orders and get on that chopper, no questions asked. I can deal with any situation that arises here. I'm a Navy

SEAL, a professional soldier. If I know you're safe I can concentrate better and I'll be better off without the two of you here."

His words hurt, but Fiona knew Hunter spoke nothing but the truth. She didn't want to give up her argument though.

At the stubborn look in her eye, Cookie eased his voice a bit. "Fee, this isn't my first mission. I know what I'm doing. Even if for some reason I can't get on the chopper, I know what to do. I'll dig in and hang out until my team can come back and get me. And they *will* come back to get me. A SEAL doesn't leave a SEAL behind, ever. It's much easier for just me to hide and wait them out than it would be if I have to look after you or Julie as well."

Fiona heard what Hunter was saying, but she didn't like it. Well, Hunter could say what he wanted; she wasn't going to leave him in the jungle if she could help it, even if his team would come back for him. Fiona knew what it was like to be left behind, and she swore she wouldn't put anyone else through it, ever.

Time ticked by slowly. The hour they had to wait was one of the longest hours of Fiona's life. Finally, *finally,* they heard the faint sound of a helicopter.

"Come on," was all Cookie said. He started off through the jungle, hacking the branches away from their path as he went. He wasn't trying to be quiet, he was trying to get them to the landing zone as quickly as possible.

"It's about a quarter of a mile through the trees, straight line distance, this way," he'd told them earlier pointing toward the west. "No problem."

It *was* a problem though. As soon as they heard the chopper, obviously so did the drug runners. While they didn't know exactly where it was headed, they had a pretty good guess since there weren't very many places it could land or get close to the ground in the area.

When Cookie, Julie, and Fiona finally reached the area where they were to be picked up, all hell broke loose. The drug runners had reached the area at the same time and easily spotted them and opened fire. Cookie didn't hesitate and returned fire. The loud sound of gunfire startled Fiona.

The noise was extremely loud compared to the silence they'd been traveling in. Cookie's teammates in the chopper began laying down cover fire. They signaled to Cookie and he urged Julie and Fiona toward a small opening in the trees. It was going to be tricky. They had to climb onto a lowered ladder and be hauled up. The chopper couldn't land, and they were going to be sitting ducks while they were being hauled aboard.

Julie went first. Cookie and Fiona kneeled down in a patch of thick bushes. Cookie was firing toward where he thought the drug runners were hiding in the jungle around them. He'd taken off his pack to have better range of motion.

It was taking a while for Julie to grab a hold of the ladder. Fiona wanted to scream in frustration. Why didn't she just grab the damn thing and get the hell out of there? Cookie was running out of ammo, he didn't have an unlimited amount of bullets. They both knew if he had to stop firing, Julie could be injured.

Cookie was surprised, but supposed he shouldn't have been, when he heard Fiona say, "Here," and thrust his original pistol at him, fully loaded again. She'd loaded it while he was firing his backup. Cookie didn't say anything, simply grabbed it and started shooting again.

Fiona re-loaded the pistol Hunter had just emptied. Her hands were shaking badly, so it was a tough job, but she knew Hunter had to concentrate or else they were all dead. She knew how to load and shoot pistols because in her world back in El Paso, she'd decided she needed to be proactive for her own self-protection. She lived alone and wanted to be sure she could handle a gun to protect herself. She'd taken gun safety lessons and actually owned a pistol herself. That simple decision she'd made so long ago was certainly paying off now.

Finally Julie was up safe in the chopper. Fiona hadn't watched her go up; she'd been concentrating on loading the bullets into the gun. It was probably a good thing. If she'd watched, it might've scared the crap out of her.

Suddenly it was Fiona's turn. Without a word, Cookie went to push her forward to take her turn, when suddenly he fell backward.

Fiona looked down in horror. Hunter was lying still on the ground with blood coming from somewhere around his upper chest. He'd been shot!

Fiona looked around quickly and made a split second decision. Hunter was going to live, dammit. He certainly didn't deserve to die out here in the fucking jungle. He'd risked his life for Julie, and for her, and she wasn't going to save herself and leave him here. Fiona knew she'd never be able to live with herself if she just up and left Hunter bleeding on the ground. She'd watched how Julie had to strap herself onto the ladder and figured she could do that with Hunter...but she had to have his help. She couldn't carry him.

She frantically shook him. "Get up, Hunter, get up!" After a few more times of her yelling at him, he finally stirred, groggily.

Fiona continued to try to get him up and moving. "Hunter, we have to get to the chopper. I need your help." She appealed to the soldier in him, in the side that saved people for a living. "Please, help me get to the ladder," Fiona begged, hoping the desperation she could hear in her own words would break through to him.

It did. Hunter staggered to his feet, with Fiona's help, and with her arm around his waist, he stumbled along beside her to the dangling ladder. Fiona tried to steady Hunter with one hand, while randomly firing his pistol with the other. She knew she wasn't hitting a damn thing, but she hoped the bullets flying would maybe make the bad guys think twice about coming out of hiding. Hunter's teammates in the helicopter were frantically shooting around them, trying to suppress the gunfire from the drug runners as well. Fiona hoped they were as good a shot as she'd always heard. She'd hate to end up dead from a stray bullet after everything she'd been through.

After what seemed like forever, but was really probably only about ten seconds, they reached the ladder. "Help me, Hunter," Fiona fake-begged him again. "Hold on to the ladder to keep it steady for me."

Fiona was completely lying to him, trying to get him near enough to the first rung so she could strap him in. "Step up, Hunter." She watched him blindly step up to the first rung. Fiona wrapped the containment rope around his back and clipped it to the ladder again. It wasn't much, and probably wouldn't hold him if he passed out on his way up, so she prayed he'd be able to hold on for the short trip up.

"Hold on," Fiona begged Hunter desperately. "For me, hold on. Don't let go." Hunter seemed to become a bit more lucid at her words, and just as his partners were hauling him up, he tried to grab her hand.

Fiona stepped back out of the way and ran back toward the break in the trees where they'd been hiding. She heard him swearing as he was lifted up toward the helicopter.

"Thank God," Fiona sobbed while still trying to randomly shoot his pistol. When she shot the last bullet, she just watched as Hunter miraculously reached the chopper and was hauled inside by several grasping hands. The drug runners were finally backing off as a result of the fire power from the chopper.

Fiona wasn't sure what the men in the helicopter would do. She knew they weren't expecting to pick up more than two people. She didn't even know if they had room for her. But they had to have seen her helping Hunter onto the ladder. Had to have seen she wasn't the enemy. Fiona wanted to see the ladder drop back to the ground for her almost more than she wanted a three course meal, but she had no idea how much weight the chopper could hold and if it was even feasible for Hunter's teammates to save her too.

Fiona grabbed Hunter's pack with the intention of slinging it over her back as she'd seen him do time after time, and almost fell backwards when she tried to pick it up. The thing was heavy! She had no idea how Hunter had been able to carry it as far as he did without seeming to be bothered by it. Fiona wanted to leave it on the ground where Hunter had left it, she honestly didn't feel strong enough to take it with her, but she knew she couldn't leave it behind. Fiona figured there was probably a lot of electronic equipment in it and probably other top secret things.

The other reason she didn't want to leave it behind was because she didn't know if there was any identifying information in it or not, and she didn't want anything coming back to Hunter. She had no time to search it to make sure and the last thing she wanted was some drug dealer in Mexico knowing who Hunter was and possibly coming after him in the States. She had no idea how likely that was, but then again she never would've thought she would've been kidnapped and taken away to be sold into the sex slave trade either.

Fiona laid the pack on the ground and lay down on her back on top of it. She snaked her arms through the straps and struggled to get upright. She put her feet to the side and shifted around. She got her legs under her and used a nearby tree to pull herself painfully to her feet. She fell back once, and luckily there was a tree there to stop her from falling on her ass. Fiona shifted her weight until she felt comfortable standing with the heavy backpack on.

Fiona looked nervously back up at the chopper hovering overhead. It was time for the million dollar question. Would they leave her behind? They'd rescued their man and the original hostage. They'd completed their mission. Would they rescue her too? Or was she too much of an unknown?

Fiona held her breath. If they left, okay, she couldn't think about that, but maybe just maybe…the seconds ticked by. Just as Fiona thought the chopper was going to take off and leave her to fend for herself in the jungle, the ladder started lowering again. Thank God! Fiona almost sobbed in relief, realizing what a close call she'd had. That ladder was literally the difference between life and death for her. Fiona choked back a sob, now wasn't the time or the place to break down. She still had to make it up to, and in, the helicopter alive.

Chapter Seven

FIONA STAGGERED TOWARD the ladder swinging crazily in the air flying around by the blades of the chopper. She couldn't walk in a straight line because of the pack on her back. She was also still trying to shoot randomly into the trees, but she was almost out of ammo. Fiona figured she looked ridiculous, but all she cared about was getting the hell out of the jungle.

She looked up. There were men hanging out of the open door still firing their weapons at the drug runners, but Fiona heard it all through a daze.

Only a little more, Fiona told herself, trying to make herself as small a target as possible, which was really laughable since she had a giant backpack on and was quite tall.

Finally Fiona grabbed the ladder, reaching it just as she started to fall on her face. She stepped up to the first rung, and hung on tight. There was no way she could get the strap around herself with the pack on, so she simply wrapped her arms around the sides of the ladder, buried her head, and hoped like hell Hunter's teammates would pull her up fast. They did.

Fiona heard a bullet hit the pack on her back and she thought she felt something hit her leg, but amazingly it didn't hurt. She was numb to everything. Her body was shaking from the adrenaline rush like it was twenty degrees outside rather than ninety. Fiona didn't think she'd feel it if a bullet had hit her in the head at that point.

Fiona opened her eyes to check on her progress in getting to the chopper and saw they were flying away from the clearing at a high rate of speed. Terrified she inhaled sharply and squeezed her eyes closed and prayed she'd make it to the chopper quickly.

After what seemed like an eternity, Fiona felt hands on her arms lifting her, practically throwing her into the interior of the helicopter. Her eyes immediately searched for Hunter. He was lying toward the back of the small space with a man dressed all in camouflage giving him first aid.

Fiona looked around for Julie, she also seemed to be fine. She was sitting off to the side with her head buried in the chest of another camo-wearing man.

The two men who'd hauled her aboard the chopper, pantomimed for her to crawl over to the side of the aircraft next to the man who was comforting Julie. Fiona gestured at her back, knowing there was no way she could move with Hunter's pack on her back. One of the men helped her remove the backpack as if she carried feathers instead of what had to be at least a hundred pounds of gear, and she made her way over to where they'd pointed.

It was too loud to talk, and no one would be able to hear her if she did try to speak anyway. Fiona saw the men all wore ear pieces, so she figured they could communicate with each other, even with the noise. She saw their lips moving, but couldn't hear anything but the motor of the helicopter. Fiona didn't care. She was out of the damn jungle and everyone seemed to be okay. At the moment that was all she could muster up inside to care about.

She watched as Hunter's shoulder was bandaged up by one of his teammates. He was unconscious, but at least they'd seemed to stop the bleeding. Fiona realized, with a start, that she'd never been so scared in her life as she was when she saw Hunter fall and the blood seep from him. Even when she'd been grabbed and had woken up to...yeah, even then. Watching Hunter fall after being shot, was scarier than even that. Fiona couldn't say why, it just was.

The chopper flew on and on and after what seemed like forever, finally landed at a dirt covered airstrip. Fiona saw a small plane and figured that was how they were leaving. Just as Fiona got the nerve up to ask about what was going on, Julie was there to ask the questions so Fiona didn't have to.

"Where are we going?" she asked nastily. "I thought we were getting out of here. Why are we stopping? Where's my dad's plane?"

The man who Julie had been clinging to, responded, "Don't worry, Julie, you'll be home soon. Your dad will be glad to see you."

And with that Julie started crying dramatically again.

Fiona turned away. She caught the eye of one of other men. She had to ask, "How will we get back in the United States without passports?" She didn't mean to be the buzz kill of the moment when they were about to get out of the country, but she'd always been too practical. Fiona had asked the question generally. She figured they probably had *Julie's* passport since they were expecting to rescue her, but they didn't even know who she was. How would *Fiona* get back into the country? They wouldn't leave her at the airport would they? She had no idea how these things worked and wished Hunter was awake. Fiona knew he'd explain everything to her and make her feel better.

"Well, we're not going back into the country the usual way." The man chuckled when he answered.

At Fiona's stricken look, he rushed on to reassure her, "Don't worry, all will be fine."

Fiona shut up. Whatever. She was glad that someone else was handling things; she didn't think she could stay upright much longer, nonetheless think about what to do next. The adrenaline was wearing off and Fiona was feeling sick again. She felt like crap, her leg hurt, she stunk to high heaven, and she couldn't get her hands to stop shaking. But she was alive. Hunter was alive. That should be all she cared about at the moment.

They all transferred to a small plane. Hunter was laid down in the back of the plane on a small cot, while Julie and the guy she wouldn't let go of, sat near the front. Two of the men climbed into the cockpit area while the two others got Hunter settled and chose a seat themselves.

Fiona climbed aboard the plane and looked around to decide where she should sit. She didn't want to sit near Julie, she was sure the feeling was mutual, and she didn't want to sit far from Hunter, so she could make sure he was okay. But she didn't want to sit near any of the other men because she knew she was disgusting. She stunk and was covered in filth. Fiona was also uncomfortable with the SEAL's obvious maleness as well. They oozed testosterone out of every pore and now that Fiona was out of the jungle and immediate danger, she couldn't help but remember what other men had done to her while she'd been in captivity.

Fiona also knew another bout with her withdrawal symptoms was coming. She couldn't control the shaking of her body, just like before. Her leg also hurt, but Hunter needed attention more than she did. She kept quiet. She'd take care of it later.

The trip to wherever they were going, took about three hours. Hunter woke up once and Fiona heard him talking to the men sitting near him. She couldn't hear what they said, but she was so far gone inside her head at that point, that it wouldn't have mattered anyway.

Fiona couldn't stop the shakes and she'd been dry heaving into the air sick bag in the seat pocket in front of her for the last hour. She knew the men thought she was airsick, and that was all right with her. She prayed Hunter wouldn't tell them anything about the drugs. Fiona was embarrassed enough as it was. If she could only get to a hotel, or somewhere, and be left alone, she'd deal with it. Eventually the symptoms had to stop. She just had to wait them out.

Cookie had woken up in the back of the plane. He tried to sit up and was restrained by Wolf and Dude.

"Settle down, Cookie, you're okay," Wolf told him in a low calm voice.

Cookie hurt like hell, but there was something he had to do, something he had to remember.

Wolf saw his confusion and tried to reassure him. "The women are safe, don't worry. You got them out. Not sure who the second broad is, but they're both okay. Only you could pick up a woman in the jungle, Cookie!"

That was it! Cookie caught Dude's arm as he leaned over him to check his shoulder wound. Wolf also leaned toward his teammate to hear what he had to say.

Looking at each of his teammates, Cookie urgently said, "Fee. Help her, don't let her go." It was all he got out before he passed out again.

Dude tucked Cookie's arm back by his side and he and Wolf looked at each other, realizing that Cookie cared for the second woman. Neither knew what had happened in the jungle, but he'd specifically been worried about the woman he'd called Fee, not Julie.

Even though Cookie couldn't hear him, Dude told him softly, "Don't worry, Cookie, we'll take care of her for you until you can see to her yourself."

The plane landed with a bump and a slide. Fiona took a deep breath. This was it. It was time to get on with her life. She didn't know where they were, but she'd figure it out. She always figured it out.

Julie and one of the men got out of the plane first, then the two pilots, then her, then Hunter was carried out by the two men who'd been seeing to him. Fiona knew the men were Hunter's team. She'd recognized their names from when Hunter had told them to her what seemed like ages ago.

One of the men who'd been in the back with Hunter had been called Wolf by one of the other men. She was so glad Hunter was with his team. They'd take care of him.

Fiona squinted as they emerged out of the plane and into the sunshine. They were on another deserted dirt airstrip, but this time there was a van waiting for them. It was hot, but the sun felt wonderful on her face. Fiona hadn't seen the sun directly in months. Besides, she was freezing. She knew she shouldn't have been, but she was. Fiona staggered and Wolf was there to catch her arm.

"You okay?" he asked.

Fiona didn't like the scrutiny the big man was giving her so she simply nodded and moved away. She just wanted to be alone.

All eight of them climbed in a van and the same two men who'd been helping Hunter before, arranged him across one of the seats and climbed in behind him. Fiona managed to crawl in without assistance, and watched as Julie and the others also settled themselves into their seats. It was all done without a word spoken. Even Julie wasn't babbling now. It was weird, but Fiona didn't have time to even care. She wasn't in Mexico anymore. That was all she cared about at the moment. They headed down the road and away from the little plane.

It didn't matter where they were going, just that they were going somewhere away from the jungle. Her feet hurt like a bitch, so hopefully they didn't have to walk far. Looking down at them, Fiona had no idea how she was going to get her damn flip-flops off. Hunter had taped the hell out of them in an effort to protect her.

They drove for a while until they reached a crappy little house in the middle of nowhere. Another van was waiting. They repeated the drill from before, and everyone got settled. The men had put Hunter in the back of the van this time and he was sprawled on the back seat. Wolf was sitting near him making sure all was well. Fiona hoped they were bringing him to a hospital. She didn't like to see him so quiet and still.

Finally, after driving for another fifteen minutes or so, Fiona started to see signs of civilization. A few houses here and there, then finally some stores. Eventually, they pulled up to another small airport, this one with an actual concrete runway spread out behind the small building. Fiona didn't have any identification so she had no idea how she'd be able to fly commercially, but again, she kept quiet and waited for the SEALs to tell her what was going on and what she should do.

When the van stopped, Fiona watched as the men all got out, except for Wolf, who was monitoring Hunter. No one motioned for her to stay, so Fiona climbed out too, but stayed close to the van...and Hunter. She knew eventually she'd have to leave him, but if they weren't going to ask her to do it right now, she wouldn't. Just being near him comforted her. She knew it was because he'd rescued her, but she also thought it was more. What more, she couldn't say...just more.

Fiona saw a limo pull up nearby. An older man got out of the limo and it finally clicked. This must be Julie's father. It was. Julie shrieked and threw herself toward the man and hugged him close. She saw the man close his eyes and embrace his daughter. As annoying as Julie was, Fiona couldn't help but tear up. If it wasn't for his man and his daughter she'd still be in that hellhole with no hope of rescue.

She stayed glued to the side of the van watching the drama unfold in front of her. A part of her wanted to thank the man herself, but she just wasn't feeling up to it. She'd have to step away from the van, walk across the space separating the van and limo, explain who she was and...Fiona stopped thinking. It just wasn't worth it.

Fiona watched as one of the men who'd rescued them, approached the Senator and Julie. The Senator had a short conversation with the military man, without letting go of his daughter, then they shook hands, nodded at each other, and that was that. The man led Julie away. They got into the limo and the door closed behind them.

Fiona sighed. She hadn't liked the woman, but it was almost anticlimactic to see her just walk away without a backward glance. Fiona shivered, put Julie out of her mind, and turned to watch the men as they headed back toward her to the van. She had no idea what would happen next. She didn't have long to wait to find out.

"Hop back in, Fiona," Wolf called from inside the van. He held out his hand to help her back inside.

"But…" Fiona said, looking between the airport and Wolf sitting in the vehicle. She shrugged. She obviously wasn't going to be flying anywhere, not looking or smelling like she did, and certainly not without any identification.

She climbed back in without Wolf's help. When the van was on its way again, Fiona finally asked, "Are we taking him to the hospital?" gesturing toward Hunter.

No one answered her at first. Finally one of the other men in the van said, "No, we have our own medical facility nearby. It doesn't behoove us to show up at the local hospital looking like we do sometimes. Don't worry; we'll take good care of him."

Fiona nodded like it made perfect sense, not knowing her furrowed brow gave away her confusion. Nothing made sense. They hadn't asked who she was, they hadn't asked where she came from, hadn't commented on the way she looked or smelled, they hadn't really asked her anything. Just took it for granted that she was there. It confused the hell out of Fiona, and that wasn't a good feeling, on top of everything else. Was she safe with them? What if they dumped her somewhere?

Just as she started to freak out, Wolf said, "Stop fretting, Fiona."

At the use of her name for the second time, Fiona started.

Wolf noticed, and tried to reassure her. "Cookie told us who you were when we hauled him in the chopper, well at least your name. He was cursing a blue-streak saying you disobeyed him. We thought he was hallucinating until he told us your name when he woke up briefly in the plane."

They all laughed and Fiona looked down at her lap. Fiona knew Hunter would be mad that she deceived him to get him on the helicopter, but honestly, it'd been for his own good.

Wolf continued seriously, "He also asked us to look after you until he got better. But it honestly doesn't matter who you are or where you came from, Fiona, you saved his life. That makes you one of us. And we take care of our own. We'll figure out the other stuff in due time, but in the meantime, we'll take of him and we'll take care of you."

Fiona just stared at Wolf. "What?" she asked dumbly. She couldn't get her brain to work right. She was tired, scared, sick, and hurting.

"Just relax," Wolf soothed, seeing how stressed out she was. "We won't hurt you and you'll soon get to rest. I know you're confused and hungry and tired, and probably scared as well. Let me introduce you to everyone, that might help make you feel better. Okay?"

Fiona nodded. What else could she do?

"I'm Wolf. Up there driving is Benny. Dude and Mozart are sitting in the seat in front of you, and that's Abe next to you. I think you probably know we're all on the same Navy SEAL team. I meant what I said. You saved Cookie's life. You're a part of us now too."

Fiona meekly nodded her head. She had no clue what the hell Wolf was talking about. She felt as if she was in an alternative world. She wasn't one of them. She didn't even *know* them. Whatever. As long as they'd take care of Hunter she didn't care what they said. Fiona just wished they'd hurry up and get to wherever it was they were going. She wanted to… no, she *needed* to lie down.

Chapter Eight

T HE VAN FINALLY pulled up to a gate, Benny punched in a code and drove through with the gate closing behind him. Fiona watched it close warily. Was this another form of prison for her? She didn't want to believe it, but the drug withdrawal was taking its toll. She felt nervous and jittery and couldn't trust her own judgment. Fiona's head was spinning and she felt paranoid. Dear God, she needed to be alone.

Fiona stepped out of the van as soon as she could after it came to a stop. She looked up at a beautiful house. It was a huge two story building with windows all around the upper floor. There was an old fashioned porch attached to the front with three rocking chairs. The front door was painted a dark red and she could see red curtains around the windows on the first floor. She had no idea whose house it was. It looked perfectly harmless, but for some reason it made Fiona nervous as hell.

Fiona watched as the men got out of the van and Wolf and Dude took Hunter into the house through the front door. Fiona took one more look around the yard, noticing the manicured lawn and bushes and slowly hobbled in behind the rest of the men. Before Wolf went down the hall behind Hunter, he took Fiona's arm and led her toward a door.

"Fiona, this is your room. It has a bathroom attached. Please take your time and get changed and clean. I'll bring some scissors down in a bit to help you get those shoes off your feet if you need it. I'll also find some clothes for you to put on after your shower. They'll probably be too big, but they'll be clean. We'll eat once you're ready." Wolf opened the door and watched Fiona walk in the room; he smiled at her then closed the door.

Holy hell, Fiona didn't know what was going on. She'd gone from living in her own filth and peeing in a bucket, to standing in the most beautiful room she'd ever seen. It was absolutely gorgeous. It was huge and the carpet was a pristine white. Fiona didn't want to walk across it to the shower. She knew she'd get it dirty. What had Wolf been thinking leaving her here?

Fiona finally staggered toward the bathroom, ignoring the dirt she knew she was tracking through the room. She entered, then closed the door carefully and locked it firmly behind her. The bathroom was as beautiful as the rest of the room. There were two sinks and a huge marble counter. There was a Jacuzzi tub and a separate shower that had at least three shower heads.

Fiona would have admired it more carefully, but she was at the end of her rope. She'd simply been through too much, and her body wasn't able to support her anymore. She sunk to the floor next to the sink, having the presence of mind to push the plush white rug out of the way, and toppled over. The last thing Fiona thought was with as bad as she felt, she hoped she would die.

COOKIE FINALLY REGAINED consciousness. Wolf had sat next to him for thirty minutes, making sure the IV was opened all the way and that the wound in his shoulder was closed up properly. Mozart had done the honors for that. Wolf knew he was the best one of them to do it. Mozart had sewn up Wolf's Caroline when she'd been hurt. Wolf could barely see the scar on Caroline's side anymore. Mozart was that good.

The bullet had luckily gone all the way through Cookie's shoulder, so Mozart didn't have to dig it out. With luck, it hadn't hit any major arteries, but had put two holes in Cookie's arm. He was on some serious pain killers, but Cookie was a SEAL through and through. He was able to be functional, even with the drugs coursing through his body, especially since he was worried about Fiona.

"Tell me what happened," Cookie demanded of his friend and teammate. "I remember Julie going up to the chopper and then only snippets after that. Fee did get in right?"

Wolf nodded. "The short version is that you were shot, Fiona half dragged you to the ladder and strapped you in, we hauled you up while she went back and got your pack. She shot at the tangos while we re-lowered the ladder. She staggered to it loaded down with your pack; we hauled her up while relocating away from there. We changed to a plane, landed here in Texas, sent Julie off on her way, and now we're here in the safehouse Tex arranged for us. Now...you tell *me* what the hell happened out there."

Cookie knew what Wolf meant. They hadn't suspected a second hostage. Cookie told Wolf as much as he knew, which wasn't much. He didn't want to tell him too much about Fiona's condition yet, as he knew it embarrassed her. But he knew eventually his teammates would have to know. They couldn't help her with the drug withdrawal if they didn't know about it. Cookie wanted to know more about Fiona and where she came from and how she'd ended up in that hellhole he'd found her in before he spoke with Wolf.

The door to Cookie's room popped open and Benny stuck his head in.

"I brought the scissors and change of clothes to Fiona's room, and when she didn't answer the door, I looked in. She was in the bathroom and when I knocked on that door to let her know I'd brought her some things, no one answered. I knocked harder and she still didn't answer. She's not in the shower and I'm worried."

Cookie immediately started to get up at hearing Benny's words. If

Benny was worried, Cookie was fucking terrified. Wolf stopped him. "I've got it," he told his injured teammate, but Cookie wasn't listening.

"Help me up," he told Wolf gruffly. All he knew was he wasn't going to lie around if Fiona was hurt. Wolf didn't object, just sighed and helped Cookie to his feet and toward Fiona's room.

Abe was at Fiona's bathroom door when the other men arrived. "We didn't want to barge in on her if she was in the tub," Abe explained further, "but we can't get her to open the door. She says she's okay, but she doesn't sound good."

Wolf knocked on the door again and when there was no answer, helped Cookie get closer. Wolf gestured at him to take a shot at getting through to her.

"Fiona?" Cookie called out, "Can you hear me? Open the door, sweetheart." The endearment came out without conscious thought.

Fiona couldn't stop shaking. Her body was rebelling against her. She couldn't breathe that well, and she knew something was seriously wrong. She thought she heard Hunter's voice, but that couldn't be right. He was unconscious…wasn't he?

Cookie tried again, his voice a bit more forceful than before. "Fee, open the door right now or we're coming in." He paused. "I'm worried about you. Come on, open the door so I can see you're all right."

Fiona roused herself again. It *was* him. "Hunter?" she said weakly. "Are you okay?" She heard him laugh.

"Hell, Fee, I'm fine, it's *you* we're worried about. Now, open the door." He said the last a bit more harshly then he intended to.

"I can't come to the door right now, Hunter," Fiona tried to explain, not really knowing what she was saying. "Maybe later." She put her head back on the cold tile floor and closed her eyes.

Cookie gestured toward Benny. He was the best lock picker they had. They could all open just about any door and any lock, but

Benny was the master at it. He could always manage to open any lock much faster than the rest of them. And this was certainly a situation where time was of the essence. Benny had the door open within a few seconds. The door swung wide and Cookie's stomach dropped to the floor.

Wolf was at Fiona's side before Cookie could move. She lay motionless on the bathroom tile, just as filthy as the last time Cookie had seen her. She'd managed to get into the bathroom, but not to clean herself up in any way. It was if she'd entered the room and fell to the ground immediately. Wolf easily lifted Fiona's unconscious body and headed back toward the medical rooms with Cookie at his back following closely.

Wolf laid Fiona down carefully on the bed Cookie had just gotten out of, and looked back at Benny and Abe. "I need warm water. Lots of it. We have to get her clean before we do anything else. Grab the scissors too so we can get those shoes off her feet."

Cookie looked on helplessly. He was feeling weak and swayed on his feet.

Wolf paused in his care of Fiona to drag a chair over toward the bed she was lying on and forced Cookie into it. "Sit, Cookie," he told him sternly, "before you fall down, you stubborn ass."

Abe and Benny came back with the water, towels, and scissors. They all started wiping down Fiona's limbs, trying to get as much dirt and crud off her as they could without a full-fledged bath or shower. They moved quickly and professionally. Fiona moaned, but didn't protest in any way.

Benny started with her feet. He cut the tape off and peeled the flip-flops off her feet. Her feet were absolutely filthy. He could see Fiona had blisters on the tops of her feet where the rubber of the shoes had rubbed against her skin. The amount of dirt and crud on the bottom of her feet was almost hard to believe. Benny dropped the shoes on the ground and carefully pulled off her shorts. He wasn't even paying attention to how she looked; he was one hundred percent concentrating on getting this woman somewhat clean so they could give her any other medical aid she'd need.

Cookie watched absently as his teammates cleaned Fiona. He wasn't upset that they were touching her and that Benny had removed her pants, he was too worried about why Fiona was unconscious and what was wrong with her.

Abe and Wolf cut Cookie's long sleeved black shirt off of Fiona, which wasn't hard to do since it was so large on her. They swore at the first glimpse they had of the metal collar around her neck. The shirt had hidden it until now.

"Jesus," Cookie heard Abe mutter under his breath. They could all see how red her neck was. The rusted metal had rubbed her skin raw. It'd probably already been sore before they'd escaped, but now, after their mad dash through the jungle, it was beyond sore. It was red and inflamed and the amount of dried blood around it was somewhat alarming.

Abe continued removing her shirt, pulling it out from under her. Throughout it all, Cookie kept his eyes on Fiona's face. She hadn't moved, she hadn't moaned, she hadn't cried. She just lay on the bed, completely out of it.

The men continued their cleaning. They had warm washcloths they were using to try to get the worst of the dirt and grime off of Fiona. With each swipe, the washcloths were becoming more and more dirty, the water they'd been rinsing the rags in was practically black with the filth that was coming off her body.

Suddenly, at the same time Benny said, "Hell," Wolf said, "Shit."

Cookie looked away from Fiona's face for the first time, wondering what they'd found. He'd clearly heard the grimness in each of his friends' tones.

Benny gestured toward her leg. They all saw what they'd missed before. The dirt and grime had hidden a bullet wound. It looked like just a graze, but it was now slowly oozing blood over her leg and onto the sheet. The washcloth had obviously removed the scab that had been forming and allowed it to start bleeding again.

Both men looked at Abe, wondering what he'd been alarmed about. He simply gestured to her arms. The inside of Fiona's elbows were covered in needle marks and bruises. Cookie had seen them before, but it'd obviously come as a surprise to the other men.

No one questioned Cookie, no one looked disgusted. They just continued to work in silence to try to wipe away this courageous woman's time in hell. And it'd obviously been a hellacious experience. Besides the track marks and filthy condition of her body, bruises were revealed as the dirt was wiped away. She had different colors of finger marks on her upper arms, and more alarming, on her waist. There was a boot sized fading bruise on her back, but the most alarming were the bruises on her inner thighs, all different colors, alerting the men to the fact that some were older than others.

The track marks on her arms were ugly, but it really didn't matter in the long run. Even if Fiona had taken the drugs eagerly, which none of them would blame her for; this woman had saved their teammate's life. She'd saved their *friend's* life. They all had questions, but they'd wait. Her health came first.

All went well until Wolf tried to put an IV into Fiona's arm. One second she was deadweight in their arms, allowing them to move her limbs wherever they needed to in order to get her undressed and clean, and the next she fighting them as if her life depended on it.

"No no no *no,*" Fiona screamed out, fighting with all she had. She kicked out with her feet and narrowly missed Abe, who was standing near her. She was obviously remembering how she'd been drugged, or worse, been violated.

"Get off me, assholes," Fiona snarled, while still twisting and turning in the men's grasps. Fiona almost managed to twist off the bed and onto the floor before Wolf and Benny got a hold of her limbs and held her down, which only made her fight more frantically.

Cookie quickly leaned down toward Fiona's head. "Fiona, snap out of it," he said harshly, trying to get through to her. He put his hand from his good arm on her forehead. She stilled. Cookie continued, leaning in until his lips were right at her ear. "It's me, Hunter. You're safe. You're back in the States; you aren't in that shack anymore. Do you hear me?"

Fiona didn't respond, but she didn't fight either.

"I'm here with you and you're in the hospital with me. We aren't drugging you. I swear on my life you're safe. Do you hear me? We're trying to put in an IV. It'll give you fluids; it'll make you feel better. We aren't drugging you. I promise."

Still no movement from Fiona. "Trust me, sweetheart," Cookie tried again. "Please, just trust me."

Fiona finally sighed and turned toward Hunter. Her eyes opened into slits, just enough to see. "Hunter?" she said tentatively. "You're really okay?"

"I'm really okay," Cookie was touched in a way he'd never been before at her unselfishness. She had to be hurting and was confused, and still, she was worried about him. Cookie moved his hand from her forehead to the side of her face. Her skin was hot and sweaty, but Cookie could feel her lean her head into his hand as he spoke. The thought that in the midst of her terror, she'd trust him, made his stomach clench with an unfamiliar, but not unwelcome, jolt. "Just relax, Fee, everything is fine. I'm here and I'm not going anywhere."

Fiona sighed and nodded. Her eyes went to Wolf and the other men and unknowingly impressed the hell out of the battle-hardened men standing around her. "Sorry guys, I'll try to stay still, can't promise though."

Abe was the first one to respond, and he did so chuckling under his breath. "No worries, Fiona. We'll take care of you. *Nothing* will hurt you here. Relax."

Wolf was able to put in the IV without further incident, but all four men watched as she scrunched her eyes closed and as the sweat popped out on her forehead. Fiona finally fell into a fevered sleep without another word.

Wolf turned toward Cookie with barely leashed anger toward the mystery men who'd drugged and abused Fiona in his eyes, and said between clenched teeth, "Spill it." They all needed to hear Fiona's story. This obviously wasn't a cut-and-dried case. They all needed to hear what was going on, and it'd have to be reported back to their commander.

Cookie sighed. "I'd hoped she was over the worst of it, but apparently I was wrong. They drugged her. I have no idea with what, but I'm assuming it was probably heroin, but her symptoms don't exactly fit. Heroin withdrawal usually includes things like agitation, muscle aches, nausea, and vomiting. She's experienced all of those, but they usually don't last much longer than thirty hours. She should be over that by now.

"But if they mixed the heroin with meth, that could definitely cause some sort of substance-induced psychotic disorder. That makes this withdrawal more serious. It has its own set of symptoms, the prominent one being delusions or hallucinations. Fiona said they'd been drugging her for weeks. She's embarrassed about it, and you can see she's fighting as hard as she can, but it's not enough. I'm afraid it's going to get bad. I'm amazed she made it as long as she did."

"She's obviously tough," Wolf told Cookie. "She'll handle this. We won't let her down."

Wolf had apparently adopted Fiona as one of their own. He'd watched her put her life on the line for one of his best friends. There was no way one of the team could've safely gone down from the helicopter to help out and to get Cookie up. Fiona had literally saved both of their lives.

"We have to figure out what we're going to do. We can't stay here forever. Tex's people are only allowing us to use this place for about a week and a half at most, and we have to report back to base. I'll call the commander and let him know what's up and that all of us won't be returning right away. We have to figure out who's staying to help take care of her and who's going."

"I'm not leaving her, Wolf," Cookie said with steel in his voice.

"I didn't think you were." It was said matter-of-factly, as if Wolf hadn't even thought of the possibility.

"I'll stay too," Benny told them. Before Abe could volunteer to stay as well, Benny continued. "Abe, you need to get home to Alabama. You know how much she stresses when you're gone. Wolf, you should probably get home too, you can talk to the commander and make sure you hold the fort down, besides, Caroline will be just as anxious to see you as Alabama is to see Abe. I'll get Dude to stay here with us."

"What about Mozart?" Abe asked, apparently having no issues with Benny's plan.

"I think he can probably go back home as well. If we need him though, we'll get in touch. We can play it by ear."

"Cookie? Does that sound all right to you?" Wolf wanted to make sure Cookie approved whatever they decided, this woman was obviously important to him, even though they'd just met. Wolf didn't question it. He'd made a connection with his Caroline just as quickly and if Cookie was feeling half of what he'd felt when he'd found out Caroline was injured, he knew Fiona was already a part of their close-knit SEAL family, even if she didn't know it yet.

Cookie ran his hand over Fiona's forehead, feeling the heat and dampness. He moved slowly and carefully, still feeling the pain of his own wound. "Yeah, I'll get her through this and we'll see where we stand." His voice lowered in pain. "I don't really know anything about her. I don't know if she has a family somewhere wondering where she is. If she's married, if she has kids…" his voice trailed off.

The mood in the room got heavy. Christ, they hadn't thought of that. Wolf cleared his throat. "The main thing is to get her well. Cookie, you can deal with all that after she recovers."

Cookie nodded. "Okay, you guys get going. Benny and Dude can stay here with me. Wolf, if you can talk to Tex and let him know we'll be holed up here for a bit longer I'd appreciate it. I'll stay in touch and let you know how Fiona is doing and what our next steps will be."

The other men left the room, each looking back one more time at the woman on the bed and their teammate. They all silently hoped she'd pull through and that she was free. It was plain to see Cookie already considered Fiona "his," and they hoped, for both their sakes, it could work out.

Chapter Nine

FIONA'S FEVER SPIKED. Cookie was in the room with her when she started thrashing on the bed. She was extremely hot to the touch. Cookie grabbed Fiona's hand to try to reassure her, but that only seemed to make her reaction worse, and it pushed her over the edge. She jerked away from him and sat up, obviously trying to get up and out of the bed.

"Duuuude," Cookie bellowed as he tried to hold Fiona still. He wasn't very effective with his own shoulder injured from being shot. The door slammed open and not only Dude, but Benny also entered the room and summed up the situation quickly.

Dude grabbed hold of Fiona's shoulders while Benny grabbed her shins. Cookie stayed at her head trying to calm Fiona down with his touch. All three men were silent while they watched Fiona twist and turn and struggle to release herself. Just as before, her efforts only exhausted her. This time when Cookie tried to gentle her with his voice, it did no good. His voice couldn't bring her out of the drug induced haze she was in this time.

Finally, after what seemed hours, but was really only ten minutes or so, Fiona fell still again. She opened her eyes, gazing duly around the room. With glazed eyes she whimpered, "Why? Why are you doing this to me?" and then fell silent once again.

"God damn," Benny exclaimed softly. "Let us know when she wakes up again," he told Cookie sadly, knowing it probably wouldn't be the last time they were needed. "We're just next door and can be here in a second."

"I will, thanks guys. Hopefully she'll sleep the worst of this off soon."

Nodding, Benny and Dude left Cookie alone with Fiona again.

Cookie slept fitfully for the next twenty four hours. Waking when Fiona woke, trying to soothe her, calling for Benny and Dude to help him keep Fiona from hurting herself when needed, and then trying to sleep when Fiona slept.

They'd actually had to put gloves on Fiona's hands because she kept trying to scratch her skin. He knew it probably felt like her skin was crawling with bugs, but it was just the withdrawal making her think that way…okay, and the multitude of bug bites as well.

Cookie had seen a lot of hard things in his life, but nothing had prepared him for the heartbreaking cries and pleading that came out of this woman's mouth. They were all the more horrifying because he knew if *she* knew she was doing it, she'd have been mortified. Fiona had done everything she could while they were in the jungle to downplay her own suffering, and there was no doubt she'd been suffering.

When Fiona was lucid enough, they all tried to get her to eat something. They knew she wasn't dehydrated because the IVs were pumping lots of life saving fluids into her nonstop, but they were worried about her caloric intake.

They frequently got her up and she was able to use the toilet. Cookie was relieved because he knew Fiona *definitely* wouldn't want them putting in a catheter. They were all amazed she was as mobile as she was. Cookie attributed that to her stubbornness and strong will. She still wasn't lucid, but they all hoped she'd soon come out on the other side of the worst of this soon.

Three days after they arrived, Fiona opened her eyes and watched Cookie sitting next to her in a chair by the bed. She didn't say anything, but waited for him to open his eyes. As if Cookie could feel her gaze on him, he stirred and his eyes came to hers as soon as he awakened.

"How do you feel today, Fiona?" Cookie asked warily, wondering what kind of mood she'd be in and how the withdrawal was affecting her today. He'd seen Fiona's eyes open before, and she'd been completely out of it, not knowing what she was saying or doing. Cookie hoped today was the day she'd break through and come back to him.

Fiona cleared her throat before she spoke. "Better."

Cookie nodded, and kept a watchful eye on her. She sounded awful, but he wasn't surprised with all she'd been through. "Do you feel like getting up to use the bathroom?"

Fiona blushed and nodded.

Cookie was thrilled to see the blush bloom across Fiona's face. In the past couple of days she'd acted like a zombie, and certainly hadn't reacted with embarrassment to anything she'd done, or that the guys had done to her. Cookie helped Fiona stand up and arranged her IV pole and walked her to the bathroom. When he went to go in with her, Fiona stopped him.

"I can do it," she told him sternly, not looking Cookie in the eyes.

Cookie was skeptical, but didn't want to hurt Fiona's feelings. "Okay, if you need my help, just say something, I'll be right here," and he gestured at the door. Fiona nodded and closed the door softly.

Cookie heard her engage the lock on the door and frowned. It wasn't as if the lock would keep him or anyone else out, but it was more the fact she felt like she had to lock it at all that bothered him. He waited not-so-patiently for her to finish up so he could put her back to bed.

Fiona didn't bother to look at herself in the mirror, she didn't bother to use the toilet, she immediately went to the small window in the bathroom. She had to get out of here. Who knew what they were planning on doing with her. She knew sometimes they liked to be nice to her to try to get her to let her guard down, then do something horrible to crush her spirits. "Never again," Fiona mumbled to herself. She wanted out. She had to get out.

Her hands were shaking, she felt horrible, but she reached for the window anyway, noticing for the first time as she did, the IV in her arm. Feeling repulsed, who knew what they were putting in her body now, Fiona tore it out, not trying to be gentle or to worry about doing it the "right way." Blood slowly oozed down her arm and dripped on the floor, but she paid no attention to it.

Fiona slowly raised the window and glanced outside. Luckily, it seemed to be night. She had lost all sense of what day it was and when it was. When she was first taken, she'd tried to keep track, but the days and nights soon all ran together. But now the darkness would help her get away. Fiona looked outside again. Unluckily, she wasn't on the first floor...she looked to her right...a drain pipe ran the length of the wall right by the window. It wasn't perfect, but it'd have to work.

Fiona paused momentarily, something was niggling at the back of her brain, something about being on the second floor rather than the first. She ignored it. Time was of the essence. She had to escape. At any time they could notice she was gone. Her only thought was to get out. Get out now. Fiona awkwardly climbed up on the toilet to get better access to the window and lifted one leg. Feeling weak and shaky, she forced her body to cooperate and eased herself out. She reached for the drainpipe and held on.

Benny was sleeping when he felt the silent alarm on his wrist vibrate. Tex had told them the house was completely wired. No one could get in or out undetected. No one had thought they'd really need it while Fiona recuperated, but it was second nature for all of them to be hyper-vigilant.

Surprised, Benny shot out of bed and threw open his bedroom

door and tore down the hall into the make-shift control room. The main control-room was actually set up downstairs in a bunker-type compound under the den, but they'd been spending so much time upstairs with Fiona, they'd all agreed to move some aspects of it up here, so it'd be closer, just in case.

Benny took one look at the television monitor and swore. Fuck. Benny whirled and raced down the hall and down the stairs. Without bothering to contact either of his teammates or disable the alarm to the house, figuring it would wake Dude up, just as it did him, Benny ran around the side of the building not knowing exactly what to expect, even after seeing it on the monitors, and looked up. "Aw, hell," he muttered.

Fiona tried to slip slowly down the drainpipe, but her hands were bloody from where she had pulled out the IV and she had no strength. She slid faster and faster toward the ground. All she could do was try to hang on. Benny grabbed Fiona just before she hit the ground. Just as he caught her, Dude came running around the corner of the building, gun drawn, ready for anything.

Fiona felt someone grab her just as she was about to escape. She'd been so close this time. She tried to throw herself out of the arms of the man who held her, but his hold was too tight.

"Let me go, let me *go*," she croaked at him while trying to hit him and scratch his eyes out. Benny grunted and grasped her closer to his chest. Dude summed up the situation quickly, looked up at the window and boomed, "Coooookie."

Cookie heard Dude yelling for him and knew something was very wrong. Yelling wasn't their usual mode of communication, so if Dude was shouting from outside at the top of his lungs, something had seriously gone wrong. He had to get to Fiona and protect her.

With one strong push against the bathroom door with his shoulder, the door slammed open as if the lock had never been engaged. His heart hit the floor. He tried to process the empty room, IV pole standing upright, and the blood splatters covering the wall and the window…and, of course, the *open* window.

Cookie strode over and looked out. "Fucking hell." He saw Benny struggling with Fiona, and Dude kneeling, trying to hold her legs. She was crying and struggling and trying to get out of their arms. A part of him saw the blood covering her arms but tried to block it out. Cookie didn't say a word, but turned around and headed down the stairs to get to Fiona.

When he got outside, Cookie saw that Benny had sat on the ground and was holding Fiona in a wrestler's hold she couldn't escape from. He had one arm diagonally around her chest and the other was locked around her head, keeping her immobile, but allowing her plenty of room to breathe. Dude was kneeling next to them holding Fiona down with his hands on her legs above her knees. Fiona's arms were trapped at her sides within Benny's grasp. She looked up at Cookie with tears and fire in her eyes at the same time.

"Let me go, you fucking bastards. You can't keep me here. Let me go, just let me go."

Benny looked up at Cookie sadly. "Guess she's still not out of the worst of it yet."

Cookie nodded grimly at his teammate's not-needed words, and squatted awkwardly down next to Benny, Dude, and Fiona.

"Fiona, it's Hunter, you're okay, you're fine. You're in Texas." He had to try to get through to her.

"Shut *up!*" she yelled viciously while trying to wriggle out of the inescapable hold of Benny at the same time. "I don't believe you, you're an asshole and I'm gonna kill you, I'm gonna tear your fucking arms off and poke out your eyes, just see if I don't." Fiona tried to spit at him, but her spittle landed a couple inches away from her hip, instead of on Cookie.

"I won't do it, I won't do anything you tell me to do, you hear me? I *won't*. You're sick. You can't *sell* people. We're not *slaves*.

Raping people and hurting and drugging them until they do what you want them to is a shitty thing to do." She paused, her breath hitching in her throat, but she continued. "I'll *never* be a 'good little girl' and let someone keep me as their sex slave. *Never.* You hear me? You might as well kill me now. Just do it already. *Fucking do it!*"

Cookie stood up. Angrier than he could remember being in a long time. Not at Fiona, but at her kidnappers. *They* had done this to her. He knew she was reliving some of the hell they'd put her through. Knew Fiona thought they were them. Cookie wanted to get on a plane, head back to Mexico, and hunt them down. They'd hurt Fiona. They'd done all sorts of unspeakable things to her. To *his* Fiona. He wanted to kill them all. Cookie knew had to get control of himself. While he might want to kill them, he had to take care of Fiona first. She'd always come first now. Always. He had no idea what the future would hold for them, he only knew he wanted to be in it with her.

"You got her?" Cookie asked Benny through clenched teeth. He wanted to be the one holding Fiona, but he knew his strength wasn't at a hundred percent yet, and he didn't want to risk either dropping her or having her escape and hurt herself further.

Benny nodded. Dude helped Benny stand up since he couldn't use his arms because they were holding Fiona. The four of them awkwardly made their way back into the house and up the stairs. Fiona hurled insults and threatened bodily harm to anyone and everyone the entire way.

None of the men said a word as they moved, as one, back up the stairs and toward her room. Not one man was disgusted, not one man pitied her. Every one of them knew Fiona's story now, with the few words she'd spat at them outside, she'd revealed everything she'd been through. They could read between the lines. The curse words and insults she continued to scream at them as they headed upstairs were a result of the drugs and what had happened to her. They all knew it and understood it.

SEAL teams are notoriously close; they have to be as they put their lives in each other's hands on every mission. It's ground into them from the first day of BUD/S training. But this, this was something new. Benny, Dude, and Cookie had never felt as close as they did at this moment. No words were spoken while Fiona was carried back into her bed and restrained. This woman had been through hell, but wasn't broken. Wasn't beaten. She was fighting until her last breath. She was outnumbered and weak, but she still fought. It was humbling and amazing. The three men had seen bravery before. They'd seen Caroline take a beating that would've broken most men. They'd seen her get thrown into the ocean; ankles tied together, and still have the inner strength to stay calm. But somehow, this was something altogether different.

They wanted vengeance for Fiona, something they knew they might never get. But all three men silently vowed to do whatever it took to make sure Fiona felt safe again. Somehow, someway, they'd make her feel safe.

Chapter Ten

FIONA STRUGGLED WEAKLY on the bed. They'd tied her down, again. At least she wasn't chained by the neck anymore. And she wasn't on the hard floor. Again, there was something she should remember...but it was gone as soon as the thought flitted through her brain. They wanted to hurt her, they *had* hurt her. They wanted to sell her. They wanted to kill her.

She watched as one of the men standing next to her filled a syringe. His back was turned, but Fiona knew what he was doing. Oh God. Not again. Not more drugs. Fiona wouldn't beg, she'd done that before and it'd done no good and had only made her feel more pathetic.

"I won't beg, you assholes," Fiona flung out recklessly, looking at the two other men in the room. She blinked to try to clear her vision, but continued, even though she couldn't see them clearly. "You can drug me all you want, but it won't help. I won't do what you say, even if I never get out of here, you'll all pay. I swear to God. I can't stop you from drugging me, but it won't help you sell me. I'll make sure that anyone you sell me to regrets it and comes to take it out on you."

Fiona's voice trailed off. The roaring in her ears was loud. She could hear her own breathing, but that was it. Oh God, he really was going to drug her again. She closed her eyes and turned her head as far to the side as she could. She couldn't fight anymore. They held her down and she felt the prick of the needle in her arm. Shit. Fiona's thoughts became more and more muddled and she welcomed the nothingness that came over her. She didn't want to know what they'd do to her this time while she was out of it.

The men sighed. Thank God. Thank God the valium Benny had given her had taken effect quickly. No one said a word. Dude got busy putting another IV in her other arm. Cookie tried to clean up the blood on her body. Benny got to work cleaning the bathroom.

Dude was the first one to leave to go back to his bedroom. Benny and Cookie sat on either side of Fiona's bed and watched her. She was breathing a bit fast, but otherwise seemed to be calm.

"Holy shit, Cookie," Benny finally said. Cookie could only nod. They both were imaging the hell Fiona had been through. The fact that she hadn't backed down, that she still wasn't backing down, said a lot about her.

"You know, when I saw you get shot from the chopper, for a moment I wondered what the fuck we were gonna do. We had one hostage rescued, you had an unknown other person with you and you were shot. I almost took her out."

Benny looked away from Fiona's face and at Cookie for the first time since he'd started talking. "We had no idea she was there too, and all I could think of was that she was expendable and you weren't. I had my finger on the trigger and I was ready to fire when I saw her stumble out of that bush with you. She half dragged you, half carried you to that ladder. As soon as I saw you were secure, we hauled your ass up as fast as we could. Even at that point I thought about getting the hell out of there. We still didn't know who she was, and we had both you and the hostage rescued."

Benny paused, then took a deep breath and continued. "I opened my mouth to tell Wolf to get us out of there when I saw her struggling with your pack. Fiona simply looked up at the chopper and waited. She knew we could leave her there. She didn't beg, she wasn't gesturing at us to lower the ladder, she was just waiting...and hoping.

God, the hope. I could see it from the chopper. Looking down at her, looking up at us, I made the only decision I could. I lowered the ladder. I could practically *see* her relief." Benny paused again.

Cookie nodded, knowing how hard of a decision that had to have been. He waited for his friend to continue.

"To know now some of the hell Fiona went through, and fuck, we both know we don't know the half of it, but to know *some* of what she went through, I feel guilty as hell that I even *thought* about leaving her there."

Silence filled the room, broken only by the slight wheezing noise that Fiona made as she slept on, oblivious to the undercurrents in the room around her.

Cookie nodded at his friend and teammate. "Believe me, I know what you mean. I had Julie all set and we were one step from leaving the hellhole she'd been held in when something made me take one last look around. I didn't hear anything; it was just *something* that made me look again. When I think about if I had ignored that feeling, when I think about how Fiona could have so easily have been left there…" Cookie's voice drifted off.

The men both knew what an extraordinary woman Fiona was. They didn't blame her for what happened tonight. In reality, they both blamed themselves. They should've known she wasn't better yet, they should've been more watchful. But sitting there with Fiona, after watching her anguish and her strength and will to live, they each made a silent promise that nothing would happen to this woman again. No matter where she went, or what she did, they'd keep watch over her. They could do no less.

TWO DAYS LATER, Fiona rolled over with a groan. Her body felt like it'd been through the wringer. She ached all over. Her head felt a little fuzzy, but she took a deep breath and looked around. She saw

Hunter sitting in a chair near her bed. His feet were up on the mattress, his arms crossed over his chest, his head canted to the side while he softly snored. Fiona wondered what time it was and why he was sleeping there.

Cookie woke up from his light doze next to the bed to find Fiona staring at him.

"Hi," he said softly, not knowing if Fiona was truly aware of her surroundings or not.

"Hi," Fiona responded. "You look like crap," she told Hunter honestly.

He chuckled. "You don't look so hot yourself," he bantered carefully. His smile quickly left his face and he sat up. He leaned forward and put his hand on her forehead. Fiona tried not to flinch away from him or blush at his gentle touch.

"How are you feeling?" Cookie asked carefully. He wanted to assess Fiona's state of mind before he let her do anything on her own so they didn't have a repeat of her escape out the second floor window.

"I feel weird," Fiona answered honestly.

"How so?" Cookie inquired, tilting his head to the side while he waited for her answer.

"I feel weak, my mouth feels like I've been sucking on cotton for a month, and I have to use the bathroom," Fiona answered honestly.

Cookie just stared at her for a moment.

"What?" Fiona finally asked. "Why are you looking at me like that?"

"Do you remember anything about the last few days?" Cookie asked quietly.

Fiona tensed. Oh shit. What happened? What had she done? She merely shook her head and waited to hear what Hunter had to say.

Cookie looked her in the eyes and merely said, "Okay, I'll help you up and we'll go from there."

Fiona wondered what Hunter was keeping from her, but she really did have to use the bathroom, so the questions could wait. She let Hunter assist her out of the bed and help her walk toward the bathroom. She gestured toward the IV still attached to her arm. "Any chance I can get this out? I'm not a big fan of needles and knowing one is imbedded in my skin, even if it's helping me, creeps me out."

"We'll see," Hunter told her without rancor.

Fiona noticed the door to the bathroom was missing. It actually looked like it'd been splintered from its hinges. She didn't remember a lot about arriving at the house, but she thought she'd remember a missing door. There was no way she was going to pee in front of Hunter though.

"Do you need help?" Hunter asked.

Fiona shook her head vigorously. "No!"

"Okay, I'll be right here next to the door with my back turned. When you're done, just let me know and I'll come in and help you."

Fiona shuffled into the bathroom. Not even thinking Hunter would peek, she quickly did what she needed to do, then turned to the mirror. Oh. My. God. She looked like the creature from the black lagoon. She almost didn't recognize herself. Fiona didn't think she'd made a noise, but suddenly Hunter was there.

Fiona watched in the mirror as he came up behind her and put his hands on the counter on either side of her hips and leaned in. She could feel him all along her back. He dwarfed her. Fiona really hadn't noticed before now how tall he really was. Her head came up to about Hunter's chin. He met her eyes in the mirror.

"How are you *really*, Fee?" he asked quietly.

"I'm okay, Hunter," she told him quietly. And she was. She was alive, she was safe, she wasn't in the jungle. She was fucking awesome.

Hunter continued to look at her. Fiona looked down at the counter. She should've felt penned in with him at her back, but she didn't. It felt...good. She could feel his strength and all she wanted to do was lean on him and let him be the strong one for once in her life. As soon as Fiona had the thought, she dismissed it and tried to stand up straighter. She was strong. She had to be.

Hunter took the choice away from her. One arm came up across Fiona's chest and the other went around her waist. He pulled her back against him. Fiona went willingly. Soon the tears started. She couldn't help it. She was weak and feeling vulnerable. The way he was holding her, as if she was made of glass, was just too much.

Cookie turned her in his arms and held on to Fiona while she cried. He hated to see her so upset, but he was glad to see the honest emotion for the first time since he'd met her.

He wrapped one arm around her back and other around her neck; he tucked her head into the crook of his shoulder. Fiona shook as she cried and Cookie could feel her tears on his neck. Her arms were curled in front of her and he could feel her fingers clutching at his shirt as if they'd never let go.

"Cry it out, Fee. You're safe. I've got you." Cookie murmured the words in Fiona's hair and knew he'd let her stand there all day if she needed it.

"I – I – I don't know why I'm crying." Her words were muffled against his neck, but Cookie still heard her.

"It's relief. I bet you were strong while you were being held, probably wouldn't let those assholes see you cry, but right now you don't have to be strong anymore."

When her tears finally tapered off and Cookie could feel Fiona's trembles subside, he carefully lifted her in his arms and took her, and her IV pole, back into the bedroom.

Cookie set Fiona on a chair in the corner of the room and kissed her on the forehead. He looked her in the eyes and ordered, "Stay put for a bit, Fee. I'm going to change the sheets before you get back in."

Cookie waited until Fiona nodded, then turned to the bed and quickly and efficiently stripped the soiled sheets and put on a freshly laundered set. He wanted to give her time to collect herself. After putting clean sheets on the bed he went back to Fiona and helped her out of the chair. He kept his hand on her elbow and assisted her back to the bed, letting her walk on her own. Cookie tucked her in and leaned down and kissed her on the forehead. He stayed close and whispered, "Sleep, Fee. I'll be here when you wake up again. All is well. I swear."

"Thank you, Hunter. Thank you for finding me. You have no idea, just thank you." Fiona closed her eyes and was asleep again in moments, not waiting to hear Hunter's response.

When Fiona woke up again, Hunter was there, as he promised. She had no idea how long she'd been asleep. She would've protested Hunter babying her, but if she was honest with herself, it felt good. Hearing a noise near the door, Fiona turned her head and saw Benny was also in the room.

"Hello, Fiona. Are you feeling better?"

"I am. Thank you for all you've done for me."

"You're welcome. It's time for that IV to come out." Benny was all business.

His attitude actually made Fiona feel more comfortable. She never liked being the center of attention.

Benny made quick work of removing the needle from her arm. Fiona rubbed her wrist where the IV had been inserted.

Another man came into the room carrying a tray with food on it. Fiona's mouth immediately started watering. She couldn't even guess when the last time she had real food was. She didn't think it'd be good manners if she snatched the tray out of the man's arms, and fell on it in the middle of the room like she was a starved feline, but, oh, how she wanted to.

"Fee, I want to introduce you to my teammates. That's Dude carrying the tray and Benny took your IV out."

Fiona wrinkled her eyebrows. "Benny? Dude? Are those your real names?"

Dude chuckled as he put the tray on the bed. "No, Fiona, they're nicknames. Just like Hunter's nickname is Cookie."

Fiona couldn't take her eyes off of the tray. The soup was steaming and the roll sitting next to the bowl looked like heaven. "Ah…okay." She didn't really know what she was saying, the food was taking all her attention.

Benny laughed. "Dude, you'd better back away from that tray, it looks like she'll fight you for it."

Fiona blushed bright red and looked down at her hands in her lap. She felt the bed depress next to her but didn't look up.

Cookie sat next to Fiona, upset that *she* was embarrassed. He put one hand at her waist and pulled the tray so it was in front of him and next to Fiona. "Dig in, Fee, don't mind us."

Fiona didn't hesitate. She grabbed the roll and tore it in half. She didn't bother with the butter which was sitting on the tray, but instead took a big bite of the bread and almost moaned. Jesus, it was even warm. Fiona forced herself to put the pieces of roll down and pick up the spoon. She leaned over so as not to spill the soup all the way down the front of herself, and slurped the delicious broth. It probably came from a can, but it tasted heavenly.

Fiona didn't care that the three men watched her eat, she was starved. When she first saw the food she didn't think it was nearly enough, but after eating half the roll and most of the soup, she was surprisingly full. Fiona knew her body would need time to adjust to eating again. She didn't want to get sick on top of everything else, so she forced herself to put the spoon down.

Fiona felt Hunter's hand at the small of her back and she suddenly realized he'd had it there the entire time she'd been eating. The warmth from his hand felt good. She hadn't been touched gently in a very long time.

Fiona tried to ignore the way Benny and Dude looked at her. She didn't want to try to interpret their looks. She was too tired and too raw for that. Finally, she couldn't stand it anymore.

"I'm sorry," Fiona said with as much dignity as she could.

"For what?" Benny asked, before Cookie could.

"For whatever it is that I did, or whatever happened that I can't remember," Fiona said honestly. She watched as the men glared at each other. "No one has told me anything, but by the way you're all acting, it couldn't have been good. What day is it?" She asked suddenly, changing the subject abruptly. "How long have I been here?" She could tell they didn't want to tell her. Finally Dude gave in.

"Five days."

Five days. Oh crap. "Wow, five days, okay then." Fiona mused out loud. "I must've been really out of it to not remember five days. So again, whatever it is that I did that's making you guys act this way, I'm sorry."

Cookie shook his head. "Fee, there's nothing for you to be sorry about. *Nothing.* Do you hear me?" He waited for her to nod before continuing. "You were sick, we cared for you. That's it."

Fiona knew he was glossing over something, but she let him for now. "Okay." She paused. "Can I take a shower?"

That made the men laugh. "I was just going to ask if you wanted a shower now or later," Cookie told her.

"Oh, definitely now."

Benny and Dude left the room and Hunter helped Fiona out of the bed and steadied her as she swayed on her feet. Fiona looked down at herself and blushed. She was wearing a button down shirt, obviously one of the men's.

Seeing her look of chagrin, Cookie hurried to reassure her. "My shirt was the easiest thing to put you in when you were sick. I can't promise we didn't see anything, but we kept everything as clinical as possible to preserve your modesty."

Fiona just nodded, wishing she could melt into the floor and never have to see any of the men again.

Cookie put a finger under her chin and forced it up so she was looking into her eyes. "Don't be embarrassed, Fee. We were all worried about *you* and not about looking at your naked body."

"I'm not sure that makes me feel any better."

"Maybe this will then. Even though you've been sick, I still think you're the most fucking beautiful woman I've ever seen."

Fiona's eyes almost bugged out of her head. "Are you kidding me?" She tried to tug her face out of his grasp with no luck.

Cookie put both hands on her cheeks so she couldn't back away from him anymore and tilted her head up even more. His thumbs rested on her lower jaw. Cookie lowered his head until his forehead rested against hers. "No, I'm not kidding. I've never been more serious about anything in my entire life. It's not just your face, Fee, it's you. I don't know the basics about you, your favorite color, where you grew up, or what you like to eat, but I *do* know you. I know you're tough, you have a will of iron, you're compassionate and you have a strong sense of right and wrong. And, most importantly, I know you won't give up. The odds have been stacked against you for a while now, but you just plowed through every obstacle in your way, and when you couldn't bust through it, you held on until you could break through with some help. That's beauty to me, Fee. You're fucking beautiful."

"Holy crap."

Cookie leaned back a fraction and didn't give her a chance to say anything further. "Now, how about that shower?"

Fiona stood in the shower spray enjoying the feel of the water sluicing down over her body. She washed her hair at least three times before she was happy with the feel of it. Hunter had wanted to help her with the shower, saying she wasn't strong enough or steady enough to stand on her own, but Fiona had firmly rejected that idea. It was bad enough he and his friends had seen her naked when she was sick and through whatever it was she'd done.

She stood in the water and for the first time really thought about all that had happened to her. It was all too much; even though she'd had a crying fit around Hunter when she first woke up, she'd been stoic for as long as she could stand. Fiona allowed herself to break down, again. She slid down the wall to the shower floor and sobbed. She cried for what the kidnappers had done to her, the hurts she'd been through, for being scared, and finally for having been rescued.

When her skin was pruned and the shower ran lukewarm, Fiona turned off the water and stepped out, making sure to keep one hand on the towel rack so she wouldn't fall on her face. Hunter had scrounged a T-shirt and sweat pants from somewhere for her to wear. She dried herself off and slipped on the clean clothes. Amazingly, they mostly fit. She didn't have any undies or a bra, but nothing felt better to her than the soft cotton against her skin. She couldn't even remember the last time she'd felt clean. She knew she'd never take it for granted again. She'd probably become obsessed with showering, but Fiona supposed there were worse things to be obsessed about. She shrugged.

Fiona walked out of the bathroom and found Hunter standing to the side of the broken door. He looked strong and fit and his shoulder wound was obviously healed enough for it not to bother him. Fiona had no idea what she should say or do, but she did know somehow he centered her and made the jumpy feeling inside her belly subside.

Cookie stared at the woman who came out of the bathroom. She was still as skinny as ever, and he could tell she'd been crying, but the shower had done amazing things for her. Her skin shone and she looked lighter than she had since he met her.

"You look great," Cookie told her honestly.

Fiona blushed and looked down at her feet. "Thanks, I'm not sure about great, but I feel a hundred percent better."

"Are you still hungry?" Cookie asked her.

"I feel like I'm somehow letting my entire gender down by saying this, but I could eat a cow," Fiona answered honestly. "I was stuffed earlier, but suddenly I'm hungry again."

"I think that'll happen for a while. I know once when my team was on a mission and some of us were captured, once we were released, I didn't feel full for weeks."

Immediately concerned for him, Fiona came toward Hunter and put her hand on his arm. Looking up at him in sympathy, she asked, "How long were you captured?"

"Not nearly as long as I think you were, Fee, but long enough."

"I'm sorry, Hunter."

"I didn't tell you that for your sympathy, but thank you, Fee. My point was, I think you're going to feel hungry for a while, even if you're full right after you eat, twenty minutes later you'll be hungry again. It's your body's way of healing. You'll be better off eating several small meals a day than stuffing yourself with one or two. Just take it easy, your body will tell you when you're done."

Stepping back a foot, Fiona was finding it hard to think straight around Hunter, she nodded at his words. "I'm sure you're right. I've always been a snacker, so it'll be nice to have a reason to snack now."

"Ready to go down?"

At her nod, Cookie took Fiona's hand and they made their way out of the bedroom silently. Cookie held on tight. Everything he'd said to her was what he felt from the heart, but he'd never opened up to any woman like that before. He wanted Fiona. There wasn't one thing about her that turned him off. Not one. If he had anything to say about it, she was his. *His.* He now understood what Wolf and Abe felt about their women. There was something inside him that knew she was meant to be his. He'd have to apologize to both of his teammates for even thinking they were crazy to tie themselves to a woman as quickly as they had to Caroline and Alabama.

Cookie knew he had a ways to go before he'd be able to officially claim Fiona as his. They had a lot to work through, there was a lot he didn't know about her, but at the end of the day, he'd fight to make her his. Forever. She didn't know it, but her life had just changed, hopefully for the better.

Chapter Eleven

W HEN FIONA AND COOKIE entered the dining room, Benny and Dude were waiting for them. The table was set with several bowls filled with delicious smelling food. There were three dishes full of pasta with different kinds of sauce, Alfredo, marinara, and meat sauce, a large bowl of salad, and a plate loaded with corn on the cob dripping with butter. The men had obviously been busy.

Fiona looked away from the food and suddenly felt self-conscious. Obviously, Hunter had arranged for the meal to be served after she was done with her shower, but being around others, she was finding, was awkward, and even a bit uncomfortable. She was the only woman, and was still a bit raw from everything that had gone on while she was held captive.

Cookie noticed her unease and squeezed her hand in reassurance. "Okay?"

"Yeah." Fiona looked up at Hunter as if she'd just thought of something. "You won't leave me will you?" She meant right then, at the dining room table, but as soon as the words left her mouth, Fiona realized she wouldn't mind if Hunter stayed by her side forever.

Hunter's eyes warmed at her words and he brought their clasped hands up to his mouth and kissed Fiona's knuckles briefly. "Never."

His words and kiss made a shiver work its way through Fiona. Could he read her mind? Fiona relaxed enough at his words to be able to continue walking into the room as if nothing was wrong, but she kept a tight hold of Hunter's hand for extra reassurance.

Cookie was once again impressed with Fiona's inner strength. He noticed the tensing of her body as they'd entered the room, and couldn't help but feel pride at her obvious effort to hold herself together. He knew she'd asked him not to leave her at the table with his teammates, but he'd answered as if she'd asked him if he would *ever* leave her.

Cookie sat Fiona on his left before taking his own seat next to her. There was a feast waiting on the table for them. Fiona couldn't remember seeing that much food in one place before.

"Did you guys make all this?"

Benny winked at Fiona and joked, "It was all us. We're not just pretty faces you know."

"I made the salad and boiled the corn," Dude told Fiona seriously, continuing to answer her question about the food, "but Benny is the chef. I've never tasted anything he's made that hasn't been downright delicious."

Benny just shrugged and commented nonchalantly, "I like to cook."

The meal was lively with everyone joking and kidding around. It was interesting to be in an atmosphere like that for Fiona, as she'd never had a big family and didn't really know how to act. She mostly just smiled at the other men and joined in the conversation when she could. She knew this happiness wouldn't last for her though. First of all, she couldn't stay in this house forever. Fiona wasn't even sure where she was; just that she wasn't in Mexico. Fiona knew she had to get back home sooner rather than later, and she figured the guys did too. This was but a short moment in her life, and she had to enjoy it while she could.

Fiona also figured, at some point, she was going to have to talk to Hunter and his team about what had happened to her, but she wasn't going to bring it up unless they did.

After finishing the meal, and eating less than she thought she would considering how hungry she'd been when she walked into the room and had seen the food, Fiona helped Hunter and the others carry the dishes into the kitchen. She insisted on helping put the dishes into the dishwasher and pack away the leftovers. The men had put up a token protest, but in the end had allowed her to help.

While Fiona kept a good distance from Dude and Benny, she noticed Hunter was by her side almost the entire time they were in the kitchen. Every now and then he'd put his hand on her waist to guide her to the side, or to get her out of the way of one of his teammates. His hand felt possessive, but in a good way. Hunter was true to his earlier word not to leave her side.

Later that evening, Fiona sat on a couch with Hunter sitting next to her and Benny and Dude across from them in two easy chairs. They were in the library, one of the most comfortable rooms in the house. Fiona knew the guys did it deliberately, giving her room and not crowding her, but she was still on edge.

"Want to watch TV, Fiona?" Dude asked.

Fiona thought about it for a second. It'd been forever since she'd last seen any kind of news, and she suddenly had a violent urge to see what had been going on in the rest of the world since she'd been kidnapped. "I'd love to watch the news…if that's okay?"

"Of course it's okay. No problem." Dude leaned over and snagged the remote that was sitting on the small coffee table. He clicked on the television and flicked the channels until he came to a twenty-four hour news station.

Fiona watched, completely enthralled, as she caught up on the politics and other news stories she'd missed out on.

Cookie kept his eyes on Fiona, gauging her mental state as she stared at the TV. Cookie didn't think about how she would feel, missing out on everything going on around the world, but it was obvious she was enjoying catching up.

Seeing Fiona gasp, Cookie turned to look at the television, just as

Benny snatched the remote off the table where Dude had thrown it and turned the volume up.

Our next story comes from Washington DC where Senator Lytle held a press conference to discuss the rumors that his daughter, Julie Lytle, had been kidnapped. Let's tune in...

Before I get into the details of what happened to my daughter, I just want to publicly thank the members of the SEAL team that were dispatched into Mexico to rescue my daughter. The men and women of our armed forces are unsung heroes, and they risk their lives every day fighting against evil all over the world. Sex trafficking is a problem that is not only a United States issue, but it's a problem all over the world. Women and children are being kidnapped, and forced into prostitution and slavery and forced labor. I'm going to use my position to lobby our government to do something about it. Now, as for the rumors, my daughter was...

The television went dark as Benny clicked it off.

Fiona turned to look at him eyebrows raised in question.

"You don't need to relive it."

Fiona simply nodded. If she'd thought about it a bit more, she probably would have been very uncomfortable listening to whatever Julie's dad had to say about Julie's time in captivity. It was the right move on Benny's part.

"With that being said, can you tell us your story, Fiona?"

Fiona swallowed, it looked like it was time. She couldn't put it off anymore.

"Tell us who you are, Fiona," Cookie coaxed gently. "How did you end up in that hellhole and where do you come from?"

Fiona took a deep breath, knowing her time here in this sanctuary was coming to an end. They wouldn't kick her out, but she had to go back to the real world, *her* real world, and they had to go back to rescuing people. It was what it was.

"My name is Fiona Rain Storme." She watched the men cringe,

then struggle to hold back their grins. "Yeah, horrible isn't it? My mother was fourteen when she had me...and she told me it was raining cats and dogs when I was born. Apparently the storm was sudden and unexpected. She'd planned to give me the middle name of Sarah, but when the storm came on right when she was heading to the hospital, and with her last name already being Storme, she decided to change it. I admit, it's not very creative, but I'm sure it seemed so to a teenager. I never knew my father; he was long gone before my mother had me. We lived with my mom's parents for a while, but it was obvious they didn't like her, or me. She was kicked out of the house when she was eighteen, and I was four. We moved around a lot, staying in homeless shelters and stuff until I was about eight. Then one day my mom never came to pick me up from school. I sat in front of the building until eight at night when one of the teachers who'd left work late, saw me and called the police. I never saw my mom again. I have no idea what happened to her and I've come to terms with that. I went into the foster care system because my grandparents didn't want me...but it was fine."

"Fine?" Cookie asked sternly.

"Yeah, fine."

Cookie knew he hadn't even heard the bad part of her story, but he was so pissed off at her mom and grandparents, he was barely holding himself together. But to hear Fiona describe her childhood and the foster care system as "fine" almost pushed him over the edge.

"What exactly does 'fine' mean to you Fee? I know how you've held up with the things that happened to you in Mexico and I suspect you'd probably downplay those to others and describe them something like 'no big deal.' So, I want to know exactly what 'fine' means to you."

Fiona looked at Hunter. He didn't look happy. She'd sworn to herself when she'd turned eighteen and gotten out of her last foster home that she wouldn't use it as a crutch or an excuse for anything bad that happened in her life. She definitely didn't want these beautiful, bad ass men to think she needed coddling, or worse, to feel sorry for her.

Ignoring the other two men in the room for the moment and taking a risk, Fiona leaned toward Hunter and put one hand on his knee and leaned her head against his shoulder. She wouldn't have to look at him this way, but it also served the secondary purpose of comforting her. Not entirely surprised, Fiona felt Hunter's arm immediately wrap around her shoulders and he pulled her closer into him and shifted until she was more comfortable.

When Fiona didn't immediately answer, Cookie prompted her. "Fee?"

"It just means that while it wasn't a fairy tale childhood full of ponies and hearts and flowers, it wasn't the hell that a lot of kids go through."

Fiona felt Hunter nod and press his lips to her hair. "Okay. For now. Can you tell us how you got to that hellhole in Mexico?"

Fiona took a breath, knowing this was the hardest part to tell. "I currently live in El Paso. I work as an administrative assistant at a local University. It's a perfectly boring job and I lead a boring life. I spend most of my days trying to help students register for classes or dealing with mad parents and students. I was getting burned out and I needed to take a break. I was on vacation in Florida when I was taken."

Fiona paused again, not really wanting to tell the guys how stupid she'd acted. She wanted nothing more than to call her story done and never think about it again, but she owed these men. They'd risked their lives to help her. She felt obligated to tell them. Fiona felt Hunter put his free hand on top of the one that was resting on his leg. He squeezed it reassuringly. It was amazing how much she relied on his small touches. Fiona didn't know why she could tolerate Hunter's touch, when the thought of any other man touching her as

Hunter was, freaked her the hell out, but she was too tired to analyze it. Fiona took a breath and continued.

"I went on vacation alone. I'd convinced myself I was an adult and it was perfectly fine and safe for me to travel on my own. No one would be interested in bothering me. I'm not gorgeous or the type of woman predators would be looking for. I'd been there three days, not really enjoying myself, if you must know. It's not that fun to be by yourself on vacation. I went to restaurants by myself, I even went snorkeling by myself, but it's not very exciting when you can't share your experiences with anyone."

"Why'd you go by yourself in the first place, Fee?" Cookie asked gently, not understanding how someone like Fiona could be so alone.

Fiona looked down, embarrassed.

"Jesus, I'm sorry, I didn't mean to embarrass you," Cookie told her; mortified his innocent question had caused her even a second of awkwardness.

"It's okay, Hunter. I was tired of my job. It's not that exciting or interesting and I just wanted to take a break. I don't have any close girlfriends that I would've felt comfortable in asking to go with me."

Dude asked the question that Cookie had been dying to ask, but had bit back. "Do you need to call anyone and let them know you're all right? That you're alive. Boyfriend? Husband?"

Fiona picked her head up off of Hunter's shoulder and looked up at him in alarm. Even though Dude had asked, she spoke to Hunter. "Oh my God, no. I'm not with anyone. I wouldn't...I didn't..." She started to sit upright, mortified Hunter might have thought she was married or had a boyfriend and was leaning against him so intimately.

Cookie gathered Fiona back into his arms and held her tight. He could feel her trembling. "Shhhh, Fee. No one thought anything inappropriate. Relax." He caressed her back and glared at Dude.

Dude just shook his head in exasperation. "Yeah, Fiona, I just wanted to make sure you knew you could contact anyone you needed to."

Fiona pulled away from Hunter just enough so she could turn her head and look over at Dude. "There isn't anybody."

At her anguished words, Cookie put his hand on her head and pushed it back into his chest. He loved feeling Fiona's arms hesitantly curl around his body, holding him back. "Tell us the rest, Fee. You're safe here. Go on. Get it all out."

Fiona nodded against Hunter's chest, not lifting her head. "Okay, so anyway, it was my fourth day in Florida and I was leaving the next day. I decided I should at least check out a club once when I was there."

Hearing Benny snort, Fiona laughed, but it wasn't with humor. "Yeah, dumb. I know. So in I went, by myself, thinking I was all that and more. I had a few drinks and watched others dancing. A guy asked me to dance, I said yes; when it was over I went back to the bar and continued drinking my drink."

Again, when Benny snorted, Fiona agreed with him. "Yeah, I know. Again, I was dumb. Really dumb. Seriously dumb. No one knows that more than me. I paid for it. Big time." The room got quiet. No one said a word, knowing what Fiona would say next.

"When I woke up, I was in that room Hunter found me in. I was still wearing the stupid T-shirt, shorts, and flip-flops I'd worn to the club. I suppose I should be glad I wasn't wearing heels, that would've made it really hard to tromp through the jungle. I'm not sure how many days had gone by when I woke up, but I was pretty out of it. They must've started the drugs before I came to. I was chained by the ankle at first, but when I attacked them whenever they got close to me, they wised up and chained me by my neck. They could control me better that way. I figure I was there for about three months, but it was probably more based on the time that I was out of it." Fiona paused. No one said a word, although she could see Dude and Benny clenching their teeth.

"What did they want you for?" Dude asked finally, knowing, but wanting to see what Fiona would say.

"They wanted to sell me as a sex slave, but I wasn't 'properly trained,'" Fiona told the men without tempering her words. "They were waiting for me to break. To beg for mercy, to beg for more drugs, to beg to die...something. But I refused. I wouldn't give in to them. They couldn't steal who I was. And I figured whatever they had in store for me would be worse than where I was, so I refused them. I don't think they would've kept me as long as they did, but they didn't know what else to do with me at that point."

"Good girl," Cookie muttered, stroking Fiona's hair.

"They were getting more and more pissed though," Fiona continued, ignoring Hunter's comment for the moment. She'd think about it again when she had time to reminisce about sitting there in his arms. "I think their buyer was getting desperate. He wanted his sex slave and he wanted her now, that's when Julie showed up. She was way different than me, so I was a bit confused. I figured their buyers would want a certain 'type' of woman, and Julie wasn't anything like me in looks or temperament. But maybe the guy was desperate and didn't care anymore. If you guys hadn't shown up when you did, Julie would've been gone soon. She caved the second they put her in the room. She begged to be let go. She went along with everything they told her to do, thinking her cooperation and 'Daddy' would save her. She was so freaked out and scared and pliable...they were going to sell her in a few days. Then I think they were going to kill me."

Benny couldn't hold back anymore and asked the question both he and Cookie were wondering. They'd talked about it together while she'd been recovering and couldn't figure it out.

"Why didn't you say anything when Cookie came into the room? You weren't so out of it with the drugs that you didn't know he was there, were you? Were you really going to let him walk out and leave you there?"

Fiona thought about how she wanted to answer Benny, but she didn't know exactly what they were looking for. She could've said all sorts of things, but she did what she usually did, she told the truth, looking up at Hunter when she answered. "You weren't there for me. It wasn't fair of me to lower your chances to get out of there with Julie alive. No one had paid to get me out. I don't have any family, no close friends, I was weak and I knew it. Something had changed with the kidnappers. They hadn't fed me in a couple of days and had even stopped giving me the drugs. They were tired of dealing with me and since they had Julie to sell, I think they were just going to leave me there, chained to the floor, to die. I figured it was better if one of us got out, rather than neither of us."

No one said a word when Fiona stopped speaking.

Fiona shifted on her seat. Hell, that had sounded dramatic, even to her. Christ. She was pathetic. "So...." she started.

"Shut. Up," Cookie said harshly, enunciating each word clearly. He was breathing hard through his nose; clenching the hand he'd laid on Fiona's leg so hard, his knuckles were white. His touch was gentle, but he looked like he was about to burst.

Dude stood up and paced the room. Fiona could hear him muttering under his breath, but she couldn't make out what he was saying.

Finally Cookie couldn't stand it anymore. The words burst forth. "Jesus, Fiona. How in the hell did you walk fifteen miles in flip-flops and shorts through the jungle, half carry me to that ladder, carry a backpack weighing a hundred pounds and cling to a rope ladder after being chained to a floor for over three months, being drugged against your will and having not eaten for who knows how long? Oh, and let's not forget, you were fucking *shot* while clinging to that damn ladder!"

Cookie's voice had steadily risen as he'd spoken and he disengaged himself from Fiona carefully and stood up. Fiona sat up as he moved. He stalked away from her, changed his mind when he got halfway across the room and stalked back. Cookie knelt in front of Fiona, not touching her, his eyes boring into hers. His hands rested on his thighs while he waited for her to answer his semi-rhetorical question.

Fiona stared back at him. Mesmerized by his eyes, not caring that Benny and Dude were in the room with them. She gave Hunter the only thing she could. "Because if I didn't, you probably would've died in that jungle trying to get me and Julie out," Fiona told him quietly, with one hundred percent sincerity. "If it was just me, I would've just laid down and died. I'm not strong like you are. It didn't matter. Don't you get it? *No one was looking for me.* I have no family, no real friends. It. Didn't. Matter. Then you came to rescue Julie and I knew you wouldn't leave me behind. Oh, I thought you might at first, and I was hoping you would, but at the same time scared you'd actually leave me there. I wanted to scream out when you started peeling back that board in the hut. I heard you loud and clear. I would've rushed across the room if I could've."

Fiona took a breath, but didn't look away from Hunter. His body was coiled with an emotion she couldn't read. She continued, trying to explain. "The first time you looked at me like I had two heads when I asked if you'd take me too, I knew you were the kind of man that would never leave someone behind. So I trudged along behind you, mile after mile, thinking about how bad *you'd* feel if I just keeled over. That you'd think it was *your* fault. So I didn't. I couldn't. I ignored how crappy I felt. I ignored how much I hurt. I concentrated on making it, one step at a time, counting down one number at a time until we were either rescued or killed."

Cookie stared at the woman sitting in front of him for another second or two, then stood up and walked out of the room without another word.

Fiona looked down at her fingers, which were cold. She'd been clutching them together tightly throughout her explanation to Hunter. She looked up at Benny and Dude. Benny had a weird look on his face that Fiona couldn't interpret.

"What?" she asked him defensively. "You would've done the same thing," Fiona told him almost accusingly.

"You're right," Benny answered without hesitation, "and Dude would too, but we're men honey. And SEALs. Trained. And I'm not sure either of us could've done it in the same circumstances."

Fiona shook her head. "Yes, you would," she said softly. "You know you would."

Benny and Dude continued to look at her. Fiona figured now was her chance to ask about what had gone on when she was out of it. She didn't want to think about Mexico anymore. Hunter's reaction to what she'd said was freaking her out. Was he disgusted, pissed, upset? She had no idea. She was nervous without him by her side, so she tried to change the subject.

"Please tell me what happened this week. What did I do that I don't remember?"

"How do you know anything happened, Fiona?" Dude asked back. "How do you know you didn't just lie on that bed out of it for the last five days?"

Fiona sighed. "I wasn't sure, but you just proved it. Please, Dude. I need to know."

The guys really didn't want to tell her, but she deserved to know. Dude looked at Benny, and saw him nod slightly.

Dude told her the basics of what had happened. He glossed over the part where she fought them and what she specifically said, but it was enough to make her pale a bit and bite her lip.

"I really am sorry. I-I-I didn't..."

Benny interrupted her. "You have nothing to be sorry for, Fiona. If you must know, we all admire you."

Fiona looked at Benny as if he was crazy.

"We do. You were clearly outnumbered, and there were three of us, and still you fought. You're strong, Fiona. You don't give up. That's a great trait to have."

Fiona wasn't sure what to say. She just looked down at her hands again. She was glad she didn't remember it, but Jesus, she'd really climbed out of a second story window to try to escape? She probably had. If she'd had the chance back in that hut in Mexico she would've done whatever she had to in order to get away. Even if that meant setting off into the jungle by herself.

"Come on, Fiona, you look exhausted. I'll take you back to your room so you can sleep." Benny came over to where she was sitting on the sofa and held out his hand.

He was big, but as Fiona came to know them, she knew they'd never hurt her. She grasped his hand hesitantly and stood up. As soon as she was steady on her feet, Benny let go of her, knowing she wasn't comfortable with casual touching yet, and gestured toward the door.

Benny escorted her back to the bedroom they'd brought her to the first night she came to the big house. The room was just as she remembered it. Big and white. The bed looked very comfortable. It was a big four poster bed that was about three feet off the ground. It even had a little step stool next to it to help people get into it. The comforter was fluffy and looked super soft. Even with her body crying out for sleep and the fabulous looking bed, Fiona didn't think she'd be able to sleep.

Remembering the look on Hunter's face when she talked about what happened to her, was killing her. She didn't know if he was mad, disgusted, impressed, or what. It was stressing her out. She supposed it didn't really matter in the long run. They now knew who she was, they knew where she lived, and that she was alone in the world. Fiona also knew she'd soon be going home. She had a life, Hunter had a life. It was time they got back to it.

Chapter Twelve

TWO HOURS AFTER Cookie had abruptly left Fiona and his teammates in the library, he opened Fiona's bedroom door a crack and peered inside. He'd tried to stay away from her, he really did, but he couldn't. He'd spent the last eight days with her; Cookie actually couldn't sleep well now without her. Even when Fiona had been out of it, he'd slept near her, holding her hand and talking to her.

After listening to her story tonight, Cookie wanted to immediately go back to Mexico and kill every single one of her captors. They were going to leave her to *die* in that pit. Perhaps worse than that, was that Fiona knew it. She would've starved to death, and no one would've known. It would've been a slow agonizing death. If she'd been left there, Cookie never would've met her. Never been awed by her strength. Hell, he might not have made it out of the jungle alive if Fiona hadn't been there to help him make it to the ladder so his teammates could haul him up to the helicopter. Cookie couldn't imagine not knowing Fiona. He honestly didn't understand how she'd made it out of her entire situation alive, and amazingly well.

He knew the human body was resilient, but Fiona was amazing. And humble. That was what got him. How the hell had Fiona grown up so humble and unassuming? Her so-called mother certainly hadn't instilled it in her, and while she hadn't told them what she'd been through in her childhood, they'd all been able to put some of the pieces together. Being a foster kid was never a picnic, and certainly not for a teenager.

Fiona honestly had no idea that what she'd done and lived through in Mexico was extraordinary. She did it because it had to be done. Period. She didn't want praise, and in fact was embarrassed by it, but she did it anyway. Fiona told her story matter of factly, whereas most other people who'd been through the same thing, would be in hysterics.

Cookie closed the door silently behind him and made his way to the bed where Fiona lay. He wasn't completely surprised when she turned over to look at him in the moonlight coming through the window.

"Couldn't sleep?" she asked softly.

Cookie just shook his head and motioned for her to scoot over.

Fiona did and watched as Hunter took off his T-shirt and let his sweats fall to the ground. He was gorgeous. In the moonlight, Fiona could see the scars on his chest, but he was built like a brick wall. Hunter was muscular, and the play of his muscles in his arms was sexy as hell. He had a light sprinkling of hair on his chest and she could see his biceps flex as he moved. His thighs looked strong and she could tell he was big...all over.

Before Fiona could take a more concentrated look at the part of him that interested and scared her, he climbed into the bed. Without a word, Hunter ran his hand over her head and brought it toward him. He kissed her briefly, too briefly, on the forehead then encouraged her to turn on her side, facing away from him.

Fiona felt Hunter snuggle up behind her as soon as she turned, pulling her back to his front. His arm came around her chest, holding her tightly against him. She sighed and snuggled deeper into his embrace. Fiona knew she should probably be freaking out that Hunter had stripped naked before joining her in the bed, but she'd felt safe when he'd held her this way back in the jungle, and she felt safe now. His skin was warm and Fiona could feel his heat soaking into her body. She wasn't thinking about what her kidnappers had done to her, and knew Hunter wouldn't push her into anything she wasn't ready for. She might never be ready, but Fiona hoped that wasn't the case. She wanted to be intimate with a man again, with this man.

"Are you okay, Hunter?"

"I'm sorry I left."

"Don't be. I understand. *I'm* sorry I upset you."

Cookie tightened his arms and put pressure on Fiona's hip until she turned onto her back. He came up on one elbow and his other hand came up to her face and cupped her cheek. Fiona had no choice but to look at him.

"*You* didn't upset me. Those assholes that kidnapped you upset me. I'm so damn proud of you I could burst. You have no idea what you mean to me." He saw the confusion in Fiona's eyes. "I know, I'm laying a lot of heavy stuff on you, but I want to be upfront with you about how I feel. Can you take it right now?"

Fiona stared at Hunter. He was leaning over her and his hand had moved from her face to brush her hair behind her right ear. His fingertips were tracing her ear, sending shivers throughout her body. She wanted to press herself up into him, even with all that happened to her, she wanted that.

"Fee?"

Oh yeah, he'd asked her a question. "I can take it." She bit her lip and looked up at the man she was beginning to think she couldn't live without. She hoped she could take it, but if Hunter needed to tell her something, she'd listen, no matter if she was ready or not.

"I know it's probably too soon, but I've never felt this way about a woman before. I've always been the one to walk away. I know I've been a jerk in the past. But I don't want to walk away from you. The thought of you being hurt, or killed, makes me crazy. The thought of walking out of this house and never seeing you again, makes me crazy. The thought of your body under mine, makes me crazy." Cookie eyed Fiona nervously. He had to finish his thoughts and stop beating around the bush.

"You're mine, Fiona. I know that makes me sound like a fucking caveman, but I can't apologize for it. I want to protect you. I want to show you off. I just want you. In every way." Cookie closed his eyes and leaned his head down and put this forehead against Fiona's. He could feel her warm breath against his face. He lowered his voice. "I know you have some stuff you have to work through, and I want to be there with you while you do it. All I want is a chance. A chance to show you that you're safe with me. That you'll always be safe with me."

Fiona's breath hitched. Hunter's words were like band-aids on her soul. All she'd ever wanted since she'd been in her first foster home was to feel safe and wanted. Hunter was offering her both.

"I..."

Cookie placed a finger over her lips lightly. "No, don't say anything, Fee. I know this is fast. Probably too fast, but I know what I want, and that's you. Sleep on it. Don't agree because I want it. Agree because *you* want it. There's more we have to talk about tomorrow, stuff that's pretty heavy, but know that I'll be there with you." Cookie looked down at Fiona. He had no idea how this woman had survived what she had, but there was no doubt in his mind that she was his. He just hoped she might want that too. "Turn back on your side again. Let me hold you?"

Fiona did as he asked without hesitation. She wanted Hunter to hold her too. When she turned over, she felt Hunter curl up into her again. His bottom arm was between them, curled up against his chest and against her back. His other arm was curled over her back and he pulled her against him by placing his hand against her breastbone.

Fiona could feel the heat from his hand against her breast. She felt a moment of panic, before consciously relaxing. This was Hunter.

She was safe with him.

"I want you, but I'm scared." she whispered as if saying the words out loud would make them have less power over her.

"I know you are. I'll never pressure you, Fee. I want you, you can feel that, but know that I'll never force you. I'll wait as long as you need. Okay? I won't tell you not to feel scared, but while you are, know that I'm here and I have your back. You don't ever have to be scared of *me*."

Fiona nodded. She *could* feel how much he wanted her. His erection against her butt was long and hard. She wished she could turn over and show him how much his words meant to her, but he was right. She needed to take things slow. Colossally slow.

"Thank you for coming to me tonight." There was more Fiona wanted to say, but those were the only words she could get out.

"You're welcome, Fee. I'll always come to you if I can."

Fiona nodded and snuggled back into Hunter's arms.

Cookie lay with Fiona throughout the night. He didn't sleep. He couldn't. Twice when she started having a nightmare, he woke her up slowly and soothed her until she fell back asleep. She was human. She might've been able to somehow make it out of the jungle alive, but she was affected. Deeply. She might always be, but Cookie knew Fiona would show a brave face to the world and fight her demons behind closed doors.

It's the same thing he'd always done. Cookie loved this woman. He didn't know how it had happened so fast, but it had. He wasn't going to let her go. He wasn't sure what their future had in store for them, but he wasn't going to let her slip away. Finally, around dawn, Cookie fell into a light slumber, holding Fiona tight and wondering how to make her want to stay with him...forever.

FIONA WOKE UP alone the next morning, but when she turned over she could see the indentation from Hunter's head in the pillow next to her. She looked around, and seeing she was alone, picked up the pillow he'd used, and held it to her face. God, it smelled good. It smelled like Hunter. Fiona put the pillow down and stared at the ceiling.

It was time to think about going home. She didn't want to, but she didn't have a choice. She figured that was what Hunter meant when he said they had to have a serious conversation today. Fiona was sure the men had to get back to their base by now as well. It wasn't as if they could stay here forever.

After showering and putting on a pair of sweat pants and a T-shirt that had been left in the bathroom for her, Fiona made her way down the stairs.

She walked into the kitchen to see all three of the guys sitting at the small table, obviously waiting for her.

"Hey, guys," Fiona said cautiously.

Hunter got up and came over to her and enveloped her in his arms. Fiona buried her head in his chest and wrapped her arms around him.

"Good morning, Fee," Cookie said softly, his rumbly voice making her feel mushy inside.

"Good morning, Hunter."

He pulled back and looked down at her.

"Hungry?"

"Uh, yeah," Fiona couldn't help the sarcasm that escaped with her words. She watched as Hunter threw his head back and laughed.

"All right, come on, Benny made us all a gourmet breakfast."

Cookie pulled away, but took Fiona's hand and led her to the small table. He waited until she was seated before heading to the refrigerator. "Orange juice okay?"

"Oh my God. Yes. Please. I haven't had OJ in…well, a long time."

Cookie took a deep breath. Jesus, Fiona slayed him with her words and she had no idea. He filled a large glass to the brim and brought both the glass and the container of juice to the table. If Fiona wanted juice, she'd get as much as she could drink.

The four of them sat around the table and enjoyed the pancakes and omelets Benny had made for them. They were mostly silent during the meal, the men thinking about the upcoming conversation they had to have with Fiona, and Fiona thinking she'd never had anything half as tasty as the food she was currently eating.

After they'd finished, Fiona grabbed her plate and stood up, intending to take her dishes to the sink.

"No, sit, Fiona," Dude practically barked at her.

She startled badly and almost dropped her plate.

"Shit, sorry. I didn't mean to scare you." Dude's tone of voice was placating and apologetic.

"No, it's all right. It's me."

"Bullshit. I was rude, and I'm sorry. What I meant to say, was leave the plates. We can do the dishes later."

Fiona nodded. She should've noticed before now, but all three of the men seemed tense. Was this it? Were they going to kick her out now? Was she going to have to say good bye to Hunter?

"We have to talk."

Fiona almost moaned at Benny's words. Yup. It was time. "It's time to go isn't it?" She might as well get the ball rolling.

Cookie took hold of Fiona's hand and held it tightly against his thigh. "Yes. But we have some stuff we need to talk to you about first."

Cookie didn't want to tell Fiona what Tex had found out for them. But she was right, it *was* time to go. They had to get back to base and Cookie wanted Fiona with them when they went.

Benny took over the conversation from Cookie. "Okay, so this house isn't ours. We have a friend, a former SEAL who lives in

Virginia. Tex works with us as well as other groups outside the military. He's a computer whiz. Once, for fun, he hacked into the FBI's computer system just to see if he could. He had the balls to call them once he was out to let them know what he'd done. Needless to say they weren't happy, but he wanted to prove a point. Anyway, Tex sort of 'manages' this house. It has a crazy level of security and he keeps its existence pretty quiet. We use it as well as some other private security people he knows."

Fiona nodded as Benny took a break. When no one said anything for a moment, Fiona nervously said, "Okay. I'll have to remember to send him a Christmas card." She immediately blushed. Jesus, she needed to control her mouth.

Cookie brought their intertwined hands up to his mouth and brushed a kiss across her knuckles. "God, you're cute. I'll be sure to get an address from Wolf for you."

Dude picked up where Benny had left off. "So yeah, Tex is one of the best computer hackers I've ever known. If it involves anything electronic, he can hack it."

Fiona had no idea why they were telling her this, so she just nodded.

Seeing Dude was confusing Fiona and not getting to the point, Cookie took over the conversation. He turned in his seat and took Fiona's other hand in his. He waited until she looked up at him.

"What the guys are trying to tell you, and screwing up, is that I asked Tex to look into your finances and circumstances back in El Paso." At Fiona's indrawn breath, Cookie continued quickly. "You've been gone for one hundred and four days. You don't have any money in your bank account. Tex hacked into the University's computer system and found that you were officially taken off the records as an employee and your landlord assumed you'd left without notice and re-rented your apartment to someone else."

There was silence in the room after Cookie's blunt words.

Finally Fiona whispered, "What?"

"I want you to come back to California with me."

Fiona just stared at Hunter, trying to digest what he'd said. Ignoring his last statement, she asked in a shaky voice, "Can they *do* that?"

"Fee," Cookie's voice was tortured. "Come here."

Fiona nearly shrieked when Hunter unexpectedly reached for her and pulled her out of her chair and into his lap. She closed her eyes to try to keep her tears from rolling down her face. It was no use. She sniffed once, then felt Hunter put one hand on her head and push it into his chest. His other hand clamped around her waist and pulled her into him. He held Fiona secure in his arms and let her cry.

Fiona heard a chair scrape against the floor and then felt another hand on her back. She turned her head to see Benny kneeling by the chair.

"You were an at-will employee at the University, hon. Unfortunately, legally they *can* hire someone to take your place." He went on, obviously answering her earlier question. "Tex is trying to track down your stuff. Your landlord had to do something with it. If it's still around, Tex'll find all of it for you. As for your bank account, most of your bills were being auto-drafted, and when your money ran out, they started bouncing. But don't worry; Tex is taking care of that for you as well. You won't owe anyone a dime once he's done."

Cookie nuzzled Fiona with his chin and she turned to look up at him. "Come back to California with me," he repeated, this time he ordered the words instead of asking them.

"But..."

"No, no buts. You heard what I told you last night. I wish I could say I'm sorry you lost your job and lost your apartment, but even if it makes me a dick, I'm not, because that means you're free to come with me, to be with me, to start over in California. I'll be honest, until we talked to Tex, I had no idea how I was going to let you walk out of this house and away from me. I have to go back. I don't have a choice, but I knew you had a life. If you can honestly tell me you want to go back to El Paso, I'll help you any way I can. But know that I don't want you to. I want you with me."

Fiona tried to focus on what Hunter was telling her. She'd heard him last night, but she obviously didn't *hear* him.

"I'm scared."

"I know you are, Fee, and that's why I'll be right there with you. Trust me."

Without pausing, Fiona immediately returned, "I do. Jesus, Hunter, I think I trust you more than I trust myself right now."

"Then come with us. Let me introduce you to Caroline and Alabama. Let the rest of my team get to know you. You'll come to trust them as much as I hope you trust me."

Dude cut in, he and Benny hadn't left the room. "You have choices, Fiona."

"What the hell, Dude?" Cookie barked out immediately, tightening his arms around Fiona protectively and glaring at his teammate.

"She has to know she has options, Cookie. If you really want her to go with you for the right reasons, you have to tell her all her options."

"Tell me." Fiona was ninety nine percent sure she wanted to go to California with Hunter, but Dude was right. She needed all the information she could get so she could try to make the right decision.

"Your bank account can have as much money as you need by the end of the day. Don't ask how, just know that Tex can make sure you have the money you need in order to rent another apartment and get settled again. He's probably already arranged to get your car out of the impound lot where it was towed from the airport parking lot. If you want to keep working for the University, Tex can arrange that too. While they were legally in their rights to replace you, it'd be a public relations nightmare if it came out you were kidnapped and the school dumped you. They'll be begging you to come back and work for them once Tex gets done with them."

"He can do that?"

"Hell yeah," Benny told her seriously. "We don't know how he can do the things he does, but we're just damn glad he's on our side."

Cookie turned Fiona's head back to him. "As much as I want to beat the crap out of Dude, he's right. You need to know you can go back to El Paso and get your life back. If you choose that option, just know it won't be the end of us. I'm not letting you go, no matter what you decide."

Burying her face into Hunter's chest, Fiona whispered, "Really?"

"Really. I already told you you're mine. It doesn't matter if you're living in Timbuktu, Texas, or in the same house as me."

Fiona looked up at Hunter and nodded.

Apparently that was all the reassurance the guys needed. "I'll call Tex and tell him to get us home," Dude said decisively as he got up from the table.

Benny also got up off the floor where he'd been crouching, and started gathering the dishes from the table. "I'll clean this up. Tell Tex we'll be ready to go this afternoon."

Cookie stood up with Fiona in his arms and without a word, headed for the door. Benny watched with a small smile as they left.

Chapter Thirteen

F IONA SHUT HER eyes and enjoyed the feeling of Hunter carrying
her. She kept them closed until she felt him bending over. She
finally opened them to see he'd brought her back to the room they'd
slept in the night before. He carefully leaned over and placed Fiona
on the mussed sheets, then put both hands next to her shoulders and
loomed over her.

"I need to touch you, Fee." Before she could say anything, Cookie continued. "We won't make love; I know that'll take time. You
need to heal physically and mentally before we go there, but I have to
hold you. I have to feel you against me. You said you trusted me
before. Please, let me show you that trust isn't misplaced. Let me
show you how much you mean to me."

Fiona could only give him a small nod. She wanted to feel him
too. As much as she wanted to be ready to take him inside her, she
knew Hunter was right about her mental state. It was way too soon.

She watched as Hunter stood up and put one hand behind his
head and yanked his T-shirt off over his head. Fiona would never
understand how guys learned how to do that. Throwing his shirt
behind him carelessly, Hunter began to unbutton his pants. He never
took his eyes off of hers.

When Fiona began to sit up to take her shirt off, Cookie quickly
said, "No, let me. Please."

Fiona lowered her hands back to her sides and continued to
watch as Hunter stripped off his clothes.

Cookie kept his eyes on Fiona's face as he unzipped his pants and lowered them. He was hard. There was no way he could control his body's reaction to Fiona lying on a bed in front of him.

"I don't want you to feel vulnerable, Fee. I'll do whatever it takes so you're comfortable with everything we do." Cookie put his thumbs in the waistband of his boxers and quickly stripped them down his legs and off. "Scoot over."

Fiona knew she was blushing. Hunter was the sexiest man she'd ever laid eyes on. He'd stripped off all his clothes so she'd feel more comfortable, but she wasn't sure that was what she was feeling. She wanted to touch him. She wanted to lick him. She wanted to snuggle in next to him and never let go. Fiona scooted over in the large bed and watched as Hunter climbed in and reached for her.

Cookie tried to control his lust. Having Fiona in bed with him, awake and willing, was almost more than his libido could handle. He'd never felt this hard and aroused in his life. Before reaching for Fiona, he needed to hear the words from her.

"Tell me you're okay with this, Fee. I need the words."

"I'm more than okay with this, Hunter. I want to touch you."

"I'm yours. Do whatever you want."

Fiona reached a shaky hand toward Hunter. He was lying on top of the covers, completely bare. His chest had a light smattering of hair and she could see scars covering the surface. Fiona lightly placed her fingertips on one of the worst scars. Hunter sucked in a breath and Fiona yanked her hand back.

"I'm sorry, did that hurt?"

Cookie grabbed her hand and pressed it back to his chest. "Hell no, it didn't hurt. Your hands on me are a dream come true."

Fiona let her hand wander over his chest, fascinated at Hunter's reaction. She kept her eyes above his waist for now, but watched as goose bumps rose over his body. As she stroked his scars, his nipples stood up on his chest. She had no idea a man's nipples got hard like a woman's. Without thinking, Fiona leaned down and took one in her mouth.

"Jesus, Fee. God yes. Shit, that feels so good. Suck hard…just like that."

Fiona could feel herself getting wet. She'd never gotten excited in the past without having a man's hands directly on her, but this was Hunter. He was completely different from any man she'd ever been with.

Cookie resisted the urge to put his hand on Fiona's head and press her deeper into him. He hadn't planned on his happening, he wanted to make *her* feel good, but now that she was touching him, he was helpless to stop her. When she switched to his other nipple he almost lost it.

"Touch me, Fee. God, please."

Fiona raised her head and looked down for the first time. Hunter was big, bigger than anyone she'd been with. She could see the blood pulsing in the vein on the side of his shaft. Hearing Hunter plead with her was heady, and almost wrong. She didn't want him to have to beg her for anything. It just wasn't right. She reached for him and wrapped her hand around him. She swiped her thumb over the tip and smeared the wetness she found there over and around the head.

"Fee, harder, hold me harder."

Fiona felt awkward for the first time. Hunter obviously needed something, but she wasn't sure what. "Show me."

Cookie immediately uncurled his hand from the sheet he'd been holding and wrapped it around Fiona's on his shaft. He showed her how hard to grasp him to make it as pleasurable as possible. He knew he was much rougher than she would've been. He threw his head back and closed his eyes.

Fiona watched Hunter in awe. He was so beautiful. She loved how he took control of his pleasure. Yes, her hand was around him, but he was clearly in charge and showing her how he liked it. When his head went back she leaned down and took his nipple into her mouth again and sucked hard.

Cookie groaned at the feel of Fiona's tongue on his nipple and when she sucked, he lost it.

"Fee, I'm gonna..." Before he could finish warning her, Cookie felt her teeth bite down on his nipple. He exploded into their hands and thrust up as Fiona continued to grip and stroke him and nibble on his nipple. Cookie shuddered and thrust one more time as another mini-orgasm went through him. He felt completely drained.

Cookie let go of her hand and let his fall to the bed with a plop. He shuddered as Fiona continued to stoke him lightly and finally she let go, only to run her hand up his body until she was massaging his release into his abs.

"You're beautiful," Fiona breathed as she stared down at Hunter. Without thinking, only knowing she wanted to taste him, Fiona brought her hand up toward her face.

Cookie caught her hand just as she got it to her face. "You wanna taste me, Fee?" At her tentative nod, he took his free hand and wiped it over his stomach, collecting some of his cum. He bought it up to her face and held one of his fingers out for her. "Taste me."

Fiona tried not to blush and leaned over and took Hunter's finger into her mouth. The taste of his salty and earthy essence filled her. She swirled her tongue around his finger, making sure to clean it thoroughly. Fiona watched through lidded eyes as Hunter's pupils dilated and he drew in a deep breath.

Fiona was surprised when Hunter suddenly surged toward her and took her mouth with his. She wouldn't have dreamed in a million years that a man would want to taste himself, and she knew he could. Fiona felt his tongue wrap around hers. They both voraciously ate at each other. After several moments of the best kiss of her life, Fiona pulled back. They stared at each other. Fiona looked away first and glanced down. He was still semi-hard. She'd forgotten about the mess they'd made.

"I should get a towel to clean you up."

"No. Don't. I want to feel you against me. I have a need to mark you. Does that freak you out?"

Fiona could only stare into Hunter's eyes and shake her head.

"Jesus, you own me, Fee. Seriously. You're perfect." Cookie looked at Fiona for a moment then fingered the hem of her T-shirt. "Do you think you can take this off for me? We won't go any further. Just your shirt."

Fiona wanted this. She didn't hesitate. She sat up and grabbed the bottom of her T-shirt and whipped it over her head quickly so she wouldn't chicken out.

Cookie didn't hesitate, giving Fiona a chance to get freaked out, and grabbed her hips and eased her over him so she was straddling his thighs. She was still wearing sweat pants, but he could only stare. She wasn't wearing a bra, and Cookie had an unfettered view of her chest. Her breasts were perfect. He'd always thought his "type" was a woman with a huge chest, but Cookie realized in that moment Fiona was the perfect size for him. Her areolas were large and took up most of her breast. She had pink nipples that were currently hard and reaching for him. She was a bit small for her size, but Cookie figured once she gained the weight she'd lost while in captivity, they'd grow a size. He didn't care. The bottom line was that they belonged to his woman, therefore, they were perfect.

Cookie picked up her hand that had caressed him earlier, and placed it on her own right breast. He made sure Fiona wiped his release on herself. Then he took both her hands in his and placed them on his hips.

"Hang on, Fee. Don't move your hands. I won't go too far, I promise. But I need to do this." Cookie didn't wait for her to agree, but maintaining eye contact, took both his hands and smoothed them over his belly, collecting his essence that she'd coaxed from him earlier. Once they were coated, he brought them up to her chest slowly and touched his woman for the first time. He finally broke eye contact and looked down. Cookie caressed and massaged Fiona, all the while branding her with his scent, with his very being.

"You're mine, Fee. No one else will touch this. No one else will get to see this. I'll protect you with my life if I have to. You're safe with me. Mine. You're mine."

Fiona couldn't hold back her sob any longer. She'd realized what he meant to do the second he put his hands on himself, and she wanted it. She wanted to feel him on her skin. It was as if his hands and cum washed away the feeling of the kidnappers' hands on her. When he'd said she was his, she lost it.

Fiona collapsed on top of Hunter, knocking his hands off of her chest in the process. The feel of his chest against hers only made her sob harder. She'd needed this kind of connection for so long. She vaguely felt Hunter's arms against her back, pulling her into him and soothing up and down her spine. Fiona wasn't afraid of Hunter, she wasn't afraid of what his hands would do to her. Being in Hunter's arms felt right.

After a long crying session, Fiona picked her head up, but Hunter wouldn't let her separate their bodies any more than that. She looked into Hunter's eyes and said what was in her heart. "Yours."

Fiona watched as Hunter's lips curled up in a satisfied smile. "Damn straight."

She smiled back, feeling content for the first time in a long time.

"Do you want to shower or sleep?"

"Do we have time?"

"Yes."

Showering meant washing his scent off. The decision was easy. "Sleep."

"Damn, woman." Cookie breathed, putting his hand on the back of Fiona's head and pulling her back into his embrace. "I love that you don't want to wash me off. Sleep then. We'll shower when we wake up. After we shower, we need to be heading out. You *are* coming back to California with me aren't you?"

Fiona could hear the insecurity in Hunter's voice and hated it. She didn't want him to be insecure about her or the relationship they were obviously starting. She hurried to reassure him. "Yes. If I have to start over I'd rather start over in the same place where you are so we can see if whatever this is…" she gestured between them, "…will last."

"Oh, it's gonna last, Fee. You're not getting away from me," Cookie said it with a smile, but he obviously meant every word. His sincerity rang out loud and clear in his voice.

"Thank you, Hunter."

"You don't have to thank me, Fee."

"I know you think that, but I do. I'll never stop thanking you as long as I live."

"As long as you aren't confusing what we have here, with gratitude."

Annoyed, Fiona propped herself up. "Seriously? After what just happened? You think that was a thank you hand job?"

"Shhhhh. No, I don't think that." Cookie put one hand on the side of her head and stroked her hair. "I just…hell. I'm gonna sound like a teenage boy here, but I just want you to be with me because you want to, not because you don't feel like you have another choice or because you're grateful."

Seeing Hunter insecure and unsure was actually kinda cute, even if she didn't like being the cause of it. Fiona knew it wasn't something she'd see very often. It was her turn to reassure him. She brushed her hand over Hunter's head to the back of his neck and put her forehead against his. "I'm here because I can't imagine being anywhere else. Even when I was out of my head with the drugs, I think I knew you were here next to me. Well okay, maybe not when I crawled out the bathroom window. But I hoped you might ask me to go home with you even before I knew about my job and apartment." At the look of satisfaction in Hunter's eyes, Fiona giggled. "Does that make you feel better?"

"Yeah, sweetheart, it does. Now, come down here and close your eyes. We'll have to get going here soon enough, but for now I just want to lie here and enjoy being with you."

Fiona closed her eyes as he asked and settled against his chest. They were sticky and it was a bit uncomfortable, but it was real, and it was a part of him. She'd stay right where she was forever, if it meant he'd be there with her.

Chapter Fourteen

BENNY, DUDE, COOKIE, AND FIONA headed toward the exit of the airport. Tex had gotten them all a commercial flight out of the Dallas/Fort Worth airport later that night. Identification was waiting for Fiona when they'd arrived at the ticket counter, as if by magic.

Cookie could only shake his head in wonder. Tex was amazing. Cookie had no idea how Tex did half the stuff he did, but he thanked his lucky stars for the millionth time that Tex was on their side. How they managed half the stuff they did without him, Cookie would never know.

"Remember, Fee, Wolf and Caroline will probably be waiting for us out in the main part of the airport. We told him we were coming back and he couldn't wait to see for himself that you were all right." Cookie kept hold of Fiona's hand to reassure her.

Fiona was quiet. She barely remembered the man Hunter called Wolf. She knew he was there in the helicopter and later, but she'd been barely hanging on, and didn't really recall anything they might have said to each other.

As the foursome exited the secure part of the airport and entered the main terminal, Fiona saw a group of people standing off to the side. Fiona knew instinctively they were waiting on them. There were three large, almost scary looking, men, and two striking women.

Benny and Dude made a beeline for the group, but Cookie pulled Fiona to a stop well away from his friends. He turned her to him and took both her hands in his. "If you don't want to meet them now, it's okay, just let me know and we'll go and get a taxi back to my place. I want you to meet them when you feel comfortable with it."

Fiona squeezed Hunter's hand. God, he was so good to her. "It's okay, Hunter. I want to meet them. I *need* to meet them. They all had a part in saving me."

Cookie brought Fiona's hand up to his mouth and kissed it briefly. "Strong as hell," he murmured under his breath, then turned them both toward his teammates and friends.

As they got closer and Fiona could see the men better, she realized she did recognize them. She didn't know who was who, but she recognized them.

One of the women detached herself from one of the men and came right up to them.

"Oh my God, we are so glad you're here! I'm Caroline and that big lug back there is Matthew." At the look of confusion on Fiona's face, Caroline sighed dramatically. "Yeah, okay, you've been hanging out with them..." she gestured toward Benny and Dude, "...so you probably have never heard everyone's *real* name. Alabama and I try not to use their nicknames, we prefer to call them by their given names. So Matthew is with me and he's Wolf. Standing over there are Alabama and Christopher, or Abe. You know Benny and Dude, but Alabama and I call them Kason and Faulkner. Then, last but not least, is Sam, who's known as Mozart by the guys."

Fiona's head spun. She'd never remember all their names.

As if reading her mind, Caroline laughed. "Don't worry if you can't remember. It took me for-freaking-ever to keep them all straight. It's like there are twice as many of them around when the guys are using their nicknames and we're using their real names."

Fiona could only nod as Caroline continued talking. "So, I haven't heard much of what happened, only that you were kidnapped and rescued in Mexico and that you were awesomely strong. At least that's what Matthew told me. I'm so happy you're all right. Will you be staying with Hunter? Do you have clothes? I'm happy to...mmmmf."

Fiona smiled as Wolf came up and put his hand over Caroline's mouth. "Jesus, Ice, give the woman a chance to breathe."

"Ice?" It was the only thing that immediately came to Fiona's mind.

Hunter leaned down close to Fiona's ear and explained, "Yeah, Caroline earned that nickname when Wolf first met her. It's a long story, and one I'm sure you'll hear sooner rather than later the way Ice talks, but for now maybe we can get the hell out of here?" He directed the last part of his words to his friends.

"Of course. Got any bags?" Mozart asked Cookie, Benny, and Dude.

"Naw, Tex arranged for our stuff to be shipped. You know how it is," Dude said, while winking at Fiona.

Fiona knew they probably couldn't have brought their bags on the plane with them since they were loaded down with weapons and who knew what else.

"Great. You and Fiona are with us, everyone else is with Wolf," Abe said, chiming in for the first time.

Fiona took a look at the woman at Abe's side. She'd been quiet, but she was very watchful. She hadn't taken her eyes off of Fiona since they'd walked up. It made Fiona extremely nervous. She'd never been good at making friends, and she really wanted these women to like her. Fiona knew if she had a chance at making whatever it was she had with Hunter work, she had to get along with his teammates' women.

Before they all left, Caroline ducked out of Wolf's hold and hugged Fiona tightly. Fiona couldn't help but stiffen in the embrace. Caroline held up her hand when Hunter took a step into Fiona. "I know, I probably overstepped my bounds there, but I'm so happy you're here and with Hunter. He deserves the best, and from the little I've heard, that's you. I can't wait to sit down and get to know you better. Alabama and I need someone new to gossip with."

"Jesus, Ice. Get out of here," Cookie scolded with a laugh, grabbing Fiona's hand and pulling her back into his side, with his hand around her waist and resting on her hip.

Caroline laughed with him and stood on her tiptoes and kissed Hunter on the cheek. "Don't keep her all to yourself, Hunter."

Cookie just shook his head as Caroline and the other men headed toward the exit. "Come on, Fee, let's get you home."

Home. Fiona liked the sound of that.

The four of them headed out the doors of the airport and Abe led them through the parking garage and over to his jeep. Alabama and Abe got in the front and Cookie helped Fiona climb into the back before heading around to the other side and climbing in next to her.

When they were on their way out of the parking area, Alabama turned sideways in her seat and spoke up for the first time.

"Fiona, I'm so glad you're all right. Christopher told me a little of what happened and I can't imagine what you've been though." Her voice was quiet and soothing.

"Thanks, Alabama. I appreciate it. I'm glad I'm all right too." Fiona smiled at the woman in the front seat. She seemed to be the complete opposite of Caroline, quiet and reserved, but Fiona liked her immediately.

"As Caroline said, if you need anything, please don't hesitate to call one of us. It can be tough being with a SEAL and we need to stick together."

Abe spoke up at that. "Hey, we're not so bad."

"Uh, yeah, sometimes you are," Alabama disagreed.

They both laughed. Fiona smiled. They seemed to be at ease. If she'd met any of the men on Hunter's team alone in a dark alley, she would've been terrified, but meeting them all together and seeing how close they were, made a huge difference.

"Thanks, Alabama. I'm sure we'll have lots of time to hang out." They smiled at each other.

The four made idle chit-chat as Abe made his way to Hunter's apartment. Pulling up, he didn't turn off the engine, but turned around in his seat to look at Fiona.

"I have to echo what the others have said, Fiona. You don't know how happy we are that you're okay. I was there, I know what I saw. Thank you for saving Cookie's life. You have no idea what that means to all of us. You're family now. You need anything, all you have to do is ask. I don't care what it is. You want a car? Just ask. You need money? Same thing. If you need a lawyer, an ear, or a way to get out of Cookie's place, we're only a phone call away."

"What the hell, Abe?" Cookie growled from next to Fiona.

Abe held up his hand to forestall anything else Cookie might say. Fiona could only look between Hunter and Abe in confusion. She thought they were friends. Why was he saying that about Hunter? Was he warning her away from him?

"I'm not insinuating you'll want to get away from him at all, Fiona. Out of all of us, Cookie is the most sensitive, and, dare I say it, caring. But I'm trying to make a point here. I learned my lesson with Alabama and the mistakes I made. My team stepped up when I let her down. I learned the real meaning of family. Family supports and trusts each other unconditionally. You aren't alone anymore, Fiona. Hell, if someone hasn't heard from you in two hours, we'll start trying to get in touch with you. Understand? *You're not alone.*"

Fiona got it. She could only nod. If she tried to talk, she'd burst into tears. No one in her old life had noticed or cared that she'd disappeared without a word. Abe was telling her that wouldn't happen here. She didn't even know these people, but they'd showed more compassion to her than anyone had since she'd been a kid.

"Come on, Fee, let's go home."

Home. Jesus, that sounded great. Fiona nodded at Hunter then turned toward Abe and Alabama. "Thanks." It was all she could say at the moment through the huge lump in her throat, but it seemed to be enough.

Cookie opened the door on his side of the jeep and didn't let go of Fiona's hand. She had to scoot across the seat so she could follow him out.

"Thanks, man. See you later." Fiona watched as Hunter and Christopher gave each other manly chin lifts to communicate non verbally, then she was being tugged toward the apartment building. She looked back once to see Alabama lean over and kiss her man passionately. Fiona smiled. She hadn't said more than a few words to the woman, but she liked her.

They stopped in front of a door on the second floor. Cookie turned her so they were facing each other. "I'm gonna apologize now before we get inside, Fee. I recently moved out of the barracks and the apartment isn't fully furnished yet." At her raised eyebrows, Cookie continued. "Okay, so there isn't much in there except for a bed, a sofa, and a huge-ass television, but whatever you need or want, we can get. Okay? Don't freak out."

Fiona laughed. "Hunter, Seriously? I don't care. I just spent three months in a damn hut in the middle of a fucking jungle in Mexico. Whatever you have is more than I have right now and it's a million times better than where I was. It's fine."

Cookie hated being reminded of the hell Fiona had been through, but understood her point. Trying to keep things light, he mock grumbled, "I'm gonna remind you that you said that when you see it and are bitching about how it's the ultimate bachelor pad."

Cookie took the keys out of his pocket and unlocked his apartment door and watched as Fiona entered his home. He watched as she glanced around the living area. It wasn't much, as he'd warned. The leather sofa was comfortable as hell, and of course the fifty four inch TV took up most of one wall. Otherwise it was pretty plain. There were no pictures on the walls and Cookie hadn't even bought a carpet to put down on the hardwood floors. There was no hall table and no knick knacks sitting around. Hell, Cookie could even hear an echo as Fiona walked across the room.

He watched as she went straight to the sliding glass door that opened to a balcony. Fiona pressed her hands against the glass and looked out without a word. Cookie locked the front door and threw the keys onto the counter as he walked past the kitchen to get to her. Cookie put his arms around Fiona's waist as he came up behind her.

"What are you thinking, Fee?"

"This is the most amazing view."

"It's why I chose the apartment. There were bigger ones in the complex, but I liked the idea of being able to sit on the balcony and have a beer or eat dinner, and seeing both the beach and the mountains at the same time in the distance.

Fiona turned in his arms and laid her cheek against Hunter's chest and snuggled into him. "It's beautiful. I didn't think I'd ever see anything like this again. I thought…"

"Shhhh, I know."

They stood glued together for a long time. Finally Cookie pulled away. "Come on, Fee, let's head to bed. We're going to have a long couple of days coming up. We need to get you settled, and I need to make sure you have what you need. If I know Caroline right, she's gonna show up here as early as Wolf will let her out of the house. She'll want to take you shopping."

Fiona looked up at Hunter and nodded. She *was* tired. She couldn't think of anything she wanted or needed more at that moment, than to cuddle up next to Hunter in his bed. How the hell she could want that, after everything that happened in Mexico, Fiona had no idea, but there it was.

Cookie's thoughts were much the same as Fiona's. He wanted to see Fiona in *his* bed. Not a borrowed bed, not on the ground in the middle of the damn jungle, but on *his* sheets in *his* home in *his* bed. Call him a Neanderthal, but he needed that.

Chapter Fifteen

COOKIE WAS RIGHT. There was a knock at the door at ten o'clock the next morning. Luckily they'd been up and ready. Cookie looked out the door and saw it was indeed Caroline, but he was surprised to see Alabama with her. He opened the door and welcomed the ladies inside.

"I'm surprised Wolf let you out so early, Ice."

"Ha, ha, very funny, Hunter. You know he forced me to stay away until now. I wanted to be here at eight."

"Oh, I'm sure he didn't have to 'force' you, Ice." Cookie laughed when Caroline blushed.

"Yeah, well, maybe he didn't have to convince me too hard."

"I bet it was hard."

Fiona laughed out loud at the comical way both Hunter's and Caroline's heads whipped around in shock at Alabama's words.

"It's always the quiet ones you have to watch out for," Fiona said, still laughing.

Caroline came up and wrapped her arm around Fiona's waist. "I like you, Fiona. I think you're gonna fit right in with us. You ready to go and spend some money?"

At her words and actions, Fiona stiffened. Shit. She wanted to spend some time with them, but she didn't *have* any money.

Seeing Fiona's body go tight, Cookie swore under his breath. He should've talked about this with Fiona already. "Can I talk to Fee for a second, Ice?" Cookie didn't give Caroline a chance to agree or disagree, and grabbed Fiona's hand and tugged her into the kitchen.

When Fiona opened her mouth to speak, Cookie covered it with his hand lightly. "Listen to me for a second, Fee. Remember when I said you were mine?" Waiting for her to nod, Cookie continued. "This is a part of what that means. I have money. I have too much money. Look around. I live simply, I have few obligations outside of my duty to my country. I have *plenty* of money, and you spending it on clothes and other odds and ends won't even make a dent."

Fiona twisted her head to dislodge Hunter's hand over her mouth. He let go immediately. "I don't like taking your money, Hunter."

Cookie sighed. "How did I know you were going to say that? Okay, here's the deal. Remember I told you about Tex?" When Fiona nodded, Cookie went on. "Well Tex is good at what he does. You're not broke anymore, Fee." When she just stared at him incomprehensibly, Cookie tried again. "Tex is a computer genius. It's almost scary the things he can do. He arranged it so you're not broke. You aren't rich, but you aren't broke either."

"Are you saying he put money in my account..." Fiona's voice dropped to a whisper as if the police were somehow listening and would barge in and demand to know where Tex was so he could be arrested, "...illegally?"

"I don't think I'd put it that way. But let's just say he decided it wasn't right that you got fired so he *arranged* it so the money you would've made over the time you were in Mexico, was deposited into your account...plus interest."

"But, I can't take that money either, Hunter. It's not right."

Cookie sighed and tugged Fiona into his arms. It seemed he was always pulling her into his chest, but he loved the feel of her there and it didn't seem to bother her. "Believe me, Fee, we've tried to rein Tex in, but he does whatever he feels is right. If you pay him back, he'll turn around and do something bigger. Believe me, we've tried.

After Tex used his contacts to find where terrorists had taken Caroline, Wolf sent him a bouquet of flowers, knowing it was lame and not very manly to send a former SEAL flowers, but not knowing how else to thank the man. Wolf sent it as a tongue-in-cheek thank you, but Tex turned around and ordered two dozen roses to be delivered *every day* for two weeks to Wolf's house. We've all learned that a simple 'thank you' is enough when it comes to Tex."

"Kidnapped by terrorists?" Fiona said incredulously.

"Focus, Fee," Cookie jokingly admonished. "It's either my money or yours."

"I can't use illegal money."

"Then please, take my card today. You won't bankrupt me. I promise. Even if Caroline takes you to Louis Vuitton and you buy the place out. Okay?"

"Do you even know who Louis Vuitton is?"

"Fee…"

Fiona nodded. "Okay, okay, but I'm keeping all the receipts and if I get too much I'll take it back."

Cookie just shook his head at Fiona. She was unbelievable, in a good way. Every girlfriend he'd had in his life had jumped at the chance for him to pay their way. Fiona was unusual in every way. "Kiss me before we go back out there. I need you."

Fiona stood on her tiptoes and didn't hesitate. She reached for Hunter as soon as the words were out of his mouth. It wasn't an easy kiss; it was raw, and sensual as hell.

Cookie devoured Fiona's mouth. He held nothing back. He wanted Fiona to know how much he needed and wanted her. Even if it was years before she'd be psychologically ready to make love with him, he'd wait however long it took.

Fiona felt goosebumps shoot down her arms as Hunter kissed her. He made love to her mouth. His tongue thrusting in and out mimicked the act of making love. Hunter tasted her, ran his tongue over her teeth and curled it around hers intimately. Fiona felt one of his hands move under her shirt and up her back.

His hand was rough and warm. The goosebumps that were on her arms, moved to her legs. As Hunter's tongue melded with her own and pushed into her mouth, his hand moved around to her side and pulled her closer into him. Fiona felt his thumb brush against the side of her braless breast, then move a fraction of an inch to brush once over her nipple. It immediately puckered at his touch. Just as Fiona arched her back to encourage Hunter to continue, Caroline called from the other room.

"Come on you two! Don't start anything you can't finish in there! I'm ready to shop!"

Fiona startled badly and pulled back with a gasp.

Cookie swore under his breath, but didn't let go of Fiona.

"Easy, Fee. It's okay." Cookie could feel her breathing hard, whether it was from being startled or from their actions, he wasn't sure. Cookie didn't immediately move his hand. Fiona was soft and warm and he wanted nothing more than to take her shirt off and worship her breasts with his mouth. He wished he'd done it before, but he knew they'd have all the time in the world to get there.

"I wish you'd go without a bra every day, but I suppose that's going to be your first stop isn't it?" Cookie laughed as Fiona blushed. "Relax. Caroline won't come in. We'll wait here until you're ready."

"If you don't move your hand, I might never be ready." Fiona laughed at herself.

"I like my hand here."

"I can tell."

They stood there looking at each other for a heartbeat before Cookie slowly moved his hand away from her breast and down to her waist. "Be safe today, Fee. Caroline and Alabama have my cell number if you need anything. Don't be afraid to ask them to call me. I'll pick up a cell for you today while you're shopping. I'll put you on my plan. And before you ask, it won't cost that much to add you. Get what you need and what you don't need. You have no idea what it means to me to know you're walking around in clothes that I paid for. It's Neanderthal, but it's the way I feel."

Fiona blushed and laughingly pushed at him. "You man, me woman." She teased.

"*My* woman," Hunter countered semi-seriously.

Fiona just shook her head and stood on her tip-toes to kiss Hunter quickly on the lips. "I'll call if I need you. I'll see you later?"

"You'll see me later."

Cookie held Fiona's hand as they walked out of the kitchen and back into the hall where Alabama and Caroline were waiting for them.

"Jeez, you guys are worse than me and Matthew ever were."

"Uh, no they aren't," Alabama countered immediately. "I remember me and Christopher once waited for you guys for twenty minutes and finally just left without you because you got distracted and ended up back in bed."

Fiona giggled as Caroline blushed. She'd have to remember not to get on Alabama's bad side. It seemed the woman had a way of remembering and throwing dead-on one liners like no one she'd ever seen.

"Anyway, let's go! I haven't been shopping in like a week!" Caroline tried to get the conversation off of her and her own sex life and back on shopping.

Everyone laughed and they headed toward the door. Fiona looked back as she left and saw Hunter standing right where he'd been when they made it back to the hall. Their eyes met and he winked at her and mouthed, 'I'll see you later."

FIONA SLUMPED ON the sofa in Hunter's apartment. Jesus, she had no idea what she'd been in for when she'd left that morning with Caroline and Alabama. She figured she'd have to rein Caroline in, but Alabama was the one that took control of their shopping. She'd dragged them from one store to another. They'd filled their cart with all sorts of clothes and the other women even insisted on including sexy undies and bras. When Fiona was ready to call it quits, Alabama insisted they visit "just one more store." Of course that one store turned into five.

Fiona had spent way more money then she'd planned on. She was going to buy an outfit or two, some jeans, T-shirts and some nice utilitarian cotton undies and bras. When she'd said as much to Alabama and Caroline, they'd objected strongly, then just ignored her wishes for the rest of the day.

Fiona had *known* it was the quiet ones she had to watch out for. Alabama was no push-over, no matter what her first impression might make someone think. When they were jostled by a man who wasn't watching where he was going, Alabama tore into him and he'd fallen all over himself apologizing before he'd slunk away.

After shopping, Caroline and Alabama brought Fiona to a place called *Aces Bar and Grill*. They said it was the team's favorite bar and that they went there all the time to have lunch, or dinner, or even for drinks at night.

They had a lunch with no nutritional value, but was delicious. The other women introduced her to a waitress named Jess, who they said was always there and was, in their words, awesome. In between serving the other patrons, Jess laughed with them and told them some funny stories about some of the other regulars who made asses out of themselves on an almost nightly basis.

Fiona had asked Caroline what was wrong with the pretty waitress, as she noticed she walked with a limp, but Caroline had just shrugged and said they'd never asked.

After being gone for most of the day, the women had finally taken Fiona back to Hunter's place. It was amazing how tiring a day of shopping and laughing could be.

Fiona closed her eyes and felt herself relax. She'd get up in just a second and see what she could make for dinner. Fiona knew Hunter would be hungry when he got home, and she wanted to do something nice for him. After all, he'd done a ton of nice things for her lately and Fiona wanted to make sure Hunter knew she appreciated him.

Cookie closed the door loudly behind him. He didn't want to surprise Fiona and scare her in the process. When he didn't hear anything, he walked carefully into the living room. He didn't see Fiona, but he did see a ton of shopping bags strewn about. He smiled. God love Caroline and Alabama. He knew they wouldn't let Fiona skimp on shopping. He had to be the only man alive that loved knowing his woman had just spent a fortune on clothes and other feminine fripperies.

He came around the side of his couch and smiled even brighter. Fiona was sprawled on the couch fast asleep. Her head was to the side and one of her arms was flung out and hanging over the edge. Cookie sat down next to her hip and massaged her back. He wanted to wake her up slowly so she wouldn't be scared.

"Fee? Wake up, sweetheart." Cookie kept rubbing her back, but put a bit more pressure on her. "Come on, sleepyhead. Have you eaten?"

Fiona slowly came awake. Without opening her eyes she knew Hunter was there with her. She could smell him, not to mention the goosebumps his hand on her back was raising. She pried one eye open and looked up at him.

"I'm awake. What time is it?"

"About seven. You hungry?"

"Oh shit!" Fiona sat up so quickly she barely missed knocking her head into Hunter's. She didn't even notice, but continued with her tirade. "I was going to make dinner for you! I'm so sorry, Hunter! What do you want? Are you hungry?"

"Whoa, slow down, Fee. You don't have to make me dinner. I'm thrilled I'll get to make it with you. I've never really done that before."

Fiona looked up at Hunter. "Really?"

"Really."

"But I wanted to thank you for all you've done for me. And I just wanted to...you know?"

"You thank me every day by being here with me. By being mine. But I do know. I want to do things for you every day too. Tell you what, if you don't ever feel bad for not having dinner ready when I get home, I'll let you do it every now and then."

"*Let* me?"

"Yup. Let you."

They smiled at each other. Cookie held out his hand and helped Fiona to her feet.

"I'll compromise with you, Hunter. I'll cook dinner with you if you help me decide what of this crap Alabama and Caroline forced me to buy today I should keep and what I should return," Fiona told him seriously.

"That's easy, keep it all."

"Hunter, you haven't even *seen* any of it."

"I don't have to. If those two forced you to buy it, I know it looks great on you."

Fiona just shook her head. "You're insane."

Cookie kissed the top of Fiona's head and sauntered into the kitchen. "Insanely happy you're here with me."

FIONA STOOD AWKWARDLY next to the bed. Hunter was already in bed and had a sheet covering his lap. Fiona knew he was naked under it and she so badly wanted to throw back the covers and attack him, but knew she wasn't going to.

She'd worn the new nighty the girls had insisted she buy, along with the matching pair of panties. Even though she was adequately covered, Fiona still felt mostly naked. She hesitated next to the bed, not knowing if she should slip into the bed next to Hunter with her nightgown on or if she should take it off.

Hunter decided for her, holding out his hand. "Come here, Fee."

Fiona put one knee on the mattress and went to lay down. Hunter grabbed her arm and pulled. She fell against him and quickly got under the sheet and stretched her legs out until they tangled with his.

Cookie could feel Fiona's heart beating hard against his chest. "Relax, sweetheart. You're safe."

"I don't know what to do."

"You don't have to do anything. Just be here with me. We'll figure it out together. Okay?"

"Okay."

After a few minutes, Fiona wiggled against Hunter. She could feel the hair on his legs rubbing against hers. It should have brought back bad memories, but instead all she could think about was the other night when he'd exploded in her hand.

Fiona slowly moved her hand against his chest, remembering the feel of Hunter's nipples hardening under her ministrations.

Cookie lifted a hand and put it over hers on his chest. "I love your hands on me, Fee, but I want to pleasure you tonight. Will you let me?"

"I don't know if I can."

"How about we take it slow, and if I do anything that makes you uncomfortable, I'll stop."

Fiona nodded. "I trust you, Hunter."

"I won't betray that trust." Cookie moved one hand up to the back of Fiona's neck and leaned up and over to kiss her. He kept the kiss light, not wanting to spook her. He used his other hand to swipe up and down her body, gentling her. He kept his touch on top of her short nightgown, which had ridden up to expose her panties, not delving under it. He could feel Fiona squirming under him. Finally when she moaned, Cookie moved his hand so just his fingertips skimmed under the front panel of her panties.

"Do you know how good you feel, Fee? You're so soft. You were meant for my hands. I can't wait to taste you. I bet you taste so sweet. You'll explode so hard when I put my tongue on you, won't you?"

Fiona shivered at his words. God Hunter felt good. His words were making her crazy. "Please, Hunter. Please." She had no idea what she was begging for, but she needed something. She needed more.

"What do you want, sweetheart?"

"More."

"More? More of my kisses? My hands on you?"

"Yes. All of it."

Cookie loved making Fiona feel like this. He didn't really want her to beg, but he also wanted to make sure she wanted it, wanted *him*. He moved his fingers back and forth just under the waistline of her panties. He could feel the heat coming from her core. He leaned down and kissed her again and moved his hand so it was covering her mound, but on top of her panties.

Cookie rubbed against Fiona while kissing her, his tongue mimicking the movements of his hand. He ground the heel of his hand against her clit and couldn't deny the pleasure her cry of delight gave him.

Fiona threw her head back and grabbed hold of Hunter's wrist while he moved his hand against her.

Cookie stilled, not knowing if she wanted him to continue, or stop.

"Don't stop. God, don't stop."

He grinned. Thank God. Cookie rubbed against Fiona harder and harder while alternating kissing her face and nibbling on her neck.

"That's it, Fee. Rub against me. You feel so good, you're so hot. You're doing fine. You're so sexy."

Cookie could feel Fiona was getting close. He'd been keeping his groin away from her, not wanting to freak her out, but now he let himself brush against her.

"Feel how hard I am. You did this. You're so sexy. I'm going to come with you, Fee. Just watching you get off makes me lose it. Feel me."

He let go of her neck with his other hand and brought it to her chest. Cookie tweaked a nipple that was already sticking up through the fabric of her nightgown. At the same time, he leaned down and blew into her ear then sucked the lobe into his mouth hard. "Come for me, Fee. Come now."

Fiona shattered. Her back arched and she cried out in ecstasy. She couldn't remember the last time she'd orgasmed that hard...or if she ever had. She could barely remember her own name, nevertheless anything or anyone that came before Hunter. When Fiona came back to reality, she could feel Hunter's face against her neck and he was breathing hard. She also felt wetness against her hip.

"Whoa."

Cookie chuckled. "Whoa indeed. Just watching you made me lose it too."

Fiona opened her eyes and stared into Hunter's eyes which were locked onto hers. "You did?"

"I did. Your smell, the feel of your heat. It's all so damn sexy, I couldn't help it. When we get together for real, we're going to be fucking combustible. We won't get out of bed for days."

Fiona could only smile up at Hunter. His words made her relax.

He didn't think she was a freak, and apparently he really *didn't* want to rush her into a deeper intimacy she knew she wasn't ready for.

"Come on, as much as I love my mark on you, you can't sleep in that wet gown." Cookie climbed out of bed, completely unselfconscious about his naked body. He went into his closet and Fiona heard him calling back to her. "Where'd you put your nighties? I want to see you in the red one."

"The second drawer on the left," Fiona called back, completely floored Hunter was getting her a new nightgown to wear. She'd never been with a guy that had bothered to take care of her in any way after sex.

Fiona watched as Hunter came back into the room.

"Come on, climb out."

Fiona pulled the sheet back and climbed out, embarrassed by the wet splotch covering the front of her gown. Why she was embarrassed, she had no idea, especially considering she wasn't the one who left it there.

Cookie grinned at her. God she was cute. "Arms up."

Fiona closed her eyes and did as Hunter told her. He'd just made her come, it didn't matter if he saw her naked, and he'd seen her boobs before as well. It wasn't anything he hadn't seen a million times on other women either. At least that was what Fiona tried to tell herself.

Cookie tried to keep his touch as clinical as possible. He took hold of the bottom of her soiled gown and pulled it over her head. He could feel his heart speed up. He wondered for the millionth time how she'd survived the hell she'd been through down in Mexico. She seemed way too fragile to have been able to come through it at all.

"Keep your arms up, Fee. Give me a moment and I'll have you covered in a second."

Knowing he couldn't prolong dressing her, no matter how much he might want to, Cookie put the red nightgown over Fiona's head and pulled her arms through the straps. It fell over her hips with a swoosh. Now for the hard part.

Once the gown was covering her hips and fell to mid-thigh, Cookie grabbed hold of her undies and slid them down her legs without warning her, keeping her covered the entire time.

Fiona squeaked as she felt the underwear fall down to her ankles.

"Step out, sweetheart. I've got a new pair for you. These are soaked." Cookie kept his voice low and controlled and unthreatening.

Fiona did as Hunter asked, knowing she was bright red.

"God, I love it when you blush. I think the red goes from your face all the way to your toes," Cookie teased, trying to keep Fiona's mind off of what he was doing. He tapped each ankle when he wanted her to step up and was able to get the new pair of panties into place. He couldn't resist running his hands over her butt cheeks and down the back of her thighs before he stood up.

"Come on, back to bed."

They crawled back into bed, and it didn't escape Fiona's notice that Hunter took the side of the bed that had the wet spot. She snuggled back into his arms and sighed.

"What was the sigh for?"

"I'm so happy. It's hard to believe two weeks ago I was…"

"Don't finish that sentence."

"But…"

"I don't want to picture you there again. It kills me."

"It's okay, Hunter. I was just going to say that I don't think I've been happier in my entire life and in some warped way, I'm glad I was kidnapped, if only because it brought you to me."

"Jesus, Fee. I can't…I don't…"

It was Fiona's turn to shush him. "It's okay, Hunter. I won't bring it up again, I swear."

That night Cookie woke up once again to Fiona having another nightmare. Not one night went by without her dreaming about her captivity and he fucking hated it. She never talked about it, but Cookie knew she had to talk to someone. She wasn't moving on from her experience as well as she could, as evidenced by the nightmares she still had every night. It wasn't healthy and as well as Fiona was doing, Cookie knew she'd break if she didn't get it out. As much as he wanted to be the one she talked to, he knew he had to get her to a professional. He'd seen a lot in his life, but he didn't think he'd be able to handle what she'd say about her time in Mexico. If she needed to tell him, he'd listen, but if not, he *never* wanted to hear it. He knew what happened to women who were taken, destined to be sex slaves, but he couldn't think about his Fee being in that situation.

Cookie soothed her as best he could, and held her as she cried. As usual, Fiona never fully woke up, but settled back into his arms without a word as he counted out loud to her. Cookie always started at a hundred and counted backward toward one. Fiona was usually asleep by the time he reached eighty.

Chapter Sixteen

THE NEXT COUPLE of weeks went by quickly for Fiona. She spent her days with Alabama and Caroline, either together or separately, and her evenings and nights with Hunter. They had more heavy petting nights in his bed, but hadn't gone beyond that. Fiona wanted to, but knew she wasn't ready because every time she thought about doing more than touching, she freaked out and couldn't go through with it. Fiona was beginning to think she'd never be ready, and that killed her. Hunter deserved so much more.

Hunter had begun to encourage her to talk to a professional. He'd told her there was a doctor on base that had experience in dealing with the type of abuse she'd suffered. He'd even given her the doctor's card. He'd spoken with her and she'd agreed to talk to her whenever she was ready. Fiona didn't know if she'd ever be ready, but she carried the woman's card with her wherever she went just in case.

One day when Fiona was hanging out with Alabama, Fiona's cell phone rang. The only calls she ever received were from Hunter's, and now her, friends. It obviously wasn't Alabama calling her, as she was sitting in front of her.

"Hello?"

"Hey, Fee, it's Cookie."

"Hey, Hunter, everything all right?"

"Of course. I'm sorry to have worried you. You with Alabama at her place?"

"Yeah."

"Okay, I'm coming over."

"Are you sure everything's okay?"

"Of course. I'll see you soon?"

"Okay, I'll be waiting."

"Bye."

"Bye."

Fiona looked over to Alabama, only to see her fingers flying on her phone. She was obviously texting someone.

When she was done, Fiona said, "That was Hunter, he said he was coming to pick me up.

"Okay, yeah, okay."

"What's up? Was that Abe?"

Fiona had never been able to remember to call the other men on the team by their real name. If anyone ever listened to them talking they'd think they were crazy since Caroline and Alabama both used the men's real names, and Fiona used their nicknames. It was as if they were talking about completely different people.

"Uh yeah, Christopher is coming home too."

"Do you think they're all right?"

"Yeah, I'm sure it's nothing."

"What? You sound funny, Alabama."

Alabama sighed. "Look, I'm sure Hunter wants to tell you himself, but I'm finding it hard to keep this from you."

"Oh my God, what? You're freaking me out."

"They got called out on a mission. They're leaving tonight."

"*Tonight?*" Fiona couldn't help the shrill tone of her voice. She took a deep breath and tried again. "Tonight? They're leaving tonight?"

"Yeah, and I'm probably going to get my butt kicked for telling you before Hunter could. He's probably nervous as hell about telling you and about leaving you. I know the first time Christopher went on a mission after we got together he was a mess. I'm only telling you this because I think you need to know now and not have it sprung on you."

Fiona nodded, even though she was freaked out, she knew whatever Alabama was about to tell her was serious.

"Christopher made mistakes on that first mission after we got together. He was worried about me and his head wasn't in the right place. When he got back...he...well he hurt me and we almost broke up for good as a result." Seeing the panic on Fiona's face, Alabama hurried on. "We got it worked out, so it's all good. I'm only telling you this so you can do whatever you need to do to convince Hunter you're good and he can keep his head in the game."

Fiona nodded frantically. "I'm sorry you went through whatever it was, and I'm so glad you two worked it out. I don't want Hunter to worry about me. What do I say to him?"

"You'll figure it out. But remember you aren't alone. He might be going on a mission, but you have me and Caroline here. We have your back. Okay?"

"Okay. Thank you for telling me. I probably wouldn't have reacted well if I didn't have a head's up. I appreciate it. Can I call you later?"

"No, don't call. Just get your butt over to Caroline's after Hunter leaves. We'll have a slumber party over there and eat too much and cry over missing our men. Then we'll go shopping tomorrow and spend a crap ton of money. That should hold us over until our men come back to us."

Fiona laughed as Alabama had intended her to.

There was a knock at the door. Alabama went to it, checked the peephole and opened it. Hunter and Abe stood there. Abe immediately reached for Alabama and pulled her into his arms.

"Hey, babe. Hey, Fiona."

"Hey," Fiona answered absently, her eyes on Hunter.

"Hey, Fee. Ready to go?"

"Yeah. See you later, Alabama," Fiona called, as Hunter steered them out the door with his hand on the small of her back.

Fiona didn't say anything as Hunter led them to his car and made sure she was she settled into her seat before walking around to the driver's side. He started it up Fiona fidgeted in her seat, but kept silent. She put her left hand on Hunter's thigh as he drove. She could tell he was tense, and knew Alabama had been right in telling her what was going on. She'd be freaking out right now if she didn't already know. Hell, she'd probably have convinced herself that Hunter was about to break up with her or something.

It was obvious Hunter was dreading telling her he was leaving. Fiona relaxed a little when he put his hand over hers on his lap, liking the skin-on-skin contact and taking comfort from it.

They arrived back at his apartment and they both were silent as they walked up the stairs.

"Let's sit on the balcony, okay?"

"Okay." Fiona kept her voice as soft and soothing as she could.

Cookie sat down on one of the wide patio chairs and pulled Fiona down into his lap. Fiona immediately settled into him and curled one arm around his neck and laid her head against his chest. "Whatever it is, Hunter, it'll be all right." Fiona wanted to settle him as soon as she could. She hated seeing him worked up.

"You know I'm a SEAL." Fiona nodded and Cookie kept speaking. "It's a part of who I am. I don't want to change it. I'm good at what I do. But if you need me to quit, I will."

Fiona sat up at that. "What the hell, Hunter? Why would you even *say* that?"

"We're leaving tonight for a mission, Fee. I have to leave today. This is how it works. Sometimes we get advanced notice, but more often than not, we have to leave as soon as we're notified." Hunter's voice was tortured and he continued. "I can't tell you where we're going or what we're doing. I can't tell you how long we'll be gone.

There's a chance I won't come back. There's always a chance I might not come back."

Fiona's eyes filled with tears at his tone of voice. This was what Alabama was talking about. Somehow she had to find the right words to reassure him.

"Hunter, I know you're a SEAL. I thank *God* you're a SEAL every day of my life. Do you think I would've survived getting out of that hell hole if you weren't? I, more than *anyone*, know how important your job is. I'd *never* ask you to quit. I'd kick my own ass if I asked you to quit. Will I worry about you? Of course. Will you worry about me? Of course. But dammit, you can't let either of those things keep you from doing what it is you do best. Am I sad you're leaving? Yes. Am I concerned that I won't know where you are or what you're doing? Hell yeah. But Hunter, I can handle it. You'll come back to me. You *will*. Every time. I believe it and *you* have to believe it. I'm not some little girl that's gonna fall apart every time you leave. Besides, I have Caroline and Alabama to hang out with and go shopping with." She felt Hunter relax a fraction beneath her. Fiona continued, trying to tease Hunter out of his doldrums.

"Besides, you did give me carte blanche to use your credit card, and I plan on using the hell out of it when you're gone." Okay, that was a blatant lie, but Hunter didn't have to know that.

"Only if you buy another sexy nightie for me to see you in when I get back."

Fiona smiled and leaned toward him. "You got it."

"I have to admit, you're taking this much better than I thought you would."

"I know. You stressed yourself out about it too. But Hunter, I have to tell you something...Alabama already told me. She wanted to prepare me."

Cookie frowned. "It wasn't her place."

Fiona could tell Hunter was about to get all worked up, so she interrupted him before he could start. "Yes, it was. You worked yourself into a frenzy. Alabama lived through something with Abe that she didn't want to happen to us. She did us a favor."

Cookie was quiet for a moment digesting what Fiona told him. She was right. Alabama had done the right thing. "You're right. Abe screwed up with Alabama and she was trying to prevent me from doing the same damn thing. But, Fee, frankly, I'm dreading leaving you."

"Since we're being honest, I'm kinda dreading it too, but you need to go, Hunter. I *want* you to go. I'll be okay. I swear."

"Before I leave, I want you to know something," Cookie said in a low voice, running his hand over Fiona's back gently and lovingly.

Fiona curled up into Hunter's chest again. "Okay."

"I love you."

Fiona's head whipped up at Hunter's words and stared at him.

Cookie said it again, "I love you."

"You aren't saying that because you're leaving and you're afraid you're not coming back are you? Because if you are, I'll kick your ass."

Cookie laughed. "No, Fee. I've known I've loved you for a while now, but I was trying to give you time to get used to me and to get used to being mine. I decided now was a good time to let you know. I'm coming back, you can bet the farm on that. I have yet to get inside you."

"Jesus, Hunter, you can't say things like that!"

"I just did."

Fiona smiled at Hunter through her tears. "I..."

Cookie put a finger over her lips. "Don't say it just because I did. Even if it takes you another twenty years to say it, I'll be here. I'm not letting you go just because you haven't said it. Say it when you mean it. When you know deep down in your heart that you mean it. Until then, I'll be here. I'll be annoying you with leaving my socks on the floor and my beard shavings in the sink. I won't let you go. If you leave me, I'll find you. You're mine. Hear me? Mine."

"I hear you."

"Say it." Hunter's words were guttural and desperate.

"Yours."

"Damn straight. Now kiss me."

THAT NIGHT CAROLINE, FIONA, AND ALABAMA sat on Caroline's huge bed. They'd watched Bette Midler in *Beaches* and cried their eyes out. Of course the movie was just an excuse to cry, and they all knew it. None of them wanted to admit they were worried about their men. Belonging to a Navy SEAL wasn't an easy thing. But luckily the women had each other to rely on and to lean on when necessary.

The next morning Caroline was the first to wake up, as usual. She elbowed Fiona and Alabama until they woke up. They took turns getting ready to go out and have some retail therapy.

Around eleven, they were finally ready. Alabama drove them to the mall and they set out, each determined to find something sexy to wear for when their man arrived back home.

They were in the lingerie shop, and Caroline was trying to decide if she should buy a black or red nighty, when something caught Fiona's eye to her right. She turned her head and saw two Hispanic men watching them. A shiver immediately ran down Fiona's spine and she felt lightheaded and sick.

She hated her reaction. The men weren't doing anything wrong. They were watching them because Caroline was loud, probably too loud for the sedate store. The men weren't trying to kidnap them, they weren't even leering at them. But it didn't matter. Just seeing them standing there looking at her, brought her right back to that hell hole in Mexico.

Fiona fell to a crouch in the middle of the store. She put both hands over her head and whimpered.

Caroline heard the sound and looked around in confusion. Seeing Fiona on the ground she immediately dropped the bra she'd been holding, and crouched next to her.

"Fiona? What's wrong? What is it?"

"They're here," Fiona whispered. "We have to get out of here."

"Who's here?" Alabama asked kneeling at her other side.

"Don't let them see you, they'll take you too. We have to hide."

Alabama and Caroline locked eyes over Fiona's shaking body. They weren't exactly sure what was going on, but they had a good idea.

"Fiona, it's safe. They're gone now, come on, get up, we'll go home and have a cup of coffee."

Fiona peeked out from under her arms and saw the two men standing there, looking at them in morbid fascination.

Whispering now, Fiona frantically grabbed her friends' arms. "Okay, they know about me, but you guys can still get out of here. I'll give myself up to them, and you guys go out that other door. Get away. You have to get away. I've already been through it, I can take it. You guys go. Just go."

Caroline saw the look Fiona had shot the two Hispanic men standing nearby. She jerked her chin up at Alabama as she'd seen Matthew do to his team time and time again. Luckily, Alabama had been around them long enough to understand. She let go of Fiona's arm and stood up to ask the men to leave. While she was telling them, she'd tell the other bystanders to leave as well. It was rude to stare.

Fiona saw Alabama start to head toward the men and jerked out of Caroline's hold. "No! Alabama No! Run, dammit, run!" She leaped after Alabama and had enough of a head start over Caroline that she reached Alabama before Caroline could stop her. She grabbed Alabama's arm and jerked her backward. Fiona then rushed up to the now gaping men. "You can't have them, assholes. You can't. Take me back if you have to, but leave them alone!"

The men, obviously surprised at the venom in Fiona's voice, took three quick steps away from her. They looked around in surprise, wondering if the crazy lady was really talking to them.

Caroline had caught Alabama when Fiona had whipped her in her direction, and ran to catch up to Fiona.

"Please, you guys, just go, she's having a flashback. You're making it worse. You didn't do anything wrong, but please, just go," Alabama pleaded with the men as she reached Fiona.

The men, happy to leave the vicinity of the crazy women, fled the store as if they'd suddenly found themselves surrounded by hungry tigers.

Caroline and Alabama each grabbed hold of one of Fiona's arms and held on tightly. She wasn't getting away from them again.

"They're gone, Fiona. They're gone. Come on, sweetie. Sit down."

Fiona collapsed on the floor in the middle of the store in relief. The men had left. They wouldn't take her friends. They wouldn't take *her*. "We have to get out of here in case they come back," she told Caroline and Alabama earnestly. "You don't know them, they won't give up. They'll be back."

"Okay, we'll go," Caroline soothed. She wished with all her heart that the guys were around. Fiona needed Hunter. "Alabama is going to go and get the car. We'll just sit here until she gets back, okay?"

Fiona nodded, closed her eyes and rocked back and forth on the floor, oblivious to the looks she was given by curious shoppers and the concerned looks from her friend.

Caroline sat on the floor of the lingerie shop holding Fiona until Alabama came back. Caroline knew Alabama was hurrying, but it seemed to take way too long for her to arrive back at their sides.

"I've pulled the car around to the back door. The manager said it'd be okay if we took her out that way. I tried to explain some of what's going on. She's worried about her too."

Caroline nodded and took hold of Fiona's head and forced her to look into her own eyes. "Fiona? Alabama has the car here. Can you walk? We're going to go home."

Fiona tried to focus on what Caroline was saying. Why was Caroline there? Was she taken too? "Caroline? Did they get you too?"

Caroline just shook her head sadly. "No, we're safe, sweetie. Come on, let's get out of here, okay?"

Fiona nodded numbly. Getting out of there sounded good to her. The men could come back any second, it was better to leave.

The three friends shuffled out the back door to the waiting car. The manager looked on with sad eyes. Alabama had told her enough of Fiona's suffering for her to feel bad about what had happened in her store.

Caroline and Alabama got Fiona buckled into her seat, and Alabama drove while Caroline sat next to Fiona and held her. Fiona shook uncontrollably all the way home.

After getting Fiona back to Caroline's house, they tucked her into bed and stayed with her until she fell asleep. Neither questioned when Fiona started counting backwards from one thousand. They even joined in when it seemed to calm her more.

Caroline and Alabama sat at the kitchen table, speechless.

"She needs help. I feel helpless. I don't know what to do," Alabama said sadly.

"All we can do it be there for her."

"Do you think she's gonna remember today?"

"I sure as hell hope not, Alabama. If she does, she's gonna be mortified."

"That's bullcrap. She doesn't have anything to be embarrassed about."

"I know that, and you know that, but I bet anything, she'll be embarrassed anyway."

Alabama then whispered softly, as if afraid she was saying something blasphemous, "I wish the guys were here."

"Me too, Alabama. Me too," Caroline agreed just as quietly.

Chapter Seventeen

FIONA ROLLED OVER with a groan. She felt like crap. The room was dark, but she was starving. Her stomach growling had woken her up. She looked at the clock, at least where the clock should be. It wasn't there. Then Fiona remembered. She was at Caroline's. She and Alabama had spent the night there because the guys had been sent on a mission.

Then Fiona sat bolt upright. Oh no. Jesus. Shopping. The men. Her freak out. Fiona buried her face in her hands. Oh my God. She'd seen those men and thought she was back in Mexico. She'd accused innocent men of horrible things. What if she'd been by herself? What would she have done? She was mortified.

She had to get out of there. Fiona looked around cautiously. She was alone in the room. She could go back home. No. She had no home. She would go back to Hunter's apartment, then go…somewhere. She couldn't stay. Hunter deserved so much better than her. What if she'd freaked out when he was there? She'd be so embarrassed. She was so screwed up in the head.

Fiona tiptoed around the room, finding her shoes and purse and checking to make sure she had everything. She cautiously opened the door to the room. Seeing and hearing no one, she made her way down the hall. When she got to the living room, Fiona saw both Caroline and Alabama sprawled on the sofa sectional. There was an empty bottle of Jack Daniels on the coffee table and several cans of soda lying around as well. They'd obviously gotten hammered as a result of Fiona's actions the previous day.

Tears sprang to Fiona's eyes. Jesus, they'd been so embarrassed over what she'd done they had to get drunk to make it through the night. As Fiona headed toward the door she knew she'd never forget the sight of her first and only true friends, passed out on the couch because of something she'd done.

CAROLINE WOKE UP and groaned. Jesus, she'd had way too much to drink. She knew better, but she'd been so worried about Fiona, she'd just kept drinking. She saw Alabama still passed out next to her, and nudged her with her foot.

"Hey, Alabama, get up. Let's go check on Fiona."

Alabama groaned, but sat up gingerly. "Why'd you let me drink so much last night?"

"Me? You were the one encouraging *me* to keep going."

"Okay, so we might have been encouraging each other."

They smiled at each other. "Come on, let's go get Fiona and get the awkward crap out of the way first, then we can make a huge breakfast, choke it down, and figure out what we're gonna do and how to help her."

Alabama led the way toward the room where they'd left Fiona last night. They stood there in shock when they pushed the door open and saw the empty bed. Caroline turned and left the room as if she wasn't feeling sick a moment ago.

"Come on, Alabama, we have to get over to Hunter's. She probably woke up early and thought she'd be polite and not wake us. She was probably also embarrassed and wanted to avoid us. We have to go get her and let her know she has nothing to be embarrassed about."

The two women threw on clean clothes and raced out of the house without a thought to their appearance. Their only focus was finding their friend and reassuring her.

Once they'd arrived at Hunter's apartment, Alabama and Caroline knocked on the door, when there was no answer, they proceeded to *beat* on the door, calling Fiona's name over and over.

When she still didn't answer they could only conclude that Fiona wasn't there. "The car!" Alabama raced back to the parking lot. Neither Carline or Alabama had been concerned about looking for Hunter's car when they'd first arrived.

Seeing Hunter's parking space empty, Alabama whispered, "Shit." Her legs folded under her and she was sitting on the ground.

Caroline slumped to the ground next to her friend, stymied about what they should do next.

For the second time in as many days, Alabama said, "I wish the guys were here."

Caroline could only nod in agreement.

FIONA DROVE FOR a long as she could. She was tired, but wanted to get as far north as possible. She shook her head. North meant away from Mexico, that was the only thing running through her head at the moment. Fiona had to protect her friends, and the best way to do that, was to get away from them.

She made it as far as the outskirts of San Francisco before she had to pull off the road. Fiona debated sleeping in the car, but then figured that would make it even easier for the kidnappers to overpower her. Then she considered stopping at a flea-bag motel that rented by the hour, but again realized if the kidnappers came for her there, most likely no one would come to her aid because they were all trying to stay under the radar.

Fiona ended up pulling into a high-end hotel. She knew she wasn't exactly dressed to blend in, her sweats and too-big T-shirt definitely made her stand out, but in the end, decided everyone would be too disciplined to say anything to her about it.

She checked in, using Hunter's credit card, and went up to her room. Fiona had no luggage, but at the moment she didn't care. She lay back on the bed and closed her eyes. She was terrified and exhausted.

Fiona tried to reason out what was going on. She remembered getting back to Hunter's apartment and seeing the Hispanic men from the mall in the parking lot…at least she thought it was the same men. She had to run, had to get out of there. She hadn't even gone up to the apartment, just raced out of the parking lot and headed north.

Fiona shut her eyes. She'd just take a short nap then get up and get going again. She fell back on what had always worked before when she was stressed out, she counted. One thousand. Nine hundred ninety nine. Nine hundred ninety eight…

Six hours later, Fiona woke up disoriented and confused. Where was she? This didn't look like Caroline's house. She sat up. It was most definitely a hotel room, but she had no recollection of checking in. Snippets of the day before slowly started filtering into her brain.

I'm losing it. Jesus, I'm losing it. Is this really happening or am I dreaming it? Did my kidnappers really find me? Fiona couldn't figure out what was real and what wasn't. She wanted Hunter, but he was…somewhere. He was off saving someone else and she had no way of getting in touch with him.

As she fell deeper into the delusion that she was being hunted, Fiona thought about Hunter… *He found me in the middle of the Mexican jungle and he wasn't even looking. He'll find me here. I just have to stay one step ahead of the kidnappers and wait for Hunter.*

"WE HAVE TO do something, Caroline," Alabama implored her friend. "We can't just sit here and wait for her to come home. It's obvious she isn't going to just come back and say, 'Hey, sorry I worried you, I'm back.'"

"Something's really wrong, Alabama," Caroline stated the obvious. "Fiona really thought those men were there to take her back to Mexico. What if she still thinks that? Is that even possible?"

"I have no idea, but, Jesus, Caroline. If that's what she thinks, there's no telling where she is. We have to call the commander. He can get in touch with Hunter. He has to know."

"But what if they can't come home right now? That would just freak Hunter out and put him and the rest of the team in danger."

"I know, but what if it was us in trouble? You know Christopher or Matthew would never forgive us if they weren't notified."

"Okay, I'll call Commander Hurt and let him know what's going on."

Caroline called the base and left a message for the team commander to call her back as soon as he could. She tried to make sure the Petty Officer who took the message understood it was literally a life and death situation and that the commander needed to call her as he got back into his office.

Alabama sat up suddenly. "Oh my God, why didn't we think of this before? What about Tex?"

"Tex! Shit! Yes, you're a genius, Alabama!"

Caroline scrambled for her phone. If anyone could find Fiona, it'd be Tex. She scrolled through her contacts and clicked on his name.

"What's wrong?" Leave it to Tex to cut right to the chase.

"Fiona's missing and Hunter and the others are on a mission."

"Talk to me."

"We were shopping yesterday and there were two Hispanic men minding their own business in the same store we were in. Fiona saw them and literally freaked. She had a flashback or something and we had to get out of mall through the back door of the store. We brought her home, but when we woke up, she was gone. She's not at

Hunter's apartment and his car is missing. We think she's stuck in the flashback or something. We don't know what to do."

"Have you contacted the commander?"

"Yeah, I just got off the phone with someone on the base and left a message for him to call us back. Alabama thought about you. You can find her can't you, Tex?"

"Yeah, I'll find her. Keep trying to get through to the commander, I'll see what I can do from this end."

"Thank you, Tex. Oh, and she's got Hunter's credit card. Hunter gave it to her to use, she didn't steal it."

Tex's voice lost its edge a bit. "I wouldn't have thought she did, Ice. That's good she has it. I'll find her and get back to you as soon as I can."

"Okay. Thank you so much. We didn't know what to do."

"You did the right thing in calling me. Later, Ice."

"Bye, Tex."

Caroline turned to Alabama and told her unnecessarily, "Tex said he'd find her."

Alabama nodded. "Okay, if he said he'd find her, he will. We just have to pray it's soon."

THE PHONE ON the nightstand rang and Fiona nearly jumped a foot. She stared at it. Was it Hunter? Was it the kidnappers? Had they found her? She struggled for a moment between wanting to answer the phone and wanting to run out of the room and jump in the car and keep driving. Fiona dug down deep to the courage she'd been missing for the last day or so, and reached for the phone.

"Hello?"

"Fiona, it's Cookie's friend, Tex. Don't hang up."

Fiona sagged in relief. She remembered Hunter talking about Tex. Thank God he'd found her. "Tex?" she whispered, "I'm so scared. They found me."

On the other end of the line, Tex sagged in his seat. Thank fuck she knew who he was, but Jesus, he had to do everything right here, and he wasn't sure what that was. Fiona was obviously stuck in the delusion she was being hunted, and all it would take would be one wrong word out of his mouth and she'd run again. Tex decided it'd be better to cater to her delusion for the moment instead of trying to convince her she was imagining everything.

"Fiona, listen to me. Cookie told you about what I can do with computers right? Well, I've got them covered. I know where the kidnappers are, and they're still back in Riverton. They don't realize you've left yet. You're safe right there where you are. Just stay put. Order room service, ask them to leave it outside your door and put everything on the credit card. I've got your credit card secured, so no one else will be able to trace it. Do you hear me? You're safe right where you are."

Tex didn't want Fiona opening the door to possibly a Hispanic hotel worker, or anyone, and freaking out again. He knew she was safe in the hotel for the moment. He'd tracked her down with one short search of Cookie's credit card. Fiona wasn't really trying to hide, she was just running scared.

"Okay Tex. I'll wait to hear from you. Am I really safe here? They don't know I left?" Her voice was low and trembled with emotion.

"No, sweetheart. They have no idea where you are." Tex was being completely honest.

"Is Hunter coming to find me again?"

Tex's heart almost broke. "I'm working on it, Fee. You know he's on a mission right?"

"Yeah, I know. That's why they came now, they knew he was gone and wasn't here to protect me."

"We're trying to get Cookie home so he can come and get you. Remember what I said, don't move. Stay hunkered down there."

"Okay, Tex. I will."

"I'm going to call you every four hours, Fiona. You be there to answer the phone. Okay? Every four hours."

"I got it. I'll be here."

"Good. Drink lots of water and make sure you order food from the hotel. Keep up your strength." Tex figured if he ordered Fiona to do things, she'd be more likely to follow through.

"Yeah, okay." She paused, and said in a child-like voice, "I want Hunter."

"He'll be there as soon as he can, Fiona. Hang on for him, baby."

Tex was reluctant to hang up, but he had some other calls to make. He had to get Cookie home. His woman needed him. Now.

"Okay, I'll wait for Hunter."

"I'll talk to you in four hours, Fiona. Four hours. No more, no less. Make sure you answer the phone."

"Okay, Tex. Bye."

Tex hung up the phone and swore long and loud. He knew Cookie hadn't expected this to happen. Fiona obviously needed help dealing with what had happened to her. His first call was to the commander. He had to get Cookie home. His woman needed him.

COOKIE SLAMMED OPEN the door to Caroline and Wolf's house. They'd been knee deep in a "situation" in a not-so-well-known country in Africa, when Wolf had pulled him aside and told him about Fiona. It'd taken both Benny and Abe holding him back so he wouldn't go running off half-cocked and getting both himself and his team killed. The team had talked it over and decided, with the blessing of their commander, to pull back and allow another SEAL team to take over.

They all knew how unusual it was for them to be even be *given* the chance to pull back. Usually when it came to Uncle Sam, there *was* no option. The mission came first, always. But apparently Tex had personally discussed the situation with the commander and convinced him for the need of an immediate withdrawal of Cookie and the rest of the team.

All six men had immediately agreed to get the hell out of Africa, and get back to California so Cookie could help his woman.

Wolf was right behind Cookie when he entered his house. Caroline and Alabama were there and Caroline immediately ran into Matthew's arms.

"I'm sorry, I'm so sorry, Hunter. I should have kept a better eye on her."

"Tell me what happened from the beginning, Ice." Cookie's voice was hard and even, as if he was holding on to his temper and sanity by his fingernails.

"Careful, Cookie," Wolf warned, not liking the tone he was taking with Caroline.

"It's okay, Matthew," Caroline reassured him. Turning back to Hunter she told him what had happened at the store and what they'd done afterwards.

"It sounds like you did everything right, Ice. You got her out of the store and you and Alabama stayed with her."

"But we got drunk and she snuck out."

"I know, but remember she got away from me too when we were in Texas. She's an adult, you couldn't have watched over her all day and all night. Even if you weren't drunk, she still could've left while you were sleeping. Desperate people can manage to do things that people who are in their right mind never can."

"She took your car, and Tex traced her to San Francisco. She's in a hotel up there."

"Yeah, he debriefed me as soon as we landed. I'm headed to the airport to get her, I just have to make one stop first."

"You're stopping somewhere?" Alabama questioned harshly.

Cookie turned to her and defended his actions, even though he didn't really feel he had to. "Yeah, I'm collecting Dr. Hancock. I wanted Fiona to see her and talk to her about everything she went through in Mexico, but she obviously never followed through. I'm not giving Fee a choice now. I don't know how to help her, but I know Dr. Hancock can. So I'm picking her up, I've already contacted her and she agreed, and we're going to fly up there and bring Fiona home."

"Sorry, Hunter. Jesus, I've been so worried about her. I know you'd never take her safety for granted. Go. Bring her home." Alabama sounded so contrite, Hunter couldn't help but take the two steps to her side and bring her into him for a quick hug.

"She'll be home as soon as I can get her here. I'm taking Benny with us, but Dr. Hancock thinks it would be best if Fiona didn't see him at all. He'll drive my car back down here while we go up to the hotel room to get Fiona. We'll fly back as soon as Dr. Hancock says it's okay. Abe will be over here to the house as soon as he can. He and the others had to debrief with the commander."

Cookie let go of Alabama and held her at arm's length with his hands on her shoulders. He watched as she nodded and he squeezed her shoulders reassuringly.

"Okay, go get her, Hunter. Bring Fiona home"

Caroline, Wolf, and Alabama watched as Cookie strode out of the house, back to the car at the curb. Benny was behind the wheel. They were on one of the most important missions of their lives, and everyone knew it.

Chapter Eighteen

FIONA ANSWERED THE phone after it rang only once.

"Tex?"

"Yeah, babe, it's me. How're you holding up?" Tex had kept his promise and called Fiona every four hours for the last three days. It had taken that long for him to get a hold of the commander, to convince him it was a life or death situation, for Wolf's SEAL team to get back to the States, and for Cookie to get his ass on a plane headed up to San Francisco.

Fiona had answered the phone every time Tex had called. They were both exhausted, but she hadn't missed one call.

"You eat yet?"

"Yeah, I ordered an omelet this morning."

"Okay, that's good. Today's the day, Fiona."

Fiona sucked in a breath. She'd been so confused over the last few days and Tex had been her lifeline. She vacillated between knowing she was losing her mind because she knew no one was after her, to being convinced the kidnappers were waiting downstairs in the lobby to snatch her if she left the room. Tex had called, just as he said he would, every few hours and helped calm her down.

"I'm losing my mind, Tex. I want to go home...back to Hunter's apartment. No one's after me are they?" The last was said in a sad whisper.

"Fiona, Cookie will be there in a couple of hours. Sit tight. He'll be there, and you'll be just fine. Don't leave now, not right before he gets to you." When Tex didn't hear any response, he continued. "I'll call you when he's standing outside your door, so you know it's him and you can let him in. Do you understand?"

"Yes." Fiona's voice was small and wobbly.

"Okay, I'll call back in a couple of hours. Stay in the room; take a nap if you need to. Cookie's coming for you, Fee. I'll talk to you soon."

Tex hung up the phone and paced the room. His prosthetic leg, for once, wasn't hurting. He could only think about Fiona and about her state of mind. She'd been through hell, and he'd been right there with her for the last three days. Tex never knew what her state of mind would be when he'd call. Sometimes Fiona seemed mostly lucid, like this last call, other times she was completely freaked out, convinced the kidnappers were right outside her door.

It was those times that had taken every bit of psychological training he'd ever had. He'd convinced her to do things like go into the bathroom and crouch down in the bathtub until they were "gone." He'd lied and told her he'd tapped into the hotel cameras and had seen the men leave the hallway, even though no one had ever been there in the first place.

He'd talked Cookie into bringing the doctor with him when he went to Fiona. She needed the help, more than anyone he'd ever met. Well, he'd never *met* Fiona, but he'd spoken to her enough over the last seventy hours, that he felt like he knew her.

Tex couldn't wait to hear from Cookie that he'd landed. It was time to end this.

COOKIE CLICKED OFF the phone with Tex and waited for Fee to open the door. Tex had said he'd call Fiona and let her know he was there and that it was safe to open the hotel door. Cookie had said good-bye to Benny in the parking lot after they'd arrived in a taxi from the airport. Benny understood why he couldn't see Fiona right now, and even if he didn't like it, he knew it was for the best. He'd wrung a promise out of Cookie to be able to come over and see Fiona as soon as Cookie thought she was well enough when they got home.

It wasn't even a minute after hanging up with Tex that Cookie saw the hotel door open an inch, then suddenly Fiona was in his arms. She'd opened the door and thrown herself at him after verifying it really was him at her door.

Cookie could literally feel every muscle in his body relax. He'd been so stressed for the last three days and it was all he could do not to dissolve into a hysterical fit of tears. One hand went around Fiona's waist and the other curled around the back of her head and he held her to him as he backed her into the room and toward the bed.

Fiona could barely say a word. Hunter was here. He was *here*.

"You came."

"I came. I'll *always* come for you." Cookie said the words as if they were the most important words he'd ever said and *would* ever say in his life.

They sat on the bed and after Fiona straddled his lap, Cookie rocked Fiona back and forth. They both needed the contact with each other. They'd each been through their own type of hell.

Finally Cookie loosened his hold, just enough to pull away to look into Fiona's face.

"Fiona?"

"Yeah?"

"Can you tell me what's going on?" Cookie had to see where her head was at. Was she still in the midst of the delusion that she was running from her kidnappers, or was she lucid enough to know she'd imagined the entire thing?

"I...I'm not sure. I think I screwed up."

Cookie shook his head and brought his hands up to Fiona's face and held her face still while he spoke to her. His thumbs caressed the underside of her jaw and he spoke earnestly to her.

"You didn't screw up, Fee. *I* did. I should've made sure I took care of you before I left. I was afraid something like this would happen. But I learned my lesson. I'm not going anywhere until I fix this. Okay?"

Fiona felt the tears start, but couldn't stop them. "I'm sorry. I didn't mean to cause so many problems. I just…they…I can't figure it all out in my head."

"Shhhh, we'll figure it out together. For now, I want you to meet someone. She's with me. Don't be afraid." Cookie gestured toward the door and a short, but kindhearted looking, woman walked in the room. She was wearing a pair of jeans and looked to be about five months pregnant. She waddled a bit as she walked, but the look on her face was open and friendly.

"This is Dr. Hancock. She came with me to help you deal with what's happening. She's with me."

Fiona looked from the woman, who'd stopped right inside the door, back to Hunter. In a low whispered voice Fiona said sadly, "They weren't ever after me were they? I dreamed it all up didn't I? That's why you brought a shrink with you. I'm going crazy."

Cookie touched his forehead to Fiona's and tried to think what he should say. Luckily, the doctor answered for him.

"Fiona, the mind is a powerful thing. I'm sure you've seen videos of people wearing those virtual reality goggles, right? They know they aren't on a roller coaster, but with those goggles on they can't stop their body was swaying and rolling as if they really *were* on a roller coaster. You've had an experience much like that. Deep down you knew those men you saw weren't after you, but based on what happened to you, your conscious mind did what it had to do to protect itself. You're not going crazy. You're perfectly normal. If you hadn't reacted as you had, I would've been even more worried about you."

Fiona looked up at Hunter again. "I'm sorry. I'm so sorry. You were on a mission…"

"Stop. You're more important than any mission. I told you that before and I'll keep saying it until you believe it. I'd scale mountains for you. I'd quit today if you needed me. You. Come. First. Period. No more "sorry's." Let's get home. Talk to Dr. Hancock. We'll figure it out. Together."

Fiona wrapped her arms around Hunter and sighed when she felt his arms surround her again. She nodded.

Cookie stood up with Fee in his arms. He'd swung her around so one arm was around her back and the other was under her knees. "Close your eyes, Fee. I'll get us out of here. You just relax. Trust me."

"I do, Hunter. I knew you'd come for me and I'd be safe." She gripped Hunter tightly and buried her head in his neck, closing her eyes as Hunter had asked.

"You're safe, Fee. Safe with me. Always."

Cookie carried Fiona into his apartment while Dr. Hancock followed close behind. She'd talked to Fiona off and on while they'd flown back to southern California. The doctor wanted to get an idea of where Fiona's head was at and the best way to go about getting her the help she needed.

Cookie wanted to cry when he'd heard Fiona tell Dr. Hancock that she'd tried to be brave for *him*. He hadn't wanted Fiona to suppress her feelings, but he *had* told her over and over how impressed he was with her bravery and courage.

He carried her into their room and put Fiona softly on the bed. She didn't stir. She'd been exhausted from trying to hide from imaginary kidnappers as well as answering the phone every four hours when Tex had called. Cookie knew he owed Tex everything. Anything the man ever needed, was his. He'd kept his woman safe. There was no way to repay that. Cookie wouldn't forget it. Ever. He kissed Fiona on the forehead and smoothed her hair back from her head gently. God, she'd scared the shit out of him.

Cookie left the room and went back to where Dr. Hancock was waiting for him.

"What do you think? Do I need to bring her in to the hospital for in-patient treatment?" It wasn't what Cookie wanted to do, but he would if the doctor thought it was what Fiona needed.

"I don't think so. She seems more lucid with you around. You can't leave her alone though, Hunter. If you need to go to work or if you're called away, you'll need to admit her for her own good."

"I'm not going anywhere. It's already been cleared by the commander. If we get called out, the others will cover it. He knows Fiona comes first."

"Okay, good. She'll need daily sessions at first. Then, depending on how those go, we can slowly taper them off. The good news is that I think she *wants* to get better."

"Of course she does," Cookie said heatedly.

"There is no 'of course' about it, Hunter," Dr. Hancock said sadly. "You'd be surprised how many women can't move past what happened to them, what was done to them. They can't get past the abuse and they spiral down into a life of drugs and sometimes prostitution. Even though they were sexually abused, they aren't able to acclimate back into society." Waiting to make sure Hunter understood her words, the doctor nodded, then continued. "Okay, stay with her tonight and bring her in to see me in the morning. I'll probably start out meeting with her alone, then I'll see if she'll allow you to come in as well. Since you were there and a big part of her rescue, I think it'll help."

"I can't thank you enough, Doctor. I should've called you long before now."

"Yes, you should have. But what's done is done. Fiona is getting help now. And if it's any consolation, I think she's going to be fine. You were right. She *is* tough. She *is* brave. That'll get her through this."

Cookie saw the doctor out and watched as she got into an SUV sitting in the parking lot. Her husband had obviously been waiting for her. Cookie stood there, as the car disappeared into the night, thinking he'd been lucky. More than lucky. Cookie turned around and headed back inside, to Fiona.

Chapter Nineteen

F IONA SMILED AT Caroline and Alabama. A week after her "freak out," as Fiona was calling it, she felt a lot better about everything that had happened. At first she'd refused to talk to either of the women, thinking they hated her. But after several meetings with Dr. Hancock, she'd finally reached out to her friends.

Thank God for true friends. Hunter had brought her over to Caroline's house and he, Wolf, and Abe had watched some sports game on television while the three women worked everything out between them in the basement.

Hunter had refused to leave her side over the last week and Fiona was inwardly glad. She'd told him several times that he didn't have to babysit her, but he'd countered, telling her he wasn't babysitting, but supporting and lending an ear when she needed it.

Fiona had only taken one step inside Wolf's house before she'd been engulfed in both Caroline's and Alabama's arms. They'd cried and laughed and that was before they'd even talked.

They'd spent hours in the basement talking through what had happened and both laughing and crying about it. When Fiona tried to apologize, Caroline lost her mind and ranted for a full ten minutes about kidnappers and nosy shoppers and sex slave rings, and Fiona hadn't had the heart to try to apologize again.

It was eleven at night when Wolf finally cracked open the basement door and hollered, "Is it safe to come down?"

Laughing, the women had answered yes.

All three men came down the stairs and went right to their women.

Cookie scooped Fiona up and plopped her into his lap as he sat on the floor by the couch. He leaned back against it and Fiona snuggled down into his arms as she usually did.

Wolf sat next to Caroline on the sofa and pulled her into him so that she was resting her head on his chest.

Abe went to the big easy chair and sat down, motioning for Alabama to come to him. She went over to him and straddled him, putting her knees on either side of his lap and folding in on him like a boneless rag doll.

"We were worried about you, Fiona," Wolf said, rubbing his hand up and down Caroline's back.

"I know, and I'm sorry."

"No, don't be sorry. It's what friends do. You do know you've got some pretty serious friends here, right?"

"I do. And you'll never know how much I appreciate it. I've never had true friends before, only acquaintances." Fiona loved the feel of Hunter's arms around her. It made talking about scary stuff somehow easier.

"I've already apologized to Caroline and Alabama, but I'm sorry you guys had to come back from your mission to get me. I honestly didn't mean for that to happen. What you guys do is important. I can't imagine if you got called away from *my* rescue."

Without raising his voice, Abe answered calmly. "You would've been rescued, Fiona. We don't operate independently. If we got called off of your rescue, another group would've been called in and you still would've been saved. Every SEAL team covers for each other."

"But…"

"No buts, Fiona. And just so you know, you're ours now. You're mine. You're Wolf's, you're Benny's…you're all of ours. If you're in trouble, we're there."

Cookie held Fiona tighter as she sobbed in his arms. He let her cry. She needed to hear Abe's words. Really hear them.

"So if you're in trouble, it's like our own women are in trouble. If you call me, I'll come running. If Alabama calls Cookie, he'll go to her. So you see, Cookie is your man, but he's actually a package deal."

Fiona looked up finally. Her face was blotchy and red from crying, but she tried to smile at Abe. She hiccupped once, then got herself together.

"I've been talking to Dr. Hancock a lot this week, as you all know. I've tried to come to terms with what happened to me, what happens to women all over the world every single day. But the one thing I couldn't do was see any good that came out of what happened to me. Yes, I met Hunter and I'll forever thank God for that, but I was having a hard time coming up with anything else for my list. Until now. Until you guys. I never dreamed I'd find a man of my own, nevertheless a family full of brothers and sisters."

"You might not like it once we all get up in your business, Fiona," Wolf warned her seriously.

Fiona chuckled. "You're right, but once I can think about it, I'll remember how lonely I was and how much better my life is now that you're in it, and I'll thank my lucky stars you all came into my life."

A comfortable silence fell over the group.

Cookie broke it with a chuckle. "If you're both done wooing my woman, I think we'll be going home now."

Everyone laughed and Fiona smacked Hunter on the arm.

Wolf stood up and pulled Caroline up with him. "It's time we headed to bed ourselves. Abe, you guys staying here?"

Abe looked at Alabama with raised eyebrows. Since Alabama had lived here in the basement for a bit while Abe was getting his act together, they knew they were welcome and frequently took Wolf and Caroline up on the offer to stay the night instead of driving home.

"Yeah, we can stay here." Alabama's words were slurred. She was already half asleep.

Cookie stood up with Fiona in his arms. He carried her up the stairs and out the door without giving her a chance to say good-bye. He knew she'd see her friends again, most likely the next day. The trip home was done in silence. Cookie hoped the night had been a turning point in her recovery.

When they arrived home, Cookie turned to Fiona and ordered, "Stay," as she reached for the door handle. She smiled at him and did as she was told.

Cookie came around the side of the car and opened her door and lifted Fiona out.

"You know I can walk. You don't have to cart me around everywhere."

"You weigh less than the pack I carry on missions. Now hush."

Fiona only smiled and snuggled deeper into her man.

Cookie carried Fiona up the stairs into their room. For what was quickly becoming a habit for them, he laid her down gently on the bed and took off her shoes. Looking into her eyes, Cookie unfastened her pants and eased them down her legs.

Fiona lay on Hunter's bed and watched as he carefully undressed her. She didn't feel even a second of unease. This was Hunter. He wouldn't do anything to hurt her. Ever.

Fiona watched as Hunter took his shirt off and threw it toward the hamper in the corner of the room. He then sat on the bed and leaned over and took off his boots. Next came his pants and boxers. Only when he was completely naked did he lean over Fiona and lift the shirt off her head. Fiona dutifully raised her arms to allow him to remove her shirt. Once that was done, he reached under her back and unhooked her bra. His actions were clinical rather than romantic, but he still made her feel cherished.

Over the last week, Fiona slowly came to terms with what had happened. As part of her therapy, Dr. Hancock had suggested she go back to the mall and the place where she'd had her "episode." She hadn't wanted to do it, but Hunter had encouraged her and promised he wouldn't leave her side.

They'd gone and walked around the mall for hours. Slowly, Fiona lost her nervousness and enjoyed the day with Hunter. Even when a group of Hispanic men walked by, she hadn't freaked out, but of course having Hunter right there with her probably had a lot to do with it.

After they'd walked by the men, Hunter had steered her into a nearby hallway and kissed the hell out of her. He'd claimed it was a reward for "good behavior." Fiona had only laughed and kissed him again.

Hunter hadn't ever made her feel guilty or bad for what had happened. Dr. Hancock had invited Hunter into their sessions and Fiona had to admit, at first she wasn't happy. She hadn't ever wanted Hunter to learn what the kidnappers had done to her, but after a few sessions she had to admit it was a good call on the doctor's part.

Hunter had to hear what had happened and she'd had to tell him. It'd solidified their relationship in a way that they didn't have before.

Cookie had guessed what Fiona had been through, but hearing it from her, hearing how she felt and how she'd endured, made Cookie realize how lucky he was that Fiona was here with him. There were so many things that could've gone differently...from the men selling her, to their hurting her, to them overdosing her by accident, to her being rescued, their trek through the jungle, the firefight as they waited for the helicopter, the flying bullets, the withdrawal...Cookie knew he could go on and on. But the bottom line was that they were here. Now. Together. Cookie knew they were meant to be together, otherwise any of those things could have ended differently.

As Fiona lay in bed next to Hunter, she knew there was no place she'd rather be.

"I love you, Hunter."

Without hesitation Cookie responded, not making a big deal out of hearing the words from Fiona's lips for the first time. "I love you too, Fee. You're my everything."

Tonight wasn't the night they'd make love, but Fiona knew it'd be soon. Hunter hadn't ever pushed her for it, and she knew he wouldn't. Fiona had talked to Dr. Hancock about sex and how she felt, and while Dr. Hancock cautioned Fiona to go slowly, she'd also encouraged her to do what felt right, when it felt right. Fiona knew she would have to be the one to make the first move, and she would. For now, she and Hunter were enjoying each other's company.

Fiona snuggled deeper into Hunter's embrace. He was always so warm, just one more thing in a long list of things that Fiona loved about him. The feel of his naked body against her own was comforting, instead of horrifying.

"Stop thinking, Fee. Go to sleep."

Fiona smiled. She loved this man more than she thought possible. As she drifted off to sleep, she smiled she heard Hunter murmur, "Mine, I'll never leave you. You'll never have another night of fear in your life."

Epilogue

FIONA LAY ON Hunter's chest panting and trying to recover. Jesus, he was going to kill her. That was the third orgasm he'd given her that night, and she'd never felt better or more loved.

"I think you've killed me," Fiona mock complained, while Hunter tried to catch his breath as he lay under her satiated body.

Fiona watched as a satisfied smile broke out on Hunter's face. She licked his nipple once more and grinned even wider at the shudder that made its way through his body. She felt him jerk inside her.

"I love you, Mr. Knox."

"I love you, Mrs. Knox."

They'd flown to Vegas and gotten married without telling anyone. Their friends hadn't talked to them for at least two days in protest, but Fiona wouldn't have changed anything about their wedding. She hadn't wanted to make a big deal out of their marriage. For her, it was a natural continuation of their love. She'd had enough of being in the spotlight, Fiona had just wanted to marry Hunter and continue on with their lives.

Hunter had protested at first. He'd wanted to give her a huge wedding and invite all their friends, and their friends, and *their* friends. It wasn't until Fiona had explained *why* she wanted a small wedding with just the two of them, that he'd relented.

Now, anytime anyone tried to complain about missing their wedding, Hunter would take them aside and bluntly explain it wasn't any of their business why they'd done what they had, and warned them not to bring it up again.

"I hate to bring up anything other than how much of a man-stud you are since we're lying still attached in our bed, but I'm worried about Mozart," Fiona said drowsily.

"I know, me too."

"Why is he so obsessed with that guy?"

"I'm not completely sure, but I think it has to do with his sister. I know she was killed when she was little and they never found the guy who did it. I think that's why Mozart joined the SEALs in the first place, so he could eventually track down the guy, since the cops had essentially closed the case."

"Do you think he'll ever find him?"

"I have no idea, but I know he sure is trying his damnedest."

"Do you think the guy he's hunting up near Big Bear is the killer?"

"I don't know, but I'd say so. Mozart doesn't make many mistakes, not when it comes to something as important as this."

Fiona nodded. "I feel bad."

"Me too. But before you ask, I'm not going to sit him down for a chat about it," Cookie told Fiona resolutely.

Fiona giggled, imaging Hunter and Mozart "chatting" about their feelings. Her giggle turned into a moan when she felt Hunter grow harder inside of her. She wiggled, urging him to do something."

"Again, Fee?"

"Oh yeah, again."

"You know, maybe you need to go and see Dr. Hancock about this insatiable need you have," Hunter teased.

"If I have a problem, so do you." Fiona sat up in Hunter's lap and swiveled her hips, loving the feel of his hard length inside her. She put her hands on his chest and leaned into him.

"You're right, I do. So let's see if we can't do something about it."

Cookie smiled up at his woman. Fiona had come so far since the night he'd found her shaking and scared out of her mind in the hotel room in San Francisco. He'd never forget the anxiety he'd felt as he tried to get to her from his mission in Africa. She hadn't had many relapses since then, and nothing like that time.

The first time Fiona had initiated sex when they'd gotten back from San Francisco, Cookie had tried to resist, not believing she'd had enough time to process everything that had happened to her. She'd insisted she was fine and it wasn't until Cookie had wrung a promise out of her to stop if she felt even an inkling of unease, that he'd continued. That first time was special.

Cookie had been with his fair share of women, but nothing in his entire life, compared to the first time he'd eased into Fiona's warm, welcome, wet body. She hadn't even flinched, just held on to his face and looked him in the eyes as he'd entered her. She'd responded to his, "You okay with this, Fee?" with words he'd memorized. She'd said, "I'm perfect, Hunter. When you hold me in your arms, I can't think of anything but you." Even with her relapse, Fiona was still the strongest person Cookie had ever met.

He rolled over so Fiona was under him. He brushed her hair out of her face and smoothed it behind her ear.

"Mine."

"Yours," Fiona immediately returned with a smile.

Blocking everything and everyone out of his mind except for pleasuring his wife, Cookie bent down toward Fiona. He couldn't ask for anything else in this world. He had it all right here in his arms.

Marrying Caroline

SEAL of Protection
Book 3.5

By Susan Stoker

Chapter One

CAROLINE OPENED THE door to *Aces Bar and Grill* and looked around for Matthew. Seeing him sitting at their usual table with his entire SEAL team as well as Fiona and Alabama, Caroline headed that way.

Waving at their usual waitress, Jess, as she passed, Caroline pushed her way through the crowd to her man. The bar seemed unusually crowded tonight, but as usual, Matthew didn't wait for her to get to him. Caroline smiled as Matthew made his way to her. It was almost annoying how the crowd seemed to part in front of him magically, but Caroline couldn't blame the patrons. Matthew was an imposing force.

Caroline analyzed her man as he came toward her. He was tall, around six foot three and had the look of a man that didn't take any shit. Matthew was wearing jeans and a short sleeve T-shirt that was just big enough to give him room to move, but didn't have any extra material either. Caroline could see his arms bulging as he moved. She stopped and let Matthew come to her. She'd never get over how lucky she was that somehow this man, this wonderfully handsome, sexy, brave, intense man, was with *her*.

"Hey, Ice. Missed you."

Caroline smiled. "We saw each other two hours ago."

"I know, as I said. I missed you." Matthew "Wolf" Steel put his hand on the side of Caroline's face and leaned into her.

"I missed you too," Caroline admitted huskily. She loved Matthew's hands on her. He always made her feel so cherished.

Wolf captured Caroline's lips with his. Not caring they were standing in the middle of a bar and were being jostled by people passing them, Wolf showed Caroline just how much he'd missed her.

Caroline's arms came up to clasp Matthew at the back of his head and she lost herself in his kiss. She could feel her body softening and readying itself for his loving, but luckily, before she did something that would embarrass herself so much she'd never be able to step foot in *Aces* again, Matthew pulled his head back.

"God, Ice. You're amazing. Come on." Wolf let go of Caroline's face and grabbed one of her hands that had crept around to rest on his chest. "I ordered for you, everyone else is here."

"Hi guys!"

"Hey!"

"Hi, Caroline."

"Yo, Ice."

The greetings were heartfelt and sincere. Caroline had never felt so lucky. Not only had she gained a wonderful man when she moved in with Matthew, but she'd gained his teammates as brothers. Now that Christopher had found Alabama and Hunter had married Fiona, she also had some sisters and best friends too.

Matthew settled Caroline into a chair next to him, and they both sat.

"What took you so long?" Fiona complained to Caroline, smiling to take the sting out of her words.

"We were having a breakthrough at work. There was this compound that we've been testing for-freaking-ever and we finally figured out how to…"

Wolf put his hand over Caroline's mouth and stopped her words. "You're off the clock, Ice. No shop-talk tonight. We're here to relax, not to hear about your chemist stuff."

Everyone laughed.

Caroline mock glared at Matthew at the same time she stuck out her tongue and licked his palm sensuously. She watched as his eyes went molten and she suddenly wished they were anywhere but there.

Wolf leaned into her, took his hand away from Caroline's mouth and put it on her thigh. "You'll pay for that tonight, Ice."

Caroline could feel the goose bumps that rose on her flesh at the feel of his words against her ear. "I'm counting on it, Matthew."

Wolf kissed Caroline on the temple and straightened, not moving his hand from her leg. He was the luckiest son of a bitch in the world. He'd never forget how scared he'd been when he watched the video of Caroline being tortured. He'd never forget how he'd held his breath praying he wouldn't have to watch her execution. The terrorists had hoped sending the tape would make the SEAL team lose their cool, but they were too well trained for that. If anything, it had solidified their determination to get Caroline back alive and to take the terrorists down.

Wolf knew he owed Cookie a debt greater than the man would ever know. Cookie had tried to tell Wolf the debt was paid when they had to cut short a mission to get back to the States and to Cookie's woman, Fiona, when she was in trouble, but Wolf knew he'd never feel the debt would ever be paid in full.

Hunter "Cookie" Knox had been the one who kept Caroline alive when she'd been thrown overboard in the ocean. He'd been the one that had held the life-saving oxygen to her face and swam them away from the terrorist boat moments before it had blown up.

Wolf didn't begrudge Caroline the close friendship she had with Cookie. And the two were close. While Wolf was a possessive man, he couldn't bring himself to care in this case. In any other situation if a man dared to touch Caroline, Wolf would be all over him, but not Cookie.

There was only one thing about their relationship that bothered him, but Wolf knew he'd most likely never bring it up with her. It wasn't worth the angst it would bring either Caroline or Cookie. Wolf would just have to suck it up and deal with it.

Tonight was the night Wolf hoped would be the night he'd make the first step toward making Caroline his, officially. He'd asked all his friends here tonight because he was going to ask Caroline to marry him. Wolf knew how much Caroline's friends meant to her, and he meant to surround her with as much love as he could, before he asked her to wear his ring.

"How are you doing, Fiona?" Caroline asked gently, leaning toward her friend. She'd never forget how scared she'd been for her when Fiona had experienced a flashback of her kidnapping and had fled Riverton.

"I'm good, Caroline. I've progressed to seeing Dr. Hancock every other week now and honestly, I'm feeling pretty good about everything. I know I'll never truly forget what happened to me in Mexico, but anytime it gets…hard, Hunter's there."

Caroline reached over the table and squeezed Fiona's hand. "Good. Hunter'll take care of you. I have no doubt."

The two women shared a glance full of understanding. Fiona understood the relationship between her husband and Caroline, and supported it wholeheartedly.

"Hey, guys! You all ready for your food now?" Their waitress stood at the side of the table. Her long black hair was pulled back into a low ponytail that cascaded down her back.

"Thanks, Jess," Benny said, looking up at their pretty waitress. "We were just waiting on Caroline, but we're all here now."

Jess nodded and turned and headed back to the bar, obviously to tell the cook their food could be served up.

"So, what's the occasion?" Caroline asked, looking around the table.

"Can't we all just get together and hang out?" Sam "Mozart" Reed asked with a smirk.

"Well, yeah," Caroline said somewhat sarcastically, "but usually when we do, you guys," she motioned to the unattached SEALs around the table, "bring some skank with you and pretend you're dating her instead of just feeding her before you bring her home to..."

"Hey!" Faulkner "Dude" Cooper interrupted complaining. "That's not fair. We *are* dating the women we bring to dinner."

"Yeah, for the night."

The men turned in shock at the words. Alabama wasn't one to speak her mind, but every now and then she'd lay out a zinger, as she'd just done.

Christopher "Abe" Powers leaned into his girlfriend and chuckled. "That's my girl," he said with affection.

"Jesus, you women are lethal," Kason "Benny" Sawyer complained. "You bitch when we date someone, you bitch because you don't like her, then you bitch when we break up with her."

"It's because we care about you," Caroline said seriously. "You all deserve better than people like Michele and Adelaide. If you'd just listen to us you'd realize we can see through those skanks in a heartbeat."

"Just because you all," Mozart gestured around the table at his teammates with their women, "have found each other doesn't mean the rest of us are all fired up to do the same."

"Bullshit." Caroline said matter-of-factly. "I think you all want what we have, and that's okay because you all deserve it. But if you continue to only look at women you meet in this bar and who only want to spend a night with a Navy SEAL, you'll never find it. You have to open your eyes and see the other women around you. The good women. Take a look at the ones who you might never 'see' otherwise."

Just as Caroline finished her impassioned speech, Jess came up to the table with a tray loaded down with food. "Hope I'm not interrupting..." she said hesitantly.

"Of course not," Benny told her gruffly, obviously glad for the break in the conversation.

Food was passed around the table and everyone dug in. After thirty minutes of good food and good conversation, everyone was relaxed against their chairs.

"So no one ever answered me. Is tonight a special occasion or what?" Caroline smiled at her friends. She didn't really care why they were there, she was happy being around her friends. She turned to look at Matthew as he stood up from the table. His hand had been on her leg throughout dinner. Of course he hadn't been still either. His thumb had caressed her thigh rhythmically and had Caroline squirming in her seat.

Caroline watched in surprise as Matthew went to his knees next to her chair.

"What the hell, Matthew? Get up."

Wolf swallowed hard. He shouldn't be as nervous as he was, but he couldn't help it. "I love you, Caroline Martin. More than anything in my life." He took both her hands in his and brought them up to his mouth. He kissed the back of both hands before putting them back in her lap. He didn't let go, and could feel Caroline trembling.

"I love you too, Matthew, but what..."

Wolf cut her off. "I've had great role models in my life. You know my parents are still together after forty years of marriage. I've seen how important it is to find the right person to spend the rest of your life with."

Caroline gasped, suddenly realizing what was happening. "Matthew..."

Wolf powered on. "I've been in a lot of shitty places. I've seen horrible things. I've done some awful things. Deep in my heart, I know you're too good for me, but I don't give a shit. You make me a better person. Every day. Every single day I think to myself, 'Would this make Caroline proud of me?' If the answer is yes, I carry on, if it's no, I try to analyze how else to get through the situation."

Caroline was openly crying now. "Matthew, seriously…"

Wolf let go of Caroline's hands and brought his hands up to either side of her neck. He caressed her jawbone with his thumbs and lowered his voice, so he was talking just to Caroline. "I love you, Ice. I love you with everything I am. The best day of my life was being seated next to you on that plane. I can't imagine my life without you, and I don't want to. I brought you here tonight to ask you to be my wife. My partner. My everything. I wanted you to be surrounded by all your friends, and my friends. I want to see my ring on your finger so every other man knows you're taken. That you're *mine*. Will you marry me, Caroline?"

Sniffing, and holding on to Matthew with a death grip on his T-shirt at his side, Caroline said, "Can I talk now?"

Wolf chuckled and leaned in and kissed her once, briefly, then leaned back. "Yes, Ice, you can talk, but the only word I want to hear is, 'Yes.'"

"Yes." The word was soft, but everyone at the table could feel the emotion behind it.

Wolf tightened his hands and leaned in to seal the deal, but Caroline put a hand on his chest and stopped him.

"Yes, I'll marry you. I've dreamed of this moment for a long time, but I want you to know that I'm proud of you every damn day. You could sit on your ass all day, every day, and I'll still be proud of you. You haven't done awful things. *Other* people are the ones who do the awful things, you and your team prevent those awful things from continuing to happen to good people."

Caroline spared a glance at Fiona, and gave her a watery smile, when Fiona smiled back, Caroline turned back to Matthew.

"So yes, I'll marry you. I love you so much. I'll wear your ring with pride. I can't wait to become Mrs. Caroline Steel."

Wolf crushed Caroline to him as the table erupted with cheers and words of congratulations. Jess was suddenly there with champagne for the entire table. The rest of the patrons were also cheering for them.

Caroline pulled back and amidst the chaos, looked into Matthew's eyes and said, "I love you."

Wolf didn't say anything, but reached into the front pocket of his jeans and pulled out a ring. He took Caroline's left hand and kissed the base of her ring finger, before sliding his engagement ring down it.

Caroline looked down at her hand and gasped. The ring was beautiful. Her eyes immediately filled with tears again. Matthew had obviously paid attention to her taste in jewelry. She didn't wear a lot of it, and had often complained to Matthew about how most jewelry, rings, bracelets, and necklaces, got in the way when she was trying to work.

The platinum ring was inset with an emerald cut diamond in the middle. It was surrounded by two princess cut diamonds. All the stones were mounded so they didn't stick up at all. Caroline wouldn't snag the ring on her clothes, or anything at work. While the ring wasn't ostentatious, the diamonds were large. Caroline wasn't an expert, but the middle stone had to be at least a carat and the two side diamonds weren't too far behind it.

"Is it okay?"

Caroline could hear the worry in Matthew's voice, and she hurried to reassure him. "It's the most beautiful ring I've ever seen. If you wanted to get me something that I never wanted to take off, you certainly succeeded."

"I wanted to get you something huge, that would definitely tell anyone that saw it that you're taken, but I know you would've hated it."

"You know me so well, Matthew. Seriously. I fucking love you so much."

Wolf chuckled. "You can show me tonight how much."

Caroline loved the gleam in her man's eyes. "Oh, hell yeah."

They had a healthy sex life, but somehow Caroline knew tonight would be a night like no other.

"Come on, Matthew, let her up for air. I wanna see that rock!" Fiona exclaimed, making everyone laugh.

Wolf stood up and took his seat next to Caroline again. He kept his hand on the small of her back and dipped his pinky into the dip at her backside. He felt her wiggle and knew she was well aware of him and his hand. Wolf smiled. The first part of his plan had gone off without a hitch, he just hoped the rest did as well.

Chapter Two

TWO DAYS AFTER she'd gotten engaged, Caroline sat across from her fiancé and glared at him.

"Matthew, it's ridiculous to spend this much money on a wedding. Seriously, let's just do it at *Aces* and be done with it."

"Ice, I want to give you the biggest wedding I can. I want everyone in the county to know you're mine, and I want to have the biggest party I can arrange after it's done."

"But Matthew, seriously, that's crazy. I think everyone knows I'm 'yours' by the way you act. You grab me around the neck and kiss the hell out of me whenever anyone even glances my way. It was really embarrassing at the grocery store when the fifteen year old stock boy happened to catch my eye and you bent me over your arm! For God's sake, Matthew, you're acting crazy!"

Wolf took a deep breath. "I know I am, Ice, but I want to give this to you."

"But what if I don't want it?" Caroline watched as a muscle ticked in Matthew's jaw. Suddenly she got it. "You need this, don't you?"

"If you don't want it, it's okay. We'll go down to the justice of the peace, or we'll go to Vegas like Cookie and Fiona did."

Caroline repeated her question, but didn't phrase it as a question this time. "You need this." Watching Matthew struggle with his thoughts made the decision for her. Matthew would do anything for her. All she had to say was "that's pretty" or "that's cool" and the next thing she knew, Matthew had bought it for her. Caroline had learned to be very careful what she said around him. She knew he'd give up the idea of a big wedding if she pushed. But it was apparent Matthew needed it. He wanted it. Caroline couldn't deny him.

"Okay. We'll do the big wedding thing." Caroline knew she'd made the right decision by the look of relief that crossed Matthew's face.

"Seriously, we can just..." He still tried to deny it.

"No. We'll do the big wedding, Matthew. But I need some help. I have no idea what I'm doing. I don't think Fiona or Alabama do either. Hell, Fiona went to Vegas and got married in a pair of jeans," Caroline's voice cracked, but she continued, "I always dreamed of planning my wedding with my mom, even though a part of me knew it would be a long shot. Since they were older, I knew there'd be a chance they wouldn't live long enough to see me get married, but I still hoped."

"Cookie."

"What?"

"Cookie can help you." Wolf put his hand on Caroline's cheek and brushed his thumb over her face tenderly.

Caroline looked at Matthew as if he'd lost his mind. "What the hell does Hunter know about weddings?"

Wolf took his hand off her cheek and ran it over his head. He was embarrassed, but needed to reassure Caroline. "Cookie held your life in his hands."

"What does that have to do with weddings?" Caroline's voice softened, knowing her kidnapping and rescue was still a very tough topic with Matthew.

"He held your life in his hands. I'd do anything for Cookie. After he met Fiona, we talked a lot about our weddings. How big they'd be. How they'd be a huge party, how beautiful you and Fiona would look in your wedding dresses as you walked down the aisle toward us…"

Caroline couldn't stand it anymore, she got out of the chair she'd been sitting in and came around to Matthew. She took his hand. "Come on, let's go sit on the couch."

They walked to the couch and Caroline pushed Matthew down and then climbed into his lap. "This is better. I love to feel your heat against me. The feel of your heartbeat against my cheek is comforting. Now, continue."

Wolf smiled. His Caroline was amazing. She knew this was hard for him, and did everything she could to make him feel more comfortable. "I was all ready to help him and Fiona plan their wedding, but Fiona told him that she couldn't handle a big wedding. That with everything that had happened to her, she simply felt uncomfortable in big crowds and would prefer a low-key wedding. Cookie agreed immediately. I owe him." Wolf's words faded out, and they both knew he was reliving the awful moments where he didn't know if Caroline was alive or not.

"I owe him, and this would be a way for him to experience a big wedding. I know he's a guy, and he's not your mom, and I sure as hell know it's not normal or traditional, but he'll do right by you, Ice. He loves you like a sister. Will you let him help you?"

"Of course." Caroline didn't make Matthew wait for her reassurance, but she continued, "I love that you want to look after your friend and I love Cookie as if he was my blood-brother, but seriously, Matthew, I'm not all into the wedding thing. If he plans something and it turns into a three ring circus, you can't blame me."

Wolf shifted until he could lay Caroline back on the couch and he was over her. He framed her face with his hands and leaned in close. "Ice, I couldn't care less if Cookie brought in lion tamers and tight rope walkers. As long as at the end of it you're mine, legally, I'll be the happiest man on earth."

"I love you."

"I love you too. Lift your arms. I think we need to seal this deal."

Caroline smiled up at Matthew and did as he asked. As he whipped her shirt over her head she said, "I love sealing the deal. Seal away my beautiful Navy SEAL."

She watched as Matthew rolled his eyes, but lost her train of thought when she felt Matthew's mouth at her breast. He pulled down the cup of her bra and immediately started sucking, with no preliminaries. Caroline pressed up into Matthew and felt how much he wanted her. Oh yeah. The last thought she had for quite a while was that she would enjoy negotiating with her man if this was how it ended.

Thoughts of a wedding and Cookie were soon lost as Matthew got busy making his woman feel loved and cherished.

"HOW ABOUT *GOD BLESS the Broken Road*, by Rascal Flatts?"

Caroline put her head in her hand and leaned her elbow on the kitchen table. Matthew had called Hunter and explained how he was now their official wedding planner. Caroline didn't think Hunter would be that thrilled, but Matthew had obviously not lied about how excited Hunter had been for his own wedding, because he was now over the moon about helping Caroline plan her wedding.

When Caroline had talked to Fiona about it, to make sure she was okay with the fact that her man would be planning Caroline's wedding, Fiona had just laughed and said, "Good luck." Caroline had smiled at the time, but now understood Fiona's implied warning.

That was three days ago. Hunter had wasted no time. He'd made appointments for them to taste different kinds of cake and to try to get the menu for the buffet locked down. Hunter had planned a day for them to go shopping for a dress and had even tortured her for hours showing her flowers.

Now they were talking about the first dance song. Hunter had a whole list of songs that he wanted to run by Caroline, and it was driving her crazy.

"I love that song, Hunter," Caroline told him honestly, "but I think it's been way overdone."

"Okay," Cookie immediately agreed, "what about *You Say it Best When You Say Nothing At All*, by Alison Kraus, or if you want something different you could go with Ozzy Osborne's *Here For You*."

"Seriously, Hunter, I don't know what I want to dance to. I don't even know if Matthew can dance."

"Doesn't matter, Ice. You'll dance 'cos that's what you do at a wedding. Pictures have to be taken, traditions have to be followed."

"Do I have to decide right now?" Caroline continued to complain. "The wedding isn't for another two months."

"Two months isn't a lot of time," Cookie admonished. "The more decisions you can make now, the better off you'll be when the day comes."

Caroline put her head on the table and whined, "I can't decide today."

"What about, *To Make You Feel My Love*, by Garth Brooks?" Cookie persisted. "It's traditional, but since the song is older, it's not done as much anymore."

"Okay, that's it. I'm done with wedding crap for the day." Caroline stood up in exasperation.

"But we have to go over the quotes for the venue and talk about what shoes you're going to wear."

Caroline just gawked at Hunter. She didn't say anything, but picked up her phone and dialed.

"Hello?"

"Hey, Fiona?"

"Yeah."

"Come and get your husband." Caroline grimaced as she heard Fiona laugh.

"Had enough?"

"Yes. I can't believe he's this into everything. It's just not right." Glaring at Hunter as she spoke to his wife, Caroline continued, "I mean, seriously, he's a big bad Navy SEAL. He can kill people by looking at them…how is it possible he's *this* into weddings?"

"I'll come and get him."

"Thank you."

"See you soon."

"The sooner the better." Caroline hung up and crossed her arms over her chest. She watched as Hunter blushed and looked away.

"Okay, look. I admit I get carried away, but I want this to be perfect for you, Ice."

"I get that, Hunter, but you have to ease up. Seriously, if I don't pick the right flowers or whatever, it's not going to be the end of the world. Why are you trying to shove all of this planning into a week?"

"Because if we're called away in the middle of the planning, I don't want anything to fall through the cracks."

Caroline's irritation melted away at Hunter's words. Of course. They were SEALs, at any point they could be called away on a mission and there'd be no guarantee they'd even be back for a wedding. She could totally understand why he was so gung-ho on planning it. "Okay, I get that, I do. I'll let you keep planning, but you have to be more reasonable about it. Work is crazy for me right now, and I can't just blow it off to go dress shopping or look at invitation samples."

"Okay. Can we plan meetings over the weekends so we can make some of the decisions and get them done?"

"Yeah, that sounds fair. I'll give you the weekends, Hunter, but please, try to tone it down."

Cookie smiled. "Of course."

Caroline rolled her eyes, knowing he wouldn't be able to tone it down. She only had to get through the next two months, then it would all be over and she'd be married to Matthew.

Chapter Three

"TURN AROUND, CAROLINE, let us see the back," Fiona exclaimed excitedly.

Caroline obediently turned around to show her friends the back of the dress she was wearing. It was what seemed like the two thousandth dress she'd tried on that day, but her friends were relentless. It wasn't as if Caroline even felt like it was *her* dress anymore. She'd heard so many "nope, that's not it" and "not quite" remarks that she'd expected them to say the same thing about this dress.

But they hadn't. Fiona, Alabama, and Hunter had taken one look and agreed that it was the one. It was, of course, white and strapless. It hugged her waist and then flared out into a bell shape. There was a train, but it wasn't obnoxiously long, thank goodness. Caroline turned and showed her friends her back.

"Oh my God. Yeah, this is it," Alabama said breathily.

Caroline turned her head and looked at Hunter. He'd done what she'd asked and backed off during the week. But the last few weekends had been crazy. He'd dragged her from one appointment to another and, even though Caroline had begged, Fiona had refused to come. She'd told Caroline, "I refused to do this for my own wedding, I love ya, but I'm not doing it for someone else's wedding either." They both laughed and Caroline wasn't upset at her friend. Fiona had been through hell, and Caroline would give her whatever she needed.

"Hunter? You've been quiet."

Cookie looked from the back of the dress Caroline was wearing to Fiona. Cookie had some long discussions with his wife about his role in Caroline's wedding, and Fiona had reassured him that she was okay with everything he was doing for their friend. He was so lucky to have Fiona in his life. Fiona understood that he and Caroline had a bond because of what happened to her in the ocean that day, and Fiona didn't begrudge him one second of wedding planning.

To answer Caroline's question, Cookie looked at his wife with an intense gaze. "The dress is perfect. The fact that there's no easy way to get you out of it will frustrate and turn Wolf on all day. But he'll know that all it'll take is one tug and the bow will come loose. He can slowly pull out each ribbon until the dress falls around your waist."

The air seemed to crackle and Caroline inhaled sharply, knowing Hunter wasn't really talking about her and Wolf, but instead seeing his own wife in her place.

"Time to go," Cookie said suddenly. He stood up and grabbed Fiona's hand. "Alabama, you can give Caroline a ride home, right? We've got things to do." He practically drug Fiona out of the small shop, but stopped to give his wife a deep kiss right outside the door.

Caroline looked at Alabama. "Holy shit. Guess he liked it."

They both laughed. The look Hunter had given Fiona was hot, and the kiss even hotter.

"Come on, get out of that thing and let's go before Hunter comes to his senses and rushes back to demand you do something else wedding related," Alabama told Caroline with a laugh. "Besides, I think I want to go home and see how Christopher is doing. I'm sure there's something I can help him with."

"Oh my God, you guys are nymphos!" Caroline griped good naturedly.

"As if you aren't!" Alabama groused right back.

Caroline just smiled. Yeah, Alabama had a point. Every time she made love to Matthew it just seemed to get better and better.

"Come to think about it, we *do* have some free time on our hands don't we?"

The two women got Caroline out of the dress as fast as they could. Caroline made sure to put a down payment on the beautiful dress and promised to call soon to make an appointment to get it altered, even though it didn't need too much done to it to make it perfect.

Alabama and Caroline left the shop arm in arm. "Thank you for coming with me today, Alabama," Caroline told her friend earnestly.

"I wouldn't have missed it."

"SERIOUSLY HUNTER, IT'S not my fault you got so turned on you had to go home and spend the rest of the day showing Fiona how much you love her."

"Be that as it may, Ice, we have to get this shit done."

Caroline didn't feel sorry for Hunter. "No, you promised me the weekends. It's not the weekend. It's Friday. I have to do this shit at work. I'll be done around four. We can do it then."

Cookie sighed. He knew he was being unreasonable, but he just wanted everything done. Once it was done, he could relax and then enjoy the wedding. "But we have to pick the food, the only time they can do it is today at one."

"Then *you* pick it, Hunter."

"Really?"

Caroline just shook her head in exasperation, knowing Hunter couldn't see it since she was talking to him on the phone. "Yeah, really. I don't care what we eat. Just make sure it's good. Make sure there's enough for everyone. Make sure there's a variety. There has to be something for the vegetarians, and the people who like meat, and then some chicken…whatever. Just don't go overboard."

"Would I do that?" Cookie asked, trying to sound innocent.

"Hell yeah you would. Seriously, just pick something, Hunter."

"Okay. What about *Inevitable* by Anberlin?"

"I'm still deciding, Hunter."

"But it's getting closer and you haven't picked a song yet. I'm helping."

"You aren't helping." Caroline could hear the smile in Hunter's voice.

"All right for now. Ice?"

"Yeah?" Caroline was ready for anything.

"Thank you."

"For what?"

"For letting me help you. For giving me this."

Caroline smiled. She loved that she *could* give this to Hunter. She might not have her parents around anymore, but Hunter was dead-set on making her wedding perfect. He wanted to make sure she wouldn't miss out on anything any other traditional wedding might have. She loved him for it. "You're welcome. Now, go and find us something good to eat at the reception."

"Yes, ma'am."

Caroline clicked her phone off and put her head on her desk. For the hundredth time she wished the wedding was over, but truth be told, she loved sharing the experience with Hunter. Even as crazy as he was acting. She would've had no idea what to do if it was left up to her.

"YOU REALLY DON'T care how much Hunter is taking over the planning of our wedding?" Caroline asked Matthew seriously that night. She'd thought about it a lot and Matthew hadn't really said much about the planning of the wedding or how much Hunter had been taking over it.

"I really don't care."

"But you said you wanted a big wedding," Caroline pressed.

"And I do."

"But..."

"I want the big wedding, but I don't give a fuck who plans it. I might have talked to Cookie about planning the wedding, but honestly, I wasn't all that into doing all the work for it. I'm happy as hell that he's getting to plan the wedding he always wanted."

"He's driving me crazy."

Wolf smiled and pulled Caroline closer. They were sprawled in their big bed after making love. She was snuggled into his side with one leg thrown over his thighs and was resting her head on his shoulder. One arm was curled up in front of her and the other was on his chest, idly playing with his nipple. He loved it.

"I know."

Caroline lifted her head and stared at Matthew. "You know?"

"Of course I know. You tell me every Sunday night how glad you are that the weekend is over. But Ice, you're gonna be beautiful, the wedding is gonna be beautiful, my parents are gonna cry. You're gonna cry, your friends are gonna cry, we're gonna party all night, then I'm gonna make love to my brand new wife all night. I think Cookie drivin' you crazy every weekend is gonna be worth it."

"You're a jerk," Caroline said with a laugh, obviously not meaning it. She put her head back on Matthew's shoulder.

Changing the subject a bit, she asked, "Do you have an opinion on a song for our first dance?" Caroline knew it was irritating Hunter that she hadn't picked a song yet, but she wasn't good at that stuff, but she knew *she* wanted to make the decision. At least in this one thing, *she* wanted to choose the song she and Matthew would dance to for the first time as man and wife.

"No."

"No?"

"No, I don't care what you choose."

"But it's our first dance."

Wolf rolled until Caroline was under him once again. He moved until his hips were in line with hers. He could feel against his hips how wet she was from their lovemaking, and Wolf immediately started getting hard again. He felt like a teenager around Caroline, and not a forty-something year old man that certainly shouldn't be able to get it up more than once a night.

"When the time comes for our first dance, I won't be hearing the music. I'll be reveling in the fact that I'm finally holding you in my arms as my wife. You'll be beautiful in your wedding dress and I'll most likely be trying to figure out the fastest way to get you out of it. We'll sway back and forth, you'll smile up at me, and I won't be able to think past the blood in my dick, trying not to get a woody in front of all our friends. So no, I don't care what song you choose for our first dance."

"Holy crap," Caroline breathed as she felt Matthew surge against her. "Okay." When Matthew didn't move or say anything further, she continued, "Glad we had that conversation…I want you."

Wolf smiled. Yeah, Caroline wanted him. He could feel how much. She shifted under him and ran her hands down his back until she cupped his backside and pressed him into her. "Anything else about the wedding you want to talk about?"

"Uh…huh? Oh…no. Matthew, please…" Caroline's back arched as Matthew slowly slipped into her wet heat.

"We could talk about something else if you wanted. The food? The decorations? The party favors?" Wolf teased as he eased back, then thrust into her harder than the first time.

"No, that's okay, I've got it."

Wolf stopped thinking about ways to tease Caroline about the upcoming wedding and instead got to work in pleasing her, not that it was hard. He loved that Caroline was always willing to do whatever he wanted. She never told him no, and was always willing to play. Wolf got to work playing with his woman.

Chapter Four

"**A**LABAMA, I HAVE no idea what song to pick for our first dance," Caroline complained to her friend. "I know Hunter would probably pick a great one, but I want to do this. But I have no idea what to choose." Caroline knew she was whining, but had no idea how to stop it. "Help me Alabama! Give me some suggestions!"

"Okay, let's see….you could go old school…*Only Fools Rush In* by Elvis?"

Caroline wrinkled her nose and shook her head. "I don't think I'll ever decide. How about this, just name some songs off real quick off the top of your head and I'll see if any of them strike me."

"*Amazed*, Lone Star; *Here and Now*, Luther Vandross; *Steady As We Go*, Dave Matthews; *You Won't Ever Be Lonely*, Andy Griggs; *Wonderful Tonight*, Eric Clapton; *From This Moment*, Shania Twain; *Your Arms Feel Like Home*, 3 Doors Down; *Grow Old With Me*, John Lennon; *Could I Have This Dance*, Anne Murray; *I'll Be There For You*, Bon Jovi; *Evergreen*, Barbara Streisand; *Loving You Forever*, New Kids on the Block; *Because You Loved Me*, Celine Dion; or *Everything I Do, I Do For You* by Bryan Adams." Alabama took a deep breath.

"Hopeless," Caroline moaned. "I mean, every one of those songs are awesome. They're all romantic as hell and would make a great first dance song."

"But none are really what you want, are they?" Alabama commiserated.

"No. But that's the thing. I don't know *what* I want."

"I think you'll know it when you hear it, Caroline." Alabama tried to soothe her friend.

"But time is running out. Seriously!"

Fiona took Caroline by the shoulders and shook her a little. "Relax, Caroline. You. Will. Figure. It. Out."

"You're right. Fuck. I mean, I was held captive by terrorists, this should *not* be freaking me out. Right?"

"Right."

"It's not a big deal. Whatever. I'll just pick one. No, I'll just have Hunter pick one for me. That'll get everyone off my back about it." Caroline saw the look Alabama gave her and sighed. "Okay, I won't do that. I don't want to do that. I'll figure it out."

"Come on, let's go and get some ice cream or something. It'll help you relax."

"Any excuse for ice cream is okay with me." Caroline smiled at Alabama. "Thanks for being here for me."

"Of course, Caroline. I wouldn't want to be anywhere else. Come on."

CAROLINE PUTTERED AROUND the kitchen working on the salad she was making for dinner. She knew she had to bring up an uneasy topic with Matthew, and wasn't sure how to do it. She'd been thinking about it for a while now, and wasn't any closer to knowing how to approach Matthew. Finally she decided just to go for it. Maybe if they were both busy doing something, it'd be easier.

"Hey, Matthew, I need to tell you something about the wedding."

Wolf looked up from the steak he was grilling on the stovetop. "Shoot."

Caroline bit her lip and looked down at the green pepper she was slicing. It was now or never. She rushed through her words. "I'mgoingtowearHunter'stridentpinasmysomethingold." Caroline could feel the air in the room go still. She'd known Matthew wasn't going to like it. She didn't know exactly why Matthew wouldn't like for her to wear Hunter's pin, but there was something about it that Caroline knew was a big deal, but she didn't know what.

She rushed on, still not looking at Matthew. "I figured since he's had it for a long time and he gave it to me, so that it would qualify for something old. I mean, since he gave it to me it can't be something borrowed so..." The knife Caroline had been using to cut the vegetables was suddenly taken out of her hand and she found herself turned around.

Wolf turned Caroline until she was facing him. He knew he needed to take care of this before now, but he hadn't wanted to bring it up. "Ice, you know what our Budweisers mean to us, yes?" At her slow nod, but confused look on her face, Wolf knew she was lying. Caroline didn't know just what that pin meant to a SEAL. He continued, "I..." Wolf's words stuck in his throat.

Ever since he'd learned that Cookie had given his SEAL trident pin to Caroline when she was in the hospital, he'd been unhappy. It should have been *him* giving her his pin. He'd been an ass and had tried to give Caroline up. Abe had prodded and poked until he'd known he could never do it, that he needed Caroline in his life. But before he'd figured it out, Cookie had claimed her in his own way. It ate at Wolf, knowing Caroline had another man's pin.

Wolf loved Cookie as if they were related, but it didn't stop the feelings. Wolf loved Fiona as a sister and knew that she and Cookie were tight, that Caroline having Cookie's pin didn't mean anything as far as a relationship other than brother/sister went, but he still hated it. Wolf even knew deep down in his heart Caroline was his, and that Cookie knew Caroline was his. That Caroline considered herself his, but her having Cookie's pin still bothered him.

It wasn't rational, but it was what it was. Wolf cleared his throat and tried to continue, tried to get his feelings across to Caroline without looking like a jealous ass. "I fucked up that day." When Caroline shook her head, he put his finger over her lips. "Please, let me finish." She nodded and Wolf continued.

"I fucked up. I'd decided you were better off without me, and my friend and teammate did what I should've. I know you belong to me, I know you love me, but it eats at me that you have *his* pin."

There was so much more Wolf knew he should say, but he didn't know where to start or how to say it. He put one hand behind Caroline's neck and the other went to her waist. He pulled her into his embrace, resting his forehead against hers. "I love you, Ice. It scares the hell out of me how vulnerable you make me. Emotionally and physically. All it would take is one person threatening your life and I know I'd lay down every weapon I had and beg them to hurt me instead of you."

"Matthew…"

"Shhhh, let me get this out. Please." At her nod, he continued. "Our Budweiser's are a fucking important thing to every SEAL. We work our asses off for the pin and when we finally get it, it's a validation of all our hard work and it's also a validation that we're a part of the brotherhood that is a SEAL. You know the saying, 'A SEAL doesn't leave a SEAL behind, ever.'"

Caroline nodded again.

"I know I left you behind and it kills me. I'm trying to figure out how to explain it to you so you'll understand. I know on the surface it sounds as if I'm just being a caveman and I'm jealous, and no lie, that's a part of it, but it's more. You having Cookie's pin is like if I wore a ring another woman gave me on a chain around my neck."

At Caroline's sudden inhale of breath, Wolf tightened his hands and then relaxed them again. He hated to hurt her, but he had to make her understand. "Yeah, no one could see it, but you'd know it was there. Even if it was given in friendship, even if it meant nothing to me other than friendship, you'd still know it was there."

"I get it, Matthew. I do. I'll give it back to Hunter tomorrow."

"No. I don't want you to do that." At the look of confusion on Caroline's face, Wolf sighed and backed up a step. He leaned over and turned off the burner on the stove. If the steaks were ruined, so be it. Wolf took Caroline's hand and led her to the couch. They seemed to talk best when they were in each other's arms.

Wolf sat, then waited as Caroline sat next to him, then turned into his arms. He curled his arm around her upper back and ran his free hand through her hair.

"I don't want you to give it back. That would hurt Cookie. He gave it to you because it meant something. The two of you went through some pretty emotional stuff in the waves. You have a connection as a result. I'd be an asshole if I tried to take that away from either of you. I'm gonna spell it out here, Caroline. I want you to wear *my* pin in our wedding. I want to give it to you and have you keep it close to your heart."

"Why didn't you tell me this before?"

"Because it makes me sound like an asshole."

"No. It doesn't."

"Well, then it makes me *feel* like an asshole. Like I'm in competition with my friend, but I know I'm not. I can't explain it, but it's like me putting my ring on your finger. That pin is the most important thing to me. Being a SEAL is a part of me, and giving you that pin is like giving you a piece of who I am."

"I won't wear Hunter's pin."

Wolf sighed. "Thank you, baby."

"I knew you weren't thrilled with me having it, but I didn't understand. I wish you would've said something earlier to me. I don't like you feeling that way and not letting me help you with it."

"I know, I should have. But the longer it got, the harder it was to bring it up. It wasn't like I could just bring it up out of the blue or anything. I love you, Ice. I'd be honored if you would wear my Trident on our wedding day as your 'something old.'"

"I will, Matthew. I promise."

"Hungry?"

Caroline laughed. "Yeah."

"Okay, then, up you go. Let's do this."

Wolf knew he'd gotten off easy, but that was Caroline. There was no way she'd make him wallow in his jealousy or guilt. She listened to him, heard how he felt, and immediately gave in. No drama. It was one of a million and one reasons he loved her.

Chapter Five

"IT LOOKS LIKE everything is set, Ice."

Caroline nodded at Hunter. They'd both worked really hard over the last month or so to make sure everything for the wedding was planned and ready to go. Okay, well, Hunter had done most of the work, but he'd made Caroline agree to most of the arrangements. Caroline had only broken down once when they'd discussed who would walk her down the aisle. Her dad wasn't around to do it, and it hit Caroline really hard that he'd never see his little girl get married to the love of her life. They'd finally decided she'd make her way down the aisle by herself. Caroline didn't mind, she'd been independent a long time.

"We just have the first dance song and the arrangements the day of, to nail down." Cookie looked at Caroline expectantly. He'd been on her for the last month to figure out what song she wanted to dance to, and she still hadn't made a decision. It'd become somewhat of a joke between the two of them.

"Hunter, I'll figure out the song before the time actually comes, don't worry about it." Caroline tried to placate Hunter, but the truth was she was nervous as hell about that first dance, but didn't want Hunter to keep harping on her about it.

"But, what if the DJ doesn't have the song in his playlist? You have to tell him before the reception so he can be sure he's got it."

"I said, I'll figure it out." Caroline's voice was testy. She was quickly losing patience.

Knowing he was on thin ice, Cookie changed the subject. "Okay, then, so the day of. You and Alabama and Fiona will come here to the church and get ready. Yes?"

Caroline nodded, relaxing now that Hunter was dropping the subject of the song choice. She freaking loved the church they'd chosen. She wasn't terribly religious, but liked the thought of getting married in a House of God. Matthew didn't have a church of choice and had told her that he'd get married in any kind of church she wanted, as long as they got married.

Caroline and Hunter had looked at several churches in Riverton before deciding. The church they'd picked had a bright red door, and that had clenched it in Caroline's eyes. There was just something about a religious building that had the guts to paint the door bright red, that made it feel right to her. Knowing it wasn't usual to allow random people to get married in random churches, Caroline and Matthew had met with the pastor and she'd agreed to marry them.

Cookie continued with describing his schedule for Caroline's wedding day. "So while the girls get ready at the church, Wolf and the rest of us will get together at his house. Then we'll take the limo…"

Caroline rolled her eyes. She still couldn't believe the big bad SEALs were going to rent a limo. It all seemed so normal, but for her man and his team, it was anything but.

"…and we'll get to the church about thirty minutes before the wedding. I don't want to risk Wolf seeing you in your dress before the ceremony. Bad luck you know."

It was supposed to be bad luck, but Caroline had put her foot down on one tradition and refused to spend the night before her wedding away from Matthew. She'd declared it a stupid tradition and told Hunter that she spent enough nights away from Matthew when he was on missions, that she wasn't doing it the night before her own wedding. Luckily, Hunter had acquiesced without further cajoling needed. But he hadn't budged on Matthew seeing her in her gown before the ceremony. Caroline had relented on that, as long as she didn't have to spend a night away from Matthew when he was Stateside, she was okay with the other tradition.

"We'll take all the pictures after the wedding while the guests are making their way to the reception. There are lots of h'ordeuvres for them to eat while they wait for us. Not to mention the open-bar. You and Wolf will take the limo to the reception and the rest of us will follow in our cars."

"How will your cars get to the church?" Caroline asked, knowing the answer, but wanting to hear Hunter spit it all out.

"We'll drop them off the night before so they'll be there ready for us."

Caroline smiled. Hunter was so funny. He had no idea she was just teasing him.

"Then after the reception, you and Wolf will go on your honeymoon."

"Yeah, about that. How am I supposed to pack if I don't know where we're going?" Matthew had refused to tell her where he was talking her. Caroline hoped it was a warm beach, somewhere like Maui, but even when she'd begged, and even after one particularly energetic night in bed, he'd still refused to tell her.

"Fiona will pack for you."

Caroline groaned. She thought for sure she'd be able to use the "I have to pack" excuse to get someone to tell her where they were going.

"The Commander gave him the week off right?" Caroline wanted to be sure she and Matthew would be able to get away and not worry about having to rush back in case something came up.

"Yeah, Commander Hurt knows Wolf is getting married. He agreed that the rest of us could have a week off as well. I'm going to have a second honeymoon with Fiona, and Abe is doing the same with Alabama. I think Mozart is heading up to Big Bear Lake and who knows what the others are doing. But the bottom line is that you don't have to worry about being interrupted, you and Wolf will have the full week to yourselves."

Caroline smiled. Thank God.

Knowing Hunter was in a mellow mood, Caroline decided now was a good time to bring up the issue of his Budweiser pin. If it meant that much to Matthew, she had to discuss this with Hunter.

"Hunter, I want to talk to you about something."

"Okay, go for it, Ice."

"It's about the SEAL pin you gave me."

Cookie turned his full attention to Caroline. "Go on."

"You know it means a lot to me…" She didn't get anything else out before Hunter interrupted her.

"Wolf finally talked to you about it?"

Caroline looked askance at Hunter. "Yeahhhh." She drew out the word wondering where Hunter was going with his thoughts.

Cookie leaned over and took both of Caroline's hands in his. "I knew this was going to happen sooner or later. Ice, Wolf was never happy you had my pin. Hell, he ordered me once to take it back, but I refused."

"I don't understand."

"Ice, me and you went through something I'll never forget in all my life. I'm a battle hardened Navy SEAL, but I've never been so touched by anything as I was with you while we were under the ocean. You didn't panic, you stayed strong, and the first thought when you came up out of the ocean was for Wolf."

Caroline nodded, waiting for Hunter to make his point.

"I gave you my pin because you proved yourself to me, and to the rest of the team. You deserved it and I was happy to give you something that meant so much to me."

"But?" Caroline could tell Hunter had something else to say.

"But now you're getting married. Wolf is your man, he isn't happy you have my pin."

Caroline got it. "Here's the thing, Hunter. Not to sound mean, but in regards to this, Matthew doesn't have a say." She held up her hand when it looked like Hunter wanted to speak. "I love the man more than life itself, but I don't think he has a right to tell you to take your pin back, or to tell me to give it back. Be that as it may, I think I need to give it back to you."

Cookie didn't say anything, just continued to look at Caroline.

"I didn't understand what it meant, or even how much it meant to the SEALs. But now that I do..." Caroline sucked in a breath. "I don't really know how to say this. And I know it's going to come out wrong."

"It's okay, Ice," Cookie soothed.

"So here's the thing. You have your own woman now. Even though I know Fiona doesn't really understand the pin thing either, now that I *do* know, it makes me uncomfortable to have your pin when Fiona doesn't. Does that make sense?"

Cookie reached over and pulled Caroline into his arms. "It makes sense." The words were spoken quietly, but with heartfelt emotion.

"I don't need your pin to know how you feel about me, Hunter. You'll always hold a special place in my heart. We don't need to give each other jewelry to solidify that," Caroline paused, and in order to lighten the mood, continued, "unless you want me to give you a friendship bracelet or something."

Her words did what she wanted them to do, lightened the atmosphere.

Cookie pulled back, kissed Caroline on the forehead and let go. "No exchange of jewelry necessary."

Caroline smiled at Hunter. "Thanks for understanding. Will you talk to Fiona and explain it to her? I can't...I don't want her to..."

"I'll explain."

Caroline sighed in relief. Hunter understood her fears without her having to say them out loud. She didn't want to lose her friendship with Fiona after all they'd been through together, especially after something that didn't mean anything to her, at least not in *that* way. "I'll return your pin the next time I see you."

"Which will be tomorrow. We still have to nail down the party favors."

Caroline rolled her eyes. "Right."

"And work on figuring out that first song tonight would ya?"

Caroline nibbled on her lip. "Okay." They both knew she wouldn't, but luckily Hunter let her off the hook.

Chapter Six

AFTER THE DRAMA with the Budweiser pin was resolved, the
following weeks moved quickly for Caroline. Hunter had
wrapped up the rest of the plans for the wedding and the day was
finally here. Caroline was more than thankful for all of Hunter's hard
work on her and Matthew's behalf. She knew she never would've had
the patience to make her wedding day as beautiful as it would be
because of Hunter.

Now Caroline was standing in the basement of the church getting
ready with two of the best women she'd ever had the fortune to meet,
to marry the love of her life.

"Turn around, Caroline, I'll lace you up," Fiona bossed.

Caroline held up the bodice of her wedding dress and turned so
her back was to Fiona. "Thank you guys for being here with me
today."

"We wouldn't have missed it for the world," Alabama told her
seriously.

"I know we haven't known each other that long, but you're the
best friends I've ever had and I'm so happy we all get along so well."
Caroline knew she was gushing, but couldn't help it. "I just hope that
when the rest of the guys find the woman they want to be with, she
won't be a bitch. I mean, some of the chicks they've been with have
been horrible. Can you imagine us trying to get along with them for
the rest of our lives?"

"Stop, Caroline, seriously, you're completely freaking me out,"

Fiona told her tugging extra hard on one of the laces she was working on.

"Can we stop talking about bitches and start talking about how awesome this wedding is gonna be?" Alabama asked matter-of-factly.

"Fiona, I swear to God, you made the right decision in eloping to Vegas to get married," Caroline told her friend seriously. "I mean, I love your man like a brother, but he's been a giant pain in my ass for the last two months."

Fiona giggled as she tied the ribbons on Caroline's dress in a big bow. "I know. The way he's been about your wedding solidified my decision to run off and get married in Vegas."

Caroline turned to Fiona as she continued.

"But Caroline, I'll forever be in your debt for giving this to him. If I had known how much he really wanted all of this, I would've bitten the bullet and given it to him, no matter how uncomfortable it made me."

Without hesitating, Caroline leaned forward and pulled Fiona into an embrace. "Well, I'm glad you didn't have to. I needed the help, and Lord knows none of us would've been able to pull this off as well as he did." She didn't say the words to be mean, Caroline was just being honest.

"No kidding," Alabama chimed in. "Seriously, how women like us can be so clueless when it comes to the girly arts, I have no idea."

The three women laughed.

"But look at us now," Caroline said seriously. "You two are absolutely beautiful. Those dresses are the bomb. Hunter sure knows what looks good on women. The lilac color really works on both of you. And he somehow picked dresses that are sexy as hell but aren't slutty. It's actually pretty impressive. Come here you guys and let's take a selfie!"

The three women leaned into each other and Caroline held out her arm and took a picture of them with her cell phone. Alabama snatched the phone out of her friend's hand and started pushing buttons.

"What are you doing?" Caroline asked.

"Sending this to Christopher. You don't think you're the only one that'll be getting some tonight do you?"

"Oh you're evil...I love it!" Fiona said, then snatched the phone out of Alabama's hand. "Give me that! I gotta send it to Hunter too."

"You guys are crazy. It's not like you won't get any tonight. Hell, if your men are like Matthew, you get it every night."

At the blushes that bloomed on both her friends' faces, Caroline laughed.

"Come on, let's finish this. The guys should be here soon. I know Hunter is keeping them on a tight schedule. I can't wait to see Matthew's face when I'm walking down the aisle."

WOLF GROWLED AND tugged at the bow tie around his neck. The medals on his breast pocket jangled as he shrugged on the white long sleeve jacket of his uniform. The full dress Navy uniform he was wearing had never felt so constricting. Wolf watched as the rest of his team, similarly attired, finished getting dressed as well. They were cutting it close, as Cookie kept reminding them.

Cookie had been a pain in the ass, but Wolf was thankful for his presence. He'd kept them all on track and had made all the arrangements. Wolf remembered Caroline making fun of them because they were taking a limo to the church, and he remembered agreeing with her that it was ridiculous, but now he was glad.

There was no way he could drive, at least safely. His hands were fucking trembling for God's sake. He couldn't wait to make Caroline his wife. She was already his, but he couldn't wait for the moment when he slid the wedding band on her finger.

"You ready to go, man?"

The words had come from Abe, but Wolf turned to Cookie to answer. "Is the limo here yet?"

"Calm down, Wolf. Seriously. We're not late. I'm the one who is supposed to be freaking out, not you."

"Cookie, I left my woman in my bed this morning, soft and sated. The last thing she said to me as I left for PT was 'I'll see you at the altar.' So excuse me if I want to hurry the fuck up and get to the damn church and claim my woman already."

Wolf watched as all five of his teammates threw their heads back and laughed their asses off at him. He just scowled. They'd get theirs eventually.

"All right, sorry, Wolf. Yeah, the limo is here. It's out front. But we can't leave too early because then we might run into the girls. Besides, the last thing you want is to be standing at the altar for too long, and if we get there too early, that's what will happen."

Wolf ran his hand over his head and through his short hair. "Tell me again why we wanted big weddings, Cookie?"

Cookie came over to Wolf and put his hand on his friend's shoulder. "Because the moment you see your woman walking toward you, smiling, glowing because she's so happy she's about to tie herself to you, is the moment you realize that all the stress, all the crap you've put up with in the last two months, has been completely worth it."

"I'm sorry you didn't get that," Wolf told Cookie seriously.

"Oh I got it, Wolf. I might not have had the church and the dress and the trappings that come with a big wedding, but Fiona still walked toward me, she still smiled at me, and she sure as fuck glowed because she was happy she was about to tie herself to me."

"Fuck man." Wolf couldn't think of anything else to say. Military men weren't known as the most romantic men on the planet, and SEALs especially weren't known for it. But it was obvious that Cookie was one hundred percent all right with how his own wedding had gone down. He and Fiona had been through Hell, and their wedding was perfect for the two of them.

"Okay, enough mushy shit, let's get this shit done." Dude had spoken. He was brusquer than the others. It was obvious he was done with the bonding talk and was ready to go.

Wolf was more than ready to agree. "Hell, yeah, let's go."

The six men walked out of Wolf's house and headed for the limo. Abe and Cookie looked down as their phones trilled with the sound of an incoming text.

"Oh yeah, just wait until you see Ice, Wolf. She looks amazing." Abe rubbed in the fact that he'd just received a picture in a text from Alabama, and Wolf wasn't allowed to see his fiancé before the ceremony.

CAROLINE SAT ON the chair and couldn't stop the nervous twitching of her leg. It was ten minutes past the time when the ceremony was supposed to have started and the guys hadn't shown up yet. She clutched her cell phone in her hands and willed it to ring.

Fiona and Alabama sat on their own chairs, staring at their own phones.

"I'm sure they're okay," Alabama said nervously.

"Yeah, they're just running late," Fiona echoed.

Caroline took a deep breath. "Something's wrong."

"You don't know that," Fiona said in a not-too-convincing voice.

"I *do* know it," Caroline argued. "You know these guys. Hell, Fiona, you know Hunter, he had this thing planned down to the last second. There's no way they're just running late. Something happened."

"Matthew will be here," Alabama told her friend soothingly.

Caroline couldn't stay still any longer. She kicked off her high heels, which were killing her, why she'd let Hunter talk her into wearing them, she had no idea, and started pacing the room. "Matthew is not standing me up. I know he's not. Hell, he fucked me so hard this morning before he left I can still feel him. He told me it had always been a dream of his to have sex with his girlfriend and his wife in the same day."

Caroline ignored the choking noise Fiona made as she tried to smother her laugh and continued on her tirade.

"Ergo, something happened. He wouldn't leave me standing at the altar. He'd know how much that would hurt me and he would never hurt me. So we need to figure out what the hell is going on. Pronto."

At her last word Caroline turned and glared at her bridesmaids. It wasn't their fault, and hell, their men were also late, but she couldn't get the sinking feeling out of her head that something dreadful had happened to their men. Caroline hated the feeling she had. It was worse than when they were on a mission, because this was *here*. In the states. In their hometown. When they were supposed to be here, on the most important day of her life.

Alabama's phone rang. The three women just stared at it for a moment, until Caroline screeched, "Answer it!"

"Hello?" Alabama's voice was low and wobbled a bit with her anxiety.

"Oh my God. Yeah. Okay. But he's all right? Yeah, okay. Where? Yeah, I'll take care of it." Alabama's voice softened and she took a deep breath. "Yeah, I did. Okay, thanks, Christopher. We'll be there as soon as we can. I love you too. Bye."

"What?" Caroline demanded as soon as Alabama clicked the phone off. "Oh my God, what?"

Instead of walking over to Caroline, as both Fiona and Caroline thought she would, Alabama walked over to Fiona. She put her hands on Fiona's shoulders and said evenly, "There's been an accident. Hunter was hurt, but he's going to be fine."

"What?" Fiona croaked. "Hunter?"

Forgetting she was supposed to be getting married, forgetting she was wearing a kick-ass wedding dress, forgetting everything but her friend, who at the moment looked like she was about to pass out, Caroline rushed across the room and put her arms around Fiona. She just made it in time to help Fiona to the ground as her legs gave out under her.

"Talk to us, Alabama. What did Christopher say?" Caroline kept her voice modulated and even, even though every part of her wanted to cry out and be hysterical. She cradled Fiona in her arms as they knelt on the ground and listened to Alabama.

"Christopher said they were in the limo and a car ran a stop light. It sideswiped the limo and hit the side where Hunter was sitting. They all have some scratches and stuff from the flying glass, but Hunter was unconscious. They took him to Riverton General to the emergency room to be safe. They're all there with him."

Caroline leaned over and looked into Fiona's eyes. "See? He's okay, Fiona. You hear me? He's fine."

Fiona could only nod, but she briefly put her head against Caroline's neck. Caroline could feel Fiona's hot breath against her skin as she did her best to pull herself together.

"Alabama, can you go and talk to the pastor and tell her what's going on and ask if she'll let everyone in the audience know? And I hate to do this to you, but can you also tell Matthew's parents? I know they'll be worried about what's going on. Just tell them I'll call them later and that Matthew is fine. Please also tell the pastor I'd like to talk to her after she explains to everyone. Then we'll be ready to head out and we'll go and see our men."

"But your wedding…"

Caroline interrupted Alabama. "Fuck it. It can wait. Nothing is more important than making sure Hunter and all the other guys are all right."

Alabama looked closely at her friend for signs she was faking it and she was more upset than she was letting on. Seeing nothing but concern for Fiona and the guys in Caroline's eyes, Alabama finally nodded and turned on her heel and left the room.

Caroline put her hand on the back of Fiona's head. "Christopher wouldn't lie to us, Fiona. If he said Hunter is okay, then he's okay."

Fiona took a deep breath and lifted her head. "I know. It's just...I don't know what I'd do without him."

"I know. Seriously, I *know*."

The women locked eyes and the sincerity and comradery Fiona saw in Caroline's eyes, strengthened her.

Fiona struggled to her feet while Caroline helped her stand. "But your wedding…"

"As I told Alabama, screw it. We need to get to the hospital."

"Should we change?"

"No, no time. We need to put real shoes on though. Grab your sneakers and I'll get my flip flops. We can't be walking around with these heels on. I'll get Alabama's shoes too. Grab our purses."

Caroline turned when the pastor walked in with Alabama.

"I'm so sorry, Caroline. I let everyone know what was going on. They're all very concerned about Matthew and the other men, but Alabama said they would be all right?" At Caroline's nod, the pastor continued, "Alabama says you wanted to talk to me?"

"Yes please. Alabama, you have the keys to Christopher's car right?" When Alabama nodded, Caroline ordered, "Okay, get Fiona to the car, I'll be right there."

Without a word, the two women gathered their purses and headed out the door. Caroline turned to the pastor to ask a huge favor.

Not too much later, Caroline hustled toward Christopher's car, holding the skirt of her wedding dress up so it wouldn't drag on the ground, her flip-flops thudding against the pavement as she walked briskly. At her arrival at the car, Alabama and Fiona's eyebrows lifted, but they didn't say a word. Caroline ignored the concerned looks of the guests who were now leaving the church, and settled herself into the back seat. She took a moment to lean forward and put her hand on Fiona's shoulder and squeeze reassuringly.

"Let's go, Alabama. Our men need us."

Chapter Seven

WOLF SAT IN the waiting room with his head in his hands. He looked down at his uniform, which was splattered with blood. This was the first time he'd really sat down and had time to think. The last hour had been horrifying, but his military training had kicked in and he'd been operating on auto-pilot.

He noticed briefly, that his hands were shaking. Wolf's team had been joking around one minute, and the next they'd been thrown around the back of the limousine as if they were popcorn kernels inside a microwave bag. After the glass had stopped flying, Wolf looked up and saw his teammates also groggily sitting up, except for Cookie.

Wolf would never forget the sight of his friend lying motionless on the floor of the limo. The side of the car where he'd been sitting was dented in and there was glass covering everything, including Cookie.

Wolf had seen dead bodies before. Hell, he'd seen way too many dead bodies, but most of the time they didn't really *mean* anything to him. But the sight of Cookie lying motionless, covered in blood, meant something to Wolf. He'd immediately crouched down in the wreck of the metal surrounding them, and breathed a sigh of relief when he felt Cookie's pulse.

They'd quickly extricated themselves from the twisted metal, checked on the driver of both the limousine and the car that hit them, and waited for emergency personnel to arrive. It hadn't taken long. A bystander had called 911 and the sirens had sounded quickly afterwards.

Wolf and Dude had ridden in the ambulance with Cookie and the cops had driven the rest of the guys to the hospital. They'd all refused medical treatment at the scene, knowing they were banged up, but not seriously injured. But Cookie had still been unconscious when he'd been loaded into the ambulance for the trip to the emergency room.

"I called Alabama," Wolf heard Abe say quietly. Wolf looked up at his friend.

"Fuck." Wolf knew he fucked up. He should've called Caroline way before now. "What time is it?"

"Calm down, Wolf, it's okay. The girls are on their way here."

"Fuck," Wolf repeated. He'd missed his wedding. Caroline would be so disappointed. She and Cookie had been planning this day for months.

"Don't even go there, Wolf," Dude warned, easing himself into the seat next to his friend. "Ice'll be cool."

Wolf couldn't get any words past the disappointment in his throat. He wasn't worried about Caroline being pissed about her wedding. He knew she'd be cool. But he'd been looking forward to this day. He wanted to make Caroline his for so long, now he'd have to wait even longer. Finally he answered Dude with a terse, "I know."

"You're disappointed," Mozart said suddenly from across the room.

Wolf didn't answer, it didn't matter if he admitted it or not, there wasn't much he could do about it now.

Benny stood up and paced the small room. "Maybe we can still make it. Mozart, call the Commander and get him over here with a car. We'll go to the church and..."

"It's fine, Benny," Wolf said with determination. "We need to stay here for Cookie. Caroline and I will get married, don't fucking doubt it, but not today."

The men fell silent. There wasn't anything they could say that would make their leader feel any better about missing his wedding.

The rest of the people in the waiting room gave the SEALs a wide berth. They were all big men and they were covered in bloodstains. Their white dress uniforms would never be the same again, they'd have to be thrown away. The flying glass, along with caring for Cookie at the scene, had ruined any chance of their uniforms being able to be saved.

The team was restless and took turns pacing the small room. Their jaws were tight and there was an aura of danger emanating from their corner of the waiting room.

"When the hell will we hear anything? What's taking so long?" Benny complained to no one in particular.

"They're waiting for Fiona. They won't talk to us, because we aren't related," Dude explained.

"The hell we aren't related!" Benny exclaimed, saying what they all were thinking.

"You know what I mean," Dude again tried to calm Benny down.

"This sucks."

Wolf could only laugh, and not in a ha-ha kind of way, but in a wow-is-that-an-understatement, kind of way.

Wolf looked up as the front door of the emergency room opened. Alabama and Fiona swept in, followed by Caroline. Everyone in the waiting room stared at the women. They looked as out of place in the hospital waiting room in their bridesmaid dresses and Caroline in her wedding gown, as a cowboy would look in a New York City dance club.

Wolf couldn't take his eyes off of Caroline. "Jesus," he muttered under his breath. She literally took his breath away. Wolf knew he'd be overwhelmed at how beautiful she'd look as she came toward him in the church, and he'd been right. It didn't matter that they weren't in a church. It didn't matter that they were in a county emergency room. It didn't matter that he was covered in bloodstains and scratches from flying glass.

It was as if he was watching Caroline walk toward him through a long tunnel. He couldn't get his mouth to form words, he couldn't get his feet to move. All Wolf could do was stare at his fiancée.

Wolf didn't hear the reunion between Abe and Alabama and he didn't hear Fiona's sobs as Mozart took her in his arms to reassure her.

Caroline finally stopped in front of him. Wolf lifted his hand and rested it on the side of Caroline's neck and he gripped her tightly. "Fuck, Ice." They weren't the words he'd dreamed of saying to his bride when he saw her in her wedding gown for the first time, but it didn't seem to matter to Caroline.

Her face crumpled and she took a step toward him, preparing to bury herself in her man's arms.

Wanting badly to take Caroline in his arms and whisk her away from the hospital, away from the pain he knew she was feeling about Cookie and about missing their wedding, but Wolf didn't want to muss her up. He put his hands on her shoulders and held her away from him. "Caroline, I'm covered in blood."

"I don't care."

"I'll get your dress dirty."

"I don't care."

"Ice…"

"I. Don't. Fucking. Care."

At her words, Wolf did what he'd wanted to do from the first time he'd seen her. He crushed Caroline to him. One hand went to her waist, and the other curled around to the back of her neck, where he held her to him. Wolf felt Caroline's arms snake around him and grab onto his white dress shirt at his back.

Neither spoke for long moments. They simply held on to each

other as if they'd never let go.

"Thank God you're okay." Caroline finally broke the silence between them. Her words were spoken into his neck, and were soft and low, but Wolf heard them.

"I'm okay, Ice. I'm okay."

"I know. I'll be okay in a second. Just…don't let go yet. Please?"

"I'm not letting go. I'm not fucking letting go."

Caroline smiled at Matthew's words. He'd never win an award for sweet-talker of the year, but he was hers and she didn't care. He was here in her arms, whole, and mostly unharmed. She'd take it.

Chapter Eight

CAROLINE FINALLY PULLED back out of Matthew's arms when a nurse called out, "Is there a relative here for Hunter Knox?"

Mozart called out, "Here," as he guided Fiona toward the nurse. The rest of the group followed behind, making quite a spectacle of themselves. Five large men, covered in scratches and bloodstained white military dress uniforms, two women dressed in lilac bridesmaids' dresses, and one woman in a strapless wedding dress with a short train trailing behind her on the dirty waiting room floor, could never go unnoticed or uncommented on.

The nurse looked at the large group converging on her in consternation. "Uh, Mrs. Knox, if you'll follow me, we'll go over here to speak in private."

"No."

"What?"

"I said no." Fiona had straightened away from Mozart and had her arms crossed in front of her chest. She was holding her elbows, so her position looked a bit more vulnerable than she probably wanted it to be, but no one said a word. She continued, "These men are as much his family as I am. They've fought next to him, they've suffered alongside him, they train with him. Whatever you say to me, you can say to them as well."

The nurse looked flustered, but didn't disagree with the obviously distraught woman standing in front of her. "Okay, well, let's still go over here to get out of the way, and I'll explain what's going on."

The nurse gestured toward an empty room to the side of the waiting room and everyone crowded in.

"Mr. Knox is conscious and doing fine. From what we can gather, he hit his head pretty hard on the window when the car was hit. That's why he lost consciousness for so long. He's got some superficial cuts and scratches, much as most of you do."

"When can I take him home?" Fiona asked. Dude was now standing behind her with his hands on her shoulders supporting her.

"He can go home later tonight, but the doctor wants to keep him here for observation for a while, just to be sure he'd okay. Because he was unconscious for so long we want to make sure he doesn't have a concussion."

"Wouldn't be the first," Mozart said under his breath.

Ignoring Sam, Fiona asked, "Can I see him?"

"Of course," the nurse said, looking glad the conversation was almost over. Obviously being in room with that much testosterone was too much for her. "Follow me, and I'll take you to him."

Caroline asked quickly, before the nurse could leave the room. "Can he have other visitors?"

"Well, I'm not sure..." the nurse hedged.

"Please? You said it wasn't serious. It'd mean a lot to of all of us if we were able to go in there and see him." Caroline pulled out the big guns. "He was supposed to be in my wedding today. He's a groomsman and we'd all like to see that he's okay for ourselves." Caroline tried to put an innocent look on her face.

The nurse thought about it for a moment, then finally agreed. "Okay, but you'll have to make it quick. It's not fair to all the other patients to have a ruckus going on in one of the rooms."

Caroline beamed at the nurse. "Promise. No ruckus. Thank you."

Wolf turned to Caroline. "What are you up to?"

"What makes you think I'm up to anything?"

"I know you."

Caroline laughed. "I love you, Matthew."

"Now I *know* you're up to something."

Caroline snuggled back into Matthew's arms and sighed as she felt his arms go around her again. She hadn't been able to breathe right until she'd seen for herself that Matthew was all right.

"Do you trust me?"

"With my life," was Matthew's immediate response.

Caroline felt her insides melt even more. She looked up at Matthew, noticing the rest of the guys had left the room. They were alone. "I want to marry you."

Wolf felt his insides seize up. Fuck. "Ice, I'd move heaven and earth to become your husband today, but I'm afraid we'll have to do it later." Wolf looked at his watch. "It's been two hours since we were supposed to exchange our vows. I know members of the church are patient, but this might be pushing it a bit far."

"I kinda bribed the pastor to come to the hospital with me."

Wolf leaned back and put his hand under Caroline's chin and forced her to meet his eyes. "What?"

At the stern look in Matthew's eyes, Caroline stumbled over her words. "Uh, yeah, well, when I heard you guys were in an accident, but that you were okay, I kinda lost it and refused to believe that we wouldn't be able to get married today. We'd been looking forward to it for so long and Hunter put so much work into everything, I really wanted to do it for him. I didn't know if he'd be okay or not, but I hoped...so I told the pastor that if she came to the hospital with me and agreed to marry us here, you'd make a 'sizeable' donation to her church."

Wolf threw his head back and laughed. He felt lighter than he'd felt since he realized they'd been hit. "You can still be my woman today?"

"I'll always be your woman."

"I mean, you can still officially be my woman today in the eyes of the law?"

"Yeah."

"Fuck." Wolf couldn't get any other words out. His throat seemed to close and he squeezed his eyes shut. He felt, rather than saw, Caroline reach up and kiss his lips, then both closed eyelids.

"I'd marry you anytime, anywhere, Matthew, but I wanted to give this to Hunter. He's almost as invested in our marriage as we are."

"I love you, Ice. You're everything I ever wished for in my life. When I was little and saw how happy my parents were, I prayed that I'd find someone like my dad had. I didn't really understand it then, and as I grew older, I realized how lucky they were. It's fucking hard to find that kind of love. But at thirty six thousand feet, I found it. I found you."

"Matthew…"

"I know I haven't told you this yet today, but you are absolutely beautiful. You in this dress? Jesus, Ice. I'm so fucking glad you're mine. I can't wait to get my ring on your finger and get you home, and unwrap you from this dress. Then I'm going to spend the rest of the night showing you how glad I am you're officially, and legally, mine."

Now it was Caroline's turn to tear up. "It might not be a traditional wedding, but you'll never find anyone more in love with you than me."

Wolf leaned down and took Caroline's lips with his own. He didn't hold anything back, but devoured her. Caroline turned liquid in Matthew's arms as she let him take what he needed. She loved it when Matthew got all dominant on her. She wasn't usually submissive, but it was obvious he needed it right now. Besides, Caroline knew she'd reap the benefits when they got home.

Wolf finally lifted his head and ran his thumb over Caroline's kiss swollen lips, now devoid of any kind of lipstick. "Can we go and get hitched in the eyes of the law anytime soon yet?"

Caroline smiled up at the man who would soon be her husband. "Yeah, let me make sure the pastor hasn't been scared away and let me sweet talk the nurse some more. We'll go see Hunter and get this done."

Wolf leaned down and kissed Caroline one more time. "I love that you want to give this to Cookie. He's my brother in all ways other than by blood. You doing this for him means the world to me. *You* mean the world to me."

"I know. You can pay me back tonight."

"You better believe it."

They walked out of the room to find the pastor. It was time for a wedding.

Chapter Nine

CAROLINE WAITED NERVOUSLY in the waiting room for Fiona. They were giving Fiona some time alone with Hunter before they all bustled into his room and sprung a surprise wedding on him. Caroline couldn't wait to see Hunter. After Fiona finished her visit, she and Matthew were going to go in and see him and explain how they were going to get married today after all...in Hunter's hospital room. Caroline hoped he'd be happy, but first, she couldn't wait to see him with her own eyes to make sure he was okay.

Finally Fiona came into the waiting room. It looked like she'd been crying, but her lips were also swollen as if she'd had the stuffing kissed out of her.

"He's ready to see you guys now," Fiona said softly. Dude came forward and put his arm around Fiona's shoulders, giving her some non-verbal support.

Caroline stood up and grabbed Matthew's hand as he held it out to her. "Ready?" he asked.

"Yeah." And Caroline *was* ready. She was more than ready. Caroline looked at the pastor who was sitting in the middle of the men and smiling. In fact, Caroline realized the woman had been smiling all afternoon, once she'd learned Hunter was going to be fine. She seemed happy as a clam to have been bribed...er...asked, to perform a wedding in a hospital room.

Caroline knocked once at Hunter's door and at his terse, "Yeah!" she pushed the door open.

Hunter was lying on the bed, wearing a scrubs shirt, the sheet pulled up to the middle of his chest. At seeing it was Caroline, he sat all the way up in bed, gingerly, and held out his hand. "Ice! Get over here."

Caroline smiled and let go of Matthew's hand and made her way over to Hunter's side.

"You look beautiful."

Caroline snorted. "Whatever, Hunter."

"Seriously. Okay, you have what looks like blood on your gorgeous dress, and your pretty hairdo is leaning a bit to the side, but for a man who saw a car coming straight for his head, you look perfect."

Caroline frowned a bit at that. But Hunter continued, "I'm pissed at the wedding thing, but don't worry, we had insurance on the reception venue, so we aren't losing all the money on that. We'll have to reassess about the flowers and some of the other stuff, but we'll figure it out. Give me a week after I get out of here and we'll have you two married in a jiffy."

Caroline sniffed and held back her tears by sheer force of will. Hunter didn't even care about himself, at the moment all he cared about was her wedding. She put her hand over Hunter's mouth. "Listen to me for a second." When Hunter nodded, Caroline took her hand away from his face and held it out to Matthew, who had been standing just behind her.

Caroline smiled at Matthew when he grabbed her hand and held it up to his lips for a quick kiss. Then she turned back to Hunter. "Okay, here's the deal. You did a shit ton of work for this wedding, and I'm not willing to give all that up. If it's okay with you, the pastor is here, I'm here, Matthew is here, you're here, all our friends are here...I want to get married now. Here. With you." When Hunter didn't say anything, but instead just lay on his bed and stared at her, Caroline stuttered, "If that's okay."

"If that's okay?" Cookie asked incredulously.

"Careful, Cookie," Wolf warned his friend, not understanding the tone of his voice.

Cookie spared a quick look at Wolf and briefly flashed their SEAL sign for "okay" to him. Wolf relaxed and put his hand on the small of Caroline's back in support.

"Caroline, come here," Cookie ordered. Caroline took a small step closer to the bed, and Cookie took hold of her hand in a death grip.

"I can't believe you'd do that. You should wait until you can do it right, until it's perfect."

Caroline sat gingerly on the side of Hunter's bed. "It's perfect today. I'm sorry the day didn't turn out like you planned it, but the bottom line is that I want to do this today. I've been looking forward to this day for the last two months. I don't want to wait. But I want *you* to be okay with it. For all intents and purposes, this is your wedding too."

Cookie reached up with both hands and brought Caroline's head down close to his. "I'm more than okay with it. I'm fucking honored you'd do this today here with me."

When Caroline sniffed with emotion, Wolf commented dryly, "If you two don't stop sniffling over each other, the doctors will discharge Cookie and all your plans for an emotional bedside wedding will be for naught, Ice."

Caroline laughed and looked up at Matthew. "Keep your pants on, Matthew."

They all laughed and Caroline stood up. "Okay, I'll send the rest of the group in. Matthew, you stay. I'll see you in a bit." She reached up and kissed her soon-to-be husband. She wasn't quick about it, and Matthew took advantage of her emotional state to deepen the kiss. Finally Caroline pulled away, kissed her fingertips, held them to Matthew's lips and backed out of the room.

"Is she wearing flip-flops?" Cookie joked to his friend.

"Yup."

"That's not what I bought for her."

"Nope."

"You okay with this, Wolf?" Cookie asked seriously.

"Fuck yeah."

"All right then."

The two men smiled at each other, both lost in their thoughts of the amazing woman that had come into their lives.

CAROLINE STOOD IN the hallway of the hospital wringing her hands nervously. The men were all inside the small hospital room where Hunter was lying on the bed. The pastor was also inside the room. Everyone was waiting for her to get in there, but Caroline wanted to have a moment with Fiona and Alabama first.

"You guys are the best friends a girl could ever have. I never had a sister, or even a close friend, but I thank God every day you came into Christopher's and Hunter's lives."

"Really? You're going to do this now?" Fiona mock-complained, wiping away her tears.

Caroline laughed and nodded. "No time like the present."

"Okay, then right back at 'cha. When I was locked inside that hut in Mexico, I didn't think I'd ever get out of there. You don't see me as broken, even when I literally descended into crazy-town right in front of your eyes."

Alabama chimed in as well, her words all the more meaningful because of her history. "I learned never to trust anyone, but you guys have shown me that people can be unselfish and genuine and I don't know what I'd have done without you, Caroline, when I was homeless."

The three women surged together as if they'd planned it. They hugged each other and sniffled. Finally Caroline pulled away and wiped at her eyes. "Okay, I know I started it, but I want to get married. Can we please put this mushy stuff away until later?"

Alabama followed Caroline's lead and wiped her face and Fiona did the same.

"Okay, Alabama, you go in first, then Fiona. It'll be just like we planned for the procession into the church, but only a much smaller aisle." They giggled, and Alabama got ready to open the door and walk in. She turned around at the last minute.

"Love you, girl. I'm so happy for you." And she was gone.

Fiona turned to Caroline.

"Oh, God, no more, I can't take any more."

Fiona laughed at Caroline. "All I want to say is thank you for grounding me back at the church. For a second my world was over, but then you were there, hauling me back to the real world and helping me get through minute by minute. Just like you did that day in the mall when I had that flashback. Thank you."

"You're welcome, Fiona. I know you'd do the same for me."

"Hell yeah I would."

"Okay, I'm going in." Fiona leaned over, kissed Caroline on the cheek, and she too was gone.

Caroline took a deep breath, she was ready. Without waiting for another moment, not even for dramatic effect, she opened the door to Hunter's room and squeezed in. It was a tight fit. The room wasn't big to begin with, but with all the SEALs, the pastor and her two friends, it was crazy crowded.

Matthew stood at side of Hunter's bed. The pastor stood by the door, ready to move into place once Caroline got to Matthew's side.

Caroline walked to Matthew and reached for his hands. Because she didn't have a bouquet, it felt awkward to just stand there, but Matthew didn't hesitate and engulfed her hands with his. The smile he bestowed down on her made her breath hitch. Matthew really was a handsome man, and in just a moment, he'd be all hers.

"We are gathered here today…" The pastor's voice droned on, but all Caroline could see was Matthew's eyes. They were locked on hers and she could see the passion lying within them. She figured Matthew could see the same in her own eyes. Caroline tried to stay in the present, but the promise in Matthew's eyes was almost too much. All she could think of was the remembered feel of Matthew's hard length sliding inside her and the feel of his hands roaming her body.

Caroline started when Matthew reached into his pocket and pulled out two rings. She'd forgotten all about their wedding bands. Thank God Matthew hadn't.

When it was time, Wolf brought Caroline's hand up to his mouth and kissed her engagement ring. He slid it off, then pressed his wedding band down her finger until it nestled against the base. He replaced his diamond and once again brought Caroline's hand up to his mouth and kissed her finger again. Wolf lingered this time, savoring the feel and look of his mark on her hand.

Then it was Caroline's turn. It wasn't planned, but she couldn't stop the words that came out of her mouth. As she pushed the wide platinum band down Matthew's finger, she told him earnestly and honestly, "I know you probably can't always wear this when you're on your missions, and that's okay. I know you belong to me, you know I belong to you."

Caroline then followed Matthew's example and brought his hand to her mouth and kissed the wedding band that lay against his skin.

Caroline watched as Matthew mouthed the words, "I love you." She gazed into his eyes and once again tuned out the beautiful words being said by the pastor.

"I do."

The strength and certainty behind Matthew's words snapped Caroline back to reality. He brought her hand up to his mouth and kissed it.

Caroline listened to the pastor ask if she would take Matthew as her lawfully wedded husband. When it was her turn, she answered, "I do."

Knowing it was coming, Caroline could only smile stupidly at Matthew and wait for the words they both longed for. Finally the pastor put them out of their misery.

"I now pronounce you man and wife. You may kiss the bride."

Matthew put both hands on Caroline's neck, a position Caroline loved. Feeling his hands surrounding her, holding her still for his kiss, never failed to make her body ready itself for her man.

"I love you, Ice." Wolf's words were spoken against her lips.

"I love you too, Matthew." Each word out of her mouth brushed her lips against his. Before the last syllable was out of her mouth, Wolf completed the connection between them. He held her head still and tilted his mouth even more until he had Caroline right where he wanted her. Their tongues dueled with each other, tasting and teasing each other. It wasn't their first kiss by any stretch of the imagination.

But it was their first kiss as husband and wife. Somehow that made it completely different from any other kiss they'd ever shared before. It took the pastor clearing her throat for the third time to make Wolf pull away from his wife. He smiled down at Caroline and ran his fingertip down her reddened cheek. "Mine."

Caroline smiled up at him. "Yours," she whispered back.

"Lean down here so I can kiss the bride," Cookie demanded, interrupting their moment.

Caroline laughed and turned to the bed and leaned over. Instead of the chaste kiss on the cheek Caroline expected, Hunter kissed her hard on the lips.

"Hey!" Wolf snapped.

Caroline laughed and playfully smacked Hunter on the shoulder. "You shouldn't mess with him like that."

"But he makes it so easy," was Cookie's response.

"My turn," Dude stated, and turned Caroline to him. He too

kissed her on the lips. "Welcome to the family."

And so it went. Each man on the team took his turn, and said how glad they were that Caroline was now officially a part of their family.

When Caroline got back around to Matthew, she could see he was holding on to his temper by his fingernails. She tried to soothe him. "Hey, husband." Her words did the trick.

"Hey, wife." Wolf gathered Caroline into his arms and relaxed when she melted into him.

"Smile!" Fiona ordered, snapping a picture with her cell phone before either Caroline or Wolf could move.

"That's a good one!" she exclaimed after checking it out on her phone. "I've been taking pictures throughout the ceremony, but I think that's my favorite."

Alabama unexpectedly thrust her cell phone into Fiona's line of vision without a word.

"Okay, I lied. *That* is my favorite." Fiona took Alabama's phone out of her hand and turned the screen to Caroline and Wolf.

Alabama had snapped the photo as Wolf was kissing his bride. The passion he had for Caroline was clear. Caroline's head was bent backward at what should have been an awkward angle, but Wolf's hands at her neck prevented it from bending too far back. Both Caroline and Wolf had their eyes shut and Caroline's hand was cupped on the back of Wolf's head.

"Wow," was all Caroline could say at seeing the picture. "I definitely need a copy of that."

Wolf just leaned down and kissed Caroline's temple gently.

Fiona gave the phone back to Alabama, and sat on the bed next to Hunter. She put her hand over his and Caroline watched as Hunter turned his hand over immediately to grasp Fiona's hand tightly.

"So, is it time for the first dance yet?" Hunter asked with a tone just short of being snarky.

Caroline knew he was still irritated with her. It didn't matter how many times she reassured him that she had the song all picked out and had consulted with the DJ. The fact that Caroline refused to tell Hunter what song she'd chosen, really irritated him. He'd asked and demanded, then tried to guilt her into telling him, but Caroline had held firm. She'd wanted one thing to be a surprise.

"As a matter of fact, I think it is," Caroline told Hunter agreeably. She turned to Faulkner and held out her hand. "Thanks for holding my phone."

Dude pulled Caroline's phone out of his pocket and handed it over.

While Caroline was searching for the correct song on her music app, Cookie turned to Fiona. "Did you know what song she was gonna choose?"

"Don't bring me into this, Hunter," Fiona told him sternly, brushing her thumb over the back of his hand lovingly. It was obvious that she couldn't muster up any strength to be truly irritated with him. "She didn't tell any of us."

Caroline handed the phone back to Faulkner. "Okay, I'm ready. Hit play in just a second."

Caroline turned back to Matthew and walked straight into his arms. She looked up at him. "It's not a conventional song."

Wolf interrupted her, "I'd expect nothing different from you, Ice."

Caroline smiled up at him and started again. "I mean, it's not a conventional wedding song. Hell, it's not really even a good song to dance to, but the first time I heard it, I thought of us. I looked up the lyrics and knew it'd be perfect. It reminds me of you and me every time I hear it now."

The music started behind them and Caroline smiled as the Goo Goo Dolls song, *Come to Me* played tinnily out of her little phone's speaker.

They swayed back and forth listening to the lyrics of a love that started with friendship. Caroline didn't look away from Matthew's eyes as they swayed back and forth, but she knew everyone was watching them with smiles on their faces.

Caroline was floored when the song came to its crescendo, and Matthew sang the words to her, but changed them to fit their own current circumstances.

"Today's the day I made you mine, I didn't get to the church on time. Take my hand in this hospital room, you're my wife and I'm your groom. Come to me my dearest love, this is where we'll start again."

"Oh my God."

Caroline heard the exclamation, didn't recognize the voice, but ignored it anyway. She had eyes only for her husband. "You know this song?"

"Yeah, Ice, I know this song."

He didn't expound.

"How?" Caroline demanded.

"Honestly? You left your phone out one night and I saw you'd been listening to it. I looked it up and downloaded it. I figured if you liked it, I should listen to it. It's a good fucking song. And now it's *our* song." He continued to surprise Caroline and semi-quoted the song again. "This is now our favorite song."

"Wow." The words had come from the nurse standing in the doorway. It was her voice that Caroline had heard after Matthew had sung to her.

"I think that's the most beautiful thing I've ever seen in my life."

Caroline smiled. She couldn't disagree with the woman.

When the song was over, Caroline turned to Hunter. "So? How'd I do?"

Cookie smiled at Caroline. "Good, Ice. You did good. I couldn't have picked a better song for the two of you."

Caroline grinned at the compliment and turned back to her husband.

"I love you, Matthew."

"I love you, Caroline."

Chapter Ten

WOLF SETTLED BACK against the headboard and smiled down at his wife. He'd kept their honeymoon destination a secret from everyone, and so far it'd been perfect. Caroline thought they were headed to a beach somewhere. As much as he wanted to see her in a bikini, Wolf had a different destination in mind. Caroline had dropped enough hints about hoping he was taking her to Maui that he vowed to take her there on vacation before too much longer.

His teammates had also tried to guess, and had thrown out ideas from Paris, France to San Francisco. Wolf had kept mum about where he was taking Caroline and he couldn't be more pleased with the results of his sneakery.

The only person he'd told was Fiona. Wolf needed Fiona to pack Caroline's bags with appropriate clothing and girly stuff. Wolf didn't expect Caroline would *need* many clothes. But he knew Caroline would want some of her own fripperies with her, so he'd told Fiona, and Fiona had sworn that she wouldn't tell anyone, even Cookie.

They actually hadn't gone far from home. Wolf had taken them to Sedona, Arizona and checked them into a cabin high in the mountains. Wolf had researched it online and booked the most isolated room he could. He had plans to keep Caroline naked and in his bed for the entire week. The resort had room service, and that was all he needed. A bed, food, and his wife.

Wolf smiled. His wife. Jesus he loved the way that sounded. He stroked the hair back from Caroline's face and smiled as she snuggled further into him. She was exhausted, and Wolf knew it was all his fault. He'd apologize, but he wasn't sorry in the least.

Wolf thought back to that morning when Caroline had checked her email. He didn't want her to do it, but knew she worried about her friends. Fiona and Alabama had compiled all the pictures they'd taken of their wedding and emailed the link to the online album to Caroline. The pictures would certainly never make someone looking at them think it was a very good wedding, but Wolf fucking loved them.

Caroline's hair was mussed in every picture. Her dress had some random black stains around the bottom of it. It drug on the ground because she was wearing flip-flops instead of heels. Her shoes were now a part of their history, because in one of the pictures he had her draped over his arm backwards and her leg had come up and hooked around his waist. Her unconventional shoes were clearly visible.

Caroline's dress was also wrinkled and had some random red stains on it. Wolf knew he'd warned her, but thanked God she hadn't cared. Her makeup was nonexistent, but again, it was how Wolf saw her most of the time, and he loved that she looked like "her" in their wedding photos.

Fiona and Alabama looked just as disheveled as Caroline did, but they were also beautiful in their rumpledness. There was one picture of Fiona lying on the bed next to Cookie, with her left hand, wedding ring prominently displayed, lying on Cookie's chest. Her eyes were closed, but Cookie had been looking down at her as if she was the most precious thing in the world to him, which she was.

Alabama had also included a picture of her and Abe. Abe was standing behind her with one arm slung around her chest diagonally, and the other was around her waist pulling her back into him. Alabama was looking up at him and laughing at whatever he'd just said to her. Even with her lilac dress mussed and with a pair of sneakers on her feet, she was beautiful in her man's arms.

Caroline's friends had done a wonderful job in catching every moment of their impromptu wedding. From the guys kissing her, to them signing their marriage license. Hell, Alabama had even snuck a picture of Wolf handing the pastor a wad of cash to thank her for the inconvenience of having to spend all afternoon in the hospital. Of course the pastor had said it was no big deal and brushed off his thanks, but Wolf smiled, remembering how she'd pocketed the check mumbling about how it would go toward expanding the playground at the church for the children.

After they'd gotten married, Wolf had called his parents and explained what had gone on that afternoon. Caroline had been worried they'd be upset over missing their son's wedding, but Wolf knew they'd be okay with it. And they were. They were pleased as hell their son was happy, and it was more than obvious he was happy. They wrung a promise out of Wolf to bring Caroline over for dinner as soon as they could after they got back from their honeymoon.

Wolf's thoughts came back to Caroline. As much as he loved the pictures, he'd soon tired of looking at them and had shoved the computer out of the way and introduced Caroline to honeymoon-kitchen-table sex. She'd taken to it enthusiastically.

Neither of them shied away from showing each other how much they loved each other through sex. Caroline and Wolf had done a lot over the time they'd lived together, but they'd never had the luxury to completely let go and not have to worry about anything other than each other. There had always been work, or some sort of drama. First it'd been with Alabama and Abe, then it had been Fiona. Neither of them would ever begrudge their friends for what had happened, but it was heaven to not have to worry about anything other than being together.

Caroline tightened her grip on Wolf and then slowly opened her eyes and looked up. "Can't sleep?" she murmured drowsily.

Wolf laughed to himself. It was the middle of the afternoon. He was wide awake and nowhere near tired enough for a nap. "No, go back to sleep, Ice. You're gonna need it later."

Not intending his words to excite her, Wolf was pleasantly surprised when they did just that. Caroline shifted until she straddled him. They were eye to eye as he'd been leaning up against the headboard of the bed.

"You're not tired?" Caroline asked again, this time running her hands over his hard chest as she spoke. Her fingers teased his nipples for a moment before they slipped further down until she could hold him in her hand.

Wolf could feel himself grow hard at the first touch of her soft fingers against him. "Jesus Ice, you're gonna kill me."

"But what a way to go, yeah?"

Caroline shifted until she could take Wolf inside, and sunk down on him. Or at least she tried to. Wolf held her hips tight and wouldn't let her take him fully inside. "Are you ready for me, Ice? I don't want to hurt you."

"I don't want to be crude here, Matthew," Caroline panted, gripping Matthew's shoulders tightly as she looked him in the eyes as she spoke, "but I've still got your last orgasm inside me. You arouse me just by looking at me with those 'fuck-me' eyes of yours. So to answer your question, yeah, I'm ready for you. I'm *always* ready for you. I'm wet, you won't hurt me."

Wolf relaxed his grip and let Caroline drop down on him. She was right. She was soaked. Hot, wet, and tight. "How does this keep getting better and better?"

Caroline treated his question as rhetorical and ignored it. She started moving, not taking her eyes away from her husband's. "I love you, Matthew."

Wolf smiled. He'd never get tired of those words. "I love you too, Caroline. Now shut up and take me."

Twenty minutes later, Wolf smiled again. It seemed he couldn't stop smiling. They were lying sideways on the bed, the covers were nowhere to be seen, and Caroline was once again snuggled in his arms.

Wolf moved his leg, which had been propped up on the side of the bedframe and shifted higher onto the bed. Caroline groaned. "Hang on, Ice." Wolf straightened and shifted both himself and Caroline until they were both, once again, lying lengthwise on the bed. Wolf leaned over and snagged a pillow from the floor, where it'd lain forgotten in the midst of their lovemaking. He settled both of them again and sighed.

Wolf heard Caroline breathing deeply and kissed her temple. Her legs were tangled up with his and he could feel the heat of her body seeping into his own. The wet spot under his ass was annoying, but at the thought of what had made that wet spot, he knew he'd suffer through lying there for as long as it took for Caroline to wake up and for them to make another.

Wolf, finally feeling sleepy, thought about what he'd order them for dinner. He wanted to make sure they kept their strength up. They had four more days hidden away from the world. Wolf picked up Caroline's left hand and admired the rings on her fingers. It made him a caveman, but he loved having his mark on her.

Wolf closed his eyes thinking about his wife. His wife. He never thought he could be so lucky in his life. Before falling asleep, Wolf thought once more about the words to their wedding song. Truer words had never been sung. Caroline was sweet, and he sure as hell was grateful.

Be sure to catch up with the team in Protecting Summer, Protecting Cheyenne, Protecting Jessyka, Protecting Julie, Protecting Melody and Protecting the Future.

Discover other titles by Susan Stoker

SEAL of Protection Series
Protecting Caroline
Protecting Alabama
Protecting Fiona
Marrying Caroline (novella)
Protecting Summer
Protecting Cheyenne
Protecting Jessyka
Protecting Julie (novella)
Protecting Melody
Protecting the Future

Badge of Honor: Texas Heroes Series
Justice for Mackenzie
Justice for Mickie
Justice for Corrie
Justice for Laine (novella)
Shelter for Elizabeth
Justice for Boone
Shelter for Adeline (TBA)
Justice for Sidney (TBA)
Shelter for Blythe (TBA)
Justice for Milena (TBA)
Shelter for Sophie (TBA)
Justice for Kinley (TBA)
Shelter for Promise (TBA)
Shelter for Koren (TBA)
Shelter for Penelope (TBA)

Delta Force Heroes Series
Rescuing Rayne
Assisting Aimee (loosely related to DF)
Rescuing Emily
Rescuing Harley
Rescuing Kassie (TBA)
Rescuing Casey (TBA)
Rescuing Wendy (TBA)
Rescuing Mary (TBA)

Beyond Reality Series
Outback Hearts
Flaming Hearts
Frozen Hearts

Writing as Annie George
Stepbrother Virgin (erotic novella)

Connect with Susan Online

Susan's Facebook Profile and Page:
www.facebook.com/authorsstoker
www.facebook.com/authorsusanstoker

Follow Susan on Twitter:
www.twitter.com/Susan_Stoker

Find Susan's Books on Goodreads:
www.goodreads.com/SusanStoker

Email: Susan@StokerAces.com

Website: www.StokerAces.com

To sign up for Susan's Newsletter go to:
http://bit.ly/SusanStokerNewsletter

Or text: STOKER to 24587 for text alerts on your mobile device

About the Author

New York Times, USA Today, and *Wall Street Journal* Bestselling Author Susan Stoker has a heart as big as the state of Texas, where she lives, but this all-American girl has also spent the last fourteen years living in Missouri, California, Colorado, and Indiana. She's married to a retired Army man who now gets to follow *her* around the country.

She debuted her first series in 2014 and quickly followed that up with the SEAL of Protection Series, which solidified her love of writing and creating stories readers can get lost in.

If you enjoyed this book, or any book, please consider leaving a review. It's appreciated by authors more than you'll know.

Made in the USA
Las Vegas, NV
19 December 2023

83126453R00361